FLAMES OF STONE

CHRONICLES OF ANNA ATTICUS STONE

BOOK 3

SEVER BRONNY

FLAMES
OF
STONE

Chronicles of Anna Atticus Stone
Book Three

SEVER BRONNY

Dedicated to our beloved cat, Buddha, who passed during the writing of this book.

We take solace knowing you were loved right to the end, and our faces were the last thing you saw in this life.

Until we meet again.

Rest in peace.

Bronny, Sever, 1979-, author
Flames of Stone / Sever Bronny.
(Flames of Stone ; book three)

Issued in print and electronic formats.

ISBN 978-1-990624-02-5 (paperback)
ISBN 978-1-990624-03-2 (ebook)

    I.   Title. II. Series: Bronny, Sever, 1979- . Flames of Stone ; bk. 3

PQ2976134885017006971   0

G329872065801801966203241
G889406827629485868302019

Version 1.1

Visit severbronny.com to chat with fans, duel in the arena with fellow warlocks, explore world lore, see character academy class schedules, peruse photos, read frequently asked questions (FAQ), and meet the author.

ALSO BY SEVER BRONNY:

THE ARINTHIAN LINE

Arcane

Riven

Valor

Clash

Legend

FURY OF A RISING DRAGON

Burden's Edge

Honor's Price

Mercy's Trial

Champion's Wrath

CHRONICLES OF ANNA ATTICUS STONE
Prodigy of Thunder
The Arcane Artist
Flames of Stone

All available from Amazon

For many a year
Through love and loss
I returned to this ledge
Sun rise and set

None that are born
Escape untorn
Yet at final bell
I fare thee well

For I declare
That I have lived

THIRTY YEARS LATER

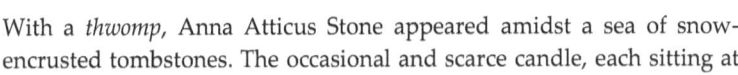

With a *thwomp*, Anna Atticus Stone appeared amidst a sea of snow-encrusted tombstones. The occasional and scarce candle, each sitting at the foot of a marker, sputtered in a bitter wind. But most had gone out.

Snuffed like the souls they try to keep alive with their flames, Anna thought, eyes sweeping over cracked granite blocks weathered so badly the names were shallow grooves. *Lives now only honored by their markers.* No one of the bloodline cared enough — or none remained — to sweep the leaves and snow away, lay new flowers, light a candle, maybe say a word or two in ancestral gratitude. For the vast many, these markers were the only evidence they had ever existed, though perhaps their names were written in some decrepit accounting ledger. It made Anna think of the old Dreadnought proverb, *Die twice we do. The first when the mortal flame expires. The second when our name is spoken aloud for the last time.* She wondered if the latter still counted if one read the name in a ledger.

Anna caught herself playing with her braided ponytail that was as long as her arm, a habit she had taken to whilst in deep thought. She smoothed her black arcanist robe, one hand running over the bulge in a pocket, the Arinthian scion, and the other over the bulge of an unlit candle. *At least you Ordinaries have your bones, even if you gamble with the possibility of one day being risen*, she thought as she strode forth, shoes crunching in the snow. While most Ordinaries craved memorialization with a coffin and tombstone, warlocks feared a necromancer raising them, and so usually consigned themselves to the sacred blue flames of memorial fires—that was, those who hadn't fallen in the field of battle, their earthly remains picked over by vultures.

"Or those who vanished into the ether," Anna added under her breath, which plumed into the frigid night air. Sometimes it happened when a dangerously inquisitive student stepped through the wrong door in the academy Hall of Rapture, or when a tired or drunk warlock accidentally teleported deep into the ground, or when an otherwise experienced warlock experimented with a new spell they did not fully comprehend.

Anna walked slowly, appreciating the solemnity of the old Blackhaven cemetery, wondering about the countless memories lying in rest here. Perhaps there was an ancient scribe in some mystical plane cataloging every thought and gesture and word and deed. Or perhaps, like a tree losing its leaves in the fall, everything decayed, to be consumed by the soil and by the great eraser that was time.

What a shame to waste all that knowledge, she thought. *Knowledge is like fire—it will extinguish if not kept fed.* She grimaced. *Except, like the candles, some knowledge is snuffed. Gone for good.*

Lurking beneath her thoughts, like a leaf floating under the surface of a pond, was the quiet horror that a part of her would rest here forever. And no amount of reflection or thoughtfulness would erase the depth of love lost. No memorial ceremony would ever dull what she still had a hard time facing.

Bare oaks creaked in the wind as she approached a man standing by a tombstone lit by a lone candle. Anna stopped ten feet behind to give him more time with his memories, imagining a boy pawing at the branches of the nearest oak, a rumpled old bear tucked under an arm, a bear that had seen much love and loss. She closed her eyes and saw the boy playing in the man's arms, their laughter echoing. She saw the whole family—daughter, son, father and mother—skipping through a field of tall yellow grass, on their way to the Plowman farm, whilst singing the tongue-twisting "Which Witch will Bewitch." She remembered a food fight in the kitchen of their Blackhaven home, proudly attending the advancement ceremony of their daughter, purchasing school supplies together for her first term, the boy eager to tell them everything he had read about the arcane arts and how he couldn't wait to one day be a warlock like his mother and father and sister.

She preferred those memories over the one of the eleven-year-old boy announcing he wanted to show his parents something amazing that they would be immensely proud of. A final smile, forever etched in time, and hardly a moment to prevent the coming heartbreak that would tear the family asunder.

Anna only opened her eyes when she heard the man quietly weeping. She rushed forth and threw her arms around his purple-robed torso. "My sweet husband," she whispered. "My love …"

Thomas Stone did not reply, nor did he move to comfort her in return. His head remained bowed, eyes closed, shoulders shaking. His hair was unruly, having turned gray after their son's death.

She placed a hand against his chest. When all he did was let his lip tremble, she pressed in against him, gifting him some of her warmth. The candle, flickering in a shallow glass pot, lit up the engraved words from below.

Samuel Sampson Stone

3274—3286

May Bear keep you cozy and warm until your eternally grieving parents hold you again

Samuel, so named after Anna's father, Sampson, and her best friend, Samantha. And for Thomas, the name was also a connection to his sister, Samantha Blackflower.

Thomas had been adamant about burying their son in the city instead of in the castle, the ancestral home of the Arinthians, declaring, "I would never leave my only son in some forgotten crypt of an abandoned castle in the middle of nowhere."

Anna had not argued, for she agreed. Her father wasn't even honored in the castle, though perhaps one day she might scrounge up the energy to place a marker there amongst all the others. She barely visited the castle these days anyway. She was a steward, nothing more. Just another name on a land registry list.

"He'd been hiding that he had blossomed," Thomas gibbered through his tears. "My only son … my only boy …"

Anna moved to brush a thumb across his cheek but he turned his face away. Hurt, she let go of him and withdrew the candle from her pocket. She brought a finger close and soundlessly lit the wick with a spark of lightning. Except her candle, unsheltered by a glass pot, quickly blew out in the wind. She lit it again, yet the wind snuffed it once more. Frowning at it, she tried to stuff the base of the candle into the pot with her husband's candle, only for him to snatch her candle from her hand and violently hurl it into the night.

She stood staring at him, hand opening and closing before her as she tried to fathom what he had done. Every year of the fifty this man had lived showed in the lines of grief and agony on his face.

"You stare at me as if you do not know me," he spat. "I gave up my noble lineage and family for you, and you dare *judge* me? You continued to advance at the academy as a teacher while I bumbled about, sifting for meaning amidst the memories and ashes. You advanced in degree while I stagnated, the dull underachieving husband next to his brilliant overachieving wife. We were *supposed* to have advanced together, and yet you have left me a whole *three degrees* behind! Now, here I am dying of a broken heart, aging by the day, and you remain young and beautiful. There is not *one* silver hair in that braid. Not one! It is wholly unnatural. You remain young and *unperturbed* by the death of our only—"

A *smack* resounded as Anna slapped him. Yet her hand remained in the air and trembled as she reached out for him. Thomas stepped away, his cheek still turned. It was true. She looked like someone in her early thirties instead of forty-nine, the seventeen-hundred-year-old artifact in her pocket having slowed her aging. But how dare he say she had not suffered! How *dare* he!

She could have easily defended herself, reminded him of the countless months of hysterical crying he had so conveniently forgotten. The long hours spent in a fetal position in a dark corner. About the silent agonies that had made her eyes distant whilst her innards burned.

"Where are you?" she whispered instead. "Where is my beloved husband, the one who made me giggle at the altar?"

Thomas looked at the sputtering candle. "I am forever here." He pointed a sternly flat palm at the tombstone, stabbing with each word. "Right. Here."

"It's been three years—"

"—and it will be an eternity!" he roared, spittle shooting forth, hands clawing at the air. "A blasted eternity!"

"We consigned him to the sacred flames. He is gone. This is but a marker. A stone of nothing but memories. We still have a teenage daughter—"

"—who is lazy and vacant and cavorts with fools!"

"Who desperately needs your guidance—"

"—who has not *one* ambitious bone in her entire body! *Not one!*"

Now it was Anna who took a step back. "How could you say such things?"

Thomas stared at the inscription. "Do you even think about him anymore?"

4

"Every day."

He scoffed. "Every day. I think of him not hourly, but *every waking moment*—"

"I have grieved until I could grieve no more, yet I *still* grieve."

He scoffed louder, pig-like, twisting in the dagger. "And oh, how it shows. We never talk about him. Not with each other, not with anyone else. As if our own son had never existed. To be acutely honest, I think we both want it that way. It is too painful. Far too painful …"

A tear rolled down Anna's cheek. "Will you ever stop blaming me?"

"I told you I do not blame you."

"Your actions say otherwise."

He turned to face her. "I *blame* you for not undoing the harm your mother did! For not undoing the curse! For not finding a way! Now it is too late. Forever too late …"

Anna scrambled. "It was a terrible accident of wild arcanery. He'd secretly advanced too fast and too far for his age and bit off more than—"

"Whose fault was that!" he roared. "Whose fault! Huh? Having failed as a mother with our daughter, you put all your hopes in my beloved and *only* son! All for what? For a crystal orb?"

Anna staggered as if struck. "There it is."

"Yes, there it is. *There it is!*" His chest heaved, lip curled as his gaze returned to the candle. "Everything I was died with him."

"Then let there rise a new Thomas—"

"Don't you dare preen like one of the enlightened Leyans in our research! Don't you *dare*. You who hides in her work, in our research, in your precious *teaching*."

"That's right, *our* research." She wanted to stab his chest with a finger. "The research *we* began after stepping into the Arcaneum!"

"Yes, we stepped inside Devil's Gate, and what did that achieve? We haven't been able to return inside, have we, despite all our research!" Another scoff. "I should have remained a Blackflower."

"You don't mean that."

"I forsook my name and what happened? My sister took everything. All the women in my life … *take* everything."

"I have given you a daughter and a son—"

"And left me with *nothing!*"

"You … you do not mean to be so cruel …" But the cold wind snatched her whispered words. For a time, there was only the sound of that wind, which gusted so fiercely that every candle in the old cemetery blew out, including Samuel's.

"I cannot look at you without seeing his face," Thomas said in the darkness. "I cannot *unsee*. Do you understand that? Your mother's prophecy has come true. The well has been poisoned. We are damned and cursed ..."

Anna closed her eyes. A deluge of painful emotions washed over her. She saw her mother angrily spit at her father. She saw the anguish on his face when he told a young Anna they were getting a divorce. The cold loneliness of the house after her mother had left. She imagined Thomas leaving her alone in the cold too.

And she remembered her mother blaming Anna for her sister's death, words that echoed to this day. "Anna Atticus Stone—I hereby denounce you in the old way! Thou art no longer a daughter of mine! I denounce thee! And I *curse* thee! Thy children shall know only woe! This I swear on the Unnameables! They shall know only woe! I damn thee! *I damn thee!*"

Anna let these moments slip through her soul. Then she opened her eyes, straightened, and smoothed her robe. "You think me of limitless patience. Allow me to set you straight. I will finish our research *with* or *without* you. I will raise our daughter *with* or *without* you. The choice is yours." She kissed her hand and pressed it against the tombstone. *I love you, Samuel. I love you I love you I love you. Give Bear a squeeze for me.*

She saw Thomas's silhouette turn toward her. "Anna, I ..."

Anna's arm briefly flared with eighteen rings of lightning that lit up the tombstone in blue. "*Impetus peragro,*" she spat, and vanished with a *thwomp*, not wanting to hear any more excuses.

THE NEXT DAY

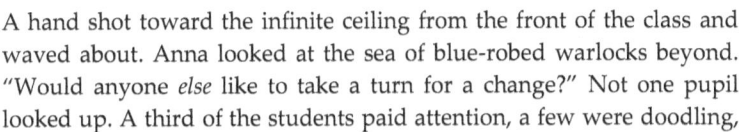

A hand shot toward the infinite ceiling from the front of the class and waved about. Anna looked at the sea of blue-robed warlocks beyond. "Would anyone *else* like to take a turn for a change?" Not one pupil looked up. A third of the students paid attention, a few were doodling, one girl telekinetically floated a note to another girl, one boy was likely asleep, and the remainder sat with glazed eyes.

"But Arcanist Stone, I know the answer," the girl with the hand up squealed, big eyes pleading. She reminded Anna of herself at that age— eager to show her smarts. Anna felt for her and, as she did with every precocious student, wanted to warn them how disastrous bringing attention to one's smarts could be. How it sometimes led to bullying and humiliation and isolation.

"Merciful spirits, girl. You keep squirming like that and your seat will fall apart beneath you."

The class tittered and the girl shrank, her hand dropping halfway. There was a fine balance between warning a student and nurturing them. The fire of curiosity must not be snuffed, but gently coaxed with kindling.

"What are you lot snickering at?" Anna snapped, the scion floating by her head flaring with an angry buzz. Anna kept it aloft in class to desensitize her students to such arcane oddities, which usually also kept the same tired old questions at bay. And floating not far away was her arcanist's satchel, an unmarked black leather affair that showcased her continued dedication to the root of arcanery—Telekinesis. She made it a point to float it through the duration of all her sit-down classes.

"Do you think it humorous that you do not know the answer to such a basic query?" she asked the class. "Hmm? Do you think it funny that half of you will hit your ceiling by the end of the coming exam quint? In this moment, if your lives depended on the correct answer to my question, only *one* amongst you would survive."

Every single head was low but one. The girl straightened with a hint of quiet pride. Anna did not encourage that pride with a smile or wink or nod, as would most teachers. Instead she strode forth from a blackboard—chalked with complex arcaneological formulas—so suddenly the entire front row leaned back, many cringing as if worried she would address them directly.

"There are half as many warlocks graduating today as there were in my day," Anna said. "*Half.* Think about that." A deep silence descended, during which she swept the room with her fierce gaze. "If you think you are special, that you can float through the exam period because Mommy or Daddy already paid tuition for the term, allow me to disabuse you of that notion. If you do not study hard enough … if you do not research the subjects at hand with every iota of concentration you can spare … You. Will. Fail. Let us not even discuss the possibility of an arcane accident happening. Unnameables know how many black-letter scrolls this academy has sent out over its thousand-year history. You think about your family receiving that black scroll and opening it up. You think about that, and consider concentrating. Do I make myself understood?"

"Yes, Arcanist Stone," the class mumbled, defeated.

After one last sweep of downturned faces, she nodded at the girl. "Matheson."

"*Arcanely ambidextrous* means a warlock can cast spells with *both* hands," fifteen-year-old Ruanne Matheson replied.

"Correct."

A boy scoffed. "That's, like, impossible."

"Who said that?" When nobody spoke up, Anna raised her right hand and made a fist. "*Kuranta spaera,*" she hissed. A lightning spear appeared in her fist, which she promptly hurled over the students' heads. People ducked and shrieked as the spear slammed into the back wall, exploding with a crackle—but only leaving a small char mark, for the spell had been tempered. Anna then held up her left hand and repeated the spell—complete with the hurl—putting a second char in the vicinity of the first.

Chest heaving, Anna smoothed her robe. "Would that person care to verbalize another useless opinion? No? Then how about that person at least identify the spell I used. No again? Can *anyone* identify the spell? Anyone at all?"

A familiar but shaking hand rose.

Anna sighed. "Matheson."

"Speared Lightning. 14th degree, off-the-books, elemental."

"Good. Now who would like to tell me the difference between a chronocast and a simulcast?"

A boy with a cheeky grin raised his hand. Anna, suspecting he was the culprit behind the earlier remark, nodded at him. "Burns."

"The latter is just a myth," Jasper Burns replied.

"Explain the difference first."

"A chronocast is, um, when a warlock casts one spell then, uh, casts a second one, but, um, the first one is still alive or something."

"And a simulcast?"

"It's a children's story. No one can cast two spells at the same time, not even you, Arcanist Stone."

"That's not true," Ruanne interrupted. "There are numerous instances in the records of high-degree warlocks casting two spells at the same time using the principle of *arcaneological splitting*, which is the bedrock principle behind a simulcast. Heck, there's even that simulcaster about, the master. *He* can simulcast for sure."

"Bookworm," Jasper muttered.

"You would do well to stuff your nose into a book now and then, Burns. It is truly by the luck of The Fates you have gotten this far." This time the class did not chortle, for there was no mistaking Anna's tone.

Some of her arcanist peers—mostly the older and stodgier ones—thought it a waste of Anna's talent to teach the lower degrees. But Anna, remembering how much of an impact her former mentor Headmistress Roth had had on her, disagreed. The coming generations needed guidance more than ever, especially since she feared the light of knowledge was slowly dimming, as evidenced by the ever-declining population of warlocks.

Jasper raised a wary hand.

"Burns."

"Can you cast Slow Time, Arcanist Stone?"

The class groaned, fearing another lambasting.

Jasper flipped his hands at them. "Oh, don't pretend like any of you aren't curious! It's like the most powerful spell there is!"

"Studying two degrees ahead is a luxury to be enjoyed by the lower degrees," Anna replied, addressing the class. "Appreciate that luxury while you have it, for the spells only get more complicated and take more and more time to master. As an example, it took me eight long years to achieve my 18th degree."

The class stirred, seemingly unable to fathom taking that long between degrees, especially considering they progressed at two a term right now.

Anna refocused on Jasper. "And then if you are lucky enough to have a family, young man, and perhaps a stable profession, you will find time a most precious resource not to be squandered with fancies."

Jasper swallowed. "D-do you still accept dueling challenges, Arcanist Stone?"

"Why? Thinking of taking me on, Burns?"

The class laughed.

Ruanne didn't bother putting up her hand. "Arcanist Stone only accepts challenges from those whom she believes will elevate her skills — and they're tempered training duels only, not like those blood thirsty things held underground."

"Mercifully I have the privilege of being able to turn down most duels these days," Anna said, going to the blackboard and telekinetically zipping a piece of chalk to her hand, the scion and arcanist's satchel floating in tow like kittens following their mother. Few intrigued her enough with their dueling smarts to warrant a private duel. But she did entertain her students now and then whilst lecturing, even taking the brighter ones on in mock duels, or when making a point. "Now enough nonsense." Anna tapped a drawing of a brain with lines showing which parts felt a tingle depending on what type of spell was cast. "Returning to the topic of Mind Armor and how it is crucial to learn the signature of every spell to aid one's mental defenses, I would like you to consider how—"

But she was cut off by the gong of the first of three academy bells, signifying the end of the day.

"Let us leave it there," Anna said whilst the other two gongs sounded and the class stuffed belongings into satchels. "You have your homework. I want details. No more rambling exposition! Burns, Matheson. See me at my desk."

Both groaned while students hurried out of the class.

"Don't look so eager to leave, Wong. You could do with additional book time yourself."

"Yes, Arcanist Stone," the boy mumbled on his way out the door.

"Jenkins, I want a better summation of principles of arcanery next time. Sloppy work today."

The girl mumbled an apology as she skittered by.

"And how's about we pass fewer notes and pay more attention instead, hmm, Poppleton?"

"Yes, Arcanist Stone," chirped a dark-haired girl. "Sorry, Arcanist Stone."

Anna watched them go before turning her attention to the two pupils hovering by her desk.

"Am I in trouble, Arcanist Stone?" Ruanne squeaked.

Anna tossed the chalk into a tray, took her seat behind the desk, and threw her long braid over her shoulder. She sat back and drummed the desk with her fingernails whilst the scion and her satchel took up floating position behind her. The two young students glanced at each other.

"Matheson, I'm going to recommend you take Advanced Arcaneology with me next term."

"W-what?"

"You are wasting your time in this class. You could do better."

"I ... I don't know what to say. Am I smart enough to—"

"Have you not heard? You are, apparently, a bookworm."

Ruanne smiled, while Jasper went red.

"Thank you, Arcanist Stone," she mumbled. "I would be incredibly honored."

"I also hope you will consider becoming a tutor next term."

"I ... I will certainly consider it, Arcanist Stone. If you think me smart enough."

Anna's lips pressed into a thin line. "What have I asked you to stop doing, young lady?"

"To stop fishing for compliments to bandage my insecurities, Arcanist Stone."

Anna flicked her head at the door and Ruanne curtsied and hurried out. Anna then folded her arms. "Which leaves me with apprentice warlock Jasper Burns, a boy who, instead of taking pride in the healing element, uses his time to daydream and muck about."

"Er ..."

She wagged a finger from her folded arms. "No, no, that wasn't a question."

"Sorry, Arcanist Stone."

"Sorry. Mmm. The path you are walking on, do you think it will lead you into hitting your ceiling this term, or the next?"

"Ne—" The boy frowned. "Wait, that's ... that's a trick question."

"So the blade is not completely dull, then."

The boy's face reddened one shade.

"You know, Burns, if you spent a quarter of the energy on your studies instead of on useless quips and questions I've heard a thousand times, I dare say you would surpass even your elders."

"W-what? Y-you really think so?"

"If you manage to pass your exams, I want you to think long and hard about your future. I believe there is potential in you. But if you're interested in hitting your ceiling relatively soon, then by all means continue on the current path of being the class jester. Gods know it's well worn, isn't it?"

Jasper looked down at his feet.

"Is there an observation, or perhaps a question, down there you wish to unearth for me, Burns?" *Unnameables help me, if it's about the scion, I will strangle myself with my braid.*

"No, Arcanist Stone."

She raised an eyebrow.

"I mean, yes, Arcanist Stone. B-but you never answered my question. Both of them in fact. *Can* you perform a simulcast? And *can* you cast Slow Time?"

Anna pressed her eyes shut.

"Right. Thank you, Arcanist Stone. I will take everything you said under serious advisement. Good day," and he hurried off.

Anna rubbed her forehead. "Unnameables give me patience," she muttered, feeling a headache coming on. That first question had been a hot one this term. Some kid had heard a rumor about her and her husband's research partner, that famed warlock the students had dubbed the simulcaster on account of performing a simulcast in some duel down south, and the next thing she knew there was a rumor she could do it as well. But the knowledge required to perform a simulcast was so complex it was oft not tackled until one achieved the 20th degree.

As to Slow Time, she *wished* she could learn the spell. Alas, finding higher-degree mentors willing to pass on that precious knowledge was like being outside in fine weather and hoping to get struck by lightning. And then there was the money. One had to make it worth their while, yet warlocks of such competence oft had greater ambitions than the pursuit of lowly riches. That was exactly the case with the man who was their research partner. He was the only living master and certainly *could* convey that knowledge, but he had met her hints at taking her on as an apprentice with an amused chortle and a change of topic. Every warlock the man came across surely asked him the same question, just as Anna, at the 18th, oft fielded the same query of apprenticeship. Alas, there was little time these days. She assuaged her guilt of not currently having a dedicated apprentice by considering *all* her students apprentices.

A knock came at the doorframe. "You look tired."

Anna looked up to find Syanda Mibukwa, one of the more amiable young arcanists, standing in the doorway. "Just ... been a long quint." She began gathering her lesson scrolls.

Syanda pressed her fingertips through a springy cloud of corkscrew spirals and massaged her scalp. "The committees want to have a word." Her family had come from Sierra when she was a young teenager, and she still spoke with a Sierran accent.

"Which ones?"

"Head and disciplinary."

"Disciplinary? Now what did that delinquent do?"

"Got caught drinking with a classmate—"

"I believe seventeen is past the age of womanhood, is it not?"

"—in the middle of the day—"

Anna stopped gathering her things.

"—in class."

Anna slammed a fist against her desk, the scion behind her flaring with a buzz. Her daughter was getting unruly, no doubt due to the trouble at home. "History repeats itself," she muttered, snatching her satchel from the air and stuffing a few scrolls into it.

"What does that mean?"

"Nothing."

"Anna?"

"Mmm?"

"You all right?"

"Fine. Just ..." Anna flapped a hand about before resuming gathering her things. "Never mind."

"You can bother me with it, you know. Talk it over a glass of wine? Ladies' night out sort of thing?"

"Perhaps another time. I have affairs I must attend to."

Syanda was thirty-four, but because Anna looked the same age—despite being fifteen years her senior—the nice woman oft tried to cajole her into joining her at the taverns. But Anna had long learned to be wary of getting too comfortable in public, or having bosom friends. She had learned what her friendship could mean to those friends. After all these years, Samantha's laughter still echoed, and she still imagined whimpers of dear friends put to the question by nefarious types eager to get her scion.

"All sorts of rumors flying around," Syanda said. "One of which is there's another illegal warlock tournament scheduled soon. The other is that some kid brought a necro book to class. I know, I know, you don't pay attention to rumors."

"Mmm." Anna threw her satchel strap over her shoulder, snatched what remained of the scrolls, floated the whole bundle before her, and tied it with a ribbon. "What does the head committee want?"

Syanda shrugged. "The answer to that probably has to do with a third rumor."

"They using you as a messenger now?"

"You know me. I'd love to get on one of those committees."

"No, you wouldn't," Anna replied as the pair started down the Hall of Rapture, with its hundred-foot-wide walls that shot up into infinity and its high sky-like light, which oft parroted the mood outside. Today it was a dark and brooding winter day, and so the light in the hall was murky and dull. "They constantly squabble and stab each other in the back."

"True, but it comes with a fat pay raise."

Anna rubbed her eyes as they walked, the scion quietly buzzing as it floated behind her. "What's this about an illegal tournament?"

"I thought you didn't pay attention to rumors."

"I don't pay attention to drivel."

"So dangerous rumors are exempt."

"Mmm." Anna, as kingdom champion, had already went once to warn those responsible for running the tournaments—which happened to be the thieves guild—that they were to stop academy students from attending. She recalled their oily leader smirkingly apologizing and saying he would see what he could do. That was months ago. Perhaps it was time to pay another visit to that seedy den of miscreants. She didn't care if warlocks battled each other—although she considered it a great waste of talent—but she did care about academy students taking unnecessary risks. Unnameables knew there were enough risks at the academy already. Those tournaments were high-stakes blood tournaments, sometimes to the death if the purse was big enough.

"I caught a kid yapping about one happening next quint," Syanda said. "Sent him to the disciplinary committee, but apparently the kid only heard it as a rumor himself, so who knows if it's actually happening."

Anna nodded.

Syanda did most of the talking as the women walked all the way to the enormous portal at one end of the hall, on through the snowy courtyard of the academy, and entered the castle-like Student Wing, one of three wings of the gigantic three-spoke structure that was the Academy of Arcane Arts.

"You should do something with your daughter," Syanda added, the pair strolling nonchalantly as students skittered out of their way, many keeping lingering eyes on Anna and her floating scion. "Maybe take her out on a hike."

"She's a drama kid, not the outdoor type. Would prefer to spout lines from some swashbuckling play than get her hands covered in sap whilst fumbling to make a fire."

"It'd particularly do her good, then. It's a wild kingdom. Besides, she's a warlock. We're not supposed to get too comfortable in the city."

Anna stopped to ponder the matter. "I suppose I *could* take her on one of my research trips." She had been planning a trip to Mount Barrow in search of an actual barrow, which legend said was hidden under the mountain—and might be tied to long-forgotten Leyan knowledge. At least, that was the hope. If fruitful, the search would be the culmination of the research endeavor of three people: Anna, her husband, and their research partner, the master warlock.

"There you go."

The pair resumed walking.

A crimson-robed young man Anna recognized from her classes stepped up to her. He cleared his throat. "Excuse me, Arcanist Stone, but I was ill and missed this quint's Dueling Club."

"So I noticed, Pedworth."

"Um, I was just wondering if it's still on next quint, seeing as it will be review quint and all that."

"Yes, but it will be the final class of the term."

"Great. Er …"

"Yes, Pedworth?"

"It's been a high honor attending your classes, Arcanist Stone. I feel like I've been part of history, what with your past and all." His eyes flicked at the scion, which had clouded over. On some days it was tinted slightly blue. On others, like today, clear.

"I see. You've been a competent pupil. Good day, Pedworth," and Anna resumed walking alongside Syanda.

"See the way he went all red receiving even the hint of a compliment? I wish *I* had that effect on my students. I look out at my class—" Syanda extended an ebony arm. "—and I see an ocean of glazed eyes."

"That happens regardless."

"At least they respect you."

"Because I'll throw them out otherwise. Or into a disciplinary committee. Or lambast them before the whole class. I would advise you to do the same."

"But you don't just rule with an iron fist. You're kind, too. Compassionate."

"I don't know who's been feeding you such nonsense," Anna said, though not without the tiniest smile in the corner of her mouth.

"Everyone knows it. My own students say so. I've been trying to learn how it's done, but ..."

"You're young. You'll figure it out."

Syanda furrowed her brows in confusion before glancing at the scion. Mercifully, she did not opine on how young Anna looked compared to everyone else, because Anna was sick and tired of hearing about it. Or maybe it was just that Thomas had thrown it in her face. At the thought of him, a wave of guilt and pain washed over her.

The two women soon found themselves in the arcanists' offices and dorms, before a pair of enormously tall doors, with a sign hung on one that read, "Meeting in Progress."

Syanda turned to Anna with a smirk. "Well, good luck in there."

"Mmm."

"Let me know if you change your mind about later," Syanda added as she continued on to her office.

Anna nodded and looked at the scion. It zipped into her pocket and silenced its quiet hum. She then placed an expectant gaze on one of the doors, which telekinetically—and silently—swung open for her. Beyond was a high-ceilinged hall of numerous doors, between which hung huge gilt-framed oil paintings depicting epic scenes from the academy's history. At the end of the hall was another pair of high double doors, both of which silently opened of their own volition when she approached.

She padded on into one of the most famous rooms in the academy—the Room of Masters, a place few students had seen with their own eyes. The walls here were filled with portraits of old men and women that went up several floors-worth of wall space before surrendering to a blank wall shooting up to infinity. But it was the far wall that drew the eye, for it was invisible, revealing the city in all its glory, as if one were a bird perched atop a small mountain. It was the highest and most majestic view available from within the academy, one imperceptible to the outside world. Like salt dashed from above by a giant, a sprinkling of snowflakes silently fell past, sometimes brushing against the invisible wall.

A slew of older men and a handful of older women, all wearing black silk robes and conversing quietly on a sprawling Tiberran wool carpet, turned to look at her. There were no chairs or tables or furniture, for the room was meant only for deep thought, high conversation, and profound decision-making.

"Arcanist Stone, welcome," boomed Headmaster Bowbrick, a tall man with a long and thin gray beard that was as finely combed as his parted silver hair.

"Headmaster."

"How are exam preparations coming along?" he asked in a gravelly voice.

"Adequately, Headmaster."

"I am sure they are. We'll make this brief." He looked to a fellow arcanist, a dour man named Corrigus, who withdrew a scroll from a satchel and floated it over.

With a mere look, Anna telekinetically caught the scroll, floated it before her, broke the crimson wax seal, and unfurled the parchment—all without so much as moving a finger.

"Your Telekinesis is the stuff of legend, Arcanist Stone," Bowbrick noted while Anna read the document, a document she had long been hoping to receive. "And your youth is the envy of every woman in this room, I am sure."

Anna flicked her gaze beyond the parchment at the stern-faced women, who looked like they would take great pleasure in feasting upon the slightest rumor about her.

"I am sure you have been expecting this proposition," the headmaster continued. "And I am sure you are thrilled. It is a big day. I am old. My time has come. Yours has only just begun."

Anna made the scroll roll itself up and slip into the pile of lesson scrolls floating beside her, which raised a few eyebrows among the committee. "I am not entirely certain I will take the job, Headmaster."

The council exchanged mystified looks.

"Surely there is no one more qualified to take my place," Bowbrick said.

"That very well may be, Headmaster, but ..." Anna halted, unsure how to explain that things in her life were about to get complicated.

"Your daughter. Yes, we know. But what family does not have their troubles?"

Some chuckles, though it sounded forced to Anna.

"If she is not ready, we should rescind the offer," a wrinkled Prigmathani said, his hair having long gone gray, yet the wisps of a rooster comb still clung to his scalp like strands of cotton.

"Agreed," the dour Corrigus said.

"I did not say I was not ready, and I am honored the committee has such high belief in my competence. With respect, I just … I will need to think on it."

The headmaster nodded. "The offer will stand until you make your decision." He looked to old Prigmathani, who pursed his lips.

"There is another matter we wish you to address, Arcanist Stone," Prigmathani said. "One I believe should have remained with the disciplinary committee, though I have been overruled." He glanced at the headmaster, who looked on, unimpressed. "A student has been caught with a most dangerous book. We want you to examine the book and speak with the student to determine if he is on a dark path."

"Why me?"

"It is well known some of your and your husband's research intertwines with the necromantic arts."

Anna's eyebrows rose a touch. "Only incidentally, Headmaster, and only out of sheer necessity. The Leyan constructs of old, the mechanics involved in ancient arcanery … you know as well as I that there are parallels and interlaced intricacies that transcend—"

"No need to get defensive, Arcanist Stone," Bowbrick said. "We are quite aware of the complexities involved. Your research is famous and has drawn many a curious eye, even from lands beyond. We are honored to host foreign scholars in this very institution as a direct result of that research. Even kings and queens follow your research." He chuckled. "Or they have their more erudite lackeys simplify it for them." He shared bemused looks with his cohorts.

"I see. I would be untruthful if I did not admit I am intrigued."

"The student is confined to a disciplinary room," Prigmathani said, withdrawing a black tome from a satchel and floating it over. "The book in question."

Anna telekinetically caught the tome midway and floated it before her face, where it slowly revolved in midair. Its cover was black and crisscrossed with red slashes, or perhaps scars. The latch mechanism was made of two clawed hands intertwined to form a lock.

"Magnificent, isn't it?" the headmaster whispered. "Probably as old as The Founding."

"Perhaps older," Corrigus said.

"At first glance, this appears to be leather," Anna noted. She tilted her head. "But upon closer inspection, I believe it is skin."

The headmaster raised his whiskered chin. "Human?"

Anna frowned, trying to make it out. "No. Some sort of beast." She closed her eyes. She'd seen this pattern before. The memory of a laboratorium surfaced, followed by a severed black limb floating in a jar. She opened her eyes. "It is demon skin."

The committee exchanged tense looks.

Anna was about to spread the fingers of a hand before the book to cast Reveal, only to refrain. "You've already examined it."

Bowbrick nodded. "We have."

"The arcanery has, of course, long sunk to permanence," Prigmathani noted. "We tried various means of discovering the contents of the book and its significance, going so far as to search the archives. No records exist of this book. The tendril geometries suggest it can only be opened by solving a runic sequence puzzle—"

"—a necromantic one," the headmaster finished.

"A kargeyasnara," Anna said. "And you've tried solving it?"

Another nod from the headmaster. "We have."

"And you've failed."

"You've solved one before, have you not?" Prigmathani broke in.

"A few. But a book like this should be in the hands of a specialist."

"There are no true specialists in the dark arts, Arcanist Stone," the headmaster noted. "Not in this kingdom. There are only arcaneologists, and of those, you are considered among the best."

"I am a teacher."

"A teacher with such unbounded curiosity she has spent many a late evening studying the arcane arts whilst her colleagues sat back with a glass of wine."

Anna flicked her gaze to the committee, who stirred uncomfortably. "I would advise you to send this to the senior arcaneologist in Antioc, who is more advanced than I am in—"

"We already did," Prigmathani interrupted. "She was here earlier."

"What did she say?"

"To show it to you."

"So she made no progress."

"That is correct."

Curious, Anna could resist no longer, and she splayed a hand before the book. "*Un vun asperio aurum enchantus,*" she whispered. A panoply of tendril formations instantly became visible, all in shades of gray and black and red. She took her time studying what she saw before passing her judgment. "Interwoven complexities on multiple geometric variances. The casting is foreign, but not of any kingdom or people familiar to me. There is fractaline scalability that suggests a nuanced understanding of—" She stopped speaking, having spotted something along a tendril path.

The committee seemingly couldn't help but gather closer, many splaying their own palms and whispering the same incantation.

"Yes? What is it?" the headmaster asked, mesmerized as much as the others.

"Interesting."

"What do you see, Arcanist Stone?" Corrigus pushed in his cold monotone.

"Intent."

"Of what sort?" Bowbrick whispered.

Anna extinguished Reveal and dropped her hand. "Malice."

The headmaster swallowed while the others shared another dark look.

"What is the context of this find?" Anna pressed.

"A young man brought it to Drama class," the headmaster replied. "It seems he wanted to appear more credible as an actor whilst rehearsing a play."

"A play?"

"About Occulus the Necromancer," Prigmathani said, observing her reaction.

"Curiosity in the dark arts is always the first step, Arcanist Stone," one of the women noted.

Anna glanced at their anxious faces. "You want to know to what degree we should be concerned."

"We look forward to hearing your report, Arcanist Stone," the headmaster said.

Prigmathani opened a palm toward the door. "Shall we?"

"Mmm."

Together they departed, bundle of scrolls and ancient book floating in tow.

TURMAN

"Miiiiisterrr Turman," Anna sang upon entering the frigidly cold brick room of a disciplinary holding cell, heavily graffitied over the generations by recalcitrant students. "Why am I not surprised it's you?"

A toothpick-thin emerald-robed student with pale skin got up off a stone bench. "I did absolutely nothing wrong, Arcanist Stone." His light blue eyes shot to the floating book and he used a pasty hand to smooth his dark hair, which was already immaculately groomed in a fashion that struck Anna as unpopular these days.

"Yeah, we did nothing wrong, Mom!"

Anna jerked her head to the right and found her seventeen-year-old daughter standing in the corner, hands stuck deep into the pockets of her emerald robe for warmth. Anna looked over her shoulder at Prigmathani. "You left them in here together?"

"The pair were caught drinking whilst rehearsing for Drama class."

"How long have they been here?"

"Seeing as they were caught at lunch, since early afternoon."

"Why wasn't I informed?"

"Proper procedures dictate—"

"That is not what I meant."

Prigmathani showed no emotion. "We think her involvement was incidental so we did not feel the need to mention it during the meeting."

Nothing is incidental with Thia, Anna wanted to say, but held her tongue, realizing the committee did not want to embarrass the potential future headmistress. She turned her attention back to her daughter. The girl was shorter than Anna had been at her age, and her hair was wild and unkempt, though the exact same rich brown, albeit cut to shoulder length.

"We didn't do anything, Mom! Honest!"

"Don't lie to me. I can smell it from here."

Thia dropped her eyes. "Was just a bit of fun."

"Just a bit of fun?"

"Oh, I *love* it when you repeat what I say."

"Arcanist Prigmathani, please take Miss Stone to a separate room. I wish to have a word with Mr. Turman."

"If you insist, Arcanist Stone." Prigmathani strode in, grabbed Thia by her upper arm, and marched her out.

"You're hurting me, you brute!"

Anna remembered Prigmathani rudely doing the very same thing to her what felt like forever ago. The man, as old as he was, hadn't changed much. Anna wanted to tell him to ease up, but she didn't want him to accuse her of favoritism or to make things worse for Thia.

"I *loathe* that name," Ralf said when Thia had disappeared from view.

"Turman?"

The teenager winced.

"It is a fine country name which speaks of subsistence and toil and hardiness. It's derived from *turmanido*, which I believe means *determined* in the old tongue, does it not?"

"I don't care. It's too close to *Turdman*, which speaks of dung, nightsoil, and stench. Do you know how much torment I've been put through because of that? Turdy. Turdling. Turd-flinger. Turd*man*. You cannot fathom. No thanks. I prefer my chosen name."

"Ralf is indeed a fine name. It means—"

"Not that one. My *self*-chosen name."

Anna opened a parchment file Prigmathani had handed her prior to entering the cell, after she had dropped off the scrolls in her office. "Ah, yes. Narsus."

The boy raised his chin proudly.

"You have not used it in any of my classes."

"That you're aware of."

"Nor have you seriously acted out in any of my classes."

"That is because I am a model pupil."

"A model pupil." Anna glanced over the file, noting the boy had bounced between foster homes until settling into an academy dorm, where he had been living ever since. "Loitering. Bullying. Drinking.

Theft of school property. Various pranks, some worse than others, though increasing in severity over the years, resulting in more than one public lashing."

"I took those like a man. But I find the practice of corporal punishment reprehensible and barbaric. In my opinion, it should be banned from the academy entirely."

"On that point we are agreed, Mr. Turman. Yet, looking at the details here, due to your smooth tongue, combined with your ability to excel in the arcane arts and in your studies, it appears to me that you have mostly managed to argue your way into lighter disciplinary actions, in many cases even having the charge thrown out. Nonetheless, an impressive, if not calculated, summary of disobedience."

"What do you mean, calculated?"

"You have been testing bounds."

"I still don't know what you mean. Besides, I was framed and people are jealous liars because I am brilliant and handsome and a far better warlock now than they will *ever* be. As to the arcanists, brutes like Prigmathani like to toy with us students. They love lording power over us."

"I see." Anna closed the file. "What will I discover if I search the name 'Narsus' in the archives?"

The young man flinched.

"Shall I take a guess?" She wouldn't bother, of course, as every boy at one time or another nicknamed himself some arcanic-tongue variant of Vanquisher or Executioner or Avenger or Justice Seeker or Punisher or whatever fashionable term was bouncing around from tongue to teenage tongue that term.

His eyes went cold. "You're going to conclude whatever you're to conclude."

Anna didn't verbalize her suspicions, choosing to let the young man speak through his actions and words—and what he did not say or do. She let the ancient black book, which she had yet to touch by hand, float between them.

"It's just a prop."

"Just a prop."

Ralf smirked. "Thia secretly loves it when you repeat what she says."

"You are poor at sarcasm."

"On the contrary, I am a 10th degree expert at it."

Anna glanced him over. His robe was as immaculately kept as his hair. His face was free of blemishes and he subtly smelled of fine rosemary oil. "You enjoy control."

Ralf scoffed. "Who doesn't?" Though he promptly straightened when her eyes narrowed slightly at him. "Er, I meant no insult, Arcanist Stone. In fact, unlike your daft colleagues, I hold you in the highest of esteem."

"Flattery will get you nowhere with me, Mr. Turman." Without breaking her gaze, she slowly rotated the black tome in midair. "The book."

"I already told you—"

"Your inability to answer the query is making me increasingly suspicious, Mr. Turman."

The young man's face went blank.

"Where did it come from? The truth, please, for I will know."

"I should remind the arcanist that it is illegal to cast Compel Truth on students. I believe *you* are the one to have lobbied for that amendment, is that not so?"

Anna couldn't help but be impressed. The young man appeared not only to be quite familiar with the student rulebook, but its history too. That explained his ability to oft weasel out of punishment. Fascinating.

"That is indeed the case, Mr. Turman, but I think it is time we talk plain as plain."

"Great, this should be good," he mumbled, smirkingly sticking his hands into his pockets.

Anna watched him for a moment. "I am of the mind to recommend to the disciplinary committee not just that you be expelled from school, but arrested on suspicion of necromancy." She'd said it so plainly that the tone could have been used in a conversation over tea. It drew the intended reaction, though, for Anna didn't think it possible that a boy so pale could go that much paler—as white as a sheet, in fact.

"You … you wouldn't dare."

"No? I am quite certain that your so-called chosen name would be proof enough of your intent."

Ralf was now breathing as fast as a squirrel. "I …"

"Choose your words with extreme care, Mr. Turman, as your future depends on them."

"I …" He fell to his knees and burst with a sob. "The academy's my only home … the only *true* home I've ever known. You … you can't take that away from me. You can't …"

"Then perhaps you ought to consider telling the truth."

"My … my name means …"

"Mmm?"

"It means *strong* in old Ohmish."

From her own knowledge of the Ohmish language, she knew *narsa* in modern Ohmish did indeed mean strong. "Is that the full truth?"

"It is. I swear."

"And the book?"

Ralf looked up at it. "I ... I purchased it."

"From whom?"

"From some old fogey's personal collection. I was selling my services as a warlock to secure his house against thievery. Instead of payment, I offered to take that book off his hands. He let it go cheap."

"Why would he do that?"

"Because he had inherited it, didn't have an arcane bone in his body, and so didn't know what to make of it."

"And you took advantage."

"I did. And ... and I am ashamed."

"I am not convinced, Mr. Turman."

"I *am* ashamed! I swear!"

"Is what you told me the full truth?"

"Yes."

"Because when the authorities follow up—"

"I swear on my soul it's the full truth! I swear, I swear, I swear!"

"Mmm."

"You're going to get the authorities involved?"

"To follow up on your claim, yes."

"Why? What's wrong with the book?"

"Don't play games with me, young man. You know the answer to that."

"I don't. Well, it's obviously arcane, but—"

"And how would a 6th degree warlock know that an object is arcane?"

"I ... I mean ... it's *obvious!* Look at it!"

"Mr. Turman, you are aware it is illegal to learn arcanery more than two degrees ahead." Anna was also fully aware she had illegally learned Reveal at a young age, yet what she worried about here was the boy learning the spells for nefarious purposes. Still, she took no pleasure from the glaring hypocrisy.

"As if *you* hadn't—" But he stopped himself, apparently aware of what he was implying.

"Did you open the book?"

"What? No! It's locked. That is, of *course* I'm curious, but who wouldn't be? Look at it! That thing is ancient and no doubt hiding something interesting. But no, I don't have anywhere near that sort of skill or power. I'd probably need to be at least your degree to open *that* thing," he added in a mutter.

"Mmm." She noticed him eyeing the bulge in her pocket. When he noticed that she had caught him, he quickly cleared his throat, blurting, "So what's going to happen to me?"

"I will submit a report to the academy disciplinary committee and they will make a determination after reviewing all the facts."

"You're going to get me expelled ..."

"If they choose to expel you, or if the authorities find something untoward, I suggest the best thing you can do for your future is take responsibility for your actions."

"I did nothing wrong ..."

"That is the opposite of my suggestion."

The teenager started rocking back and forth where he sat, hands writhing in his lap.

"I believe there is some good in you, Mr. Turman. You have had a difficult life, but it is the choices you make now that will distinguish you." Anna felt for him, wanted to comfort him further but refrained. She had a responsibility to the academy, to the warlock community, and especially—

"I am going to ask you something else. What have you to do with my daughter?"

"What? Nothing! We bonded because we share the same element of earth and a love of Drama class. We're just friends."

"Is that so?"

"Yes. I swear!"

"Mmm." Anna tilted her head, voice factual, cold. "Be wary with my daughter, Mr. Turman."

Ralf bit his lower lip. He said nothing, but Anna suspected he got the message. She stepped out of the cell, clanging the door shut behind her.

"The sound you just heard, Mr. Turman, I suggest you do not make it a familiar one. History, the warlock community—and especially Ordinaries—have little tolerance for warlock criminality. You hang by a thread, yet you have the potential to be a great man. Do not squander it."

The teenager's lower lip trembled as he continued to rock back and forth. Anna watched him only a moment longer before walking down the long hall of cells.

"Your assessment?" Prigmathani said when she came upon the cell that housed her daughter.

"He is hiding something. Start an inquiry. Check his story."

"That is my assessment as well. I think he is a prime candidate for arcastration."

The bars rattled as Thia shot to them. "What! You can't do that! No! Mom, you can't let them arcastrate such a brilliant and creative soul!"

Anna furrowed her brow at her daughter. "Please do not interrupt. We shall speak in a moment."

"Do you wish to take custody?" Prigmathani asked.

Anna nodded while she stared at her daughter, trying to comprehend her.

"Very well, then. The committee will recommend a two-day suspension from classes."

"Lenient. She is lucky."

"Lenient? *Lenient? That* is all you have to say on the matter, *Mother*? About your own daughter?"

Prigmathani glanced between the two women. "I shall leave you to it."

"Oh, yeah, leave us to it, you evil son of a—"

"*Thia!*" Anna snapped so suddenly that even the usually unmoved Prigmathani raised an eyebrow.

Anna's lips thinned. "Apologize to the senior arcanist."

"I'm *sorry*, Arcanist *Prigmathani*," Thia sneered.

"I shall leave you to it," Prigmathani said again, and departed.

Anna waited until the man was out of sight before turning on her daughter. "What in *Sithesia* were you thinking!" she hissed, making her daughter retreat into the dark cell.

"We had lunch together in an empty Drama classroom and then imbibed a little to add some excitement to the play—"

"In the middle of the day? *Between classes?*"

"All right, maybe it wasn't the smartest thing I've ever done—"

"Mercy, child, and that's just the beginning. What do you have to do with this boy?"

Thia fussed with the front draping of her robe whilst staring at her feet. "Nothing. We're just friends."

"And what about the book?"

"What book?"

"Don't play daft. The one floating by my head."

"It's just a prop, Mom."

"You *know* it's not just a prop."

"What are you *talking* about? It *is* just a prop!"

"So you know nothing about it."

Thia threw her arms skyward. "What am I *supposed* to know about some stupid book we happened to be using as a prop? You *know* I don't care about books like *you* do, *Mother*."

Anna remembered herself sneering at her own mother the very same way. "Don't say it like that."

"Like what? *Mother?*"

"Yes, like that."

The women stared at each other, one with hurt in her heart, the other with a face twisted with rebellion.

Thia folded her arms. "Enjoy seeing me in here, don't you? Want to teach me the lesson that I'm a criminal, that it?"

Anna opened the cell door. "You're not a criminal. Don't be dramatic. And I'm taking you home. We have a lot to talk about."

"Oh, great. I can't wait." Thia marched by—and started walking down the wrong way, toward the boy's cell.

"Where are you going?"

"To see him."

"You will not see him."

"Am I free to go?"

"Yes, but—"

"Then I am going to see him."

"You can't. He is under suspicion of dabbling in necromancy." Those words halted Thia in her tracks. "Is that what you want to get yourself involved in, Thia?"

Thia kept her back turned to Anna. "Whatever. I hate you," and she marched back the other way, storming past Anna, who closed the cell, sighed, and walked after her.

"Are you going to tell Dad?" Thia spat as she stomped on ahead.

"Do you not think he has a right to know what his daughter is up to at school?"

"He already thinks I'm a huge loser. What did he last call me? Oh, yeah, *degenerate*. 'My degenerate daughter,' he said. So I'm sure telling him will be a massive help. Can't wait to hear what Dad has to say."

"Your sarcasm is tedious. Your father loves you—"

"He *loved* Samuel. He *loved* you."

"What is *that* supposed to mean?"

Thia twirled about, face stained with tears. "You know *exactly* what it means. *Now* who's playing dumb?"

"Thia—"

"Oh, stuff it, *Mother*. The only thing Dad loves these days is drinking and gambling and criticizing. Gods, I hate you, you're so blind. Leave me alone," and she ran ahead.

But Thia waited for her nonetheless in the dark academy courtyard, for she didn't want to have to march all the way home in the windy cold and snow.

Anna stopped beside her daughter, glimpsing tears before Thia turned her back on her. "I fear for you, Thia. You know how dangerous it is even being my daughter."

"I bet you do, considering how much you love meddling in my life."

"I'd go to hell and back for you. We Arinthians *must* take care as—"

"Yeah, yeah, because kidnapping is a real threat and everyone and their stupid dog want to take a bite out of you for the scion. Ugh, I get it, *Mother*. Sure, we're lucky to be living in the city—but that's only because Dad insisted on it! Had it been up to *you* we'd be living in that abandoned old castle in the middle of nowhere. You're so paranoid it's stifling. And stop reminding me that I'm an Arinthian! I don't want the stupid scion! I'm not as ambitious as you are, all right? I don't care about it! I don't care if I hit my ceiling soon! I don't care if I'm not a perfect student. I don't *care* if I'm not on the student council like you were, or a dueling champion, or any of that useless bunk! It doesn't mean anything, you understand? It doesn't *mean* anything!"

Anna stared at her daughter, who reminded her of herself at that age when she had thrown tantrums at poor old Panza. "What *do* you care about?"

"Being left alone to live my *own* life. I'm a woman grown, and I don't have to do what you say. You're just an old woman who loves her books and is pretending to be young because she *looks* young. But it's all fake. You're so fake, Mom. Dad's right." Thia swept a hand from Anna's head to her feet and back again. "It's unnatural. *Unnatural*."

Anna saw Thomas standing before her in the cemetery, his expression merging with the one her daughter wore in that moment. "You … you do not mean to be so cruel," she whispered, echoing the same words she had said to her husband.

"Ugh, you're so naive it's gross, *Mother*."

Anna scrunched the robe over her heart in a vain effort to dull the pain. "You are upset. We will pick this up later, when you've calmed down."

"Pfft."

Anna sighed for the umpteenth time that day and, in readiness to cast the 17th degree Group Teleport spell, offered her arm to Thia. "Take my hand, and let us go home at the very least."

Thia stared at it with utter revulsion. At last, she snatched Anna's hand, squeezed overly hard, and snarled, "Fine, whatever."

THE STONE FAMILY

Anna and Thia appeared amidst a small forest of snow-encrusted and gnarled oaks, towering pines, hulking cedars, and blue spruces, located in the heart of the Rose Quarter, the most affluent neighborhood in Blackhaven. Hanging on a large maple barren of its leaves was a sign painted with the crimson words, "Danger: Warlock land. Thou hast been warned."

The locals knew not to step into the forest. Even robbers thought it cursed—rumors Thomas, wary for his family's sake, had encouraged by posting mysterious signs on the property. Another one read, "Have you seen Clifford? Last known trying to stalk this forest," and a third read, "Robber mysteriously vanished here. Do you know anything?" Such rumors were of course helped by the occasional trespasser finding himself in a different part of the city, confused and unable to remember what had happened. The most common interloper was the occasional drunk, oft found paralyzed in place after having set off an alarm, and who would thence wake up in an alley also having no memory of how he had gotten there.

As was her habit, Anna immediately splayed her hand. "*Un vun asperio aurum enchantus,*" she whispered, searching for any sign of arcanery that should not be there. Although they owned the entire block, one could never be too careful.

The area lit up with all the usual tendril geometries from various castings. Prior to moving into their new home, Anna and Thomas had worked together to enchant a large circle within the forest with powerful arcanery, including the 10th degree Area Alarm; the 14th degree Major Illusion, which made it appear to be nothing more than an ordinary forest; and the 15th degree Sanctuary, which made it so no one could see the true purpose of the area unless they were invited by either of them. The scion had further amplified all of Anna's castings so that only the most advanced and determined warlocks would stand a chance at bypassing them.

Even so, as a final line of defense, Anna had spent a great deal of money hiring an expert warlock to cast the incredibly complex 18th degree ritual Area Conceal, which synergized nicely with her Major Illusion casting. Being 18th degree, she could have cast the spell herself, except she had only achieved the degree three years ago, and thus was not as experienced with the spell as someone who had been casting it, say, for twenty years. To her mind, the expense had been worth it, not only to protect her family, but also as a case study of the spell, for opportunities to study the work of those more adept than her came few and far between these days.

"Ugh, Mom, you're so paranoid," Thia muttered. "I bet you the neighbors think freaks live here. Oh, wait, we don't even *have* neighbors, do we? Whole block's a forest the locals think is haunted. Did you know they think that? Mom, are you listening to me?"

"Mmm." Anna was now busy listening for potential enemies, having found nothing untoward enchantment-wise.

"No, it's not haunted, kids. It's just filled with warlock *freaks*."

"Thia."

"Yes, *Mother*?"

"I'm trying to listen."

"She's trying to listen," Thia whispered to no one.

Anna couldn't help but recall talking to herself—to Bun-Bun and Bear—in the very same way. Except Bear now watched over her son in the Great Beyond after having been consumed in the sacred blue flames with him, and Thia stopped talking to Bun-Bun after her brother's untimely death. It was then that the slide into apathy began.

"Any veegrants aboot oot there, Muther?" Thia drawled in a smooth northern twang, no doubt learned in Drama class.

Anna dropped her hand and placed a flat gaze on her daughter.

"I know, it sucks having such a degenerate daughter, doesn't it? You'd love to trade me in for someone more ambitious. I know Dad would. Well, you know what sucks even more? Having a teacher for a mother. Yeah, try dealing with *that* all your life."

"Thia."

"Mother."

"Stop it."

"*Stop it.*"

"You're seventeen. Cease all this whining and act your age."

"I *would* if you'd let me grow up."

"Your father and I have repeatedly asked you if you would rather live in the academy dorms."

"I *told* you I want a place of my own."

"Then get to work and raise the monies. We paid your tuition and even offered to pay for the dorms."

"Pfft."

"Really, girl, I cannot fathom you sometimes."

"Feeling's mutual," Thia muttered.

On this subject, Anna was somewhat glad that Thia was a bit lazy, for she suspected the girl would get into all sorts of trouble living on her own in the city—and become a prime target for kidnapping and extortion. Anna and Thomas had considered every scenario they could think of on how to track her down should someone kidnap her, resorting to such crude and demeaning tactics as enchanting tiny parts of her satchel and shoes and clothing in anticipation of that unthinkable day should some nefarious fiend got to her. And in the worst-case scenario, Anna had long decided that she was fully prepared to hand over the scion to save her daughter, a tricky proposition considering the scion would not tune to the new owner unless she was killed. Not to mention she would still be able to track the scion, as Object Track was an inherent and permanent ability between the scion and its tuned owner. She would have to surrender the scion consciously, which was an arcaneological process that involved letting it go in the language of arcanery—the same mechanism used in bequeathment.

The pair wordlessly crunched along in the snow until they came upon the ruins of a stubby square tower built from ancient stone blocks. Besides the forest itself and some old leftover enchantments, the tower was all that remained of the warlock family that had built it centuries ago, a dynasty that had slowly withered over the eons, until only one inheritor remained—an aging Ordinary that had reluctantly sold the entire block to the Stone family to pay a long-overdue land-tax bill. The cranky old man had spat on the floor as he had signed the deed over, barking, "The land be cursed anyhow, woman. But if there be anyone worth taking keep of it, I supposed it ought to be you. But damn you for heapin' the first shovel of soil upon my grave." Anna had inspected the land thoroughly but found no such curse, only old stories that came with every piece of old warlock land. Those stories at least helped keep the curious at bay.

"Can't even invite my friends over because *someone* won't give me the key to my own home."

"You can come and go as you please," Anna said, coming up to the old iron door.

"You know what I mean. None of my friends can so much as enter the forest, let alone into my room! Are you even *vaguely* aware of how isolating that is for someone my age trying to survive the social ladder of society? 'Woe to the lonesome chick wandering the henyard with foxes watching.' "

"I am not entirely sure that quote aids your cause. The precautions your father and I put into place are for your own safety."

"Ugh, if I hear that one more time ..."

"You are welcome to mingle with your friends all you want in the safety of the academy."

"For a kingdom champion who's supposedly in line to become the next headmistress, you can be quite daft, *Mother*."

Anna threw Thia a glare that told her to watch herself, and Thia shrank back a little. Despite her age, grounding was not off the table, though Anna and Thomas avoided it at all costs as it resulted in an uproar, with Thia ignoring her studies out of sheer spite. Were Samantha still around, Anna would have tearfully confessed to her that she thought herself a horrible and incompetent mother who was continually and inadvertently committing the same mistakes as her parents. But Samantha was dead and Anna kept all those doubts and fears bottled up inside, along with myriad other injuries and grievances.

After staring her recalcitrant daughter down, Anna pressed a palm against a runic oval. "*Shyneo*," she incanted, and her hand burst with lightning. "Anna Atticus Stone. Fourth floor."

A black oval appeared before the doorway, blowing wind that ruffled their robes and hair. Ever on the lookout, Anna stepped aside, allowing her daughter to march through the portal with folded arms, mumbling, "This is so stupid ..."

Anna stepped through after her, emerging into a spacious castle-like room—the Stone family living room, filled with plush floor cushions on a high-pile Tiberran wool carpet. As the portal vanished behind her, she glanced around to make sure all was as it should be. Inset into the right-hand wall was a gigantic marble fireplace with an overhanging mantel stuffed with books and candles. On the left, surrounding a second equally large fireplace, was a library of books and scrolls. Anna had eventually liberated her parents' library and brought it here, with Thomas adding in his own collection. Her old home by River's End had been consigned to nature, which had steadily consumed it over the years.

Directly off the living room was the couple's sleeping and bathing room. Ahead was a dining area, which led to a kitchen leftward, while a rightward hallway led to two offices, one for Anna and one for Thomas, as well as two unused bedrooms, one of which had belonged to Samuel and the other to Thia. The third floor was now entirely Thia's, as the teenager had insisted on some semblance of privacy, the second served as a pantry, and the first was ruined and filled with traps and alarms. Each floor was an entire dwelling in and of itself, for the tower had been built as a generational home for multiple families at a time. There was even a decrepit old cellar complete with a well, which served as a training room and storage.

Being a true warlock tower, there were no stairs, meaning portals connected all the floors, including the cellar. Everything was castle-like, from the seven-foot-thick walls crafted with irregular gray blocks, to the ancient archer alcoves with their crosshatched stained-glass windows, to the battered iron-strapped oaken doors, to the arched doorways, to the thousand-year-old soot buildup above the fireplaces.

But it was home, and a safe one at that—or as safe as Anna and Thomas could make it. The rare visitor who understood the enchantments involved might even call it a keep.

Anna removed her shoes and placed them side by side by the wall near the portal etching. "Would you please get the hearths going and set the heat, Thia?"

Thia kicked her shoes off without unfolding her arms. "Why can't *you* do it?"

"I want you practicing the runes."

"You can take off the arcanist hat, you know. We're at home. Bad enough you call me out in class." Thia winced and pressed a hand to her stomach.

"No more than I call anyone else out."

"That's what *you* think. It's embarrassing."

"You think everything I do is embarrassing."

"Because everything you do *is* embarrassing."

Anna rubbed her eyes, trying to find the energy to deal with her unruly daughter. "Why are you so angry with me?"

"Why do you *think*?"

"Could you please just do as I ask? Are you not cold?"

"Fine. You do that one and I'll do this one," and Thia thumped off to the closest fireplace, but before she got there, she slapped a hand over her mouth and ran into a nearby privy, where she retched.

"That's what happens when you drink and teleport," Anna sang, freeing her scion to float away from her pocket alongside the black book. She went to the library fireplace and pressed a hand against a rune, vividly imagining the effect. "*Igniato.*"

The fireplace burst to life, the heat pluming forth. Anna stood by it, taking shelter in its warmth, until a groaning Thia stumbled out of the privy, hair askew, face pale.

"You've been acting out a lot lately. Is there something going on I should know about?"

"Don't you think you control my life enough as is? I'm a prisoner here."

"You know that's not true. Your father and I have a duty and a responsibility—"

"Oh, will you stop it already? I don't care, all right? I just want to live my life." Still holding her stomach and looking quite peaky, Thia shuffled over to the unlit fireplace and slapped the rune. "*Igniato.*" When nothing happened, she shouted, "*Igniato*, you stupid thing! *Igniato!*"

"Your anger is clouding your concentration."

Thia pressed the fingertips of both hands against her scalp and took a deep and angry breath.

"If you calm down and focus, you can—"

"Can you *staaahp*? I'm trying to concentrate."

Anna fiddled with her braid as she watched. There was something off with her daughter. She had been cruel of late, which was different from the usual lazy but rebellious spitefulness.

After a few deep breaths, Thia pressed a hand to the rune. "*Igniato.*" This time the hearth roared to life, and she spread her hands above the flames before turning around to warm her backside. Finding her mother watching her, she promptly turned back around.

Anna, seeing her daughter was in a fragile place, decided not to press her and to finish the heating task herself. She imagined three of the four main floors heating evenly—there was no sense heating the floor with the pantry—and declared to the house, "*Net sukio seko.*" There was a *click*, followed by a quiet hiss and the room warmed up even more. It was one of the benefits of living in a sorcerer's tower—it had already been enchanted with some warlock amenities, and precision arcane heating was a luxury few could afford.

"When are you making food, Mom? Mom?"

"Mmm?"

"Food, Mom. When are you making it?"

"I'm exhausted. Do you think you could—"

"That's *your* job."

"You're seventeen and need to learn how to—"

"We should have hired servants like Dad wanted. But noooo, because then we'd be deprived of the holiness of doing manual labor ourselves. Heavens forbid a *poor* should claim a wage from us. What is it you always say, Mother?" Thia stiffened, adopting a nasal tone as her head wiggled about. "We ought not to bathe in pretentiousness."

Anna almost snorted. "Ridiculous. I do not sound like that." *Do I?*

Thia ignored her as she dragged a hand through the air. "Herald headline, Mother—*we live in a freaking tower!* We have whole floors to ourselves, yet we can't have servants to make our lives easier? Of course not! Why? Because that would be turning the poors into slaves." She returned her attention to the fireplace, poking and prodding the logs to coax out the flames, all while muttering under her breath.

Anna blinked. "If I may say so, Drama class has truly taught you the art of performance." Yet for once, she wanted to admit she secretly agreed. She and Thomas had only gotten busier over the years, and both had been particularly exhausted of late, making food a daily struggle. They had worked hard to make enough money to purchase the tower, its lands, and its arcane security additions, and pay for Thia's tuition, hire quality mentorship for all three of them, and put aside a small nest egg for their children.

"It's about the only fun class there is," Thia muttered. "And it's not even a class but an *after* class. This kingdom has zero appreciation for the arts. Pathetic."

"All right," Anna said.

Thia whirled about, eyes narrow with suspicion. "All right, what?"

"All right, we can hire servants."

Thia blinked. "What's the catch?"

"No catch."

"You're lying."

"Thia."

"Seriously, what's the catch?"

"I suppose only that they are thoroughly investigated."

"Is this your way of making peace with Dad?"

"What do you mean?"

"You two have been acting weird of late. Bickering about inanities. Snapping at each other."

"Your father's having a difficult time."

"Oh, you mean because my brother blew himself up in front of all of us? Imagine that." But after seeing the hurt look on her mother's face, she dropped her eyes, mumbling, "Sorry."

Anna nodded stiffly despite her daughter not seeing this small gesture of forgiveness. Whilst hiding her face, she made the scion zoom back into her pocket, set the big black book on a mahogany parlor table, and strode through the dining area and on into the kitchen, singing, "I'll fix us up something to eat." Yet her voice cracked just enough for Thia to surely know she had deeply wounded her once more.

Anna fumbled around the old kitchen, remembering her mother and father doing the very same thing in her childhood home. It was the sort of nonsensical plodding that tried to make sense of the world by creating order out of the chaos of misaligned cups and plates and tableware. And so instead of fixing up food, she started organizing—grouping jars of beans and roots and rice and seeds with like jars, telekinetically straightening the variously sized copper spoons hanging on the old walls, and putting a wet cloth to the old copper tap above one of two giant stone basins. The taps had been enchanted with pressure, probably by an earth warlock who knew how long ago, allowing them to draw water from the well in the cellar.

Her daughter padded into the room. "I'm sorry."

"It's all right. I understand."

"No, I've been mean."

To Anna's great surprise, she felt her daughter's arms slip around her waist as she pressed herself to her back. "I'm sorry for hurting you, Mom."

Anna stopped her tidying to press her daughter's hands against herself. "I love you, Thia."

"I love *you*, Mom."

Anna closed her eyes and savored the peace of the moment. She could hear the crackle of the flames, smell the ancient stone and spices of the kitchen, and feel the loving touch of her remaining child. As Thia had once quoted, what gentle joy know the quiet moments …

"I want you to accompany me on an adventure tomorrow." Anna felt her daughter's hands slip away.

"An adventure? What sort of adventure? Not another trip to a library, is it?"

"No, not that sort of adventure. I want you to come to Mount Barrow with me."

"Ugh, you know I hate climbing." Thia made her hands tumble. "I'll just end up turning into a snowball on my way down."

Anna snorted a laugh, which was enough for her daughter to smile, lighting up Anna's heart. Anna covered her mouth and tilted her head, seeing the beautiful girl she had raised as if she were free of all the blemishes of character that had built up over the years.

"Stop looking at me like that."

"Like what?"

"All ... lovey-dovey. It's weird. You're weirding me out, Mom."

"Right. Sorry." Anna couldn't help smiling though as she set to fixing up supper. "You're dawdling."

"I was wondering ..."

"Mmm?"

"Er ... want any help?"

Anna whirled about and pressed two hands to her chest. "Gods be merciful, did I just hear—"

"Never mind," and Thia tried to skitter out of there, only for Anna to snag her telekinetically and drag her daughter back into her embrace, where she showered her head with kisses, singing, "I love you I love you I love you I love—"

"Ugh, stop it," but Thia barely put up a struggle. "Er ... you'd still love me if I did something stupid, right, Mom?"

Anna froze. She extended her daughter at arm's length to face her. In that face she saw herself and her parents and her sister and her husband and her deceased son.

"I mean I didn't *do* anything stupid but if I *did* do something stupid, then—"

"Of *course* I'd still love you. Don't be daft. Now what's this about?"

"Nothing. I was only wondering, that's all. Let's just get on with it. I'll carve the potatoes. We're making potatoes and chicken, right? Let's do potatoes and chicken."

"Thia."

"Mom, I don't want to talk about it, all right?"

"Thia? You're scaring me."

Thia stared at her mother. She swallowed, as if pondering what to say, then blurted, "Fine, I *may* have skipped a few too many classes and *might*, uh, fail the term ... again."

"That's it?"

"That's it. I swear."

"My word, child, that is not the end of the world. You can try again next term. Yes, that is disappointing news, but for a moment there ..."

"For a moment there you thought what?"

"Nothing. I don't know what I thought."

Thia studied her intently. Then she grabbed a sack of potatoes and tumbled a few out onto the pockmarked basalt counter. "This is why I don't tell you things. You're constantly disappointed in me. I can't ever do right by you, let alone Dad. If you're going to tell him you might as well spill it all. Guess it's best to get the shouting over with all at once."

There came the *whoosh* of a portal from the living room. "I'm home!" Thomas called.

"Oh gods, he's going to kill me," Thia squeaked. "I changed my mind. Don't tell him anything."

"Your father has a right to know. You just leave him to me."

"Yeah, like *that's* going to work."

"Hey," a purple-robed Thomas said, walking into the room and dumping a basket of carrots, potatoes, garlic, leeks, and broccoli onto the counter. "Unnameables, what a long day. Spent it crafting a custom enchantment on a clunky elevator mechanism probably out of Rivican times in some stuffy manor for someone who turned out to be far pickier than he had let on." He took a breath. "I must have cast and recast that enchantment three times before he was happy. And then he had the sheer audacity to argue over my fee. Can you believe that? I had to threaten to dissolve my enchantment altogether before he finally coughed up what he owed. What a loathsome toad of a noble. What's with the book back there, anyway?" He ran a hand through his gray hair before noticing the women working steadfastly away. "And what's with you two? Not even a hello for your father? Not a peep?"

"Hi, Dad."

Thomas pressed his fists to his waist, eyes flitting between Anna, who was seasoning three chicken breasts for the fire, and Thia, who was chopping potatoes as if her life depended on it. "Now what happened?"

Anna saw no point in stalling. "Your daughter got caught drinking in class."

Thomas slammed a fist against the counter, making both women jump. "Unnameables, help me. Thia, what were you thinking? It's one thing after another with you, isn't it? And what is your punishment to be? Tell me it's not a full suspension. Heavens, I think I'm going to be sick."

"Just a couple of days," Thia blurted. "It's fine, Dad. They let me off lightly. I'm sorry. Won't happen again."

"Won't happen again? *Won't happen again?* Look at me when I'm talking to you, young lady!"

Thia stopped cutting and turned to her father, who she feared far more than her mother ever since Samuel's death, as his temper was susceptible to bursting like a dam.

"What have you to say for yourself? Huh? I imagine the answer is not going to be found through the window, is it, Thia?"

"I said I'm sorry—"

"Sorry? What, you think you can simply say sorry and get to do it again?"

"As if *you* never had a glass of ale before class, *Dad!*

"Of *course* I never had ale before class! I never drank in school, *period!*"

Anna, remembering time spent drinking ale in the Basting Brisket in the academy's Shoptown when they had been not much older than Thia, could have corrected him, but chose not to.

"Yeah, well, I'm a woman grown who can make—"

"Then make your idiotic decisions in your *own* place when you get your *own* job!" Thomas roared. "You lazy, incompetent, selfish, stupid girl!"

"Enough!" Anna roared, whirling on her husband. "She *is* a woman grown and she *is* taking responsibility for her actions. She doesn't need any more browbeating from either of us. Now, you either support her in this difficult time, or clam up."

The pair glared at each other.

Thomas's lip curled. "You excuse her behavior."

"I do no such thing—"

"You enable her when she needs a firm—"

"She needs love and support, not your fool temper making things worse. And where do you get the nerve calling her a *degenerate*? Are you aware of how hurtful that is? You're her father—*act like it!* Support your daughter in her time of need."

Thomas's gaze flicked between his iron wife and his wilted daughter. He rudely sucked air through his teeth. "Bah," he spat, and strode out.

"Oh, great. Just great!" Anna shouted after him. "Hit the tavern when the fire gets hot, why don't you! Very responsible fathering!"

Thomas said nothing more, other than to bark commands at the portal, which were followed by a *whoosh*.

Thia abruptly threw her arms around Anna again, this time bawling into her robe. "You heard him he thinks me lazy and incompetent and selfish and stupid and he hates me and he'll disown me when he finds out the full truth …"

Anna turned and cuddled her daughter close. "Nonsense, child. Your father loves you very much, just as I do."

"You don't understand …"

"He needs a bit of time. Still, perhaps tomorrow's adventure might be best served done together, eh?"

Thia nodded into Anna's robe. "I guess …"

THE SLOPES OF MOUNT BARROW

"You keep looking up at it like it's special," Thia noted between huffs, struggling to keep up with her mother. "Does the mountain mean something to you beyond being a subject of your research?"

The women plodded through deep snow, each carrying a rucksack and holding a staff to help on their journey. They wore winter coats, boots, and mittens, and their breath steamed in the crisp winter air.

Anna stopped in a pine glade and nodded at the snowy peak, gleaming in the bright morning sun. "When I was a young girl, just after I had blossomed in the arcane arts, my father—your grandfather—took me to the very top of that mountain."

Thia caught up to Anna and bent over to rest her hands on her knees. "I bet you he used Group Teleport," she muttered.

"Er ... yes, but that is because we were not on an expedition."

"Pfft. You could have teleported us closer, admit it."

"Exercise is good for the soul and mind, Thia."

"So is loafing by a fire in peace. Why'd he take you up there, anyway?"

"To show me the kingdom. And to tell me a poem your grandmother wrote to him back when their own love was young and vibrant." Anna stared off into the distance.

"You going to repeat it to me or stand there gawking?

"It wouldn't make sense to you. Mercy, it made no sense to me when I first heard it."

"Mom, I'm a drama kid. Try me."

"Very well." Anna closed her eyes. " 'None where grow the hard granites. The spires that tangle with the clouds. So flieth the bird, so gentle … and free.' " She looked at her daughter, who was grimacing as if having smelled something foul.

"You're right. I don't get it," Thia declared, and the two women burst with laughter.

"It speaks of mountains without a human in sight," Anna explained after their laughter had died. "And of a bird flying amidst that freedom. And of …"

"Loneliness?"

Anna nodded. "And of loneliness."

Thia leaned on her staff, pressing her cheek to it. "What was he like?"

"Your grandfather? He was a kind man. A wise man. A loving man." Anna snorted as she plodded onward in the snow. "And could be just as temperamental as your father."

"I wish I'd known him," Thia said, trundling along after Anna.

"I wish you had known him too."

"How come we don't ever visit Grandma? She's still alive, so … I don't get it."

"Because."

"Because why?"

"Because your grandmother said some awful things. Unforgivable things."

"Did what she say have something to do with your sister?"

Anna said nothing.

"Come on, Mom. Dad told me about my aunt. Said Grandma condemned us all after her death. The whole lineage. He said it's because of that very curse that my brother … you know. Is that true? Mom? Hellooooo? Why don't you talk about this stuff?"

"Because."

"Because why?"

"Must everything be explored, Thia?"

Thia scoffed. "We're on *your* expedition. So allow me one of my own. Go on, Mom, spill the soup."

Anna whirled on her daughter. "The past is not to be turned into a source of drama for your amusement, Thia."

Thia stumbled back a step. "I didn't … I didn't mean it that way."

Anna glared before resuming the trek, jabbing her staff into the snow as she walked. "It was the second-worst moment of my life. Forgive me for not wanting to talk about it."

"Well, maybe you *should* talk about it, Mom. Might be good for your soul."

"Or it might open up old wounds."

"Which could then be allowed to heal."

Anna stopped. She turned to face her daughter, who had stopped well back of her and was wincing as if anticipating a scolding. "Where is all this wisdom when it comes to your studies? Hmm? Where is the thoughtful Thia when she is needed? You are fully capable of applying yourself, yet you choose to cavort with hoodlums who—"

"They are not hoodlums, Mom!" Thia shrugged. "All right, maybe one or two cast questionable shadows, but still …"

"I want you to stay away from him."

"Who?"

"You know who."

Thia dawdled, head low. "You can't tell me who I should and shouldn't befriend. I'm a woman grown—"

"—who still lives at home. And as long as you still live at home, your father and I will continue to advise you—"

"—and meddle in my affairs."

"And meddle in your affairs, yes. And trust me I take no pleasure in it. I would much rather not have to worry about you, but you have been making that impossible." Anna sighed. "We won't be around forever, Thia, so I suggest you listen to our advice. Believe it or not, we too were once young and foolish, but we have learned from that foolishness, and we expect you not to repeat our mistakes."

"You *still* look young, Mom. You look like you're thirty, maybe thirty-two, when you're *forty-nine!* It's Dad who's aged, especially after …" Thia fell silent. Like her parents, she rarely talked about Samuel. "What did you say in the report? Are you going to expel Ralfie?"

"School reports are private affairs, Thia," Anna replied, continuing the trek.

"Just be honest with me, Mom. Is he going to be expelled or not?"

"That is for the committee to decide."

"Well, what did you tell them? Everyone knows your word is like gold around there."

Anna stopped, but did not turn around. "There was not enough evidence to pursue the matter further."

"See? Then you have no reason to stop me from—"

"Suspicion ought to be enough to make you think twice about—"

"It's my business who I befriend, not *yours*, Mom!"

"Enough, Thia. I will not suffer another word on the subject."

"Fine, whatever. But you can't make me stop seeing my friends."

Anna sighed again and resumed walking. She had written the report last night and dropped it off prior to their trek, recommending to the committee that Ralf Turman be put on probation, with the additional suggestion that he be watched closely for signs of necromantic interest. Truth be told, she was not sure the committee would do much beyond send him a sternly worded letter of warning, which would be about as useful as a wag of the finger.

"What are you hoping for us to find, anyway?" Thia pressed as they squeezed by a pair of pines so laden with snow that a bunch of it cascaded when Thia accidentally smacked the trunk with her staff. The women casually summoned their shields to ward off the small avalanche—lightning for Anna, earthen ivy for Thia. But whereas Anna's shield was thick and as large as a barrel, Thia's was thin and barely the size of a buckler.

"Gah!" Thia squealed once they were free of the pines. She scrabbled at her back, wincing.

"What's the matter?"

"Some snow went down my back."

"I thought you had your hood raised."

"I *did*. I accidentally knocked it back raising my shield."

Anna shook her head. Her daughter was clumsy and incompetent in the arcane arts, something that troubled Anna greatly. She had pushed and cajoled and tempted and begged her to try harder, to focus on the arts, yet that had only made Thia rebel more. It was a miracle she had gotten to the 6th degree, and that was solely because of Anna's highly competent mentoring. It was near impossible to train someone who had little to no enthusiasm to push herself.

"You're looking at me a certain way again."

"Like what?"

"Like I'm Sithesia's greatest disappointment."

"You cannot truly think I look at you like that …"

"It's that dopey sort of look, too," and Thia made the exaggerated face of someone who had lost their beloved pet, completed by fists twisting beside her eyes. "Boohoo," Thia whined in mock weeping. "Oh, woe is me, my daughter is a complete fool. A doorknob of a girl who plods about in a daze. I simply *cannot* fathom her. She is quite the clod."

"Really, Thia, you do go on."

"Just … stop pitying me all the time, would you? I'm sorry. I know I'm a failure and I'm letting you down every day, but I will never be perfect, and I will never be competent enough to wield—" She flicked a hand at the bulge in one of Anna's pockets. "—*that*."

"It's been a family tradition for almost two thousand years—"

"Yes, except I'm sure there's been plenty of times when an Arinthian offspring was too dumb to receive it, and so whoever was trying to bequeath—is that the right word, bequeath?"

"That implies I would be dead, and I would rather pass on the scion while I am still very much alive."

"Oh. Well, not that, then. You know what I mean. Anyway, whatever Arinthian was trying to dump the scion onto their daft offspring probably had to compromise. In fact, I bet if you checked the records, you'd find loads of examples of doorknobs like me getting passed over."

Anna frowned, but had to concede her daughter might have a point.

"Come on, Mom. I'm not like you. I'll never *be* like you, nor do I *want* to be like you. I'm not a dueler or a bookworm or a teacher. I just want to lead a simple life. Recite some quality prose on stage. Gossip with my friends. Use the arts to, I don't know, start a garden or something. Is that really so bad?" Thia strode past, only to turn about some ways on. "You coming, or are you going to stew?"

"Please do not use my words against me."

"As if you don't use my words against me all the time."

Anna had to smile at that. If there was one thing her daughter possessed that she did not, it was a playful and sharp wit.

"You never answered the question," her daughter, now in the lead, said as she batted aside a large pine bough with her staff, knocking its snakelike clumping of snow to the ground.

"Which one?"

"I asked what you're hoping to find, remember? You said this morning it was something to do with your research on Devil's Tower."

"Devil's *Gate*."

"Whatever."

"Do you remember learning about Vilnius Vivictus in History class?"

"All those *V*'s sound vaguely familiar."

"He was a master builder in the time of Occulus and Atrius Arinthian, your great ancestor."

"He's your ancestor too, Mom."

"Yes, obviously."

"Didn't he, like, build stuff? And wasn't he super fond of puzzles?" Thia repeatedly snapped her fingers, trying to jog her memory. "Fractaline! That's the word."

Anna did not want to say that, considering he was a *master builder*, of *course* he did "build stuff." Instead, she pointed ahead and telekinetically bent a rather huge pine bough out of her daughter's way.

"Ooh, you should be doing that for every branch, Mom."

"I would rather you practice your Telekinesis yourself."

"But you're so much better at it than I am!"

Anna's lips thinned at the poor excuse, but she did not push the point, wanting to preserve her daughter's relatively good mood. They stepped past the branch and Anna continued with the story. "And yes, he was fond of fractaline spellcraft, crafting large tapestries of patterns that never repeated. He was quoted as saying, 'patterns within patterns.' It's even on his personal crest."

"Was he the one who was also quoted as saying, 'puzzles within puzzles'? I remember it from a play."

"Yes, that's quite correct! Good memory."

"Thanks, Arcanist Mom."

Anna ignored the sarcasm. "As to building things, Vivictus arcanely sculpted Castle Northspear out of sheer rock."

"Oh, yeah, I totally remember that part too," Thia said unconvincingly. "What's that have to do with Mount Barrow?"

"Vivictus, besides being a master builder and an Arcaner, was also a notable scholar. During his research, he supposedly came across ancient knowledge on how to construct portals to other planes. There is a theory that he created a hallway of such portals, or doors, if you like."

"You mean like the Hall of Rapture?"

"I suppose, yes, especially because one story says that some of these doors, at least the wrong ones, led to oblivion."

"What does that mean?" Thia huffed, having slowed down now that they had begun a gradual climb up the gentle lower slopes of the mountain, with its moraine of boulders and rocks that had tumbled from up high, interspersed with slightly stubbier pines.

"No one knows. The thing is, two of these doors are specifically said to open to two notable planes. Can you guess which ones?"

"Ley is obviously one."

"Correct."

"And … Hell?"

"Exactly."

"So again, why Mount Barrow, Mom?"

"Legend says Vivictus constructed himself a tomb here. Being a master warlock, he enchanted his body to teleport itself to its own tomb at the moment of his death, with the tomb sealing itself behind him."

"And that included the map?"

"An astute guess. Yes, and that included the map. Again, if legend is to be believed."

"Is that why it's called Mount Barrow?"

"Actually, no. Mount Barrow—at least the name as a landmark—is in fact older than the kingdom itself. No one actually knows why it is named so, though arcaneologists speculate it was named in Rivican times because the word *barrow* comes from *barros*, meaning *burial ground*."

"So you and Dad have been searching for this map?"

"For years. But uncovering a burial ground would be a momentous find too. And we aren't the only ones looking, either. A famed scholar by the name of Ottentus also searches for it."

"The simulcaster! Ralfie won't stop talking about him. Isn't he, like, the only living master warlock with a full sleeve of rings?"

"Yes."

"Have you met him?"

"He is our research partner."

Thia stopped in her tracks. "Really? How come you haven't introduced us?"

"He is a rather private and focused fellow."

"Because he's a 20th degree master?"

"It can be argued one cannot attain such a rank without being private and focused." Anna took the lead and the pair resumed the labored ascent. "But there is something else supposedly buried with Vivictus, you know. A way back into Devil's Gate, and therefore into the Arcaneum."

"Which you and Dad supposedly already entered."

"Not supposedly. Your father and I genuinely did enter the Arcaneum, but that's a whole other story."

"Which I've heard about ten thousand times. Dad's been obsessed with trying to get back inside for forever." Thia chuckled. "I think he wants to become Leyan. Transcend and all that. Find meaning. I jestingly said to him, 'Welcome to the hunt, good sir.' It was one of the rare times he actually laughed at something I said."

"Your father wants to extinguish the pain that burns inside him."

Since it had to do with Samuel, Thia did not comment on this, and Anna did not elaborate—not that she needed to.

"Let us keep up our training by remaining watchful for anything suspicious," Anna said, and splayed her hand, incanting, "*Un vun asperio aurum enchantus*." But there was not a tendril in sight.

The two women trooped on until Thia dumped herself on top of a snowy boulder, panting heavily. "Mom, I'm exhausted and starved. Can we eat lunch already?"

"I suppose some nourishment would liven things up." Anna squinted at the peak, shining brightly in the early afternoon sun. "And I know just the spot."

ATOP MOUNT BARROW

"Wow, must have been a heck of a duel with this Reaper fellow if it ended a whole war," Thia noted, munching on a banana and squinting against the sun. "You should write a book about your adventures, Mom. Or at least let someone else do it for you."

Anna swallowed a bite of buttered and salted bread, the last chunk of which she held in partially wrapped linen. "I have no interest in fame."

"Where's my chocolate?" Thia muttered, reaching into her rucksack, only to stop and frown. Then she withdrew a rumpled bunny. "Mom, why is Bun-Bun in my rucksack?"

Anna shrugged. "He was lonely, and I thought you could use his company."

Thia scoffed, muttering, "And you tell *me* to grow up ..." She stuffed him back into her rucksack, exchanging him for a linen-wrapped bar of Canterran chocolate. Then, when she thought Anna wasn't looking, she dragged him out, kissed him on the forehead, and gently pushed him back inside. Anna had to look away to hide her smile.

The women sat on a thick woolen blanket atop Mount Barrow, Anna having recounted much of those tumultuous days when she had been only two years older than Thia was now. She had also told her more about her grandfather, Sampson Jeremiah Stone, and how he had done his best to prepare Anna for the scion. She had touched on her sister and how she had coveted the scion, how Anna had berated Thia's father for his cowardice back before they started dating, which Thia had a good chuckle at, and how Thomas ended up overcoming that cowardice by not only joining her on the quest into Devil's Gate, but eventually offering to marry Anna as a Stone, forsaking the powerful Blackflower lineage. What she did *not* mention to Thia was that Thomas apparently regretted forsaking his inheritance, and that he blamed Anna for their son's death.

"Mom?"

"Mmm?"

"I said isn't this view beautiful?" Thia pressed, taking turns biting into her banana and chunk of chocolate. "Not a cloud in sight, so you can see the whole kingdom."

"Mmm."

"You all right, Mom?"

"Mmm."

"Stop that."

"Stop what?"

"Pretending like you didn't just get lost in thought."

Anna looked about, soaking in a snowy kingdom gleaming in the sunlight. "It truly is beautiful."

Thia scrubbed the cuff of her emerald robe. "Ah, shoot. Why's chocolate so hard to get out?"

"You're smudging it."

"Bah. Anyway, it's Dad, isn't it?"

When Anna said nothing, Thia nodded to herself, muttering, "Definitely Dad." She finished her banana and tossed the peel over Anna's head. Anna, who had been sitting by the edge protectively in case Thia got curious, as she was wont to do, watched the peel fall down the mountain and splat against a ledge. She tilted her head toward that ledge, curious.

"Let's finish up. I want to have a peek at something," Anna said. They finished their lunch and folded the blanket up, working together to stuff it back into Anna's rucksack. Mother then turned to daughter. "Can I trust you not to come too close to the edge while I'm gone?"

"What? Where are you going?"

"Just a little ways down. I'll be right back to fetch you."

"Is this another dumb test in the old way?"

"Thia, I won't leave you atop a mountain."

"Uh-huh. Should I start searching for game? For a spot to shelter? Oh, right, I'm a degenerate who can't discern her butt from her elbow. If anything, I'd probably—" She made her hands roll over each other. "—slip and tumble." She shielded her eyes from the sun as she made a show of peering over the edge. "Do you think I would form a large snowball on the way down?"

"Thia."

"I think I would. I think it'd be hilarious. People would point and say, 'There's that clod girl. She's now a snowball.' I'd be a warning to the kiddies to take their studies seriously."

"Thia!"

"All right, all right. Go and … do whatever it is you do."

"Thank you." Anna turned her attention to the ledge. She imagined standing atop it, the crunch of snow underfoot, the exposed black rock nearby. "*Impetus peragro,*" she snapped, and vanished and reappeared with a *thwomp* on the ledge. She looked up to see her daughter looking down at her. She cupped her mouth with her hands, shouting, "Stay away from the ledge, Thia!" and even made a shooing motion for Thia to step back, which she of course did not obey. "Contumacious girl," Anna muttered.

She had a look around the wide ledge and noticed that, although it was a natural formation, it also perfectly served as not only a lookout spot, but also as a shelter against the weather, for there was a hollow in the rock, forming a bit of a roof overhead. Most interestingly of all, there was a large boulder stuck into the mountain at the concave apex of the wedge.

Not wanting to leave her daughter up top too long lest she do something stupid, she snapped off the Teleport incantation and appeared behind Thia, who was so startled she slipped and fell. Anna lashed out telekinetically and grabbed her daughter before she tumbled to her death.

"My word, girl. What have I told you about standing too close to the edge?"

"You startled me!"

"Really, Thia. Sometimes I wonder if those hoodlums you cavort with pushed out all your good sense."

Thia folded her arms. "And you *really* want to ruin such a nice day with another argument?"

Anna pressed her lips together. Instead of replying, she opened her hand. "I want to show you something."

Thia blew hair away from her face in a huff before slapping her hand into her mother's. Anna then envisioned the exact same spot and incanted, "*Impetus peragro grapa lestato exa exaei.*" The pair appeared on the ledge together, with Anna immediately yanking Thia away from the edge.

"Easy, Mom. I'm not a total dolt."

Sometimes I beg to differ, Anna thought, though felt guilty for thinking so. "What do you make of that?" she asked, nodding at the boulder.

Thia approached the boulder. "Kind of looks like it's hiding something, doesn't it?"

The women exchanged a wondrous look before Anna told her daughter to step clear. When Thia did so, Anna raised her right arm and latched on telekinetically. The boulder did not budge. Anna put more arcane strength into the spell, until the scion in her pocket buzzed loudly and the space around her warped fishbowl-like and all eighteen lightning rings exploded around her forearm and her eyes burst with lightning.

"Give me a hand here," Anna said through gritted teeth. "Thia?"

"All right, all right," and Thia raised her left arm, muttering, "Don't know what you expect me to accomplish here."

Still, the little telekinetic strength she had to give was enough to get the boulder to start rolling. Once it started, it kept going, and the women had to jump aside lest they be flattened. The boulder rolled by—and right over the ledge. Anna glanced over the edge, instinctively grabbing Thia's arm to prevent her from falling over a second time. They watched the boulder smack into the mountain and cascade down its face, gaining ever more speed.

"Huh, look at that," Thia noted. "It isn't making a large snowball after all."

The boulder smashed into the trees far down below with a great *crash* that could be heard even from their height.

Thia smacked her hands together, shouting, "*Kablooey!* All right, now *that* was fun!"

"Not so much for those poor trees."

"We burn trees in our fireplace, Mom."

"Dead ones."

Thia shrugged. "I guess …"

Anna turned her attention to where the boulder had rested and found her eyebrows rising up her forehead, for behind the boulder was a small cavity, and inside that cavity was a small wooden box.

Thia jumped up and down whilst clapping. "Oh my gosh oh my gosh oh my gosh we've found *treasure!*"

Anna grabbed her before she could touch it. "Wait." She raised a hand. "*Un vun asperio aurum enchantus.*" But the area, or the box, showed no signs of arcanery. Nonetheless, Anna made Thia stand behind her as she summoned her shield and used her staff to poke open the lid.

The only thing inside the box was a yellowed parchment note.

Thia burst out laughing. "No one's half as paranoid as you, Mom."

Anna let her shield vanish. "Hmm." She strode forth, picked up the note, and read it.

Thia crowded close. "Aww, it's a poem. 'For many a year, through love and loss, I returned to this ledge, sun rise and set. None that are born escape untorn, yet at final bell I fare thee well, for I declare'—" She paused to sigh wistfully. "—'that I have lived.'"

For a moment the women stared at it before both turned to see the grand view once more. Anna felt the sun on her face and the gentlest of breezes ruffle her robe. She listened to the deep silence, imagining someone standing in that very spot, thinking about life, love, loss. She saw Samuel running up to her with a broad smile. She saw Samantha handing her tea. She saw Suala Raga painting her face with charcoal and blowing fire smoke at her. And she recalled that old Dreadnought proverb about two deaths.

"We should come here together again," Thia whispered. "It's beautiful."

Anna could only nod. She could imagine spending a lifetime on that ledge, thinking, reflecting, studying, transcending …

"There's people!" Thia exclaimed, pointing down. "They're investigating the boulder."

Anna squinted and indeed saw small figures plodding about the last tree the boulder had smashed into. Curious, she put the old note back into the box, secured the box with loose stones, and returned to the ledge. "Shall we investigate?"

"What happened to all that paranoia?"

"Curiosity is what happened to it," Anna muttered.

"I don't know … what if they're bandits?"

"Then I shall step back and watch you disarm them." Anna felt a wry smile creep into the corner of her mouth as she recalled Panza once doing the same when she had been learning to play constable.

Thia blanched. "Let's go home. It's a study day. I should be studying."

Anna snorted. "Since when do you study?"

Thia pressed the fingertips of a hand into her chest. "I'm offended! I study! I do, just … not as much as you, that's all. What if they really *are* dangerous, though? What if—"

A suspicious Anna ignored her daughter and focused on returning to the spot they had already walked through. She grabbed Thia's arm and incanted, "*Impetus peragro grapa lestato exa exaei.*"

The pair appeared back amidst the snowy pines, on a path of their own footprints leading up the mountain. Anna tossed aside her staff, wanting to be as limber as possible in already deep snow. Besides, she could always summon a staff if need be. Her daughter hesitated but did the same.

"D'you hear that?" a man hissed from nearby.

"Aye, that was a 'port," said another man.

"Who's there?" the first called. "What business have you with the dig?"

Thia, who was holding her mouth, face green from the teleport, cowered behind her mother. Were it not for the men, Anna would have asked what in Sithesia was the matter with her as she hardly ever got sick from teleporting.

"We 'ave crossbows!" the second man warned as a pair of burly men clad in furs, one bearded and the other scruffy, emerged from between two snowy trees ahead. "Don't you try nuffin'!" Both had their crossbows up and pointed at Anna.

"We don't mean any harm," Anna replied, palms open. "We're just passing through. Don't make any sudden movements," she whispered to Thia, who was holding on to the back of her robe. "What sort of dig is it?" she asked the men.

"Ain't none of yer business, 'lock."

"It is illegal to mine without a permit from the king."

The bearded one spat into the snow. "So happens we 'ave a permit. And we ain't minin'."

"Forgive me if I do not believe you."

"We do," the scruffy one said. "The master has it in 'is possession."

Anna had a hunch she knew who they were referring to. "Your master wouldn't by chance be Ottentus Maledius Anavictus?"

The bearded one's eyebrows crossed. "Aye, that's 'im. Who be askin'?"

"He is digging based on my research. Which I shared freely. With the caveat of being kept abreast of where it led."

"An' who you be?"

"She is Kingdom Champion Anna Atticus Stone," a voice with a thick accent boomed from behind them, dying quickly in the snowy forest. "And I would lower those crossbows lest she skewer you with a pronged bolt of lightning."

The men immediately lowered their crossbows and stiffened to attention. "These two women was creepin' up on the dig, sir." Neither man seemed to know where to look, so they simply kept their chins high.

"Escort them here, and mind your foul tongues, yes?"

"Aye, sir." The bearded one inclined a thick-necked head. "After ye, ladies."

Anna exchanged a look with her daughter before the pair trundled past the men, who followed close behind. Curiously, Ottentus did not yet appear.

The lot trooped around the mountain, walking through a heavily forested area of tall pines and firs. They soon arrived at a short valley that sloped down into the mountain, and there sat a freshly dug cave. Eight dirty workers at a time pushed stone-filled carts up a steady incline, dumped them in a burgeoning pile off to the side, and returned to the cave with the empty cart. Heads turned toward the women, who appeared like princesses compared to the grubby workers. But it was the wrinkled bald man in the highly coveted opalescent-white robe of a master who caught Anna's attention. He stood before a desk of books and scrolls underneath an open tent, moving parchments about, brow furrowed in concentration.

"I suppose it was only a matter of time," Anna said, approaching the tent, her daughter sticking close by.

The man turned his attention to them, strode forth to meet Anna halfway, hand extended. "Arcanist Stone, what a sincere pleasure to see you again, yes?" he sang in a melodious voice thick with a Franterran accent. The Franterrans were a minority populace living in southern Canterra, stubbornly refusing to integrate fully into Canterran culture by clinging to their own customs and traditions. They had their own language too, one the Canterrans considered crude. Ottentus thus oft pronounced his *S*'s as *Z*'s, for example, and his *W*'s as *V*'s, so Anna had heard, "Vut a sinzere pleazure to zee you again, yes?"

"Ottentus," Anna replied cordially as she shook his hand, recalling the firm handshake from when they'd last spoken at a symposium of arcaneologists at the Library of Antioc a couple tendays ago. "I see you've beaten us to the chase. Is this one real?"

"Still too haughty to call me Ottie, I see," he smilingly jested. He was tall, heavily wrinkled, and completely without hair of any sort, not even eyebrows. He also animated his words with elaborate hand gestures, for he was the sort to speak with his hands as oft as with his tongue. "And yes, this is the real tomb of none other than Vilnius Vivictus. But we shall get to all that." He extended his hand to Thia. "Your daughter, I presume? But who is younger? Your mother does not age, but we know why, yes?" He winked, hairless brow dancing up and down.

"Thia, this is Ottentus Maledius Anavictus, a famed scholar, arcaneologist, and the only living master in all of Sithesia. Ottentus, my daughter, Thia."

Thia took the man's hand and gave it a firm shake. "Deeply honored, sir."

"I know we ice warlocks have a reputation for being cold, but I assure you, I am warm as sunshine, yes?" Ottentus smiled as he bobbed his head about. "And your mother's making me blush, but she also speaks the truth. I am indeed—" He let go of Thia's hand to flex his right arm, and a full sleeve of pure ice exploded from his wrist to his shoulder, hovering just over his opalescent robe sleeve. "—a master."

Mother and daughter gaped with equal awe. Known as The Sleeving, it happened when all twenty rings merged into one—and it happened on its own, when the craft itself considered the warlock deserving of mastery. For Anna, that full sleeve represented the pinnacle of her lifetime's ambition. One day, she hoped to have her own full sleeve.

"I've heard a lot of stories about you, sir," Thia said. "Is it true that you once fried two villains on the spot with a simulcast?"

The man chortled.

"I apologize for my nosy daughter," Anna said, flaring meaningful eyes at her.

"That is a question I have heard a lot of late," Ottentus said. "Alas, it is a rumor that bears some truth. A gang of brigand warlocks, eager for wealth and the high honor of slaying a master, had put me in a position that forced my hand. I simply did what had to be done. The survivors fled and spread the tale, elongating it with each telling."

"Can I be even nosier and ask another awkward question, sir?"

"*Thia—*" Anna hissed, only to be stayed by an open hand from the man.

"Please, call me Ottie," Ottentus coaxed. "Or Uncle Ottie, if you like. I have a lot of nieces and nephews. Now what is your question, dear child?"

"Er ... why the, uh—" Thia flicked a finger at her own scalp and eyebrows.

Anna sighed. "Really, Thia ..."

"Now, now, Arcanist Stone. All teenagers are curious beasts, as they rightfully should be. I am hairless because I am training myself to become a Leyan. The research your parents and I are involved in here, once complete, should theoretically allow anyone fit enough to make a simple query—" He knocked against an imaginary door, clicking his tongue with each knock. "Hello, Ley? I would like to enter, yes?" He laughed at his own antics. "I jest, but once one passes a test, perhaps, or a review of one's life, maybe one will be allowed to become Leyan." The brow danced. "*Yes?*"

"But isn't that, like, a myth?" Thia asked.

"No myth, no, but an age-old dream. The Arcaneum is proof, which is, of course, your mother's word. And your father's. But I believe them. You believe them too, yes?"

Thia shrugged. "I guess."

"Your mother and I are friendly research competitors, dear child. I think your mother wanted me to be her mentor, but she—" He made a gesture as if rubbing a coin between his fingers. "—couldn't afford me, yes?" He laughed, but after seeing the unimpressed look on Anna's face, quickly added, "I jest, I jest. Your mother is far too proud to be my apprentice." He slapped his knee, apparently finding this hilarious, only to scrub the air with a hand. "No, no, no, I lie, I lie, I lie. The truth is she never asked to be my apprentice, even though I could teach her much. Perhaps you ought to think about it, Anna?" His head bobbed up and down. "Yes, yes, yes?" Then his head bobbed left and right. "No, no, no?"

"Perhaps," a confused Anna replied with another placating smile. She had hinted many times, and had even considered formally asking him what his annual fees would be to mentor her, though wanted to take further measure of the man first. Yes, he was the only living master, and thus more than qualified to tutor her on her path to the incredibly difficult 19th and 20th degrees, but he was also a research competitor who could claim her ideas, as lethargic mentors oft did to their energetic apprentices.

"But, Thia, oh, my girl, that is such a pretty name! Were you named after someone special?" He raised a finger. "Let me guess. Thiassa, of Narvissa, Soa."

"Quite right," Anna said with an appreciative nod.

"She was a warrior queen," Thia said with a snort.

"You snort. Why snort?"

"Because I'm about as far as one can get from a warrior, let alone a queen."

Ottentus clasped his hands before his chest, wrinkled brow performing its own little play as it wobbled about. "I see the wheel has rolled away from the wagon, yes?" He boomed a laugh, which the women patronized with placid smiles. "Ah, if only our children were as inclined as we are in the arts." He sighed deeply. "Life would be simple, yes? But kids—" He pinched Thia's cheek between two knuckles. "—love to rebel, don't they?" He nodded. "Yes, they do indeed."

Thia chortled awkwardly, letting him get away with the pinch, though not without leveling a *He's kind of lame* look at her mother. It was a look Anna knew all too well as her daughter oft deployed it whenever people groveled to Anna, which happened so often in public that Anna rarely accepted invitations to anything these days.

"As I was saying, Thia, your mother and I are friendly competitors, for each of us wants to be the first to uncover the mythical Hall of Sacred Doors."

Anna raised an eyebrow. "You discovered its name? Where? How? What's the origin?"

"Ah, but I cannot share all my research secrets, no?"

"Surely the origin at the very least can be—"

"All right, all right. I suppose I have gleaned more than my fair share from you and your husband's research." He chortled. "Your mother is most persuasive, yes? The idea itself is Rivican, as they were thought to be able to travel between the planes. My theory is that an arcaneological framework of this knowledge had been rediscovered in history."

Thia, seemingly tired of the man already, stifled a yawn, earning her another disapproving look from her mother.

"I know, I know, boring, boring." Ottentus stepped aside and opened a welcoming hand toward the cave. "Would you like a tour? I have much to reveal. And where is that excitable husband of yours?" he asked as they walked down the slope toward the cave. "He should be here. It is his research too, ya?"

"Ya," Thia replied, nodding vigorously whilst trying not to crack a laugh. Anna telekinetically flicked her daughter's ear. Thia pressed a hand to the side of her head and dramatically cried out, "Ouch, Mom! Why'd you do that?"

"Let us dispense with the theater," Anna replied, "and show courtesy to our host."

" 'Lost winter child, oh, woeless is I.' "

"That counts as theater."

Thia rolled her eyes.

They entered the cave, the interior of which was around twenty by twenty feet, supported by large timber trusses, and lit by sputtering torches that stank of oil.

Ottentus, vigilant with how Anna and her daughter interacted, chuckled diplomatically. "Perhaps your daughter would like to aid us in the excavation, yes?"

"I'm not getting my hands dirty digging stupid holes in the side of a—"

"Ah, but what if I told you, dear child, that there is a teenager your age here?"

"What? Who? Where?"

"Hey, Thia," said a familiar voice from the darkness.

Anna looked over at an adjoining shaft and saw an emerald-robed Ralf Turman emerge, wiping his hands on an apron. His pale cheeks were smudged with dirt, but his hair was as perfectly smooth as ever.

"Ralfieeeeee!" Thia squealed, shooting forth and enveloping him in a hug. "You all right? They didn't expel you?"

Ottentus smiled. "He is a rambunctious one, no?"

Thia pressed a hand to his chest. "He's utterly divine and *so* funny, but in an ironic sort of way, you know? What are you doing here, anyway?"

"Archaeology Club. I *told* you that you should have signed up."

Thia shrugged, muttering, "I thought it'd be boring."

"Oh, it's *far* from boring, my princess of the dramatic." He noticed Anna watching him and cleared his throat. "Greetings, Arcanist Stone."

"Mr. Turman." Anna's lips remained in a thin line.

Ralf straightened. "Er … the academy officially informed me that I am under investigation. I am completely confident they will find nothing untoward."

"Ah, but you have the heart of a rapscallion, no?" Ottentus said with a chuckle. "Good, old-fashioned labor. *That* is the remedy. You will work very hard for me and make something of yourself. Yes, young man?"

"Yes, sir."

"Ya, ya." Ottentus made his hand talk as he elbowed Anna. "They yap and yap and yap, but we know the truth, don't we?" He frowned at the boy. "You get into trouble and I—" He kicked forth with a boot whilst making a clucking sound with his tongue. "—kick you right on out, yes? You are to refrain from any weaselly shenanigans, my boy. I mean it." His brow danced in a fun uncle fashion.

"I promise to be on my best behavior, sir."

"Good. Now come, my fair ladies. I have something to show you."

The group walked down the main shaft, which sloped ever downward, Ottentus and Anna at the front and Ralf and Thia in the rear. The pair of teenagers purposely walked slower, whispering and giggling often, while Ottentus described the excavation.

"Of course, I could have hired earth warlocks, but—" Ottentus once more made a rubbing coins gesture with his fingers. "They fetch quite the price in this kingdom, not to mention they can be a nosy bunch. The Sierrans and Abrandians are cheaper, but few would travel this far for grunt work." He flicked a hand at a passing group of men pushing on a cart, all of whom kept their heads low. "Ordinaries are by far the best bargain, providing manual Telekinesis. Oh, spare me that look, Arcanist Stone. It was a clever jest, and they are far from slaves! I pay them a respectable wage, thank you very much. You should see their outdoor mess hall. They even have privies."

"Tell me about what you've discovered," Anna pressed.

"It is most remarkable, Arcanist Stone. Most remarkable! And all thanks to your research. Sure, I had my part to play, but much of the mental labor was due to—" He pointed both index fingers at her, sliding them back and forth. "—you, you, you. And, of course, your husband. Speaking of that rabble-rouser, is he not wanting to join us?"

"He is engaged at the present moment, but I am sure he would find all this fascinating."

"So diplomatic, Anna. So diplomatic! He is a busy bee, yes? Perhaps fixing another clunky elevator or enchanting a burglar alarm?"

"Perhaps," Anna muttered, slightly offended by the implication that such work was beneath her husband. Sure, it wasn't *proata mentora*, but it was honest labor that helped those in need. And it was certainly better than spending time in the tavern grousing to fools.

"But you will be enthralled. See over there—" and he thrust both arms ahead, pointing toward a gigantic partially excavated slab of stone carved with runic symbols.

Anna stopped in her tracks. "Unnameables, is that what I think it is?"

"Indeed it is, my dear lady. Now I insist you bring him here immediately, yes? You leave your daughter with us and fetch that inquisitive husband of yours. Husband Thomas must see with his own eyes what his work has helped uncover."

"I am afraid he is quite busy mentoring the king's son—"

"Ah, the owl boy." He briefly smiled at the teenagers. "Imagine being that young and receiving tutoring and mentorship from the finest arcaneological minds in Solia. The Ridian princeling is a lucky, lucky boy. And I feel no shortage of gratitude for the monies the royal lineage has in turn heaped upon our research. Now you leave that delightful daughter of yours with us and fetch that curmudgeonly husband. The young prince can come too if he likes. The Ridians know Ottie. They like Ottie. Everyone likes Uncle Ottie!" he boomed, laughing.

"I'll be fine, Mom. You go ahead and fetch Dad. He'll want to see this."

Anna glanced back to see her daughter nodding and smiling toothily. Ralf stood beside her, fiddling with his apron, avoiding eye contact.

Seeing she had lost this little battle, Anna sighed. "Very well. But behave, Thia."

"Or Uncle Ottie will kick you right out, yes?" Ottentus sang, laughing. "Come, my children. Let us inspect the column, for I challenge you to decipher the runic glyphs. Let us feed those inquisitive minds, yes?"

When he turned toward the slab, Thia and Ralf shared a secret look about Ottentus's lameness. Anna pressed her lips together before striding off. She wanted to leave the cave to avoid teleporting through solid rock, which carried a slightly higher risk of an accident happening, the sort of accident that was most unforgiving. Once outside the cave entrance, she glanced at the toiling men entering the cave, none of whom would meet her gaze, envisioned the mammoth tar-covered walls of a portcullised drawbridge, and snapped off, "*Impetus peragro.*"

THE BLACK CASTLE

❧

"It is an honor to receive you again, Arcanist Stone," said a stout warlock guardswoman in a crimson robe, one of a slew of heavily armed soldiers and warlocks stationed by the drawbridge gate. "We were not expecting you. How can I be of service?"

"I would like to speak to my husband."

"Of course. He is with the prince. I shall take you in myself."

They strode through the vast grounds and on into the keep. Guards were posted everywhere, both warlock and Ordinary. All were attentive and professional, though many, as usual, chanced a glance her way.

"It is always an honor for us to see you here," the woman repeated. "We take great pride in hosting the kingdom's champion. I hear it on good authority that the king is quite fond of you."

"Mmm." *Could we speed this along, perhaps?* she thought, not wanting to leave Thia alone with that boy for too long. Even though they shared classes together, she did not trust him after what he had brought to class. She had fiddled with the book late on the previous evening, using Reveal to study the lock mechanism and the book itself, but had not attempted to open it as she had been too tired.

"And I am sure you do not remember, but I was present during the honorship ceremony," and the woman droned on about that ceremony, which had honored Anna for various *proata mentora* services she had performed on behalf of the kingdom over the years, including chasing off brigands, representing the kingdom in parlay during conflicts and minor wars, and raising the morale of soldiers simply with her presence. She had received a medal, which sat on a bookshelf gathering dust alongside various similar accolades.

"That's very nice," Anna only replied, trying not to sound dull as the woman launched into how she had attended some of Anna's classes back when she had been in the academy over a decade ago. Anna, having seen thousands of student faces over the years, couldn't remember her in the slightest, this despite the woman professing she'd had a terrible facial tic that she eventually mastered with the help of a soothsayer, who foretold that gargling salmon water during their spawning season would cure her.

"And it worked too, Arcanist Stone! I got so sick I fell into a coma and when I woke up the twitch was miraculously gone! The soothsayer was right!"

"Mmm."

After delivering a cheerful goodbye complete with a deep bow, the guardswoman finally handed her off to a powder-faced attendant who held his nose higher than his forehead as he walked, repeatedly saying in a silky voice, "This way, Lady Stone," as he led her down gilded hallways decorated with lush carpeting and marble statues and towering gilt-framed paintings of royals of old. "This way." The man stopped before a pair of golden doors. "Aaaaand here we are, my lady." When a raucous laugh shared by two men came from within the room, the attendant hesitated. "Perhaps my lady would like to return another time?"

"Why would I do that?"

The man rubbed the thumb of a white-gloved hand against his fingers. "It seems your husband and His Highness are quite consumed in their conversation."

Anna gave him such a disapproving look the man swallowed, mumbled an apology, and skittered off. She glared after him before flicking a hand at the handle, which turned with a *click* that, were it not for the boisterous laughter, would have alerted everyone inside that the door had opened.

Anna slipped into a grand parlor filled with the usual royal accouterments—statues, vases, gilded paintings and armchairs and plush couches and countless overly ornate tables of various sizes. By one of those tables, a burgundy-robed Prince Richard Ridian the Third was playing with a tiny brown owl, one foot of which was leashed to a nearby chair. And on one of the couches, with its back facing her, was her former pupil, King Power Ridian the Second, who she had mentored off and on since he was a sullen teenage bully, transforming him into a proper man—until the trappings of royalty spoiled him like fruit left in the sun too long. On the other end of the couch sat her husband, Thomas Stone. Both men were in mirrored poses, holding wine goblets, their legs crossed and one arm draped over the couch.

A young powder-faced servant, wearing a curly wig and standing against the wall, noticed Anna enter. He opened his mouth to announce her, only for Anna to raise a stern finger in warning at him, and he stiffened instead.

"And that's how she responded, is it?" the king boomed, big belly undulating as the chortling petered out. "I say, women are all the same, regardless of station." He made his hand talk in the same manner Ottentus had. "Never cease with the nagging, do they? The queen gives me no end of grief about the servants, I tell you. This one's unfit, that one's too slow, that one's too ugly. She wants them powdered and wigged and prim and proper. Reminds me of my mother, I tell you. My word, and she wonders why I spend all my time hunting."

"At least you *have* servants," Thomas muttered. "Anna's too paranoid for servants. Yesterday she said she's willing to allow one, maybe two, but they have to pass a series of hurdles so challenging they have to practically be acrobats. So you know what that means …"

"Thou art not getting servants," the king declared, and the men broke out in laughter again.

Anna folded her arms, listening.

"What am I supposed to do with her?" Thomas pressed. "What am I supposed to do? She dotes on our daughter and keeps her nose in her research and doesn't seem to have the faintest idea that we just lost our one and only *son!*"

The king wobbled his bearded head. "To be fair, that was three years ago, my dear chap."

"Yes, but one does not simply get over the death of a child!"

The king nodded along, taking a sip from his goblet.

"She outshines me at everything—absolutely everything! I am but a pale candle next to a beacon fire. And our daughter is a complete dolt. You would think, having such a brilliant mother, that some of it would have rubbed off. But no, she likes plays and poetry and—at least when it comes to matters of sheer practicality—can be as daft as wood." Thomas expelled a great sigh as he rubbed his face. "I miss the court intrigues, you know?"

"I find them tedious and boring," the king replied. "But your sister manages quite well."

"Getting fat on her fortune," Thomas replied, poking the king's belly. "Like you," and the pair laughed again.

"Papa, can I go outside and play?" the young prince asked. He was thirteen yet looked nine, a boy stunted by a near-death bout with mousepox. He had blossomed in the arcane arts, yet his progress had stalled only months into his training. Thomas had told Anna he had overheard the servants saying the boy was a simpleton who would probably end up in an asylum, but all Anna had seen was a lack of proper attention to coax him out of his royal-coddled shell.

"No, Son," the king boomed. "Sit and play with your feathery friend." He burped long and loud, thumping his chest with a fist. "He loves owls," he said to Thomas. "And I don't care what the lickspittles around here say," he added loudly for the servant to hear. "My boy's smart, and wiser at his age than his old man was."

"That's certainly apparent," Anna snapped, striding forth.

The men shot up from their seats, both spilling wine onto the carpet.

"Anna—"

"Arcanist Stone—"

"Like a pair of school chums caught smoking leaf in the privy," Anna said, swooping in closer to the boy. "Has he taught you anything today, young man?"

"To be quiet," the boy whispered.

Anna folded her arms at the king and Thomas, both of whom looked down like scolded boys. "The second afternoon bell has yet to toll and you two are swaying like cat tails in the wind. What have you to say for yourselves?"

Both men started mumbling at once, the king scratching his beard and Thomas the back of his head.

"Hmm? I cannot understand you with all that slurring."

"I told you she'd make a good headmistress," the king muttered.

"She certainly acts one at home," Thomas muttered back, and the pair burst out laughing, which they desperately tried to suppress. They had to hold on to each other as if fearing they might tumble to the ground—yet even then, the king rolled onto the couch, his belly threatening to burst through his gold buttons like an overcooked sausage.

"Oi, that wine does hit quick upon standing, don't it?" he wheezed, face cherry, wine spilling all over the couch and his fine breeches.

Thomas tried to haul the big man to his feet, laugh-wheezing, "Get up, you fool! Don't leave me to my devices here!"

Anna extended a hand to the boy. "Come, let us find your governess."

"Yes, Arcanist Stone."

"Don't forget your owl."

"Come on, Hootie." The boy unclasped the owl from the chair, let it climb onto his arm, and took Anna's hand.

"I apologize, Arcanist Stone," the king wheezed through his laughter, trying to get himself level on the couch. "I fear we may have imbibed a wee bit too much …"

"That is most apparent," Anna snapped.

"Oh dear, I may have done you in, good sir," the king muttered.

"I'm used to it," Thomas said.

Anna took the boy to the servant. "Please take him to the governess. I have words I would like to say that he ought not to hear."

The young servant bowed. "Certainly, Champion Stone." He flashed the men a smug look and lingered only a moment, as if he wanted nothing more than to hear them scolded, before taking the prince by the hand and leading him out.

"Bye, Arcanist Stone," the boy sang, flapping a hand at Anna.

Anna gave him a pained smile, watching him plod along, recalling how Samuel had walked the same way. *They should still be friends*, Anna thought, remembering the boys playing with each other despite Samuel being the elder. Samuel had been so kind too, so caring and understanding. She remembered him showing the boy Bear, and then having Bear talk with the boy's owl. He would have made great counsel for the young prince, for all princes needed bosom friends.

"Ohhh, we're in trouble now," the king wheezed. "Who would have thought someone who looks so young could be so fierce. You married a lioness, sir."

"That I did, but you'd think—"

Anna whirled on the men. "I have a good mind to deliver a tongue thrashing," she hissed, and the pair of men, who had clambered back onto their unsteady feet, fell silent once more. "But I fear it will do no good."

"That's a relief," Thomas muttered, trying to keep his crimson face plain despite wanting to continue wheezing with laughter.

"You revile our daughter to the *king*? Shame on you. What manner of man have you become?"

"You certainly stepped into a pile this time," the king whispered, holding onto Thomas's shoulder.

"And you, the ruler of our great kingdom, whose head is on the coinage, entertaining the cup instead of his son and heir. Do you not recall how you, too, were ignored by your own father?"

"Yes, m'lady, I do," the king squeaked.

"Yet you parlay like an oaf with my husband, the pair of you hounding your wives like they should be good servants. On this day, I am ashamed of you *both*."

The men silently weaved in place, each holding the other for steadiness. But the king's gaze soon wandered, searching for his cup. "Dear me, I may have spilled a bit of wine," he cooed, and the pair burst with renewed laughter.

"Nothing a proper servant couldn't solve with a good cleaning cantrip," Thomas declared.

"Your presence is requested," Anna hissed through gritted teeth.

"Better be in a tavern," Thomas replied, holding his stomach and leaning against the king.

"Ottentus's latest excavation struck true."

Thomas did a double take. "What did you say?"

"And your daughter is waiting there with him and a certain boy who I think she should keep well clear of."

Thomas sniffed, smoothed his robe, sniffed again, and was about to march forth, only to point at his cup, which shot to his hand. He downed what remained, sniffed a third time, and clasped the king on the shoulder. "I leave you to your governess and wife and servants, my lord."

"What joy," the king replied tonelessly, and the men burst with yet another round of wheezing laughter.

"I will be in the hall," Anna said, and strode off.

"Good to see, Arcanist Stone!" the king hollered after her. "I mean, good to see *you*, Stone! Arcanist Stone! And my apologies once more!"

"Save it for your queen wife," Anna muttered, flicking a hand at the closed door. It burst open, the handle breaking with a *crack*, and slammed against the wall. In the hallway, Anna whirled about and waited, arms folded across her heaving chest.

"I better tend to the wounded hen," Thomas sang, stumbling toward her.

Even the king winced at that and busied himself with his golden tunic.

Thomas presented himself in the hall and bowed. "My lady—" But he bowed so low he lost his balance and tumbled forth. Anna stepped aside, allowing him room to fall to the floor. "Whoops," he slurred, clambering back to his feet.

Anna simply began marching down the hall.

"Wait for me, sweetums," Thomas sang, stumbling after her.

"I am having a difficult time recalling a more humiliating moment," Anna hissed when he had finally caught up to her.

"Nothing a strong Sierran coffee couldn't right," Thomas slurred. "Hey, whoa that horse, would you?"

She slowed only a bit, allowing him to catch up.

"Do you realize how stuffy you talk whenever you're around royal halls like this? For that matter, you talk like this in the academy too. Where is the Anna I married? The grill—I mean, girl, ha! Dear me. Anyway, where is the girl who nuzzled close and laughed and made merry?"

"That *girl* still sits atop the grave of our *son*."

Thomas stumbled to a stop.

Anna halted and dropped her head. She ran a hand over her braid and fussed with the tail of it. "I apologize."

"Not at all," Thomas said. "I am glad to hear the truth for a change."

"We both pulled back. It wasn't just you."

"No, it wasn't just me."

She turned to him. "You ought to rest. I should take you home."

"Nonsense. I need to see this. I'll splash my face and down a coffee from a street stall." He grinned.

"You will make a fool of yourself if you come in this state. Embarrass me *and* your daughter."

Thomas clicked his heels and saluted. "Sir! I will do no such thing, sir! I mean, m'lady!"

"You are drunk, *sir*."

"Just a—" He pinched two fingers together and squinted. "I need to see this. I earned it. You cannot erase my contributions to the work."

Anna shook her head. "This goes against my better judgment—"

Thomas clapped his hands together with a *smack*. "Then it's settled. But, uh, you will have to teleport me there."

"That is the first prudent thing you have said this afternoon, Husband."

"Thank you, Wife."

The pair walked out into the courtyard, where Thomas—to Anna's dismay—dunked his head in a horse's trough. With his hair still dripping, he purchased a mug of coffee from an ebony-skinned woman with two curved blades on her hip. He did indeed down the cup on the spot, burning his mouth in the process, before clapping his hands and saying, "That's that." Husband and wife then moved on to the gate, where the anti-teleport boundary ended. There Anna opened a hand, which Thomas accepted, and incanted the 17th degree Group Teleport incantation.

Once at the dig site, they entered the cave and hurried to join Ottentus, Ralf, and Thia. The teenage pair were chortling over a jest while Ottentus oversaw men excavating around the stone slab with pickaxes and chisels.

"Careful now!" Ottentus barked at the workmen. "Do not dare disturb the runes!"

Ralf was the first to notice Anna and Thomas. "Your father's here," he whispered to Thia, who promptly stepped away from him whilst muttering, "Why's his hair wet though?"

Thomas paid them no mind. "It's a Vivictus," he blurted, striding forth. "I recognize that rune there." He moved past Ottentus to tap a squiggle in the slab.

"Yes, yes, go on," Ottentus said, shooing the workmen, who scampered off, taking their tools with them.

Thomas brushed aside dust that had built up from the work. "And this rune here … this too is a classic Vilnius Vivictus rune. Note the sculpted workmanship. This was not carved by hand, but—"

"—by arcanery, yes, exactly!" Ottentus said. "By the master builder himself." His brow danced at Thia. "A fun anecdote, which I like to tell around the supper table—both of our surnames share the old-tongue word for *victor*. Alas, we are unrelated."

"How fun," Thia mumbled tonelessly.

"Anna and I studied his workmanship up in Northspear." Thomas rubbed his scraggily chin. "I don't suppose you have some coffee on hand, do you, Ottie?"

"I hope you like Sierran black."

"Like it? Dad loves it," Thia said to Ralf.

"You there," Ottentus barked at one of six workmen trundling in with an empty cart. "Fetch us a pot of Sierran and mugs from the kitchens."

"Yes, sir," the young man replied, and hurried away, while his cohorts remained on standby to resume their excavating.

"Sharpens the focus," Thomas muttered, frowning at the runes before turning to beam at his wife. "I *knew* the work would yield something. This is the place. He found it."

Anna smiled tepidly, glad to see Thomas distracted by something that mattered for a change.

"But what is it, Uncle Ottie?" Ralf asked.

"It has to be his tomb, right?" Thia asked, cringing as if trying to impress Ralf, though Anna suspected it was approval she was seeking.

"Not necessarily," Thomas replied, rubbing his chin as he appraised the runes. "Could be anything, really. A hideaway, a chapel, a labyrinth, a home—"

"But it could be his tomb, right?" Thia pressed.

"Obviously," Thomas said. "But it is not his body that is of interest."

"It is what he hid," Ottentus said, nodding along.

Thia, who Anna saw as only seeking her father's approval, wilted. Anna considered saying something to her husband, but thought to leave it for the moment, for something had caught her eye. While the two men waxed on about the possibilities, she stepped up to the slab and glanced about for a chisel.

"Allow me," Ottentus said, and opened his left palm and pointed a finger at it. The finger drew a tiny squiggle and a chisel *sizzled* into existence in his palm.

"Did he just cast a 13th degree spell … *wordlessly*?" Thia whispered as Ottentus floated the chisel to Anna's hand.

Ralf nodded proudly. "Well, he *is* a master."

Anna, not wanting to show how impressed she herself was with the man's non-verbal Create Simple Object casting, began gently chipping at the rock that had consumed the slab like moss growing over a paving stone. Yet her mind lingered on that coveted skill, for although she could pull it off with certain elementary low-degree spells, she wanted to be able to perform it with higher-degree spells too. The only thing was that she noticed it sometimes came with a tradeoff in potency of casting. It was why competent warlocks rarely cast spells non-verbally in duels.

Her chipping echoed in the chamber. Except instead of continuing to work at revealing the slab bit by bit, she chipped in a leftward line, away from the exposed portion.

The men looked on as she worked.

"Anna, what do you see?" Thomas asked. "Anna?"

"Don't know yet," she mumbled, fixated on a hunch. The master builder's workmanship in Northspear never contained a mere slab. There was always a purpose to the runes, whether it be an elevator or drawbridge mechanism or a relatively simple torch rune.

"She is looking for an edge to the work," Ottentus said.

At last, due to her chipping away, a long chunk fell off, exposing a vertical groove. *I need more light,* she thought, and twirled an index finger, incanting, "*Shyneo lampa.*" A floating ball of lightning *sizzled* to life above her, casting bright blue light on the slab. She used the chisel and a work brush to expose more of the groove, until its implication became obvious.

"And there it is," she whispered, stepping back.

Ottentus stepped near, a hand pressed to his cheek. "By gods, Arcanist Stone. This is no mere slab." He turned to the assembled throng, opening his hands. "This is a door."

AMIDST SNOWY WOODS

The excitement after that discovery was palpable, and Ottentus had a workman fetch more chisels from his cohorts so that everyone, from Thia to Ottentus, could chip away at the rock. Much coffee was consumed, yet the work was slow and tedious, for Anna insisted on casting Reveal upon each rune in case one was booby-trapped. Despite their combined efforts, they barely got through uncovering a tenth of the mammoth door, and it remained difficult to see its true size, for even using ladders they had yet to find the top edge.

"It'll take tendays to get through this," Thia said, wiping her sweaty brow before tossing aside her chisel. "Ugh, I'm pooped."

"Then there's all the protective arcanery Master Ottentus saw that the master builder had placed on the door," Ralf muttered, throwing his chisel up and catching it. "Which we will have to contend with."

"Luckily that 'we' doesn't involve us," Thia muttered, side-glancing at Ottentus and Anna. She elbowed Ralf. "When's supper? Go snag us a bite, would you?"

"I am not your servant!"

"Then why are you grinning like that?" She whapped him on the shoulder. "Go fetch, boy. Remember that one play?" She stuck out her tongue and curled her hands into paws. "Was I the dog? I was, wasn't I?"

"Really now," Thomas snapped. "What is the matter with you? Have you no sense of propriety?"

"Dad, I was just reminding him about some stupid play —"

"Enough. Go fetch us some supper."

Thia snorted. "Fetch." She elbowed Ralf again. "Get it?"

"Too funny," he said, though without mirth. "Come on. We'll both go. I'll show you where the mess hall is," and he and Thia departed.

Anna watched them go, uncomfortable with how familiar they were with each other. And the way Ralf looked at her, with that expression that warmed up when she paid attention to him, but died the moment she looked away, unnerved her. She wondered if it was a flaw in his character, perhaps related to the same decision-making that had brought in a potentially necromantic book.

Ottentus, meanwhile, was frowning at a series of runes, a thick book on ancient runecraft floating open before him.

"It could be a recombination puzzle hiding a kargeyasnara," Thomas muttered, taking another sip of coffee.

"Yes, yes, but I do not believe that to be the case."

Anna raised her chisel to opine on the matter when it vanished with a *pop*. Unsurprised that the Create Simple Object casting had finally timed out, she reached for Thia's chisel when an alarm sounded in her head.

"Please excuse me. I think another rodent just got into the cupboards," she said, the code she and Thomas used for whenever someone trespassed across their land. Mostly they were kids simply exploring the "haunted forest," sometimes city folks on a stroll, or even messengers trying to deliver a message to Anna instead of to the academy, where she told everyone to send their letters.

"Mmm," Thomas and Ottentus toned at the same time before continuing the conversation.

"Right, I'll leave you to it, then," Anna muttered, and strode off. They had a lot more chiseling to do before the really interesting work began anyway.

Once outside, she glanced around in search of Thia, but couldn't see her and Ralf, and she wasn't sure where the mess hall was. Knowing she was safer here with her father and Ottentus than in most other places, Anna turned her attention to home ground, choosing a spot away from the alarm so as not to give herself away. "*Impetus peragro,*" she incanted, and appeared with a *thwomp* in the snowy forest surrounding the tower.

After making an initial sweep and finding nothing untoward, she imagined her soul and body becoming like water with water, air with air, and then one with the arcane ether, as demanded by the notoriously difficult-to-cast 15th degree Invisibility spell. With her thoughts aligned, she carefully dragged an open hand down her body whilst whispering, *"Arcan persona visinabla balan."* Silently, her entire person became invisible.

Unlike the Chameleon spell and its famous extension which allowed for movement, a properly cast Invisibility spell emitted no shimmer even while moving—at least to the naked eye. However, were the watcher to cast Reveal and the invisible person moved, the watcher would see a shimmer. It would take a warlock highly trained in Reveal to spot an invisible person standing absolutely still.

Anna was one of the few warlocks able to cast the Invisibility spell to full effect. Most warlocks, even high-degree ones, learned the bare bones and avoided casting it in the field, all due to its sheer complexity—and the occasional misfire, which sometimes resulted in a warlock making themselves permanently invisible, a fate far more tragic than hilarious, especially for the loved ones in the warlock's life.

With the spell cast, Anna strode forth, splaying a hand. *"Un vun asperio aurum enchantus,"* she whispered, and swaths of familiar tendrils lit up. She passed oaks and pines and cedars and spruces, sticking close to thick trunks, keeping to tracks already laid in the snow, and only slowed once she heard two male voices speaking in rough Abrandian. Ever wary of the history between herself and that kingdom, and how many an Abrandian cursed her to this day for how she had dared to vanquish their champion, putting a halt to their invasion of Ohm, Anna prepared her mind to cast Tongues.

"Translateo commona linguino Abrandian," she whispered, and was instantly able to understand them.

"Place is trapped foot to head, so let's wait 'ere."

"This has got to be the spot, though, right? Look at them tendrils. They're practically masterworks. And that's just the ones we can see through the footprints. What if we stepped on one already?"

"She'd have come by now."

"What if she cursed us without us knowing? Are we aiming too high here?"

"Will you shut up? We only get one crack at this."

There was a pause. "You're sure the brat walks this way?"

"Positive. She's lazy and takes the same route."

Anna's blood flash-boiled upon hearing this. These men were after her daughter, no doubt to hold for ransom! And oh how she would make them *rue* conjuring such a plot …

She crept forth, placing one careful foot before the other, keeping her movements molasses-slow. She soon spotted the men hiding behind the trunk of an oak, their bodies covered with tendrils that showed a Chameleon casting enhanced with the movement extension. Her Reveal casting also allowed her to see clear silhouettes, which showed they were dressed in the Ordinary clothes of the nobility, no doubt to blend in with the crowds of the Rose Quarter. One man was bearded and much larger than the other. Their hands were splayed, each having cast Reveal, their eyes on alert. They had chosen a good spot too, for the oak was gigantic and had few trees near it, giving them plenty of room.

"It'll be just like the last job."

"A quick snatch 'n' 'port."

"Right."

So you're professionals, Anna thought, moving forth into an opening amidst the trees, wanting to get within Telekinesis range.

One of the men looked right at her. "Oi, what's that?" he whispered.

Anna froze. *Competent ones at that.*

"You see that? Right there."

"I don't see nothin'," the other whispered.

"I'm tellin' you I saw something. What if she cast Invisibility?"

"Do you know how hard it is to get that spell right?"

"Yeah, but she ain't no normal warlock."

The men stared right at her, and Anna kept absolutely still. She could hit them from there with most spells, but she suspected they could still get away as they had likely rehearsed what to do. All they needed was a moment to duck behind a trunk and teleport elsewhere. If they got away, she would have to deal with them again in the future, a chance she did not dare take. She had to get this right—she, too, would only get one crack at this.

For Thia, she thought, standing rock still. *Fifty feet. Ten more to go. Don't breathe.*

"Sorry, but you was seeing things, chum. Nerves and all."

"Yeah, I reckon so."

Don't breathe. They're still suspicious. Stay. Abso. Lutely. Still.

"High-value target."

"High-value target," the other repeated, and they chuckled.

"What's the first thing you is goin' to buy?"

"A manor and my own gang of slaves."

"I'm goin' to retire."

"That's what you said about the last job."

"Aye, but this is the big one."

"Aye. The big one."

While the two men bantered about what they would do with the money they would earn ransoming her daughter, Anna readied to start moving again. But just as she raised her foot to take the next step, there came a *thwomp* from behind her, followed by two pairs of feet tromping in the snow.

The men fell silent and stared directly at her, forcing her to stay absolutely still once more.

"Mom's going to be angry with you for teleporting while …"

"While what? Spit it out, girl."

"You know …"

The footsteps halted. Anna imagined Thomas glaring at Thia.

"Fine. It's none of my business," Thia said with a heavy sigh.

"Damn right it isn't. Unlike you, Daughter, I have *earned* the right to imbibe."

"Ugh … I … I think I'm going to be sick."

"You *still* get sick from teleporting? Are you jesting me?"

There came the sound of someone briefly running, followed by a retching noise.

"Disappointing," Thomas said. "And I am not speaking about you getting sick. I am speaking about your slothful ways. Had you studied harder, you wouldn't be sick right now, would you?"

"Just leave me alone, Dad."

Refusing to get distracted, Anna watched the men with iron resolve. They, too, were absolutely still, biding their time.

"Get in the house. We are going to have a talk."

"House?" Thia scoffed. "More like a prison."

The pair marched on as they argued, coming closer and closer.

Anna waited, a viper ready to strike. When the footsteps were practically upon her, the men moved. Anna struck, slapping her wrists together and roaring, "*Annihilo bato!*" A crack of thunder rent the air as two bolts of lightning shot at the men, who were peeking out from opposite sides of the trunk. The brigands, however, had excellent reflexes and, combined with the distance involved, had *just* enough time to roll aside and simultaneously snap, "*Impetus peragro!*"

Anna, now visible from the sudden movement—Invisibility was as prone to failure as Chameleon—bolted to their position, hand splayed with Reveal, which she was strong enough to have kept lit.

"Mom? Mom! What's going on!"

"Anna? What happened? Who was that?"

Anna ignored her family and focused on the wispy remnants of tendrils that remained from the teleport, which swirled like a whirlpool.

The majority from the man on the right drifted eastward, and judging by depth of drift, the distance was around three leagues, too far for an accurate teleport. But when she switched to examining the ones from the man on the left, the majority swirled westward, with a distance of perhaps a league. By the time she realized the men had planned opposite escape routes, the tendrils were gone, and she had failed to analyze a more accurate distance measurement, which could have allowed her to teleport after the second man, who had been closer. She evidently needed more practice sniffing out direction.

"Shoot," she hissed, slamming a fist into her thigh.

"Mom!" Thia ran up to her, face pale and sweaty.

Anna leveled her gaze at Thomas. "Why didn't you cast Reveal as we had trained?"

"I forgot, all right?"

"And why would you forget something so vital in keeping our daughter safe!" Anna roared, losing her temper. "Do you realize what those men wanted? Huh?" She stabbed a finger at Thia. "That's right! They were here for *her*."

"How do you know—"

Anna patted her chest. "Because I heard them! You understand? I *heard* them."

Thomas paled as much as their daughter.

Anna ran a hand through her tightly woven hair and down her braid as she began pacing. "We'll have to take extra precautions now. No more walking in and out. Thia gets an escort to *and* from the academy, and by teleportation *only*."

"Oh, great," Thia muttered. "Why don't you just chain me up while you're at it."

"Quiet," Thomas hissed. "This is serious."

"I know, Dad, but I don't want to—"

"Would you rather be kidnapped? Huh?"

"Maybe they'll put me out of my misery," Thia muttered.

"We ought to be prudent and hire a bodyguard," Anna added.

"Don't even think about it, Mom! I barely have any privacy as is! No. Way! *No way!*"

"It would be for your own good, Thia," Thomas said.

"I can handle being escorted like a baby back and forth but I won't put up with some—" Thia flapped her hands about. "—*goon* watching me every moment of the day! You can forget it. And if you try to smother me like that, I'll sneak off. Besides, who's to say the people you tried to shoot weren't merely exploring the forest here?"

"Didn't you hear your mother? She heard them talking—"

"Maybe that's what she *wanted* to hear! Maybe she entirely misread the situation. You know how paranoid Mom is. I just want to be normal. Ugh, I wish I was born an Ordinary."

"You'd still be our daughter and in even more danger," Anna replied, hurt by her words. "For you would not even be able to defend yourself."

"I meant something else."

After a stunned pause, Thomas and Anna talked at the same time, both gesticulating at Thia and at the spot the men had hidden.

"Utterly foolish of you to think your mother would make something up like that—"

"Thia, we are trying to protect you—"

"Have you no sense of self-preservation, girl—"

"Do you not understand what just happened—"

"How could you say you would prefer to have been born into another family? How could you say that?"

As they went on, Thia merely folded her arms and rolled her eyes, head bobbing about in a *Talk all you want, I've heard it all before* manner.

Thomas finally faced her and gripped her arms. "Do you not comprehend that your foolery will get you killed?" He jostled her. "Do you not comprehend that?"

Anna grabbed his arm. "Stop it! Let go of her!"

Thomas stepped back. "I have had enough! You are getting a bodyguard."

"No, Dad—"

"It's final. And forget servants! *Forget them!*" he roared, face crimson as he took a turn pacing.

"Dad, no, I swear I'll be good and I won't try to leave the academy or home or—"

"Plain as day that you do not respect us, let alone yourself."

"Dad, please—"

"We'd need someone with a lot of time on their hands. Someone who can be trusted. Someone with honor and integrity and, above all, skill. What's the name of that Black Eagle who retired?" Thomas repeatedly snapped his fingers, trying to jog his memory. "You know the one. She was our Dueling Club teacher back in the day."

"Niterra Bladesong," Anna replied. "But she is too old."

"She was a kingdom champion. Besides, it is obvious this one needs some elderly guidance."

"Dad ... Mom ... please ..."

"Do you want to approach her or should I?" Thomas asked, stomping about. "I have had it! Do you hear me? *Had it!* They will try to kidnap her and maybe kill her and I could not live with myself if anything happened ..."

Anna sighed. "Leave it to me. I'll check the property is secure and go right away." As her husband ranted on about Thia and the situation, Anna stepped before her daughter. "Thia, you are all we have left. Do you understand?"

Thia merely held herself, face cross, reminding Anna of not just her sister, but of herself. "I'm sorry. I know how you must feel, I do, but—"

"Stuff it, Mom."

Thomas abruptly whirled on Thia. "They could come back. Get in the house. *Get in the house!*"

"Ugh, I hate you both," and Thia stormed off, with a still-ranting Thomas following, but now he was also watching the trees like a hawk, hands raised in attack formation.

Anna watched them go, feeling utterly helpless. How could she govern her students so well, manage her studies and research, take out the occasional corrupt village warlord or help the city arrest a notorious wanted warlock—such things were expected of a kingdom champion, after all—but she could not, for the life of her, get a grip on her own daughter? Or her own husband, for that matter? How had it come to this?

She sighed again and began to check the property, with the plan to reinforce or add enchantments as she saw fit.

* * *

An hour later, as dusk settled, and after reinforcing her own property and teleporting off to another, Anna walked up to a grove of gnarled oaks caked with snow. Overseeing those oaks, like a cantankerous captain of the guard, loomed a large vine-encrusted manor so black with tar it reminded Anna of her ancestral castle. She'd asked the king's retinue for the favor of divulging the famed Black Eagle's address, and was told the woman had been granted an estate just behind the Black Castle.

Anna almost pressed on before realizing who she was about to visit. She instead splayed a hand, incanting, "*Un vun asperio aurum enchantus.*" Sure enough, a whole field of tendrils lit up before her—colorful and complex enchantments of every make and sort, from paralyze and sound trap to, what appeared to Anna, a portal trap. She imagined some hapless fool getting teleported to a lake or, worse, some dungeon.

"Likely a dungeon, knowing the old warrior," Anna muttered. Then the sound trap gave her an idea. Poorly enchanted, sound traps sent an alarm at every noise and could be triggered by something as innocuous as a bird call. But a properly enchanted one only sent an alarm when a human was nearby. The difference between the two was what separated a mediocre warlock from a great one. Few could properly cast a sound trap, and Niterra Bladesong, the former kingdom champion and Black Eagle, was one of them.

Anna twirled her finger. "*Shyneo lampa*," and out popped a pumpkin-sized ball of lightning, bathing the area in blue light. With another flick of the finger, her scion floated out of her pocket, remaining nearby like a floating puppy, dutiful in its silence. Then she stepped up to the enchantment, leaned forth, and said, "Hello, Bladesong."

There came a *thwomp* behind her. "Who seek death?" croaked an old voice with a choppy Nodian accent Anna still associated with getting lambasted for her slovenly performance in Dueling Club all those years ago. "Speak!"

Not wanting to spook the old woman, Anna did not turn around. Instead, she slowly raised her hands for Niterra to see. "And they tell me I'm paranoid."

"Who are you? Turn so I see face!"

Anna slowly turned, palms still open, and saw a hunched old woman in a cream nightgown, hands in attack position, nineteen rings of air around her right arm. Her hair was gray and unruly, ebony skin blotchier than Anna recalled, for the Black Eagle suffered from the skin pigment condition known as skiniligo. But the diamond chin and angular face were the same, as was the fierceness in the eyes.

"My successor." The woman did not lower her arms. "A fancy trick."

"I am no doppelganger," Anna retorted. "Nor am I someone who cast Metamorphosis. By all means, see for yourself."

"This I do. You move, you die." Watching Anna like a hawk, the woman splayed the fingers of a hand, hissing, "*Un vun asperio aurum enchantus.*"

While she examined her, Anna extended a thumb, aiming it over her shoulder. "Where does the portal go, anyway?"

"Quiet! I focus." The woman's head tilted this way and that. She kept grunting as she examined Anna's tendril evidence, visible in the floating lamp and scion. "Maybe high-quality casting. If you Stone woman, you say what happened between us under shadow of Devil's Gate."

"You found me cowering behind an illusory wall I had cast. You told me I had been betrayed and to keep out of sight of your lot."

The Black Eagle grunted and lowered her arms. "So it you. Thirty years since you face Abrandian champion. *How* you beat him say to me you deserve to be next Solian champion."

"Honestly, I found managing your class after you much harder."

Niterra blurted a chuckle, which she quickly suppressed. Then a short laugh escaped her wrinkled lips, followed by a long, wheezing laugh that had her slapping her knees. Anna couldn't help but join in on the laughter, for there were few women in Sithesia who could understand the toils of shepherding unruly teenage warlocks eager to prove themselves in clumsy mock duels on a muddy training yard.

When the laughter settled down, Niterra flicked a hand at the manor. "I have good Sierran wine. Strong. You come?"

"Thought you'd never ask."

"Come, come, Stone."

"But I'm not much of a drinker. Have something lighter?"

"Titan wine good for health. You come. Mind step. Do not want to appear in dungeon."

So I was right, Anna thought, eyeballing the portal trap as they passed it, for she had kept Reveal lit. "You know those are illegal, right?" She asked it amusedly, for no one in all of Sithesia would challenge the famed Black Eagle—not to mention warlocks protecting their property were given a lot of leeway.

Niterra scoffed. "Age has its privileges."

"Mmm."

They walked up to the manor, which was as dark as the night. Its old brick was crumbling, the vines long dead, the roof shingles askew.

"Looks as haunted as my castle," Anna muttered, snuffing her large floating lamp in favor of lighting her palm, which didn't feel as obtrusive.

"Previous Black Eagle head owned it. They give to us until we die. Then pass to next victim. Call it an honor. I call it a tomb." Niterra walked up to the old plank door emblazoned with the Black Eagle crest. It creaked open before her without any gesture given. "You speak of your castle, Stone, but you no live in it." She stepped out of the way to allow Anna to pass. "Why that so?"

Anna noted the door enchantment's complexity as she stepped inside, the planks creaking underfoot. "Long story." The hall was dark and smelled of mold and old books.

"Husband. Daughter. Loneliness. No story needed."

"I suppose," Anna muttered. She had visited Castle Arinthian less and less over the years. Some time ago, after Panza had died, having bequeathed his scion to a worthy Ohmish champion, and after a particularly turbulent time arguing with Thomas as to where they should bring up their newly born daughter, Anna had boarded the old castle up, then sat out front of it for a whole day. It had been a meditative practice to honor Panza, her old mentor and friend. Though she still paid the pricey taxes and checked on the castle, fearing that some hoodlum or nefarious fiend would break in to learn or steal its secrets.

"No teenager want to live in middle of nowhere, castle or no castle."

"Mmm."

The hunched old woman tottered onward into the darkness, planks creaking beneath her. Anna followed, wondering if the old Black Eagle used light at all.

"How is your arcanery?" Anna asked as they entered a musty parlor of mahogany bookshelves and dusty settees surrounding a gigantic bear-hide carpet.

"Stiff, but can still—" She snapped her fingers. "—snap the neck of anyone, man or beast." Niterra glared at Anna a moment, and in the flash of her eyes, Anna saw the fierceness had not dulled over the years. Then the woman turned her attention to a series of candles, which she lit the old-fashioned way—with a flint and steel striker.

Anna moved to help with her lightning. "May I?"

"You may *not*," Niterra replied, efficiently lighting each candle with one strike. "You smell?" she asked, closing her eyes and inhaling. "Burnt metal remind Niterra of old duels. Of fighting."

Anna inhaled and saw what she meant, although for her the metallic burnt smell was more synonymous with lightning frying armor-covered flesh.

"There was a time I also thought of that smell as lighting candles," Niterra said, watching Anna.

"There was a time it made me think of fireplaces and pipe smokers." After Anna snuffed her palm to allow the cozy candle glow to prevail, she saw that the bear carpet was a rich crimson, meaning it was a Nodian bear.

"Not my kill," Niterra said as she went to a towering shelf of cubbyholes, a quarter of which were filled with large dark bottles. She picked out a bottle near the top and floated it to a rickety cart, on top of which sat a lone glass goblet. "Hmm," she toned, glancing about in search of something before livening up. "Ah, there." She flicked at a second goblet sitting upside-down on a distant shelf and made it float nearby.

Anna stepped near the floating goblet. Jewels glinted around an inscription, which she read aloud. " '*Loyaltos, creatos, vira.*' " Loyalty, ingenuity, strength—the motto of the Black Eagles. "I really don't need something this fancy."

"Nonsense. You honored guest."

Anna, not wanting to make a fuss, looked on as the woman floated the gigantic bottle over. Niterra then raised a finger and wiggled it and the giant cork in this giant bottle of old Titan wine began wiggling along with the finger, until there came a *pop* as it shot free. With a tilt of her head, the floating bottle tilted above the bejeweled goblet and poured out wine as black as pitch, filling it near to the top before filling the other goblet—all without a single drop falling to the cart.

Sharp as ever, Anna noted, accepting the floating goblet.

Niterra floated the bottle to a table and raised her liberally filled goblet. "To old days."

Anna raised hers in turn. "To the old days."

The pair of women took a sip, and Anna immediately coughed, for the wine was like acid.

Niterra snorted a laugh. "Strong, yes?"

Anna could only nod as she clapped her chest.

Niterra took a long gulp before raising her goblet once more. "And to Headmistress Roth, may Unnameables let rest in peace."

After regaining control, Anna raised her goblet to the woman who had been her former headmistress and mentor. "To Roth," and she took a tiny sip.

The woman had passed quietly in her sleep at a ripe old age. She had been so respected that foreign dignitaries, the king and queen, and the entire academy had attended her memorial ceremony, one of the grandest in a decade. Anna had even delivered a speech about how Roth had been a virtuous example of passing knowledge on to the next generation of warlocks.

Niterra drifted to an old armchair and sank into it with a groan. "Now what does current kingdom champion want from former kingdom champion?"

"You protected the royal lineage almost all your life."

"Fifty years."

"Fifty years," Anna echoed, shaking her head in disbelief.

"And how quick they passed, Stone. How quick they passed ..."

"Mmm."

The pair of women mulled this over in the thick silence before Anna reanimated. "I was wondering if you still had an appetite for protecting."

Niterra smiled cheekily. "I eighty-four years old but feel as young as you look, Stone."

"Except I *feel* much older than I look."

"That because ..." Niterra made a show of glancing down at Anna's pocket.

"That is indeed the reason. A side effect, if you will, and one that is not always welcome. One that ... causes tension for my husband."

"One would think husband happy wife not grow wrinkled like old apple."

"Mmm." Anna paced the room, swirling the goblet in her hand as she examined the old books. "My family is in danger, Champion Bladesong."

"All who wield scion have danger as companion."

"My daughter. They've threatened to kidnap her to get at me."

"Who is this 'they'?"

"Probably men wanting quick riches, but I cannot know for sure."

The old woman grunted and took another sip.

"I was wondering if you would be interested in watching our daughter. I would of course pay you ... that is, *we* would pay you—"

"I do it free."

Anna, who was inspecting the spine of a thick tome titled *Famous Feats of Legend*, turned around. "I'm sorry?"

"I do this—" Niterra chopped a flat palm left to right. "—no charge."

"But that is preposterous—"

"What, Stone think Niterra Bladesong need money in her old age? Stone look with eyes. See this place? Big. Useless. Niterra Bladesong forced to retire because Niterra Bladesong look old." Niterra made a claw of her hand and drew it to her chest. "But fire burns bright. Big bright. I do this for you, Stone ... my successor." She stood, giving a firm nod. "I do this for kingdom."

For the first time in a while, Anna was left speechless.

LATER IN THE NEXT QUINT

Anna hovered over a snoring dark-haired girl whose head was resting on her folded arms on her desk. She snapped her fingers. "Jones!"

The girl bolted upright, eyes wide, "Huh? Yes? What's happening?" As the class snickered, she rubbed her red eyes and looked up. "Oh, gosh, I'm *so* sorry, Arcanist Stone. I must have fallen asleep again …"

"You've been groggy for a while now. Is anything the matter?"

The girl fiddled with her thumbs. "M-my sister was born last quint and she's been crying non-stop so none of us have gotten much sleep at home and it's gotten so bad I fell asleep over breakfast and —"

The class chortled, only to be silenced by a single look from Anna. "I see," Anna said, still eyeballing her students. "And what classes do you have left today?"

"Arcane Servitude. After lunch, that is. And then Dueling Club."

"Would you perhaps like to leave early to catch up on sleep?"

The girl blinked. "Really? But … but it's a review quint. I can't miss anything."

"I can have a student bring you the lecture notes." Anna raised an eyebrow at the class in invitation.

Her daughter's hand shot up. "I volunteer my bodyguard."

The class burst with laughter as heads swiveled to glance up the rows of tiered seats at the old woman sitting in the back.

Ralf, sitting beside Thia, snickered as he elbowed her. "That old crone could barely sweep a broomstick, let alone some baddies."

Anna folded her arms. "I suppose you have no idea who that is, do you, Turman?" The famed Black Eagle had retired prior to his generation entering the academy, so few knew of her fierceness and prowess.

Ralf shrugged. "She's an old bag. So what?"

"Ooh," went the class, egging him on.

"Mmm. Let me tell you something, Turman. At eighty-four years of age, that 'old bag' could sweep the floor with you, one hand tied behind her back, while *blindfolded*."

"Ooh!" went the class again, louder.

Ralf folded his arms as well. "I would like to see her try."

"I accept challenge," Niterra barked from the rear of the class.

The class gasped, with a few slapping their hands over their mouths, as heads turned to the rear. Niterra, wearing the famous gold-fringed crimson robe of the Black Eagles, sat with poise, her face showing only a hint of the fierceness that had made her a legend back in her day.

Anna gave a nod. "It's settled. Former *kingdom champion* and retired *Black Eagle* Niterra Bladesong—" She made sure to emphasize the woman's various titles. "—who I had already scheduled as a guest arcanist to teach today's Dueling Club alongside me, will demonstrate to the class how a warlock who practices their art as they age can still be most formidable."

Ralf swallowed, started sinking into his chair, and promptly straightened. He shrugged, muttering, "Whatever."

"Mom, what are you doing?" Thia mouthed.

"Whatever indeed, Turman," Anna replied, ignoring her daughter. She strolled back to the blackboard as the class jostled each other and whispered excitedly. "Now then," she said, flicking a piece of chalk to her hand and using it to tap the blackboard, already filled with her neat writing. "Who can tell me the tongue-to-tendril ratio of Minor Illusion? And look lively, people. This question will be on next quint's exam." She glanced over her shoulder at the dark-haired girl. "Jones, what are you still doing here?"

"Are you kidding, Arcanist Stone? I'm wide awake now. Ain't no way in hell I'm missing Dueling Club now!"

Anna didn't let her smile show.

* * *

There came a knock at Anna's academy office door.

"Mmm?" Anna toned as she marked a student's scroll with a quill tipped with crimson ink. Two squat bottles of ink sat beside her on her desk—green and red. The green was almost completely full, but the red was nearing empty. Levitating beside the desk was a small cask filled with stones.

The knock came again.

"Yes, come in!" Anna called, realizing her grunt hadn't been heard through the thick old door.

That door opened and Syanda poked her head in. "Did you hear anything about something happening after classes?"

"Another unsanctioned fight?" Anna asked without looking up.

"Not exactly. Apparently, a certain retired Black Eagle and former kingdom champion is going to take on a 6th degree kid in the arena with both hands behind her back, blindfolded, and hobbled."

Anna tossed her quill at the red inkwell, taking minor delight in telekinetically lifting the lid and nudging the quill through the gap at the last moment. "Niterra is merely going to make a short demonstration in Dueling Club. She's a surprise guest lecturer."

"Word's spread like wildfire and everyone thinks it's going to be the butt-kicking of a generation. They're expecting a full-on duel to the death."

Anna stared flatly at Syanda before snorting a laugh. Syanda snuck inside to join Anna, closing the door behind her. Together the pair laughed at the absurdity of the student populace, which could *always* be counted on to twist things out of proportion.

Syanda smoothed her black arcanist robe that matched her thick curls and sat on Anna's desk. "Do you remember that time what's-his-face was scheduled to be whipped in the courtyard and everyone showed up thinking he was going to get hanged?"

Anna nodded through her chortling. "Wasn't that the one where some kid—who had been bullied by what's-his-face—put up hastily made posters declaring it would be the academy's first official hanging?"

"Oh, yeah, I forgot about that." Syanda sighed, still smiling. "Forgot that little detail. I think that was when I first started teaching and met you. Now look at us."

"Now look at us."

Syanda nodded at the floating cask. "Pushing ourselves today, are we? How long?"

Anna shrugged. Now and then she liked to push her telekinetic muscle. Perhaps inspired by Niterra's presence, today happened to be one of those days.

"I'd have a nosebleed by now." Syanda picked at her teeth with a fingernail. "Come on, did you take the head job or not?"

"Haven't decided yet."

Syanda threw up her hands. "Are you jesting me? What's there to decide? Anna, really now."

Anna expelled a deep breath while flapping a dismissive hand.

"You can't ignore it forever, you know."

"Just … got a lot on my mind."

"Then take me up on the offer for a goblet!"

"Too much on my plate. There's the excavation now too."

"Ooh, have they finally excavated the door?"

"Yes, and Thomas and Ottentus have been plucking away at it non-stop."

"How's that husband of yours doing, anyway?"

"When he's not at the dig, he's interrogating constables about a pair of goons with Abrandian accents."

"I'd be doing the same thing. That is, if I had a kid." The woman shrugged. "But then I don't have a kid so instead I drink." She laughed at herself, got up, and sashayed to the door. "I'm going out dancing later. You should come."

Anna tossed her braid over her shoulder and snorted. "I'd rather eat chalk."

"I know, I know. You don't dance. Work, work, work. That's all our future headmistress does."

Anna looked up, lips pressed together, to see Syanda's head lingering through the door. "The door for fun is clooosing, Anna. You better enjoy yourself while you still look youuuung …"

Anna couldn't help but smilingly shake her head at her cohort's antics.

"Fine, have fun marking essays!" and Syanda's head vanished, leaving the door partly open.

Anna grunted, flicked a finger, and the door shut. Then she picked up the quill, scraped the excess red ink off on the lid of the bottle, and returned to marking.

* * *

Anna glanced about the snowy courtyard. Her class was assembled in a wide circle, their shields raised, creating a colorful display of the seven elements, with the white shields of healing being the least prominent, seeing as they served in the capacity of healers instead of duelers.

Gawking over their shoulders was what felt like the entire academy of students—including some arcanists. One of those students was her daughter, an anxious-faced Thia. The girl had been incensed with her mother for letting this "charade" happen. But Anna needed to prove a point, not just to Thia, but to the class—and the school as a whole.

Anna raised a hand between the two combatants and waited until the chatter died down. For a long moment, time dragged. The sky was overcast and gray, and the air smelled as if snow would fall soon, just as it had for Anna's final victory at the Antioc Classic, a victory that cemented her run as unbeaten champion. She remembered the hush of the crowd prior to her own duel kicking off. The master of ceremonies raising her arm in victory after she had vanquished her foe. She remembered falling to her knees in the snow-covered sand to burst with a cry of victory and sorrow, grieving for those she wished could have been there to witness the historic moment. That was decades ago, and Anna had not stepped foot in an official arena since.

With silence achieved, Anna chopped at the air and sprang back, shouting, "Fight!"

The emerald-robed Ralf, six earth rings around his arm, slapped his wrists together, roaring, "Annihilo!"

Old Niterra, blindfolded and left hand tied behind her back with a leather cord, merely hopped aside and yanked with her right arm, encircled with nineteen airy rings. As a thick vine punched by the woman—smashing into a student's fiery shield with a *hiss*—Ralf flipped backward, his foot snagged by an air tendril. Niterra swiped sideways, hissing, "*Gosa!*" The usually two-armed off-the-books 13th degree air spell was still powerful enough to send Ralf rolling into the wall of shields, which shoved him back, much to the crowd's delight.

Ralf slapped his wrists together from the ground, shouting, "*Annihilo!*" Another thick vine shot at Niterra, who summoned a shield on her primary arm. As the vine thunked against an airy shield, the crowd cheered in awe, for switching shield arms was a tough thing to learn.

"Still zero-zero, but keep it tempered, Turman!" Anna shouted over the noise of the throng, reminding the young man of his responsibilities. She monitored from a perimeter around them, keeping a hand splayed with Reveal to ensure the tendrils aligned with the rules.

Niterra let her shield vanish, her gray hair bobbing as her head jerked about with the next spell, performed by throwing her arm toward the ground and shouting, "*Dawo draffa!*" A downdraft pressed Ralf into the snowy ground—and flattened a few students behind him. She kept her arm low, letting the wind pummel him for a moment before letting go. As the draft weakened, Niterra swirled her one free hand with surprising grace, incanting, "*Ipulato aero marjorus!*" A different gust, this one from below, picked a scrambling Ralf up and lifted him into the air.

"*Flustrato!*" Ralf shouted, flailing. But his casting was way off, and the Confusion spell slapped an innocent burgundy-robed girl upside the head. The girl, standing behind the shield wall, wobbled and began trundling away, mumbling inanities to herself.

"Watch your aim, Turman!" Anna called. The girl would be fine, but she was lucky he had not cast a more dangerous spell. Despite being tempered, stray spells could still hurt those who were not ready to defend themselves. Sure enough, after seeing the girl, many more students raised their shields.

Niterra listened to the wind before cupping her hand before her lips. "*Hooza,*" she incanted, dragging out the final vowel, making a long "Ahhhhh" sound. A strong wind plumed forth from her open mouth, fogging in the crisp air. It slammed into Ralf and threw him past the audience, raising cheers—and laughter.

"That's a point for Bladesong!" Anna called, raising a finger with one hand and making an *O* with her other. "One-zero."

As the crowd jostled Ralf back to the arena, Niterra shook out her shoulders and took a few rapid breaths, one ear always turned toward her opponent.

"Watch your footing, Turman," Anna said when the red-faced young man neared the outer shield wall.

He clucked his tongue at her and broke through the shields, sweeping both arms along the ground whilst roaring, "*Fiuria girata fissura!*" There came a deep cracking as the ground split with a fissure that shot forth, snaking toward Niterra.

The blindfolded woman only flashed a brief smile as she ran to the right and along the shield wall, using the mere sound of the students to keep herself clear of them, proving her nimbleness.

Ralf pointed ahead of her and the fissure veered straight at Niterra. This surprised Anna, who did not think any of the usually randomly meandering off-the-book elemental spells of the 7th degree were controllable. She had underestimated Ralf's ingenuity.

The students shouted in alarm and pushed to get out of the way, for the fissure headed right toward them too. This prompted Niterra to jump. Her timing was perfect as the crack shot underneath her—and continued into the crowd. A slew of students fell into it, forcing Anna to react. She shot her arms out and snagged them telekinetically before they fell too far. Luckily the fissure halted and other students grabbed on telekinetically to haul the unfortunates back up. She'd get him to repair the damage to the grounds later, a challenge that posed little trouble for an earth warlock.

"Irresponsible casting, Turman!" Anna shouted as the boy angrily launched a bevy of lower-degree spells—Fear and Deafness and Sleep and Confusion—at Niterra. Niterra danced about, though her head snapped back upon one landing.

"Physicals only get a point here!" Anna reminded the crowd when they cheered the hit. "Keep it confined, Turman," she added, seeing yet another of his spells smack into an innocent blue-robed boy.

Unbeknownst to Ralf, Niterra had been using the time dancing about to whisper a string of arcanery whilst subtly spinning a finger—"*Portus ea ire itum combata lina.*" It was the core ritual preparation to a certain spell Anna was all too keen to observe, for although she already knew the 17th degree root, having cast it in her own home, this was the legendary 19th degree standard version that elevated the spell to a whole other level. Anna's Reveal allowed her to see that the finger-spinning wound arcanery up or, in strict arcaneological parlance, "charged it up."

When Niterra appeared to stumble after getting hit with a second Confusion casting, Ralf pressed his apparent advantage and slapped his wrists together, shouting, "*Annihilo!*" Another vine punch shot forth at the blindfolded Niterra—and smashed into her chest, exploding into earthy shards. It had been properly tempered this time, and Anna raised a finger on each hand, shouting, "One-one!"

As the crowd roared, Niterra readied to unleash what she had been preparing, telling Anna the old woman had been strategic in which spells she let hit her and which she dodged, with the aim of keeping her concentration intact. The woman first bought time by viciously making a whipping gesture at the ground, roaring, "*Grau!*" causing a roar of air that sounded like a hundred wagons bearing down on everyone. It was so sudden and so deafening that not only did the entire crowd flinch or duck or cover their ears, but so did Ralf, who was the focus of the cacophony. Meanwhile, Niterra pointed at the sky above Ralf and drew a quick oval, shouting, "*Portus da!*"

"Portal there," Anna whispered out of reflex, following every nuance of the spell.

As a pitch-black oval burst to life above Ralf, lying flat like a plate, Niterra then drew a second oval *underneath* Ralf, incanting, "*Ata ei portus da!*"

"And a portal there," Anna translated as a second portal opened up beneath him. Ralf, who had just recovered from the 2nd degree Slam spell, cast at full 19th degree strength, was about to slap his wrists together—only to plummet through the portal. He instantly emerged from the one above and zipped right into the ground portal, only to reemerge from the top one to repeat the process, quickly falling faster and faster, until he was flailing like a plucked chicken and screaming, "Ahhhh!"

The last time Anna heard a crowd go that wild was when she had first run along the arena wall at the Antioc Classic.

Meanwhile, the blindfolded Niterra, one arm still tied behind her back, casually picked up a handful of snow, crushed it one-handed into a snowball, and tossed it at Ralf. The snowball slapped into his chest as he flew by with a scream.

Anna raised two fingers on one hand and one on the other. "Two-one!"

As Niterra packed another snowball, laughter spread through the crowd.

Splat! went the second snowball, smashing into his back. "Three-one!" This happened two more times, with the final snowball sent into Ralf's face.

"And that's five-one!" Anna called, pointing both arms at Niterra. "We have a victor!"

As the crowd roared and Ralf was now a falling blur, Niterra sliced at the air, shouting, *"Portus null!"* Before Ralf became a Canterran pancake, she expertly snagged him telekinetically, slowing and then halting his fall entirely, so that he remained floating just above the ground. Niterra held him for a moment before yanking her hand back. He fell with a *thud*, and the old woman, still blindfolded, one arm still tied behind her back, bowed toward him in the old way.

The crowd stormed inward. People helped her remove the blindfold and the cord around her arm so they could congratulate her and pester her with questions.

Anna stepped up to Ralf to offer him a hand up, but he only scowled at her and searched about in the crowd until Thia ran to him to help him up herself. Anna instead went to quell the crowd by waving her arms.

"For mercy's sake, people, let the woman breathe! Shoo. *Shoo!* And watch your step!" When they gave Niterra space, Anna stepped around the fissure and placed her hands behind her back. "The spell you just witnessed, one of only perhaps two people in the whole kingdom could cast competently." *The other person being in an excavation at this very moment*, she thought. "Its name?" She pressed a finger behind an ear, angling it forward.

"Combat Portal!" a bunch of older students shouted, faces split with glee.

"Correct. As with many spells of legend, the 19th degree spell you witnessed has been the bane of many a warlock. It is one of the most difficult spells to cast in battle, yet you saw that it can be done. Not just by a woman of eighty-three years of age, but blindfolded and with one arm tied behind her back."

The crowd cheered and clapped and whistled as Niterra stood proud, face just as fearsome as when Anna had been the woman's young student.

"Niterra Bladesong taught me many things," Anna continued, turning slowly in a circle to address the throng. "One of those things is, no matter how old one gets, one must always practice the rudiments. I thus charge you witnesses, you stalwart souls of the academy, to go home and practice those rudiments. Practice, practice, *practice!*"

As the students broke up and began departing, Anna flapped a hand at the ground. "Dueling Club class stays for a moment." When her students had assembled around her, some still holding their shields up, having gotten caught up in the moment, Anna raised her chin. "Note that, although Turman is the best in his degree, he could not take advantage of his hobbled opponent. Why was that?" When people remained mute, Anna raised an eyebrow at Ralf, who stood beside her daughter. "Turman? Care to comment?"

He shrugged. "She got lucky."

This caused people to boo.

Anna raised her hand, silencing them. "Would anyone else care to comment on what happened?"

Something amazing transpired. Her daughter, not even part of the class and hardly known for volunteering an answer, blurted, "She kept him off balance."

Disbelieving eyes turned to Thia. Ralf flashed her a look that would have curdled fresh milk.

"Exactly right," Anna said, giving a subtle and proud nod at her daughter. "The difference in this battle was timing, choice, and delivery," she went on, noting that Ralf shrugged off Thia's hand. "Experience counts for a lot more than spell strength. Wisdom allows one to end a battle with the least amount of energy expended."

"And she didn't even cast a spell like Slow Time," someone blurted, and people laughed, though there was tension in the laughter, with a few catcalls thrown in expecting a demonstration of the mythical 20th degree spell.

Anna raised her hands and cut them off before they got carried away. "Such spells are not for trivial occasions, and certainly not to be cast in jest or for impatient students eager for a show. Let us instead show our gratitude by lending a round of applause to my esteemed predecessor, former kingdom champion and Black Eagle Niterra Bladesong." Anna clapped along with the throng, nodding at the old woman, who allowed everyone to see the hint of a genuine smile before hiding it in another bow.

"All right, get to studying, people, and good luck on your exams next quint!" Anna called. "Now off with you! Shoo!" She smiled and the class chortled and dispersed. "Turman—fix the grounds, would you, please?"

Ralf smacked his lips, stepped up to the fissure, and muttered an incantation, guiding and tugging at the earth until it closed fully. When Thia approached him to talk, he glared at her for so long she dropped her head as if ashamed. "You can forget about later," he hissed before storming off.

Anna walked up to stand beside her daughter. "What was happening later?"

"Nothing anymore, Mom. And stop spying on me."

"I was hardly spying." She gave Thia's arm a gentle squeeze. "It is very difficult to speak one's mind when one feels the weight of loyalty pressing for silence. For that, dear daughter, I am proud of you."

Thia looked up at Anna and her face melted. "Oh, Mom," and she threw her arms around her mother—and burst into tears.

Anna was so stunned she stood there, gawking down at her poor daughter, before embracing her with a hug and patting her back.

"That was most refreshing," Niterra said, looking on. "Thank you, Stone."

"Thank *you*, venerable one," Anna replied.

The woman winced as she rubbed her sides. "I very sore."

"I can imagine." She continued patting her daughter's back before the girl stepped away.

"She troubled girl," Niterra noted quietly as the pair watched Thia stroll about, kicking the snow whilst mumbling angrily at herself. "I watch her all quint. Something bother her."

"Any idea what it is?"

Niterra shook her head.

Anna sighed. Then she recalled what she had seen. "I don't suppose you, uh, would be open to teaching me that spell, would you?"

Niterra glanced Anna up and down. "Stone think she can use this old fart of a woman for her gain ..."

"No, I'm sorry, I didn't mean—"

Niterra burst with a choppy laugh.

"You were jesting," Anna noted, adding in a mutter, "Didn't know you had a sense of humor."

"Few know Niterra. But I teach. I teach you spell. We work when girl sleep or study."

"How can I ever repay you for this great service to me? The gods know how expensive 19th degree mentorship is."

"Stone be honest with Niterra. Be friend to this old woman. Deal?"

Anna could hardly believe what she was hearing. Niterra had to be lonely and bored indeed in that decrepit old manor. Not having had a friend quite like her before, Anna smiled bittersweetly and reached out a hand. "Deal."

AFTER SUPPER

"There's been a breakthrough!" Thomas's voice floated in after a portal *whoosh*.

Anna, Niterra, and a mopey Thia, all of whom were having mugs of honeyed pine needle tea in the dining area, raised their heads.

"It's indeed a kargeyasnara!"

"What's that again?" a sheepish Thia whispered.

Anna leveled a *You ought to know that* look at her daughter, but upon seeing the hurt that remained from earlier, she added in a whisper, "A slip-rune sequence puzzle."

"It old arcanery," Niterra whispered with a wink.

"Oh. Thanks."

"And probably the most complex kargeyasnara I have ever seen," Thomas called, throwing off his boots and mitts. With his stuff scattered on the floor about him, he intertwined his hands to rest on top of his gray-haired head, staring off at nothing in particular. "Not even Ottentus has seen a puzzle *this* complex. Could take months to work it out." After a thoughtful pause, he wiggled two fingers. "But we managed to excavate the remainder of the door. That's how motivated we've been. Oh, and guess what?"

"A raccoon popped out and sang everyone a verse from 'The Goon that went too Soon'?

Thomas blinked. "What? No! And spare me that nonsense, Thia. This is an exciting time! Don't ruin it with your usual …"

"My usual what?"

"Pessimism. Gloominess. Sarcasm. I don't know, pick one."

"I choose sarcasm then."

Anna patted her daughter's hand, winking and cheekily whispering, "It's an exciting time for your father."

"And for your mother too. This is *her* research as much as mine. Anyway, we've found a runic inscription bearing *three* candles in triangular formation."

"The witch's mark," Thia said, adding in a mumble, "I know *that* one at least."

"Do you recall the history of the mark, though?" Anna asked, encouraging her daughter with a smile.

Thia frowned in thought. "Arcaneologically speaking, three candles in a triangular formation usually refer to the dark age between the years 500 to 1500 after The Founding, but many scholars believe the actual mark is much, *much* older."

Anna opened a bewildered hand at her daughter. "Look at that. Totally capable of brilliance." Suddenly Thia reminded Anna more of herself than ever.

A red-faced Thia took a sip of her tea and, to Anna's surprise, went on. "It was a time when many innocents were declared as witches and burned at the stake in groups of three. Warlocks were persecuted by Ordinaries—" Thia raised a finger. "—and even by fellow warlocks posing as converts, greatly setting arcanery back and forcing warlocks as a whole to hide and take precautions. To this day, the number three is considered bad luck." She shrugged. "At least by the more superstitious sort."

As Anna shook her head at her daughter, smiling proudly whilst trying to fathom why she could not apply herself when it mattered, Thomas wiggled his fingers and growled in a witchy voice, "Oooh, an evil omen doth cometh! Bad luck for *aaalll* …"

"What about the family curse?" Thia asked. "I thought you believed in curses."

Thomas wilted. "Oh. Right. Perhaps I ought not to tempt the Fates with blasphemy. But returning to the topic at hand—"

"Is Ralfie still there?" Thia interrupted, revolving her earthen mug to warm her hands.

Thomas dropped his arms. "Who? Oh, the kid. No, he left. Probably got bored again while the adults worked."

"He's not a kid, Dad. We're woman and man grown!"

Thomas scoffed. "Then maybe you two should act like it."

"Ugh, I'm so sick of this." Thia shoved her half-finished tea away and stomped by her father, muttering, "I'll be in my room."

Anna raised a hand after her. "Thia—" but dropped it upon seeing her summon the portal to the third floor, where her room was, and step through it with a huff. "Really, Thomas. Your daughter was demonstrating her hidden brilliance and you chastised her!"

Thomas merely rubbed his scruffy chin, ignoring his family. "The witch's mark could mean anything in this context, though. Hell, witches, demons, arcanery, secrets, ancient knowledge, a warning, a source of power ... truly anything."

"Perhaps you ought to focus on making amends with your daughter."

"What? What amends?"

"You hurt her feelings."

"Her feelings get hurt when a street cat saunters away instead of letting her pet it, or when you don't recognize one of her cryptic quotes, or even when you breathe wrong. Remember when she accused me of maliciously making my nose whistle every time I breathed in? Her feelings are like—" Thomas waved a hand about, mimicking wavy air. "—the weather. Or a flock of birds."

Anna wanted to share a look with Niterra but did not want to disparage her husband to someone watching over their daughter.

"We'll need your help solving the kargeyasnara, I think," Thomas went on. "You're brilliant at these sorts of things. Ottentus even said so."

"Did he now?"

Thomas drifted to the kitchen and began banging around. "Don't sound so unenthusiastic. Where are the mugs, anyway? There's still tea, right?"

"Where they always are. And no, you have to make some."

Thomas cursed under his breath as cupboards banged. Meanwhile, the women sipped their tea at the supper table. Anna felt Niterra's gaze but did not meet it. Seeing Thomas act so callously at home was one thing, but doing it in front of someone else was humiliating—and eye-opening. He hadn't so much as said hello, let alone pecked her on the lips as he used to do. And she couldn't remember the last time he had yanked on her and laughingly carried her to the bedroom.

Niterra watched Anna, but instead of commenting, she pointed a hand toward the floor.

Anna raised an eyebrow.

"She still home," Niterra reported, withdrawing the hand. They had each enchanted a pebble, with Anna respectfully asking Thia to carry them on her person at all times in case she were kidnapped. Anna had further considered enchanting something of hers in secret, but did not want to disrespect her daughter any further than she already had.

"You think you bad mother," Niterra noted as there came the sound of a pot being filled with water from the kitchen.

Anna said nothing, only kept revolving her mug of tea like Thia had.

"Remember deal."

"I *am* a bad mother," Anna confessed. "A horrible mother," adding in a mutter, "just like my mother was to me." She plopped her face in her hands, resting her elbows on the table. "The blasted cycle is repeating itself, and it feels like, despite my very best efforts, I'm just along for the ride."

Thomas slid out of the kitchen. "Want to work on it tonight? The kargeyasnara?"

Anna spoke through her hands. "I'm exhausted and I have classes tomorrow."

"Oh. Too bad."

She heard him slip back into the kitchen, where the banging continued along with mutterings of, "What does a man have to do to get some grub around here?"

You should hit the tavern! Anna wanted to shout, for he had once again missed supper with his family. To be fair, she had done the very same thing countless times—many *more* times in fact than he had, all in pursuit of her own studies and research, with the eternal aim to advance in the degrees. And that was when Samuel and Thia had needed her most, during their formative stages. In that sense, she felt like she did not deserve his attention if she herself had not given him—or her family— much of it. And oh how she regretted not having spent more time at home with Samuel …

Niterra seemed to sense this. "After son die. You both withdraw?"

Anna rubbed her face before folding her arms onto the table. She nodded.

"How you grieve?"

"Grieve?" Anna snorted. "I don't know. I—" She flipped a hand at the library.

"Stick nose in books? Study and research and train?" Niterra briefly flashed nineteen air rings around her arm. "Make more rings?"

Anna nodded again.

"This common." Niterra took another sip of tea before nodding past Anna. "That book. Your work?"

Anna glanced back at the big black book she had confiscated from Ralf, sitting on a table next to a stack of notes and research books. The book looked primal in comparison to the everyday objects nearby, with its crimson lacerations and demonic skin and passive ill intent.

"Something like that."

"Remember deal, Stone."

"Right. Sorry. I suspect it's necromantic, but I haven't gotten far in the historical and arcaneological analysis. Hard to tell for certain without cracking open the cover and seeing what's inside."

Niterra opened a hand toward the book, silently asking, *May I?*

Anna flapped a hand at it in a *Be my guest* manner, and Niterra got up with a groan and went to the book. She splayed her hand, cast Reveal, and inspected it like Anna had countless times. "A kargeyasnara."

"Yes. And no, I haven't solved it yet."

"Binding not leather."

Anna fiddled with her mug. "Demon skin. At least, as far as I can tell." She hadn't bothered to turn around, for she doubted there was anything new the woman could tell her. Sure enough, Niterra soon returned.

"Too advanced for old Niterra," she said with a cluck of her tongue. Instead of sitting back down, she went to stand by the fire. "Now Niterra turn to honor deal. Come, Stone. We work on spell."

Anna almost jumped out of her chair. Fewer things in life excited her more than learning a new spell, especially a challenging one. Despite already knowing over a hundred spells, she eagerly skittered to stand before the old woman.

"Let us switch to my tongue. You know enough Nodian?" The question carried the implication of Anna casting the 12th degree Tongues spell.

"Enough to understand you, but I am weak at the language myself," Anna replied. She closed her eyes and thought of a kingdom of a proud, charcoal-skinned people warring for their tribes—Moonclaw and Jadefire and Wolfhowl and Warblade. She thought of the Nodian smile, of boys and girls training to become warriors from birth, a boy hunting a red bear to become a man. Of Nanukin, the god of the hunt, Konkorra, the god of war, Anwama, the goddess of love, among others. Then she focused on the harsh language itself and incanted, "*Translateo commona linguino Nodian.*"

Anna opened her eyes. "You are Moonclaw, yes?" Yet she heard her mouth say, "*Ibakwa Klamomo, kwekwe?*"

Niterra's already creased face wrinkled further with pain. "Your Nodian hurts my ears," she replied in her native tongue. "But it is my words that are important right now."

Anna wanted to ask Niterra how she had come to serve another kingdom, but she had long learned—back in her teenage years—that no one who wanted to keep their head ever asked Black Eagle Bladesong such personal questions, and so she instead said, "Understand."

"*I* understand," Niterra corrected, saying, "*Kiki druku.*"

Anna repeated the words.

"But let us leave the lessons of my tongue for someone more patient than I," Niterra continued, bringing her callused old fingers together before her gold-fringed crimson robe, with its Black Eagle crest. "What do you know of the spell thus far?"

"Besides its root?"

"Besides the Portal spell, yes. Tell me."

Thomas, holding a steaming mug of tea, strolled to the supper table, threw a *Blackhaven Herald* scroll onto it, and pulled up a chair. "Hearing my wife speak a different tongue is always—" He whistled seductively, smiling so genuinely Anna would have almost laughed were it not for the many unaddressed pains drifting between them like a fog. He ruined it anyway by adding, "Too bad you couldn't save that focus for the puzzle."

Anna ignored him and replied to Niterra in Nodian, "There change direction root principles."

Niterra stopped her by scrubbing at the air with a palm. "No, no, I can't take your butchering of my mother tongue. I will speak Nodian. You stick to Solian."

"Fair enough." Anna kept the Tongues spell lit to understand Niterra but stuck to Solian when she spoke. "The core rudiments of Portal apply, but whereas Portal has established, stiff boundaries, *Combat* Portal bends those boundaries." She had already been studying Combat Portal off and on for years now in preparation for truly delving into it—and for the day she had a qualified mentor to guide her. Such spells, were they cast purely using knowledge gleaned from books, almost always resulted in catastrophic failure, often with gruesome results. "The other root involved is the Teleport spell. The drawing of ovals must complement the visualizations of target locations and be properly situated in the ether."

"Excellent. We have a strong underlying framework to start with," Niterra replied in Nodian. "Now let us work, step by step, on combining those visualizations with gestural precision, timing, and arcane draw."

And so the women worked, diving deep into the nuance of the spell.

An hour later, Thomas excused himself to return to the dig, wanting to put in a couple more hours before bed.

"Aren't you going to eat?" Anna asked.

He shrugged. "I'll catch a snack in the city on the way," and he summoned a portal and stepped through it.

"Bye to you too," Anna mumbled, conscious of Niterra watching her. Still the woman did not comment, something Anna was thankful for. It was embarrassing enough having this legend witness the turmoil of her home life with her daughter. Having the woman also witness the turmoil between Anna and her husband was almost too much to bear.

Like a sixteen-year-old trying to pretend she wasn't heartbroken, Anna bounced on the balls of her feet and forced an awkward smile. "You were talking about how to keep the tongue-to-tendril ratios balanced whilst tuning the geometric arcane lensing properties …?"

"Yes, but 'properties' is not the best word here," and Niterra dove into another nuanced discourse on how semantics factored heavily into every facet of the spell.

As a testament to the sheer complexities involved, after another solid hour of training, Anna felt like her knowledge of the spell had barely advanced. This was the norm of spells of high degree, and she knew it would take months, perhaps years of focused study to get the spell to a point where she could competently cast it in the heat of battle, the true challenge.

Anna rubbed her forehead. "We ought to stop here. It's late, and I still have a cycle to perform." As was her habit, she intended to perform every spell in her arsenal, and tried to practice them every evening, a precarious balance with a family, her myriad school duties, and the expectations that came as kingdom champion. This she usually did in the dilapidated cellar, which absorbed the cacophony of violent spell casting. These days, with how many spells she knew and including time for meditative stamina recuperation, it took at least two hours.

"Yes, my bones are creaking," Niterra replied in Nodian, groaning as she rubbed her back with both hands. "I fear the day fast approaches when I will need a staff to walk about."

"It is not very Nodian of you to admit weakness," Anna said with a cheeky grin.

Niterra snarled and Anna promptly mumbled an apology. Nodians loathed weakness. It was practically a cultural edict.

"Er … would you like to start sleeping here?" Anna offered. "I'm sure the manor gets lonely."

Niterra raised her eyebrows. For the first time, it appeared she was speechless.

"Mirko got your tongue?" Anna asked, quoting a rather dark proverb, for mirkos, vicious beasts about the size of deer, were known to tear out their prey's tongue before feasting on their face.

"That … that would be nice, thank you. I will fetch my things."

"And I will make accommodations. Thia's floor has a lot of room." Anna chortled. "I suppose I should warn her," she added, already wincing at the coming fight. She stepped aside, allowing Niterra to take the portal first—she had been granted portal privileges upon first arriving at the tower. Anna then took her turn, incanting, "*Shyneo.*" Her palm burst with lightning. She pressed it against the runic oval. "Anna Atticus Stone, third floor." A portal burst to life, its wind ruffling her robe and making her braided ponytail bounce. She stepped through, emerging in darkness.

Poor girl must be asleep, Anna thought as the portal vanished behind her with a *whoosh*. She was about to resummon the portal, but something bothered her—the total silence. Thia was a light snorer, and that gentle wheeze always calmed Anna. She thus padded to the closest door in the castle-like hall, but found it closed.

"Thia?" Anna asked, giving a double knock. "Thia? You in there?" When no answer came, Anna's heart skipped a beat. She quickly raised a hand and focused on the pebble. The tendril tug led right into the room, indicating it was still inside.

"Thia? Are you all right? Answer your mother, please!" Anna listened, but the silence only deepened, broken by the pounding of her heart. "I'm coming in!" she warned, stepping back.

Thia had been allowed to bolt her door for privacy, a battle her parents had lost years ago. Anna had never broken the door before, but this, quite possibly, was an emergency. Familiar with the mechanism on the other side, Anna knew only brute force would do it. In a blink, three spells scrolled by her mind—1st degree Telekinesis, 2nd degree Push, and 8th degree Strength. The first couldn't reach the bolt through the door, and the third would take too much time, and so she shoved at the air, specifically aiming at the door handle, roaring, "*Baka!*"

The door rattled, the frame cracking. Dust fell from the old ceiling. *One more should do it.* Anna repeated the shove, channeling the scion in her pocket, which gave a brief buzz, and there came a metal-splitting sound as the door flew open and slammed against the wall on the other side, the planks splintering.

"Thia!" Anna shouted, running inside, lit hand bathing the room in lightning blue. She saw an outline on the bed and shot to it. But after throwing the covers back, she found only pillows.

"Damn it, girl!" Anna hissed. She splayed her hand again, sensing for the pebble. The tendril wisps led her to the bedside table, where the pebble sat under a book. Anna picked it up and gaped at it, incredulous that her daughter would be so reckless.

As if you weren't ten times more reckless at her age, said a voice in Anna's head. But it was quickly trampled by an army of visuals of her daughter's feet scraping against the snowy ground as she was dragged away, shouting for her mommy.

Anna shot to the lone window, its parapet deep and pointed, the window a thin slice, for it had been originally built to be an archery slot. The window was not openable—or so Anna had thought, for upon closer inspection, she saw small chunks of mortar at its base. She felt the window frame—and it dislodged.

Anna yanked it aside and looked down three floors. At the bottom was a thick winterberry bush—and its buildup of snow had been disturbed. For a moment, she gaped uncomprehendingly at the bush like she had at the pebble, trying to work out how her daughter had squeezed through the thin gap, how she had been planning to get back inside with the door bolted shut, or even how she had survived such a long fall— unless she had used her arcanery in a clever manner. Having seen flashes of her brilliance, she no longer put anything past her.

Studying the snow told her it was possible still that she had been kidnapped. Though the odds of someone getting through the myriad enchantments that littered the grounds were slim, they were not zero.

"I'm coming, Thia," Anna whispered. "I'm coming ..."

NOTORIOUS

Anna stormed back to the hall, slapped the portal rune, and snapped off the incantation to summon it to the top floor. There she quickly scribbled out a note that Thia was gone and she was going to look for her. She left this note on the carpet before the portal, only to realize it would be swept away by the wind the portal generated. So instead she summoned the portal, slipped on through to outside, and jammed the note into the old doorframe that led into the ruined first floor, knowing Niterra would certainly find it before her husband.

Anna then ran to the bush. To her immense relief—and frustration—she found one set of tracks leading out. Being 6th degree, Thia did not know Teleport, and Anna had not trusted her to learn it—even illegally, as was Arinthian tradition—due to her demonstrated lack of interest toward advancement. But in classic Arinthian tradition, she *had* offered to illegally teach her the 11th degree Reveal, strictly to learn how to spot evil enchantments aimed at her person. The girl had only scoffed at her mother, throwing in her face that "It is illegal and you should know better." There had been no discussing the subject since.

Now Anna wondered if her daughter had learned the spell behind her back anyway, for as Anna raced along the footprints, she saw how they carefully wove around her outer enchantments that triggered when even she would pass—and in a very clever manner, utilizing tree branches.

"Did you get help?" Anna wondered aloud. "Or did you study the enchantments to get by them without triggering anything?" Thia had been granted arcane privileges that allowed her to pass through all but the final ring of enchantments, which Anna had only recently put into place as a last line of defense in the event her daughter got kidnapped.

Anna raced past that line and on through the forest, skidding to a halt on the ice of a deserted street. It was lined with four-story stone domiciles decorated with fancy plaster scrollwork and iron-balustraded balconies and gargoyle waterspout grotesques, all typical of the Rose Quarter. She searched the ground but quickly found it impossible to discern Thia's footsteps from the public's.

"Where would you have gone?" Anna kept muttering to herself before coming upon the likeliest answer. "*Impetus peragro*," she snapped off, reappearing with a *thwomp* at the foot of the Steps of the Crescent Moon of the academy. She raced up the icy basalt steps, on through the courtyard and the gigantic portal that led to the Student Wing, and farther on to the student dorms.

Throughout, she passed the occasional student keeping late study hours. Out of respect, every single one bowed their head and said, "Good evening, Arcanist Stone," as she passed. But Anna, singularly focused on her quest, ignored them all, and soon slid into the men's dorm. Arcanists, of course, were allowed in both dorms, but a female arcanist entering a men's dorm was unusual enough for the few young men loitering in the plush and spacious common room to straighten, eyebrows rising.

"Excuse me," Anna muttered, and raced up the steps toward the 6th degree dorm hall. More than one boy followed, certain someone was in big trouble. Despite looking like she was in her early thirties, the forty-nine-year-old Anna had cultivated quite the no-nonsense reputation.

"Initiate!" she called after a portly emerald-robed teenager whose name she vaguely thought was either Chappie or Fungal. What she did know about him was that he was part of Drama class with Thia and Ralf. "Where can I find Ralf Turman's room?"

The young man pointed. "Er, that door there, Arcanist Stone."

"Thank you," and Anna sped to the door, giving it a quick double rap. "Turman?" No answer. "Turman, it's—"

"He's gone," said the young man she had asked earlier.

Anna turned. "Where to?"

The boy hesitated.

"Do not play games, young man. This is a grave matter."

He glanced back at a small assembly of fellow emerald-robed boys. "I ought not to say as—"

Anna took a step forward, voice acid. "Unless you want to explain the boy code of honor to the disciplinary committee you will *promptly* divulge the whereabouts of—"

"He went to a tournament," the young man blurted, hands wringing. "A bunch of them did." He added in a theatrical mutter, "Now doth done it have I …"

Anna stared at him. "Where?"

"Er, I really—"

Anna took another step forward, hissing through clenched teeth, *"Where?"*

"Shanties," he whispered, again glancing over his shoulder at the boys. "The big old warehouse."

"The abandoned one?"

"That's the one. The basement. B-but please don't tell anyone there I told you."

Anna snarled and shot off. Eyes fell to the floor as she passed. *They probably know all the details of the tournament, including which combatants are involved*, she thought. *Despite me warning them how dangerous these tournaments can be.*

Kids always seemed to know such secrets, something Anna couldn't relate to. Having never fraternized with academy cliques as a teenager, she had been left out of the gossip and intrigues and secrets—nor did she much listen to rumors, as she had been the subject of too many. She had been that rare creature who came perhaps once in a generation—the over-achieving bookworm valedictorian dueling champion. But such creatures paid a social price.

Once outside, Anna raced to the Steps of the Crescent Moon, the Teleport boundary for all but a select few arcanists. Even at her age, experience, and fame, she still felt like an outsider in some ways.

"*Impetus peragro,*" she snapped, soon reappearing amidst a grubby street surrounded by dilapidated homes and shuttered storefronts. A group of men standing around a low fire and wrapped in layers of mismatching garments glanced at her.

"'Lock on a walk," one of them muttered, spitting on the snow.

The others mumbled their agreement, nodding like chickens.

Anna glanced down at her black arcanist robe and realized that word would quickly spread if she got any closer. She had to blend in, and so she strode in the opposite direction from her destination, which was only three blocks away, and entered an alley. Once out of sight, she switched her mindset to casting a spell she rarely employed, one that came with a mountain of tedious ethics studies. It was a complicated 15th degree spell that, if used for ill gain, could easily result in a serious investigation by the warlock constabulary.

It was also a ritual, and in the context of this spell, that meant performing certain gestures and their accompanying visualizations. Usually, these rituals took anywhere between a quarter of an hour and half an hour. She began by hovering her right hand over her left arm, visualizing it being a youthful sixteen years of age. She swept her right hand up and down that arm, including the underside, mimicking the motion she would complete during the actual incantation, preparing the visualizations ahead of time. Those visualizations were critical and set up the actual arcanery. Already she could feel the invisible tendrils aligning, readying for the trigger phrase.

Her left arm done, she moved on to her entire left leg, including underneath her foot, imagining how the flesh had looked when she was sixteen. Then she moved to her right leg, and steadily worked her way up her body, switching hands to complete her right arm. Once she had completed visualizing her face and hair, always the hardest part, she did a second sweep, this time focusing on clothing—a royal blue robe to match the degree.

At last, feeling that the arcanery was properly aligned, and with about a quarter of an hour having passed, she swept a final hand down her body whilst incanting, *"Persona morpha mat agateo kipat,"* simultaneously drawing on the prepared visuals. Her entire body and robe morphed before her eyes. Long hair sprouted from her head and fell like a curtain around her vision, reminding her so much of her youth. The veins of her hands softened, the skin paling and smoothing.

With the ritual complete, she flicked a hand and the scion floated out of her pocket. She glanced at its curved surface. Visible in the dim light was the reflection of her sixteen-year-old self—long brown hair, blue eyes, and the comely face of a teenager who had recently celebrated her womanhood ceremony.

She returned the scion, which she rarely had to deploy these days, to her pocket and strode out of the alley, a 4th degree warlock studying her 5th degree.

When she strode by the huddled group, she received a catcall whistle. "Off to the tournie, are ya, lass?" sang a man. "Don't get 'urt now, little girlie!"

"I remember that part too," Anna muttered. But whereas Ordinary girls had to come up with myriad clever tactics to keep such calls at bay, all Anna needed to do was briefly flare her lightning eyes. That promptly silenced the men, who did not know enough about the arts to realize that such a skill was for the higher degrees.

She made her way down the winding street until she came upon an empty warehouse surrounded by animal pens of various sizes. But instead of animals, there was refuse—wood, twisted metal, debris, old barrels, broken-down carts, and the like. All rotting under piles of snow.

Two burly men in indiscriminate dark robes—a highly suspicious deviance from warlock culture, for all warlocks were expected to wear their degree color when performing duties in public—stood at the entrance, checking over a line of thirty well-dressed Ordinaries and no less than twenty warlocks wearing academy robes.

"Gods," Anna whispered. If there were that many waiting in line to get in, how many were already inside?

Incensed by the brazenness of the organizers, she strode to the back of the line behind two burgundy-robed girls, both blond, with a single golden band on their upper arms, indicating they were 2nd degree.

"Oh my gosh, this is, like, *so* exciting?" one gushed.

"But, like, feels *so* wrong?" replied the other. Both sounded identical, making questions out of statements.

One of them turned to Anna. "Oh my gosh, isn't this, like, *so* thrilling?"

"Mmm," Anna toned. Then she realized she ought not to act like her arcanist self and ran a hand through her long hair. "Yeah, I guess it's pretty thrilling. Like, looking forward to seeing who's competing," she added, awkwardly blurting, "You know?"

"Don't know who's all competing, but I *do* know it's a big purse," said a blue-robed boy with olive skin ahead of the girls. He snapped his fingers at Anna. "Hey, you kind of look familiar. Have we met? Do we have a class together or something?"

"Nope."

"You sure? You look crazy familiar."

Anna, not knowing what else to say, flipped him a hand in a *What can you do* gesture.

The boy scratched his head, but turned forward again.

The line moved along, until Anna heard the sound of coins. *Shoot, there's an entrance fee!* she realized. She tapped one of the girls in front. "Er ... how much?"

One of the guards answered for her, barking out to the line, "Crown a head, people. Have it ready so we can move things along."

The girl pointed at him, cheekily mouthing at Anna, "Crown a head."

"Right." In her haste, Anna hadn't thought to bring any money. *What to do, what to do?* She glanced about, wondering if there was an alternate way to slip inside. Then she noticed that the guards weren't checking the money with Reveal, no doubt not expecting any complicated tricks from low-degrees, a laziness she could exploit.

With the idea in mind, she stepped out of the line, mumbling something about having to run to use the privy.

"What privy?" one of the girls muttered at the other as Anna whisked herself off to a nearby alley. There, with her back turned, she opened her left palm and positioned her right hand over it. Using this spell for her intended purpose most certainly broke an ethics law. After visualizing a golden crown in her hand, with the crown on one side and King Power Ridian's chubby face on the other, and with teeth marks included from people biting it to ensure it was real gold, she whispered, "*Obiectum minfassa koina,*" the incantation to the heavily restricted 13th degree Create Simple Object spell. A golden coin sizzled into existence in her hand. Although she could have teleported home to retrieve a real crown, she wanted to locate her daughter as soon as possible.

The novelty of seeing her former pupil's face on coinage having long worn off, she lifted it up and down, weighing it. *Just about right,* she thought. She recalled Ottentus using the spell non-verbally, and knew she would have to put in a lot more practice if she was to ever get to that level—and she already underutilized the spell, for she was responsible enough to usually have things she needed at hand.

With the arcanely crafted crown weighing her pocket down, she hurried back to the line. As the line crawled forward, giant drums began to pound from deep within the warehouse in anticipation of the first duel. That pounding echoed Anna's heart, which threatened to burst through her chest from nerves. If caught, she risked arcastration—if there was one thing the kingdom did not tolerate it was warlocks making fake coins or jewelry or arcane items or documentation or anything used to deceive others. As with many ethics laws, the academy drilled into students' heads to turn in any warlock who contravened those laws, for they risked warlock-kind as a whole.

And rightly so, Anna thought. But this was an emergency, and she believed her transgression could fall under an exemption clause. She could further argue the establishment itself was an illegal gathering, and she was there to investigate as kingdom champion, which was true. Ethics law demanded she report every instance of an unethical casting, which would then be considered in balance with the actions performed, something she would think about later. Still, she did not like breaching ethics laws she herself taught, nor did she like risking her career—and everything she had worked for. But for her daughter, she would break any and every law, and kill any and every villain.

At last, she reached one of the bored guards, who stood across from the other, leaving a gap for several students to walk through at once. The bearded brute of a man beckoned with an index finger. "Cough it up, girl."

Anna reached into her pocket with a sweaty hand and handed over the coin. Just in case, she readied a certain other spell on her lips, one that would be another huge ethics breach if performed.

As with every coin, the guard telekinetically lifted it before his half-lidded eyes. The coin revolved once—before vanishing with a *sizzle*.

Anna's heart jammed into her throat. But just as the man's face melded into a vicious—and triumphant—scowl, she pointed two fingers at his head and snapped off, "*Hoodvinka*," quickly followed by her saying, "The coin is real."

The man's face went plain as he focused on the spot in the air where the coin had been floating a moment before. "Looks good," he said dully, and he grabbed at the air, placed the non-existent coin into a pouch, and waved her through, as if having not heard the incantation, a mark of a successful casting. Luckily, the pounding drums had drowned out their conversation, and everyone else had been too busy yapping excitedly with each other. Done properly, the subject would not even remember the spell being cast.

Anna hurried by, not meeting his gaze lest he realize he had been hoodwinked. That had been one of the rare instances of her using the highly unethical 14th degree Bewitch spell out in the field. It was a spell usually taught for the exam only, with certain parts left out to minimize its casting strength. But Anna, being the clever and curious warlock she was, had uncovered those missing pieces from the archives, filling in what remained with Roth, who had known Anna needed every arrow in the quiver to defend herself against those coveting her scion.

Anna followed a loose group of students through the mostly empty warehouse to a wide stairway. She descended two flights of stairs to the basement, which was filled with people. The room was vast, filling ten barns' worth of space, the ceiling high, perhaps twenty feet. The ground sloped with crude tiered seating, though everyone was too excited to sit, choosing to stand instead. Down in the bowels, in the center, was certainly an arena, though Anna couldn't see it through the crowd. She guessed it had been built sometime after Arcaners had been outlawed, allowing such lawless behavior to go unchecked.

She pushed her way through the crush, which chattered loudly over the drums that rhythmically went, *Boom! Bah-bum-bum-boom!* over and over. They reminded Anna of her tournament days, and the nerves of combat slipped into her veins. Conscious of the scion in her pocket, she searched for her daughter, her reflexes keyed. There was a wide mix of people here, from academy students to Ordinaries to nobles. All had the same expression on their oily face, a mixture of excitement and anxiousness. Violence was in the hot and humid air, which stank of ale and sweat and bad breath. No one knew what might happen, and that was what thrilled them. In a time of peace, they wanted to feel the excitement of being close to death.

Anna pushed forth, keeping her face hidden behind a curtain of hair, not meeting anyone's gaze to lessen the chance of being recognized. Nonetheless, an ebony-skinned boy of her fake age managed to lock gazes with her as she searched for her daughter.

"Whoa, whoa, whoa," he said, gently taking hold of her elbow. "Has anyone ever told you that you look like the spitting image of a young Anna Stone?" he shouted over the blasting music, for the drums had now been accented with a rolling *rat-a-tat-tat* snare. "Cherry, check this girl out," he said to a pale-skinned girl with blue hair, holding onto Anna's elbow. "Remember that old poster you had before your dog chewed it up?"

"Holy Unnameables, you look *just* like her," the girl squealed, clapping twice. "Seriously!"

Anna, recognizing the pair of blue-robed students from her classes, chuckled nervously. "Yeah, I get that all the time." She looked down at the boy's grip and he finally let go.

"Wish I'd been alive to see her fight in the arena," the boy said. "She's my teacher for a couple of classes, you know. So strict, but *so* smart."

"Are you related to her?" the girl asked.

Anna shook her head, searching beyond them for Thia.

"I once asked her about one of those duels—" The boy repeatedly snapped his fingers. "Who was it again she wupped? Endius? Totillus?"

Anna recalled flashes of light as she'd teleported around during those two duels, letting off bolts of ripping lightning. "I think both," she replied absently.

"Totally. Anyway, I asked her about one of them and she just shut me down with this grumpy look." He chortled. "I thought she was going to have me whipped."

The girl slapped his shoulder. "It's 'cause you don't ask people about duels that end in death."

"Oh. Yeah, that's probably why. But I also asked back when I didn't realize she ain't the sort you can just strike up a casual conversation with. Even still, that one look stalled a whole bunch of questions I had about her other legendary duels—" He counted fingers on a hand. "—Apoc's Forfeit, Snix the Speedsword—"

"—Sabius The Reaper," the girl threw in.

"Oh, yeah, legendary—*legendary!*"

Anna saw herself flying through the air above an arena surrounded by two massive enemy armies. She remembered a huge elemental waiting for her down below alongside a man flinging air spells up at her, before she had been sucked into a violent tornado.

"You should make coin on that resemblance somehow," the girl added, snapping her back to reality. "Like, you could be rich reenacting her famous duels."

Anna forced a chortle. "That's funny. Thanks for the tip," and she pushed on.

"Wait, you should hang out with us!" the boy called. "You're so fiery looking!"

Fiery was the buzzword of the term. Every term, there was one that drifted to the top. Being a former student and now an arcanist, Anna had lived through a wide assortment of them—cruel, blazing, wicked, fiendish, ripping, villainous, scathing, awesome, 'mazin', crazin', hellas, and countless others, all coming in and out of fashion like cuts and sizes of robe. This term, robe fits were loose, lending students the appearance of wearing their older siblings' clothes.

At last, Anna squeezed into an aisle and began descending the wood bleachers, which were sticky from spilled ale. Down at the bottom was a half-sized arena pit, with a floor of sand sodden with old blood stains. It sank ten feet below the lowest bleacher, its stone walls marked up with gouges and blood and blast marks. Above those ten feet of wall there was no protection whatsoever—no fencing, no balustrade, nothing.

Anna kept searching, looking for her daughter, or even Ralf Turman, who might be with her. But there had to be a thousand people there at least, and the faces kept melding together. Further, many had their hoods up, making it hard to tell the warlocks apart. Here underground, they looked like hoodlums, the word having derived from nefarious warlocks who would keep their hoods up so as not to get recognized whilst breaking the law.

The nobles, who were mostly on the younger side, were stylish, with some wearing ostentatious peacock-plumed hats, others big sashes, others still colorful beadwork. At forty-nine years of age, and despite looking like her young self, Anna felt like the oldest person there.

Until she spotted a gray-haired man, one whose eyes went wide upon seeing her face. He was down in the hallway that led to the arena, milling with the other combatants, the only turquoise robe of the bunch. His face was scarred and brutish, a dark bottle of ale clutched in a thick-fingered fist.

Anna was trying to place that face, which looked remarkably familiar. But from where?

Then, strangely, the man, who hadn't torn his eyes away from her, cupped his mouth with a shaking hand—and burst into tears.

It was in that moment that Anna recognized him. Flashes of practice and arena duels zipped through her memory; cuddling by an infinite window in her dorm room; kissing, talking, arguing; and then catching him with another girl.

Standing in the pit, as a fifty-year-old competitor, a notorious dueling champion, was none other than her ex-boyfriend, Scadius Von Edgeworth.

A LOW FLAME

Anna tried to vanish in the crush of the crowd, but Scadius soon caught up to her anyway, for people quickly moved to make room for him. The old warrior grabbed her by the arm and flung her about. All around, people gawked, most too in awe of him to notice his treatment of Anna.

"Look at me," he growled, eyes red and wide and searching her face. "Who are you?"

"No one," Anna replied, struck by how he had aged, how his face had soured over the years from wear and tear. Too much ale had permanently reddened his nose and the arena had left countless scars, from burn cuts to lightning trees to black ice marks.

He shook her. "Liar! Who are you!"

With people staring, Anna could not afford a scene. "We can talk, but not here."

Scadius was breathing rapidly. "Come with me," and he manhandled her through the crowd with a tight grip on her arm.

Anna let him drag her away only to avoid drawing more attention. He used a guarded side door to take her down to the arena back area. There he spun her about to face him once more. After looking her over, he raised a shaking hand to cup her cheek, his chin trembling.

Anna stepped away from the hand, leaving it to waver in place. Her face was impassive and plain. She did not feel for this man, nor did she respect what he had become.

"Are … are you her daughter?" he whispered.

Anna shook her head.

"Are you related to her?"

Anna stayed quiet, watching him.

"Gods, you look like her. I … I can't believe it. I can't." His Canterran accent, once lilting and smooth and beautiful, had decayed to a raspy growl. He splayed the fingers of that wavering hand. "Dare I?"

Anna, seeing the single golden band on his upper shoulder that, combined with his robe color, indicated he was the same degree as her—18th—knew he could see through the Metamorphosis. An inexperienced lower degree, who would not know what to look for, might not.

"You know what you will see," Anna said.

The man staggered back as if struck. "Gods …"

"What are you doing here, Scadius?"

"Making a living. Providing for my son."

"You were warned never to return." Years and years ago. But how he had changed since!

"*You* should have been his mother."

"Those days are long gone."

"I … I heard you married him. That worthless noble. It broke me. You know, I still rage at you sometimes for what you did. Giving away my lineage's scion like that …" He shook his head, eyes distant. "There are holes in many a wall from my fists."

"You have a son, a family, yet you risk them with this foolery?"

"I … I do not have a family. Only my son. My precious boy, Zigmund."

"Named after the great Canterran dueler of old. Your choice, or hers?"

"Mine of course." He took a swig of the ale still gripped in his fist and sniffed with that red nose. "She left me. Caught me out with a girl, like you did. Except the girl was half her age. She did not take it well."

Anna didn't know what to say. Although his appearance had changed drastically, who he was inside hadn't changed at all, and he was suffering for it.

Scadius turned his back on her. "You … you don't know how much I loved you. *Still* love you. Yet … yet I still sometimes rage in the night. I rage about what you did. I loathe you more, I think. Yes. I cannot forgive you. Ever." Then he whispered, "You should have been his mother …"

"I *am* a mother."

"So I heard. A son and a daughter. They must be beautiful children. I wish they were mine …"

"You do not mean that."

"Oh, I do. You have no idea." He sighed. "I also heard your boy died."

Anna swallowed, unable to speak of her son with this man.

"I am sorry. It must have hurt." He turned back to her. "But I also hope it hurt *deep*."

There was a *smack* as Anna slapped him.

Scadius, head averted from the slap, kept it there. "Yeah." He nodded. "Yeah, I remember what that felt like."

"You deserved it then too."

"I probably did." He grabbed her arms with such violence it startled her, the ale bottle digging into her right arm beneath his punishing grip. "What is this game? Why do you play with me still?"

Anna's scion buzzed angrily in her pocket.

He let go of her and stepped back, his eyes shooting to the bulge. "Gods, it's here. In my presence. Of course it is …"

"Scadius Von Edgeworth, the king explicitly warned you never to return. You are a vicious dueler, a taker of arena lives, a scoundrel, a gambler, a drunk. Out of respect for our past, I give you this final warning." She lowered her chin, voice menacing. "Dispel yourself from this kingdom."

He scoffed, guzzled down the rest of the ale, and tossed the bottle aside. It shattered against the filthy ground. "Are they here? The constables? I reckon I could smite them all."

"You're drunk."

"Oh, darling. Sweet darling. You haven't seen me drunk. And I pray you never do." A crooked smile splayed across his chapped lips. "I bet you've grown soft over the years. Sure, I heard about some of your duels and tricks. But holding class isn't the same, and you know it. Neither is training alone. Shadows put up no fight. The instincts and arcane muscles wither. The strength ebbs. But I—" He tapped his chest with a fist. "—I am strong. A mighty Von Edgeworth. The kids in my kingdom have *my* poster on their walls now. I have become the greatest dueler of my time."

"A dueler who makes his money fighting weaker opponents? Taking extra purse if they die a gruesome death? Pissing that money away on ale and bad bets?"

"Then battle *me*, Anna. Face me, if you dare. We can finally settle that old score."

"I have no score to settle with you. On the contrary, I wish you only peace. But a peace not in this place, but in your own kingdom, in your *own* home."

"You're afraid. I can see it in your eyes. You fear I would lay siege to the castle of your mind. And you would be right." He raised his chin. "I like you afraid. Gods, but you're so beautiful still. And you look as mighty as you did in those posters of you in your prime. It gives me goosebumps, Anna." He pulled back a sleeve to show a scarred arm riddled with bumps. "Goosebumps." He dropped the arm, letting the sleeve cover the scars. "Show me what you look like. I heard you have hardly aged. I want to see if you have scars or remain as unblemished as you did then. But I suppose your healing saved your countenance, didn't it? You always had that over me, your dual element. I hadn't bothered trying. Didn't want to weaken my primary. You know what they say—focus is strength."

"Go home. Go to your son. Make something of him. Become decent. I know it is within you." She'd almost called him by his old pet name—Scadie—and that made her cheeks color with shame.

The man laughed, but it was a laugh that masked great pain. "You stand here and say these things with such ease! You, a bookworm who got lucky with the lottery of bequeathment. A teacher, a nosy busybody. You dare judge me after what you did?"

Anna walked to the stairs, turning at the foot of them. "Go home, Scadius. Let us never lay eyes on each other again."

Scadius stood with glassy eyes. Behind him, down a long hallway of doorless openings from which emerged the silhouettes of competitors, awaited the arena. The rhythmic sound of drums and snares and now a bagpipe was reaching a crescendo, indicating the first duel was about to begin.

He gave her a bittersweet smile, voice lost to the din. Yet she could see him mouth, "I can't." His head shook as he repeated, "I can't …"

"So be it," Anna said, and she turned her back on him and strode up the stairs.

* * *

Anna at last spotted her daughter amidst a group of teenagers. Yet when she drew near, she saw that some of the men were in their mid-twenties, their hoods concealing their age. She grabbed her daughter's arm and whirled her about. "Thia—"

"Who the hell dares to—" Thia's eyes widened upon seeing the young countenance. "*Mom?*"

"You're coming home. *Now.*"

"Arcanist Stone," exclaimed Ralf, hand shooting away from Thia. Then his face split with a smug smile. "It is illegal to cast Metamorphosis with the intent of subterfuge, Arcanist Stone."

"Not if the intent is reconnaissance-oriented, Mr. Turman," Anna snapped.

Upon hearing this, the older men promptly scattered.

"We're doing nothing untoward, Arcanist Stone. And I would like you to know that I have been cleared of any wrong-doing by the academy. The disciplinary committee rightly decided that my intention with the book had merely been to show a convincing prop. Nothing more. Further, and I am sorry to remind you of this, Arcanist Stone, but Thia *is* seventeen." He slipped an arm around her daughter's waist and gave it a squeeze. "Under kingdom law, she is a woman grown."

Thia wiggled away from him, withering under her mother's glare.

"Is that what you will tell the constables when they show up?" Anna asked. "That you're a woman grown who was playing innocent whilst watching a bloodbath? Is that what you want to see here? A person die?"

"Death is a part of life, Arcanist Stone," Ralf chimed in.

Anna ignored the boy, focusing only on her daughter. "Because that sort of thing never leaves you, Thia. *Never.* You will see it again and again. When you're eating. Studying. Walking. Between thoughts. In your nightmares ..."

"Mom, I ... I don't know. I don't know. I just want to have fun without feeling like I'm not allowed. Do you understand?"

"It's not about being allowed, Thia. It's about prudence. Wisdom. There are risks worth taking and then there is recklessness."

Thia looked down, kicking one toe with the other. She looked up to shake her head. "Gosh, this is so weird. You look younger than *me.*"

"How could you take this risk, Thia? After what happened? Why would you do it?"

"They were probably just some hoodlums," Ralf said with a shrug.

"I told him about the attempted attack," Thia muttered, head once again low.

Anna cupped her daughter's cheeks, raising her face to look her in the eye. "I already lost a child," she said. "I don't want to lose you too. You are indeed a woman grown, and I cannot make you do what you do not want to do. But I beg you, please come home. Please ..."

The crowd abruptly cheered as an announcer's amplified voice boomed, "One-zero!"

"Oh, Mom ..." Thia mouthed.

"Please," Anna mouthed, a tear rolling down her cheek. "Come home ..."

Thia tilted her head, face once more reminding Anna of Thomas and Samuel and her mother and father and her sister and herself, especially in that tilt. She was everyone, including an Arinthian, yet herself too, her own person. She wiped her mother's tear away with a thumb and nodded, mouthing, "All right, Mom. All right …"

Anna breathed an immense sigh of relief. She took her daughter by the hand and, without so much as a glance at Ralf, led her away.

"I'll see you later, Thi!" Ralf called after her, using a shortened version of her name—a *pet name*, Anna realized.

"Are you really going to report them?" Thia asked as they left the bulk of the crowd.

"As soon as I take you home. It is my duty."

"You're going to make me a pariah amongst my friends."

"If you become a pariah doing the right thing, are they really friends?"

Thia didn't reply to this. "*So* weird seeing you as your younger self," she again said as they ascended the stairs. "We look like sisters."

"There she is!" barked a voice from the entrance. "That's the one who hoodwinked me!"

A group of burly warlocks ran at her.

"Get behind me," Anna snapped.

Thia didn't need telling twice.

"Come here, kid!"

As the men neared, Anna ran a hand down her body, incanting, "*Morpha null*," and reverted to her normal self, a black-robed arcanist champion who looked in her early thirties but was forty-nine. To warn them off, she flicked a hand forth, tossing the scion into the air among them. Everyone watched its arc, the moment punctuated by the muted pounding of drums and a crowd cheering a momentous victory. Anna then splayed the fingers of her hand, incanting, "*Infusio marjorus laitna inti obiectum*," casting the 11th degree off-the-books Major Lightning Infusion. The scion, already buzzing angrily, burst with a gigantic spiderweb of lightning. This lightning connected with everything around them—the ground, the high ceiling, and everything in between, including the people, forming a vast lattice of crackling energy. The entire warehouse lit up blue.

The men skidded to a halt.

"It's zero-tempered," Anna said, eyebrows furrowed hawk-like. "But I can change that in a heartbeat—and I can focus it on certain targets. I suggest those targets step aside."

The men hesitated.

Anna tilted her head, voice lethal. "Do you require a demonstration?"

The men immediately hopped aside, one slipping in a puddle of ale in his haste to move.

Anna walked forth, daughter pressed tightly to her back, the gigantic spiderweb of lightning moving along with the scion, the crackling fingers probing every surface. None dared follow her outside, where she promptly cast Group Teleport to whisk her daughter home.

"Gods, Mom, that spell was scary as heck," Thia said back in their home grove, steadying herself against an oak to ward off the queasiness. "I don't think I've ever seen you use the scion like that."

"That wasn't your first time, was it?"

"What are you talking about? I've seen you use the scion hundreds of times—"

"I was talking about you attending an illegal tournament."

Thia blinked. "Well, I'll have you know it actually *was* my first time going to one of those!"

Anna flicked a hand toward the tower, hidden behind the trees. "And what about you sneaking out?"

Thia deflated. "Oh, Mom. I just want to go to bed." Thia plodded onward, only to halt. "Am I going to get blown up walking through this part?"

"Come here."

"Whaaaaat?" Thia whined, but shuffled over. Her hair was askew, her face a little peaky. Anna tried to smooth the hair but Thia flinched away, averting her gaze.

"Such a beautiful girl," Anna said.

Thia clucked her tongue, arms folded, foot tapping at the snow.

Anna gave Thia's shoulders a double tap with each hand. "You *are* a woman grown. And it's time for me to trust that you will show prudence when it counts." She splayed a hand.

"What are you doing?"

"Making you immune to the outer ring alarm enchantment. You no longer have to sneak out. I just ask that you tell me where you are going, that's all."

Thia grabbed her mother's wrist. "It's all right. And I promise, I'll carry the tracking pebbles from now on."

Anna raised a questioning eyebrow.

"What? It all actually *does* make me feel safer, Mom."

Anna dropped her hand. "Very well. Then I'm proud of you," she said as they began walking.

Thia averted her face, as if she felt like she did not deserve the praise.

"I am, you know. You might not be class valedictorian when you graduate, but you're my little girl, and you're growing up right before my eyes. And you *are* showing signs of wisdom and learning."

"Mom, stop it, ugh."

"All right, all right."

"And I hate to spoil it for you, but I'll be lucky to hit my 7th, let alone my 8th. I can feel the ceiling coming."

A bell rang in Anna's mind, indicating Thia had crossed the outer perimeter.

"Have patience, Thia. Have patience. I have to ask, though. How'd you get past the outer perimeter?"

Thia shrugged.

"Thia? How'd you do it?"

"You're going to get mad again."

"I won't get mad."

Thia stopped to face her. "Promise?"

"Promise."

Around them, the snowy grove of mostly oaks creaked in a gentle breeze.

Thia mumbled something.

"What? Speak up, please."

"I, uh, I disenchanted a tiny, *tiny* section."

Anna stood dumbfounded. "You *what*?"

"See, I knew you'd get mad," and Thia resumed walking, albeit hurriedly.

Anna grabbed her and flung her about. "On the contrary." She was beaming. "Do you know how proud I am of you right now?"

Thia blinked. "Huh?"

"Thia," Anna began in a whisper, "you learned Reveal and Disenchant *on your own*."

"*Illegally*," Thia whispered.

"In Arinthian tradition. Why didn't you tell me? We could have trained together! I could have taught you so much!" Was there hope for her daughter and the scion after all?

"I didn't want you to know I was sneaking out and—" Thia swallowed, looked away.

"But your training is so much more important! Why do you not apply yourself like this at school? My enchantments are *incredibly* difficult to disenchant. Even seasoned casters struggle. Do you not realize you are a *brilliant* warlock?"

Thia shrugged.

"Why do you cavort with such hoodlums and fools? Why do you care so much about Drama class yet so little about Arcaneology?"

"I'm tired, Mom. I just want to go to bed. Please."

"Fine, but tell me one more thing," Anna said as they arrived at the foot of the tower, looking up at her daughter's room. "How'd you get down, and how did you plan on getting back up?"

"That part's easy. I jump out and use Telekinesis to lower myself down. It's *just* strong enough to prevent me from breaking my tailbone."

"And how do you get back inside?"

"I use the portal."

"What about the door?"

"I rigged it. There's a hidden thread I pull to raise the latch." Thia lifted a finger. "But you're not allowed to use it to get into my room."

Anna grabbed her daughter and whirled her about like she used to do with her as a child.

"Mom, stop!" Thia said, letting out a tired laugh.

Anna set her down. "Thia. I. Am. Amazed. *Amazed!*"

"You can't tell Dad."

"What? Why?"

"About any of it."

"Well, we have to tell him what you've been up to."

"Fine, but not how I got out. Not about Reveal or Disenchant. None of that."

"Very well." Anna snorted and snapped her head sideways. "Get inside, you pest."

Thia smirked as she stepped up the old stairs, but she lingered by the portal rune. "You haven't told Dad yet, have you? About how I'm going to fail the term."

"I have not had the opportunity."

"You mean you haven't caught him in the right mood."

"Actually, I was rather thinking … what if you and I sat down together and got you ready for the exams?"

"Mom, I'm *way* too far behind."

"It'd be better to try than repeat a whole term, don't you think? Imagine leaving your friends behind."

Thia dropped her gaze to mull it over before mumbling, "Yeah, I guess, but I still feel like I don't have a chance …"

Anna raised her palms. "I am just telling you, the offer stands. It is not too late. You ought not to give up."

"Is that why you haven't told Dad yet? You're hoping I suddenly get the overwhelming urge to study my brains out and pass the final exams?"

Anna shrugged. "Maybe."

"Ugh, Mom, you're incorrigible. *Shyneo.*" She slapped the portal rune. "Thia Stone. Third floor." A portal flared to life. "*Good night, Mom,*" Thia mouthed over the wind before stepping through.

"*Good night, Thia,*" Anna mouthed back.

No sooner had the portal vanished than another portal flared, and out stepped Niterra Bladesong. "The kid alive?" the woman asked, eyes darting about.

"Yes, yes. Come, I have quite the story to tell," Anna said, walking back down the steps. "Has Thomas returned?"

"No. He still at mountain. Where we go?"

"To the constables. There's an illegal tournament we have to shut down."

She'd fix the enchantment alarm and write an ethics report tomorrow.

STUDY DAY, A QUINT LATER

"Annihilo! Baka! Annihilo! Voidus occa!"

Anna slipped left then right, dodging the twisting column of air and a powerful shove. She raised her shield in time for the second First Offensive column to slam into it, and finally ducked behind the shield as the Blind spell tendrils zipped overhead.

The slaps of Niterra Bladesong's wrists continued. *"Annihilo! Annihilo! Annihilo!"*

Anna jumped behind an ancient stone well the family drew water from, which blocked a couple blasts, before she sprinted to and alongside the wall, against which were stacks of cobwebbed furniture—chairs, tables, settees, along with some old crates.

"Annihilo! Annihilo! Annihilo!"

While pieces of dusty furniture tumbled to the floor behind her, Anna jumped against the corner of the room. Just as she was about to telekinetically lash out to a spot ahead of her, her foot slipped against the peeling paintwork and she caught a blast right to the chest. She slammed against the wall and slid to its base with a grunt. As one last chair smacked into the ground with a dull *thunk*, Niterra lowered her arms with a sigh.

"You all right, Mom?" Thia absently asked from a nearby desk brimming with school books and scrolls, her hand lit with green ivy-laced light. She was studying for the coming quint's final exams, which began tomorrow. The group was in the tower cellar, having started hours ago after breakfast. The only light came from their lit palms, for candles had the habit of going out around an air warlock. Besides, Anna had insisted it was good practice to keep up a Shine spell whilst studying or training.

"Fine." Anna hauled herself to her feet, feeling sorer than she had felt in some time. "Guess I'm not as agile as I was at nineteen," she muttered, wincing whilst rubbing her back. She had been attempting a maneuver she used to perform in the arena. "Just a little rusty."

Niterra folded her arms. "Perhaps Stone try with less legs?"

"I can perform the maneuver. I just need to train up again," Anna insisted, Scadius's words about withering drifting about in the back of her mind like a stubborn fog. She wanted to see if she could regain some of her more advanced dueling skills, but so far, it had been one miserable failure after another—and this was against someone who had been mostly standing in one spot, firing off mostly tempered spells. But Anna knew all she had to do was persevere. From now on, she would step her game up, not just here in the cellar, but also in Dueling Club—take a more aggressive stance when dueling the more advanced students instead of mostly playing teacher. She planned on also studying Scadius's past duels. Not just in case he came back and she had to put her foot down, but out of sheer interest. She did not like even the perception of her growing rusty, for such a perception lent confidence to the bold—as exampled by hoodlums daring to attempt kidnapping her daughter from her very home.

"Is that … is that your old school trunk?" Thia got up from her spot and went to a large trunk, uncovered by the chaos.

Anna rubbed her forehead. "Perhaps we ought to take a short break, Niterra."

"I boil us pot of tea," the woman said, and tottered off to a nearby wall etched with a portal rune.

"That would be grand, thank you. And then we'll work on conditioning my Mind Armor," Anna added, thinking of that "lay siege to the castle of your mind" line Scadius had deployed on her.

Niterra only grunted as she stepped through the portal she had summoned.

Thia blew dust off the trunk lid before raising it with a groan. "Oh, wow, neat sword," she said, picking up Burden's Edge, sheathed in its scabbard. "Would make a fine prop for a play."

"I would prefer that you not use that particular blade as a mere prop."

"What? Why? It's just a sword that sort of looks like—" Thia froze. "Oh. *Oh*." She gingerly slipped the blade back into its scabbard and returned it to the trunk. "That's the blade that is tainted with the blood of my aunt, isn't it?"

"Yes." Anna remembered placing the sword before Samantha's parents. That was the last time she had used it for anything. For thirty years since, it sat in storage, waiting for an unknown future.

Thia stared at the blade. "Dad told me about it. He said it's a family heirloom as old as the lineage itself."

"That it is."

"Said that Atrius Arinthian wielded it."

"That he did."

"And that the Dreadnoughts had gifted it to him for allowing them sleep."

"That they did."

"Sounds a bit like a children's tale."

"I once thought the same."

"What made you change your mind?"

"History. The study of history made me change my mind. And visiting the Arcaneum. Seeing things beyond all current understanding … changed my perspective forever."

Thia shivered. "I'd never want to wield it. Too *much* of that history. Too much violence. And I'm just not the violent type."

"And that is a great mercy," Anna said. Yet she was torn. Not wanting to wield a blade also meant her daughter would not be as adept at defending herself. Her dueling skills were so subpar that she actively avoided mock duels with friends in safe surroundings. There was currently no situation in which Anna envisioned her daughter receiving the scion, not even in the event of Anna's death. It would be an instant curse, a deadly hourglass with precious few particles of sand. Right now, were Anna to die by accident or due to natural causes, her will explicitly stated for the scion to go to the crown and be handed to a worthy Solian warlock champion. And a violent death would, of course, mean someone killing her to capture the scion for themself.

"Wait, is that your academy satchel?" Thia lifted the well-worn leather bag. " '*Omnio incipus equa liberatus corsisi mei.*' " She drummed the back of the satchel with the fingernails of both hands. "Why does that sound so familiar?"

Anna, stuck thinking about her disappointing performance, telekinetically righted an overturned chair and slumped into it. "It's a motto." She had let her skills slip to an embarrassing extent. What if she had to face someone far more competent than teenagers at school, or street thugs, or a sparring partner? Let alone someone like Scadius?

"A motto of our family?"

"Of the Library of Antioc."

"And what are these etched lines for?"

"They represent my tournament wins."

"Oh, right. It even says so right above. You were unbeaten, weren't you?"

"Mmm."

"Fiery." Thia put the satchel aside and continued digging.

All begin equal but only the curious thrive, Anna thought on her daughter's behalf, finding sad irony in the fact that Thia had not asked what the motto meant. She did not have the curious streak her mother possessed.

"Whoa, Mom, there's, like, a treasure trove of stuff here! Got all your old school robes, and look at all these trophies! Wait, what's this?" Thia lifted a long-sleeved and bell-skirted dress that sparkled in the light of her lit palm. "Ooh, pretty." She pressed it against herself. "Oh my gosh, it's like moonlight! When did you wear this? And why is there a splotch of blood on it?"

"My first academy dance, before I dated your father. And that's tomato juice. Your aunt purposely shoved a lordling into your father, spilling our drinks on it. I think I bawled all the way back to my dorm room."

Thia gave a twirl with the dress, face turned upward. "Mmm," she toned.

"It wasn't nearly as dreamy a time as you are imagining it. It was … lonelier."

"I could wear this dress to the Endyear dance. It's a bit out of fashion, but if I had it cleaned and loosened a bit … gosh you were thin."

"I was lean." Anna, supporting the side of her head with a hand, smiled. "You'd look lovely in it."

"I'd look *dazzling*. Can I have it? Pleaaaaase?"

"On one condition."

Thia slumped. "Come on, Mom … I told you I don't stand a chance."

"I guess the dress will have to wait until you do."

"Ugh, you're horrible," Thia said, dumping the dress back into the trunk.

"Folded, please."

Thia folded the dress, muttering how she'd be lucky to pass a single class.

Anna stood. "Let me give you a hand."

"With what?"

"With studying."

"Ugh. If you have to."

* * *

From across the room, Anna watched her daughter poring over a book on the myriad nuances of 7th degree spells. The afternoon sun streamed in through the old stained-glass window, making a halo of Thia's frizzy hair. The only sound was the quiet roar of the pair of hearths flanking Anna and Niterra, who sat on cushions, books in their laps.

"You think our efforts will pay off for her exams?" Anna whispered.

"Not know," Niterra whispered back. "But she distracted."

"With what? Friends? Drinking? Partying? Boys?"

"This I not know. She no talk. But she have many friends at school."

"Mmm."

Thia was indeed a popular girl, at least amongst a certain crowd who enjoyed Drama class. It was the quirky type of popular, for she wasn't a bookworm, nor was she a social butterfly who attended all the lavish parties, preying on the latest gossip like a mirko hunting children. Mercifully she also wasn't the Drama type who threw out lines from plays or poems every single chance she got, but rather the type who enjoyed the camaraderie of learning a play together and exploring its meaning and story. She'd had plenty of boyfriends too, all insecure but interesting-to-her boys, short flings that usually ended in arguments.

Yet watching her study was so intimately familiar to Anna, as if she were seeing a reflection of herself. Except this girl fiddled with her quill a lot more, chewing on the feather portion, and oft whilst staring out the window as if daydreaming.

"Stop staring at me, Mom. It's freaking me out," Thia said without looking up. "And stop whispering about me. I can hear you, you know."

"Sorry," Anna blurted.

"Old buzzards," Thia muttered, though with a cheeky grin.

Anna flipped a page in a musty book about kargeyasnaras. Niterra, meanwhile, ran an ebony finger along a page from a book titled *The Intricacies of the Common Tongue of Solian: A Discourse on Language*.

"Solian language dumb," the Black Eagle declared.

"I'm sure you know the old proverb, 'Better late than never.' "

"Hrmph."

Niterra had taken to doing some learning of her own of late, though it was more of an amusement to those around her than anything else, for all she did was complain. About how the Solian tongue loved to play coy. How it was cowardly and soft and without honor, with its ambiguities and false niceties and concessions and cheap proverbs. Above all she hated sarcasm, calling it "Oily humor," for there was no such thing in Nodia.

"What about that Ralf boy?" Anna pressed in a quieter whisper, unable to help herself. "Is she fraternizing with him much?"

"A little," Niterra whispered back. "They act … in a way."

"In what sort of way? Funny? Odd? Secretive? Lovey-dovey?"

"Lovey-dovey?" Niterra's face scrunched as if she'd stepped in dung. "What this … horrible word?

"Do they secretly embrace? Kiss? Hug? That sort of thing."

"I not know. But she secretive. Yes, secretive."

"You two clucking old hens can stop talking about me anytiiiiime now," Thia sang, head propped on one arm as she studied.

Anna and Niterra cleared their throats and pretended to be busy with their books. Thia shook her head, muttering something about nosy busybodies.

Anna's gaze wandered to the parlor table, on top of which sat the black necromantic book confiscated from Ralf. She suspected it was a spell, but she couldn't be sure. Until she found a way to crack the kargeyasnara, it could be a recipe for demon cake for all she knew.

The winter sun crept across the room. Pages turned, tea was sipped, few words were said.

Deep in the book, Anna frowned with concentration at a particular passage. She circled it with a finger and gave it a double tap.

"You find something?" Niterra asked.

"Not sure yet. We know there are various kinds of kargeyasnaras. The basic kargeyasnara, which is a slip-rune sequence puzzle; a kargeyasnara *ciphera*, a password puzzle rune; a kargeyasnara *locka*, which is a key-lock puzzle with a key that needs to be put together before insertion; and various others. But this, this one I have not heard of …" She tapped the page again.

Niterra leaned over like an eager schoolgirl. "What it say?"

" 'One of the first slip-rune sequence puzzles to go out of favor was known as a kargeyasnara *arcana*, which required the casting combination of certain spells to unlock the puzzle stage. This was because it was one of the more complicated kargeyasnaras to craft, and therefore teach. The arcaneologist should watch for complicated key-lock patterns on the leading edges of the tendrils, which indicate equally complicated spells may be required to fit the patterns, much like a key inserted into a lock.' Obviously, hence the word key-lock," Anna muttered, smoothing the page with a hand. "I think that's why we haven't been able to understand the door puzzle. We've been thinking we can decipher the geometries, but the reason we haven't broken through might be because it's not a question of complexity, but simplicity."

"Stone talk riddles."

"We've been trying to understand the pattern of waves after drops have fallen in the pond. What we *should* be looking at is what the drops are made of." Anna stood up. "I'm going to the excavation."

Thia bolted up from her book, having taken a short sunshine nap. "Ooh, can I come? Will Ralf be there? I'm coming."

"You ought to study. Exams start tomorrow."

"Mom, I need a break. Been studying all quint. Besides, it's a Study Day. I *deserve* a break."

"A Study Day is named as such for a reason, Thia."

"If I study one more word my poor brain is going to explode." She knocked on the side of her head. "Hear that sloshing? It's already a puddle of ooze. Come on, Mom, you *know* how hard I've been working. I earned a break. Don't be stingy. Besides, I'll take some of my books with me."

Anna, out of excuses, could only purse her lips. Thia had indeed been studying harder than she had ever studied before, so why not reward her? Besides, Anna had promised to be more trusting of her daughter.

"All right. But dress warm."

* * *

"That is a *fantastic* revelation, Arcanist Stone!" Ottentus exclaimed in his Franterran accent, which they heard as, "Zat iz a *fantastic* revelation, Arcanizt Ztone!" He twirled like a kid, Anna's book on kargeyasnaras, floating open before him, coming along for the ride. "Of course, of course, of *course*! Why had I not seen this before, yes?"

Thomas, standing by the giant slab door, massaged his scalp. "So this whole time we've been thinking wrong? It isn't one of the standard kargeyasnaras, but some obscure variant that went out of fashion a few centuries ago? And the only way to solve it is to cast specific *spells* at it?"

"A little more than a few centuries ago, but essentially, yes, that's my theory," Anna replied, striding over to the slab, hand splayed with Reveal. "Look here, at these specific tendril geometries. The saw-like pattern seems random, yet it concludes in a definite dip before—"

"—restarting, right. And here we were thinking it was fractaline."

"Deceptively complicated," Anna continued, "when in fact there's a definitive beginning and an end to the tendril path. So now we know that casting certain spells leaves a tendril imprint that—"

"—also looks deceptively complicated," Thomas finished, nodding. "I get it, I get it." He beamed at her. "My brilliant wife solves another puzzle."

"Not quite solved. Got a long way to go here. We don't know which—or even how many—spells create the opposite pattern."

"Creating an exact key-lock mechanism," Ottentus sang, spinning about once again and laughing. "Oh, Anna, Anna, Anna! She is such a brilliant arcaneologist, yes?"

Thomas did a little shoulder wiggle. "I married a smartie, eh?"

Anna forced a smile at her husband. How she wished he showed her this sort of attention outside their research! And that certain look almost made her blush, for suddenly she was conscious of how young she still looked. So why wasn't he showering her with affection?

Then, like a curtain, a distant look descended over his eyes, as if he were seeing their son in her face, and he cleared his throat and returned his attention to the runic slab, one arm folded across his chest, a finger tapping his chin. "So now … which spells slip into the tendril pattern?"

"And how many?" Ottentus asked, arm folded the same way, a finger tapping his bald chin.

"Just cast all of them at it," Thia blurted. "Everything you know."

The three adults turned to Thia, who sat cross-legged beside Ralf. The pair were playing cards, their study books open beside them. It irked Anna some that their knees touched. She still remembered the boy's caustic words to her and how he had squeezed Thia's waist. She had wanted so badly to slap his hands away, then slap his face for his gall.

Ottentus snapped his fingers. "Perhaps you ought to focus on your studies, yes, boy?"

"Yes, master." Ralf elbowed Thia. "Let's leave the old fogies to it."

The pair got up, dusted off their behinds, grabbed their books, and trundled off to the furthest table that was still within sight. Niterra, who sat reading a book near a half-filled cart laden with rubble, stood up and tottered after them, her chair floating alongside. Once the teenagers had settled down, keeping their backs to her, she put down the chair, smoothed her robe underneath her, sat, and resumed reading.

Thomas cracked his knuckles. "Shall we?"

And so the three accomplished warlocks began casting spell after spell at the slab from their arsenal. Anna kept her fingers splayed and studied not only how the tendril patterns of the slab and their spells fit, but how Ottentus's 20th degree master tendril work looked. What she saw astounded her. Unlike an average warlock, or even an advanced warlock like her, his spell casting was pristine and precise. It was like she and

Thomas were carving wood with chisels, whereas Ottentus was carving with a scalpel. Sure, Anna had caught glimpses of perfect castings, but she had never *seen* them cast back-to-back like this, over and over. And Ottentus was himself a smooth caster, his gestures accurate and graceful.

They continued throwing spells at the slab, steadily working their way up the degrees, yet nothing altered the tendril geometries.

Until Ottentus cast one of the most heavily monitored and restricted spells in the standard arsenal, a spell none of them thought would do anything—the 13th degree Memory Wipe, a highly controlled, deeply unethical, and almost always illegal-to-cast spell.

"The tendrils danced!" Anna exclaimed, shooting forth, hand splayed open. As if they were chords strummed by a lutist, a full third of the tendrils had vibrated. "There are three spells, and we just found one of them," she announced.

Thomas, studying the same patterns, grimaced. "How do you know it's three?"

"Two-thirds of the key-lock geometries remained dormant."

"Yes, well deduced, Arcanist Stone," Ottentus said, bald head nodding. "This continues the pattern of the witch's mark. Three spells. One found, two remain. Let us resume." He shivered. "Oh, how exciting! I suddenly feel quite young, yes?"

They continued casting spells, with Thomas having to bow out at the 15th degree, where his arcane progress had stalled. As he looked on with a curled lip, fingers splayed with Reveal, Anna's and Ottentus's castings slowed due to many of the spells, being rituals, requiring more time to cast. Anna soon bowed out at the 18th, her current degree. Ottentus continued on alone, face scrunched with concentration as he took his time getting each 19th degree spell right. Doppelganger—nothing. Combat Portal—no movement. Possession—

"Ye, gods, they jumped!" Thomas exclaimed, shooting forth to study the tendrils alongside Anna.

"It was a perfect marriage," Anna said, watching the vibration of the tendrils die to stillness. She took note that it was another spell that came with heavy ethical concerns, ones addressed by every responsible warlock body, from the high council to the governing academy committee.

"Slow Time will be useless," Ottentus concluded, almost enjoying seeing the disappointment on Anna's and Thomas's faces. No warlock, no matter how high in degree, passed up an occasion to watch the casting of such a legendary spell.

"But I think I know which final spell is required," he added.

Anna and Thomas could hardly breathe as Ottentus cast the complicated and lengthy ritual that was the infamous 20th degree Arcastrate. Each held their breath, hands splayed before them in anticipation. When the spell hit, the tendrils leaped to life, and Anna and Thomas squealed and embraced, for much of their research had led to this point.

"Wait, why didn't anything happen?" Thomas asked.

Anna instantly knew the answer. "They have to be cast simultaneously."

"It's impossible to simulcast two rituals," Ottentus said. "Your friend—" He nodded to Niterra, who was sitting, reading as if nothing interesting was happening. "She can cast the 19th, yes?"

"As a matter of fact, she can," Anna said, and waved Niterra over when she happened to glance up, sensing they were talking about her. When she came over, Anna explained what they wanted to do, and Niterra merely nodded her understanding as if having expected to be called upon all along. Unlike Anna and Thomas, the castings had not impressed her, no doubt because she had seen many such castings in her eighty-three years.

"Memory Wipe, Possession, Arcastrate," Ottentus noted, pacing before the slab. "Interesting."

"Why interesting?" Thomas pressed. "Are we talking about ethics again?"

"All three spells have necromantic roots," Anna replied on Ottentus's behalf.

Thomas folded his arms. "And what is the relevant context?"

"It's arcaneological history," Anna said. "The spells Vivictus chose to solve his puzzle all happen to have necromantic roots, which might be his way of warning us."

"We know necromancy has been corrupted over time, yes?" Ottentus threw in. "And therefore, much like certain parts of ancient healing, it became—" He interlaced the fingers of both hands together. "—*verbatten*."

"Forbidden," Thomas whispered, translating.

"But not necessarily forbidden in an evil way. More like …" He rubbed two fingers together. "Like healing. Maybe advanced healing, yes? Advanced arcane arts. See? Oh do forgive me, I am thinking too fast for my clumsy tongue to keep up."

Thomas looked at Anna to clarify, which she promptly did.

"The study of death and life were once thought to be two sides of the same coin," Anna explained. "So, in *context*, this could also serve as a reminder that much of our current knowledge is a misunderstanding of old knowledge."

"I still don't understand." Thomas glanced at Niterra for reassurance and received only a flat look.

Ottentus stacked a hand on top of the other, then slid the bottom hand out and slapped it on top. "Misunderstanding on misunderstanding—"

"—creating layers of obscurity through time," Anna concluded. "Presumptions built upon older presumptions, creating a cloud of knowledge that is simply—" She flipped open her palms. "—wrong."

Ottentus wiggled two fingers at the slab. "Master Vivictus argued *against* banning necromancy."

"And he was vilified for it," Anna said. "The original knowledge that made up The Founding came from a time prior to the formation of the degrees. We have to remember it was an era of wild arcanery. But, importantly, back then necromancy was considered the eighth primary element. Vivictus, sensing where the wind was blowing, might have felt he needed to preserve ancient knowledge."

She made circles in the air with both palms, excitedly adding, "Remember that this slab—this chamber—was built after Occulus was defeated." She was barely conscious that Thomas was glancing between Ottentus and her with a confused frown. "Occulus, being a necromancer, solidified in people's minds that necromancy was a blight never to be trifled with. But the knowledge was *already* intertwined with arcanery on a fundamental level."

Ottentus was nodding along with a proud smile.

Thomas's frown only deepened. "I hate feeling this dense."

Ottentus clapped him on the shoulder. "Nonsense, my man, you are a great help."

"Or condescended to," Thomas muttered under his breath, which Ottentus ignored or pretended not to hear.

Anna, needing to focus on the challenge at hand, began pacing, extending one finger after another. "4th degree Fear. 5th degree Darkness. 7th degree Blind—"

"—the 9th degree Frenzy," Ottentus threw in.

Anna pointed at him in acknowledgment as she continued pacing. "12th degree Tongues is fabled to have originally been created to commune with demons."

"Now we stray into mythology," Ottentus said.

"Memory Wipe, Bewitch, Metamorphosis—"

"I get it, I get it," Thomas said, turning to the slab. "You're saying we're on the right path. If your assumptions are correct—"

"Theories," Anna corrected.

"If your *theories* are correct, this furthers Master Vivictus's argument that *all* knowledge should be preserved. And that should—at least in theory—lead us to The Hall of Sacred Doors."

Anna stopped pacing before the slab, where she nibbled on the end of a fingernail. "There's only one way to find out."

Niterra glanced the slab over. "Those three spells. I do not like combination. Could spawn monster."

"Forgive me, venerable one, but there are a whopping *seventy-two* degrees between the four of us," Thomas said. "I hardly think anything stands a chance against such competence."

This silenced Niterra.

"If the old master builder *did* protect it with a guardian," Anna noted, "that is proof that whatever he is trying to protect could potentially be used for nefarious ends."

"The Hall of Sacred Doors *is* supposed to have a door to Hell," Thomas said. He shrugged. "Or so goes the legend."

The group exchanged looks before hurrying to take up attack positions.

Anna considered telling Thia and Ralf to vacate the cave, but also didn't want to let them out of her sight—and not just because she was wary of what they were up to, but in case something supernatural happened that could endanger them.

Thomas took up a position behind Anna, for it was assumed she would be the one to cast the 13th degree Memory Wipe. But because all three spells had different casting lengths, everyone had to start theirs at certain times. Arcastrate taking the longest, Ottentus had to begin his first. This was later followed by Niterra beginning the Possession ritual, and finally by Anna starting the Memory Wipe spell.

Generations ago, Memory Wipe's ethical use became limited to erasing a horrible trauma, and was thus more useful to the healing element than anything else. Mostly, it was taught for the exam, and in a limited, underpowered fashion that greatly tempered its effect. It was no longer used as a punishment, for it had been found that those whose memories had been wiped tended to repeat their crimes in one form or another, sometimes with catastrophic results. Also, the wipe, if done incorrectly, could be undone with the 14th degree healing spell Rectify Memory.

Anna went through the motions of thought, which had to be precisely aligned—and were quite malignant—if examined from afar. Each thought built on the prior, starting with *I wish to erase this precise memory of the subject*, continuing on with, *This memory will be extracted by eliminating the following foundations*, and after some in between steps, ending with, *I will now utter the final incantation that will trigger the destruction of said memory and its roots.* Of course, usually one would have an idea of the memory involved, but in this case, Anna cast the version taught for the exam. The variant was always cast against a special ancient training dummy that only lit up if the spell—any version of it, no matter how tempered or watered down—had been properly cast.

With the requisite thoughts aligned, and as her cohorts readied their final steps, everyone slightly slowing or speeding up to match each other's casting pace, Anna raised a hand and twisted it, incanting, "*Erassa memora au o minad.*"

The three spells struck simultaneously, and there resounded a great *Gong!* as the entire slab rippled like a wave. That wave continued through the surrounding rock—and strengthened, making the ground rumble.

"What's going on?" Thia called from the far table.

"Stay back and raise your shields!" Anna shouted, raising her shield above her head to protect it from falling debris.

The ripples abruptly ceased, leaving behind a ringing silence. Then the rock of the cavern surrounding the slab jumped forth. It hung in the air as a loose bundle of stones before it began coalescing into a form.

"Ye gods, what is *that*?" Ralf shouted over the grinding noise.

Anna glanced back to see him and Thia standing shoulder to shoulder, each with their earth shield raised above their head, dust and pebbles falling on them.

She returned her attention to the slab and saw a rocky behemoth take shape, its head scraping the ceiling. Then … silence.

Everyone gaped.

"Is it … is it a *statue*?" Thomas whispered, hands raised before him, fiery shield on his left arm.

Anna shook her head, unsure. She was about to splay the fingers of her hand to cast Reveal, when a pair of crimson eyes opened up on its head.

Someone immediately shouted, "Golem!"

BEHEMOTH OF ROCK

Niterra, Anna and Thomas all slapped their wrists together, roaring, "*Annihilo ito!*" with Niterra saying *dio* in place of *ito*. Anna's and Thomas's third offensives shot three prongs apiece—lightning and fire, respectively—whilst Niterra's shot four twisting blasts of air. All slammed into the golem, knocking it back a rumbling step.

When the smoke from Thomas's fire prongs cleared, it became apparent that the spells had done no damage whatsoever, leaving behind only char marks. Anna, realizing the thing was immune to arcanery, shouted over her shoulder, "You two—ruuuun!" whilst she, Thomas and Niterra retreated a bit.

Then the golem did something Anna had never seen a golem do—it reached out with a huge paw and made a pulling motion. As if snagged by an invisible rope, Thia and Ralf were sprung backward with a yelp.

Anna, seeing her daughter shooting toward the behemoth, felt bile rise up her throat. Blood raced through her veins as every motherly instinct kicked in. She lashed out telekinetically, halting Thia only ten feet away, while Ralf careened through the golem's legs.

Ottentus, meanwhile, finished casting the formidable 17th degree Incarnate, a spell that infused him with ice and exploded him to be the same size as the golem.

"Elementals!" Niterra shouted, and she and Thomas drew five-pointed shapes in the air, roaring, "*Summano elementus marjorus!*" with Niterra saying *kampiona* in place of *marjorus*, for she knew the 19th degree version of the spell whilst Thomas only knew the 14th. The difference between the two spells was girth and power, with Niterra's air elemental vastly bulkier than Thomas's.

"Elementus—attack!" the pair shouted, pointing at the golem.

As both elements launched forth to pummel the golem with their fists, Anna drew a circle around her daughter, incanting, "*Sfaera au praentergo buboa!*" encapsulating a screaming Thia in a protective ball of lightning. A brief memory, forever seared into Anna's brain, saw herself looking at her old friend Samantha lying dead within such a bubble.

Behind and underneath the golem, a shaking Ralf made a raking gesture, voice quivering as he shouted, "*Infermi!*" a spell Anna was unfamiliar with. Students learned all sorts of off-the-books spells in their spare time, and there was hardly a moment to wonder or care which one this was, especially seeing as it was ineffective.

Above him, the golem shuddered from thudding blows delivered by the pair of elementals. Then the behemoth reared back and, with one powerful punch, obliterated Thomas's elemental, showering them all with sparks and bits of flame.

Niterra and Thomas threw a volley of spells at the golem, with Thomas keeping close to Thia's bubble.

"Master-level golem!" Anna shouted above the cacophony, trying to figure out how to destroy it whilst standing protectively before Thia's bubble.

Niterra's elemental exploded with another punch, forcing Ottentus, brimming with ice that made sheets of cold air plume forth from his gigantic body, to take its place. The golem punched and Ottentus swerved aside. The golem punched with its other fist and Ottentus parried with an icy arm, but the punch was strong enough to send cracks rippling up the icy exterior.

All able warlocks then launched another volley of spells at the golem, none of which had any effect whatsoever. Ottentus even tried opening up a giant combat portal underneath it, but the golem was immune to that too, as it was immune to being teleported away, something Ottentus tried by snatching its wrist and snapping the Group Teleport incantation.

Anna's mind raced. How did one defeat something immune to arcanery? Then she remembered—*the scion!* As spells continued to slam into the golem, she drew it out of her pocket. She considered casting Incarnate to make herself just as large, to bring her physical staff skills into play, when the golem kicked out. She instinctively jumped aside, simultaneously yanking on the blue bubble. It shot away—but not enough, for the golem's toe caught the bubble's edge, punting it. Anna and her encapsulated daughter were sent hurtling, the pair spinning around each other, joined by Anna's telekinetic tether, until they slammed against a cave wall with a sickening *crunch*.

The women yelped in pain, Anna tumbling to the ground like a ragdoll and Thia doing the same inside the bubble. Anna dazedly scrambled to right herself before noticing her daughter lying limp. Anna's worst nightmare became true as she again saw Samantha's lifeless body lying inside her bubble of lightning. "No, no, no, not again—" Anna gibbered, heart threatening to shatter forever.

As spells whizzed and banged and exploded behind her, she slashed across the air, hysterically shouting, "*Sfaero null!*" The bubble vanished, leaving behind her still daughter.

The ground rumbled, but Anna did not care. With a shaking hand, she raised her palm above her daughter's head, incanting, "*Examino potente morbus aurus persona.*" The 1st degree healing spell Diagnose showed a heartbeat, and Anna expelled an immense sigh of relief. Her daughter had merely been knocked out.

She turned her attention back to the golem and narrowed her eyes. No spell was doing damage, not even the four physical ice bolts of the Fourth Offensive, cast by a 20th degree master warlock, left more than a scratch. Ottentus was back to his regular size, reduced to telekinetically keeping the thing off balance while Niterra and Thomas blasted it with the occasional spell they thought might work. Like Thia, Ralf lay unconscious by the opposite wall, having apparently been knocked out in the same manner.

With the scion buzzing before her, Anna strode forth. She raised an arm and lashed out telekinetically, catching the golem's right fist just as it exploded a giant ice elemental Ottentus had cast. Then she lashed out again and caught the other arm. The golem pulled back, dragging Anna along like a leashed dog, but she dug in her heels and pulled with all her telekinetic might. The space around her warped as the scion strobed with silent lightning.

Thomas, Niterra and Ottentus, seeing she had slowed the golem to a molasses-like crawl, joined in with their Telekinesis, until the thing stood frozen in place. Only its pitiless crimson eyes moved, looking from warlock to warlock, all of whose arms were outstretched holding Telekinesis.

"Now what?" a panting Thomas asked.

"Try melting," Niterra said, wincing from the strain.

Thomas let go of his hold and whirled his hands about in a whirlpool fashion, incanting, "*Summano fiero virli!*" The air spun before him and burst into flames, creating a tornado made of pure fire. Thomas used his arms to keep the tornado centered on the golem's torso, but all it accomplished was to heat their faces, for the golem did not so much as start to glow, indicating the spell did not possess nearly enough heat to melt its rock.

"Snuff it! It's too hot!" Anna shouted above its whirling roar.

Thomas slashed at the air and the tornado vanished with a fiery *whoosh*. He quickly resumed his telekinetic hold.

"We cannot defeat it, yes?" Ottentus yelled, his chest rising and falling from the exertion.

"Need a battering ram," Anna said through gritted teeth.

"An amplified one at that," Thomas added.

"Your army has one, yes? But I will need permission."

"Leave that to me," Thomas said. "King's a friend."

"I can't hold it forever," Anna said. "But I can hold on while you lot escape. I don't think it'll follow us out of the cave." It was too big to fit through the tunnel and would likely stick around to guard the slab until its casting duration ran out, which, considering the originating caster, could be days, even months.

"I'll grab Thia," Thomas said.

"And I will take the boy," Niterra offered.

"I shall hold it with you until we both go, yes?" Ottentus said.

Anna nodded. "On three, you two let go. One … two … *three!*"

Thomas and Niterra let go and the golem's limbs slowly ground forth, this despite Ottentus and Anna's combined telekinetic might being easily over fifty degrees, though both were tiring quickly. Such was the raw power of ancient arcanery cast at the master level. Historically, golems were always a tricky thing for warlocks to deal with due to their invulnerability to arcanery. Simply casting one into existence was once considered a pinnacle achievement for a 20th degree, at least when it came to summoning a guardian. That was before the knowledge of how to cast one had been lost to time, of course.

Anna and Ottentus struggled to hold on, but their telekinetic strength steadily waned, and the golem began to win ground. It slowly reached out an arm toward Ottentus and splayed its fingers. The man sensed its telekinetic hold and snapped off, "*Impetus perago,*" vanishing with a *thwomp*, leaving Anna to deal with the behemoth alone.

The golem's arm swiveled toward her at a faster clip now. But Anna, seeing Scadius's sly smile as he told her how the arcane muscles wither, redoubled her efforts. With a groan, the fishbowl around her expanded. The scion flashed even faster, strobing now. Her teeth ground against each other and she scowled up at the golem. For a moment, miraculously, they were at even strength. Anna remembered finally winning the boulder tug-of-war at the Plowman farm, a few years before the old man passed on.

But the hold could not last, for Anna felt the rapid approach of the arcane horizon. Overdraw loomed, and with it would come arcane sickness or perhaps death. Refusing to take such a needless risk, she wrenched free with a jerk, visualized the cave entrance, and as a mighty fist sailed her way, incanted, "*Impetus peragro!*"

With a *thwomp*, she reappeared outside and quickly shot to her daughter, being seen to by Thomas, who held one of her hands.

"You all right?" Anna asked, taking her daughter's other hand, her chest heaving from the telekinetic exertion.

Thia nodded groggily. She and Ralf had come around, though both moved snail-slow.

"Get ready to Group Teleport," Anna ordered, linking hands with Ralf as well before looking over her shoulder at the cave entrance along with everyone else, all surely wondering the same thing—would the golem pursue them outside the cave?

But all they heard was a deep silence.

"It's protecting the slab, yes?" Ottentus noted, and everyone relaxed a little.

Anna took another moment to look her daughter over, moving her chin left and right and staring deep into her half-lidded eyes.

"I'm *fine*, Mom," Thia croaked, withdrawing both hands from her parents.

Anna raised a palm at Ralf, readying to cast Diagnose.

"I'm fine too, Arcanist Stone," he said, wincing. "Just have a headache."

"I take girl home?" Niterra offered.

"Can't let either of them out of my sight," Anna said. "Both of you need to be monitored, so don't wander." There had been instances of people getting hit hard on the head and later dying, usually from brain swelling or bleeding. If either of them suddenly passed out, she would have to immediately teleport them to a high-degree healer.

"Can we go home now, Mom?" Thia whispered, voice weak.

"Not yet. I don't like the look of you."

"I'm fine, Mom. Just … just need to rest."

"I'll get to petitioning the king," Thomas said, standing. "The army has a small arsenal of arcanely amplified ballistae, catapults, and battering rams. The trick will be to talk them into lending us one." He shook his head. "That was a close one. *Too* close. We'll have to get you kids out faster, or keep you away altogether. Anyway, off I run. You do as your mother says, Thia."

Thia only closed her eyes and lay back to rest, hands holding her stomach as she took long breaths.

"I'll be back soon," Thomas said. "*Impetus peragro.*" He vanished with a *thwomp*.

"You and me are going to have a little talk, *Apprentice*," Ottentus barked.

"What did *I* do?" Ralf whined.

"Come here. Come. Here!"

"Ugh." Ralf hauled himself to his feet and shuffled aside with Ottentus, who proceeded to berate him for his reckless behavior inside the cave, specifically when it came to spell casting. The man's voice soon lowered to a hissing whisper, and the boy dropped his head and nodded, mumbling an apology.

Anna, surprised the young earth warlock had become an apprentice to the ice master, nonetheless returned her attention to her daughter, sweeping her frizzy hair aside from her forehead, shiny with sweat.

They waited for a time, but when Thomas finally reappeared, he informed them that the battering rams were being used in military exercises, and one would not be available for another quint at least.

"I think the commander was lying," Thomas added. "He doesn't much like outsiders taking possession of military weapons. But I also think he doesn't like me personally because the man does not drink."

That settled the matter for now, with Ottentus and Thomas agreeing to research how to destroy the golem while they waited for the battering ram to become available. In the meantime, Anna resolved herself to overseeing exams, which would take place all quint at the academy.

"Come, Daughter," she whispered, giving her hand a squeeze. "Let's take you home."

OLD CUSTOMS AND
ANCIENT THINGS

❧━━━━━━━━━━━━━━━━❧

Up on stage, Anna straightened before Ralf, conscious that her daughter would be tested by the stern Prigmathani, who stood nearby. She and Prigmathani were two of a slew of arcanists who were testing the 7th degrees, having already administered the first six degrees over the course of the quint. Each time, the stage was reset for the next degree, as each degree required different challenges. A fat golden hourglass sat on a tall table beside each arcanist. Emblazoned into the top of each hourglass was a rune, which reset the hourglass with a touch and the trigger word, *resetio*.

"Initiate Turman, you will now demonstrate competency in the four compulsory spells of the 7th degree," Anna began, reciting the traditional phrase all arcanists used. "Failure to perform or failure to follow my precise instructions will result in disqualification. Nod if you understand."

As Ralf nodded, Anna heard Prigmathani, ever the efficient arcanist, cast Reveal in anticipation of Thia's crucial test.

Anna stepped aside. "We shall begin with the standard 7th degree Slow spell. Before you is a moving target. When I give the go-ahead, use the spell to slow it down." She splayed her hand, incanting, "*Un vun asperio aurum enchantus*," and the old practice dummy's tendrils lit up with ancient arcanery, for they were from a bygone era in the academy's early history. The helmeted dummy walked left to right in a clunky fashion, its steel surface charred and pockmarked with hundreds of dings and cuts. Inside the pot helm floated a pair of white lights, representing eyes.

Ralf rolled out his shoulders and took a deep breath.

Anna pressed a finger into the rune atop the still-trickling hourglass, incanting, "*Resetio.*" With a white flash, it instantly reset so that all the sand particles were at the bottom. "You will have until the hourglass runs out to cast the entirety of the 7th degree to my satisfaction. Do you understand, Initiate Turman?"

"I do."

She flipped over the hourglass. "Go!"

Ralf drew a figure S in the air, incanting, "*Effectus xadius!*" The dummy slowed to a crawl.

"Nullify it, please."

"*Effectus null.*"

The dummy resumed its awkward march.

Ralf turned to her with a smirk.

"You have one more attempt before disqualification, Initiate Stone," Prigmathani declared.

Thia hopped from foot to foot, face pale, hands wringing.

You can do it, child. Come on! Anna found herself thinking.

"Arcanist Stone?" Ralf cut in.

Anna caught herself and cleared her throat. "Initiate Turman, you shall now demonstrate your proficiency with the 7th degree Blind spell. When I give the go-ahead, use the spell to blind the dummy. Go!"

Ralf made a gouging gesture with two hooked fingers and yanked back, shouting, "*Voidus occa!*" The pair of white lights were instantly snuffed.

"Nullify it, please."

"*Voidus null,*" Ralf said, reversing the gesture, and the dummy's eyes flared back to life.

Anna pumped her fist, hissing, "Yes!"

"Didn't think it was that big a deal," Ralf muttered.

Anna, having witnessed her daughter finally slow her dummy down, once again cleared her throat and tried to refocus on Ralf. "Initiate Stone—I mean, Initiate Turman, you shall now demonstrate your proficiency with the 7th degree Minor Illusion spell. Your task is to craft an illusory stool."

Ralf swallowed, glancing about. Nobody else had been asked to craft something so large. Most had been asked to make illusions of plates or cups or quills or bottles. But Anna suspected he could handle it. Despite distrusting his intentions with her daughter, she wanted to nonetheless challenge the boy, to better him.

"Go."

Ralf hesitated. After a long think, he began to meticulously draw the entire outline of the stool.

"You have one more attempt before disqualification, Initiate Stone," Prigmathani declared, once again tearing Anna's focus away. Thia was now whimpering, rocking back and forth. All Anna wanted to do was rush to her daughter and embrace her and shower her head with kisses whilst cooing encouragements. She well remembered how cold Prigmathani had been toward her when she was Thia's age, so her heart particularly panged for her in that moment.

"Arcanist Stone?"

"Mmm?"

"I completed the spell."

"Oh. Yes. Good." Anna nodded at the stool. "Nullify it, please."

"*Illuseea null,*" and the stool vanished.

"Initiate Turman, you shall now demonstrate your proficiency with the 7th degree elemental spell Summon Minor Wall. It is to be cast precisely along that line there." She indicated a long rope behind her, one of a slew of parallel ropes that had been strung between two poles, one behind the arcanist, and the other at the very back of the stage, the curtains having been raised to reveal the back wall, full of ropes and stage props and battered academy testing equipment.

"Go."

As Ralf performed the complicated gestures, incanting, "*Summano valla minimus girata barricada,*" Anna expelled a sigh of relief upon seeing Thia's ability to make an illusory tankard, probably because Anna had spent the most time on that particular spell with her, grilling her on its arcaneological peculiarities and pronunciative semantics.

Come on, Thia. One more to go! she thought.

Prigmathani demanded she cast Summon Minor Wall, and Thia, in her haste, bungled her first attempt.

"Uh, my time is trickling, Arcanist Stone."

Anna glanced at Ralf's earthen wall of clay and mud and branches, which had the requisite height and thickness. She leveled her chin and shouted, "Pass!"

Now it was Ralf who pumped his fist as he walked off stage, and with plenty time left in the hourglass. But Anna's attention had already returned to her daughter, who was on her final attempt. Then it happened. As another 6th degree student made her way to Anna, Thia managed to summon an earthen wall.

Prigmathani inspected it. Anna could see it was a touch too thin and short, making her sure he would fail her on the spot. He checked the hourglass, which in that moment trickled out. He too leveled his chin.

"Pass!"

* * *

"Really, I was sorely tempted to run to her, pick her up, and twirl her about then and there," Anna said to Syanda as the pair strolled through a bustling Shoptown. It was lunch, and anxious students streamed in and out of shops. Those who noticed them gave deferential nods or acknowledged them with the greeting, "Arcanists."

"I think she gets teased enough because you're her mother," Syanda said.

"Yes, yes, an arcanist is expected to keep their composure at all times."

"Especially one who might become headmistress."

"Mmm."

"Still pondering, are we? Job not interesting enough?"

They passed Emma's Enamels, and Anna recalled painting her nails opalescent what felt like a lifetime ago. The shop window had changed some over the years. In her day it had showcased sparkling enamels in beautifully shaped bottles. Now it showed dull colors in plain bottles. Perhaps it was merely the style of the day.

"It's not that," she said.

"Then what?"

"It's … bah." Anna waved the matter aside.

"Fine, but I'm determined to get it out of you over a glass of wine sometime. You there—" Syanda snapped her fingers at a hooded burgundy-robed warlock smoking a pipe on the outskirts of Shoptown. "—what are you doing?"

The warlock whirled around and descended into a fit of coughing so violent his hood slipped off, revealing a mousy boy of no more than fourteen years of age.

"Ugh, it's so gross," he wheezed, and dumped the pipe into a nearby refuse barrel. "Can't believe they think it's fiery," he muttered, shuffling off, still coughing.

"Some things never change," Syanda said.

Anna spied the old sign, Delia's Dresses. The shop was empty and dark, for the woman had passed away some years ago, and no one in the family had been interested in taking her place. *But some things do change,* she thought. Some of the shops had indeed changed hands or gone to next of kin, but many had also closed down, others sold to new vendors.

"I got essays to grade," Syanda said, "but that was a good lunch. We should visit the Basting Brisket more. See you later?"

Anna halted by another empty shop, Quinion's Quills, Inks and Sands. "Mmm." As Syanda wandered off and the occasional student walked by, bowing their head and saying, "Arcanist Stone," Anna closed her eyes and recalled her and Samantha drooling over all sorts of wonderful quills. The shop had closed long ago after the crotchety old Quinion had died of ridge fever.

Sighing, Anna resumed her wandering and soon came across the Academy of Arcane Arts Artifacts and Arcane Accessories shop. "Arcanist Stone!" sang the squat but beefy man behind the counter, practically barreling over a couple of blue-robed girls in his haste to grab her hand. "What a pleasant surprise!" he said, vigorously shaking her hand before rubbing his giant hands together below his beard. "Are you in the market for an enchanted item, or perhaps a ring recharge?"

"Hello, Bartholomew, and no, but thank you," Anna said with a polite incline of her head, her eyes already poring over the arcane marvels—an enchanted two-hundred-crown ball of fur that could morph into a hat, fifty crowns per parchment that absorbed all ink and could only be revealed with a secret activation word, an enchanted dictation quill for seven and fifty crowns, and a long spyglass for a whopping two thousand crowns. Who could afford such things other than the nobility? There were spell scrolls up to the 10th degree, priced exorbitantly, of course; enchanted spell books; a shimmering and ethereal cloak that could cast Chameleon on its wearer for a limited time; a waterskin that melted snow into water; a shirt that refreshed itself with a vanilla scent when its rune was triggered; and a ring of limited teleportation, the latter pair for an ungodly sum.

"Oh, you young ones missed out on the pleasure of seeing Champion Stone here in the arena," Bartholomew boomed to the remaining students in the shop, a few of whom giggled behind their hands at his ostentatious manner.

"She was a sight to behold, let me tell you." He slapped his wrists together at imaginary opponents. "*Zip! Zap! Zoop! Kaploowee!* Blew opponents apart with her lightning while walking on thin air, I swear to you. You know she's the only one in the kingdom with a scion? That's right. It's the most powerful artifact in the whole kingdom, and can turn anyone into a turnip—" He snapped his fingers. "—like *that*."

"I think you have rather taken to exaggeration over the years, Bartholomew."

Bartholomew pretended like he hadn't heard, eyes sparkling as he continued to entertain his student audience. "We used to sell hundreds of her posters here. *Hundreds.* In fact, I think I still got one." He shot to a wall, reached up to a high shelf, retrieved a scroll and, after blowing the dust off, unfurled it. "Yep, there she is. Look at the fierce pose. The casual yet confident way she holds the staff. The slightly open right hand, ready to cast a potent spell. The eyes of steel that made opponents cower in their boots. You can almost feel the rage in the lightning coursing over her body. But it's not all youthful deadliness, for there is a grace and dignity in the face, is there not?"

Anna quietly slunk away to peruse the rest of the shop, hoping he'd stop.

"And what a headline—'Unbeaten Champion Anna Atticus Stone.' I think this was after her final victory in the Antioc Classic. She'd performed some serious feats of legend in that whole tournament. She didn't just run along the wall, she practically *flew!*"

One of the students went, "Ooh," as Bartholomew recounted fictitious maneuvers Anna didn't bother disputing, for her gaze had focused on a golden object she thought she recognized.

"That's quite a curious little gargoyle statue, is it not?" Bartholomew sang, gliding right over, leaving the students to gaze in amazement between the poster and the woman sharing shop space with them. "I don't know what to make of it. The arcanery is old, likely ancient, but it's also broken—you can see a wing is missing there—making it nothing more than an ornament. The person I bought it from said it stopped working after it was in a fire."

"A building fell down on it," Anna mumbled.

"Really? How can you tell, Arcanist Stone? Then again, I suppose you are advanced enough to be able to identify such things with ease. I'm a mere 11th degree, a candle flame compared to the mighty bonfire of the 18th." He boomed another laugh, but Anna barely heard him through the echoes of spells being flung and the cacophonic fall of a brick building and a gigantic water elemental smashing a blue bubble against the ground.

Before all of that, she saw this little creature moping about on Samantha's desk. *Yes, that was its name—Mopey the Gargoyle!*

"How much?" Anna asked, cutting Bartholomew's spiel about yet another of her legendary duels, which happened to be against Totillus the Turncoat Monk, the man responsible for murdering Samantha.

"For you?" Bartholomew flapped a dismissive hand at the gargoyle. "Twenty crowns?" He winced.

Anna reached into a pocket, realized it was the one with the scion, then reached into the other one, withdrew a pouch, and counted out twenty crowns.

"Why, thank you, Arcanist Stone. I hope it makes a nice trinket."

"Mmm." She drifted to the shop door, wondering if she could perhaps repair the gargoyle. She'd have to inspect it with Reveal to assess the damage, but in theory, the 11th degree Greater Repair might stand a chance, though it would be quite the challenge working on ancient arcanery.

"And I didn't kill Totillus," Anna said, one foot halfway out the door.

"No? But I thought you painted the streets with his guts —"

"A friend spared me from carrying the burden of his death. He died by the rope in Ohm for his crimes. Good day, Bartholomew."

"Good day, Arcanist Stone," Bartholomew murmured, face slack.

* * *

A polite knock came at Anna's office door.

"Just a moment!" she called absently, one Reveal-lit hand splayed above Mopey the Gargoyle and the other pinching at arcane tendrils. She had been neglecting marking student exams, lost in the attempt to fix the gargoyle's ancient arcanery. Besides, the exams could wait. Getting Mopey to work again couldn't, though, as Anna couldn't stop thinking about the little thing.

The sixth academy bell began to gong, and the knock came again.

"A moment, please, I'm casting!" Any warlock would know that meant she needed to concentrate and come back later.

Anna refocused, carefully fitting a crafted tendril sheath onto a new wing segment she had incanted into existence using the 13th degree Create Simple Object incantation. Before casting that spell, she had taken half an hour simply formulating what the wing should look like, what to make it out of — she'd chosen fool's gold — and how it should fit back into the break, a task made much easier by the fact the other wing was still intact. She only hoped her object casting wouldn't fizzle, and so took great care into making it as perfect a casting as she could, which gave it a higher chance of permanence. After conjuring the broken wing into existence, she set it in place and used the intense heat of highly focused and sustained lightning to fuse it in place. Then she moved on to studying the other wing's arcanery in detail in preparation to cast the 11th degree Greater Repair, which allowed her to repair arcanery.

Usually, it'd be almost impossible to recreate an ancient spell of this sort, especially because the knowledge to craft complex animated creatures had been lost to time. But Anna had theorized that all she had to do was copy the other wing's arcanery—and mirror it onto the new wing. The still-intact wing's arcanery was relatively simple compared to the body of the gargoyle, which was dense with complex tendril geometries not even her brilliance could recreate.

The challenge with ancient arcanery was that it had sunk to permanence, meaning it was not pliable like ordinary arcanery. One could not stretch, tear, or move the tendrils unless the entire tendril web had come loose from the object. Although usually when that occurred the web fell back into the arcane ether, vanishing forever, as had happened with the separate wing portion. Thus, the only thing to be done was to recreate the entire wing's arcanery, tendril by tendril, mirroring the geometries, the weaving, and myriad other subtleties of the intact wing, a process that took hours of pure concentration.

With the carefully constructed tendril sheath slipped snugly over the previously conjured wing segment, she used a finger to gently press the base of the tendril web to the tendril body of the gargoyle, spread her other hand over the webbing for additional stability, and whispered, "*Apreyo enchantus delicato obiectum roa.*" She allowed herself one breath before adding a complicator. "*Fusio ata synerga ata kolesh ata apreyo tei komplet.*" The connection sealed with a small white light.

Fuse and synergize and coalesce and repair to completion, Anna thought, translating the complicator literally. She admired the extension's arcaneological beauty, particularly the robustness of the framework that combined multiple aspects, allowing the mind to use each like a tool as needed. In this case, it was the fusion aspect that she had mostly drawn upon to enhance the original repair. Complicators were highly advanced extensions that allowed multiple avenues of discovery—a sort of arcaneological toolbox. Complicators were why arcaneologists spent decades mastering spells like Greater Reveal; there were simply that many variables involved in the craft.

"Come on," she whispered, poking Mopey with a finger. "Wake up."

Then something amazing happened. The gargoyle, stuck in a seated position, opened its beady eyes for the first time in over thirty years.

Anna shot to her feet, hands cupping her mouth. "Unnameables, it worked," she said through her hands. "I can't believe it worked …"

Mopey looked up at her, grimaced, and slouched off to a corner of her desk.

"Mopey, fetch me that quill."

Mopey's small gargoyle shoulders drooped as he shuffled his way to her quill. He picked it up and dumped it before her. Then he folded his arms and turned his back on her, his wings opening and closing like a butterfly's.

The polite knock came again. "I'm finished! You can come in now!" Anna absently said, hands resting on her head as she recalled beautiful memories of her and Samantha giggling while the little creature poked at Bear and Bun-Bun to ascertain if the stuffies were a threat.

The door opened. "Anna?"

Anna, recognizing that voice, was jarred from her reverie to find a thin ebony-skinned man with gray hair and a wrinkled face, a pair of square silver spectacles perched on the end of his nose.

"Jordan?" Anna said, shooting up from her chair. "Jordan!" She rushed over and threw her arms around her old friend.

"Hello, Anna," Jordan said, giving her a tight squeeze before drawing her back to have a good look at her. "My gosh, woman, you look almost as young as you did on graduation day. Unbelievable …"

Anna pressed a hand to the side of his head. "And you have gone gray, my old friend."

"The courts will do that to you." He was a senior barrister now, defending warlocks accused of serious crimes.

"My gosh, how long has it been?" Anna asked, hands on her hips.

"Since the funeral, I think."

"Right, right." Three years.

"I tried visiting you, but you were always busy."

"I'm sorry I didn't come to visit you in turn." Anna waved a hand about vaguely. "Things got … complicated."

"Completely understandable." Jordan glanced around her office as if searching for a topic of discussion. He lit up upon spotting an old herald clipping hanging on a board filled with other such clippings. "Look at that. You kept it."

Anna stepped up beside him and saw a yellowed parchment herald with the title, "Former Academy Student Sells Ingenious Windblower Rune to Solian Navy."

"That was one complicated piece of arcanery," Jordan muttered.

"We were all very proud of you. *My* thesis spell was too complicated to sell to anyone."

"But you can still perform it, right?" Jordan pretended to scrape one arm with the other. "That *peeling carrots* spell, wasn't it?"

"Burst is it's name. And yes, I can still cast it, but it hasn't gotten any easier over time. I *may* have made it a bit too—" She waved a hand about vaguely, searching for the right word.

"—complicated?"

She chuckled, surrendered a nod, and returned to stand behind her desk. She was about to ask what the occasion was for his visit when he spoke first.

"How's that old fool Thomas, anyway?"

Anna shrugged. "He hasn't been the same since … you know."

"Since Samuel. Of course. And Thia?"

"We're awaiting the results of the rest of her exams, but she passed the core spell trial."

"Oh, that's great. That's really great. You must be very proud."

"Immensely."

"You heard from Will?" Jordan pressed.

"Not in years. Last I heard he was carousing about the kingdoms in some caravan."

"Typical."

"And how's your wife?"

"She's with the kids. Probably teaching them the Henawa way to skin a squirrel or something."

The pair chuckled, but Anna sensed a somberness in Jordan's tone.

"Why do I get the feeling you're not here with good news?" Anna asked.

"Sharp as ever." Jordan scratched the back of his head. "It's, um …"

"Spit it out already," Anna said with a nervous chuckle.

"It's your mother."

Anna froze. Jordan had worked near her mother for decades, for she had been a magistrate. "What *about* my mother?"

"She wants to see you."

Anna's mouth hung open. She didn't know if she wanted to rage or cry or run.

"I know, I know. You haven't spoken in, what?"

"Thirty-five years."

"*Thirty*—that long, huh? Wow."

"Thirty-five years, Jordan."

"Yeah."

"Not since renouncing me after the death of my sister and cursing me and my future children."

"I know."

"And now she wants to see me? *Now?*"

"Yes, well—"

"After I begged her to talk to me? After she had her new family slam the door in my face? After she missed my wedding, the birth of my son and daughter? After the *death* of my son, her *grand*son she never got to know? *Now?*"

"You're shouting, Anna. I understand how you feel, but—"

"I don't think you do." Anna was shaking her head. "I don't think you do at all."

Jordan sighed, nodded at his feet. "I suppose I don't."

Anna folded her arms. "What does she want? And why now, after half a lifetime of bitter silence?"

"You know I worked with your mother. She was a hard magistrate, but generally a fair one. She knew I was close to you, though never mentioned anything of it. But after your son's death, she made me promise that, when the time approached, I would fetch you." He looked up at her. "That time approaches."

Anna's arms slipped to hang. "So she's dying."

Jordan gave a solemn nod.

After staring at him, Anna couldn't hold her emotions in anymore. The carefully crafted exterior, honed over decades of practice, cracked, and she burst with a cry and fell. Jordan shot to her, grabbing her before she hit the floor. He lifted her onto her chair, where she slumped.

"It's all right, Anna," Jordan kept whispering, brushing her ponytail away from her face after it had awkwardly flopped over her head. "It's all right …"

Anna hunched forward to rest her face in her hands, elbows on her knees. She sobbed for a time, feeling like the fourteen-year-old she had been when she lost her entire family in the space of days. As he had then, Jordan rubbed her back before she sat up, sniffing and repeatedly smoothing her arcanist's robe. "Right. Right. Right …"

"She's at Mercy of the Unnameables."

Anna nodded, well familiar with the infirmary, having taken plenty of injured people there when her paltry 6th degree healing skills did not suffice.

He offered her a hand. "Allow me to take you to her."

Anna stared at the veined ebony hand. How her friend had aged, yet she had stayed the same. But just as it had been in their youth, when he and William had been quite the pair of rabble-rousing misfits, she felt older than him.

After a nod, she took his hand and allowed Jordan to haul her to her feet.

"Right," she said, smoothing her robe for the umpteenth time. "Right …"

BEDSIDE

Jordan led her down a green-tiled hall filled with withered old people wearing blue hospice gowns. All sat in iron-wheeled chairs made of well-worn wood and cane. The occasional warlock or Ordinary checked on someone or entered a room. The former wore the robe of their degree and a healer's armband, which depicted a serpent coiled around a staff, and the latter wore a white gown embroidered with the infirmary crest over the heart. Patients blubbered inanities or moaned or talked to themselves. Most sat silently, staring at nothing in particular. Small torches flickered behind cages. A third were out, giving the hall a calm dimness.

"The healers don't know how much time she has left," Jordan said as they passed a cart full of empty porcelain bedpans. "Maybe months, maybe less. She wanted to be sure you heard what she had to say, before … you know."

Anna nodded as she released a shuddering breath.

"The thing is, I don't know if she will be able to now. She took a turn of late, and, well, you'll see what I mean …"

As they walked, Jordan looked over to see her still repeatedly smoothing her robe. Mercifully, he said nothing.

An old woman recoiled in a wheelchair. "Watch out, here cometh the reaper!" she called, clumsily signing to the gods with both hands and baring her teeth and hissing at Anna.

"Ignore the loon," Jordan said.

"Right." But Anna suddenly found the black of her robe vulgar against all the white. "Is her family here?" she asked.

"No. I suspect they don't know she wants to talk to you."

Anna wondered what they looked like now. "The kids have to be in their forties. And that means the husband must be—"

"He passed two years ago. Failure of the heart."

"Oh. I see."

Jordan stepped up beside an open door and turned to her. "Here we are. Want me to wait here for you?"

"No, it's all right. You go on home to that family of yours."

"I'd like to have you all for supper sometime."

Anna nodded, sniffing as she whispered, "That'd be lovely."

Jordan nodded as well. "It's nice to see you."

"Nice to see you too."

They briefly hugged. Jordan gave her a kind smile, and left Anna alone. She released another shuddering breath, nodded to herself, said, "Right," and entered the room.

There were four beds, only one of which was occupied. A wispy privacy curtain hung halfway around the bed, showing feet underneath a white blanket. Stacks of towels sat on a nearby shelf, along with neatly folded patient gowns. A single dirty window was closed. The room smelled strongly of eucalyptus and mint, typical of infirmaries and healing wards everywhere.

The hall noise abated at the door, and the room felt like a tomb. But it was not silent. Murmurings came from the bed, a croaking ramble that never ceased.

"… nothing but and untoward displeasure … you never cease to disappoint me, child … I do not care for your tongue, girl … then you should pick it up … do not presume to lecture me … gods be merciful how you soil your mind with inanities … you do beat all, child …"

Anna, hearing herself getting chastised anew, almost turned about on the spot. But something drew her to the voice. Wary of what she was about to see, she padded forth, hands wringing. At the foot of the bed hung a parchment nameplate that read, "Thelma Atticus Riverwood." Anna surmised Riverwood was the surname her mother had adopted from her new family. She looked up and found an old woman she barely recognized. A woman with closed eyes and gray hair and deep wrinkles, the sort earned from a lifetime of frowning. Her hands were prunes, chest rising and falling shallowly. The mouth was moving, spewing words that made little sense.

"… you are a wicked man … a wicked, wicked man … I sentence you to arcastration and death by guillotine …"

Anna watched this old woman who was her mother, slowly seeing the resemblance in the face. She remembered being castigated for not washing the dishes, or her father being lambasted for pushing the sisters too hard in training. She remembered her sister being praised and cuddled while Anna sat watching, wishing she were being cuddled as well. Instinctively she reached for her pocket, thinking to give Bun-Bun a squish, when instead her hand felt the cold outline of the scion.

The woman opened her eyes, yet the rambling never ceased. "She's a horrible girl … a damned girl … certainly my greatest disappointment … should have been her … *should have been her* …"

"Hello, Mama," Anna whispered, voice cracking. She straightened her back and smoothed her robe, refusing to show weakness.

"… she skewered her … skewered my precious baby like she was a rabbit to be cooked over flame … she preens … oh how she preens … in the arena … in the heralds … in the academy …"

Anna bravely drew closer, and the woman's eyes followed her.

"I know that face … wicked girl comes close … cannot forgive her … she's damned … *I* damned her …"

Anna reached out a hand and, for the first time in three and a half decades, touched her mother's arm. The woman's eyes widened as she froze. Anna thought she had stopped breathing, but then her face softened, the frown vanishing. "Is that really you, Anna?" she whispered in a sweet voice.

"It's me, Mama. It's me."

"Anna … Anna, I'm … You have to know something …" Suddenly her face creased with foulness again as the rambling returned. "Arrogant witch shouldn't have had children … knew they were cursed … had them anyway … and look what happened … *look what happened* …" The last she said in a devilish hiss.

Anna tried to harden her heart, but the spears of her mother's words punched through anyway.

"… dragged to Hell … she will get dragged to Hell …"

"I know you don't mean—wait, what did you say? Mama?"

"She will die sooner than you think … and then her soul will go to Hell … and it will be trapped there for all eternity …" The face abruptly softened again. "Oh, Anna … I'm so full of regret … I cannot depart this life without telling you how deeply sorry I am for what I did. How I acted. I was too proud."

"You just said my daughter is going to die."

"What? I … I said no such thing."

"You said it mere heartbeats ago."

"Did I …? I … I don't recall … There's something wrong with me … I'm too old … Please, listen to me—" The frown returned, curdling. "… going to burn for all time …" The woman's head tilted, the voice lowering to a demonic growl. "Her death approacheth, girl … a sin for a sin … one daughter for another … a curse as old as time …"

"What? What are you saying?"

The face softened, the voice sweet once more. "Please, Anna, I don't know what's happening, but you need to be wary. There is a shadow over my heart. I could not take it back, as much as I wanted to."

"Lift the curse, Mama. Lift it. Reclaim me. Say I am your daughter once again. Do it in the old way."

"I … I already did … I already did …"

Anna burst into tears. Her mother had accepted her as a daughter once more without her knowing.

"But the shadow remains, Anna … The shadow remains …"

"Back up, though. What about Thia? What about my daughter—your lone remaining grandchild?"

"Thia … she m—" Her mother's face twisted mid-word, the growl returning. "She will be embraced by the land of rock and fire… There she will be held … purgatory … for all time … a sin for a sin …"

Anna jerked her hand away. "Who are you?"

"I am the sacred Karma you have always dreaded … I took your son … and I will take your daughter …"

Anna splayed her hand. "*Un vun asperio aurum enchantus.*"

"Anna?" her mother asked sweetly. "What is it, my daughter?"

"I see no sign of possession, but curses can be hidden in the body and mind." The finest ones, cast to be tiny and undiscoverable, sometimes required surgery to discover. Anna shuddered at the thought, and was ashamed to consider asking her mother to be opened up by a warlock surgeon. How selfish of her!

"Anna, I'm sorry. I'm so sorry. I was too proud." Her mother closed her eyes, the words a whisper. "Too proud … too …" A gentle snooze began, the chest rising and falling rhythmically.

"She's been like that for a quint now," said a soothing female voice, startling Anna. At the door stood a young milk-skinned woman with long milky hair. A beaded Henawa necklace hung over the crested white robe of the infirmary, and she wore the armband of a healer. Since she lacked an accent, she was not a Henawa outcast, but born into Solian society.

The woman drew the curtain back. "Let's give her some breathing room."

"What's the matter with her?"

The healer sat opposite and rubbed Thelma's hand. "She suffers from age-related delusions. The mind has slipped beyond the reach of our abilities."

"Who has seen to her?"

"We've had a 16th, a 17th, and a 19th degree diagnose her condition. All three concurred. Mania brought on by old age."

"I would like to have someone else look at her. Someone I know."

The woman gave a bittersweet smile, the knowing sort that had seen Anna's reaction many times. "Of course." She looked at Thelma's face. "She spoke of you, Arcanist Stone. In her lucid moments, she kept trying to take back a curse she had inflicted upon you after—" She swallowed, not wanting to verbalize the circumstances involving Anna's sister. "I believe she has tried every variation she could think of, but nothing made her feel different. The poor thing has carried the guilt of your son's death on her shoulders. Strangely, the dementia has both softened and hardened her, as you witnessed."

"How long were you watching?"

"I've already heard everything she said to you. She is …" The woman patted Thelma's hand. "… quite the talker now."

"How long does she have?"

"She is lucid less and less. In fact, the lucidity you saw was the most I have seen in days. The majority of her waking time she is … rather cruel, unfortunately."

"Did you check for—"

"Every variant. Nothing. If it *is* an internal possession, you know that would mean—"

"I know." Anna sniffed, wiped the underside of an eye with a finger, then wiped the other. "I know …"

"It would have to be an off-the-books Possession that my distinguished colleagues could not find. A variant beyond the reach of Diagnose. As you probably know, such occurrences are … more than rare, as they would have to be obscured and made infinitesimally small."

Anna stood. "I will return with my expert."

"As you wish, Arcanist Stone. And although I am honored to meet you, I am sorry it is like this."

"Thank you for trying to comfort her in her final days," Anna whispered. She looked at her mother's troubled face, lips already moving with silent inanities, before striding out of the room.

* * *

"Just beyond, Champion Stone," whispered a gray-robed junior arcaneologist, stepping before a gigantic pair of oaken doors depicting a crimson gargoyle reading a book. Behind the gargoyle teetered a pile of tomes and scrolls.

The mid-twenties young man bowed. "It is a great honor to have you visit our library, Champion Stone. If there is anything we can provide you, anything whatsoever, my office is over there." He bowed again and walked off.

"Mmm," Anna toned absently, looking up at the gargantuan doors. She leveled her head and sighed before projecting the thought, *It's me.*

There was silence. Then came the reply, also in thought form, *You only come when you want something.* The doors remained closed.

Don't play games, Anna replied. *It is beneath you.*

Seven years doing wondrous research without a thought to my own research, and you have the gall to tell me not to play games?

Anna sighed impatiently. *Fine, I'll share our discoveries.*

Another thoughtful silence. *If only you had such an attitude in the first place.*

I don't want to rehash the scion. We've discussed it to death.

Your friend Panza barely shared his despite you promising otherwise.

I made no such promise. It was a suggestion, nothing more.

It was not enough. You did not have enough sway.

He had a kingdom to protect.

That may be so, but the healing arts protect all.

Just open the damn doors already. When they remained closed, Anna smacked her lips and turned on her heel, about to walk off, only to feel the wind of the doors silently opening. Digging her fingernails into her palms in irritation, Anna turned back around and walked into a vast round room, the walls of which were made of glass-fronted bookcases that rose a hundred feet to a glass-domed ceiling. Floating just below that glass dome, before an open bookshelf, was a throne-like chair with a figure sitting in it.

"Games," Anna said aloud, her voice echoing around the chamber. "You love your games. A waste of everyone's time, all to show how *brilliant* you are." She couldn't help the caustic tone. She had had enough of Ning's antics over the years.

The doors silently closed behind her as the chair drifted down toward the floor where there stood a giant desk littered with scrolls, parchments, wax, inks, and quills. High above, two bookshelf cabinet doors silently closed. Sitting in the chair was a sixty-three-year-old Lien Ning, black hair neatly put up in a bun, almond eyes as alert as ever. She was thin, yet she too looked youthful for her age, perhaps in her late forties.

"Two bookworms trying to stem the flow of time," Ning declared as the chair drifted over the desk, parking in front of it.

"Unlike you, I am not afraid of aging. My youth is incidental to the burden I carry."

Ning gave a derisive snort as she stepped out of the chair and smoothed her gray robe. Embroidered over the heart was the emblem of the Library of Antioc—a gargoyle reading a book, the pages of which turned now and then, a wonderful arcane trick that had the threads neatly reweaving themselves over and over.

"You get too comfortable in that thing and you'll never leave it."

Ning turned to ponder the throne-like chair, carved in the shape of a miniature castle complete with battlement supports that connected to drawbridge arms and a backrest that made up a castle tapering to a series of minarets, with various runes carved throughout the chair. "Considering how useful it is, that's a tempting thought. You know you could soil yourself on it and no one would know?" She shook her head in wonder. "Ancient arcanery is a marvel."

Anna avoided thinking about how the specifics of the arcanery involved worked and instead thought of Mopey.

Ning turned to her. "You repaired an artifact that once belonged to the library."

Anna, realizing she had left her thoughts open, pressed her lips together.

"Relax, I won't ask for it back. Though I think you ought to consider donating it to us when you're done playing with it. Its value is in the tens of thousands of crowns, although I of course consider it priceless."

Anna raised an eyebrow.

"That little gargoyle has no known use," Ning added, clasping her hands behind her back. "If that's what you're wondering. It's just one of a precious few rare animated artifacts still around from the old eras."

More games, Anna thought, this time keeping her mind guarded.

"Yes, I could break in. I have advanced that far," Ning said. "But I have honor."

"Aren't I fortunate," Anna muttered.

"I did not achieve the esteemed position of Senior Arcaneologist being a dolt."

Anna grunted. She clasped her own hands behind her back and began pacing, staring up at the wondrous stacks of towering bookshelves in the spacious and circular room. "You always wanted the scion to help with your research. That favor I cannot grant."

"You have a family to protect, that I understand."

"But I can offer something better."

"You have my interest."

Anna stopped and turned to face the famed arcaneologist. "The Hall of Sacred Doors."

Ning unclasped her hands. She took a step forward, whispering, "You named it?"

"We *found* it." Anna shrugged a shoulder. "Well, *he* found it."

"By gods." She blinked several times before frowning. "But Ottentus only found it due to your research. You and your husband's, that is."

"Mmm."

Now it was Ning who paced, eyes trawling over the towering bookcases. "To be granted access to all of written history, even the forbidden texts and tablets. All knowledge … all known spells and their variants … the ultimate dream …"

"The ultimate dream," Anna echoed.

"Assuming all—even *some*—of the doors are complete."

"Mmm."

"Speculation is the master builder ran out of lifespan. Have you verified how many he—"

"We have yet to gain entry. For all we know it could be an empty tomb."

"But it looks promising."

Anna nodded.

Ning paced in thought, eventually halting before Anna. "Your price?"

"There are protective hindrances."

"I'm sure there are."

"Help us unlock them."

"Done."

"Also …"

"Also …?"

"Examine my mother. Thoroughly."

Ning raised a stern finger. "I do not do that anym—" The finger wilted. "Your mother?"

Anna pointed two fingers at her own head, inviting Ning to read her thoughts. She then closed her eyes and went over the entire encounter in the infirmary.

"So your mother says," Ning said, having read her mind.

"What do you mean?"

"She *says* she tried everything, but she did not accept you as her daughter in front of you."

"She might be too far gone for that."

Ning's head bobbed. "Perhaps."

"But you do not do that anymore."

"I spoke hastily."

"Because the reward is worth making the exception?"

"Of course it is. When do you want me to look at her?"

Anna stared at Ning.

"Now?"

"Now."

The doors silently opened. "Sweetums, I've—"

"I'm busy, you fool!" Ning roared over her shoulder.

A man in his mid-fifties halted, an open scroll before him. He looked up with a salt-and-pepper beard, hair wild and frizzy and as gray as his robe. Upon seeing who was there, he let the scroll roll back up with a *shloop* as his face split with a broad smile. "Anna!"

"Hello, Herzog."

"Aye, how is my favorite teacher of the arcane arts?" Rafael Herzog sang in a lilting and springy accent, jogging forth with an exaggerated bounce to his shoulders, arms out in welcome.

"Roll that slobbering tongue back, Husband," Ning snapped. He and Ning had married many years ago, and have always had a tempestuous relationship. Anna had no idea why they bothered with each other at all. Perhaps his kindness complimented her harshness.

The man ignored his wife and kept coming. "Come, come, come, how are you, lass?" Anna let the man embrace her, giving him a couple of pats on the back in return. "Now don't you patronize old Herzog, young lady. And oh how young you look indeed! Incredible what that scion does, eh, lass?" He patted Anna's shoulders. "Your family is still in our thoughts, yes they are. We are eternally sorry for your—"

"Spare her your sentimental drivel," Ning said.

"You ignore my grumpy wife, lass, you ignore her. Turned into quite the grouch over the years, hasn't she? I fear she is not sweetening either, no she is not," and he chortled, though it was a kind chortle that lacked any malice.

"I ought to have you thrown out on your ear," Ning muttered.

"As the resident historian, you should lend your opinion too," Anna said.

Ning folded her arms. "Absolutely not."

Herzog perked up. "On what? Your research? *The* research?"

"Two husband-and-wife teams would work well together," Anna said. "And yes, *the* research."

"Under no circumstances will I allow this blubbering oaf to partake in—"

"We know its name," Anna interjected. "The Hall of Sacred Doors."

"The Hall of Sacred Doors," Herzog mouthed. "Aye, of course …" He turned away from them, eyes searching the skylight. "Of course, of course, of *course*!"

"I would imagine you know your history of the occult."

"Indeed I do, lass, indeed I do. Dating back to the days of the witch. Time before time. But The Hall of Sacred Doors … my, oh my, oh my … wait, wait, wait. Tell me that you—"

"Yes," Anna interjected.

"Yes?"

"Yes."

"Where?"

"We are expecting the battering ram to arrive tonight."

"Tonight? Battering ram? Alas, I don't have the gift my wife lords over us all. Feed my starving curiosity, my dear woman. Where, oh where, oh where?"

"First, I would like your opinion on something else—rather, some*one* else."

Herzog tucked his scroll under an arm and raised his nose. "I am most intrigued, yes I am indeed. Who is this creature, lass?"

"My mother."

* * *

Ning withdrew a splayed hand after hovering it over Thelma's sleeping body. "I see no sign of Possession whatsoever. Further, her mind is too jumbled to read clearly. It's impossible to know which thought is delusion and which is real. She is haunted, but I am not sure it is of the sort you think."

Anna, who had been pacing beyond the bed with folded arms, stopped to look at Herzog. "What say you about the ramblings?"

"They only loosely align with the demonic sphere of influence, but I tend to agree with my unruly wife and declare they are most likely … if you will forgive me, lass … mere ravings."

"But the curse. My son—"

"Did you find any evidence of tendril interference on his person?" Ning broke in.

Between silent screams, Anna remembered checking over the boy with shaking hands. "No."

"Any unusual behavior prior to the fateful moment?"

Anna recalled Samuel's beaming face as he readied himself to show off his arcanery. "No."

"Any quiet ramblings in his sleep? Any violent or strange or unexpected behavior toward his sister or peers?"

Anna saw Samuel laughingly tossing a ball of twine with his friends. Being chased by his father, who pretended to growl menacingly while the boy giggled. A birthday party. Silent, diligent studying.

Anna shook her head. "No."

"Then we must conclude there is simply a lack of evidence of any arcane meddling."

Anna resumed her pacing. "Let us talk about evidence, then. There is a theory that some curses can transcend the body and get lodged in the arcane ether because the wound was so poignant, lending power to the curse. As a warlock, my mother, hysterical from the death of her daughter, cursed me and my progeny. My son has already perished. And now my mother, in a demonic voice, has warned me of my daughter's coming death."

"Excuse me, my poor lass, but as I am sure your mother would say, that is all circumstantial. Your son died as so many other lightning warlocks have died—suffering an uncontrolled surge. It was an accident, lass. Nothing more, nothing less. To add to that—and you must forgive me for saying what I am about to say, my dear—but some would argue it was a natural death."

Anna stopped pacing to bristle.

Herzog went to her and gently grabbed her shoulders, whispering, "Think with your head, lass. You're a trained warlock of the 18th degree, yes you are indeed. One of the finest minds in all of Solia."

"We understand you fear for your daughter," Ning threw in. "But the evidence is simply lacking. That said, it would be prudent to take precautions. Is she guarded?"

Anna nodded. "Night and day."

"Tracked?"

"At first she refused, but now she is open to it." Anna clutched the foot of the bed frame. "My mother also said something about my daughter getting dragged to the land of rock and fire. I am unfamiliar with this phrase. What could she mean by it?"

Herzog exchanged a look with Ning.

"What's that look for?" Anna pressed.

"I grant you that is a point of interest," Ning said.

"You are unfamiliar with it, lass, because the land of rock and fire is a phrase that comes from an obscure and ancient tale long predating The Founding."

"An allegory, really," Ning threw in.

Herzog's head bobbed. "Aye, aye, aye. It is known as The Allegory of the Dull Man, which goes as such. A man, called stupid all his life, wants to be smart. He thus steps up to a door beyond which he thinks is the fabled Library of All Knowledge, located in the land of rock and fire. He knocks on this door three times. Upon the third knock, a voice thunders from the other side. 'How have you suffered to earn the knowledge I contain?' " Herzog said in a deep voice.

"The man replies, 'I have been called stupid all my life and wish to become smart. Even my own wife and children mock me so.' The door says, 'You may enter, but only because you have suffered so. Yet hark! Warn I thee that the knowledge contained within me may hold unbearable truths. Knowing this, do ye still wish to enter?' The man, of course, said yes. So the door opens and he enters and is immediately overwhelmed by the countless tablets contained within. Towering shelves stuffed with ancient knowledge. Excited, the man delves deep into studying, learning secrets he never thought to consider. But after reading every tablet contained within, he runs out of new things to learn and decides to return to life. And so he leaves the library a smart man—" Herzog raised a finger. "—the most brilliant man to have ever lived, in fact. Except when he returns to his home so that those he knew can at last bask in his brilliance, he finds that the streets and people and culture—and even the language—have changed. No one understands him. His wife and children have long grown and died, as have their children, and their children's children. Nothing but dust remains of them, and no one has even heard of his name, nor can he communicate with anyone. For you see, so enraptured was he by this great knowledge, in the pursuit of wanting to be brilliant, that he forgot to live in the first place. He traded all he knew for all he did not know. The allegory is about wanting to know more than is good for you, and the land of rock and fire is a plane where knowledge that was forbidden in Ley is kept—for good reason."

"But it goes by another name," Ning added.

"Yes, another name. The phrase itself hints at it."

"Hell," Anna whispered. "But then … but then how would my mother know about this obscure phrase if she's delusional?"

"A mystery indeed," Ning said. "But your mother was an accomplished warlock and could have stumbled across it in her own research."

"My mother cared little for the arts after she hit her ceiling," Anna countered. "She threw all her efforts into her family and profession as a magistrate."

"That very well may be so, but delusions manifest in unpredictable ways." Ning opened a hand at Anna's mother. "Listen now, for example."

"… but I gave you back the doll … you cuddled it … *I* never got to cuddle it …"

"She may be speaking of her childhood, of your childhood, or of your sister's childhood. It is difficult to know without context."

"But you can read her mind if you choose to. You can *see* the context."

Ning pondered the point.

Anna pressed, "Therefore if we could get her back to the topic of the land of rock and fire, you could see what she is thinking. Is that not so?"

"I am uncomfortable with the ethics involved—"

"This is my daughter's life we're speaking of," Anna declared. "My daughter's *life!*" She marched past them to her mother's bedside. "Mother? Mama, are you there? It's Anna. Your Anna."

"Careful now, lass," Herzog said, but Anna ignored him.

"Mama, please, it's Anna. Your youngest daughter. I'm here."

Thelma's eyes opened and her face softened, voice still a feverish murmur. "My daughter … my Anna … I tried … I really did …"

"Tell me about this land of rock and fire, Mama."

"Land of … of what? I don't know …"

"The land of rock and fire. Tell me about it and how my daughter is involved. Your *granddaughter.*"

"I'm sorry. I don't—"

"My word," hissed a new voice from the doorway. Everyone turned to see the Henawa healer sweep into the room. "Are we throwing a party here? You are disturbing the patient with your badgering—"

"I'm afraid I must insist," Anna said, returning to her mother.

"I am sorry but you have no jurisdiction here."

"Mama, tell me about the land of rock and fire. Please …"

"No, this will not do at all. I cannot have you upsetting my patient like this. I'm fetching the guards," and the woman rushed out the door.

"We don't have much time, Mama. Your granddaughter is in danger."

"The land … my land … the house …"

Anna shook her head. "No, no, not the house. The land of—" but just as she was going to reiterate the belabored point, her mother's face went foul.

"Her soul dragged, kicking and screaming," she hissed, eyes darkening. "There she will be chained in the land of rock and fire, your precious daughter, for all time …"

Anna looked at Ning. "Did you see?"

Ning's face had gone pale. "I did."

Her mother's voice went soft, whispering, "… unless you take her place …" Then the woman's eyes closed and she fell into a troubled sleep, for her hands twitched and her brow furrowed and she gave the occasional whimper.

The young healer reappeared with two guards at her side. "Leave," she ordered. "Now."

The group of distinguished warlocks, chastened by this young woman, mutely filed out of the room.

"We're sorry for the intrusion, lass," Herzog murmured as he passed her.

The woman flared meaningful eyes at Anna that said, *You should know better.*

Anna ignored her, for her daughter's life mattered more than a moment's worth of her mother's discomfort.

After being escorted off the premises into the snowy courtyard of the infirmary, with some muttered apologies by the guards to Anna, whose fame preceded her, Anna turned to Ning. "And?"

"I did see … something," Ning said, though quickly raised her palms. "You have to understand it could still be part of the delusion, a manifestation of the dementia."

Anna beckoned. "Show me."

"It is disturbing imagery, and would certainly contravene myriad ethical concerns as to the privacy of—"

"*Show me.*" Anna softened her tone. "Please. For my remaining child." *My precious baby girl. My Thia.*

Ning studied Anna with folded arms before dropping them. "Damn you. Very well. But I must warn you, it will not be easy for you to see."

"I understand." Anna closed her eyes and relaxed, or tried to. Soon imagery flooded her mind. It began with fire. A hearth. A room. Was it a home? An infirmary? Like a dream, the visuals kept shifting, making it hard to tell. She saw stone. Shadows leaping like flames. Or perhaps flames leaping like shadows. The echo of a scream, a girl in pain, followed by darkness and the quiet ruffle of flame, accented by a muted sound. A puppy? A kitten? A baby? The warble of a bird? Again, hard to tell.

Then, plain as day, she saw her son, smiling. "Ready, Mama?" he squealed. She wanted to reach out and stop him, but he raised his hand and, with that brilliant smile he got from his father, incanted, "*Shyneo!*" Time slowed as the moment ripened. She saw the spark at the base of the wrist turn into a creeping cluster of lightning. It snaked up his palm before flaring around the small fingers. She saw herself and Thomas looking down with pleasant surprise. Then she saw, fleetingly, a shadow slip into the wrist and explode the lightning. She *felt* her son scream and—

"No!" Anna shouted, trundling forth with an extended arm, eyes flaring open, only to realize she was standing before Ning.

"I warned you. And that is only half of it."

"You all right, lass?" Herzog whispered.

"My son ... I saw a shadow ... It was the curse ..."

"That could be a manifestation of guilt," Ning said. "The mind works in mysterious ways."

"How could my mother have seen my son? That's impossible."

"It's possible she could have read about it—"

"Except the nuance of his death was never published."

"Then she could have heard about it second-hand. Perhaps your husband may have spoken out of turn at some point, as husbands are so oft to do."

Anna, envisioning Thomas, sloshing tankard in hand, commiserating to someone like the king, acceded the point with a nod. The story could indeed have reached her mother in that sense. "But it was so vivid, so clear ..."

"I repeat, the mind works in mysterious ways," Ning said.

Anna released a shuddering breath. "Show me the rest."

"Fine, but I will spare you the imagery of your son."

"I am grateful," though it wasn't like Anna did not see her son perish on an almost daily basis anyway. She closed her eyes again. This time, she saw her daughter, pale and sweaty and weak, as if she were fighting a fever, getting dragged by a shadow through a fiery landscape. Thia barely put up a fight as the shadow stepped onto a black floor. Ahead loomed a cell writhing with souls moaning in pain. The cage door opened, ready to accept Thia for eternity. The shadow yanked Thia forth. Her daughter screamed.

Anna whirled about, tearing herself away from the vision. She clutched her chest, mangling the arcanist's robe between her fingers as she rapidly breathed in and out.

"Lass?"

"That was too vivid," Anna blurted, trying to keep herself together. "It had to be implanted."

"Not necessarily. Again, it could easily be a visual manifestation of your mother's guilt for cursing you and your children. A nightmare of the consequences of her actions, amplified and clarified by the happenstance of your son's accidental death. I repeat, delusions manifest in unpredictable ways."

Anna, digesting what she'd seen, said nothing. Fat snowflakes began to fall, settling on her shoulders and arm sleeves. At last, she turned around. "Before we enter the excavation, I would like you two to join my family for supper."

Herzog smiled. "Oh, lass, that would be divine! Of course we will!"

"That's unlike you," Ning muttered.

"Really, Wife, a bit of decorum."

Ning cocked her head. "You wouldn't, by chance, want me to glance over your daughter's thoughts, would you?"

Anna hesitated.

Ning scowled. "I am not in the business of snooping, and have already transgressed my bounds. You above all know that I must always be wary of my gift lest the high council decide I am a threat."

Anna raised her hands in surrender. "Fine, fine. I apologize. But come for supper anyway. Let us mend bridges. I insist."

Ning sighed. But after a long think, she surrendered a nod.

BATTERING

Thia shot to her feet, her fork clattering onto a dish of steak, potatoes and gravy. "I can't *believe* you saw Grandma without me!"

Six people sat around the supper table—Anna, Thomas, Thia, Niterra, Ning and Herzog. Herzog and Thomas, sharing a corner of the table, had been conversing about various delectable meads they had each tried, whilst the older women had been talking about a coming winter fair. The table was set with the Stones's finest flatware and porcelain, the tablecloth Dramask silk from Tiberra.

"Calm down, Thia," Anna said. "I received a message that she wanted to see me."

"You could have picked me up at the very least! She's my grandmother! That I never got to know! Because you wouldn't *let* me!"

Thomas dabbed at his lips with a cloth. "I do apologize, everyone. She is most uncouth. I suppose I have only myself to blame for her poor upbringing." He placed stern eyes on his daughter. "Thia, your mother hasn't seen her mother in thirty-five years. You cannot expect—"

"Bah!" Thia slumped back down, picked up her fork, and repeatedly stabbed the steak.

"You cannot expect your mother to bring you on her first visit, Thia," Thomas finished.

"She went twice. *Twice!*" Thia flipped a hand at her mother. "Well then? What did Grandma say?"

Anna opened her mouth to reply, only to close it. She had no idea what to say to her daughter.

"Did she at least ask about us?" Thia pressed. "About me? About Samuel? Does she even *know* about Samuel?"

Ning folded and refolded a white napkin embroidered with the initials *AT*, for Anna and Thomas, a wedding gift from Jordan. "Your grandmother suffers from dementia, Thia."

Thia narrowed her eyes. "You went too? Wait, aren't you that—" She stiffened, then shouted, "I don't give you permission! You're not allowed!"

"I do not read people's minds willy-nilly, girl."

"Good." Thia folded her arms, face crimson. "Because I don't want you snooping." She tapped two fingers at her temples. "Private. You understand? *Private.*"

"Nor do I read minds without explicit permission."

"Please forgive her behavior," Thomas said with a nervous chuckle before hissing at Thia, "What in Sithesia is the matter with you? You are embarrassing us!"

"I guess I just don't like surprises." Thia glanced from face to face, eyes narrowing. "Why does it feel like you're all conspiring together? Why do I feel there's a plot afoot?"

Anna watched Ning, secretly hoping she would pick up something from Thia—and feeling guilty for it. On the one hand, she wanted to respect her daughter's privacy, and on the other, she wanted desperately to protect her from the evils of the world.

Ning kept playing with her napkin. "Would you *like* me to read your mind, Thia?"

Thia reared up. "What? No!" Her eyes shot to Anna, then Thomas. "I mean, of *course* not! Are you *mad?*"

Anna glanced between Thia and Ning. Had Ning picked up Thia's secret already? *And do I want to know?* Anna thought, wanting Ning to read her thoughts.

I wouldn't tell you even if I had snooped, Ning said into her mind. *Teenage secrets hidden from their parents are for the teenagers to share. Your daughter is no exception.*

Nicely cryptic of you, Anna snapped back in thought. *So she does have a secret she is hiding from me?*

I never said that.

Anna picked up a hint of hesitation. Thia was hiding something.

Thia leaned forward, glaring at her mother. "It's enough you imprison me in my own home and track me like a bloodhound, but now you want to read my mind too? Are you serious? *Are you serious!*"

Anna, not knowing how to explain herself, white-knuckled her knees underneath the table.

"I don't trust you scheming buzzards," Thia hissed, standing. "I'm going to my room," and she stormed off.

"You are not excused, Thia!" Thomas called after her. "I am talking to you, young lady!" But he might as well have been shouting at a footstool for all the good it did, as Thia simply summoned the portal to her floor and stepped through it.

Niterra groaned as she stood. "I shall resume my watch," and shuffled after the girl, no doubt to stand in the hallway of the third floor or even inside the doorway of her room. As someone who used to spend countless hours standing in silence, watching and guarding royalty, Anna thought Niterra had to take some pleasure in the task. Perhaps it reminded her of the old days, or perhaps it was meditative. Who knew?

Thomas rubbed at his brow. "I do not understand my own daughter," he muttered to Herzog.

"Lads and lasses of that age have stumped the most seeing of mystics," Herzog replied diplomatically.

Thomas snorted. "I suppose." He picked up his fork and resumed shoveling potatoes into his mouth, prompting the others to continue eating. For a time, everyone ate in silence, until Thomas asked between mouthfuls, "What *did* your mother have to say, anyway?"

Anna didn't know what to tell her husband either. In fact, she thought this whole supper had been as bad an idea as she had ever thought up. *What the heck was I thinking?*

In a habit learned from his noble upbringing, Thomas neatly folded his napkin and placed it in the center of his plate. "Why do you hesitate?"

Anna fiddled with her glass of water, turning it in place on the tablecloth. "Husband, did you by chance ever tell anyone—anyone at all—of the details of our son's death?"

Thomas ballooned, only to wilt. He cast his eyes into his lap. "Perhaps I may have. Around the cups. It was the only way I knew how to deal with it." He looked up. "Why?"

Anna, a little relieved that Ning's theory held some weight, nodded. "You have a right to know."

Thomas glanced around at them. "Know what?"

Anna considered telling him outright, but knew it would come out clumsy and form a partial picture. She thus placed eyes on Ning. "Show him."

Thomas forced a nervous chortle. "Show me what? What game is this?"

"No game, Mr. Stone," Ning said. "I offer you a vision of what transpired when visiting your mother-in-law. Nothing more, nothing less. Do you wish to see it?"

Thomas picked up the neatly folded napkin and repeatedly scrunched it. After seeing their grave faces, he swallowed and surrendered a nod. Ning closed her eyes, and Thomas followed suit. After a tense silence during which Thomas stiffened more and more in his chair, he abruptly shot up, the chair falling backward and clattering against the floor. "No, no, no, no …"

"It is most likely a result of dementia," Ning tried explaining, but Thomas was hearing none of it.

He paced back and forth, repeatedly mumbling, "No, no, no, no …"

"There is no evidence of tendril castings," Ning went on. "No curses or hidden enchantments."

"That *you* could see," Thomas countered as he paced. "And how did she know the details of our son?"

"We theorize she heard a story about it second-hand."

"Because of my big mouth. Fine, whatever. First she took my son, and now she wants to take my daughter. I won't allow it. *I won't allow it!*"

"It's the land of rock and fire phrase she used that intrigues us," Herzog noted. "Sit down, lad, and let us put our arcaneological heads together on it."

Thomas reluctantly did sit down, but after parsing the history and potential meaning behind the phrase, he shot right back up. "Ottentus— he's also a scholar of the occult. Maybe I'll ask him—"

"I would much rather you do not broach our private affairs with our research partner," Anna countered, not feeling comfortable with the idea of a master diving into their private life.

"I guess we *will* be busy with the battering ram tonight. Still, if a master warlock doesn't know, no one will know. Maybe when things have calmed down I could—"

"I think I have made my position quite clear, Thomas." She gave him an imploring *Please respect it* look.

After glancing about the table, he chortled nervously, muttering, "Of course," and settled back down.

They finished the meal in thoughtful silence, sharing tea and small talk before readying to visit the excavation.

* * *

"You dare bring a *telepath* into our midst?" Ottentus hissed in his Franterran accent when they'd joined him outside Mount Barrow, where he had been talking with the captain of a gigantic battering ram that stood in stark outline against the starry sky. "Without asking *permission*?"

The moment he said this, Ralf, his apprentice, cleared his throat. "My mind has a right to privacy," he snapped, and he strode off at a brisk pace. Ning had once told Anna it was a common reaction, especially amongst teenagers. After about ten paces, Ralf placed his lips to a golden ring, incanting, "*Impetus peragro*," and vanished with a *thwomp*.

"Where did he get a teleportation ring from?" Anna asked.

"I crafted one for him," Ottentus said. "It is a weak one, limited to two locations—here, and the academy. I do such things for all my apprentices. But let us not stray. You brought a telepath here. How in Sithesia did you think that was a wise proposition?"

"She does not read minds willy-nilly," Anna said, echoing Ning.

"Anna is correct," Ning said. "I am bound by honor and ethics. You need not fear me."

"Honor, ethics—hah! If I had a copper every time someone said such a thing. I am a 20th degree master, yes? I *must* be allowed to concentrate!"

"They are a husband-and-wife team of arcaneologists who I think will be an excellent addition—"

"That very well may be, Arcanist Stone, but I cannot allow distractions to interfere with the work. I must be allowed to concentrate fully, not waste precious energy guarding my mind. I cannot concentrate if I fear someone is snooping! Do you understand? The telepath goes, or you *all* go. Make up your mind double quick," and he went off to continue speaking with the warlock captain, a man in charge of twenty soldiers in plate and chain mail who idled nearby, jesting and prodding each other as to who would be brave enough to wander into the dig on their own to catch a glimpse of the golem. More than a few took notice of Anna, with many inclining their heads at her out of respect.

Ning looked up at the outline of rock against the starry night. "Mount Barrow. An apt choice for a tomb."

Anna turned to Ning. "I apologize. I thought he would feel more secure about you."

"He is one of the greatest researchers in all seven kingdoms. I am not at all surprised he wants to jealously guard his find. In fact, I thought you naive to have invited us."

"I am surprised he even let *you* near it, lass," Herzog said to Anna.

"Her research is the sole reason he found it," Ning added. "Probably still needs her."

"He needs *both* of us," Thomas said in clipped tones. "Who do you think convinced the king to lend this behemoth in the first place?"

"Yes, how nice that you have pull with that man," Ning said, though a nodding Thomas missed the sarcasm. She sighed. "We could have had some of the finest minds in Solia in one place working on a legendary problem. A true shame." She leveled her gaze at Anna. "I expect privileges should you gain entry into the hall."

Anna could not possibly make that sort of promise at this early stage, and so kept her mind and mouth shut, something Ning took notice of with a single raised eyebrow. Anna wanted to press the recalcitrant woman again about Thia, but realized, without that promise, it would amount to nothing except another lambasting. In truth, she had been disappointed in Ning's insights. The woman seemingly refused to believe that her mother's curse was real, which frustrated Anna to no end. Did Ning not realize how Anna put her daughter above all other considerations? Was it because she herself was not a mother? Or did she resent that Anna *still* refused to share the scion?

They thus said curt but cordial goodbyes which a distracted Thomas mumbled his way through, and Ning promptly teleported herself and her husband away.

"I see wisdom prevailed in the end, yes?" Ottentus said, rejoining them. "No good to have a telepath about. They are a snoopy bunch by nature. Come, let us speak with the captain about this most intriguing contraption."

After taking them to the ram, Ottentus, utterly captivated by the arcanery of the machine, continued to pester the captain about it.

The soldiers had nicknamed it The Javelin. It was composed of a gigantic central log that must have been cut from a thousand-year-old tree, for it was thicker than a grain silo. The round tip was capped with heavily dented steel and enchanted with massively amplified explosive arcanery. The launch mechanism itself was amplified, which theoretically resulted in a force so great it could puncture through thick castle walls. There were forty wooden wheels in total, each banded with iron. The total length was a staggering one hundred and twenty feet, and the height a whopping thirty feet.

"The only challenge is it needs to be close to the point of impact," the captain explained. "Something easier said than done in a siege."

Ottentus chortled. "The last part will be a tight squeeze, yes? My worker bees have been cutting a path in the ceiling all quint, but they will only go so far. Little creatures fear the golem."

"Who wouldn't," Anna muttered under her breath.

"It's much bigger than I thought," Thomas noted, looking up at it. "So what's the plan, Captain?"

"Sir, if all goes well, it will roll down the hill, through the tunnel, and upon gaining close proximity with the golem—" The captain smacked a fist into an open palm. "—smash it to smithereens."

The group of listeners nodded in appreciation at this, Ottentus most of all.

"Has it ever taken out a golem before?" Thomas asked.

"No, sir." The captain patted the side of the ram. "But she has had some historic success in obliterating an ancient guardian of a similar nature that guarded a laboratorium deep under the Black Castle. Golems are physical structures immune to arcanery, but not to sheer force."

"So what odds do you give it?" Thomas pressed.

"Judging by everything I have been told about your golem, about one in three, sir."

"Oh, I cannot wait another heartbeat," Ottentus said, rubbing his hands together in glee. "Let us get it rolling, yes? Go, go, go!"

"Yes, sir." The captain placed two fingers in his mouth and whistled. "Men—assemble!" A team of men split into two groups, one on each side. Each grabbed onto a handhold and leaned forward. Every man was sculpted with muscle, a longsword hanging down by their hip. The captain raised an arm. "Ready, men? Aaaand heeeeeave!"

The men groaned as they struggled to get the mammoth ram rolling. The moment it began to trundle downhill, the captain opened a hand and incanted an arcane phrase. The last thing they saw before the gigantic thing ran away from the men and vanished into the excavation site was the tip of the battering ram beginning to glow red-hot with explosive arcanery.

Everyone stood with bated breath. From inside the tunnel emerged the screeching trundle of the wheels, made ever more into an echo, much like a stone clanging about in a deep well. Then there came an enormous *twang* and *thwoom*, followed by the *boom* of a massive explosion that sent everyone shooting for cover. Ahead, the cavern shook. When the rumbling ceased, the soldiers threw up a resounding cheer, whilst their captain stayed mute.

"Let us see if we struck true," the captain said, and flicked two fingers forward. The soldiers jogged forth as one unit into the darkness, with the lead men grabbing two wall torches on their way.

Anna wanted to tell the captain to be careful with his men, all Ordinaries by the look of them, in case the golem was still active, but thought better of it as they were surely well trained in fighting all sorts of things, from enchanted castle walls to summoned beasts.

Once they went in, Anna, Thomas and Ottentus jogged in after them, with Anna casting her floating lightning lamp to light the way better. Rubble started appearing halfway in the tunnel, hinting at the power of the explosion. At the mouth of the chamber entrance, lodged into a wall, they passed the wheelbase, more than a few wheels completely free of their mounting. The chamber itself was a pile of rocky ruin, in the midst of which sat the giant battering ram, its tip still smoking and glowing red from the heat, the glow steadily fading. None of the debris moved, though one piece was identifiable—the head of the golem, sitting apart, the eyes dark.

The soldiers, seeing the head, loosed a mighty cry of victory.

Ottentus, Anna and Thomas each congratulated the captain, who allowed himself a smile before ordering his men to begin reassembling and repairing the ram, an effort that would apparently take hours.

Meanwhile, the three warlocks began arcanely lifting boulders and rubble aside. The workers, who had been waiting outside in their mess tent, were summoned to help with the endeavor. The combined effort resulted in the three esteemed warlocks once more standing before the slab.

Except it hadn't moved. Nothing had changed. As Ottentus and Thomas discussed what to do next, Anna noticed the shape of the eyes of the golem matched two indentations in the slab, indentations they had assumed were old unidentified runes. She telekinetically picked up the head and floated it over to the slab, cutting Ottentus and Thomas off mid-discussion. The pair gawked as Anna fitted the giant head against the slab. There was a red flash, followed by a deep grinding noise.

The slab ground open.

SILENCE BROKEN

The slab opened inward, revealing a descending spiral stairwell caked with ancient and undisturbed dust. The height to the ceiling and the width of the opening were as large as the gigantic slab, creating an inviting void. Carved from the solid rock of Mount Barrow, the stairwell descended into dark and unknown depths.

"By gods, no footprints," Thomas said. "We are the first."

"Remarkable," Ottentus whispered, hands open in reverence. "One can live lifetimes without finding something so important."

Thomas nodded along. "We might be staring at the entrance to the lost tomb of none other than the master builder himself … or something greater."

"Or something not at all what we expected," Anna said. "Master Vilnius Vivictus was an Arcaner who also had a deep love for puzzles." *Patterns within patterns, puzzles within puzzles*, she thought.

"And Arcaners tended to be secretive to a fault," Thomas replied. "Good point."

They had to be, Anna thought, recalling Panza, one of three secret-keepers charged with keeping the order's secrets safe.

The soldiers stopped their ram work and gathered alongside the excavation workers to gawk at the discovery.

"Everybody quiet now!" Ottentus hissed at them. "And stay back, yes? We do not know what we are facing here." The soldiers and workers gave them plenty of space, with more than a few taking shelter behind rubble. "Shall we, Mr. and Mrs. Stone? Quietly now."

Anna, Thomas and Ottentus splayed their hands and whispered, "*Un vun asperio aurum enchantus.*"

Anna froze. The entire stairwell down—the ceiling, the spiral steps, the walls, all lit up with red tendril weavings long sunk to permanence.

Ottentus threw up an urgent hand. "Nobody move!"

"What is it, sir?" the captain whispered.

Thomas, having crouched to splay his hand to inspect whatever arcanery he would find, edged away, whispering, "The entire thing is enchanted with an explosive trap …"

"We don't know how sensitive the triggers are, yes?" Ottentus added, edging away as well.

Seeing the master warlock retreat made every single person— Thomas and Anna included—scurry away like rats fleeing a fire. Everyone backtracked until they were at the mouth of the tunnel to avoid accidentally setting it off.

"Captain, I suggest that your men avoid working on the ram for the moment," Ottentus said. "We do not want to set those enchantments off with accidental tremors now that the door is opened, yes?"

The captain turned to Thomas. "Sir, if I may, what devilry have you gotten us into?"

"I have paid you handsomely, have I not?" Ottentus interjected.

"Yes, sir, but—"

"Did that sack of crowns imply anything about prying, Captain?"

"Er … I guess not."

"Good. We understand each other. But to show goodwill, we will help you put your javelin back together, yes?"

The captain glanced somewhat longingly past him at the open slab. "I suppose …"

"Rest assured there is nothing beyond that door for men such as you, Captain. What lies down there is solely reserved for warlock minds that can comprehend it. By design, no Ordinary or lowly warlock could fathom—or survive—the knowledge contained within. That I guarantee you. The king has entrusted this excavation to the kingdom's champion. I hope you do too, yes?"

The captain glanced between Ottentus, Thomas and Anna. "If you say so," adding with a stiff jaw, "sir."

"I do, Captain. And men who have not believed such warnings have suffered gruesome deaths, so I would advise against curiosity. Now just stay clear until we ascertain how to move forward. Once we deem it safe, we will help you put the battering ram back together, yes?"

The captain pursed his lips but nodded and returned to his men.

"Well played, Ottie," Thomas said, clapping him on the shoulder, something Ottentus did not seem too amused by, but forced a smile nonetheless. Thomas looked at Anna. "What's the arcaneological theory on permanence when it comes to traps?"

"Most are one-time use and expire after being triggered. In this case ..." She shrugged. "He was a master builder. It's anyone's guess, and I don't want to spend time near it, trying to understand the tendril geometries."

"It will reset," Ottentus declared, a hand clutching his mouth, the fingers drumming his cheeks. "Yes, it will reset."

Thomas folded his arms. "How do you know?"

Anna thought about it. "It's intended to only allow the most knowledgeable through. Anyone else would trigger an explosion. But the knowledge would then be exposed, so it would have to reset itself to allow preservation. That is, assuming what this is hiding is *worth* preserving once disturbed."

Thomas nodded along. "Some things are indeed intended to be uncovered fully after discovery." He flicked a hand forth. "Except there is no way to get through that, is there? We can't fly, and if you try grabbing onto something telekinetically, the whole stairwell will go off."

They both looked at Ottentus, who kept drumming his cheek and mumbling ideas to himself in Franterran. If anyone would know a way through, it would be a 20th degree with a full sleeve.

"We can try digging around it, yes?"

Anna and Thomas gaped. Thomas was the first to crack with a laugh, and Anna almost followed, but suppressed it out of respect for the distinguished man.

Thomas slapped his knee. "The only living master warlock ... and that's his idea ..."

Ottentus looked at him, eyes narrowing. That was all it took for Thomas to straighten and clear his throat. "Sorry, Ottie. I forget myself sometimes."

"You have a better idea, yes?"

"Actually, no. I guess I was hoping you had a way to, you know—" Thomas wiggled a hand, mimicking the movement of a snake. "—weasel our way through somehow."

"There are obscure spells out there, ghost spells and spells of an ethereal floating nature, but look how silken threads of tendril webbing attach themselves between the floor and walls and ceiling. Like jungle vines, yes? I suspect they too would set it off were they disturbed. No, no, no, this is difficult. Very, very difficult …"

"A problem that vexes a master," Thomas muttered. "Great."

"I say we set it off," Anna said. When they looked at her, she shrugged. "Might as well get that out of the way and see if it resets."

Ottentus stared before swishing a pointing finger. "Agreed."

They set about making preparations, first by summoning multiple arcane walls of ice, fire and lightning, which would serve as blast walls, then helping the captain and his men move the giant battering ram head away from the entrance and back onto its mount, a process that, using their mighty telekinesis, took only half an hour of careful movement.

The workmen and soldiers were then excused. Unfortunately for Ottentus, the captain insisted the battering ram be teleported back to its military compound immediately, as he did not want his men wasting time and energy guarding it overnight. Ottentus grumbled but agreed, not wanting to pony up for another night—he had already sunk a fortune into simply hiring them in the first place.

"What an odd fellow," Thomas noted, watching a still-grumbling Ottentus depart up the tunnel to see the soldiers off. "Something tells me he doesn't have a wife and kids. How else could he devote all of his time to this? He did say he's an uncle though. I could see him being a fun uncle, in fact."

"How else indeed," Anna muttered, turning her attention to the three layers of summoned elemental walls that rose to near to the ceiling. The first and smallest was Thomas's, a fifteen-foot-high wall of solid fire that quietly ruffled like a long hearth. The second was Anna's, twenty feet and pure lightning. And the third was Ottentus's, shooting right to the ceiling and made of solid ice that slowly exuded cold mist.

"What's that supposed to mean?" Thomas asked.

"Nothing."

"Don't 'nothing' me. I know that tone. You're displeased." Thomas sat on a nearby boulder in the torchlit cavern and folded his arms. "Go on then. Out with it."

"I do not wish to argue."

"Too late for that. Something's on your mind, and you know how it bothers me when you hold stuff in for later. We have a moment, so out with it."

Anna turned away from him. "The truth is … I miss you."

A moment passed. "What? I'm right here—"

"I miss my husband. The man I married. The man who used to show me affection."

"But you don't show *me* any affection either!"

They fell silent, listening to the *whoosh* of the flames and the *crackle* of lightning, accented with the occasional *crack* of ice. The full truth was that it had been hard for both of them since Samuel's death.

Anna rubbed her forehead. "And now the specter of that curse, of the life of our daughter, hangs between us as well …" She turned around to find Thomas nodding at the ground.

"If something happened to her …" He pressed a fist to his mouth, swallowing hard. "If something happened to her, I wouldn't be able to cope."

Anna came to him, enveloping his broad shoulders. "My dear husband," she whispered. "Let us not ever let it get to that."

They stayed embraced until they heard the *thwomp* of a teleport, and almost jumped apart in surprise. It seemed Ottentus was all right taking the risk of teleporting through rock.

The accomplished warlock saw them, grunted, and strode toward the wall of fire. "Let us continue, yes?"

Thomas patted Anna on the back and walked past her. He swiped at the air with an arm, saying, "*Summano null,*" and his wall of flames vanished with a loud *whoosh*. Anna did the same with her lightning wall, and Ottentus with his ice wall, and they found themselves standing twenty feet in front of the yawning entrance.

"I suppose we can just toss a pebble in and it will go off?" Thomas asked.

"Why not?" Ottentus flicked a finger and a stone shot to his hand from the rubble-filled cavern.

"Come, Husband. Let us take up position," and she took his hand and led him to the entrance of the cavern, where they summoned their shields before them, Teleport on their lips.

Ottentus, meanwhile, tossed the stone up and down while he stared at the entrance. He looked back at them. "Ready, yes?"

When Thomas shouted that they were ready, Ottentus threw the stone past the slab and summoned a giant shield of ice. There was a long silence filled with anticipation. The moment the stone connected with a wall, there was a blistering flash. A wall of sound louder than anything Anna had ever heard blew forth so violently she and Thomas did not even have a chance to utter the Teleport incantation.

In a fraction of a heartbeat, everything went black.

* * *

Anna saw Thia's face twist with horror as flames leaped into a vast horizon. Thia pleaded for her mother.

"Mom … help me. Mom … please …" Her feet kicked against a black floor as she fought the iron grip of a merciless and unfathomable shadow. Ahead waited a cage filled with screams of pain.

Anna added her own scream to that chorus as the shadow stuffed a ragdoll Thia into that cage. She screamed so shrilly she began to black out. In the darkness, she heard the door clang shut, leaving behind nothing but an echo … and a high-pitched ringing.

* * *

Anna startled awake in pitch darkness. Lying on her back, she groaned from the splitting headache that threatened to tear her mind apart. The headache was accented by a high-pitched ringing, as if her head were a bell and someone had struck it with a crystal hammer.

"*Shyneo lampa*," she croaked, and a ball of lightning shot out of her hand. It floated above her, revealing a passage full of rubble, and a bloody and shaking hand—her own—in front of her face. It was the catalyst for her to bolt upright, allowing pebbles and rocks and dust to slide off of her chest.

"Thomas? Thomas! Ottentus?"

But the only response was silence. She was alone, surrounded by nothing but rubble. The explosion had brought the entire ceiling down on them.

"Gods," she whispered, scrambling to her feet. A quick check revealed only cuts and bruises, but no serious abrasions or punctures. Her shield had taken the brunt of the blows.

None of that mattered, for she shot to the rubble, only to realize she had no idea which direction she was facing. She pressed a hand to her throat, incanting, "*Amplifico*," and felt her vocal cords strengthen arcanely. "Thomas!" she roared, the noise so loud inside the small chamber it made her wince. "Thomaaaaaaaaaaas!"

Yet the silence was all-consuming. It was a thick, tomb-like silence. The silence of eternal burial. Another noise permeated it—the shrill *hiss* of blood raging through her head, each pulse of her heart sending a jolt of pain through her body. The headache was almost unnatural in its severity, making it hard to concentrate. It seemed to pulse with the crystalline ringing that had taken up lodging deep in her ears.

Panicking now, Anna considered teleporting out, yet also realized that performing the spell through solid rock was risky as it was, let alone while panicked and tormented by such a headache. Instead, she searched the ground for clues—and found a few footsteps under the rubble.

Further, she noticed a gentle incline in one direction, and used both clues to deduce which way to dig down—and which way to dig up.

"But which way are you?" she muttered, glancing between the two walls of rubble. Instinctively, she felt her pocket—and discovered the blast had torn it open. The scion was missing, no doubt thrown by the sheer force of the blast. Thinking about the violent forces involved, she hoped wherever the scion had gone, her husband was also near. She focused, and felt the scion's pull directly downslope—and judging by the strength of that pull, it was close. She began telekinetically working her way through the rubble pile, moving boulders aside or behind her. The panic increased with each heartbeat, and she could not stop her thoughts from spiraling. *Don't you dare leave me alone in this life, Thomas! Don't you dare!* Tears rolled freely as she dug with bloody hands.

At last, she uncovered a foot, then a leg, and then the chest of her husband. After checking his chest, she found him to be still breathing. The reason why became apparent, for when she frantically dug out his head, she saw there was a small pocket around it.

"The Fates were not ready to let you go, dear love," she whispered, readying her mind for the healing ahead. A Diagnose casting revealed nothing untoward—he had merely been knocked out.

Thomas's eyes fluttered open, floating orbs amidst a dusty face. "You look a little worse for wear, my love," he croaked, raising a shaking hand and gently brushing her cheek with his dusty fingers. "Took a knock to the head, eh?"

She leaned into his hand. "I did."

"Nothing your healing can't fix."

She smiled.

He wiped a tear of hers away. "Don't cry."

"I thought I'd lost you."

"You didn't lose me. I'm right here."

They hugged, and he whispered, "With all that dust, I may have smudged your cheek a tad."

She blurted a laugh, and he laughed in turn, and they held each other for comfort before turning their attention to digging their way to the scion, which they found only feet away. Ottentus was another matter. As they telekinetically dug down the slope, neither said aloud what both were thinking—was he alive? He had been frightfully close to the blast and hadn't taken the extra precaution of summoning elemental armor, something Anna recognized she and Thomas should have done. But if anyone could have survived, it would be a master warlock.

They eventually broke through to the main chamber, only to find Ottentus pacing back and forth before the giant doorway that opened to the spiral stairwell, a huge swath of rubble having been cleared from the explosion and pushed against the walls—a testament to his skill with Telekinesis.

"Ah, there you are. It is still here, and as potent as ever."

"What? What is?" Anna mumbled, trying to think through the splitting headache.

"Your hunch was right, Arcanist Stone. The explosive traps have renewed themselves."

Anna and Thomas exchanged a look. Not only had he survived, but he'd survived unharmed.

Husband and wife hobbled forth. Ottentus didn't even glance them over, despite their torn robes and bloody faces. He, on the other hand, had not a scratch on him.

Anna's pride fought with her inquisitiveness. She wanted to ask him how he had escaped the explosion unscathed, but she also did not want to seem *too* curious. There was nothing more unbecoming than having one warlock beg another for knowledge they had not earned. She also wanted to know why the man had not searched for them. Then again, perhaps he had trusted them to stay safe just as they had trusted him to do the same.

Anna healed Thomas and herself, noting that much of the blood had already coagulated, meaning they had to have spent some time in that rubble. Then she set to repairing her torn robe while Thomas repaired his. Unfortunately, the headache refused to budge, telling her it had been a harder knock to the head than she had presumed. In the mean, Ottentus kept pacing and muttering about various ideas on how to get through.

After repairing his robe, Thomas joined Ottentus, acting more as a provoker of thought than an originator, asking questions like, "What about trying this?" and "Have you thought of …?" Anna, on the other hand, thought the obstacle was a little *too* difficult. Even two thousand years ago, with greater knowledge of ancient arcanery, warlocks did not have the ability to fly. As the men talked about brute-forcing their way in, Anna drowned them out by talking to herself.

"Could require a ghost spell to get through the stairwell," she muttered, a hand feeling the cool crystal orb once again secure in her pocket. "There is evidence such spells existed back then, hinted at in the records, now all but myth in the eyes of arcaneologists …" Her eyes fell on the runic slab door. Amusedly, she supposed the only way to close it would be to once more stick the golem head against it, which meant finding the golem head in the rubble.

Then something else caught her eye, the three candles that had intrigued them earlier. She positioned herself to the side of the opening—in case one of them set off another blast from inside the stairwell—and studied the slab door, which rested against the far wall of the interior of the stairwell.

The triangular formation of candles was upside down, with two candles being at the top instead of at the bottom. Underneath each candle was a runic sequence. The first runic sequence under the top-left candle was shaped in the form of a coiled snake, underneath which was an oval, within which was a tiny key. Underneath the top-right candle was a snake-like Z pattern beside a figure so small one had to look closely to see that the figure wore a robe. At the end of that Z pattern was another tiny key, but without a surrounding oval. Underneath the third candle, located at the bottom, was a blank crest, or perhaps a shield.

Anna studied the sequences in whole, going so far as to include the proportions between each. Suddenly, it all came together, and the light of understanding shone on Anna's thoughts. As if sensing this, the men's chatter cut off.

"Why are you smiling like that?" Thomas asked.

"Because we're not meant to come through *this* door first."

"Arcanist Stone will explain her epiphany to us simpletons, yes?" Ottentus said with a wry smile.

Anna pointed, careful to keep her hand outside the doorframe. "The coiled snake underneath that first candle, which we assumed was an expression of ancient witchcraft—or perhaps a symbol of ancient healing—actually represents this very stairwell. The key within the oval underneath it represents a conclusion."

"A final destination," Thomas translated, shooting to stand behind her.

"I believe so. The second runic sequence depicting a Z-like squiggle and a key seems to represent a means to unlock that first oval."

"Like a key opening a lock," Thomas muttered.

"And the empty crest?" Ottentus asked, having joined them. "What is your analysis of that symbol, Arcanist Stone?"

"I do not believe it is a crest but a means to protect us from the explosion in this stairwell."

"A shield ..." Thomas slapped his forehead. "Gods, how did we miss that?"

"Your wife's brilliance reveals itself to us once more ..."

"We stand in but one of three chambers," Anna declared, ignoring the flattery. "There are two others. I propose that they must be found and solved before we can safely enter this stairwell."

"Great," Thomas muttered. "And I bet they'll take all year to find."

LESSONS IN FEAR

"But I *already* saw it," Thia said, plodding in the snow behind Anna amidst the towering pines of Ravenwood.

"You did indeed—when you were a *baby*," Anna replied, using her staff to test the deep snow ahead. Both women were clad in furs, for the air was frosty, their breath pluming in clouds. A light flurry of snow fell from a cloudy sky, settling snowflakes onto their shoulders and hoods. A piercing headache bothered Anna, and she was rather tired, for she had not slept well, having suffered from nightmares about Thia.

"I was seven. I remember it enough. Besides, it doesn't mean to me what it does to you. I'm cold and hungry and I just want to get to tonight's Star Feast."

"I wanted to bring you here as part of your advancement gift." What Anna *actually* intended to do was hand her daughter the deed to the castle. That was how proud she was of her. And with that she hoped to spur on her daughter's interest, not only in the lineage, but in arcanery itself.

But all Thia said was, "Pfft."

"I don't know why you are being so sour. You achieved your 7th degree! That is a *momentous* achievement!"

"By the skin of my teeth," Thia muttered. "But didn't I look pretty in your old dress? I felt like a pearl."

The prior evening, Anna had dropped her daughter off at the academy for the school's end-of-term dance, which Thia had made Anna promise *not* to attend. "I am sure all the boys were enchanted," Anna said diplomatically.

"Darn right they were." Thia twirled awkwardly in the snow. " 'Eyes aglow, eyes wide, eyes on me, sublime.' " She sighed wistfully.

"Must have been quite the affair indeed if you're quoting a play."

"Not a play. Just a poem I thought up to honor the occasion."

Anna wanted to ask her daughter if she had danced with a certain boy, but suspected she already knew the answer. What mattered was that Thia had had fun, and she had come home safe, instead of ending up drunk out of her gourd who knew where, as oft happened with young men and women celebrating advancement.

They trekked on, with Anna following a slight indentation in the snow, an old deer trail she had used before.

"You always do this, Mom."

"Do what?"

"Make us work."

"Walking is work?"

"Would have been a thousand times easier had you simply teleported us to the doorstep."

"I thought today we could walk up on it as if we were just discovering it for the first time. Like two explorers."

"Sometimes I think you never grew up."

"I'll take that as a compliment."

After a lengthy slog, the women stepped up to a wall of winter brambles.

"I don't remember *this* being here, though," Thia said.

"Mmm." A suspicious Anna cocked her head as she splayed a hand, only to change her mind. "Since you know the spell, give it a go."

"School's done, Mom. We're supposed to be *celebrating*, remember?"

"Learning and training will be a lifelong endeavor. Let's go, missy."

"Ugh." Thia plodded by and splayed a hand. "*Un vun asperio aurum enchantus.* There, no arcanery. Are you happy?"

Not wanting to ruin the occasion, Anna did not chastise her daughter for such a poor attempt that had likely failed. Instead, she splayed her own hand and repeated the spell. Indeed, there was no sign of arcanery.

"You happy you checked on me?"

"You cast it so quickly. I only thought—"

"—that I'm totally incompetent? Hardly a surprise."

"I don't understand why you're so grumpy," Anna said as she used her staff to clear away snow from the base of the brambles.

"Because."

"Because why?"

"Just … because."

Anna continued poking about as she thought to take a chance. "Does it have something to do with the thing you don't want to talk about? The thing you're hiding from me and your father? The thing you let Ning read about in your thoughts, but are too ashamed to tell your parents? *That* because?" She turned to find her daughter staring at the snow. "Whatever it is, your father and I will always love you. We will *always* be here for you."

"How did you know I let Ning read my thoughts?" Thia mumbled.

"Because I think you wanted to be judged for it."

Thia looked up and narrowed her eyes. "You're too smart for your own good."

"Not the first time I've heard that," Anna muttered, recalling Thomas throwing that in her face multiple times after she had cornered him in an argument.

"Anyway, I don't want to talk about it. When I want to tell you, I will, all right?"

"Fair enough. Your father and I will wait until you are ready. I just hope … I just hope you're not in any trouble."

"Ugh, Mom, drop it already. Can we just—" Thia flipped a hand forward. "—get this over with?"

Whatever it is has taken the joy of life from you, though, Anna thought. She sighed. "Very well, then. Look here." Anna tapped at the soil. "See anything interesting?"

"I see dirt. What do *you* see?"

"That the brambles have not embedded fully into the soil, meaning …?"

"Meaning you like wasting my time with inane questions?"

"Incorrect. Meaning this was the work of an earth warlock."

"Did some pesky local rats take up lodging once more? Will you have to rid it of *another* infestation? Because you know I abhor violence. I'd rather you take me home if you're going to play constable again."

"Mmm."

"Mom, are you even *listening* to me? Ugh, I wish I could learn Teleport so I wouldn't have to fall prey to people's stupid whims."

"Artfully spoken. Is that Drama class flair?"

"I'm going to become a mime just to see how you react." She placed hands against an invisible wall, lifting them and pressing them again with each syllable as she mouthed, "He … llo … Mo … ther …"

"Whatever profession you choose I am sure will suit you well," Anna said as they walked parallel to the bramble wall in search of a way through. "And this is no whim. I've been wanting to bring you here for a while. At last, you have truly earned it." She didn't want to resort to teleporting in just yet, and was rather curious to see how long the wall was.

"*You* don't even come here anymore."

"I still make my rounds, just not as often as I used to."

"Yeah, like once a year. You don't come because it's boring and stupid and did I say boring?"

Anna didn't take the bait and they trekked on along the wall, yet the brambles did not end. Anna stopped to ready a teleport to the other side.

Thia bundled herself in her fur coat. "I know that look."

"What look?"

"That *I'm going to kick some butt* look. Violence, Mom. It's not always a solution."

"What makes you think this will end in violence?"

"Because *you're* violent. You're, like, the only violent scholar there is."

"Really? I don't think of myself as a violent person."

"That's because you're oblivious." Thia counted on her fingers. "You're a former arena champion, you're now *kingdom* champion, they teach about some of your duels in school, you used to play constable all the time—and still do. *Ahem*, example being a certain harmless warlock tournament you shut down—and you even teach Dueling Club. Every evening before bed, you train being violent. Oh, and you carry an ancient artifact with you that, in your own words, 'Has a long history stained with blood.' You're, like, the epitome of a violent person."

"That's one way to look at it. What you do *not* hear about is the countless times I have defused situations. But I suppose those occasions are not nearly interesting enough to make the heralds. Besides, you forgot the greatest example of my so-called violence …"

"Which is?"

"Abrandia's invasions of Ohm. Violence sometimes is a solution to prevent further violence."

"Fine, you stopped a war with one duel. I'll give you that."

"How gracious of you. Now hush for a moment. I need to focus."

"*She needs to focus*," Thia whispered to no one.

If I'm the epitome of a violent person, you're the quintessential teenager, Anna thought, keeping that thought to herself.

"If you don't want them hearing us, maybe we should cut our way through."

Anna, about to cast Group Teleport, let go of Thia's hand. "That's a good idea." The *thwomp* of a teleport was much louder than conversation, and was a sound warlocks were highly attuned to. She stepped aside. "Let's see you get through without making noise."

"Mom, I don't *care* if we get through. Can't we just … leave it be for another day? You can come back with like a whole army of constables or whatever."

"Indulge me."

"You're the worst," but Thia stepped up to the wall. She sighed as if it were the last thing she wanted to do, raised an arm, and incanted, *"Minimus ipulato planta."* The bramble slowly split apart, leaving behind a hole to walk through. She smirked. "What, did you think Minor Shape Earth was the only interesting off-the-books earth spell of the 2nd degree?"

"So there's Minor Shape Plant and Major Shape Plant. Huh." Thia had cast the former.

"You seriously didn't know that, Mom?"

"This might shock you, but much of what happens in those elemental halls stays within."

"Unnameables bless my troubled soul, did I just teach my own mother, the smartest of the smart, something new?"

Anna gave her daughter a warm smile. "You know what? I would love it if it happened more."

"I bet you would," Thia muttered, stepping through the bramble. "You coming, or are you going to gawk at your daughter, who continually shows you how secretly brilliant she can be?"

Anna joined Thia, smilingly shaking her head. "Now let us be quiet as we creep onward."

They trooped on, with Anna keeping Reveal lit, and thankfully too.

"Stop," Anna whispered. "What do you see ahead?"

Thia, apparently sensing the change in seriousness in her mother's tone, did not even complain before whispering, *"Un vun asperio aurum enchantus.* Whoa, it's a giant alarm."

"Go ahead and identify it."

"Can I inspect it first?"

"Just be careful."

Thia slogged forth, stopping feet away. "Area Alarm. 10th degree. Standard."

"Good. Proficiency?"

Thia adjusted her hood and crouched. "Can't tell. Not as good with that stuff."

Anna went over to crouch alongside and point with a finger. "See the edging on the thickest tendril there? The fractaline pattern of the jaggedness? Look familiar?"

"You call that tendril thick? It's needle-thin. But …" Thia grimaced. "But I guess they're the same as the brambles …?"

"It is indeed the same caster, and based on the competence of the casting, my best guess is he is a 14th degree."

"Could be a woman, Mom."

Anna had been about to say she had yet to come across a woman who coveted the scion when she realized she knew two—Ning, and Veruca Valence, the Skull Stalker from her youth. "Nonetheless, *someone* wants to be notified of intruders," she noted. "Now what should we do about this alarm?"

"Go home."

"Thia."

"What? I'm starved, and I don't want to get into a fight, let alone die a screaming death over a stupid wall of brambles. You closed that castle up, right? So what's the worry? You said yourself you're tired and you have a headache."

"Concentrate. Your life could one day depend on decisions you make in situations like this."

"I don't plan on putting myself *into* situations like this, Mom."

"Sometimes situations have a way of finding you. You are an Arinthian and the daughter of a scion holder. You need to come to terms with the fact you will always be a kidnap threat. I would think the most recent example outside our home would have woken you to that danger."

"My plan is to become so meek and useless that no one will ever want to kidnap me."

Anna stared at her daughter.

Thia rolled her eyes. "That was a *jest*, Mom, yeesh. Besides, I stopped sneaking out, I have a bodyguard at all times, and I even carry these—" She jammed a hand into a pocket and withdrew two tracking pebbles, one enchanted by Niterra and one by her mother. "So I don't know what else you want from me. I'm never going to be a dueler like you, all right? Oh for—stop looking at me like that. The scion thing will resolve itself. I don't have to be the one you give it to. I'm sure you'll figure something out, being the brilliant witch you are."

"We don't use that derogatory word."

"Get with the lingo, Mom. The students call each other witch all the time."

"Doesn't change its derogatory nature."

"You know what? I'm wrong. You *are* getting old. Ugh, my Reveal snuffed talking to you."

Anna opened a hand at the enchantment, drawing her daughter's attention back to it. "My question stands. What should we do about the alarm?"

Thia tapped her lip with a finger. "Well, you can disenchant it, or we can find a way around."

"Let us learn from the wall of brambles. We can deduce from its length that this enchantment, too, is cast all the way around. Both were laborious castings, meaning we ought to be doubly suspicious of the intent."

"Spare me the litany and just say what you want to do."

"I suggest a short hop."

"Oh, no. I'm not a ragdoll to be thrown around."

"Come, come, it'll only take a moment. And it's part of the adventure."

"Fine, but since you seem to be all right with learning illegal spells under certain conditions, I *insist* you teach me Teleport. To escape, of course. From enemies. Right." She nodded, surely knowing Anna could see right through her and that she wanted to learn to Teleport to escape from her mother.

"I don't blame you," Anna said, continuing their conversation in a whisper. "When I was your age, I also wanted to escape the responsibilities thrust upon me. I am acutely aware I can be stifling. Truly. And I'm sorry. I wish there was a better way. I promise to teach you Teleport when you demonstrate better competence in the arts. Don't roll your eyes. It is not a trifle to teleport. Even *I* had trouble with the spell. One wrong thought and—" Anna snapped her fingers. "—your foot is fused with a rock, or your hand with a branch—which might I remind you happened to your brother when your father was being careless with the casting nuance."

As a 15th degree, Thomas had had his struggles while learning the 17th degree Group Teleport spell. Took years for Anna to trust him again after that incident. "My point is that, unlike me, Thia, you cannot heal your way out of a mistake. Do you know how many times I had something like that happen to me when I was learning Teleport?"

"On second thought, maybe I'll wait," Thia muttered.

"Prudent, but I admire the drive. Now latch on. You're going to experience the legendary Teleswing."

Thia grabbed her stomach. "I'm not sure. Don't want to get queasy and barf again."

"Stop making up excuses and latch on already."

"Just like when I was a little girl," Thia grumbled, grabbing onto her mother.

"If only your skill in studying got as much attention as your skill in sarcasm."

"I passed my degree. That should be enough."

"Yes, and I am mighty proud. *We* are mighty proud. Now hold on tight. Not that tight," she wheezed when Thia purposely squeezed too tight.

"What about the falling snow? Won't it trigger the alarm?"

"Not a competently cast alarm like this one. Anyway. Here. We. Go—!"

Having already picked out her route ahead of time, Anna lashed out at a high pine branch. With the ropey tendril secured, she made it go taut—then rapidly shortened it, yanking the pair of them up and forth. They rose quickly, the wind ruffling their robes and throwing off their hoods. At the apex of the swing, both received a face full of snow before descending, landing and rolling in the deep snow on the other side.

Thia wiggled about as she tried to shake out the snow that had found its way down her robe. "Thanks for that, Mom. Really fun."

"Not my most graceful, but still a thrill, was it not?"

"I was being sarcastic. I don't enjoy these things like you do. My idea of a good time is reciting a play with friends and trying to find quality props. And if it were up to me—" But she froze, for the distant sound of a pair of male voices reached them, and they were steadily approaching.

"How is your Chameleon extension?" Anna whispered.

"Barely exists," Thia whispered back.

"I'll use mine." She ran a hand down Thia's body. "*Armari obscura chameleano traversa othra persona.*" After Thia had completely melded with the snowy background, Anna ran a hand down her own body. "*Armari obscura chameleano traversa,*" making herself vanish in the same way. "You know how it works—"

"Yeah, yeah. Keep it slow. No sudden movements."

"Mmm."

"Except you forgot one thing—"

"That I did *not* forget." Anna reached back and, using Telekinesis, which she had honed over the decades, smoothed over their snowy tracks.

"They'll see the ones on the other side."

"Only if they look carefully."

They walked a short way onward, until they could see movement ahead between the trees. The women stopped. Anna smoothed out the snow, making sure to hide their standing footprints, then went totally still. The voices soon reached them, and they were not speaking in Solian, but in *Abrandian*.

Anna, realizing Abrandians here could only spell trouble, quickly ran through the mental requirements to the 12th degree Tongues spell, brushing up on a language she associated with war and pain and anguish. Then she touched her throat with one hand and pressed three fingers to her temple with the other, whispering, "*Translateo commona linguino Abrandian.*" Instantly their words became understandable, and the headache subsided, pushed aside from the excitement.

"… no, just *admit* the captain is not as smart as he thinks he is," the taller of the men said to the shorter. Both were noodle thin and carrying crossbows, their bulk coming from thick winter furs. And both had the same pinched faces. "He made it thinking he would trap all the animals inside, but I've only found a rabbit and a squirrel. No other animal can get through. He's still stuck in that war mindset. What are we going to eat tonight? Go cannibal? Eat each other like those poor bastards on those long voyages?"

"The cap will think of something," the shorter one said, his voice more high-pitched. "Always does. You know what I think? He didn't cast it for animals to get in. He cast it for us not to get *out*."

The taller one laughed. "You say ridiculous things sometimes."

"It wasn't a jest. You really think he'll pay out after? Think about it."

"He's paid out three times already."

"Small-town robber gangs are relatively easy marks, evidenced by the fact we had little trouble shaking them down. Besides, his stupid brother failed to catch the daughter with that ham-handed attempt at her own house. How do you know this won't fail either?"

Anna's blood went cold. The brother of the so-called captain was one of the men she had caught trying to kidnap her daughter!

"Because they brought us in to help them plan, and we did a good job. The truth is you're paranoid. You've *always* been paranoid. Honestly, I'm sick of it."

"You go on licking his boots, but if I even have the *slightest* inclination he won't pay up, I'm out. This is the big one. He won't need us after this."

The men trundled by, unaware that Anna and her daughter stood only feet away.

"And you'd leave your own brother behind?"

"In a heartbeat."

"I don't believe you."

"Better believe it," but the tone was a bit warm, indicating he was trying to scare his likely older brother.

So there are at least two pairs of brothers, Anna thought. The question was, would the captain's brother be at the castle as well?

She watched as the men walked by the spot Anna and Thia had teleswung over to bypass the Area Alarm enchantment, oblivious to the fact that two sets of footprints mysteriously ended just on the other side of the bramble wall.

"Abrandians, great," Thia whispered when the pair of men had disappeared into the woods. She gave a nervous chortle. "These better not be more kidnappers. What were they talking about, anyway?"

"Hunting."

"That's all? Because it sounded like a lot more than that."

"Something about robbing other robbers."

"Oh. Wonderful. You said my attempted kidnappers were Abrandians and I should keep an ear out for that language and now here we are and—" She flashed both hands. "—surprise, surprise—I'm getting the impression you want to confront these goons. Remember how I said you're obsessed with violence? Need I say more? I got a bad feeling about this, Mom."

"You say that every time."

"I'm not used to risk and danger like you are. *Nobody* is. You, like, live and breathe it."

"I'm a teacher. My life is boring relative to what it used to be, especially before you were born."

"Oh, I've heard the tales, so that I can believe. Can we please go home now?"

"Soon."

"*Mom—*"

"Soon, I promise."

"And you say *that* every time. Then there's going to be some big kerfuffle and you're going to summon the constables from way out far and everyone is going to have to write a long and boring statement and we'll miss supper."

Anna didn't want to tell her daughter that the constables wouldn't come out this far unless it was for something very serious. These kidnappers weren't the type to give up and would thus have to be dealt with, even if she had to do it on her own.

"Soon," and they walked on, with Anna keeping Tongues alive. At last, they glimpsed the black-tar minarets, ancient stonework, and stained-glass windows.

"That is what almost two thousand years of family history looks like," Anna whispered, conscious of the deed to the castle in her pocket. Rather selfishly, she wondered if the moment of offering it to her daughter could still be salvaged after she took care of the would-be kidnappers.

"It's an old castle in the middle of nowhere. Just because it belongs to you doesn't make it any different from any other castle."

"Ah, but this castle *is* different. It has secrets and mysteries and history and maybe even treasure."

"I'm a city girl. I'm never moving out here. I don't want to get to know it."

"Because you might fall in love with it?"

Thia pondered her retort. "*You* never fell in love with it. *You* never moved us in."

Anna couldn't argue that point. Thomas would have balked, but also rearing a family in the middle of nowhere was a difficult thing to pull off—not to mention horrendously isolating.

More voices reached them.

"No, put that one there, you fool!" a man shouted in Abrandian. "This is the big one. If you want a bonus, you'll do *exactly* what I say. No detail left undone! We only have a day."

Anna almost gasped. Tomorrow was the day she would usually arrive to honor her ancestors and check on the state of the castle! But how had they discovered that? Also, what exactly did they have in store for her? *This I have to see for myself*, she thought, advancing.

"Slow and easy now," she whispered.

"Mom, I'm not sure about this. Please, it's dangerous."

"Exposing you to a little danger will help your confidence should you ever face it again." Might even scare her daughter straight and motivate her to take learning the arcane arts more seriously. The girl had yet to learn how to truly defend herself, and Anna worried what would happen should a day come when someone wasn't around to protect her—her daughter even panicked in mock duels, for mercy's sake! Besides, if things *did* go awry, Anna was confident she could defend them both, especially seeing as Niterra had been helping her brush up on her dueling skills after Scadius had accused her of going soft over the years.

"I want you more familiar with danger so you can make better quality decisions instead of panicking like you usually do," Anna added.

"You're going to get us killed, I swear," Thia muttered.

"I'll teleport us out if need be."

"Hardly reassuring, Mom …"

"Just pay attention and think about how you would react."

Anna stepped onto a well-traversed trail of footprints that would obscure their own steps. The trail led them to an open plain full of ruins, what remained of an ancient village from back in Atrius Arinthian's day. Behind that village loomed a magnificent and ancient castle that tapered into a series of minarets. Its walls were black as tar, its battlements thick and slotted with archer murder holes. A large and round window near the center looked like a watcher.

But it was what was amidst the ruins that caught Anna's eye, for a circle of tents sat clustered together, eight in all. Beyond, through the run-down walls of what might have once been an old tavern or manor, Anna caught a glimpse of four men wearing furs, jabbing the last of a line of thin and sharpened logs into the snow at a steep angle, as if bracing for a siege. All had a crossbow slung across their back, the best weapon available for those who could not match arcane wits with their opponent. One of them, a broad-shouldered boy of about Thia's age, perhaps an apprentice, was piling up more snow and making the logs look like they were part of a snowdrift. All the men occasionally flicked a hand at obtrusive sticks or stones, which moved aside on their own, indicating they were also warlocks, but mostly used brute muscle or the heavy logs.

What in Sithesia are they doing? Anna thought, creeping closer, Thia so close behind she stepped on her heel. Anna stopped to brace her daughter, murmuring, "Careful now."

"Mom, *please*," came a murmur back, with Thia refusing to let go of Anna's hand, gripping it with both her own.

"I'll have Teleport on my lips. It's important that you pay attention and learn." Anna had far more confidence in her abilities than her daughter did, that was for sure.

Allowing her daughter to keep a tight hold of her hand, Anna led them through the ruins, and upon clearing them, spotted the leader, a purple-robed warlock with a single golden band on the upper shoulder — 14th degree, exactly as she had guessed. An animated fellow who gesticulated this way and that, barking commands at the men, he looked in his late forties, had a chubby face, and was the only one without furs. Perhaps the barking was his way of compensating for an insecurity about his height, for he was also short and stubby, at only about four and a half feet tall.

Who she did *not* see was either of the men responsible for the attempted kidnapping of her daughter back at the tower.

"Do a better job camouflaging!" the captain barked in a goonish Abrandian accent, the sort Anna had heard spoken in the Abrandian army a long time ago. He flapped both hands about, fingers glinting with bejeweled rings as he tottered around the construction. "More snow! Pile it on, son!"

"I'm working as fast as I can, *Dad*," the teenage boy retorted with heavy sarcasm, which sounded more potent in Abrandian. Despite wearing ruffian Ordinary clothes under his furs, his hair was swept into the latest style. By all measures, he was a handsome young man.

When a bearded mountain of a man made some comment about the boy being lazy and playfully mussed that stylish hair, the teenager flared seven earthen rings at him and feigned slapping his wrists, making the mountain man summon a lightning shield and say, "There he is! There's our feisty boy!"

"I'm not a boy anymore," the young man muttered, allowing his rings to vanish.

"You'll always be a boy," his father said. "Now keep working."

Anna drew closer still, her daughter practically dragging her feet in the snow like a human snow anchor. Anna came as close as she dared — within twenty-five feet. Not optimal, but close enough for lethal strikes should the need arise. There she halted, Thia clinging to her back like a toddler.

The man crouched and checked the sight line along the sharpened logs. "Move a hand's width that way!" He gesticulated wildly. "That way! All must rise exactly together. See? When she comes—" He jabbed forth at the air with all his extended fingers. "—skewered like a rat! You remember what we call this?

"The Pitchfork!" the men shouted in unison, telling Anna they had served together in the Abrandian army. She was also now aware of what they were doing—setting a trap, but not for an army, for *her*. The logs were aimed at the usual spot she teleported in from, a clearing in the west, and would probably be enchanted to shoot forth much like the battering ram, creating ballistae-like projectiles. If done correctly, she would have little time to react. And anyone she traveled with would get skewered as well.

Great job, Anna, she thought. *You got complacent over the years. Should've varied your route like you used to.* She had been far more paranoid back when she was younger. But as her legend had cemented, the attacks had slowed to a trickle, perhaps happening every few years or so, and even longer after Thia's birth, as if her daughter had served as an amulet of protection.

The mountain man rested a hand on a large crossbow he had stuck into the snow beside him. "When are you going to enchant them, Cap?" The huge spiked club on his back, combined with the thick furs, gave him the appearance of a caveman.

"Tonight, tonight, tonight." The captain shot a hand out as men moved one of the logs. "Hold it there! Yes, that's it." He jogged well back of the spears. "And I stand here. She teleports in there—" He pointed. "—sees me, I pull the arcane trigger, and—" He smacked his hands together. "—*bam!*" He dusted his hands, nodding proudly. "I have to say, this is my most brilliant trap yet. A fitting grand finale to a career of wickedness and debauchery," and he laughed, prompting the others to laugh along.

The warlock captain returned to jab his son with an elbow. "Eh, boy? Your mother would be proud."

"Mother left you because of these sorts of stunts."

The man, having to reach due to his shortness, thumped his son on the back of the head with a bejeweled fist. It was such a hard blow that the teenager crumpled to the snow, crying out in pain. There he lay, sobbing the sob of a boy in more than just physical pain.

"Take it easy there, Cap," the mountain man said.

"Mind your business, you oaf." The captain glanced about. "We get one shot at this. She comes only *once* a year to check on the castle. I've been working on this for a long time. Do you know how much I spent on bribes getting that information?"

So that's how you did it, Anna thought. *Bribery. Typical.* She recalled mentioning her trips to senior officials at various times, usually because she ordered maintenance from the city afterward for things that could not be arcanely repaired, such as rot and decay. There were also yearly tax considerations that had to be kept up, all of which were reported. It would not take much to deduce timing from such records, and countless bribery-prone administrators had access to that information. She had to hand it to the Abrandian—he had been clever and tenacious, and it perhaps would have paid off had she not come a day early.

"Even if it fails, every thrust and counter-thrust—" He tapped his temple. "—all up here. All orchestrated for maximum success."

"That's why you're an arena champion, Cap," the mountain man said, yet his eyes were on the crumpled boy, and there was sadness in his voice.

"That's right. I beat the best of them back in the motherland. Now I will return glory and honor to our kingdom and heal an old wound. That woman will suffer for the humiliation she caused our people."

"And we will become rich," a voice called out from behind Anna. Slowly, so as not to fizzle the Chameleon spell, she turned her head to see the two brothers returning from the woods. "Still no game, Cap. You want to 'port us to a city or something? We can pick up a few chickens to roast over the fire."

Anna felt her daughter stiffen as the two brothers walked by only feet away. That made seven men now.

"What happened to *him*?" the older brother asked, nodding at the broad-shouldered son, still weeping quietly in the snow.

"He's a weakling who needs to toughen up," the father said. "Haul his lazy butt up."

The mountain man picked the son up. "Get it together now, boy."

"I'm so sick of this life," the teenager gurgled. "I hope she puts me out of my misery."

"Hush now, boy, and do as your father bids."

"I think I'd rather live with Mom," the teenager muttered.

"Your mother already told you she doesn't want a sniveling weasel of a boy who can't hunt and keeps sticking his head in books. She hates us warlocks, Son. Better get that through your thick head. Be grateful you have me as your mentor. I have to rear you myself, which ain't no easy thing. Now shut up and get back to work, and if I hear you whine one more time, I will box those ears, that I promise you, boy."

As the teenager returned to shoveling snow into piles with his bare hands, the captain nodded at the older brother. "Chicken will do fine. I'll 'port you to Antioc as soon as this is done."

So he knows illegal Group Teleport, Anna noted, not surprised in the least. Almost all outlaw warlocks knew illegal spells of one sort or another. It also likely explained how a 14th degree had brought his gang over from Abrandia.

"Mind if I go right now, Cap?" the older brother asked. "We're all starved. Missed breakfast already." The other men nodded along with this.

The captain glanced about at them. "Bunch of whiners, all of you. Fine, but keep your heads down. That means no arcanery, not even to grab a coin. You hear me? They don't take too kindly to our sort in the cities."

"You're the boss, Cap."

But Anna had no intention of letting them get away. She withdrew the scion from her pocket and tossed it into the air. It became visible as it floated, catching the attention of the mountain man. In reaction, Thia's grip turned to iron.

"Uh, Captain—is that yours?"

All seven men turned to gape at the scion, floating only twenty feet away and clouding over. It seemed none of them knew what to make of it, or what to do.

"Is that a castle defense mechanism?" the older brother asked.

"You must have tripped one walking in," the mountain man said.

The captain, who had been frowning, went ashen. "Abrandia, help me. I think I know what that is—"

"*Extingui*," Anna snapped just as all their arm rings lit up. Most were 2nd or 3rd degree, except for the young man, who was 7th, the mountain man, who was 8th, and of course the captain, a 14th. But those rings only had a moment of life before the scion snuffed them, leaving the men gaping like fools.

The younger brother fell to his knees, weeping like the son had. "Gods, we're dead. We're dead. I knew it'd end like this. I knew it …"

"Put them down," a still-chameleonic Anna barked in Abrandian.

The younger brother immediately hurled his crossbow to the snow, repeatedly blubbering, "I don't want to die. I don't want to die …"

His older brother, glancing at his gibbering younger brother, tossed his crossbow ahead of him, along with everyone else. When the mountain man hesitated, Anna glanced at the scion and it floated near him, flashing angrily with silent lightning. He took a step back and fumbled at his crossbow before throwing it to the ground as well.

"You moron!" the boy shouted at his father, tears streaming freely. "You got us killed! I *told* you this was a stupid plan! I *told* you!"

Anna felt Thia shaking against her back. She gently pried her hands loose, which took some effort as her daughter didn't want to let go. But Anna insisted and Thia finally allowed them to be removed. Only then did Anna run a hand down her body, incanting, "*Chameleano null*," making herself visible—but leaving Thia chameleonic.

She locked eyes with each of the men, all of whom dropped their gazes upon seeing her iron stare—all but two, the mountain man and the captain, whose lip was curled with loathing. *Yet your eyes show fear*, she noted. Some lessons from the arena were eternal. One of them was seeing fear in the eyes of an opponent. Her final tournament in Antioc had been the culmination of that, when she had stared at her opponents with the confidence she had earned defeating The Reaper.

"An interesting contraption," she said in smooth Abrandian, honed better over the decades. "I teleport in there—" She nodded ahead. "—and then you, how did you put it, skewer me like a rat?"

The captain glared, defiant, while his son dropped his eyes in shame and resignation.

Anna cocked her head. "Under kingdom law, a trespasser has few rights, let alone a foreigner. So I will ask you the following question *only* once. You there," she said to the younger brother. "What did you plan to do had I appeared with my daughter? Be warned, for I have means to discover if you are lying." The ethics involved gave her much leeway here.

"He ... he would have ..."

"Shut your fool mouth, boy," the captain hissed. "You say another word and—"

Whilst keeping her gaze on the younger brother, Anna calmly clenched a fist. "*Voidus lingua*," silencing the captain on the spot. "Go on, son. You need never fear him again."

Those words caused the men to stir.

"He ... he planned on slitting her throat."

"No witnesses," the older brother said, stiffening with bravery on behalf of his brother, despite shaking like a leaf himself. "That was his order, and we follow orders. He was our commander in the field."

Anna tried not to wince from a sudden headache pulse, as if the very pulp of her brain were threatened any time her daughter was in danger. She allowed the scion to buzz menacingly in their midst. "Turning you all into cold-blooded murderers. Is that how it was in the army together?"

"I never murdered anyone," the younger one blubbered.

"Neither did I," the older brother said, chin held high.

"Same here," the broad-shouldered son blurted, earning him a wicked glare from his father.

"But you robbed many a soul," Anna countered. "All of you." When the accusation went unchallenged, she placed her gaze on the captain. "I should peek into that foul mind and see for myself how many innocents you have murdered."

The stubby man stood rigid, refusing to utter a word.

"Alas, I do not want to soil my thoughts with yours. Let us instead work on tying you lot up and presenting you to the proper authori—"

"Mom—look out!"

A *twang* came from behind a ruined wall.

Anna instinctively whirled and summoned her shield. But there was a reason crossbows were such a common weapon against warlocks, for what felt like a hot poker jabbed into her upper left arm *just* as her lightning-crust shield appeared—and promptly flickered out. After a yelp of eye-watering pain, the first thing she glimpsed—beyond the bolt sticking out of her arm—was her daughter. She had become visible, eyes saucer-wide, hands covering her lower face in terror. The second was a man loading another bolt into a crossbow from beside a ruined wall twenty feet away. A hunter, judging by the bear trap on his back, who must have crept up on her.

Too late, she realized why there were eight tents and only seven men about. But there was no time to worry about him, for the sound of feet crunching on snow told her she had a heartbeat to react before that mountain man plowed into her and bashed her head in with his ham fist. The other men too were rushing at her—all but the son, who seemed stuck in hesitation, glancing between Anna and her daughter.

Despite the pain and her left arm being useless, Anna knew she had to be precise. Scion-deprived of their arcane powers—and thus their Mind Armor—the villains had a critical susceptibility to all spells. She chose a classic—an extension of Confusion she had learned on her own time a few years back.

"*Flustrato grapa seko!*" she incanted, whirling and jiggling a hand at six of the closest and most dangerous attackers—the captain, the mountain man, the two brothers, and the two fur-clad men reaching for their crossbows. Confusion was ordinarily a powerful spell, but she had split it six ways, substantially diluting it. The power of the scion would still amplify the spell enough to at least cause hesitation.

The two brothers and the pair focused on their crossbows had their heads snapped back. But the captain and mountain man, seasoned warriors in their own right, both ducked. The captain—seemingly by instinct—beckoned at a crossbow in the snow, only for nothing to happen, an old habit spurned by the scion's secret power.

The mountain man, movements surprisingly graceful for his size, closed in fast, aiming to bowl Anna over. She flicked her hand, using his momentum to telekinetically nudge him aside. He clawed at the air as he stormed past, sausage fingers brushing her robe, before he slammed into the brothers, sending all three tumbling to the ground.

As the two brothers glanced down at their crossbows as if trying to figure out what they were holding, the other pair of fur-clad crossbow-wielding men bumped into each other like children playing some clumsy game.

Meanwhile, the stubby warlock captain's arm abruptly flared to life with fourteen rings of fire.

Anna's heart skipped a beat. The one thing she hadn't practiced much over the years was ring snuff, which the scion allowed to be cast once daily, for the ring snuff power was sun-tuned. She thought she remembered it lasting longer.

Grinning victoriously, the man slapped his wrists together, roaring, "*Annihilo ito!*" Three fireballs *whooshed* at Anna, who realized they would hit her daughter if she let them through. She thus spread her hand and, as if trying to bring a dog to heel, made a downward movement. The scion flared with a loud buzz as all three fireballs, which she had grabbed telekinetically, slammed into the ground at her feet, melting the snow with a *hiss*.

Her daughter next surprised her by screeching, "*Armari elementus totalus!*"

Anna chanced a look back to see thin armor made of bark appear around Thia—only to fizzle out, demonstrating for the umpteenth time it was one thing to cast a spell for an exam, quite another to cast it in the midst of battle.

As the mountain man scrambled to unlatch himself from the still-confused brothers, eight lightning rings lit around his arm. But he wasn't the one to give her pause, rather the crossbowman who had emerged from behind the ruined wall, his crossbow aimed directly at Thia, standing only fifteen feet away.

"Stop or she dies!" he shouted. "You saw that I'm a dead shot, so don't you move, woman!" He was focused on Thia, but his words were for Anna.

Chest heaving, Anna realized the harrowing truth. As fast as she was, the man's trigger finger was faster, and the odds of telekinetically snagging a crossbow bolt were way too small to even risk an attempt. Further, that one strike had immobilized her left arm, making certain critical offensive spells unusable.

"Lower your arm!" the man barked. His trigger finger tensed and Thia closed her eyes and yelped. "*Now*, woman!"

Anna dropped her arm—and felt a huge body plow into her. Her head snapped back as her body smashed into the ground. The last thing she glimpsed before everything went dark was her daughter's ashen face.

A RECKONING

Amidst a raging headache, Anna's eyes fluttered open to see enormous flames leaping before her, burning her face and body.

She was in Hell.

The men had killed her.

Back in Solia, her daughter lay in the snow, covered in her own blood. Somewhere, a shadow was dragging her daughter's soul to its final destination … a metal cage.

All was lost. *All was lost!*

At least, that was her impression. Her throbbing mind wandered from thought to thought, confused as the day it had first become aware of itself. She sensed something was terribly wrong, yet she did not know what. There was acute pain in her left arm and her stomach roiled with vicious nausea, making her desperate to vomit—if she could move. Something iron kept her in place. Only her eyes could rove about to make sense of things. She was lying on her right side in the dirty snow. No, that wasn't dirt. It was bloody snow. *Her* blood.

It was dark out. Thomas would be enjoying supper with Samuel and Thia, waiting for her to come home. She would be late again. Why did she study so much, neglecting them both? It was an absurd thought she took guilty shelter in.

Men were near. Eating, talking in low voices, the words making no sense to her. A foreign language that sounded cruel and demonic.

Demons had drugged or poisoned her, befuddled her mind, and secured her in place. All common tactics to keep warlocks immobile.

But her mind wouldn't let her focus on any one thing for too long. She tried to see beyond the fire, but her peripheral vision was murky, thoughts a painful, pulsing blur that matched the irregular beats of her heart, as if her own blood were an enemy battering at the castle gates of consciousness. She saw Thia's ashen face morph into Samuel's. Her son lay with his arms over his stomach, in the final pose, a bear tucked under one arm. She watched helplessly as blue flames enveloped his body. Felt herself clawing at Thomas to let her by and save their precious son from the fire that would claim him forever. Yet as much fight as she gave, Thomas was unrelenting, and the flames that reflected in his eyes spread to Thia. She lay beside Samuel, except her hands were covering her ashen face, exposing only the eyes, which stared open with the horror of seeing something beyond the grave.

Anna's mother stood nearby. No, she was in a bed. No, her shadow fell over a young Anna, the back of the woman lit with flames. "I curse you," she growled in that demonic voice. "I curse your son. I curse your daughter. I curse your entire lineage …"

Anna wanted to scream. To curse her*self*. To sob. To do anything. But all she could do was let tears roll down her cheeks as her eyes unfocused, seeing only fire.

The demons spoke back and forth. The voices were familiar. One was younger, that she could recall.

But where was Thia? *My precious baby girl …*

Even through the confusion, a fundamental truth burbled like a vat of acid—getting captured had been her greatest blunder. A blunder no one would ever forgive her for, least of all herself.

Consciousness wafted about like the smoke of the fire. Throughout, a question echoed. Where was Thia? *Where was Thia!* Steadily, that consciousness clarified, though the nausea and pain refused to abate.

The voices got angrier. An argument broke out in a language she now recognized as Abrandian. She had the sense that men stood up to face each other across the fire. *Do with me what you will, but I just want her to live. Please save my daughter. Please let her live. Please …*

A horror of a thought intruded. Was her daughter even alive? Had they already slit her throat? "No witnesses," she heard the brother say. No witnesses …

The argument devolved into a fight, shadows moving before the fire. Someone bumped into her, nudging her enough to glimpse a girl sitting with her legs crossed, arms tied behind her, a gag over her mouth, face tight with fear. *Thia!* Their eyes briefly met before a rough hand shoved Anna, breaking their gaze. The argument abated. Someone had triumphed in an argument that surely would prove decisive. Even though she did not understand the language, Anna nonetheless knew it was the most important argument she had ever had the misfortune of hearing.

An argument that was answered with the fiery glint of a knife.

Thia squirmed, trying to shriek through her gag. If Anna could only thrash. If she could do anything at all other than move her blasted eyes. *Take me instead. Unnameables, help me and grant me this last wish. Please take me instead. Please …*

Miraculously, in place of Thia, the knife, held in a meaty hand, drew near Anna. *So these are my final thoughts. Let me be at peace knowing my daughter will survive me.* Yet the brother's words shattered that illusion — no witnesses. *No witnesses!* Those two words crystallized her thoughts. She was immobile — Paralyze spell, no doubt — but her mind, attacked repeatedly with mind spells to collapse the fortress, was slowly gaining freedom. *Too late. Too late!*

As the knife hovered before her, the man holding it gathering the courage to do the deed, she ignored the panic and closed her eyes, searching deep, hoping they had made the error others had made.

Sure enough, she felt it nearby. The scion was close — close enough to allow her to draw from its vast reservoir of sheer arcane power. They should have separated it from her with distance, yet few knew the secrets no holder of the sacred artifact dared share. Most assumed simple possession was enough to stop it from amplifying the warlock it was tuned to — and most also didn't know about the tuning itself.

Another argument broke out, and the knife moved toward Thia. Anna knew that knife would perform a deed nothing could undo. Seeing her daughter's terror-stricken face, a clarity beyond panic seeped into Anna's throbbing mind, one that cut through the numerous Confusion castings leveled against her and the nausea caused by whatever concoction they had poisoned her with. In her mind's eye, she saw the master warlock Ottentus effortlessly casting spells without uttering a word or moving a muscle. Latching onto that concept, she used the power of the scion and the immeasurable love for her child and channeled both into a clear phrase, imagining performing the precise gesture needed — the whirl of an arm. A tremendous buzz flared nearby, so close Anna could see lightning flashes of the orb glint off the knife coming at her daughter's throat.

Sfaera au praentergo buboa, she thought. The knife thudded against a protective blue cocoon which had appeared around Thia—a result of the 10th degree Sphere of Protection. Anna then summoned a monstrous shield made of a thick black lightning crust, one that curved almost completely around her, opting for a shield instead of the more complex Elemental Armor. Had she had the time to think about it, the teacher in her would have been proud, for she had wordlessly cast Sphere of Protection on her daughter and then summoned a strong shield to a wounded arm, an example of experience and determination overcoming adversity.

Shadows moved as the men panicked. The knife repeatedly stabbed at Anna's shield—*thunk, thunk, thunk*—but it might as well have been a stick trying to pierce stone. Next came the telltale slap of wrists. "*Annihilo ito!*" Three balls of fire slammed into the shield, the flames briefly merging with the fire in front of her and licking around the crust edge before subsiding.

Anna knew she needed mobility and clarity, and that meant fighting off the Paralyze enchantment and dispelling whatever poison they had forced her to ingest. First she needed to battle through the Mute spell that prevented her from casting. Aided by sheer force of will and mental acuity, Anna vanquished the casting in mere moments—the spell had luckily been a relatively weak casting. Next she battled through the Paralyze spell that kept her rigid like a statue, another weak casting. Finally, she drew upon everything she knew about the 6th degree healing spell Remedy Poison Infection Venom, incanting, "*Remedia rexo excella vindiv infecta poisa venoma extracta.*" She focused it on poison, dispelling it in her own veins as if she had swallowed a potent antidote. Immediately her thoughts clarified and the weakness abated somewhat—it would take time for the remainder of her strength to return.

The problem was that casting the spell had nearly finished off what remained of her stamina—the warlocks had done something right; they had used the 11th degree Arcane Drain to rob her of that precious invisible nectar.

Anna peeked over her shield and, seeing Thia's bubble roll across the ground from an incidental fireball, knew her daughter was safe for the time being, if only for heartbeats. Her actions would have to be precise. Not wanting to risk another massive failure, she righted herself into a crouch, closed her eyes, and focused on the only thing that could save them—a brief meditation. This she did by using her willpower to ignore the spells walloping her cocoon of a shield, coaxing the panic to subside by feeding it imagery of her arena victories. Running along a wall. Launching herself over an opponent. A final punch to the face, drawing a roar from the crowd. Confidence surging, she next worked on the throbbing pain in her arm, using the age-old monk principle of acceptance. The throb quickly consumed her. When her body became the throb, it subsided. Last, she harnessed her stamina, the raw arcane power drawn from the reservoir of the sacred ether, renewed at four times the usual rate.

Throughout, the villains tried lifting her up, but their Telekinesis was not nearly strong enough. They tried yanking on the shield with the 2nd degree Disarm, but her 18th degree Shield stubbornly held on to her wounded arm. *You will not vanquish me*, her iron mind said to them. *You will not prevail.*

With that renewal, her hold over the scion strengthened. Her vision improved, and through the fire and lightning blasts she glimpsed not only her daughter's protective blue bubble — still intact! — but the scion, flashing repeatedly in the fist of the warlock captain, even as he slapped his wrists together, hurling offensives.

The son was frantically tugging at the father's robe, cheeks stained with tears, yelling at him in Abrandian what Anna thought was a call for them to run. But the man's face was twisted with a combustible mix of rage and fear and indignation.

Anna at last stood, elongating her cocoon shield to cover her legs, careful not to disturb the crossbow bolt in her arm as even the slightest move made her wince. She created a schism in the shield, peeked through it, and saw the captain's eyes widen with the realization that he was in serious trouble. He grabbed hold of his son with one hand, the scion clutched in the other, and began the incantation that would get the two of them to safety. "*Impetus peragro grapa —*"

Anna, her mind gripping the scion with an iron fist and knowing what was about to happen, shook her head sadly at the boy through the schism, mouthing, "Don't."

"*—lestato exa exaei!*" the father roared. There was a *thwomp*, accompanied by a gut-wrenching tearing sound as the man's body shot off — whilst leaving his arm behind. That arm hung onto the scion, a lone and swinging appendage amidst the chaos, before slipping off to the snow with a *thump*.

Standing there behind the scion was a son gaping at his father's arm. Miraculously, he had listened to her and jerked free of his father's grip at the last moment. The scion had remained along with the severed arm, the injury due to the latter almost certainly foiling the Teleport. The father's chances of survival were grim. If he was lucky, the man had reappeared underground, instantly dead.

The wallops of spells halted. The mountain man, the two crossbowmen, the hunter, and the two brothers gaped at what remained of their captain. They glanced at each other before the hunter, the two crossbowmen, and the mountain man bolted in separate directions. The older of the two brothers initially did the same, only to return when his younger brother remained, head bowed in what appeared to be remorse. The son simply dropped to his knees before the arm. There he cupped his face with his hands and sobbed.

"No," Anna said to those who had fled. Her arm, rippling with eighteen lightning rings, shot through the schism of the shield, telekinetically lashing out. "You will not go free to murder again," she hissed, eyes bursting with The Settling, the lightning crackling viciously. Her Telekinesis snagged them all in a web and jerked them back. Even the mountain man fell. They were dragged kicking and flailing back to the fire.

While the older brother hissed urgently at the younger brother, who simply kept shaking his head, the five men thrashed about at the brothers' feet. Every time they broke free of the telekinetic web, Anna simply flicked a finger and reattached it. But she wavered, suddenly dizzy from the loss of blood and still weak from the poison they had given her. She had to sit down again lest she lose consciousness. Having triumphed, she felt the excitement fade a bit, enough for loss of blood to take hold—and she had lost more than she had realized. Throughout, Thia had pounded against the inside of the bubble surrounding her, her frantic yelling partly muted by the barrier.

Be precise, Anna, she told herself, and thought to try a more complex spell. She drew a quick outline of all five thrashing men, choosing to trust her instincts about the two brothers, even though those instincts had led her astray in this sojourn. Still, she needed to conserve energy for what was to come.

"*Paralizo carcusa cemente dio.*" The relatively low-degree men, unable to defend against her 18th degree spell strength, froze in place, paralyzed. A usual group spell would require the conjunction *grapa*, but the 14th degree Paralyze Group was an exception to this general rule, among its many other exceptions, including its name, which was reversed.

One of the many quirks of the decision-making process behind those responsible for The Founding, Anna thought, unable to help her inquisitive mind from indulging in such academic fancies.

Feeling it safe enough to do so, she let her cocoon of a shield vanish, giving a reprieve to her aching arm. Then she locked gazes with the brothers. "Be calm. I wish to talk," she said in Solian. *For the moment*. The Abrandian brothers seemingly understood because they quickly nodded. While the younger brother squeezed the shoulder of the captain's son with empathy, Anna turned her attention to her left upper arm wound. She raised a shaking palm over it—her body was weak, but not her mind—and, after performing the requisite mental preparation, she incanted, "*Examino potente morbus aurus persona.*" Diagnose told her that the bolt had penetrated the muscle and jabbed the bone, but no tendons had been severed. It was repairable yet would require focused work and an iron stomach, both of which she was too weak to muster. For now, the wound would have to be dressed.

She flexed her body, causing exquisite pain to shoot through her left side, and incanted, "*Virtus vis viray.*" The 8th degree Strength instantly amplified her muscles. She grabbed her left sleeve with her right hand, girded herself, and in one swift movement tore the sleeve clean off, making her grunt in pain as the cloth had briefly snagged the bolt. Then she grabbed one end with her teeth and tore the tube of cloth, creating a rough rectangle. Next she tore that rectangle into two strips, all while keeping a stern eye out in case someone got cute.

"*Virtus null,*" Anna said, nullifying the spell to conserve precious stamina. She also snuffed her lightning eyes and arm rings for the same reason, even though they drew upon a minuscule amount of stamina. She then used one strip to tie a tourniquet above the bolt and the other to secure the bolt in place, an Ordinary healing practice for those who did not have access to the healing arts, which were rare outside the cities.

Throughout this ordeal, the brother, the paralyzed men—at least those who had fallen facing her—and Thia all looked on with wide eyes. For her daughter, this was the first time seeing her mother in true combat outside of training duels.

Anna took a shaky breath and fought back the black walls of unconsciousness. "I will now set my daughter free." She focused on the older brother. "Be warned that I will have little patience for foolery of any sort." The look she gave him was the kind that said *And by that I mean I will obliterate you if you so much as blink at me wrong*. "Do you understand?" The man and his younger brother nodded and sat down, unprompted.

Anna swirled her good arm in reverse at her daughter. "*Sfaera null,*" and the bubble vanished.

Once free, Thia lunged to hug her. "Oh, Mom, are you all right?"

"Mmm."

"Good, but I hate you for getting us into this!" She pummeled Anna's back with the sides of her fists whilst still clinging to her. "I *told* you this would happen! Told you, told you, *told* you! Ugh, I can't believe you almost got us killed, Mom!"

Anna winced from the pain in her arm. "We shall discuss that later." *And I will have much to atone for.* "Right now, let us tie these men up." She gently pried Thia off and looked at the younger brother. "You have rope. Where is it?" She hoped stating it as a fact would deter lying. "You understand *rope?*" She pinched two fingers of each hand and drew them outward in a straight line."

"Yes, understand," the younger brother said in clunky Solian, raising a shaking finger to the tents.

Anna nodded at her daughter, who ran to gather restraints. "And bring gags!" Anna called, keeping a careful eye out until Thia returned, not wanting to be surprised again. She had a limp arm, was weak, and would have to wait until she got a little stronger before attempting a Group Teleport. Worst case, she would have to paralyze them all as she attempted emergency arcane surgery.

Thia soon ran back with rope and socks.

"You know how to tie a—"

"I'm in Drama class, Mom. Of *course* I know how to tie a proper knot."

Anna didn't know what Drama class had to do with knots. "Can you handle tying them up?"

Thia glanced at the mountain of a man. "I … I can try."

"I can help," the son blurted in an Abrandian accent, looking up at Anna with tear-stained cheeks and repeating in a whisper, "I can help."

As earnest as his face and eyes were, Anna was not foolish enough to trust a boy whose father she had vanquished. "Thank you, but we can manage. You speak Solian well."

"I much prefer this kingdom over mine. Mine is full of criminal brutes."

Thia got to tying the men up, stuffing socks into their mouths. "They're filthy, but I guess you deserve that, don't you?" she hissed. She finished with the crossbowmen and hunter but stalled with the mountain man. "Mom, what do I do if he refuses?"

"Cast Fear on him. Potency will be increased with infusion." She looked to the brothers and the son. "What does he fear?"

"Lions," the son blurted.

"Wolven," the younger brother offered in clunky Solian.

How quickly they turn on each other, Anna noted.

"You going to let me shove it in, you beast?" Thia asked. "Or are you going to force me to make you a training dummy? Oh, look, a single blink. Smart man." She used one hand to squeeze his jaw and open his mouth and the other to jam the sock in good, muttering, "Cretin tried to kill my mom?" She kicked him in the ribs. "You can eat your own stink."

"Enough, Thia. The courts will judge them."

Thia flashed her mother another angry *I told you this would happen* look. Anna did not disagree, but would discuss it with her daughter later. For now, she needed to deal with everyone in a way that would effectively deter any future attempts.

Thia, on her way back, came across a scroll in the snow. "What's this?" she said, picking it up and unfurling it. "And why does it mention the castle?" Her eyes widened the further she read. "Mom, why is my name put in at the bottom?"

"That is the deed to Castle Arinthian, a gift from me and your father for hitting your 7th. It has yet to be notarized, of course, but that can be arranged any time you are ready."

Thia stared at Anna, eyes watering. "Oh, Mom … I … I cannot accept this."

"We'll discuss it later."

"Is my father dead?" the son asked, wiping the tears from his cheek with a sleeve, tears that had fallen for an entirely different reason than Thia's.

"Alas, that is most likely. Even if he survived the teleport, he would quickly bleed out. And he most probably teleported somewhere without healers, ensuring the latter."

"I hope he is. And I know what you're thinking, but he was never a father, only a tyrant. Just last month, he broke my ribs with a kick because I wouldn't fetch him his stupid coffee."

The young brother nodded along to this.

"So I hope he's dead. I hope I never have to see him again. He kept me as a slave—him and that brute there. At least *he* was a little kinder. But I knew this day would come. I knew it in my bones."

"What do you mean by 'this day'?" Thia asked, having tucked the old document into her rope belt.

"A day of reckoning." He looked up at her with big doleful eyes.

"W-what's your name?"

"Jonah."

"That's a nice name."

Anna could swear her daughter blushed. If the boy was genuine, Anna suspected they would have some things in common.

"Earlier in the month, two men tried to kidnap my daughter. Would you know anything about that?"

Jonah and the younger brother dropped their eyes while the older brother swallowed. Anna turned her attention to him. "You know, the 12th degree Compel Truth is highly unethical—*except* in this very circumstance."

"We would have heard such thing," the older brother said in clunky Solian, earning him a warning look from the younger brother.

You're lying, Anna thought. "Then you leave me no choice." She raised her palm at the older one.

"One of them was *his* brother," the younger one blurted, nodding at the mountain man.

"And the other man who went with him?"

"My uncle," Jonah offered. "Just as vile a man as my father," confirming what Anna had heard.

The gang contained three pairs of brothers—the captain and his brother, the mountain man and his brother, and the two younger crossbowman brothers. It was an arrangement that ensured loyalty, not untypical amongst brigands.

"Where can I find them?" Anna pressed.

"Don't know, but they will be looking for you," Jonah replied. "My uncle will want revenge. You should be wary."

Thia tossed her arms skyward. "Great, and they know where we live too. Juuuust great."

You really did place your family in danger this time, you arrogant fool, Anna thought. But recriminations would come later. For now, she recomposed herself.

"You came all this way to strip me of the scion," she said to the lot.

"They all struggle to make a life for themselves at home," Jonah said. "They're dirt poor, and even when they *do* make money—usually from robbing people—they lose it gambling. Father offered them a fortune if they came along on his plan. He was at the Ohmish front thirty years ago as a fledgling warlock. Saw you duel The Reaper. A lot of men like him took it personally when you, a teenager, bested the kingdom champion. He is the same age as you, yet he was behind in the arts back then. His hatred of you only festered over the years, and his dream became to steal your scion like you supposedly stole ours—even though we had two already."

"Many hate evil Anna Stone," the older brother added in his clunky Solian. "You big enemy at home. Big enemy." Then he turned to the son. "Would your papa leave after get scion?"

The boy shrugged. "Probably. He was a thief and a liar and I'm surprised you all followed him as long as you did."

His words made the shoulders of the brothers droop.

Anna felt another bout of nausea come on and had to sit back down. "What concoction did you feed me?"

The older and younger brother exchanged worried looks—a sign that gave Anna a sinking feeling—before the older nodded at the mountain man. "He give maledite."

"Blue toad venom," Anna muttered, that sinking feeling deepening. It meant her condition would eventually take a turn once the venom infiltrated the brain. No wonder the Remedy Infection Poison Venom spell hadn't worked very well—she had focused on poison instead of venom. All the spell had accomplished was to stall for time. Now she was too weak, her mind too foggy, to recast the complex spell a second time.

Her eyes unfocused on the fire as her mind dipped into a reservoir of healing knowledge gleaned from Ning's academy healing classes. "Ketelinothasia," she blurted. "Does he carry any?"

"Is that the antidote?" Jonah asked. When she nodded, the three of them either flipped a hand or wobbled their heads in an *I don't know* manner.

Anna looked at Thia, who blurted, "I'm on it." She jogged off to the tents, shouting over her shoulder, "Which one's his?"

"The big one!" Jonah shouted back.

"They're all big!"

"Can I help her, Grandmage?"

"Sorry, but I do not know you."

"Of course. I understand."

As the weakness made her face flush and the nausea wormed its way up, threatening not just vomiting but a blackout, Anna realized time was of the essence. She flicked a finger at the teenager like she would at a student asking to leave class. "All right, you may give her a hand."

"I promise you can trust me," and Jonah shot off.

The scion floated lower too, as if mimicking how she felt. The older brother watched it. "It not allow be stolen. That fool think he could take and go, leave us to rot in foreign kingdom." He looked to the bloody arm lying in the snow and shook his head. "Now he pay big price. Big, big price."

Anna ignored him, not wanting to discuss the scion. Instead, she watched from afar as Thia and Jonah worked harmoniously together, soon returning with a tiny blue vial. Thia kept glancing over at Jonah and sheepishly smiling, making Anna recall a fellow arcanist saying how teenage crushes were like anonymously cast fart clouds—they came without warning and left everyone confused.

Thia delivered the blue bottle.

Anna turned it about in her palm. "It has no label."

"It's all there was," Jonah said, shrugging. "Except for more poison."

Anna stared at the tiny vial. Not seeing much of a choice besides taking a horrendously risky teleport, she uncorked it and tipped it into her mouth. The taste was medicinal and acidic, but the effect immediate—her stomach began to lighten. The flush retreated, and the weakness subsided, leaving behind that perpetual background headache. When she gave a nod, Thia pressed a hand to her chest, whispering, "Thank the Unnameables …"

Anna then sat back and let the antidote complete its work. While she recuperated, Thia and Jonah remained standing side by side, poking at the fire with sticks as they bantered back and forth about school and parents and their ages—Jonah revealed he was eighteen, a year older than Thia—and how Thia was in Drama and how Jonah always wanted to try Drama and that he dreamed of attending the academy as the Abrandian academy was a foul place where people treated each other horribly and myriad other things, until Anna had had enough and, probably before she was ready, blurted, "We can go now."

"Oh, but, don't you think you need a little more rest, Mom?"

"I can rest later. We still have to drop this lot—" She nodded at the three crossbowmen and the mountain man. "—off at a constabulary."

"What about us?" the older brother asked.

"You will explain yourselves before a magistrate, who can decide what to do with you."

The older brother dropped his head while the younger brother hissed something at him.

"What did he say?" Thia asked Jonah.

"He said, '*Told* you he wasn't nearly as smart as he thought,' referring to my evil father." He rolled out his shoulders and jumped up and down. "I've never felt freer in my life." He placed a hateful gaze on the mountain man. "I never have to see these bastards again, right?"

"The proper authorities will see to you," Anna replied.

"Oh, no. No, no, no. I know what that means." Jonah looked to the dark horizon. "I'm not going back to Abrandia. I refuse. I hate the people, the culture, and my mom would never take me back anyway. She loathes warlocks and their shenanigans." He looked into Anna's eyes. "I want to attend the Solian academy."

"You have to do something for him, Mom. Please."

Anna sighed. "We'll see. Now let's get you all ready to teleport."

REVELATIONS

❧ ⸺⸺⸺⸺⸺⸺⸺⸺⸺⸺⸺ ❧

"Sign here, here, and here," the junior constable, a young woman with a large forehead and pinkish hair, said. She had watched Anna with unconcealed awe throughout the recitation of events, taking feverish notes whilst the senior constable, a gray-haired captain in his fifties called Peters, asked questions.

"The word of a kingdom champion will be more than enough to convict the men," Peters said from behind the desk, setting another form in front of Anna. "And there too, please. My predecessor had quite the high opinion of you, Grandmage," he said as Anna signed the last form. "As does my kid."

"Captain Mera Blight was a fine woman," Anna replied, sliding the parchment back. "And she is missed." The grotesquely corrupt thieves guild had assassinated the woman some years ago after she had dared to bust a slave house. An investigation failed to find the perpetrators, but Anna always suspected the investigators themselves had been bribed. To this day, she carried a chip on her shoulder against the guild, even though they had left her alone.

She looked at the row of prison cells. Thia mingled before one, chatting in giggly whispers with Jonah, who clung to the bars with one hand, the other constantly maintaining that hair sweep. Seeing the way Thia acted around the boy, Anna almost didn't say what she said next.

"Captain Peters, I would like the teenager considered for an academy entrance exam."

"Are you sure, Grandmage?"

"No … but he deserves an entrance trial for possible acceptance. He's already achieved his 7th degree, earned in the Abrandian academy."

"If he is found innocent of any wrongdoing, I will be sure to pass him along to the academy."

Anna looked farther down the row of prison cells, spotting the mountain man. "Do you mind if I have a word with the big fellow there?"

"Feel free to question him however you like. I assure you that you will find no quarrel from us."

Anna returned a nod.

"It was a real honor, Champion Stone," the young woman blurted, earning an unimpressed look from her senior.

"Mmm," Anna toned as she walked down the line of cells, passing Thia and Jonah on the way.

"We don't have to leave yet, do we, Mom?"

"In a few moments," Anna absently replied.

"We still have some time," Thia whispered to Jonah, giggling.

"Still can't believe you're going to own a whole castle."

"No way. I'm not going to accept it. Last thing I want is to be a bigger target." And Thia giggled again.

My word, girl, was all Anna thought.

She soon stopped before the large man's cell. He sat on a bench, back against the wall, legs outstretched on the dirty hay, hands shackled with special manacles that prevented arcanery. She rolled out her left shoulder, still sore from the healing. Peters had summoned a city healer upon her arrival, meaning she did not have to do the work herself, which she had not had the stomach for anyway after such an arduous encounter. Even now, that blasted headache, which had started in the excavation, refused to abate completely.

The man watched her, a smirk floating amidst the bushy beard. Anna pressed three fingers to her temple and a hand to her throat. "*Translateo commona linguino Abrandian.* I'm hoping I only have to ask you this once," she said in Abrandian. "Where is your brother hiding?"

The man shrugged, the smirk widening.

"I thought that's how you'd react." Anna narrowed her eyes. "Do you think I will let your brother have another go at my daughter? Hmm?"

When his smirk did not subside, she flicked two fingers, telekinetically hauling the man up. He kept smirking, forcing her to do the work of floating him forth. His feet dragged along the hay floor like he was a recalcitrant boy not wanting to go to bed, albeit a giant one.

"Unlucky for you, I have a tool I have been granted permission to use," she said, conscious of the two brothers looking on from the cell over. Whilst telekinetically holding him up with an outstretched right arm, she reached out with her left and grabbed his mangy head of hair. The man snarled and tried to wriggle away, but Anna held him firm with her telekinetic might, the scion buzzing loudly in her pocket, amplifying an already mighty Telekinesis.

She prepared her mind for the controversial spell. "*Kompella o minad veta honesta.*" She knew the tendrils had penetrated his Mind Armor and latched onto his brain when his eyes went wide with struggle. An 8th degree stood little chance against an 18th degree casting of the 12th degree Compel Truth spell. "I ask again," she repeated in Abrandian. "Where is your brother hiding?"

"Shan ... ties ..." he growled through gritted teeth, referring to the roughest quadrant of Blackhaven.

"Where in the Shanties?"

"Plank ... building ... big ..."

"Be more specific."

"Don't ... know ... more ..."

"Then on what street?"

"Don't ... know ... street ..."

A warlock more practiced with the spell could get a subject to be more eloquent. Alas, Anna had very little experience with Compel Truth in the field—and was glad for it, as it was a spell for questioners. She thought about casting Empathic Transmission but, considering that was a two-way street of communication, did not want to expose the security enchantments around her domicile.

"What were their intentions with my daughter had they captured her?"

"Exchange ... for ... scion ..."

"What would happen to the scion?"

"Captain ... use ... make ... gold ..."

"The most worthless use of a scion there is," Anna muttered in Solian before switching back to Abrandian. "Not to mention that a stronger warlock would find him and murder him for the scion long before he made his riches. Now tell me, when did you expect to meet your brother again?"

"He would send word ... only if victorious ... otherwise ... would go home ..."

"To Abrandia?"

"Yes ..."

"So he and Jonah's uncle are still here in the city?"

"Yes …"

"Hatching a plot to kidnap my daughter, unaware you have been captured."

The man loosed a raspy breath, and Anna realized he did not have to answer for she had not asked a question. But it did not matter—she had gotten enough, and let go of his hair and body with a spiteful jerk. The pair glared at each other before Anna turned on her heel and marched off, snapping, "We're going home, Thia."

"Ugh, got to go. I hope we see each other again," she cooed.

"Bye, fair castle-owning princess."

Thia waved with both hands. "Bye, bye, bye!" and hurried to catch up to Anna.

Back at the desk, the senior constable interlaced his fingers on top of a pile of work. "I assure you, Grandmage, that everything those villains have done will be extracted and judged. I suspect most will never see the light of day again."

Anna thanked them for their time and left with Thia. Outside, she abruptly embraced her daughter in a hug, whispering, "I apologize. I was trying to teach you a lesson, but the reality was that it was *I* who needed the lesson. I am deeply, deeply sorry."

"Oh, Mom." Thia squeezed back hard. "I love you so much."

"I love you too."

"What should we tell Dad?" Thia asked, letting go to take her mother's hand in readiness for a teleport.

"The truth."

"He's going to explode at you."

"And I will deserve every harsh word."

"For once, I agree. You will. But …"

"But what?"

"I'd rather not see you two fight for the umpteenth time. Can we not tell him?"

"We're going to tell your father what happened. All of it. And we will not varnish a single word."

"Ugh, Mom, you're such a …"

"A what?"

"Nothing. Never mind. Let's just go home. Oh, and you can have this back—" and she thrust the deed to Castle Arinthian back into Anna's hand.

"Thia, I really think you ought to reconsider—"

"No, Mom. All right? No. I truly appreciate it, but I cannot accept this gift. You and I both know it would only make me a bigger target, and this little adventure has only proven to me how much I despise violence. Maybe when I'm thirty and I'm bored out of my mind with the city and I get some stupid yearning for country life … maybe then. Until that day comes, though, I'm afraid it's an emphatic no. I'm sorry."

"Emphatic. That's a good word."

"Told you I'm brilliant."

"Your father will be happy."

"Why's that?"

"He hated the idea of giving you the castle in the first place."

"And on that I would have to agree with him again," Thia muttered.

* * *

Thomas did indeed explode, shooting up from the end of the table and roaring, "You *what*?" The table was laid out with their fanciest dishware, all empty. The flame of a fat Endyear candle wavered above the mantel.

"Calm down, Dad. We're fine," Thia interjected, sitting beside her mother.

"Yes, I almost got our daughter killed," Anna continued, and resumed the story. Throughout, Thomas stood, white-knuckled fists pressed into the table as he glared at her.

"… so they're in the city, waiting for us to slip up," she finally concluded. "And the building could be any one of thousands."

Thomas's lip curled, his face puce.

Thia shrank in her chair. "Dad's about to explode," she murmured under her breath.

"Here I was thinking your little jaunt was simply taking a little longer than normal. That you would return to help with supper. Instead, you decide to play hero—*with our daughter*," he hissed, "who has hardly a *fraction* of the field experience *you* have! Correction—she has zero—" He made two *O*'s with his hands, thrusting them forth whilst roaring, "—*zero* experience! And in your hubris, you didn't even bring Thia's guard!"

Anna sat rigid, hands together before her, head level as she stared at his chest, feeling too guilty to look him in the eyes. "That is the way of it, yes."

"You risked killing our only remaining child for … for what, exactly?"

Anna opened her mouth to say she had wanted Thia to learn what danger felt like to prepare her better, but such an explanation did not feel remotely adequate, and so she remained mute.

"You arrogant woman! You could have teleported her home and *then* gone on a hunt! How could you gamble with our daughter's life like that!" Thomas slammed the table with his fists. "I ought to divorce you!"

Thia slapped both hands over her face and burst into tears. "Dad … stop it …"

Anna wilted in her chair, feeling as if Thomas had speared her in the gut. She would have preferred that as it would at least be healable. His words, however … there was no healing them.

"I have never had cause to say this to you, Anna Atticus Stone, but you were an idiot. An *idiot!* Do you hear me?"

Anna, hearing her mother scream at her father with the same threat of divorce—a threat she would eventually carry out—only swallowed, stomach roiling worse than when she had been poisoned.

"This is how you killed Samuel," Thomas added, making Thia burst with a more pained sob. "He wanted to make you proud. We don't need your mother cursing us—*this* is the curse! It's the curse of you Arinthians and your blasted scion! It's the curse of ambition and arrogance! This is how it all happens, over and over and over." He threw his arms up, head shaking. "I can't. I just … I can't. And what have you to say for yourself, huh? Or are you going to just sit there like a mute scullery maid caught stealing milk money?"

"Mom's already apologized to me, Dad," Thia whimpered.

Anna swallowed, throat dry.

"Apologies don't bring people back from the dead!" and Thomas stormed off, slapping his chair out of his way. It fell backward, bouncing a few times against the floor before settling. As the portal flared and Thomas stepped through it, Anna stared at the chair, remembering many a knocked-over chair from her youth when her own parents had argued. Here she was repeating the same patterns. How did that happen? *How!*

Thia's sobs calmed down to sniffles. "I *told* you you shouldn't have said anything to Dad. I told you …" She fiddled with a spoon. "Mom. Why are you staring off into space like that? Mom. Hellooooo."

"You haven't eaten. Let me fix you something up."

"Ugh, I lost my appetite."

Anna ignored her as she went into the kitchen.

"Some Star Feast," Thia muttered from the dining area. "The *one* day I'm without that old crone eyeballing me and—" There was the sound of two hands smacking together. "—*bam!* Almost got fried to a crisp. Maybe I *should* accept the castle … bring my friends there … hole up for eternity in a fortress …"

As she muttered on, Anna fumbled in the kitchen, ladling a bowl of the stew Thomas had spent hours preparing, stew that was supposed to have been served with a dish of turkey and potatoes she had charged herself with making, only to realize her hands were shaking and tears were streaming freely. She was failing as a wife and mother. Failing miserably. And Thomas's words kept ringing alongside that cursed headache. *I ought to divorce you! I ought to divorce you!* She pressed a hand to her mouth to stifle the sob that wanted to burst out and declare she had been wounded deeper than any wound she had received in the field.

Thomas's other words echoed about in her head as well—apologies don't bring people back from the dead. His words could not have been more potent.

A memorial ceremony had failed to wash away the guilt of their son's death, which remained like a mountain scar. Always there. Always visible. She had encouraged Samuel in his pursuits of the arcane arts and it had cost him his life. And now she had almost paid the same ultimate price again, simply because she had wanted to encourage her daughter to face danger and become adept at handling it. Oh, what had she done! Such arrogance was inexcusable. *Simply inexcusable!*

Anna felt Thia's arms close around her from behind. She pressed them close to her with one hand whilst keeping the other pressed tightly over her mouth. She didn't want to let her daughter see her like this. To see her so weak and wounded and humiliated and beaten.

"I'm sorry for blowing up at you, Mom ..." she whispered, adding in a murmur, "Please stop beating yourself up. Even kingdom champions make mistakes. I love you ..."

That was all it took for Anna to lose it. The sob breached her emotional walls and her shoulders heaved. Thia only held her tighter, and for a time, mother and daughter stood in the kitchen embracing.

"I have an idea," Thia finally whispered.

Anna slipped away to repeatedly dab at her eyes with the sleeves of her robe. "What's that?"

"Let's make the turkey."

Anna snorted. "It's late—"

"—and we haven't had a proper Star Feast. We'll just throw a chunk of the—" She flapped a hand at a bucket of ice, inside of which was wedged a giant turkey. "—thing onto a fire and make just enough portions to get roasted through for tonight. And we'll make one portion for Dad for when he gets back."

If he gets back, Anna thought.

Using Telekinesis, Thia lifted the turkey out of the bucket and floated it to the stone counter. "Wait, I need a cutting board."

"Coming." Anna pointed at a cutting board hanging by a loop above the hearth, and tried to shoot it underneath the bird, only for Thia's Telekinesis to fail. The turkey, which had already been wobbling, fell. The cutting board knocked into it and sent it rolling off the counter. The turkey landed on the floor with a squishy *splat*.

Both women slapped a hand over their mouths. Burbles of laughter escaped through those hands, first from Thia and then Anna. Then Thia laughed full-throatedly, followed quickly by her mother.

"The sound it made ..." Thia gurgled through her tears. "*Splat!*" She slapped the counter. "*Splat* ... stupid turkey ..."

"There's only one stupid turkey here," Anna wheezed through her laughter, once more dabbing at her eyes with her sleeve with one hand whilst tapping her chest with the other. "Me."

"Oh, Mom, you're not a stupid turkey. You're more like ... a pigeon."

"A pigeon? A *pigeon*?" Anna lost it. She laughed so hard she had to prop her hands against her knees.

"A pigeon," Thia said, nodding repeatedly through her laughter. "Definitely a pigeon," and she mimicked the back-and-forth neck motion pigeons made, reinforcing the laughter.

For a time, mother and daughter continued teasing each other and laughing about the turkey and the squishy sound it had made, with Thia even saying she could write a whole play around such a moment. For Anna, the mirth was a balm that soothed the burn of the self-inflicted wound her arrogance had caused.

Anna eventually calmed down enough to lift the turkey back to the counter. While she cleaned it off and the pair strategized how to attack the thing with a cleaver—neither were very good cooks—the banter went on. They even managed to boil some potatoes, finishing them off by roasting them in a griddle over the fire with butter and herbs and turkey breasts. As the women chatted on about this and that, keeping things light, the place filled with the mouth-watering scent of roast turkey.

"Gravy!" Thia blurted at one point, running to the kitchen. "We need gravy!"

"Flour!" Anna called after her. "Get the flour and we'll use the juices from the pan!"

Thia waddled back with a huge sack of flour swinging between her legs.

Anna flipped a hand. "My word, girl, why did you bring the whole sack? We have a canister in the bottom cupboard."

Thia stopped, eyes wide and unblinking. "I … I don't know." She proceeded to keep that same dumbfounded look as she turned around and waddled back, prompting Anna to laugh once more. Her daughter was such a goof. An adorable goof.

"I'm *definitely* going to write a play," Thia declared from the kitchen amidst the sound of cupboards opening and closing.

"*Bottom* cupboard!" Anna sang, rolling the turkey and potatoes about in the sizzling pan.

"Right. Found it!" She drifted back into the room. "It's going to be about our little adventure together."

"Gods help me, please no."

"It'll be fine, Mom. People will love it." Thia popped off the wide cork that plugged the ceramic canister, stopped to paint a headline in the air with a hand, and said, "Play opens about the mysterious Anna Atticus Stone, and how she fouled up big time and everyone yelled at her." Thia sprinkled the flour onto the pan juices to thicken them up. "They'll love seeing you muck up for a change. I'll even include a bit about pigeons."

After Anna finished chortling, she said, "I am not sure such a play would be wise as—"

"Mom."

"Mmm?"

"I was jesting. Did you seriously think I was going to write a play about us?"

"Well, it's you, so—"

"*Seriously?*"

Anna shrugged. They yapped on, ribbing each other, mother and daughter at ease. Anna cherished every moment, for it had been a long time since she had seen her daughter so comfortable and kind and merry. Not one word of sarcasm, not one jab. It was heavenly.

When the meal was ready, they sat in their usual spots, with Anna at one end of the table and Thia beside her, the plates steaming before them. They dug in like famished beasts, and for a time, there was only the sound of forks scraping against dishware, the flames of the two hearths, and the creak of the windows as a wind had sprung up outside.

"Did you *really* cast two spells wordlessly whilst poisoned and immobile?" Thia asked, munching on a potato. "Isn't that, like, a feat of legend?"

Anna shrugged. "That boy caught your eye."

Thia blushed something fierce. She covered her mouth with a hand as she chewed and looked away.

"What happened to—" Anna thumbed at the black book on a nearby table. "—what's-his-face, the sullen boy? Ralf."

Thia froze, eyes distant.

Anna, stuffed, put down her fork, arranging it neatly beside her plate. "Thia, is there perhaps something you want to tell me?" she gently prodded.

But her daughter stared off at the library hearth with glazed eyes. A hand wandered to cup her belly.

A stark thrill zipped up Anna's spine. It was then she knew. That simple cupping gesture. The nausea after teleportation, her coyness, her moodiness, her avoidance of certain activities … it all added up.

Thia started, catching herself, and smiled. "It's nothing, Mom. I was just—" But she realized her mother had a hand over her mouth. For the longest moment, the pair stared at each other. Thia, a deer caught, Anna, trying to fathom what she had deduced.

Thia placed her fork beside her dish and shrank in her chair. "You know," she whispered.

Anna could only nod.

"It … it was an accident," Thia said. "And now I … uh … I … I am …"

"You are with child," Anna said through her hand.

Thia swallowed and surrendered a nod.

Anna felt a clamminess she had never experienced before. She repeatedly wiped her hands against her thighs, trying to wipe it away. Her daughter was going to have a child, and she was going to become a grandmother and Thomas was going to be a grandfather but Thia was only seventeen and barely scraping by in the arts and who … who was the father? Oh gods, who was the father?

But she already knew who the father was. Thia had just told her.

Ralf. Ralf Turman was the father of her grandchild.

Another thought also intruded, one she did not want to admit existed … that the Arinthian line would continue. That this child would likely be the one to inherit the scion.

The headache raged, and Anna glimpsed a cage amidst an inferno. Unable to bear such thoughts, she shoved them away so strongly that she jerked in her seat, startling Thia anew. Her daughter opened her mouth, no doubt to ask if she was all right, when Anna blurted, "Does he know? Ralf?"

Thia nodded again.

"How far along?"

"Um …"

"Thia? *How far along?*"

"Two months," Thia mumbled.

Anna gaped. "Two months? *Two months!*"

"Please don't raise your voice. This is hard enough as it is."

Anna forced herself to calm down, but barely managed to keep herself from hyperventilating.

"I knew I'd have to own up to this eventually," Thia continued, "especially when I started showing. But I couldn't figure out how to tell you yet."

"So what was your plan when you *did* start showing?"

Thia shrank. "I was going to wear a bigger robe …"

Anna blinked. She couldn't believe her daughter.

Thia swallowed. "But, um … I don't want him to be the father. He's not … he's not a good person."

"Explain. Thia? *Explain*."

"Stop repeating yourself. It's annoying."

"Stop stalling and explain, young lady!"

Thia fiddled with her hands in her lap. "He might, uh, have a, uh, passing interest in …" She nodded at the book.

Anna glanced between the black book and Thia. "In—" She dropped her voice to a whisper. "—*necromancy*? Do I understand that right? The father of your child is infatuated with …" The clamminess returned, the throb in her brain hardening to an anvil strike.

Thia nodded.

Anna didn't know if she wanted to rush over to console her daughter or scream at her like Thomas had screamed at Anna. She had hidden something of vital importance from them, something they would have learned about anyway, but then this … this necromancy business was an entirely different sort of thing.

Then the dam burst. "He made us go through some ancient ritual about him being a father and me a mother in the old way some sacred way and I thought it was all a play really hokey and all that but I think with this whole excavation thing I saw another side of him and I think …" She leaned forth, whispering, "I think he was serious."

Anna bolted up from her chair, ready to swoop out of there, track down Ralf, and throttle him until he cried. Yet she did not move.

"Mom? Mom, stop it. You're scaring me. Sit down. Please, sit down. And make that thing stop buzzing."

Anna, not realizing the scion was buzzing like a swarm of raging hornets, glanced at it and it instantly silenced. She then reluctantly sat down.

"This isn't something you can fight your way through, Mom. Oh, and you can't tell Dad." Thia raised a finger, stalling Anna from speaking. "You know how traditional he is. All he ever wanted from me was to be a proper girl. You don't know this, but he once told me he looked forward to seeing me have a traditional wedding with a proper boy. That's his vision of me. To be a proper wife to a proper fellow in a proper manner." She twisted her fingers in her lap. "But I've never been a proper girl …"

"Well, you *have* to tell him."

"I know, I know, just … when I'm ready."

"What, when you're *really* showing? Do you not think that will be *worse*?"

"No! I mean … yes. I mean … I don't know."

"Two months."

"Uh-huh."

"Two months …"

Thia rested her elbow on the table and held her forehead. "Ugh, you thought *you* screwed up. Look at *me* here."

Anna wanted to laugh, but not so much as a smile escaped her lips. "This necromancy business. You need to tell me about it."

"I just did."

"No, I mean everything."

"Everything?"

"Everything."

"All right, but it's weird stuff, Mom. And I swear I thought it was just a thing he was messing with. You know how kids get into things. The pipe, the bottle, catchphrases, acting a certain way—oh, you know that craze a few years back when a bunch of kids started wearing black makeup to be ironic?"

Anna nodded, recalling all too well Thia emerging from her room as a fourteen-year-old wearing black lipstick and black eyeliner and with her hair dyed black. Anna had thought it was for a play, but then a bunch of the kids at the academy were wearing the same makeup, all on account of The Fated One, a traveling play that had run through town about a necromancer who became the victim of his own whims, losing his family to the dark arts. It was a parable, and an important one at that, but also one that took root in the young.

"But that was all harmless," Anna said. "As an arcanist, I see that sort of thing every term."

"Exactly. That was all a necromantic fancy. We were all being ironic. That's all. Ironic. Just kids trying to express themselves. To find a place amongst you adults by creating our *own* thing …"

"Go on …"

Thia turned her spoon round and round on the tablecloth. "Anyway, he has a name. It's his dark name. His ironic name. He calls himself Narsus."

"Narsus." Anna recalled the boy gloating about that very name in the academy cell.

"Narsus, yes. It means …" Thia closed her eyes as she stopped revolving the spoon. "I don't remember, actually." She continued playing with the spoon.

"Did he involve you in any other rituals?"

Thia shook her head. Then she shrugged. "He's always messing around with spells, so I don't know. Maybe."

"Maybe? *Maybe?*"

"Stop getting hepped up, Mom."

"Hepped up?"

"It's slang."

"Cut it with the slang and speak plain to me."

"Right. I'll try."

"How far is he into the, uh—"

"The necromancy? How am I supposed to know? I thought it was ironic."

"So what makes you think it's *not* ironic?"

Thia shrugged. "I don't know. A feeling."

"A feeling."

"Gods will you *please* stop repeating everything I say, Mom? It's *so* annoying."

"This is serious."

"I *know* it is."

"He could get arcastrated for this. So is he or is he not involved in necromancy?"

Thia kept turning the spoon.

"Thia? Is the father of your child a budding necromancer or not?"

"I don't know, all right!"

Another loud buzz emanated from Anna's scion as it repeatedly flashed with lightning.

"Will you shut that thing up already, Mom?" Thia shouted over the noise. "Yeesh."

Anna ran her hands through her hair, wrecking the careful braid. She smacked her gums at the scion, silencing it once more, before shooting up from her chair, slamming the table with an open hand, and roaring, "Tell it to me true! Is the father of your child a necromance or is he not!"

"Is who the what now?" a voice, slightly slurred, asked from the portal area.

The women looked over to see Thomas arm in arm with none other than the king. The pair wavered, and the king clutched a bottle of Sierran Titan wine by the neck. Anna went ashen. The buzz of the scion had masked the sound of the portal.

Thomas now knew.

Thia slapped both hands over her mouth. "Oh gods oh gods oh gods oh gods ..."

Thomas unspooled his arm from the king's shoulders, staring at Thia with a wild look made all the more crazy by his unruly hair from a night of drinking.

King Power eyed the bottle in his fist, looked around for a table to set it on, found none nearby, and took a swig instead. "I, uh, apologize for the intrusion, ladies," he mumbled in the thick silence. "We could have that Endyear drink another day, old chum," he mumbled to Thomas whilst glancing back at the portal. "My guards wait for me outside. I ought to see to them and—"

Thomas grabbed him by the arm, hissing, "You're not going anywhere, old chum."

"Or I guess I'm not going anywhere," the king mumbled. "I suppose my guards can idle outside." He forced a chortle. "They're paid handsomely anyway to do that all day."

Thomas grabbed the bottle and took a big swig. He raised a single rigid finger, lowered it, raised it, then lowered it again.

"I was going to tell you," Thia squeaked. "I swear. I just ..." She dropped her head. "I'm sorry, Dad. I didn't want you to find out like this."

"You were going to tell me."

"Yes."

"You were going to tell me that, at seventeen years of age, you are going to be a mother."

"Yes."

"At seventeen. When you struggle focusing on your arts. When you can barely protect yourself."

"Please, Dad ..."

"And what is this necromancer business? Huh?"

"Nothing. It's a figure of speech. Truly, Dad. Calm down. Please."

Thomas clenched his jaw as he looked at Anna. "I suppose *you* knew since the beginning, didn't you?"

"Mom only found out tonight," Thia blurted. "She figured it out on her own."

Anna stood, not knowing what to say or do. She had suspected something was different. If only she had had the courage to follow up on those suspicions earlier! Yet she did not know if that would have changed anything …

"Who is he?" Thomas asked.

Thia started breathing hard. "No one."

"Who is he!" Thomas roared.

Thia dropped her head. "I'm a woman grown who has the right to—"

Thomas loosed a spiteful laugh. "A woman grown …"

The king elbowed him. "Perhaps we ought to go back to the tavern and—"

"We're not going anywhere."

"Yes, you are," Anna said.

"I beg your pardon?"

Anna marched forth, saying, "You will either speak in a civil tongue or you can sleep in the tavern."

"How dare you—"

She stopped before the pair, placing a flat gaze on the king. "You—" She flicked her head at the portal. "Out."

"Yes, m'lady," the king mumbled like he had when he had been the pupil she had chastened many a time. He scuttled to the portal, fumbled summoning it, but finally managed to depart, leaving Thomas standing with the bottle of Titan in hand.

"Our daughter is at a critical point," Anna said, staring at Thomas with narrowed eyes. "Either you support her, or you can find somewhere else to sleep tonight, where I suggest you ponder on the fact that you will be a grandfather. Choose your words carefully."

"A grand—wait, me sleep somewhere else? *Me?* Even though this is surely *your* doing? The free and fanciful way you've been bringing her up?"

Anna, having had enough, ballooned.

"Stop it!" Thia shouted. "Stop fighting! All you two *do* lately is fight! I'm sick of it!"

Husband and wife glared at each other.

"Theeeeere's the famous killer you read about," Thomas whispered. "There she is, staring me in the face. The dueling champion. The holder of the scion. The *Arinthian*."

Anna's eyes danced between his. *You mistake resolve for lethality, sir*, she thought. Yet knowing she shouldn't make things worse—but certainly wanting to—she whirled about and returned to the table.

Thomas took another swig. "You know what? I *am* going to sleep at the tavern." His head bounced with a nod at Thia, lips pressed so hard together they bulged. "Of all the disappointments …" The nod turned to a shake. "Setting aside the challenges of being an *unwed* mother who spends her time daydreaming about silly plays, do you know what they'll say about us when people find out? What civil society will think? We have responsibilities. People look up to us. Of all the disappointments …" He turned, slapped the portal rune, and whisked himself out of there, leaving behind a deafening silence.

Thia shakingly fumbled about for a chair.

Anna went to her and enveloped her before she collapsed to the ground, stifling her sob in her robe. "It's all right," Anna whispered, lovingly stroking her daughter's back. "It's all right. We'll get through this."

Thia clung on tighter than she had during their adventure. "He'll never forgive me. He'll never look at me the same. He's going to put me out in the street. He's going to disown me."

"He's just in shock. Your father's a stubborn fool who lets his emotions run his temper. But he has a heart, and he will learn. He always has." Or so she wanted desperately to believe. "You are loved. Your father loves you. *I* love you. Now let's get you some tea and then to bed. You've had a trying day. We can continue the discussion tomorrow."

SOTO NEI SOTO

Anna stared at the *Blackhaven Herald* headline. "Abrandian Warlock with Missing Arm Found Half Embedded in Shanties Building. Suspected Teleport Misfire."

"Would you like to take it free of charge, Champion?" the stallkeeper asked with a toothy grin.

"Not today, thank you," Anna replied, handing the scroll back.

"Bless you, Champion. May the Unnameables watch over you and your family and keep you safe from harm."

"Thank you, gentle sir."

She moved along, eyes darting about, watching, anticipating. It was another overcast and snowy day, with flakes gently tumbling onto an already inundated street. Not the slightest breeze stirred the air, the blanket of snow muting the city with a soft, white calm. She ignored the headache that pulsed in the back of her mind, and the visions, left in the afterglow, of a nightmare—a shadow, a daughter, a cage.

Anna kept her hood down, not wanting to miss anything. An old woman carrying two buckets of buttermilk tottered by, head covered with a scarf. A blacksmith wiped his sweaty brow before returning to working on the hoof of a palfrey. A girl chased a boy, lobbing snowballs at his back as the pair giggled. They reminded Anna of Samuel and Thia when they were little and Samuel had learned to run. He had stumbled often, Thia letting him get up before continuing the chase. They had generally been kind to each other, which had been an immense relief to

Anna, who had grown up with an adversarial relationship with her sister.

As she walked on, eyes taking in every building, the neighborhood steadily worsened — she passed abandoned and boarded-up buildings and droopy characters mingling in dark alleys and heaps of snow-covered trash. Soon she heard the call she had been expecting.

"'Lock on a walk!"

"'Lock on a walk!" someone echoed half a block away, the call parroted down the street. Some groups of men promptly broke apart. Others came together.

Whereas she had been mostly anonymous in her youth when doing such patrols, those who now saw her did a double take. Many knew of her, just had not laid eyes on her in the flesh.

So many of them were young. Too young. Rabble-rousers, runaways, throwaways, outcasts. They gaped from the filth and squalor as if seeing a princess. A few whispers trailed. Is that the one? Is that *her*? It can't be …

Anna eyed building facade after building facade, wanting one to fit the description of the mountain man. But she might as well have been searching for a specific pebble on a beach. That was what shortcuts were for. When she had played constable all those years ago, the streets had taught her that someone always knew something. And it was that someone for whom she searched.

"'Lock on a — gods, that's *her*," a boy hissed, quickly slapping another boy's crossbow aside. "She'll bleedin' turn you into a snake before you blink, you idiot." They melded back into the shadows, whence they watched her like all the others. So many wary eyes.

Like a creeping fungus, corruption had grown over the decades since the annihilation of the Arcaner order. Who would've thought that so-called outlaws were needed to keep real outlaws in line. That was all the underworld ever understood. Strength. Power. Fear.

Anna stepped up to three boys loitering before a shoddy old door guarding a brick alley. She recognized the hinges, of all things, and the dinged-up iron brazier. She remembered a man whose face was tattooed with spears. Another with a crossed-out line tattooed down his face. Beyond the door loomed the weathered basalt blocks of the Temple of Cadrius. And within, perhaps an answer to her query.

"Y-you ought not to be h-here," the oldest boy, no more than fourteen, stammered. "I c-can't let you in. W-w-we'll get in t-t-trouble …"

"They will understand." She opened a palm between them and nudged it toward the door. "Excuse me."

The boys hesitated before stepping aside.

"Thank you." Anna slipped by. Politeness held surprising power, especially against the powerless.

After closing the shack-like door behind her, she paced on through the narrow alley, her steps quiet in the snowfall, the scion bulging in her pocket. She stopped before the stonework, with its pillars and high beam carved with the word "CADRIUS," ancient graffiti that had given a name to the temple when its original had been long lost to time. In the snowy silence, she recalled throwing down the gauntlet in this very courtyard, the first awakening of a long line of awakenings of the woman she would become. "The no-nonsense sort," as her students liked to describe her, though not without some affection. But they knew a side of her the streets did not, and vice versa.

Now the lioness returned, and the hyenas awaited, surely already aware of her presence. Their servants watched from the shadows, fearful of what she might do, hopeful she would simply go away.

Anna spread the fingers of a hand, incanting, "*Un vun asperio aurum enchantus.*" Ancient tendril enchantments lit up all about the temple floor and walls, all sunk to permanence, all connected to warlocks who had long turned to dust. There were no new ones. So brazen were the current occupants, so enmeshed and protected by bribery, that they need not fear intruders like they used to. There were no lions or lionesses about anymore … except for her.

Anna walked along the lines of a faded blue tendril web, conscious it was trying to alert its master of a presence. As she had done thirty years ago, she wondered if some combination of dirt and ash somewhere underground received a *ping*. A flare of arcanery, perhaps the ether hoping for consciousness where none remained to be found. The last remnant of a decision made eons ago.

She stepped through a central chamber, remembering a certain fallen monk holding a gathering to hunt her down, not realizing she was waiting for him outside, ready to call him out by name. Like so many others through the years, he had fallen to her arcane might. But unlike the others, he had been the lioness's first big kill. So to speak, of course, for he had later died by the rope. Yet she might as well have been the one to place it around his neck.

"It was a worthy duel," she whispered to herself, pacing on through the chamber, reaching a back wall with a huge hole in it, damage sustained in a bygone era. The edges still had char marks, and as was typical when it came to ancient charring, local legend said it was the work of dragons. Yet the evidence pointed to a mighty catapult, perhaps from a siege when the city was not much more than the Black Castle and a surrounding village, with this temple a mysterious remnant from even earlier times.

Anna stepped through the hole, entering a hallway of makeshift doors, shanties added over the years to make a small fortress of another sort. Here there were indeed fresh alarm enchantments, upon which she stepped on purpose, triggering them. They vanished, indicating weak castings. The last door was already open. Beyond were stairs carved out of the clay earth and stiffened with rotting planks. Anna descended these squeaky stairs, conscious of the narrow clay walls, the musty smell of mold, and pipe tobacco reminding her of her old mentor, Panza.

The scent grew stronger as she neared the noise of a room filled with quietly chattering people. Some had already started shushing each other in anticipation of her entrance. All that remained was a finely carved door, the door of a noble, no doubt stolen from its home.

Anna nudged a finger and it began to creak open. But the noise annoyed her and she flicked her finger, making the door swing hard — and slam against the wall with a *bang*. She stepped through, entering a dark and smoky underground tavern full of rough men and women with hard faces. There had to be a hundred of them. She was unsurprised to see so many at this hour of the morning. Some smoked pipes, some held tankards and others tall glasses of wine. Some wore robes, some leathers, some chain mail. Nearly all were armed. The daggered ones were night stalkers, initiated loyal agents of a certain guild that had caused the city much trouble since the fall of Arcaners. Pipe smoke billowed from within many a hood. Candles and torches flickered, hearths crackled, pots boiled. No one stirred.

They watched, waited, until a raspy and confident voice rang out from the crowd. " 'It is not the mice who stir when the lion enters —' "

" '—but the sheep who crave its protection,' " Anna concluded, cutting the voice off.

A wide man in a silk doublet of patterned brocade, the buttons of which strained against his bulk, puffed on a thin pipe as long as his arm. "I suppose being a teacher has its advantages."

"Proverbs are cheap in academia."

"And worth gold underground."

"Mmm."

The pipe waved about. "No men storm. No shouts. No orders. No chaos."

"This is no raid."

"Nor would there ever be one, considering we own the city."

Chortles rang out as heads nodded and knowing elbows were exchanged.

Anna waited for them to die down, but the man spoke first and the chortles ceased.

"What can the thieves guild do for our illustrious kingdom champion?"

"Two men—Abrandians—tried to kidnap my daughter."

The man puffed on his pipe and blew out a large ring. "So?"

More chortles.

"A simple query."

"Favors here beget favors."

Anna had expected this. "What do you want?"

"We find these men for you. Deliver them to you …" He idly turned a skull-shaped glass with green liquid about. "… wrapped in meekness. In exchange, you keep those clean hands off our tournaments."

"I would not have a problem with those tournaments if they were held only amongst the lot of you. But you let our students in. You let them compete. Gamble. Perhaps you even encourage these activities. And that I *do* have a problem with."

"It is dangerous for a mime to forget she is a mime," the man opined to much snickered amusement. "You are a figurehead. A symbol for the poors. You have no real power." He opened his ham hands. " 'Arms, arms. Arms all and everywhere, so as eyes they see … let us beware.' "

Anna tilted her head, recalling watching one of Thia's plays. Luckily the line was famous enough to quote. " 'Then let us see these arms. Let them be numbered one to true. A head for a mount … should none come to account.' "

The man grinned, hands still splayed. "Good sirs and ladies!" he boomed. "Please indulge our guest. Let the banners rise."

Arms began to light up with rings. Warlocks of fire and water and earth and ice and air and lightning and even two warlocks of the healing element, all showed off their rings, numbering from a single band to sixteen at the highest count. Forty or so in all, a full third of the gathering.

The crowd chortled, the sound strengthening to laughter as the man kept his palms open, a bemused smile around the pipe.

"What can a single wolf do against an entire pack?" he boomed over the laughter, taking a puff of his pipe.

Without glancing down, Anna answered by letting the scion free itself from her pocket. It drifted forward, its lightning flashes pronounced against the darkness, its usual buzz as silent as the looks it received. Keeping her Reveal lit, she tilted her head the other way. She had lost some of the edge that came with being an arena dueler. It was time to test her bounds once again. Training was not enough.

"*Extingui*," she whispered, and saw the invisible tendril bubble burst out into the throng from the scion. One by one, arms snuffed. Warlocks shot up, crossbows rose, and swords and daggers were drawn.

Anna stood motionless, the smoke drifting between her and the wolf pack. Taking a calculated risk, she sauntered forth to the table, conscious that a crossbow bolt was quicker than her fastest reflex.

She halted before the table. " 'In the land of the speechless, the mime is queen.' "

"I am not familiar with that one." He was uglier up close. Blotchy skin, wine-stained teeth, gaudy rings on tobacco-stained fingers, middle-aged zits. He was but a wheezing pustule of a man.

"That is because my daughter wrote it." Anna grabbed the rim of the skull cup and turned it so that its empty-socketed face stared at him. "Besides, '*yestus aro o sureka au mirthus.*' "

"Jesters are indeed the source of mirth. And we respect our jesters, as we respect our teachers. Do we not, my gentle-hearted friends?" The throng of hard-faced men and women chortled on cue. "For our teachers scorn us before the class. Lead us by the ear to a corner. Drag us out into the yard to be whipped."

"Two men not of this kingdom. That is all I ask."

"Look around you. We are of every make and sort here. And we are not parrots, repeating on command. You have been told the price. Take it or leave it, Champion. And if you decline but truly want to shut the tournaments down—" He reached out and turned the glass back the other way, so the skull faced Anna once more. "—do it yourself, *Champion.*" This time the title was said with a mocking twist.

"You are asking me to sell my principles. Everything I am."

"Spoken like an Arcaner of old. Yet you yourself are no Arcaner and the order is dead. So what say you, Champion?"

She pressed her hands amidst the pipes and drinks and cards and crowns on the table, leaned forward and mouthed into his oily face, "No deal."

The man's grin vanished, his eyes going hard. "Then perhaps we ought to aid these men in finding your precious little girl."

Anna's face remained close, the scion stirring with a buzz. "Then perhaps the king's men should storm this hovel and drag each and every one of you, by the ear, into a corner." *Where you will never be heard from again.*

The man glared before breaking with a smile. " '*Soto nei soto*,' " he said, slicing two fingers through the air. Everyone relaxed their weapons, for *Sword no Sword* meant, "Come and leave in peace—no harm sent, no harm returned." It was the old way of de-escalation, and a foundation of a parlay. The man knew that should violence begin, he would be the first to die.

Anna straightened. "Mmm."

"We own this city, Champion. Remember that. And do not come again. Not every heart here …" He smiled a smile that did not reach his eyes. "… beats gently."

Anna lingered a moment longer, disappointed at the results. But she could not sell her soul. She would have to find the men herself.

She turned on her heel and strode out of there, the scion floating in tow, every eye following its silent lightning flashes.

CURLS OF SMOKE

In the afternoon of this special day, there came a *thwomp* as Anna appeared amidst a snowy forest of conifers she knew all too well. The first thing she did, as she had always done over the years, was take a deep breath and inhale the crisp air, letting the strong aroma of pine needles infuse her soul. The snow here tumbled as it had in the city — slowly, with no hurry to settle on the thick white blanket that covered every branch, boulder and bush. She lingered, taking deep breaths, watching her breath plume, the silence so thick she could hear the flakes settling on her shoulders with the gentlest of pats. The only thing disturbing the peace was that cursed headache, a perpetual annoyance she could not shake, despite trying many variants of spells and Ordinary remedies.

After taking her usual bearings, she walked forth through undisturbed thigh-high snow, the trail just ahead. One of the critical tests of a novice warlock was being able to teleport amidst snow without fusing with it. It was the same with rain. And the deeper the snow, the greater the chance of accidental fusion. It was a lesson she hammered into students when teaching Teleport, yet every year a student overextended, discovering just how painful snow fusion could be.

After she found the trail — nothing more than a dip in the snow, with a clearing of bushes as a guide — she splayed the fingers of a hand, whispering, "*Un vun asperio aurum enchantus.*" Old and fading tendrils the color of lightning lit up all around. As she did every year, she stepped on the Area Alarm enchantment, triggering it.

"I'm home, Papa," she whispered, hoping somehow he got the message. "I'm home. And I bring glad tidings." She walked across the thirty-five-year-old enchantment, cast so competently it stood a chance of sinking to permanence. A few others lingered, one of Panza's make, an illusion spell that, when triggered, made the house vanish. But it could never be triggered again, for its owner was no more.

Anna stepped into a clearing, hearing the laugh of a little girl chasing a still smaller girl, the latter crying. She heard the voice of her father echo, "Stop it, Dey-Dey! Stop chasing your sister! She doesn't like it!"

When her eyes fell upon the ruins of an old house, she heard the clank of dishes as her mother fussed in the kitchen. She saw Panza sitting on a chair, the spindles of which had now fallen to the ground. He gummed his pipe thoughtfully, watching the girls play, his mind elsewhere. She saw her sister chasing her, knocking her to the ground, giggling how funny it was. In the snowy silence, she heard and saw a whole childhood pass before her eyes like a finely crafted illusion.

But the erosion of the house, with its eaves long fallen, its roof invaded by hibernating vines, its windows smashed from wind and decay, was no illusion. She had refused to repair any of it, wanting the wilds to reclaim what was owed. No monument need exist here, for it would only perpetuate the tragedy that lingered in Anna's mind as fresh as if it had happened yesterday.

She stepped before a certain spot in the clearing, a spot unmarked, where she withdrew one of two tiny candles, sticking its end into the crystal blanket of snow. She touched the wick. Wordlessly, her finger sparked with lightning until the wick caught. The candle flared before settling into a steady flame.

"Hello, Dey-Dey. Thirty-five years ago today, you died in this spot, in my arms, with a heartfelt apology on your lips, your eyes seeing the stars for the last time. I wish things had turned out differently between us. I truly do. But I have honored your memory as best I could. You are and forever will be my sister. When my time comes, I hope we can reconcile in death what we could not in life."

She took a shaky breath. "Enough of that. I bring you tidings. You will be a grandaunt! Your niece, whom I wish you could have met on your best day, continues the line. And she's brilliant in her own way. A drama kid. Has lots of friends. But she's lonely, too. Like I was. Yet I am the one thrusting that loneliness upon her. In that way, the curse continues. No, not that curse. The other one," she said, tapping her bulging pocket. "She should have had cousins. They should have played together in their youth. Your kids with my Samuel and my Thia. Perhaps he would still be alive." She sighed longingly. "Alas, The Fates had a different plan. I miss you. That is, I miss the person you could have become. I miss the idea of you maturing into a decent woman. I know, I know, but allow me my lingering fancies." She sighed a second time. "Now let us linger together."

She watched the candle expire, ruminating on the countless memories that surfaced like boulders in a dropping tide. When the candle died out with a quiet *hiss*, its smoke wafting lazily into the air, she kissed her hand and tapped the snow beside the candle, whispering, "Mama will join you and Papa soon. Please make her a comfy bed and prepare her some pine needle tea. You know how she likes a nice dollop of honey. I love you, I love you, I love you."

She turned about to face the house, took another shaky breath, and stepped up to the old door, hanging only by a single hinge. She pulled on it, unsurprised that it came free. She set it aside without the intention of putting it back, inviting the wilds in.

The floorboards creaked as she stepped into the old hall, her eyes falling on a certain bench. She saw her feet dangling off that bench, yet how tiny it looked now! She must have been so small back then. She saw Panza sitting beside her as her parents argued in the kitchen, heard a telltale *slap* before her father walked in and crouched before her. One of her proudest moments, marred by bickering. No one alive had blossomed with the arts at ten years of age, yet there she was, the precocious bookworm, gripping Bun-Bun tight, trapped inside an old house, the future inheritor of a legendary seventeen-hundred-year-old artifact that would in time destroy the family it protected.

"Your spirit is free now," she said to the little girl she was, letting the silence of the hall wash over her. "Yet here you are once again …" As with the castle, it was a pilgrimage she made every year. But this one would always fall on the same day. She had taken great care to erase its location from any and all records—not that many remained, for her father had been rightfully paranoid in that regard.

Anna moved on into the kitchen. Its cupboard doors hung loose, the wash basin thick with grime, the floor covered in dead leaves and acorns and pinecones and mouse poop.

Anna kneeled on the floor, withdrew the second tiny candle, placed it on a certain spot, and lit it. The scion floated from her pocket and lingered nearby. "Hello, Papa. Can you believe it's been thirty-five years?

Yet I remember that day as if it happened moments ago. I miss you. I miss you more than words could ever express."

Her head fell, eyes closed, as she paid homage to her father's memory before she reanimated. "I bring glad tidings! Your granddaughter is with child, making you a great-grandfather. Isn't that incredible? The circumstances are not ideal, sure, but it's something, isn't it? Despite the questions, I know how proud you would be. I know it ..."

She sniffed. "So, uh, I will not be the last Arinthian after all. The ancient line does not die with me, as had been your greatest secret fear. But a challenge still remains ..." Her eyes fell upon the scion, clouding over, as silent as the house. Today, as if in honor of the ancient lineage, it was tinted blue. "I cannot give it to my daughter. She is not strong enough to wield it. It would be a death sentence. But perhaps her daughter—or son ... my granddaughter or grandson ... perhaps they will accept the challenge."

Her head bounced with a hopeful nod, eyes unfocused in the deep silence. "It's doing to my family what it did to us. It's destroying us. My husband, he ..." She couldn't do it—couldn't reveal how her marriage was failing in a similar fashion as her father's had. "Momma cursed us. She sent Samuel to you, and now she wants to send you Thia. All because of an accident. You know what happened with Dey-Dey. You know it. I know it. But Momma loathed me in a way that bled through. Now I am afraid. So terribly afraid. I have these dreams ... nightmares. There's a shadow ... a cage ..." Her chin trembled, but she forced it to stop. "I worry about Thia. Someone might kidnap her, or the shadow of the curse might take her." She expelled a shuddering breath. "I had more to say, but I have a headache that refuses to die. So let us linger."

As with her sister, she watched the candle burn. When it at last expired, she watched its smoke curl around the scion, as if embracing her father's heart.

"The line continues, but I have not fulfilled the sacred quest. The scion remains unclaimed in the next generation, and I have not bridged the gap between the past and the present, between Ley and Sithesia. But I am working on it. An excavation shows promise. I know the arcaneologist in you would be intrigued."

She kissed her hand and pressed it to the plank boards, whispering, "Mama's coming home soon. Please don't fight. Take care of each other, like I remember you doing so in the days of my early youth. I love you, I love you, I love you. Forever and ever."

AMIDST THE WHITE

Thia paced back and forth in the dimly lit green hall of the infirmary, one hand holding her tummy, the other scrunching her robe. "What if Grandma doesn't *want* to see me? What if she throws us out? What if her other family's there? What if—"

"We'll deal with each as it comes," Anna replied, leaning against the wall, eyes reflexively following every white-robed healer and attendant as they padded from room to room.

"Why is this taking so long? Why do they make us wait?"

"They have many to attend to."

"And why isn't Dad here?"

"He refused to come."

"Did you make him feel terrible first? Guilt him in the way you are so good at? Is that why?"

"No, Thia. He …" But how could she explain Thomas's cruel words to her, ones that still echoed around in her brain? Particularly the final ones, "You disgust me!" which he had roared in her face before storming out last night. Another argument, the same yet wholly different. No resolution, only a digging in of heels.

Thia resumed her back-and-forth pacing. "He's at the excavation, isn't he? Keeping himself occupied."

Or drunk with the king or in some hovel, Anna thought. He had not been coping well with Thia's news of being with child. His world was cracking like his mind. No matter how soothing the words she spoke, they acted not as a balm but as tinder to a slowly building fire. Despite her efforts, she could not douse the flames, nor know what that fire would consume.

"Your father is still coming to terms with—"

"Oh, save it, Mom, would you? It's *your* fault he loathes me."

"I understand why you feel that way." As if mirroring her father, Thia had only gotten more volatile, blaming Anna for whatever came to mind. It was everything Anna could do simply to keep her in the house with the retired Black Eagle as she searched for the men who threatened to kidnap her, bolstered the enchantments around their tower home, and searched her heart for what to do and how to survive. It felt like the family was hanging on by a thread.

"It is vitally important that you—"

"Yes, yes, beg Grandma into taking back the curse. How exactly do you expect me to do that again? Oh, yeah—" Thia flipped her hair about as she twisted one finger against another, adopting a babyish tone. "Hey, Grandma, it's your estranged grandchild here. You don't know me, but could you think about maybe, you know, lifting that superstitious curse you cast on the family? Oh, don't worry. Samuel wasn't your fault. He blew himself up all on his own trying to impress his parents."

"Thia, really, such nonsense need not—"

"Oh, and you'll never believe the news, Grandma! I'm with child! Out of wedlock! Isn't that exciting?" She sarcastically clapped whilst jumping up and down, squealing, "Yippee! Your granddaughter's a disaster! A degenerate of the lowest breeding! Yippee!"

"Thia, that's quite enough—"

"And Dad's lost his mind and is drunk half of the day and we're digging about in some ancient hole pretending all's normal and since you're on your deathbed could you, like, please lift that curse already?"

"She is ready to see you now," cut in a voice, the same Henawa healer Anna had offended on her prior visit. The woman folded her arms across her white-robed chest. "Perhaps you ought to consider returning another day?"

Thia reddened and looked away while Anna smoothed her robe. "Now would be fine, thank you."

The healer's eyes flicked between mother and daughter before she unfolded her arms. "Follow me. She is not well," she said as they got underway, "so you would be mindful to watch your tone. Her family—"

"Great, they're here," Thia muttered.

"—have just departed."

"Oh. Good."

"She has delved deeper into the delusions since you last saw her. You may be kingdom champion, but I need remind you that the infirmary will not tolerate another fracas."

"I assure you we will be on our best behavior," Anna replied.

"Fracas?" Thia mouthed. "What fracas?"

Anna only waved the matter aside, not wanting to get into it.

The healer led them to the same room, and Anna found herself once more staring at the partially curtained-off feet of her mother. But this time it felt like her family's entire future rested on how this encounter went. She was not a believer in superstition, but the curse had rung true thus far, what with the death of her son, the words the woman had employed, and now the vivid nightmares. And how could her mother have used the phrase "the land of rock and fire" in particular? The allegory …

"I will be nearby," the healer whispered, and left the room.

As before, Thelma Atticus mumbled under her breath, but her words were quieter, more feverish. Thia drew closer first, moving around the wispy curtain, with Anna in tow. Upon seeing her grandmother's face, Thia shakily inhaled—and held that breath. Despite less than a month having passed since Anna had last seen her mother, her face was more sunken, blotchier, and paler than Anna remembered. Time was rapidly taking its toll.

The woman's eyes were closed, yet the murmurings never ceased.

"Hello, Grandmother," Thia said, taking the woman's frail hand between both of her own. "Do you know who this is?"

Thelma's eyes fluttered open. "Thia …" she whispered, surprising Anna. "You will never replace her …"

"Replace who, Grandma?"

"My daughter. You will never replace her …"

"I …" Thia glanced back uncertainly at her mother.

The old woman's voice strengthened—and deepened with a certain growl. "I am referring to your aunt, Deya, whom your mother murdered in cold blood. Cold, *cold* blood …"

Thia reflexively pulled her hands back, and Anna saw goosebumps rise on her forearm where her robe sleeve had slid back from the sudden movement.

Then the voice sweetened. "Oh, my sweet child … I lay eyes on you at last … I am so sorry … I was too proud … just like your mother …"

"It's all right. I'm here now, Grandma."

Thelma looked past her granddaughter to her sole remaining daughter, voice surprisingly strong and lucid. "Your father got his wish in the end. But now you must contend with the same curse. Are you training her like he trained you?"

Anna shook her head. "No."

"I will never accept the scion, Grandmother," Thia interjected.

"Smart girl." The woman patted Thia's hands. "Smart girl …"

"I have come to share some glad tidings, Grandmother—"

As if a lever had been pulled, menace once more infiltrated Thelma's voice. "You will be dragged … kicking and screaming …" prompting Thia to retreat from the bed. "… to the land of rock and fire … and there you shall remain … condemned to suffer the flow of time … forever …" Her face softened. "Where did you go, sweetie? Please come back and tell me of these glad tidings …"

Thia looked uncertainly back at Anna, who only nodded at her. Thia drew close, once more enveloping Thelma's hand in both of her own. "The tiding is that you will be a *great*-grandmother."

"You are with child … oh, my, how beautiful! How lovely indeed!" The other hand reached out to shakingly cup her granddaughter's cheek. Thia leaned into it, and for a moment they held each other in that tender manner. "Have you thought of a name?"

"Lividia if it's a girl. Lividius if it's a boy."

"Liver of life in the old tongue."

Thia smiled warmly, whispering, "Yes, Grandma. Liver of life."

Anna stirred, for this was the first she had heard of names. Thia had already thought that far ahead, without sharing it with her—choosing instead to share it first with her estranged mother, perhaps out of spite. Anna buried the hurt, for the task at hand was too important for such things to sully.

"And who is the father? Who will be the papa of this child? And when did you marry? I fear I cannot remember. Forgive me, I must have been ill …"

"Er …"

"The Lord of Demons is the father," the woman growled, face twisting with a vicious scowl.

Thia recoiled, hands slapping over her mouth. "Stop it, Grandma. You're scaring me."

"Cursed and damned … the fruits of one sister murdering the other … the babe is damned … *you* are damned, daughter of the kinslayer …" The wild eyes fixated on Anna. "And as for you, your suffering has yet to even begin …"

"Stop it, Mama!" Anna blurted as if she were the teenager, unable to stop the tears rolling down her cheeks. Suddenly her head pounded. She saw feet kicking at a black floor, a shadow dragging her daughter toward an eternal cage. "You ... you need not be so cruel ..."

Thia, face slack with surprise, hugged Anna consolingly, whispering, "It's all right, Mom. It's all right ..."

Thelma's vicious scowl faded as the sweet voice returned. "If only I could live to see the newborn babe. Alas, the hourglass is almost empty ... the Great Beyond waits for no one."

Thia swept to her side. "Grandma. Please, *please* lift the curse."

"The curse ... I ... I tried, my sweet child. I tried. I hope it worked."

"Try again. Please. Here. Now. With us. Say the words that need to be said. Say them for me and for your coming great-grandchild. I beg you, Grandma, say them."

"Very well. For you, for the next generation, I will try." The old woman took a deep breath. "In the old way, I, Thelma Atticus Riverwood, hereby withdraw—*no!*" she suddenly growled, face twisting once more as the eyes settled on Anna. "You will never beat back the darkness that awaits! Black as pitch. Black as your heart. Black as the soot this old lady will soon know. The shadow awaits ..."

"All right, Grandma, all right," Thia whispered, patting the withered hand, having stayed nearby this time. "All right ..." And thus she coaxed the sweetness to return.

Thelma's eyes closed, her voice weak. "You tell your father to stir the stew ..."

Anna, profoundly defeated and brain throbbing, hung her head, whispering, "I will, Mama. I will ..."

"... as the flavors have to mingle ..."

"Yes, Mama. He waits ... he waits for you at the table with Deya and Panza and Samuel and Bear. It will be a fine feast."

"I will not be late ... just make sure to keep the candle lit about the hearth, for 'shouldst the candle dieth after Endyear ... all ... all would be clear. Shouldst ... shouldst ...' " But her voice weakened beyond the reach of even a whisper.

" '... it dieth prior, the house would know naught but ire,' " Anna concluded for her, slipping in beside her daughter to take the old woman's hand. "I will not forget, Mama. I will not forget ..."

* * *

A black-draped husband, wife and daughter stood side by side, with the daughter between her mother and father. They were three amongst many, having formed a large circle made up of the other family and friends and acquaintances and old colleagues from the profession of law, which included Jordan Winters and family. In the center, a sacred blue fire leaped above a body. Throughout, a woman in black cloth sang a fragile melody that soared over the procession, guiding the departed soul to the Great Beyond.

Anna's gaze focused on the blue flames, allowing the sacred Memorial Ceremony spell to take root. Through the smoke, all went white. Out of the white stepped forth her youthful mother, smiling kindly. She was not alone. By her side were Sampson Jeremiah Stone, Deya Atticus Stone, and Samuel Stone, Anna's father and sister and son, all holding hands. Her mother's round face was simultaneously youthful and weathered with stress, her dark hair coursed with strands of silver. As if she had come straight from holding court, she still wore her magistrate robe. Sampson's curls were brown and bouncy, and with those chiseled features, he looked every bit like the marble busts of old — an appearance prior to the wrinkles of dealing with two teenage girls, a failing marriage, and the pressures of being a secret scion-carrying outlaw, which had aged him beyond repair. His smile was full of love and empathy, with a tinge of bittersweetness.

As for Deya, she was the teenager prior to her death, with the same face shape and eyes and hair as Anna and with little trace of the loathing that had so tormented her soul. She too was smiling kindly, perhaps the first Anna had ever seen on her sister's face.

Most touchingly, Deya held on to Samuel's hand. The boy, having inherited Thomas's black hair and Anna's vibrant blue eyes and his grandmother's round face, smiled proudly, as if he had indeed achieved that great achievement of becoming a warlock, as if he had lived through a certain moment instead of it taking his life. Oh how Anna wanted to squeeze her little boy one last time! She would trade the scion in a heartbeat for just one more precious moment together …

One by one, all four raised a hand in goodbye. Anna raised a hand in turn, whispering, "Goodbye, Mama. Goodbye, Papa. Goodbye, Dey-Dey. Goodbye, Samuel. I love you, I love you, I love …"

The waving continued for some time, with Anna whispering those last words over and over, until her father took his wife and daughter gently by the hand and led everyone back into the white, leaving Anna alone, the fingers of her still-raised hand slowly folding into a loose fist. As the white faded, that hand lowered, and she became aware she was amongst a now broken circle, for many people had already departed the yard of snowy oaks and maples. Memorial Grove, used for just such occasions, was a tranquil spot located in the heart of the city.

Anna glanced about and saw her daughter speaking with the *other* family. These men and women, who had been kids when she was a teenager, now had children of their own. They seemed to take Thia's condolences with grace, if not with some aloofness. Anna took shelter under a gnarled oak, which offered a little protection against the bitterly cold wind. A few straggling acorns fell, joining those already split and rotting in the snow. Watching that other family from afar, she soon heard a sound behind her that she was expecting—that of footsteps.

"My deepest condolences, my old friend."

Anna turned to see a gray-haired Jordan offering a hand, which she took. "Thank you." His Henawa wife and son and two daughters mingled in the background with people Anna did not know.

"I'm sure William would have liked to have been here," he mumbled.

"He always had the heart of a traveler. For him, the allure of a life out there—" She nodded at the horizon. "—is stronger than a life in the city."

"That and his profession prevents it."

One of the last Arcaners, Anna thought, nodding along.

Jordan adjusted his square spectacles. "You haven't been sleeping, have you?"

"It's been … a long Endyear."

"How is Thomas?"

Anna shrugged as she glanced about. "Not quite sure where he crawled off to, actually." She folded her arms, trying to regain some dignity from having been abandoned once again by her husband.

Jordan folded his arms as well. "I think I saw him depart earlier with a royal page."

Of course he did, Anna thought. *No doubt summoned by his bosom friend the king for another bout of sloppy drinking and complaining*. The bottle was how Thomas dealt with things these days, but she did not have the strength to confront him right now.

"I heard he and your former pupil are close."

"Mmm."

"Must be odd to be friends with a king."

Anna said nothing, only watched as her daughter struck up a conversation with a girl of her own age from the other family. She wondered what they spoke about.

"She is growing to be a fine young lady," Jordan noted.

"Mmm."

Jordan dawdled as if unsure what to say.

"Not like you to be tongue-tied," Anna muttered.

"Just wondering if you're all right. Beyond this, of course. I didn't see you at the Antioc Classic. They always call you out by name when you come in honor of your achievements there. So ... *are* you all right? Because you don't look it. You look—"

"I look what?"

"Troubled. You look troubled, Anna."

Anna wanted to tell him the truth. That her home life was falling apart. That Thia was with child. That men wanted to kidnap her to get to Anna. That those men also wanted revenge for their brothers, recently locked up for crimes discovered during questioning. That the family curse remained unbroken. That she was repeating the errors of the past. That she lost sleep from all the worrying and the nightmares and the headaches.

"I'm fine," she said instead, just as she had when they were teenagers in the academy together.

Jordan nodded in that knowing way of his. Mercifully, he said nothing more, only patted her arm, mumbled another condolence and how he would always be there for her, and rejoined his family. His children glanced her way. She knew that questioning look all too well. It was the *Can we talk to her?* look. But Jordan guided them all away, sparing Anna once again. Their families had last suppered together while Samuel had been alive. Anna hadn't had the strength since to continue that tradition, for a chair at the table would forever remain empty. What mirth could possibly be enjoyed while seeing that empty chair?

Thia eventually traipsed back, holding herself to ward off the wind, which threw about her hood and kicked up a swirl of snowdrift. "They're nice, I guess," she said, standing by Anna. "The slightly aloof but polite type that didn't want to get to know me better. I got the sense they were sad that Grandma left this life in our presence instead of theirs."

Anna nodded, watching them from afar. How dignified they all were, accepting handshakes with solemn nods, their children dressed in the finest silks, their friends some of the highest nobles of the land.

"Dad left."

"Mmm."

"He hasn't said a word to me in forever."

"Give him time."

Thia scoffed. "Do you know what he did when I told him what I am going to name my child?"

Anna tried to ignore the stabbing pain from the wound Thia had perhaps inadvertently inflicted back in her mother's room.

"We were in the kitchen and he carefully put down his tea and gave me this long look. I can't even describe it." Thia pondered the matter. "Actually, I can." She made claws of her hands. "It was a look of utter, *profound* disappointment. Like I had let him down in the worst way possible." Her hands fell. "And then he … he just left. He turned his back and left. He didn't care about the name at all. I stood there gawking like a fool before bursting into tears. I wanted him to come and hug me, but he just kept going. I … I don't understand Dad, you know? I cannot fathom him."

Cannot fathom … It hurt Anna to hear her daughter use the same language as her. She imagined Thomas walking until he found a bottle. She needed to find the strength to confront him, to coax him back, but she couldn't. And she didn't know why either. She, who had triumphed over great adversities, in the arena and out, felt defeated in the face of this onslaught.

"I wanted a cuddle from Dad. You know who I instead ended up cuddling? I'm embarrassed to admit it, but I almost squeezed Bun-Bun to death."

Anna's heart melted. "I am sure he was very happy to be of service once more."

"Yeah, he's … he's been a good companion of late."

Then Anna's heart fell, for that meant, like herself at that age, her daughter was getting even lonelier.

"You should go visit the excavation," Thia blurted. "*We* should go."

"Why?"

"Do you not read your letters? Ottentus made a breakthrough."

"You opened my letter?"

"It was sent by Ralf. I'm sorry. I was curious what he had to say. I thought he'd …"

"So? What *did* he have to say?"

Thia adopted a deeper and detached voice. " 'Dear Arcanist Stone, Archmage Ottentus Maledius Anavictus has asked me to pass on that your presence is requested at the excavation at the strike of the sixth evening bell on the 5th day of the second month, to discuss an expected breakthrough. With regards, Initiate Ralf Turman.' "

"You memorized it?"

"I was angry. *Seething*, in fact. He hasn't reached out once, not *once* since—" She fell silent.

"Mmm." Anna had many questions for Ralf Turman, the one who had given himself a teenage nickname. The one who dabbled in necromantic rituals and who had dared to try to involve her daughter in them …

"Maybe that's a bad idea, though," Thia mumbled. "Besides, school's about to start up again."

Sever Bronny

Her daughter glanced at Anna's knuckles, which had gone white from having balled her fists. She unclenched them and smoothed her robe.

"The 5th is the day after student council elections," Thia added.

"Were you thinking of running to represent your degree?"

"Of course not. Well, no. Maybe. I mean, I *wanted* to run. It's just …" She patted her belly. "You know … but *you* were head of student council, right? I saw your plaque and all."

"Mmm."

"You should talk about that stuff more, Mom. You don't always need to be so …" Thia gesticulated at Anna from foot to head.

"So what?"

"Tight-lipped."

"Tight-lipped?" Anna scoffed. "I didn't think you'd be interested."

Thia shrugged. "I might be now. Make something of myself before I hit my ceiling. It's coming. I sense it. I seriously doubt I'll hit my 8th." Her eyes unfocused as if she were seeing something in the distance. "Actually, I know it …" she whispered.

"You say that every term, and look at you now. A preening 7th."

"I'm not 'preening.' I don't preen, Mom. Yeesh."

"I was good at it, you know. Being head of student council, that is. Changed the way a few things were done. Made some enemies. Caused some trouble, to the point they called me a mischief-maker." Anna shifted her weight to one foot, reminiscing. "Student Council is exciting but a *lot* of work. You get your own special room, sure, but there's twice-quintly meetings, tons of new responsibilities like—"

"Twice-quintly meets? Forget I even brought it up."

Anna shook her head in resignation.

Thia sighed. "Can we go home?"

"Yes. Yes, we can go home now."

CONFRONTATIONS

Having completed the core ritual, including spinning a finger to charge up the spell, Anna pointed at the ceiling and drew a quick oval, roaring, "*Portus da—*" Midway through she swiveled the hand to draw another oval at the feet of a straw dummy, concluding, "*—ata ei portus da!*" The first portal flared to life, but the second fizzled.

"No, no, no," Niterra said in her thick Nodian accent, slapping her knee with each word. She sat on a crate, one of a few in the cellar—and the perfect spot to critique from. "More fluid," she added. "Smooth, smooth, smooth." She made an elegant motion of a pointed arm. "*Portus da …*" That arm gracefully swiveled to the dummy. "*… ata ei portus da.* See motion? Must repeat smooth here too—" She tapped her temple with a finger. "Repeat smooth."

"Repeat smooth," Thia echoed absently. She sat on a blanket on the floor, surrounded by books of famous plays, a quill in hand as she scribbled out ideas for next term's Drama class. She hadn't even looked up, but had developed the habit of mimicking certain words or phrases she found interesting, sometimes between humming a stage melody to herself.

Anna, forehead beaded with sweat and a subtle headache ever present, nodded. It was not so much the motion that was troublesome, but the accompanying thoughts. Creating a single portal with so few arcane syllables to employ in so short a time was difficult enough, but repeating the maneuver and *linking* the portals made the spell sometimes feel impossible. She was still far too slow with the casting. In combat, an opponent would have time to react, maybe even step away. In that sense, she was nowhere close to getting the spell combat-ready.

Niterra nodded as if reading her mind. "Yes, that 19th degree. You feel pain yet?"

My brain is squealing that it's going to break, Anna thought. They had been at it for hours already, and she needed to hop to the academy to take care of some administrative errands. It was their tenth lesson, with Anna having spent countless hours in between practicing the nuance of the spell on her own. But as brilliant and studious as she was, as many hours as she had already put in, she had yet to successfully cast the spell. To be fair, Combat Portal oft took much longer a time to learn; it was just she demanded perfection quicker than others. Her strength was the sheer determination to protect her daughter, and the willpower to continuously work at a problem until she solved it.

She organized her thoughts so they would flow more fluidly, and that included the imagery and the mechanics of the spell, which in turn included pronunciation and syllabic precision, gestural precision, and arcane draw from the ether. When ready, she spun her finger about whilst incanting, "*Portus ea ire itum combata lina*," charging up the spell. Then she snapped a hand forth, quickly and efficiently drawing an oval a few feet from the dummy. "*Portus da—*" Her hand moved a little to the right, drawing another oval underneath the dummy. "*—ata ei portus da!*"

Both ovals appeared. The dummy began to fall, with its wooden feet appearing from the upper portal, only for the portal underneath the dummy to fizzle, eviscerating its top half, which thunked against the floor, while the bottom half dropped onto the floor beside it from above with a second *thunk*.

Anna's arm dropped. "Well, that would certainly take care of the opponent, wouldn't it?"

"And what if Stone cast spell on friend?" Niterra asked.

"Or myself," Anna muttered, rubbing her eyes.

"Disaster, yes."

"Disasterrrrrr," Thia sang mid-hum, nib scratching away on a parchment.

Anna stepped before the two halves of the dummy and opened a palm, envisioning them becoming one. "*Apreyo.*" The two parts jumped back together, fusing with a sealing light. With a movement of Anna's hand, the dummy righted itself and floated back to its spot.

If only people were as easily repairable, she thought, returning to the starting location. Just as she readied herself to try for the umpteenth time, an alarm rang in her head. "Perimeter alarm!" she said, and ran for the portal etching in the wall. Niterra, meanwhile, groaned as she stood and wandered over to protectively stand behind Thia, who didn't bother looking up as she sang, "Probably only a messengerrrrrrr."

"*Shyneo*," Anna said as she slid to a halt before the portal etching. She smacked it with her lit palm, snapping, "Anna Atticus Stone—ground floor." The portal flared to life and she shot through it, emerging on the snowy stoop of the old warlock tower. She flared a hand. "*Un vun asperio aurum enchantus*," before fluidly running a hand over her body whilst incanting, "*Armari obscura chameleano traversa*." The first was Reveal, which would allow her to see any malignant casting, and the second was Chameleon with the travel extension, allowing her hidden movement.

She shot forth as fast as she dared through the snowy forest, careful to evade certain enchantments whilst striding over others, notably Area Alarms that did not go off when touched by those preapproved to wander through. She soon heard a voice she thought was repeatedly calling her name.

"Arcanist Stone? Arcanist Stone, are you there?"

Anna crept up to an oak and peeked around it. She saw a young man in an amber robe standing between the edge of the wood and the street. He was smoothing over a cowlick that simply refused to stay pressed, forcing him to lick his hand and mash it down. That one gesture made Anna recognize him. He had hit his ceiling two terms ago, graduating to help run the family business of tax collection. Reveal indicated no abnormalities like Possession or Doppelganger—such a gesture with the hair was usually the best way to tell, for mannerisms unique to the personality were the hardest to mimic.

Anna thus strode forth. "Mr. Slimwealth. What can I do for you, young man?"

"Arcanist Stone!" he blurted, mangling a scroll he kept turning in his hands. "I was warned you were of the … protective sort."

"Forgive me." Anna swept a hand down her body. "*Chameleano null*," making herself visible. "One can never be too careful these days," she added, eyes sweeping the street in search of threats.

"Yes, of course. Bentley Reginald Stafford Slimwealth at your service, Arcanist Stone. You may remember me from class."

"Mmm." He had been a mediocre student with mild ambitions and a questionable reputation with women.

He unsuccessfully tried to press the cowlick down. "B-but of course you do. It's just they make us formally introduce ourselves on formal occasions."

Anna raised an eyebrow. "The occasion being …?"

He extended the scroll, which she accepted.

"What's this?" she asked, cracking the large seal.

"I regret to inform you that the taxes on your estates are overdue."

Anna's eyes pored over the ornate document. "That's ridiculous. I had my husband pay them last month during the winter head tax."

"I am afraid he may have perhaps forgotten the, uh, additions involved."

"Wait, this is *twenty thousand* crowns! Surely there has been a mis—"

"Twenty thousand crowns and one hundred and thirteen spines, to be precise," the man muttered, "and seventeen castles if we're being absolutely—"

"Twenty. Thousand."

"I understand it is a substantial sum, but the books are quite clear."

Anna stood staring at him.

"Please forgive me for saying so, but as I am sure you are aware, Arcanist Stone, the treasury has been more than forgiving regarding your … situation."

"My situation." She couldn't help her indignance from repeating his words back to him.

"Yes, er … the castle is, uh …"

"Is what? Use that tongue, Slimwealth. I am in no mood for dilly-dallying."

"Of course, Arcanist Stone. My apologies. The castle's debts are overdue. A generation overdue, in fact. Your father paid them. Your husband staved off the majority for a time, using his pull with the king, but alas …"

"Alas, what? I've been paying the taxes. *We've* been paying them—"

"Yes, but the general sum has been nonetheless accruing on the higher ledger. It has merely been … suppressed."

"Suppressed?"

His voice dropped to a whisper. "I am surely out of line divulging this, Arcanist Stone, but your husband's pull with the king has deferred the greater payments from being, well, paid. Alas, the threshold has been pushed to a point that I am afraid my office, uh, can no longer ignore." He raised his palms. "Please do not get upset with me, Arcanist Stone. I am merely doing my duty in service to the treasury. The maintenance of roads, the institutions, our armies—all have to be paid for. Usually a castle has employment, crops that yield an income, but in your case …"

"In my case it sits forlorn because I am an irresponsible castellan."

"I certainly did not mean that you are—"

"No, no. It is all right. It is the truth, after all." She sighed, one eye poring over the document anew whilst another remained trained on the street.

The young man glanced over his shoulder. "Er … are you expecting someone, Arcanist Stone?"

"Kidnappers."

"Kid—" He chuckled nervously. "Surely that is a jest …"

"I am afraid it is not," she muttered, reading the fine print. "This is due by the end of next quint?"

"The first payment, yes. We have already sent letters warning to that effect, but received no reply."

"My husband usually deals with the mail." Did Thomas know?

"Due to your stature, we thought to make a courtesy call in person, something usually quite outside our purview. Of course, certain people deserve special attention, and the kingdom's champion—"

"Yes, yes, thank you, Mr. Slimwealth."

"Is, um … is your daughter still …?"

"Still what?" Anna absently asked, flipping the page to the next parchment. The base sum, which had not been addressed for some years, had nonetheless compounded over that time. Now if she did not pay in a timely manner, there would be substantial fines. The sums involved pointed to the castle eventually being confiscated by the treasury. Where in Sithesia had their savings gone?

"Forgive my impertinence, Arcanist Stone, but I-I-I am quite the eligible bachelor, and-and-and would be honored to—"

"She is with child," Anna said, not looking up from the parchment.

"Oh. *Oh!* I see. And-and-and may I ask who—"

"You may *not*."

"Yes, of course. How presumptuous of me. Please forgive my—"

"How am I supposed to come up with such a sum in so short a time? I have bills to pay. My daughter's tuition—"

"I sincerely apologize, Arcanist Stone, but I am not permitted to advise upon such matters. You understand, of course." He glanced about, voice dropping to a whisper once more. "That said, I can call in a favor and ask—"

"No, thank you. I do not wish special treatment on account of my station."

"Ah. I see."

"I suppose the army is always looking for scroll work," Anna muttered.

"Yes, yes! That is quite right. A high-degree scroll fetches thousands, if not tens of thousands, for the right sort. The nobility pays even more. Rich warlocks unable to craft at higher degrees pay handsome sums to be able—"

"Will that be all, Mr. Slimwealth?"

"Oh. Yes, Arcanist Stone. Although I am sorry to see you again in such a circumstance, I would like you to know I have always held you in the highest esteem and I am deeply honored to serve you and if you need anything you can reach me at any time at my office at the treasury, or if you like at my home estate at—"

"Thank you, Mr. Slimwealth. Good day to you," and she walked off, eyes reviewing the documents.

"And good day to *you*, Arcanist Stone! *Champion* Stone! Please say hi to Thia for me!"

I'd rather not, thank you, Anna thought as she paced through the forest, recalling having to speak to the young man about the way he treated women at the academy, specifically telling him they were not chattel. She rolled the scroll back up and sighed, muttering, "It's one thing after another, isn't it?" She summoned the portal, knowing she would have to address this tax business immediately.

* * *

"Your husband is with the king's entourage watching the tournament, Champion Stone," the young guardswoman said at the drawbridge to the Black Castle.

"What tournament?"

"An Ordinary's jousting and sword and archery tournament, hosted by order of the king."

"Ah. Of course." For a moment there she thought the lot of them were watching an illegal warlock tournament, which would have destroyed her hope for the kingdom's ability to tackle corruption, a hope already in dire straits.

"Shall I take you to him? It is being held just beyond in the outer ward."

"I can find my way, thank you."

"My honor, Champion." The chain-mail-clad woman bowed so deeply that her long hair almost grazed the muddy puddle at their feet.

"Mmm," Anna toned absently as she walked by, wanting to confront her husband. She passed into the tunnel of the great tower portcullis gate, from which many a person had been hanged, receiving head bows from burly guards along the way. The *clang* of sword-on-sword and the *thwoot* of arrows and the *clop* of heavy horses echoed off the block walls of the thick gate. Greeting her on the other side was a sprawling outer ward lit with torches and buzzing with activity. Archers shot at targets, knights in full plate armor jogged their horses around a low jousting fence, and soldiers in chain-mail and surcoats squared off with swords and bucklers. Watching the fray, on a central wooden platform, was the upper crust of the nobility and royalty. Men and women in the finest cloth, with servants at their beck and call. The tower, the grand hall, and the jagged keep of the famous Black Castle loomed beyond, the keep being one of the oldest buildings in Solia's history as a kingdom, having been erected by King Solin Northsword the great.

Anna strode toward the platform, mindful of the mud, much of which was already freezing over with the evening frost.

"Ho!" a man boomed.

Anna turned to see a huge warhorse bearing down on her. Her reflexes kicked in so sharply that, instead of jumping away as she had intended, she slipped in the mud. Luckily the rider was competent and veered his horse just shy of her.

"Excuse me, m'lady," the knight boomed over his shoulder as she smacked her gums in annoyance, for her lower robe was now filthy with mud.

She thought to use a cleaning cantrip, but something about the fine cloth and the constantly bowing servants and the glitter of so much jewelry made her leave the dripping mud well enough alone.

People took immediate notice of her as she neared, with men nodding at her or elbowing each other, and women whispering behind their hands, not an unfamiliar sight for Anna even amongst the nobility. The servants bowed deeply as she stepped onto the platform, while the nobles inclined their heads, most barely so. Anna acknowledged them all with one nod, her focus on the king's entourage, which sat under a raised enclosure.

Three powder-faced women stepped before her.

"Anna Stone," oozed the silky voice of a fifty-year-old woman wearing a crimson square-neckline gown and a matching ruby necklace. Her hair, dyed blond to hide the gray, was up in a twist and studded with jewels. Her once porcelain skin was speckled from age and glossy with cream.

Anna pursed her lips, giving only the slightest of nods. "Mayda." Mayda Madeline Haught had been Thomas's academy love interest. They were supposed to have been married, but Thomas had found the courage to pursue Anna instead.

The other two women gave small curtsies, which Anna returned out of expectation more than politeness, everyone muttering each other's first names. One was Lady Samantha Blackflower, Thomas's older sister and head of the House of Blackflower. In her mid-fifties and wearing a black velvet gown with a diamond necklace, she was a dark-haired woman with an imposing visage. Her name always reminded Anna of her academy friend, Samantha Brownsoil, long deceased. But that was the only thing those two women ever had in common.

The other was none other than Lady Triana Taylor, now head of the *Blackhaven Herald*. A woman also in her early fifties, she wore an emerald dress that complemented her dark skin. Her hair was made up in a tight bun that was pierced by a golden clip in the shape of a quill. Anna still remembered dueling—and defeating—her when Triana had been a 6th degree and Anna a mere aspirant. She also well remembered how close Triana and her sister had been and how they had plotted against her.

All three women held tall-stemmed goblets of wine.

"Now *this* is a rare pleasure," Mayda cooed, delicately swirling her goblet. "Are we not horrendously jealous of how young she looks, my queens?"

The three women chortled, the sort of laugh that lacked any true mirth.

"The power of the scion, no doubt," Triana said, taking a tiny sip of wine.

"How *doth* my sister-in-law fare?" Lady Blackflower asked, raising an imperious eyebrow at Anna's soiled robe. "Perhaps getting a wee bit too close to the mud baths, it seems?"

"Rumors abound," Triana added, joining in on the goblet-swirling.

Anna, seeing Thomas in deep conversation with the king and a group of moneymen, no doubt readying to make bets on the tournament, thought she should wait before trying to take him aside. She looked to a passing tray, searching for a glass of water. When none was offered, she resigned herself to a tall flute of champagne.

"Rumors and flies have much in common," she noted, taking a tiny sip herself.

"Charming," Mayda simpered.

Triana cocked her head. "I speak of the House of Stone, of course. Word is it will be graced with a new addition. You and Thomas must be very proud. How shall I quote you?"

"My daughter ought not to be any of your concern." Her innards went cold. The last thing the family needed was the heralds writing about their inner struggles.

"How *scandalous*, though, is it not?" Mayda oozed to the other women. "And no one knows the father." She clucked her tongue, shaking her head. "All that arcane might cannot prevent ill-repute from falling on the infamous House of Stone ..."

Anna glanced about in search of some—any—other distraction. "Mercifully, reputation concerns me little these days," she feigned, for the truth was, although she cared little for herself, she desperately wanted to protect her daughter from these vultures, and from the condemnations of Solian society as a whole, which could be fickle, the repercussions grave.

"Not if you want that headmistress job," Mayda noted.

"I am not sure I am at all suited for it anyhow," Anna lied, hating herself for getting ensnared in this horrid conversation.

"But My Lady Herald, have you not heard how her brother—" Mayda nodded at Lady Blackflower. "—has racked up quite the gambling debt?"

Triana opened her mouth with a scandalized gasp. "Oh, do tell, Lady Haught. Do tell."

You obviously know, you meddlesome buzzard, Anna thought. Yet her cheeks burned with the implication. So *that's* what happened to the monies! It was exactly what she had feared. How could he have been so irresponsible! How!

Except she had to pretend like she knew all about this gambling debt, and so she gave a false smile and swirled her own glass, showing interest.

Lady Blackflower pursed her lips at her brother, his garrulous laugh booming from the king's platform. "Yes, he has been quite the sloth of late. He ought not to fraternize with a purse full of debt. I did warn him how the Blackflower name had power that could keep him out of trouble." She shrugged. "Alas, he chose ..." She cleared her throat as she eyed Anna up and down, her gaze lingering on the sullied robe.

"Oh, we *all* warned him," Mayda sang, eyes rolling as she took a long sip of her goblet.

"Yes, I really did saddle him with a life of mediocrity, did I not?" Anna threw in. "I suppose he would have been far happier with a full purse, cronyish company, and a simpering wife. Excuse me." Having had enough, Anna slipped by the women, setting her nearly untouched champagne on a passing tray.

The women clucked behind her. "How base ... utterly unsuited for high society ... besmirches our good names by sheer proximity ... a kingdom champion with the manners of a stable hand."

Anna ignored them, for of all the people in the nobility, she cared least about what those three vultures thought of her. Only Triana worried her, for the woman loved a salacious story, and was certainly not above slander. It had been some time since a *Blackhaven Herald* piece took a shot at her, and Anna now dreaded that big judging eye focusing on her daughter instead.

Her former pupil, King Power, was the first to spot her approach. "Ho!" he boomed, face cherry from drinking wine. "Your wife approacheth, good sir, and she has quite the serious face today."

Thomas did a double take. He wiped his hands on a cloth before picking up a tankard and taking a long swig, then groaned as he stood. "No doubt to deliver yet another tongue thrashing. I better see to the querulous woman then." He extended a hand to the nobles around him. "Good sirs," all of whom shook with lame holds, which told her they hardly respected him.

He gave her a hard look as he made his way past finely dressed nobles. "Excuse me, good sir. Excuse me, my lady—and what fine cloth you wear on this eve! How well it matches your eyes! Shooting tomorrow, Lord Drapes? Great horsemanship, Sir Sethmyer." At last he stepped off the crowded platform, sneaking a chocolate from a tray.

"We need to talk," Anna hissed.

"You look like you got kicked by a horse," he said, tossing the lump into his mouth and chewing loudly. "Why didn't you clean yourself up before coming to such an esteemed event? You are embarrassing me."

"I have other concerns at the moment," Anna replied, returning a polite nod from a high-powered noble on the high council who oft fraternized with the academy council.

"Did you make your presence known to my sister? I'm sure she'd be delighted to see you."

"Your sister loathes me."

"Maybe you should ingratiate yourself more into high society instead of—" He flipped a hand at her muddy robe. "What are you doing here, anyway? Thia get herself into more trouble? Maybe finally revealed who the father is?"

"Actually, she is reading. And do not throw such barbs at your daughter lest I carry out that tongue thrashing."

Thomas scoffed.

"I have many things to say to you on many topics, but let us stick to one. I just received a visit from the treasury."

Thomas, who was reaching for a pastry from a tray-carrying servant, froze.

Anna glanced at the servant, who took the hint and wandered off, before drifting close to her husband. "Tell me you didn't gamble it away. Please, say it isn't so."

Thomas swallowed.

"Lady Stone!" a knight with a twirling mustache and scuffed armor crooned, sliding in beside Anna and putting a drunken arm around her and Thomas's shoulders. "How do the Stones fare? What joy to see you both enjoying the fruits of the poors." He laughed at his own jest. "Quite the sorry pigs we are stuffing our faces here while the commoners rot, eh?"

Anna cleared her throat. "Sir Gallows."

"Have you met my son Eldric yet?" He glanced about. "Where did that little turdling go now? You there—give me that pastry lest I skewer thee!" He veered off in chase of a tray-carrying servant.

Anna folded her arms. "And this is the company you keep."

"All you do is judge."

"What have you done, Thomas? What have you done?"

Thomas forced a smile at a passing noble as he said out of the side of his mouth, "Can we talk about this later?"

"You will speak with me now or I shall make a scene."

"Then walk with me, *dear wife*." He placed an arm around her, raised his tankard at those they passed, and escorted her off the platform onto a raised wooden footpath that led to the Great Arcaner Hall.

"Take your arm off me," she snapped as they walked. "I have little patience for your antics at the moment. In fact, I am in a most foul mood."

Thomas glanced back at the crowd. Anna could still feel their eyes following them. His arm slithered off her shoulders.

They entered the hall, with its carved fluted columns and tapestries and ancient paintings of Arcaners of old. The hall had once served as Arcaner headquarters. Now it felt like a tomb.

Anna rubbed her brow and leaned up against a column. "How much?"

Thomas leaned against a column opposite and stuck his hands into the pockets of his robe. "I …"

"How much do you owe? Tell it to me true."

"Er …" He mumbled something.

"What? I didn't hear you."

"Fifty."

"Fifty. Fifty thousand? *Fifty thousand!*"

Thomas raised a palm, eyes darting. "Don't shout. There're ears everywhere."

"Whose ears?"

"The nobility's."

"I don't give a hoof at this point."

Thomas pointedly looked her up and down. "*That's* evident."

"Choose your words carefully, sir." She glared, and his eyes dropped. "So in sum we owe seventy thousand crowns and you, who act as if nothing were wrong whatsoever, want me to keep my voice down."

"It certainly won't help to shout, will it?"

"When did the gambling truly start? And I'm not talking about dabbling. I'm talking about throwing crowns into the pot. When?"

"After Samuel. I … I promised I'd protect our family from financial ruin after taking your hand in marriage. I carried over a tidy sum from the Blackflower name that I had protected from my father. But the children … the house … the purchase of the tower … it all started to add up. Then the tax came due for the castle, and I thought I could cover the sums with, er … with a bit of luck."

Anna folded her arms. "With a bit of luck."

"I thought I got good at making fair judgments with cards and games of guessing. Then … I don't know …" He rubbed his forehead. "I guess it got away from me."

"The castle was never your responsibility," Anna snapped. "It was mine. *I* thrust that burden on us." She triple-stabbed her own chest with a finger. "*I* did that."

"But I am the man of the house and I—"

"Had you come to *me* instead of trying to play the fool hero, we could have dealt with the sum together! How could you hold that from me? How could you do that to us, to our family?"

"Keep your voice down, would you?"

"I would, had you not let me down in such a … such a … manner!" she roared.

"I know. I *know*, all right? Just … don't make things worse."

Anna didn't know what to say.

Thomas ran a hand through his greasy hair. "I was hoping to get the king to absolve my debts, but as it turns out, the crown doesn't really do that. They keep strong books, and …" He chortled nervously. "I guess I don't quite factor into their accounts."

Anna chewed on a thumbnail. "What time is the armory open until?"

"It's open day and night. Why?"

Anna placed her gaze on him.

"That's demeaning—"

"You can help, or you can find a new home. Crawl back to Mayda, for all I care. It is your choice."

Thomas clutched at his heart. "You do not mean to be so cruel."

Anna did not, but she also did not want him to know that. "Your daughter, who craves your respect, hasn't heard a kind word from you since revealing she is with child. Instead you, a grandfather-to-be, have chosen to piss the family money away on frivolities while fraternizing with fiends who have nothing better to do than gossip about us. All the while, the debt has grown … and now it has come due."

Thomas opened his mouth to reply, only to spot the tears rolling down her cheeks.

"You leave me to fend for myself," she whispered, "not realizing how much I miss you. How much I miss my husband. My Thomas. Do not approach me, sir. Don't you *dare*."

He retreated from his advance, eyes on his feet.

"Our daughter needs us, and we have *both* let her down. We have a child who is in danger and I cannot find her pursuers. And I … I have placed her in danger with my own arrogance. We have dug a hole, and it is time to either start digging our way out of it, or …"

"Or what?" he whispered, unable to look her in the eye.

"Or we walk our separate paths." It broke her heart to admit that her marriage might fail, especially considering the failure of her parents' marriage.

Thomas nodded to himself. He looked up, tears running down his own cheeks. "I suppose I always knew this would all come to an end." Anna, thinking he meant an end to her marriage, was about to burst with a cry, when he smiled. "I meant the gambling. You know what I intend to do? Seek a monk. I think what is lacking in me is *spirit*. I will find a guide to lead me from this path of confusion and darkness and wanting. I promise I will find my way out, Anna. I promise you that."

"No sweeter words have I heard this year."

"Good. Good … Now come, my love. Let me take us to the armory." He took her hand and led her away. "Is that headache still bothering you?"

"Ugh. Night and day. What torment."

"We should get that looked at."

Anna, having tried everything she could think of and then some, only sighed.

Thomas nodded, then shrugged. "If there is one thing I am sure of in this day and age, it is that scrolls—particularly *your* scrolls—will fetch a high price."

This time, Anna let him drape his arm around her waist as they walked. Yes, he had let her down, but she wanted to fight for the marriage. How easy it would be to throw the life they had built together away, as her parents had done!

Yet some things were worth saving ...

ENCHANTMENTS

Although an armory was situated amidst a sprawling underground labyrinth underneath the Black Castle that included an arena, barracks, a wine cellar, arcane Trainers, and myriad other structures — including the entrance to a vast and ancient subterranean complex Anna once partly explored with Jordan and William — the *Royal* Armory was a whole other complex. As it was the power behind the throne, it was heavily guarded and sealed from the outside. Even to get to the doors required special permission. Luckily, Thomas's royal contacts paid off in this regard.

"Why's the passage so ridiculously large, anyway?" Thomas asked as they walked down a monstrous tunnel carved out of sheer rock, his voice echoing. "Practically made for giants, of which I am pretty sure we have none in the reserves."

Risper Katroon, the 14th degree ebony-skinned captain of the Royal Guard, chuckled amiably. "No children's stories come to life, I am afraid." He threw a gentle elbow at Thomas. "But that's what we have us warlocks for and our Incarnate spell, isn't that right?"

"Those of us mentally equipped enough to cast such spells, that is," Thomas mumbled.

Both men wore the same color of robe — purple, worn by the 13th through the 16th degrees, denoted further by golden bands on the upper shoulder. The captain had one band whereas Thomas had two, the difference between a 14th and a 15th.

"I'm too old and tired and too unambitious to get there myself," the captain countered. "But you're still relatively young. You have time."

"So no giants," Thomas prodded. Anna sensed her husband was trying to avoid the topic of progression in the arts.

"No giants. Siege engines, on the other hand, we have plenty of, and they require substantial height clearance, especially the high siege towers, trebuchets, and the larger catapults. Some of the engines are so old though that the knowledge on how to work them has been lost to time. But the real challenge is coordination." The sixty-something-year-old captain, famous for his skills of strategy and cunning, having earned the nickname "The Whisper" back when he had dueled in the arena, nodded sagely. "You can only teleport so many, usually the most powerful and largest ones first, and you only have so many warlocks with so much stamina in the pool. Thank the Unnameables sieges are generally slow affairs. It's the sudden onslaughts that cause trouble."

"Coordination," Thomas repeated, nodding along.

"And that's just one facet. You won't get to see it, but let me tell you, the full breadth of this place—" The captain shook his gray-haired head. "—it's *massive*. The army has a great many secrets, as you can no doubt imagine."

"No doubt," Thomas muttered.

Anna was curious about the arcanery involved. "I'm assuming there's a reason why we have to walk instead of teleport."

"Security is why, Arcanist Stone. There are anti-teleport enchantments infused into every square foot of the complex that can only be unlocked in emergencies."

"In a time of war," Thomas said.

"Precisely. Sure, some have Teleport privileges, but those lucky souls are few and far between, and mostly in high command. You know, very few get to see this." The captain thumbed over his shoulder. "Usually they make you dump your scrolls with the steward. But I guess it pays to have friends, eh?" He punched Thomas's shoulder. "The honor goes both ways. To have the kingdom's champion here—mmm, mmm, *mmm*, sir! A rare treat indeed. Everyone else is gushing it up above, so it's nice for the rank-and-file to have their routines broken up a bit. It can be painfully boring down here, you know?"

Thomas and Anna nodded along, their heads craning to take in the immense arched ceiling.

"You get one guess who built it," the man said.

"Vilnius Vivictus," Anna replied.

"The master builder himself, that's right. Why am I not surprised that you know that, Grandmage?"

"He has been a source of study for us of late," Thomas threw in.

"Mmm."

"Well, what he built protects the kingdom's secrets. And those who are not authorized to see those secrets get their minds wiped. I am quite serious in that regard." The man winked. "But you two need never worry about that."

They walked up to a hundred-foot-tall pair of black doors engraved with enormous runes, and the captain rapped on it with a knuckle. "Solid steel. Legend says the master builder tried to convince the Dreadnoughts to make them from Dreadnought Steel, but they simply didn't have anywhere near that amount of steel—or the manpower." The captain shrugged. "That and they apparently served another master at the time, but who's to say what was true two thousand years ago, eh?" He made a frilly gesture with a hand. "It's all … speculation, isn't it? Hearsay, I believe is the word the magistrates like to use."

"Much of history is our best guess," Anna said.

The man nodded in agreement as he stepped up to one of the doors. He placed a palm on it, incanting, "*Shyneo.*" His hand froze over with ice. "Captain Risper Ekron Katroon. Open right." There was a deep mechanical *click* and the right-hand door slowly ground open outward. They stepped aside and watched as the edge of the door finally became visible.

"Eight feet thick and weighs as much as a mountain. Even using ordinary steel, the forging took a whole year—and that's per door. They used the old Dreadnought forges under the castle. Even with the master builder's help, it took a small army of warlocks to teleport them to this level."

Anna's interest was piqued. "How do you know all this?"

He shrugged. "The plans. The crown commissioned it, after all. The documents are in the archives."

Anna and Thomas exchanged the same look.

Thomas gripped his chin. "You think he …?"

Anna shook her head. "Almost certainly not."

"Almost?"

"Highly, *highly* unlikely."

"But if anyone *would* have it, it would be the crown. In case …" Thomas nodded down the tunnel.

The captain glanced between them, eyes slightly narrowed as he tried to piece together what they were talking about.

Anna grimaced. "In case of war? But how would the knowledge—" She froze. Of *course* the knowledge would be pertinent!

The captain raised a finger, moving it between Thomas and Anna. "You're referring to that dig of yours, aren't you? The one that involved you borrowing The Javelin."

Thomas grinned. "That quick mind must be why you made captain. And that battering ram certainly did the trick."

"Deduction is one of my greatest strengths. It allows me to see the bigger picture. Move pieces about. Make critical decisions in critical moments. Alas, there aren't too many wars these days. I fear my talents will go to waste before I see this life through."

Anna's mind worked quickly, putting her own pieces together. "Knowledge is a weapon."

"The champion *too* can deduce. No surprise. But let me clarify for you, Arcanist Stone. Knowledge *is* the weapon. A real shame your earlier research into Devil's Gate—the Arcaneum—has led us nowhere. It is still closed to you, is it not?" He leaned closer, eyes narrowing with hope.

"Alas, that it is," Thomas grumbled. "And barring some miracle breakthrough, probably will remain so for the foreseeable future … if not a generation or two."

The man deflated. "Ah. That is most unfortunate. It has been quite the source of debate amongst the scholars, who will continue to devour any parchment you publish on the matter." He indicated for them to enter. "Please."

They stepped by, entering a vast sanctum from which diverged numerous giant corridors.

"We call them The Branches," the captain said proudly, flicking a hand at various hallways. "Armor. Weapons. Siege engines. Arcane artifacts. Archives. So on and so forth. All unmarked, of course." He said all this as he led them to a desk manned by a slew of bored guards who perked up upon seeing Anna.

"Soldiers. May I introduce Thomas Stone and, someone who hardly needs an introduction, Champion Anna Stone."

The men and women thrust their hands out, eager to shake Anna's hand, while Thomas stood by looking diminished.

After some small talk on what an honor it was to meet them—without asking what they were doing there—the guards had Anna and Thomas sign their names in the middle of a blank ledger using a peacock quill. The moment they finished, their names vanished from the page.

The captain smiled as he closed the ledger. "Secrets must be kept. This way." He led them on toward one of the smaller corridor branches.

Anna exchanged a look with Thomas that said, *Ask him.*

Thomas cleared his throat. "Captain, forgive us, but we must inquire about the master builder's catalog of works—"

"I can absolutely give you access," the man replied, making Anna and Thomas exchange a look of excitement. He raised a finger. "But only after you finish. I have never seen a scroll made by our illustrious champion. Please allow me that honor."

"It will be the least I can do," Anna said, trying not to get her hopes up. Even if it led nowhere in relation to the dig, seeing the master builder's original plans would be an incredible experience.

The corridor, about fifty feet high and twenty feet wide, was filled with iron doors, each marked with what appeared to be a random number.

"They are identifiers—but only if you know how to read them."

Anna glanced over the dully painted numbers. "Cryptographic arithmetic?"

"We cannot speak more on the subject," he replied, the man's slight grin telling her she was either right or very close.

They passed the occasional guard or black-robed attendant or warlock, every one of whom did a double take upon seeing Anna. Yet none said a word, and all looked away the moment the captain laid eyes on them. Anna had the impression questions that did not concern one's business were frowned upon here, perhaps even forbidden.

At last they stopped at a door no different from the others. The man relit his palm and placed it against the iron, this time saying only his name. It opened inward, and they entered a wide and rocky cavern, the walls of which had a crystalline structure.

"The master sometimes liked to preserve original ambiance," the captain noted with a hint of irony, taking them to a wide desk, behind which stood long rows of shelves filled with books, scrolls, and tablets. Two people stood behind the desk, one an old warlock in the black attendant robes of the armory, who looked like someone's grandmother, and the other one, perhaps bizarrely to an outsider, in a full suit of armor.

Except Anna, recognizing ancient arcanery, nodded at the suit. "What's its name?"

The old woman pressed the fingertips of veined hands into the desktop. "Thesper. But he does not work, and hasn't for as long as I have worked here."

"Forty years, is it now, Mertha?"

The woman gave an almost imperceptible nod.

The captain opened a hand. "Mr. and Mrs. Stone, may I introduce Mertha Abalone, Senior Keeper of the Scrolls."

The woman acknowledged them with a nod before using a fingernail to flick the old suit of armor with a *ting*. "Apparently a warlock misfired while crafting parchment."

"Our lingo for creating spell scrolls," the captain threw in.

"The spell hit old Thesper and he has not worked since."

"Would you like me to look at him?" Anna offered. "I have had a bit of luck reanimating an ancient trinket."

"We had our best look at him to no avail."

"This isn't just anyone, Mertha."

"Fair, and I suppose if anyone can repair old Thesper it is one of our famed arcaneologists."

"Alas, I am but a humble teacher these days." Although people liked to call her an arcaneologist, in her case, it was more of an honorary title. A true arcaneologist pursued arcaneology as a profession. Though some argued a teacher of the arcane arts—an arcanist—was not far behind, particularly a teacher that taught complex arcaneology and studied it in their spare time, as was the case with Anna.

"The greats all say such things." The woman opened a palm. "It would be our honor."

Anna walked through a partition in the wide desk and splayed a hand over the suit of armor. "*Un vun asperio aurum enchantus*," she incanted, a spell the others also cast to monitor what Anna did. The suit burst with ancient tendril geometries, all faded and sunk to permanence. Anna muttered as she examined the nuance. "Third, fourth, fifth leading order tendrils ... the weavings are highly interwoven ... advanced arcanery, even for the era ... approximately two thousand years old ... exquisite workmanship ... signs of a master."

"They're all master works," Mertha noted. "All such creations. Only masters can craft them. Or used to be able to. But you are working with one, are you not? What is he like?"

"Ottentus? Quirky," Anna muttered, absorbed in the observation. "Yes, here is the damage. The plates got misaligned, forcing a break in the bonds between the surrounding enchantments, which were crafted to be malleable so that they could move along with the plates." It was the same with Mopey's wing. "As a result, a crucial tendril portion fell back into the ether." Even arcanery sunk to permanence had its limits, usually stemming from inherent weaknesses in the original casting, or more commonly, in the structure they adhered to.

"Vanishing forever," the captain muttered. "And there is no known way to retrieve that portion?"

"None that I am aware of," Anna replied. "Must have been quite the blow."

"It was an explosive failure," Mertha said, "one that sent poor Thesper here slamming into a wall and the offending warlock into a wheelchair."

They let her ruminate, until she snuffed her palm, concluding, "This is no trinket. I would have to study the neighboring geometries in depth and have to be able to perfectly mimic the master's weaving before I even took a stab at repairing it. I'd have to recreate the crafting from scratch."

"And it would have to be a perfect casting," Mertha added, "so that it could sink to permanence. To add to the challenge, Champion, you would receive no payment in the event of failure. Only a working replacement tendril weaving with a high probability of permanence will guarantee payment, as judged by the resident arcaneologists."

"How much would a job like that pay?" Thomas asked.

"Twenty-seven thousand crowns, which is actually a pittance considering this hunk of metal knew every cubbyhole and the contents therein. Now we employ a small army of attendants just to keep things organized." She indicated down one of the rows, lit with dim ensconced candlelight. A young black-robed attendant—one of several scattered about in the rows—looked up from a tablet before returning to her work.

"Those young'uns are a *lot* more expensive over the long run, as you can imagine," the captain added.

Thomas glanced at Anna with a *Think you can manage it?* look.

Anna sighed. It would be a massive gamble of her time, taking her away from her family—and that's *if* she were successful. But seeing as it was a huge lump sum ... "I suppose it *would* advance my own knowledge on the subject," she said.

The woman cracked a smile. "Ancient arcanery is the least understood of the myriad reservoirs of the arts. It will be interesting to see if you succeed."

Thomas leaned over to whisper, "I will of course do my part and support however I can, and that includes extra work."

Anna gave him a *Yes, you will*, look.

The captain rubbed his hands. "Wonderful. But it will not be too low a task for the kingdom champion, will it?"

"Work is work," Anna replied, mind already working on the problem at hand. But she was soon forced to shelve the project as the captain turned their attention to what they had come for.

"Scrolls!" he declared with open arms. "These two have come to craft us scrolls. What are we short on, Mertha? Give them something juicy."

Mertha nodded at Anna's arm. "19th?"

"18th," Anna corrected.

The woman looked at Thomas.

"15th," he said, adding in a mumble, "Making it illegal for me."

"Really a shame Create Scroll is 18th, isn't it?" The captain clapped Thomas on the back, whispering, "Military exceptions *can* be made under the right circumstances ... *if* you know the spell, that is."

"Alas, I do not. In this regard, Anna's knowledge of the arts far outstrips mine. And you wouldn't want a 15th degree fumbling about with such a complex spell anyway."

"Wise words." Mertha turned to Anna. "There is only one spell at the 18th that consistently causes us trouble when crafting into scroll form, Champion—and that is *Voidusarcanatis*."

"Area Spell Void," Anna muttered, translating its ancient name. "I had a feeling it'd be that one."

"And by trouble, the Keeper of the Scrolls actually means near impossible," the captain threw in. "We have, what, one in the archives at the moment?"

"Zero, Captain," Martha said. "We have zero at the moment. The last one was used to secure a new wing of the king's palace when the caster in charge of the project failed to cast the spell in a way that would get it to sink to permanence, forcing us to use the scroll variant, which was certified to sink to permanence as the casting had been perfect. No surprise considering Roberta Roth crafted it."

"She was an excellent headmistress and a fine contributor to the vault," the captain said, nodding at Anna and Thomas as if expecting them to continue the tradition.

"The scroll is yet to be replaced," Mertha went on. "The spell is notoriously difficult to render into scroll form."

"And notoriously difficult to cast," the captain added, eyes sparkling.

Thomas fidgeted. "Uh, regarding the rate ..."

Mertha slid a wrinkled chart before the couple. "Standard rates apply. But if the casting is deemed of high quality—meaning close to perfection—we add fifty percent."

"Gods, look at those numbers," Thomas muttered, a finger sliding down the list of spell rates that rapidly increased with each degree. "I knew I should have worked harder to advance in degree." He tapped the Area Spell Void scroll fee. "And if the casting is perfect?"

"Then the payout quadruples."

Anna and Thomas exchanged looks.

"Not an insubstantial amount of money, is it?" Mertha noted. "But the knowledge to make a perfect scroll casting is about as rare as it comes. And Spells of Legend are the hardest to come by. Warlocks of such skill — and forgive the implication — they —"

"—hardly ever need the money," Thomas finished. He patted his chest. "Alas that is this fool's fault. I am a degenerate gambler, and now my wife is forced to help save the day." He smiled at Anna, who was so surprised by his candor that she blushed.

"Please, we must witness this casting," the captain said.

"Do you have a whole quint?" Anna asked as she perused a series of blank parchments Mertha had handed her. "Because that is how long this will take." She chose a fine vellum, the margins of which had already been painted with exquisite gold scroll work. "Perhaps longer, considering I have never infused the spell into scroll form before."

Now and then Anna would craft scrolls for rich merchants, the most oft requested being Repair (for common breaks), Unconceal (to find stuff hidden by servants and employees), Object Alarm (to protect expensive items), Object Track (to track thieves), Amplify (to make bold announcements), Strength (to lift heavy things about), Teleport (for personal and business travel), Area Alarm (to protect the storefront or home), Sanctuary (to provide security, used mostly during travel), and especially Group Teleport (to move workers about). She charged high fees as her scrolls were pristine works, limiting the chance of a misfire. And she never accepted work—no matter how much money was offered—if there was a hint of nefarious motivation in requesting a scroll. Nor did she render offensive spells into scroll form except in rare circumstances, like for well-intentioned people trying to survive in the wilderness. If anyone so much as dared to ask her to craft a Bewitch scroll, she threatened to report them on the spot. Ill-intentioned people would be forced to seek out the scroll on the black market, notorious for shoddy workmanship and fake scrolls. Many a hapless fool had been found fused to an object after purchasing a Teleport scroll in the black market—and that was if the scroll worked in the first place.

"And it is rather dull work at that, Captain," Mertha threw in. "Every gesture, every thought, every nuance of the spell must be infused, all while casting the spell again and again, sometimes into a single letter, sometimes into a sentence."

"Forgive me. I show my ignorance at last." The captain clapped his hands together. "Let me make it up to you by escorting you to a certain ancient cubby in Archives."

AN ANCIENT CUBBY

Anna and Thomas stared up at a giant box the size of a shed, one of countless many, all stacked in rows that shot up to a hundred-foot ceiling.

Thomas snorted. "Cubbyhole. More like a house. How do we even get to it?"

"With this." The captain placed two fingers in his mouth and whistled before shouting, "*Summano formaplat!*"

Thomas and Anna winced from the loud whistle.

"Was that really necessary?" Thomas muttered, sticking a finger in an ear and wiggling it.

"I'm afraid it was. Ancient gestural casting quirk of the spell. You should hear the one that closes one of the vaults." He made an exaggerated wince. "Piercing stuff. Ah, here it comes."

They turned to watch a stone platform silently float down the dimly lit alley of cubbies.

"By the look on your faces I would say you have never seen such arcanery. It is impressive, is it not? Only a few handfuls were crafted, all inside this complex. Ancient arcanery at its finest."

The platform stopped to float overhead. It was ten by ten feet and studded with bronze poles and chains so caked in verdigris they almost looked like moss. Every bit of the stonework and the poles was engraved with fine runes, creating a geometric tapestry.

Anna splayed her fingers. "May I?"

"By all means. Archives has been trying to understand the arcanery for generations." He chortled. "You unravel the mystery of this casting and you'll own the kingdom."

They stepped aside as the platform silently lowered to the ground, coming to a floating rest just above the highly polished stone floor.

"*Un vun asperio aurum enchantus*," Anna incanted as they stepped onto it. She almost gasped, for it was some of the finest craftsmanship she had ever seen. Tightly packed, pristine, and nearly undulled by time. There was only one object that reminded her of the work, and it rested in her pocket.

"*Formaplat quadrat dio*," the captain commanded, and the platform slowly rose. "Are you impressed or are you impressed?"

"Interesting how the tendrils connect to the super structure, and how they change based on their position in space."

"It's all connected, yes. There are tangential synergies and Rivican-like mechanisms within the arcanery itself. It's excruciatingly fascinating stuff—and unfortunately well beyond my oafish understanding."

"Consider me most impressed indeed, Captain," Anna said, crouching to inspect the tendrils closer.

"I have to see this for myself," Thomas muttered, and also cast Reveal, joining Anna in a crouch. "Gods, look at the weaving. The depth—"

"The interconnectedness," Anna threw in. "The leading edges—"

"—the miniscule castings, the coloring. Each property perfected." Thomas shook his head. "A master work." He looked up. "Who—"

"None other than—" The captain splayed his arms at the gigantic cubby before which they came to float.

Anna and Thomas stood to marvel at the sight before them, keeping Reveal lit in case they spotted artifacts. The room-sized cubby was stuffed from bottom to top with documents, scrolls, tablets, wooden chests strapped with rusting iron, and objects like statues and paintings and jars of plant and animal specimens and large bones on stands and countless other oddities. There were four thin aisles a single person could squeeze through. Everything was labeled, much of it wrapped in archival linen.

Thomas's mouth hung open. "This will take a lifetime to get through ..."

"*Several* lifetimes, in point of fact," the captain said. "We've had children of parents who were themselves the children of parents who had worked on this very cubby, translating the old tongue, deciphering lost nuance, applying the latest arcaneological discoveries to the master builder's thinking, which itself was far ahead of its time, as evidenced by what we stand on. Yet there's still stuff we find. Now imagine this problem across all of Archives. There's untold knowledge waiting to be rediscovered." He folded his arms. "You two ought to consider becoming resident arcaneologists."

"We have plenty enough work, thank you," Thomas muttered, running a hand over the toothy and monstrous skull of some ancient predator. "Though the offer is tempting."

"I bet it is, especially to a pair of arcaneologically minded souls such as yourselves."

Anna peered down one of the dark aisles barely wide enough for a child, let alone an adult. "Is there a cataloged portion that deals with structures he built?"

"You are talking about a master builder, my dear champion. That's almost the entire cubby. You will have to be more specific."

"Right. What about structures built near the end of his life?"

The man consulted a brick of a book as thick as it was tall, sitting on a wedge in the outer perimeter of the cubby. "Section 7398. But you need to decide which document you wish to see." He indicated that she look for herself.

When Anna squeezed in beside him, she saw a very long list of documents under section 7398, each labeled with a letter followed by a number. The master had worked on some fine establishments near the end of his life—a cellar in the king's palace, a formidable vault in the armory, various mercantile estates, a huge dam, and a new wing of Castle Northspear, the work he was most famous for. With that wing, the castle had taken him a decade to complete. But it was one of the last entrants that intrigued her.

" '*Barrus au Ito*,' " she said, circling the three words with a finger, beside which was the letter designation *V* followed by the number seventeen.

"Barrow of Three," the captain translated. "Is that of significance because of your Mount Barrow excavation?"

"There's only one way to find out. Where would this be?"

"Seven three nine eight dash *V* seventeen is near the back of aisle four, about seven feet in and on the right-hand side. Judging by the number, it's probably ankle height, so be ready to stoop."

Anna, wondering how she was supposed to do that in such a tight space, snuffed Reveal and lit her palm instead. "May I?"

"By all means."

She squeezed in through the crush of documents and artifacts of aisle four, trying to keep the stifling beast of claustrophobia at bay. The edge of every document and item was numbered with a tiny white script that stood out nicely in the glow of her lightning palm. At last she found the section labeled 7398, which ran from top to bottom in a thin and uneven slice, much like a teetering pile of documents sitting on a desk, albeit one jam-packed from all sides by similar towers. At the top was the *A* designation, meaning the *V* designation was indeed near her feet. But as she was sideways and barely able to move laterally, this proved far more difficult to reach than simply leaning down.

"You have to perform a sort of cartwheel maneuver, Arcanist Stone," the captain called from the back. "There's an art to it, really."

Anna, feeling every bit her age of forty-nine, grimaced and groaned as she awkwardly wedged her way downward. After a few tries, during which she had to back up to reach the spot, she finally grabbed hold of document 7398-V17. Except there was a problem.

"It's stuck!" she called back. "Won't budge!"

"Oh, careful, careful, careful! There's a trick to that too," the captain exclaimed, chortling nervously. "Don't want to wreck anything, do we? You have to lift the stack above."

"Are you jesting me? I'm practically upside down in here."

"Not at all. Our archivists are all superior in Telekinesis for this very reason. We suspect lifting stacks of documents was how the resident arcaneologists and helpers trained their Telekinesis up in the old days. And yes, we recognize it is not an ideal organizational system, but it's all connected with the animated suits of armor that break down when stuff gets misplaced."

"What do you mean by the suits break down?" Thomas pressed.

"I'll give you an example. One of our juniors moved a crate of Rivican terracotta pots a whole ten feet. Well, one of the rickety buckets of animated old tin worked itself into such an angry tizzy that one of its arms fell off. Just … clunked to the floor. Not the first time it's happened either. I guess we got lucky in that the enchantment hadn't slid off into the ether because the arcaneologists managed to fix the thing in the end."

Anna grumbled at the mess of it all but hooked on telekinetically to the stack above, which slowly rose, allowing her to scoot the parchment out from underneath. It then took some effort to extricate herself from the stack.

"Was that buzz what I think it was?" the captain asked. "I have heard it makes such a sound."

"Mmm," Anna toned, delicately unfurling the archival linen that wrapped the document.

"Forgive me, Champion, but … may I see it?"

She rarely gave in to such requests these days, but seeing as the man had been so helpful, she idly flicked a finger and the scion floated free of her pocket. The captain gasped upon seeing its cloudy interior flash with silent lightning.

He splayed a hand. "May I?"

"By all means," she said in echo of him.

He cast Reveal and gasped a second time. "The weavings are even tighter than the platform! This is beyond a master work … one could live many lifetimes without laying eyes on such craftsmanship. Countless lifetimes …"

"Leyan workmanship is quite the marvel, isn't it?" Thomas muttered, his eyes trained on the same thing Anna's were—the document. But it wasn't any ordinary document.

It was a map.

A FRIENDLY COMPETITION

Anna's eyes pored over the parchment herald, each line making her knuckles go whiter. *Although rumors continue to circulate that Arcanist and kingdom champion Anna Atticus Stone has been offered the position of headmistress of the esteemed Academy of Arcane Arts, there are other rumors that have yet to be addressed. This humble herald has it on good authority that Arcanist Stone's husband, the noble-sniffing Thomas Stone, formerly of House Blackflower, has racked up quite the gambling debt—we are speaking in the tens of thousands here, far beyond a layman's purse. Rumors swirl that the couple's relationship is strained due to this account. Some people are even saying the couple is heading for divorce, which would not be an unfamiliar tradition in the Stone household. But hark! There is more! Most salacious of all is the news that their daughter, the rabble-rousing drama kid Thia Stone, is with child—and no one knows who the father is. It is rumored not even the girl's own parents know who is to be their son-in-law. For a house that purports itself to be a model of kingdom citizenship, that house now besmirches the honor of the kingdom and—*

"Bah!" Anna hissed, telekinetically crumpling the *Blackhaven Herald* into a tight ball and slapping it off the table. It was such a sudden implosion that her arcanist friend, Syanda Mibukwa, sitting across from her at one of a slew of tables in the Arcanists' Mess Hall, flinched.

The woman patted her curls as if worried they had been mussed and leaned forth. "It's gossip, Anna. Just people yapping. You should be used to it by now. And hasn't this—" She flicked a hand at the crumpled ball. "—Triana Taylor had it out for you since you were a student here? She's the one you bested in a duel when you were an aspirant and she was like a 3rd degree, right?"

6th, Anna thought, but didn't bother correcting her colleague. Her eyes bounced from arcanist to arcanist, many of whom averted their gaze the moment she glanced their way. As was arcanist habit, every one of them had at least one herald before them, sometimes even three—from the *Antioc Herald* to the *Academy Herald*. Some even peeked at the *Youth Herald*, though deciphering student irony and in-jests was like trying to see through a Darkness cloud.

Anna sighed as she glanced up at the infinite ceiling, a staple of the academy's most renowned rooms. The mess hall was already a large room made all the larger by that ceiling. Whereas at one time in its history it had been filled with arcanists to manage a burgeoning student warlock population, in this day and age there were only scattered handfuls of arcanists sitting alone or in small groups, quietly chatting over morning tea or coffee, forks picking at a breakfast of eggs and bacon on porcelain plates emblazoned with the academy crest. Historical portraits and paintings hung on all four crimson walls, the paint matching the fine Tiberran carpet, which had been teleported into the mess hall, being as it filled the entire floor. Every chair was gilded, every table leg ornate. Even the white tablecloths had the academy crest, offset with silver thread. It was fine dining fit for nobles.

Anna fiddled with the end of her braided ponytail, tightening the weave as she went. "I suppose I should find Thia before she runs for the hills." *Or drops out, gods forbid*.

"Doubt you'll have time before class begins."

"I actually have her *in* my first class today. Just hoping to catch her prior." It was the end of the first quint of a new term, which meant every class started with a bit of orientation.

"It's a zoo out there. You wouldn't find her if she were wearing a jester's outfit."

Anna didn't want to confess that Thia carried a tracking pebble.

"Which class is it, anyway?" Syanda pressed as the other arcanists started to rise from their places—after being in the academy for so long, including their student years, most arcanists developed an innate sense of time, giving themselves enough of it to get to class prior to the first bell. As they left, servants—older Ordinaries granted special worker privileges to be able to access certain portions of the academy—quietly saw to their tables, bussing the fine porcelain with academy-crested silver trays.

Anna slid her chair back and stood. "Sword and Sorcery."

"Nothing like starting the day off with a bit of violence." Syanda tucked in her chair. "Looking forward to the new batch. I've got the aspirants all morn."

"I envy you." Anna loved aspirants. Their doe-eyed gazes full of wonder, their as yet unbroken optimism, their curiosity and politeness.

Syanda snorted. "These ones are a twisted lot. And I mean that literally. Did you see the latest trend? They're wearing their belts backward."

Anna's face curdled. "Why?"

"Because they want to appear fiery. You know every generation must have its thing—practically every term, too. How else are they supposed to tell each other apart?"

"I would think the robe colors would be enough," Anna muttered as the pair walked toward the doors.

"I suppose. Oh, and hey, I still want an evening glass. I know you're busy these days—"

"You don't know the half of it."

"—but I request—no, *demand* a glass of wine. Let's do our own gossiping for a change."

"If this headache ever goes away, I might take you up on it."

"I'll believe it when I see it," Syanda muttered.

Anna only grunted. She politely thanked her colleague for breakfast and the pair parted ways. The halls were indeed a zoo, with students hurrying this way and that. And the younger the student, the greater the hurry. All took notice of her, but whereas she was used to the attention, these particular looks were the sort that also quickly glanced away, sometimes even as they mumbled a "Good morning, Arcanist Stone." Triana Taylor, having latched onto a particularly juicy piece of gossip, had struck true once again.

"Some things never change," Anna muttered as the sea of students parted around her like clouds cleaved by a mountain. It was the final day of student council elections, which meant the halls were plastered with posters. "Introducing Aspirant Mathy Childs—a young noble with respect for the underprivileged," read one. "What council needs is a good dose of cynicism, so if you're 4th, vote for Jasper North," read another. "A vote for 9th degree George Spigot is a vote for competency." Absent were any posters of her daughter, who had been putting posters up all quint for her own bid to represent the 7th degrees. It had read, "Let none fear, for Thia Stone is here! Ever in the shadow of her famous mom, she knows what it's like to fight for those of a more average bent." Anna thought it in poor taste, but students had thought it cheeky and clever.

As luck would have it, just as Anna stepped into the snowy courtyard with the intent to head to the Elements Wing, she spotted an amber-robed warlock hurrying toward the academy gates. She knew it was Thia because of the way she waddled a bit like a goose, one hand on her tummy, the other holding her hood tightly lest someone see her face.

Anna quickly caught up to her daughter. "Thia!"

Thia whirled about, satchel flying around her. "*Mom?*" Her face was red from crying.

"Tell me you weren't going home."

"Well, what did you *expect* me to do? It's even in the *Youth Herald*, Mom! I'm a pariah. I'll never be able to show my face in school again!"

"Nonsense. Do you know how many pieces like this I had to contend with all my life?"

"Yeah, but you grew up being slagged! They've never done this to *me* before. I can't deal with this sort of thing, Mom. I'm not nearly as strong as you are. I just want to go home and die."

"What about your campaign for student council?"

"Are you jesting me? *After today's news?* I spent all morning tearing my posters down and ripping them up!"

"And where's Niterra?"

"I left the old bag behind in my haste to—oh, there she is." Thia nodded past Anna, who turned to see Niterra grimacing as she hurriedly tottered forth, one hand up, no doubt tracking Thia's other pebble.

"You cannot run from your problems, Thia," Anna continued. "You must face them. It is the path of least suffering."

"Stop regurgitating stuff that old monk told you. You're not a monk, Mom. You'll *never* be one."

Niterra finally caught up to them. "Ah, these bones creak like old trees," she wheezed. "I too old for this." Her face twisted with ferocity at Thia. "You must obey elders, girl! Cannot run like weasel. Must wear decisions like clothes and honor them."

Thia rolled her red eyes. "Ugh, more monk gobbledygook."

Anna opened her palm. "Thia, please come to class. There's someone quite hopeful of seeing you."

"Is it a man with a guillotine? I'll take a guillotine. That would be nice."

"Actually, today happens to be a certain boy's first day of class as a Solian student."

Thia blushed, whispering, "*Jonah's* here?"

"He needs a friend to protect him from the vileness that will surely be thrown his way as an Abrandian." *And you could use a distraction from that horrid boy Ralf*, but Anna didn't voice that thought aloud.

Thia muttered something under her breath.

"I didn't quite catch that," Anna said.

"Ralfie's not going to like that," she muttered a little louder.

Anna's mind was abruptly clogged with so many angry thoughts she didn't know what to say. Was the boy controlling Thia? But she thought they were hardly speaking? Was another necromantic ritual involved? She wanted to roar, *I don't give a flying hoof what that crazy boy thinks!* Instead she forced her head to flick at the giant portal to the Elements Wing. "The matter at hand is no one else's business, and I encourage you to take responsibility for your decisions and hold your head up, Thia. Besides, people will quickly get distracted by the next juicy morsel. It'll settle down as it always does."

Thia gave the academy gate a longing look before her shoulders slumped. "The guillotine it is, then," she muttered, and joined her mother and the old Black Eagle on the walk to class.

* * *

"Satchels away, people," Anna barked the moment she entered the classroom, which was nothing but a giant square with an infinite ceiling. The floor was padded, one wall lined with carts full of dull training weapons, another with practice dummies, and the rest with various moveable obstacles.

The group of amber-robed 7th degrees, many of whom greeted her with, "Good morning, Arcanist Stone," picked up on Anna's no-nonsense tone and quickly did as they were bid. Niterra took up a position by the door as usual, while Thia looked about the throng of students, finding Ralf and Jonah standing obliviously beside each other.

"I hate coincidences," Thia muttered under her breath.

As Anna put away her own satchel, a girl ran up to Thia who Anna recognized as Kimani Taylor, Triana Taylor's daughter—and friend to Thia.

"Hey, I'm *so* sorry about that horrid piece in the heralds today," Kimani blurted. "I'm going to give my mother an earful when I next talk to her. But, yeah, I'm *so* embarrassed and ashamed and—"

"Come here," Thia interrupted, dragging Kimani into a hug and patting her back. "I already know how you feel about your mother. Don't even give it a second thought."

Kimani squeezed, awkwardly giving Anna a brief and nervous look, back before letting go. "You sure?"

"Of course," and Thia gave a flap of the hand. "'Tis but a minor laceration."

The girls chortled before Kimani elbowed Thia. "He says he knows you. The new boy."

Thia glanced past Kimani to look at the boys. Upon seeing Thia, Ralf's face split with a sneer whilst Jonah's face warmed with a smile. "Uh, yeah, we had a run-in of sorts already."

The two teenagers couldn't have been more different. Ralf's dark hair was so perfectly groomed he looked like he was preparing to sit for a portrait, whereas Jonah's chestnut hair was swept in the latest unruly style, hanging loosely down to his square jawline. Ralf, seventeen, was short and thin with narrow shoulders, and the eighteen-year-old Abrandian was tall, with broad, muscular shoulders.

"Enough chatter," Anna said, motioning for the girls to join the circle.

"Yes, Arcanist Stone," Kimani blurted, and ran to a spot not far from the boys.

Thia, head high despite the stares, boldly moved to stand between the boys. Although she acknowledged Ralf with a thin-lipped and small nod, she blushed upon seeing Jonah, and seemingly made an effort not to smile too broadly at him. Some of the other students made meaningful eyes at each other, but Anna was proud that Thia paid them no mind. Perhaps she had taken Anna's advice to keep her head up after all.

Anna brought her hands together. "First things first, people. Welcome to 8th degree Sword and Sorcery. In this class we will focus on applying the lessons you will be learning about the 8th degree. As always, you will also be applying the entirety of your arts in your efforts. I don't care if your aim is to become a guard captain, a cobbler, or a scribe—I want you fluid in every spell in your arsenal, so expect to perform many arduous repetitions and cycles."

There were some scattered chortles as students relaxed a little.

"We also have a new addition to the class, Jonah Ivanov. He is from Abrandia—" Some hisses rang out, and Anna raised a palm. "—but I suspect you will find him to possess the soul of a Solian."

"And I speak Solian well too," the young man blurted, making many a girl do a double take. He was the most handsome boy in the class, and had already drawn some side looks from the girls.

"He comes from struggle, so I trust you will make him feel as comfortable as possible as he transitions into academy life."

After a smattering of polite applause, Anna delved into a more in-depth outline of the class, which included expectations of the students and herself. Throughout her spiel, she saw Thia throwing side-long glances at Jonah, who would look away. Jonah would then do this to her, with the same result. The pair kept missing each other, but apparently on purpose, for both would smile out of the corner of their mouths. Of course, it didn't take Ralf long to spot this behavior, and his face soured like a pickle.

"Now that you have a good idea of what to expect, and before we dive into discussing how 8th degree spells will fit into your repertoire, let us begin with basic cycles. I want to see who's been diligently practicing over winter recess and who's been lazy." Anna raised a finger. "We're going to start by working *backward*. Summon Minor Wall on three, lined perpendicular thataway—" She pointed two fingers past the students to a wide-open space beyond them. "One, two—three!"

Students, unprepared for the sudden demand, fumbled with the gesture, with many a *slap* coming from the sound of a fist hitting an open palm, the final motion uttered during the "*Summano valla minimus girata barricada*" incantation. Walls of crackling lightning, splintering ice, rustling fire, crumbling earth, slopping water, swirling air, and white-sun healing *whooshed* into existence, creating a cacophony of noise Anna had to shout over.

"Nice and even, Krishnan," she called, pacing behind the students. "That's it, Pedworth, but work on the height. Weak and wispy, Nakamura. You can do better. Too irregular, Fungal. Straighten it out next time."

One wall of water, instead of being perpendicular so that they would all fit, appeared horizontal, cutting off the entire field of play.

"Null it, Taylor, and try again!"

Kimani smacked her lips before scraping a hand across the air, hissing, "*Summano null.*"

"Excellent, Ivanov."

The teenager mumbled a sheepish, "Thank you, Great One—" only to be cut off by Anna snapping, "Arcanist Stone will do, young man."

"Yes, Arcanist Stone. My apologies."

"Competent casting, Turman," she said, not wanting to give too much praise despite Ralf having cast the strongest wall in his degree. His skills had greatly increased since becoming the apprentice to the master warlock Ottentus.

"You are having way too much trouble, Stone," she said to Thia, never afraid of calling her own daughter out. "And that goes for too many of you. The spell wasn't to be practiced just for the exam, but for real life. Too much lollygagging during the recess and not enough studying. Get it together, people."

An awkward moment came when Ralf and Jonah tried to coach Thia at the same time, the former snapping at her and the latter calmly explaining she had rushed the gestures. As a result, she turned away from Ralf and beamed at Jonah, nodding along to what he was saying. Ralf's pickle expression curdled to sour milk.

"A poor showing all in all, but we won't linger. I want quicker castings from now on. Minor Illusion—make me a boot!" She clapped thrice, each time shouting, "Let's go, let's go, let's go!"

And on it went, spell after spell, utilizing the obstacles and practice dummies as needed, with Anna pushing for a balance of speed and competency. She called out those whom she deemed had not practiced over the winter recess, and only complimented those who achieved or surpassed her high expectations. After cycling through seven degrees, Anna flicked a hand at the carts, simultaneously giving them a telekinetic shake, subtly hinting at what she was about to do.

"Go ahead and pick one out." The now sweaty 7th degrees rushed to grab a weapon, most choosing the smallest and lightest. Ralf did the same, picking a wooden dagger, until he saw that Jonah had picked out a tall spear, at which point he switched to a club.

"Line up. Go, go, go!" Anna called, pacing the floor in a wide circle. "Ten feet. Aaaaand—rise!" Students either let go of their weapons or tossed them into the air before raising them telekinetically. "I want ten feet off the get-go. Move it, people. None of that wobbling, Schmidt. Watch that angle, Fisher, lest it get away from you. Nice and steady, Sutton. Keep it even as a keel, Taylor. All right, everyone's in the air, good. Now we're going to do something different—a little competition. You're going to repeat casting the entire cycle of degrees, but this time, *while* holding your weapon aloft."

More than one student gasped.

"I don't want to hear any complaints from 7th degrees. Chronocasting should be part of your regular cycle repertoire by now. But judging by your grumbling, I'll be surprised if any of you will even manage to get to the 2nd degree in the competition. We'll start with a simple one—Repair." She beckoned at a battered wooden cart full of chipped cups, which trundled over on squeaky wheels. "Grab and smash, but keep your weapons aloft. Let's go, people, and keep an eye on falling objects. I don't want any accidents in our first class together this term."

Chaos broke out as a slew of weapons fell, forcing students to jump aside to avoid them. Anna calmly pointed at the occasional item to flick it aside or halt its fall. "Reraise, smash, and repair. We're not moving on to Push until everyone has at least attempted the feat." Anna planned to skip the spells that weren't suited — or even possible — to chronocast with, like Unconceal and Object Alarm, and would push only the doable ones.

Less than half managed to smash the cup whilst keeping their weapons aloft. Ralf was the most competent chronocasting Repair, with Jonah close behind, both able to smash their cup and repair it, their weapons wavering above them like wooden guillotines. Everyone else struggled, and in some cases, like with Thia, struggled mightily.

"Not even close, Stone."

Thia flared her eyes at Anna in a *Stop picking on me, Mom,* manner.

"We're going to start eliminating people as we go."

"I'm not sure the academy condones murder, Arcanist Stone," Kimani jested, prompting laughter from some. She smiled as she kept glancing between her floating wooden sickle and her broken cup, which lay in pieces below her hands, splayed open in readiness to repair it. The index finger from each hand pointed up, keeping a connection with her weapon.

"Hope that wit won't get in the way of a quality repair, Taylor, as we're all waiting for you now," Anna countered, grateful the daughter was as different from the mother as their elements of water and fire. Unlike her mother, the girl never seemed to fall prey to gossip or slander.

"It won't, Arcanist Stone. *Apreyo,*" the girl incanted, and the pieces began to reform, only for the sickle to slowly descend. Anna held her tongue, waiting to see if Kimani would finish the repair in time. The cup sealed with a light and the girl quickly looked up, halting the sickle only feet from her head.

"Excellent, Taylor. Next one should be easy — Shine. Light 'em up."

All students kept their gazes aloft whilst raising a hand, incanting, "*Shyneo.*" Palms lit up left and right, but the *thud* of falling weapons increased as castings failed. They were hitting their concentration and stamina limits.

"Now for a challenge," Anna said, bringing one group of dummies forth with a sweep of an arm, not bothering with the others. She lined them up before certain students who were still in the fight whilst chiding the rest to raise their weapons back up. Every single weapon that was still aloft wobbled now, and the remainder had exhausted their nerve or stamina. Fewer than a handful remained, those being Ralf, Jonah and Kimani.

"Push!" Anna called.

The three quickly transitioned to a shove, roaring, "*Baka!*" sending the dummies tumbling. Sickle, spear and club descended, only to be caught before reaching their heads.

"This is something everyone can practice on their own time," Anna said. "The goal is to not let your weapon lower even a little."

"Great work, Jonah," Thia said. "Keep it up."

Ralf's club wavered as he flashed her an angry scowl, one that quickly dissipated when he noticed Anna watching him.

"Let's up the stakes and jump straight to a 4th," Anna said, still staring at the side of his red face. "I want to see you slap your dummy with a quality Fear casting. Ready? Hit 'em!"

All three twisted their hands at the dummies, roaring, "*Dreadus terrablus!*"

As they had been enchanted to do, the heads of all three dummies glowed red, indicating a successful casting.

"Now I want you to lift your dummy whilst keeping your weapon aloft!" Anna called, with many a student gasping or talking behind their hand to a neighbor. Anna ignored them. "You can do it! I know you can! Push yourselves!"

Kimani was the first to raise her dummy, and fail both castings, barely dodging her sickle before it cracked her head open—not that Anna, with a hand ready to intervene, would have let that happen.

"Higher, Ivanov! Turman has you beat!"

"She means *Turd*man," someone muttered, and snickers rang out. One of those snickers had come from Jonah, who promptly cleared his throat and held up a quick hand in apology to Ralf. But Ralf's already foul expression turned to loathing.

"Next person to make such a jest wins a trip to the disciplinary committee," Anna snapped, searching for the perpetrator. But everyone avoided her gaze. "You two stay focused and keep them aloft as long as you can," she said to the boys, pacing back and forth behind them. Both quivered as much as their weapons from the strain. The spear, being taller, rose higher than the club. But Ralf, seemingly not wanting to be bested even on that account, raised his club higher, doing the same with the dummy.

"We're going to see a decisive victory in a moment if you don't push it, Ivanov," Anna said, stepping between the two boys and taking turns looking straight up and at the faces of the students, making sure everyone was paying attention. She suspected Jonah was only doing so well because he desperately wanted to impress Thia—and by the look on her face, he was succeeding.

"Careful, Jonah," Thia whispered. Everyone's eyes were trained high above, where the main action was.

Jonah's spear tilted toward the club. Ralf in turn smacked it back with his club, dislodging Jonah's already weak telekinetic grip. Jonah gave a groan of surrender as both his dummy and the spear fell. By the angle, Anna knew the spear would safely miss him, and so she turned to face Ralf to congratulate him, only to find that he was making eye contact with her, which was unusual as his gaze should have been trained aloft on his club. Suddenly there came a collective shout of alarm followed by a sickly *squish* and a cry of pain.

Anna whirled about. What she saw sent a thrill of horror zipping down her spine. The spear had jammed into Jonah's left shoulder. He fell to his knees, wide-eyed with shock.

The students screamed.

FORMS OF ARCANE ART

All hell broke loose as Anna shot to the boy, catching him as he fell back, his eyes still saucer-wide. Healer-trained to ignore calamitous events in order to get things done, Anna tuned the hysterics out as she lowered him gently to the ground. She then splayed a hand over the wound, incanting, *"Examino potente morbus aurus persona."*

Diagnose revealed the severity of the injury—the tip of the spear had jammed in much farther than was apparent, piercing the lung and outer heart region. Already Jonah wheezed, his breathing raspy, with a slight whistle to it. If he was to survive, he would need urgent attention from the most senior healers the kingdom had to offer. Luckily the academy, used to dealing with the most gruesome injuries, was one of three places in the kingdom that could handle it, the other two being the Blackhaven and Antioc infirmaries.

"Calm down, people!" Anna shouted at the panicked throng. It was then she realized Niterra Bladesong was holding Ralf, tongue-thrashing him in Nodian as she practically throttled him about with an iron grip. But there was no time to consider either of them. Anna snapped her fingers. "Taylor—look at me. I am going to carry Jonah to the healing ward."

"B-but d-don't you have emergency teleport privileges?" Kimani asked.

Anna didn't waste time explaining she was not on the disciplinary committee or on the academy council. "I need you to telekinetically guide the end of the spear so it doesn't bump into anything on the way. Can you handle that? Don't look at the injury. Look at me. Can you handle that?"

The girl quickly nodded.

"Thia—keep the rest of the class calm."

Thia, who'd gone ashen, gaped.

"Thia! Did you hear me, child?"

Thia, finally seeing her mother, jerked into awareness and nodded. As she moved to get people out of the way, Anna readied to move Jonah. "On three. One, two—*three*," and she telekinetically lifted Jonah. "Keep up now," she told Kimani as she hurried as fast as she dared toward the doors, leaving behind a trail of blood.

Jonah gasped as the spear wobbled about.

"Don't let it move!" Anna said, ignoring the gawkers.

"I'm trying. I'm trying!" Kimani replied, running with a hand outstretched.

"Am I going to die?" Jonah whimpered between wheezes.

"No, you'll be fine. But don't talk. Clear the way, people! Move!"

Students lunged aside as the group swept past glass displays of historical treasures and statues of notable people that made up the famous Hall of Heroes portion of the Elements Wing. They burst through an arcane membrane that kept the cacophony of the element halls at bay and hurried toward a pair of doors at the end of the healing hall, the only one accessible to all elements. The other elemental halls kept up a steady onslaught on the ears—lightning thundered, flames roared, waves crashed, ice cracked, air shrieked, and earth rumbled, a stark juxtaposition to the serene wind-chime sounds of the healing hall.

Anna used her free hand to slap at the air first left then right, and the pair of doors ahead burst open.

A young blue-robed girl with thick dreadlocks and a healer's armband shot from behind a counter. "How can I help?"

"Summon the seniors to surgery room three. Left lung and outer heart penetration."

"On it, Arcanist Stone," and the girl shot off. "Call them in and get ready to prep three!" she shouted at aproned attendants. Men and women of various ages and creeds—Ordinaries and warlocks alike—burst into action, causing a beehive of activity.

Anna slowed to fit the boy through the doors that led to the surgery ward. "Watch that tip."

Kimani, face squinched with focus, only nodded as she scooched the end of the spear by the doorframe.

"Easy now. Here we go."

"I'm going to die …" Jonah wheezed. "I don't understand what happened … one moment I was ready to congratulate my opponent … the other … gods, that is a ghastly wound—"

"Don't look at it. Keep your eyes on me, young man." Anna's head swiveled between the final doorframe and surgical room three, filled with cabinets and gurneys and steel trays brimming with malicious-looking instruments. The room was dark, and it had been so long since Anna was an apprentice healing student that she no longer remembered the specific phrasing to light the various arcane lamps up.

She thus twirled a finger, incanting, "*Shyneo lampa*," and a pumpkin-sized globe of lightning crackled into existence. "Onto that gurney there," she said, placing Jonah on a large wooden bed fixed with cart-like wheels.

"Unnameables that hurts," Jonah mumbled, face white as a sheet and lips blue, indicating to Anna that he was rapidly losing blood.

Anna, seeing that the spear was secure, summoned a linen gauze to her hand and quickly wrapped it around the wound to at least slow the bleeding. Then she splayed a hand whilst saying to Kimani, "Hop out there and see what's taking them so long."

"Yes, Arcanist Stone," Kimani said as she sprinted off, crashing through the pair of doors.

Anna took a concentrative breath as she placed a hand near the wound. "*Reducto poina persona*."

When the boy sighed in relief, she pressed the linen tight against the wound with both hands. She had chosen the relatively weak Reduce Pain over Anesthetize as she did not want his heart rate to drop too much.

"W-what happened?" the boy wheezed. "I … I don't understand …"

"Hush, son. We'll worry about that later. Right now, you focus on relaxing as best you can."

"I don't … I don't feel so good."

"I know. They're coming." Anna splayed her hand for a second round of Diagnose. "*Examino potente morbus aurus persona*." Blood was filling the chest cavity, and his heart could stop at any moment. The sand of his hourglass was almost empty. He required a warlock who could competently cast the 17th degree healing spell Arcanic Surgery of the Lung Humor and the 18th degree Arcanic Surgery of the Heart Humor, which usually required a 19th degree in practice. That narrowed it down to two people in the kingdom, one being the head of the academy healing ward, and the other a certain woman in a certain library who practiced surgery part time.

Anna glanced back at the silent doors, thinking, *Come on, come on, where are you?* She remembered the seniors being quicker. Then again, everything felt slow in an emergency, the humans clumsy and all too fallible. Time itself seemed to slow to a horrid crawl.

At last Kimani burst in with a slew of attendants.

"Where's the senior?" Anna asked as they swarmed around Jonah.

"He's performing surgery at Mercy, Arcanist Stone," an attendant replied, referring to Mercy of the Unnameables, the infirmary her mother had passed in.

Anna, realizing that left only one choice, knew what she had to do. "I'm fetching a second. Hold this. No, more pressure." When Kimani had properly taken over holding linen to the wound, Anna let go. "Be right back."

"But Arcanist Stone, we have warlocks—"

"Not for this you don't," Anna muttered as she crashed through the doors. She sprinted through the halls, cursing herself for not pushing to have emergency teleport privileges. The panel of cantankerous geezers that made up the academy council was a stickler for the rules, worried she would be a risk to the institution should she ever get captured. She ran all the way to the Stairs of the Crescent Moon, already envisioning the majestic Library of Antioc, before snapping, "*Impetus peragro.*"

With a *thwomp*, Anna appeared on Gargoyle Bridge, an ancient brazier-lit drawbridge named because of its imposing pair of winged gargoyle statues, mouths perpetually aflame. At the end of that bridge was an open spiked portcullis gate that only closed in times of war. The Library of Antioc, circled by a sludgy moat, loomed above under an overcast sky, with its stained-glass windows and gargoyle-shaped drainage spouts. Its founder, Theodorus Winfield, had converted the castle into a library in a bygone era.

She shot by gray-robed attendants and onlookers who gasped or yanked on colleagues upon seeing who it was. Whispers and exclamations followed her down to the front desk, where she slapped the counter and barked, "I need to see the senior arcaneologist immediately! It's an emergency."

A stone-faced young man in an attendant robe gave her the once-over. "I really am sorry, miss, but the senior arcaneologist is extremely busy and cannot simply see any warlock who wanders through—"

An older man in a gray robe emerged from a nearby office, drawn by the commotion. His eyes widened upon seeing Anna. "Fool, do you not know who this is?"

"Er … no … should I? Who is she and—"

"She's needed in surgery," Anna blurted to the older man, ignoring the blathering of the younger one. "Penetration of the left lung and outer heart membrane. Boy has moments to live. Other senior is already in surgery."

"This way, Arcanist Stone."

The younger man swallowed. "Did you say *Stone*?"

But Anna and the older man left him behind as they raced to the portal room.

"I came to you because she is not always in her office," Anna explained. She could have run up herself but hadn't wanted to risk it.

"Glad you did, Arcanist Stone. Senior Arcaneologist Ning is hosting foreign healers in the laboratorium on the topic of dissection," he said as they skidded to a halt in a spacious high-ceilinged and black-stone room filled with nothing but torches and barely visible oval etchings. He lit his palm up with airy light, slapped a particular portal rune, and blurted his name, which Anna did not catch as she was too in her head. A portal flared to life, from which *thwoomed* a sharp wind, rustling their robes. The pair stepped through, emerged in a hall, and raced on. Between marble busts and paintings and statues, Anna glimpsed the city below through castle windows.

They barged in through Ning's giant doors into the round inner sanctum with its glass-domed ceiling and desk, and shot on through another pair of doors that had them navigating a series of rooms before finally stepping into a wide and bleak room filled with bodies under gray sheets. Surrounding one of these bodies, lit by ancient floating bronze torch lamps, was a slew of purple- and turquoise-robed warlocks, each wearing a shiny guest sash made of white silk. Men and women from various kingdoms looked over at Anna and the attendant.

Ning emerged from amongst the group wearing her usual gray robe embroidered with the gargoyle over the heart. In one hand she held steel shears and the other a bloody scalpel. Behind her lay a large man, chest open with a steel implement. "Who *dares* intrude when I specifically warned—" She halted upon spotting Anna, almond eyes narrowing.

"Left lung vertically pierced by spear and outer chamber north aortal pierced by spear tip," Anna said as she hurried over, the man excusing himself behind her. "Vertical impalement above the left shoulder blade. Internal bleeding. The boy has moments and requires—"

"—surgery of the lung and heart humors. Yes, yes, girl, I can hear that plain. Where's your—"

"—senior's in surgery at Mercy."

An olive-skinned man with spectacles tilted his head. "Is that *the* Anna Atticus Stone?" he asked in a thick Tiberran accent.

"Is she not a dual-wielder of healing?" a woman asked in a Sierran accent.

"None other," Ning said, tossing the scalpel into the open chest cavity. "And that she is. But don't think *too* highly of her. This one—" Ning nodded at Anna like she had nodded at countless other students who had disappointed her over the years. "—hit her ceiling at the 6th." She sighed as she also tossed the shears into the chest cavity. "You lot wanted to see the academy. Well then, I suggest you keep your aprons on as we're about to perform heart surgery."

* * *

"How long have they been at it now?" Headmaster Bowbrick asked in his gravelly voice, joining Anna in the dimly lit hall outside Surgery Three.

Anna stood to greet the man. "Five hours straight, Headmaster."

The tall man idly stroked his long beard. "This is the Abrandian boy?"

"Yes, sir. Eighteen, father deceased, mother in Abrandia. I have already dispatched a messenger to alert her, with the offer of a multi-hop teleport if she chooses to come, but from the boy's own account, I don't anticipate a response."

"At academy expense, of course."

"Er … yes."

"I did not mean that as a judgment. It is what it is."

"Yes, Headmaster."

The old man placed his hands behind his back as he stared thoughtfully at the pair of doors, beyond which could be seen the flicker of bright arcane lamplight, typical of surgery. "I have prepared a black letter scroll in case of the worst. I hope I do not have to deliver it." He looked down at his shoes and sighed. "There's going to be an inquiry, Anna."

"Of course."

"By all accounts, you were performing your duties as expected. But there has been an accusation against a student. It seems the Black Eagle saw him nudge the spear toward the victim."

"I failed in this regard, Headmaster. I judged the spear to be falling well clear of—"

"And that is corroborated by student witnesses who saw the spear change course during the descent." He shrugged. "Do not fault yourself, Anna. You were doing your duty."

"I should have been more vigilant."

"These things happen. The academy has and always will be a dangerous place. One day, you too will be in my place, preparing a black letter scroll … and perhaps sending it."

Anna looked at the doors. "I have not made up my mind yet, Headmaster."

"And I refuse to give up on you. I need someone worthy of the post to take my place. Someone who can care for the academy during their tenure. Someone who can water its soil and help it grow." He looked at her. "I need a good steward, Anna. As far as I am concerned, there is only one person alive who can truly be that steward, and I am looking at her now."

Anna felt it wrong to receive such high praise when she felt so much guilt over Jonah. "I … I am honored you think so highly of me, Headmaster, but—"

"No buts." He patted her on the shoulder. "No buts, Anna. You are who you are, and nobody will ever be free of sin." He walked past her, only to stop. "The disciplinary committee will want a full report of your recollection."

"I will start on it immediately."

The man nodded before walking off, leaving her alone. Anna was about to walk to the front desk to fetch some parchment and a quill, when the doors burst open, and out streamed attendants and warlocks alike, each sweaty, many mumbling to each other in arcane healing parlance. All nodded or bowed lightly before Anna, muttering, "Arcanist Stone."

"So? How did it go?" Anna asked, annoyed no one was saying anything.

"The senior will be right with you, Arcanist Stone," a young woman said, rubbing puffy-ringed eyes and following after her colleagues.

Ning soon emerged, wiping her brow with a cloth.

Anna opened her palms in a *Well?* fashion.

Ning took her time folding the cloth before giving the barest hint of a smile. "He'll live."

Anna could have hugged her. Instead, she thrust an open palm forth. Ning stared at it before taking it, and the women shook hands.

* * *

"I did no such thing, child," Anna replied, pinning a long-sleeved linen shirt to a drying line. The pair stood atop their home, the tower, surrounded by crenellations that allowed defenders to attack an invading force. Judging by the random pockmarks on the outer wall, such a thing had repeatedly happened in the tower's history. The sky was sunny and cloudless overhead, and birds warbled below, flitting between bare-branched trees. A perfect day for a bit of laundry. "The disciplinary committee—"

"—hangs on every word of yours!"

"—took into account the word of *all* the witnesses. That included you, your classmates, myself, and Black Eagle Bladesong."

Thia kept hold of her head, shaking it. "You don't understand …"

Anna plucked another shirt from the laundry pile and turned to her daughter, folding her arms. "Then explain it to me."

"The academy is all Ralfie had!"

"The academy was all Jonah had as well, and Ralf wanted to take that from him with one spiteful action."

"You got him expelled because you don't want him around me."

"What I want or do not want had no relevance in the proceedings—"

"Horse crap!"

"Don't you use such language with your mother. Come back here! Thia!"

But Thia marched to the top hatch and, careful of her belly, awkwardly climbed down the ladder without acknowledging her mother, leaving Anna flustered.

"I do not understand you, girl," Anna muttered to herself, returning to hanging laundry. If only Thia had had the strength to hang in there, she would have been on student council. In Anna's opinion, Thia had the wherewithal to potentially become head of student council one day—if she applied herself. "And that's the trick, isn't it?" Anna added.

She moved on to hanging clean robes—today had been her turn to do the family laundry, with Thomas and Thia taking theirs in the quints prior. If there was one thing the family did well, it was splitting some responsibilities. Anna had insisted, though sometimes secretly mused about servants during menial tasks such as this. Alas, what with the gambling debt, that was impossible now.

After making sure every piece of clothing had proper spacing and saw some sun on the wide top of the tower, Anna nodded to herself in satisfaction and climbed down the ladder, closing the hatch above her. The tower top was fortified with strong arcanery, so she had no concerns about someone coming in from above.

The family used to do laundry arcanely, with Thomas using his fire element to dry everything, but the clothes had oft been stiff and smelled like charring. The open air did a far better job—weather permitting.

"She go to her room?" Anna asked Niterra Bladesong, who sat having her morning tea at the table, a ray of sun streaming on a *Blackhaven Herald* before her.

Niterra nodded without looking up. "That boy trouble."

"I am not sure if he would be more trouble in the academy or outside it."

"That boy trouble wherever he go. We see him again today."

Anna poured herself a cup of tea and sat across from Niterra. "Mmm," she toned, taking a sip, enjoying the flavor of pine needles and honey and lemon, a perfect balance of tartness and sweetness. Ralf Turman, the secret father of her grandchild, would still be around, albeit at the excavation, tutored by a master warlock.

Niterra let go of the herald, allowing it to roll itself back up with a *shloop*. "What will you say?" she asked, leaning back, cup in hand.

"To Ottentus? The full account of what happened."

"That the boy know he send killing blow. You must say this, or I will."

"The boy's intent will certainly be the prime topic of discussion."

"Thia say she come too. Want to talk to boy."

Anna, eyes on the dust particles slowly tumbling about in a ray of sunlight, only nodded.

"You want work on *Combataoraporta*?"

"Combat Portal can wait," Anna replied. "I plan on finishing the Area Spell Void scroll today and delivering it." They were expected at the excavation at the sixth evening bell, after supper, giving her all day to complete a task she had been working on ever since taking on the assignment. Most of the rest of her spare time had been spent in the bowels of the armory studying the nuance of Thesper's tendril weavings.

"I make that scroll once. Sell it high price to armory. Never again. Too difficult. Too dangerous. I drained whole day. Unable to complete duty." She used the table as a support as she stood with a groan. "Now I go play guard."

"If I run into trouble, I will be sure to ask you."

The old woman grunted as she tottered off. Anna wanted to thank her again for watching her daughter, but she had already done it so many times that Niterra only scowled in response now.

For a time, Anna enjoyed the silence, sipping on her tea now and then, watching the ray of sun crawl across the table. She enjoyed its warmth on her bare hand, the aroma of the tea, the warbling birds, and the distant gong of nine morning city bells, muted through the stained-glass window of the tower. The peace helped with the piercing whine of the headache she had yet to shake. She must have taken quite the knock indeed when that stairwell exploded. Time had dulled it somewhat, as it had the nightmares, but not completely. She still had puffy eyes and longed for the peace she felt in that moment to enter her sleep.

After she took her last sip, she cleared the table and went through a door and hallway that took her to her office. The sun greeted her there too, this time at a forty-five-degree angle. It streamed across a leather-inset desk, on top of which sat an eagle-feather quill in an inkwell alongside a single document—the vellum scroll she had picked out at the armory, the corners of which were secured with small lead bricks, its intricate and golden margin artistry shining in the sun. The rest of the office looked like a tornado had come through. Scrolls were tightly packed into cubicles, and thick books were jammed into shelves as well as on top and teetering in piles all about. Yet as disorganized as it all looked, Anna knew where everything was. She just didn't have the time or the energy to deal with it.

The room smelled of parchment and history. Every time she came in, she imagined the tower's predecessors doing the same thing—coming to this room and studying or writing or enchanting scrolls. She enjoyed continuing that beautifully lonely tradition of old, a tradition reserved only for the current owners of the tower.

She sat down on a cushioned spindle-back chair and smoothed the parchment before her. Three-quarters of it was filled with neatly written script, each word infused with potent arcane energies that, when combined into a verbal reading, would unleash the mighty power of the 18th degree *Voidusarcanatis*—Area Spell Void. As was her habit, she went over the scroll as a whole, starting with the instructions she had written for the potential future caster—the pronunciation, the myriad shortcut symbols and what they meant, the gestural forms distilled into mere words, the complex thought process that the reader had to be handheld through, and how all of it synergized into an effect. Every scroll was different and dependent on the caster's ability to translate the arcane tongue into a readable form that could ideally be triggered by almost anyone. And the higher in degree one went, the more difference and complexity one saw.

There were standards of wording, of course—such and such gesture written in such and such a way, for example, sometimes replaced entirely by one runic symbol if the gesture was repetitive enough. The same with thoughts and pronunciation. The remainder—unsettled terms, interpretations based on language changes, optimized thought processes—were subject to fierce debate amongst arcaneologists.

But that was how the arcane arts grew—and it was also how it withered, particularly with knowledge that fell by the wayside or became too complex for the next generation to manage. Allowing change thus had its drawbacks. Regardless, how all the parts of a scroll added up to a whole was always left to the caster.

Once Anna refamiliarized herself with the work of the scroll and settled on which portion she would work on next, she dipped her nib into the inkwell, brushed it against the edge to draw off the excess ink, and set to writing the words, *Ia deklarus iasafa dominus au tio dominia bi forsisi ei exio au o aformentedia dimensiona del o ancro arcan enerva*, which translated to, "I declare myself master of this domain by forcing a hole of the aforementioned dimensions in the sacred arcane ether."

Once that phrase had precisely and neatly been written, she set the quill aside, took a deep breath, and readied for the most critical aspect— the infusion of arcanery. With thoughts of the entire framework of Area Spell Void in mind, she began the hour-long ritual of the spell itself by first incanting the deceptively simple words of the Create Scroll spell— *"Infusio skrul,"* which would allow the arcanery of Area Spell Void to be infused into the vellum. Then she raised a hand and went through the complicated motions of the entire Area Spell Void ritual.

At the crucial moment that required the thought process of the sentence she had written, she leaned forth, pressed a finger on top of the first word, and drew her finger along the sentence as she continued with the arcane incantation of the spell, *"Ia deklarus iasafa dominus au tio dominia bi forsisi ei exio au o aformentedia dimensiona del o ancro arcan enerva."* This was one of the trickiest parts of crafting a scroll, for what she had written were the instructions to the spell, whereas the words she spoke were the incantation to the spell itself. The purpose was to inject a small portion— a thought process—of that incantation into the written words. If one's intellect strayed by one thought or word, causing the slightest mispronunciation, the spell could misfire when the reader got to that portion, sometimes resulting in catastrophe. Most casters could manage one or two, *maybe* three words at a time. Anna could do a whole sentence, saving precious time.

During the casting, she felt the continual cool and immense draw of arcane stamina depart her soul, amplified and buttressed by the scion— a great aid in such marathon efforts. It buzzed in her pocket as each word flashed in sequence, indicating a successful casting—one of multiple castings of the same spell, performed sentence after sentence, sometimes even on a single critical word. Luckily, Anna did not have to finish the ritual, and halted it then and there. Beginning a scroll was the easiest part as one only needed to infuse the very first part of a spell. *Finishing* a scroll was a whole other matter, and the longer the spell took, the longer the scroll took. Many a half-finished scroll sat in the archives, or in a warlock's office, waiting for someone to step in and conclude it. Yet few casters enjoyed finishing someone else's work and sharing the credit.

With the task complete and that sentence infused into the scroll, Anna contemplated the line that would follow. After a long time of organizing her thoughts and the precise wording to be used, she picked up the quill and readied to do the whole ritual over again.

* * *

Anna slid the scroll, tied with a crimson ribbon, across the desk. Mertha, Senior Keeper of the Scrolls, gingerly picked it up with both hands as if it were a delicate treasure.

"I have been looking forward to this very much," the old woman said.

"As have they," she whispered, giving the slightest nudge backward.

Dawdling behind her, pretending to be busy with nearby shelves despite a whole room of them, was the entire staff of apprentice scroll keepers, young men and women eager to see and hear about *the* Anna Atticus Stone's workmanship.

"Are you all right, Grandmage?" the woman whispered. "Surely the casting must have taken a toll."

"It was ... quite the challenge," Anna wheezed, trying to force the nausea to subside. There were two drawbacks to crafting scrolls — the effort was physically exhausting, and, for some unknown reason that had to do with the way arcanery interacted with the sacred ether, arcane stamina renewed at one-*tenth* the usual rate after crafting a scroll. Meditation did not aid this rate, nor did the effect go away until the caster got at least seven quality hours of sleep. In that sense, crafting scrolls was dangerous, especially at the higher degrees — and especially during wartime, when scrolls became as scarce as mercy. Hence the increased values involved. Anna, having pushed herself to finish the scroll today as it was the deadline she had given herself, had nearly depleted her reserves even teleporting to the Black Castle. None of it had helped her headache, which raged to the point of wincing.

Should have walked, Anna thought.

Mertha placed the scroll before her, ceremonially untied the ribbon, and unfurled the vellum. She pointed at lead paperweights in the shapes of miniature crest shields, which hovered over and touched down on the corners. Then she held her hands together before her so that the sleeves of her robe covered them, giving her the appearance of a sage. "*Un vun asperio aurum enchantus,*" she incanted, and began to silently read whilst analyzing the tendril geometries.

Anna found this scholarly way to cast Reveal a pleasant visual. But feeling peaky and wanting to lie down, she also wished the woman would have done the assessment on her own time. Alas, too much money was involved, and the whole thing felt ritualistic anyhow. The senior keeper, the apprentices in the rear—none of them moved. They barely even breathed, waiting for the judgment to come down.

At long last, just as Anna was going to ask for a cup of water, the woman closed her eyes and took a deep and meditative breath, allowing the apprentices to do the same. They stirred, sharing meaningful looks.

"Arcanist—Grandmage—Stone. This—" A hand slipped out from the wide cuffs, hovering five fingers over the writing. "—is one of the *finest* works I have ever had the privilege of seeing. And that is doing it a disservice, for this is no mere common work. This is the work of a *master.*"

"Ah, my dear woman, you speak too highly of my talents. I have a long way to go before I—"

"And you sell your efforts far too short, Arcanist Stone. This—this work here—is a wonder. The wording you have chosen, the phraseology, the sheer *clarity*—" She shook her head. "The way your mind works, how you craft and place pieces into a whole … it is simply marvelous."

"Yes, well, er … thank you."

"And I hope you will forgive me for saying so, Grandmage, but you simply *must* take that headmistress position. The kingdom needs your intellect, your skill, your judgment. Warlock-*kind* needs it. I know you would push your arcanists to a whole other degree—pun intended."

Anna pressed her lips together. "Mmm." She did not take too well to being pushed into things she was not ready for.

Mertha stepped aside. "You buzzards, come see what true focus can achieve."

And like buzzards they did indeed descend on the parchment, feasting on it with their eyes as if it were a carcass. They whispered things like, "Look at the way she simplifies the lensing effect," and, "The tendril geometries are so smooth and precise," and "With the right pronunciation guidance, a *child* could trigger this scroll," amongst other arcaneological jargon.

While they fawned over the work, giving quick sidelong looks of awe at Anna, Mertha withdrew a piece of rectangular parchment marked with the royal emblem and the armory crest, and wrote a number. She signed it with neat and loopy script and slid it forward.

Anna picked up the note. "This … this is quintuple the stated amount. Perhaps a little too generous—"

"A master work like that is perhaps seen once in a generation. Besides, I want this to be the beginning of a long and fruitful relationship." She leaned forth, whispering, "*You* are the future."

"Thank you. I am honored," Anna mumbled, still staring at the ridiculous sum of 20,000 crowns before her.

"Please know, Grandmage, that you are more than welcome to drop off your scroll work at any time, day or night, year-round. It will *always* be accepted and paid for appropriately."

"Thank you." Anna tucked the treasury note into an empty pocket. It was a relief to know she could make money in this manner, but she would also have to be extremely choosey lest she find herself dueling for her or her daughter's life with zero stamina.

When she glanced back at the apprentices, every one of them was staring at her with unadulterated awe. Then something interesting happened—Mertha bowed. Seeing her lead, the apprentices did the same. A silence befell the room as they held that bow, and Anna, judging by the way one of the girls whispered to another girl, "Can you believe this?" suspected they had never performed such an honor before.

"I am honored," Anna repeated to them, and walked out in a daze. She continued walking toward home, feeling strangely light, albeit still a little nauseous from the repeated casting. A scroll like that she could maybe do once or twice a year, and next time she would stagger the work so it did not drain so much stamina, leaving her exposed like this.

On the way, she stopped by the Black Bank and handed in the promissory note, paying off the entirety of the 20,000-crown castle estate taxes. That left Thomas's 50,000-crown gambling debt, and she'd put a huge dent into that if she could repair Thesper. The remainder Thomas could chip away at doing odd warlock jobs.

"And maybe laundry for a year on top as atonement," Anna muttered as she left the bank, chortling as she imagined him grumbling atop their tower quint after quint.

Winter darkness had descended by the time she got home for a supper of roasted spiced lamb, ginger-buttered potatoes, and steaming peppered carrots, all covered in a sumptuous mirko gravy, and all made by Thomas. The family feasted alongside Niterra, with Anna whispering to Thomas the amount she had been paid. He went wide-eyed, shot to his feet, and raised a toast to his "brilliant wife." Thia smiled for the first time in what felt like forever, and for a tender moment, the family felt as one—despite Thomas having yet to speak more than a word or two to his daughter.

The most incredible thing? As if he had read her mind, Thomas offered to slave away for whatever remained regardless of how things went with Thesper, *and* he offered to do laundry and cook meals at home.

"As restitution," he whispered, winking at her.

"Have you been yapping with Ning?" Anna whispered back whilst Thia and Niterra had a lively conversation about Nodian Endyear traditions, which apparently involved the sacrifice of snakes and scorpions.

"I have *not*. Why do you ask?"

"Nothing." She smiled at him.

"Oh my, I haven't seen that cheeky smile in some time. Young lady, we might have to have a talk about such cheekiness this eve in the bedroom—"

"Ew, you two," Thia said.

Thomas ballooned, only to catch one of Anna's eyebrows rising at him. He promptly cleared his throat, nodded as if to say, *Fair enough*, and resumed eating—though not without throwing Anna a sly wink, making her blush.

Anna took it all in. The aroma of food, the warmth of family, the security of having a Black Eagle watching over her daughter, who had even cracked a jest at her father's expense, something about him ogling her mother most inappropriately, which Thomas again took in stride. And Anna allowed herself to take solace from the fact she would be a grandmother and Thomas a grandfather. She took this all in knowing how fleeting it would be, for shortly after supper Niterra—on account of Anna having expended her stamina crafting a scroll—would teleport them to the foot of Mount Barrow, where they were expected to meet Ottentus at the excavation.

For now, though, she allowed herself the pleasure of simple joy.

THE SECOND SLAB

"Ah, and it is your priceless map that will finally allow us to start on the third shaft, yes?" Ottentus said, rubbing his hands gleefully, his usual Franterran accent most pronounced today, with its harsh *z*'s in place of *s*'s, among others. "But I have to ask, Arcanist Stone, why is there no more on the subject? Is the archive not more … how can I put this in such a way that does not lend offense to your kingdom … is the archive not more organized?"

"It's all the documentation we could find on this particular subject," Anna replied.

"At least in the spot we checked," Thomas added. "There's a treasure trove of other documentation there that could be pertinent."

"Surely the authorities—perhaps even your dear friend the king— could be persuaded to allow me to visit these archives …" He drummed the fingertips of each hand against the other, hairless brow bouncing. "… yes?"

Thomas gave a sheepish chortle. "I am afraid they do not allow foreigners access, Ottentus. It's a miracle *we* were even allowed inside. And their checks are thorough, so don't even think about sneaking in or bewitching me," he added, laughing at his obvious jest.

But the man did not so much as smile. Instead he flicked a finger at a workbench and telekinetically procured an expensive and rare piece of Ohmish bronze workmanship—a magnifying glass. He snatched it from the air without looking and held it above the map, which was a detailed—and expensive—copy of the original, made by a resident artisan of the Archives.

"Ach, this third chamber is deeper than we had thought, yes?"

Thomas expelled air through flapping lips. "*Much* deeper."

Anna said nothing, for she had already suspected as much long before laying eyes on the map. The original triangular formation of candles depicted on that first slab door showed that the lowest candle was noticeably lower—at least when factoring in the proportional distances between all three candles.

"Was there anything else in the archives on the excavation?" Ottentus pressed. "Perhaps a means to get to the other chambers quickly?"

Thomas shook his head. "We searched but the documentation on the build itself was either hidden or misplaced."

"Or lost," Ottentus muttered, sucking air through his teeth in annoyance. "And let us not even mention theft and plunder over the eons ..."

Thomas tapped the lowest chamber on the map. "Have you considered teleporting directly in?"

Ottentus only scoffed, as if the answer was obvious.

"I suppose even *if* you managed it, you could end up getting blown up on the spot ..."

While the men discussed the subject, Anna noticed her daughter fidgeting as she glanced about in search of something—or more likely, some*one*. Niterra caught Anna's eye and the women shared a knowing look before both returned to their tasks—Niterra as watchful guard, and Anna as arcaneologist, or at least playing the part for now.

"That depth could mean anything," Thomas said.

"It could be a hidden Rivican chamber," Anna offered, folding her arms. "Perhaps a chamber the master builder wanted to protect."

"Perhaps even his tomb," Thomas threw in.

"That is my thinking as well," Ottentus said, rubbing his hairless chin with the bronze edge of the magnifying glass. "Or it could be a magma chamber, yes?" and he glanced about the chamber they were in. "It is possible this entire mountain could be an ancient dormant volcano."

Thomas glanced about in the same manner, grimacing with skepticism. "One without a caldera? Without porous rock or obsidian?"

Ottentus returned to examining the document. "Certainty will come when my diggers reach the chamber."

"How long do you suppose that will take?"

"At that depth?" Ottentus tossed the magnifying glass onto the map. "Months." He sighed and used both hands to squeeze husband and wife on the upper arm. "Come, come. Let me show you what fruits our efforts have wrought in the mean."

He led them past men moving large carts full of rocks and on down a second passageway that diverged sharply from the main. The sound of chiseling and pickaxe striking got louder as they neared. At last, they found themselves standing before a second gigantic slab of a door engraved with runes.

But it was not the door that Anna and Thia stared at, rather a certain boy who had spotted them and was obviously trying to hide behind a huge workman with a wheelbarrow.

"Ah, there is my young apprentice. Come here, boy!" Ottentus called. "I know you hear me, son. Stop playing coy and make yourself known, you are embarrassing me."

"Stupid oaf can't even hide me right," Ralf hissed, elbowing the workman aside. Despite the man being three times Ralf's weight, the man mumbled an apology and skittered off, barely able to keep his wheelbarrow from toppling in his haste to get away. Ralf sauntered over whilst repeatedly smoothing his hair with one hand and his soot-stained robe with the other.

"Greetings," he said, chin held imperiously high.

"I must confess that my young apprentice here has been most helpful of late. I am very grateful that the academy has given permission for him to perform some of his studies in the field in lieu of the classroom. He has been most diligent in keeping his nose in those books, pestering me about that which he does not understand. And he is learning to command the workers, sparing me such efforts. He is doing the academy an honor. His contributions have been a true *proata mentora*, yes?"

Anna, suspecting she knew what had happened, brought her hands together. "I am afraid I have no idea what you are talking about, Ottentus."

Ottentus furrowed his hairless brow as he glanced between her and Ralf. "Forgive me, but I was under the impression you have generously given my young apprentice leave from the academy to spend extra time here. Is this not the way of it?"

"Mr. Turman was expelled from the academy for gravely wounding a fellow classmate."

Ottentus gaped. "Surely that is a jest ..."

"I am afraid that it is not."

Ottentus turned to face the boy, who dropped his head. "Get. Out. Of. My. *Sight*, boy. I will deal with you later."

"Yes, sir," Ralf mumbled, and dragged his feet as he schlepped away. He glanced back once—and flashed a manipulative grin.

"I want to speak to him," Thia blurted.

"As a concerned school colleague should," Ottentus replied. "Maybe you can talk some female sense into the daft boy. Go on, young lady. And feel free to—" He made a mocking strangling motion. "—thrash him a little, yes?" He laughed at his own jest, one Anna did not find particularly amusing. Something felt off to her, but she couldn't quite put her finger on what it was, especially because the headache had reared up like a neighing mare, as if sensing its place of birth. She made eye contact with Niterra, who understood her meaning to follow Thia.

"Like a Canterran mastiff, that woman," Ottentus said. "Overly protective and with a big bite."

"We wouldn't need her if it weren't for the threats," Thomas countered. "Not to mention the blasted curse."

"Ah, yes, the curse. We speak of that later, yes? Come, come, let us examine the findings so far."

Anna flashed Thomas a *What have you been telling him?* look.

"What's with her and that boy, anyway?" Thomas asked, ignoring Anna. "I know how easily things can go awry in class when it comes to spell casting, but I don't want her being friends with someone who was expelled for attempted harm. See the way he looks at people? Like we're prey? Kid gives me the creeps."

Anna almost told him the truth, that Ralf was the father of their coming grandchild, but held her tongue on account of Thia making her swear that she did not, under any circumstances, want Thomas to know who the father was. Anna, sensing how Thomas might fly off into an irrational rage—or even harm the boy—honored that request. Thomas did not even seem to suspect the boy, likely because his vision was clouded by a dream of his daughter eventually marrying a proper boy of reputable station. An arcaneologist, or magistrate, or scribe, or healer …

They stepped up to the slab with Ottentus, who gesticulated at the entirety of the door. "Incredible, yes? Absolutely incredible. The runes are defensive, as expected, which your husband and I eventually solved, Arcanist Stone. But these lines here in the center have managed to elude our understanding."

Thomas rubbed his chin. "A runic zig-zag, perhaps a sequence of some sort. Anna, what say you?"

The two men looked to her. She cocked her head, already deep in thought. "The rune is cubic in nature, indicating dimensions. I suspect it's a tunnel. What interests me is that rune there—" She pointed at two matching squiggles, one substantially larger than the other. "That circle represents a head, those lines arms and legs. I think these two runes are human forms, which in my estimation means the entire runic sequence—" She made a circle with her palm. "—represents the spell Shrink."

The 9th degree spell was now only taught for exams—all that was expected of students these days was for them to go through the motions. As with many spells, the knowledge on how to make oneself tiny had been lost just before Arinthian's time, around the year 1452. It was a period scholars called The Third Horror on account of mass deaths, attributed to a harrowing plague of unknown origin said to have slowly turned people inside out.

Unless knowledge of the spell was somehow retrieved, it was only a matter of time until it was booted out of the standard spell set. It was theorized some scrolls of the spell still remained, locked in private collections or forgotten in old chests. But even if that were the case, it would take a master-work that covered critical missing portions for the spell to stand a chance at resuscitation.

Anna, and other scholars, believed there was only one real way to retrieve the full complement of that knowledge—and that was getting it from the library in the mystical plane known as Ley. Not a trivial problem considering the Leyans withdrew from the world after Atrius Arinthian vanquished Occulus, closing themselves off since. Hence why The Hall of Sacred Doors was such a big deal. If that connection could be reestablished, it could change arcanery itself … and thus the very course of history.

"Shrink, huh? I feared such a thing," Ottentus said, shaking his head. "This is most disappointing news indeed."

Thomas shook his head right alongside. "I suppose we should have guessed that spell expectations would be quite different two thousand years ago." He glanced between Ottentus and the slab. "But surely you can manage a basic version of it, Ottie …"

"Alas, Shrink is a most confounding spell, the nuance of which has eluded me thus far. In that sense I am as average as a student attempting it for an exam. And forgive me, but I cannot risk suddenly becoming large in the confines of a miniature tunnel."

"Of course, of course, forgive me for the assumption. Where is the entrance to this miniature tunnel, anyway?"

They glanced about, with Ottentus barking orders at nearby workers to look for anything unusual in the rock.

Anna once more merely cocked her head. "You needn't bother," she declared after a long think analyzing the runic patterns. "The slab itself hides the entrance. This puzzle is composed of three parts." She pointed. "The defensive portion, the portion that solves the opening of a small door-within-a-door, and a way to get inside the tunnel to retrieve what is on the other end."

"The third puzzle piece being the Shrink spell," Thomas muttered.

"Yes. And the actual entrance a shrunk person would enter should be that square near the center."

Ottentus stepped up beside her. "So the opening sequence we observe in these runes here—" He pointed at the relevant impressions. "—you have translated as accounting to that square, meaning the little door, and not the slab as a whole, yes?"

Anna, sensing a rhetorical question, gave a nearly imperceptible nod.

Ottentus smacked his gums as his bald head bounced up and down. "Yes, I see it. I see it. Well deduced, Arcanist Stone. Well deduced indeed. And most astute. This is why I have teamed up with the *both* of you. And what a team we make, yes?"

Thomas wagged a finger. "But even if we manage to open that small door, we still don't have a way to get inside without the ability to safely cast a Shrink spell."

The group fell into thoughtful silence.

"I could go on a quest to find a Shrink scroll," Ottentus said after a time. "But it could take months, if not longer."

"I may have a quicker solution," Anna offered.

Ottentus impatiently revolved a hand as if spinning wool. "Please share your idea, Arcanist Stone."

"I'm not sure it would work but I could fetch it and try. Before I do, you mentioned the protective runes and that you solved them. What do they summon if activated?"

"Another guardian. That is my best guess. If it's another golem, I will pay to bring back that captain again."

"Then I would rather hold off on solving it tonight, if you do not mind."

"She just finished crafting a scroll," Thomas explained, earning him another *Why did you tell him that?* look from Anna, which he also ignored.

"You underestimate me, young Anna Atticus Stone." Upon seeing the reproving look on her face, Ottentus *tsked* at himself. "Oh, but you are not as young as you look. This I forget, yes? Then again, you can always lend me the scion and I will be young too." He laughed, yet Anna once more found one of his jests unfunny, especially because it involved the scion. This was the first indication of him having any interest in it— but that was always how it began.

"I tease, I tease. You let Uncle Ottie worry about the guardian, Arcanist Stone. Now please do go on and fetch this thing that may help us, yes?"

Anna, feeling a bit defensive, wanted to call him out on using the word *fetch* due to its implication.

Ottentus seemed to pick up on this. "Ach, forgive me. I need to learn to be more eloquent in Solian. My mind—" He knocked twice against his temple with a knuckle, making a clucking noise with his tongue. "—it sometimes reverts to male Franterran thinking, which can be as crude as a dockside tavern, yes? I apologize most sincerely for my ill manner and inconsiderate jests, Arcanist Stone."

Anna noticed he was struggling a little with the Solian language today, his accent thicker than usual. Ottentus was odd like that—when he was in deep concentration, his language skills suffered. She suspected it was because he thought in his native Franterran tongue, and thus accepted his apology with a nod.

"I am most relieved that you can look past my many faults, Arcanist Stone." The old Franterran looked on with an almost teenage hope.

"Very well then, I shall return shortly," she declared, and strode off. After all, she was rabidly curious about the puzzle, not to mention tonight would be a good time to open the slab as she would be busy with the academy tomorrow.

A ways up the tunnel she passed Thia and Ralf, who were in a hissing match that went quiet upon spotting her. Niterra glanced at Anna and nodded, telling Anna all was under control. But before she could ask Thia if everything was all right, her daughter folded her arms and spat, "I'm *fine*, Mom. Could you please give us some privacy?"

"I'll be back shortly," Anna grudgingly said, and moved on. Once outside, she teleported to the academy, padded through its empty halls, quiet in the evening hours of a study day, and stepped into her office. As usual, Mopey the gargoyle sat slumped in a corner of the desk, looking as grumpy as if he were stuck in the rain without shelter.

"Need a favor from you," she said, picking him up. He looked at her and scowled. "And if you do it for me, I will do *you* a favor. So think about what it is you want. Do you understand?"

Mopey's beady little gargoyle eyes narrowed.

"Something tells me you understand. Come on. It'll be an adventure."

She held him by his big belly without him putting up too much of a fuss, though he did try to free his wings. "What do you need your wings for when you're too heavy to fly?" Anna asked, readjusting her grip as she walked him to the Stairs of the Crescent Moon. "You can't even float seeing as you're practically a lead brick."

Mopey curled his lip, folded his arms, and looked away.

"Anyway, this will be fun. Now hold on for a ride—*impetus peragro!*" She vanished and reappeared with a *thwomp*, conscious of her still critically low stamina reserves from the Craft Scroll casting. After checking Mopey was all right—he did seem a little dizzy, head roving about as if drunk—she walked back to the excavation, with Ralf and Thia once more falling silent upon her approach.

Anna tried not to think about grabbing the boy by the scruff and forcing him to answer her questions with the 12th degree Compel Truth spell, choosing to instead focus on something constructive, like the history of the dead Shrink spell and how that pertained to the challenge ahead. It yielded a nugget.

"I thought of something else," she said upon walking up to Ottentus and Thomas. "Shrink was dying in his era—" She nodded at the runic slab, referring to the master builder Vilnius Vivictus. "—and he was the sort who would have found it a test of skill to be able to competently cast the spell."

"On this I agree," Ottentus said. He looked at the miniature gargoyle. "Is that what I think it is? An ancient animated beast?"

"His name is Mopey and he's a bit grumpy, but he might be up for exploring on our behalf."

"Excellent thinking, Arcanist Stone. And I did not even know they made them so small." Ottentus stuck two fingers of each hand in his mouth and whistled sharply. Then, with a brief fluid gesture across his neck, he boomed with an amplified voice, "Everybody out!" He flicked a finger across his throat to kill Amplify and made a shooing motion with both hands at Anna and Thomas. "Husband and wife ought to depart as well. I cannot predict what may happen once the guardian is summoned."

"Wait until we're clear, please," Anna said, and turned to walk off, only to realize Thomas wasn't coming.

Her husband folded his arms. "I'm staying."

Anna flipped a hand that mimed, *Are you crazy? Do you know how dangerous this might be?*

"You have to let me have my fun too. Go on and make sure Thia's protected. I'll be fine."

Anna swallowed, fearful for her husband. But it was only fair, seeing as he had to deal with the danger she was in throughout their marriage.

And he was a relatively competent warlock, though not nearly as seasoned as she was when it came to battle.

Anna placed an expectant gaze upon Ottentus.

"Worry not, Arcanist Stone. This mighty warlock here—" He tapped his chest with an open palm. "—will protect your husband, yes?"

Thomas grimaced at this and turned his back on the both of them.

"You be careful, Thomas," she said.

He flapped a hand. "Yeah, yeah."

Anna walked off with a sigh. She found Thia and Ralf and Niterra already outside, the former pair standing with folded arms and looking away from each other. A slew of workmen drank water by the main tent, jesting about what was going to happen.

Anna looked at Ralf.

"I have nothing to say to you," he spat. "You took my only home away, and now you're turning my future wife against me."

"We're *not* marrying," Thia hissed. "That's the *last* thing that will ever happen. Do you understand that, you vicious little fiend?"

"We'll see."

Anna was about to roar at him that how dare he presume such a thing, when there came the *crack* of a monstrous explosion from within the excavation. As everyone else hit the ground, Anna and Niterra reflexively summoned their shields of lightning and air. A plume of dust billowed forth from the entrance, consuming everything in its path. Anna crouched behind her shield, which covered her and Thia. As the dust cloud rolled over them, she couldn't help but fear the worst for Thomas.

The moment the rumbling subsided and the air calmed, Anna thrust Mopey into Thia's hands. "Hold him and stay with Niterra. I'm going after your father." She sprinted into the tunnel, lighting her palm along the way as the blast had blown out all the torches, and soon arrived at a giant pile of rubble.

"Thomas!" she shouted. The only reply was the trickle of stones and pebbles. "Thomaaaaaas!"

A portion of the rubble moved—a *large* portion, sloughing off a bulbous surface that steadily rose. Anna, breathing rapidly, backtracked, hands at the ready. When the rubble fell off, she saw fur. Then the creature rose up on its hind legs, opened massive jaws, and roared.

Anna found herself facing a twenty-foot bear.

Except this time, it was not made of stone, but looked very much like a normal bear, albeit a gigantic one with demonic teeth and claws. It snuffled a couple of times and barked—or that was what it sounded like, the noise more like a horn blast—before dropping to all fours to charge at her.

Anna, acutely conscious of how little stamina she had to play with and that she might need it for healing, slapped her wrists together, roaring, "*Annihilo dio!*" The scion in her pocket flared with a loud buzz as she threw everything she could spare into the spell. Four thick bolts of lightning, amplified mightily by the scion, smashed into the beast, obliterating it on the spot. Again out of reflex, Anna summoned her shield to protect herself from the bits of flying flesh. They slapped into her shield and the surrounding rubble and walls with squishy *sloops* and *splats*, before fading into nothingness—the beast, after all, had been a summoned creature.

Anna didn't miss a beat, shouting, "Thomas! Thomaaaaaas!"

There came a *thwomp* from her right as Ottentus appeared.

"Where's my husband?" Anna snapped, rage building at the ineptness the so-called master warlock was displaying.

"There was an unexpected explosion—"

"That is plain as day but does not answer my question, does it! Where is my husband!"

"Let us search for him, yes? Come, come. We move quick."

The pair swept their arms about and large piles of rubble began to telekinetically sift themselves. Anna worked with frantic speed, using up what remained of her stamina, betting it all on simply finding Thomas.

At last, a bloody hand emerged. "Here!" she shouted, shooting to him and scrabbling at the rubble like a rabid cat. Ottentus came to her and helped, telekinetically shoving the whole pile off Thomas in one go. Anna then flipped her husband over, calling his name.

He coughed a cloud of dust, wheezing, "Gods, woman, need you screech my name like a banshee?"

"Oh thank the Unnameables," Anna blurted, squeezing him tightly. "That's the second time in here I thought I lost you." She let go to pat him down. "Are you injured?"

He moved his limbs. "Just a bit sore. What the heck happened?"

Anna looked at Ottentus for an answer.

The man shook his head. "I glimpsed it too late. A hidden pressure plate we missed prior to the summoning, which the bear stepped on just after being summoned, as if that was its entire purpose. It was so unexpected that when the *click* of the trap sounded, there was an almost instant—" He smacked the heels of his palms together. "—*boom!* The plate is hidden under that rubble there, at the initial spawn point. I suspect we had not triggered it because it required the weight of the bear, and we hadn't found it because the arcanery was hidden underneath in the mechanism. A very clever contraption that would have had us defending against a simple bear when in reality it was the explosion we ought to have worried about—"

"I don't care about that! Why didn't you protect him?"

"Arcanist Stone, please, there was no time, only pure reflex. You of all people should understand this, yes?"

Anna, unable to argue with such naked truth, nonetheless scowled her displeasure at her husband being left to fend for himself. At the degrees and complexities involved, Ottentus should have protected him.

"I'll have my workers cordon off the plate. You vanquished the beast, yes? I know it survived the explosion."

Anna ignored the question, the answer to which was rather obvious, and instead helped her husband sit up.

"Feel like I got run over by an ox cart," Thomas mumbled, wincing and rubbing his lower back. "We had our shields up just in case, but I wasn't prepared for the suddenness of it—or the sheer force."

"The good news is the guardian question is settled," Ottentus said, moving to the slab door. "I will now get to work on solving the door-within-a-door puzzle, yes?"

"I'm through trusting his instincts," Anna whispered to Thomas as the man began to mumble to himself about the puzzle. "From now on we rely on each other here, all right?"

Thomas nodded.

She wiped his sooty face with her sleeve. "Oh, Husband, look at the state of you," and she gently drew him into a hug.

He patted her back, whispering, "I'm all right, love. I'm all right …"

"Next time we leave him to deal with the guardian on his own," she added, to which he nodded again.

Anna let go and was startled to find Ottentus standing nearby, staring at her. "I solved it," he said flatly, making her wonder if he had heard her. "Bring the little beast and bring the kids and workers, for we are about to make history, yes?" He turned and walked back to the slab, the center of which was now open with a small stone door.

Thomas nudged Anna along between coughs. "Go on. I'll be fine."

Anna, having lost a lot of faith in Ottentus, almost didn't want to leave her husband's side. Yet he seemed fine, and in truth she was more angry with the incompetence than scared some new beast might emerge. Without another word, she went to fetch everyone.

"Dad all right?" Thia asked, holding a depressed Mopey as she and Ralf waited separately from the workers and Niterra, who looked on from nearby like a shrewd vulture.

"He's fine."

"You sure? Because that was a big blast. Last time we all almost got killed."

"He's just dusting himself off." Anna looked to a scowling Ralf and opened her mouth to snap at him.

"We talked about it," Thia interrupted. "I have made my feelings *abundantly* clear. He is well aware we are not going to marry."

"My daughter has made herself abundantly clear," Anna repeated, more than a hint of steel in her voice. She had never threatened a student before. Then again, this boy no longer *was* a student. "I expect you to give my daughter space."

Ralf, biting his lower lip, only averted his gaze.

She gave her daughter a *I suggest you stay away from him* look, which for once was met with a nod.

Satisfied for now, Anna gathered everyone up and returned, the curious workers muttering amongst themselves as they straggled in tow. Upon reentering the chamber, Ottentus immediately made those workers cordon off the pressure plate with sticks and rope, a task Ralf helped with by bossing the poor wretches about, barking, "Move that rubble first, you fool! And you—tighten that rope up!"

Thia, meanwhile, took one look at the scratches covering her father and the fact that he was repairing the tears in his robe, and said, "Dad *did* almost get blown up, didn't he?" Her face softened toward her father as she held onto a squirming Mopey.

"Nothing of the sort," Thomas blurted, hastily dusting himself off for the umpteenth time. "It was entirely expected."

"That true, Mom?"

But Thomas interrupted. "You ought to have as much faith in your father as you do in your mother, Thia." There was clear hurt in his voice and he avoided eye contact with her.

Anna sighed, not knowing what to say. Now was not the time to start another argument, and things were already threatening to spill over if Ralf so much as *hinted* about marrying Thia. It was a miracle Thomas hadn't caught on about them as it was.

Niterra, looking on, shook her head—not in disapproval, but rather sadness.

"I think he wants to explore or something," Thia muttered, barely able to hold Mopey.

"And exploring is exactly what we had in mind for him," Anna replied, grateful for a distraction. She took Mopey from her daughter and brought him to the slab, where she held him up before the runes. "See this pattern here?" she said to the little creature. "It's a map of the tunnel. There is something at the end of it. If you can fetch it for us, I will grant you whatever wish you desire. Do you understand?"

Mopey blinked at her.

"It doesn't understand you, woman," Ralf snapped, instantly earning himself a snakish hiss from Ottentus, who had raised the back of his hand as if threatening to smack him, which Ralf recoiled away from. With the workers now toiling away at clearing more debris, the pair had joined the group at the slab.

"I apologize for my apprentice's rudeness," the man said. "Please do go on, Arcanist Stone," he pressed, still glaring at Ralf, who had withered like a chastened rat.

Anna placed Mopey into the opening, small enough that the gargoyle had to tuck in his wings. He looked about, bored, before settling into a squat. Anna poked his belly. "Go on. I know you want something. You can tell me what it is. Eh? What is it you want? Point." She pointed at him. "See me pointing? Now you point. We'll start there."

Mopey raised an arm and, to her great surprise, did indeed point. She followed that point down to her pocket. It was clear what Mopey wanted.

The scion.

STEAM

Anna gaped, unable to believe that Mopey, that little beastling, wanted the *one* thing she could not give.

"Surely there must be something else …" she whispered, wilting.

Mopey turned around and folded his arms.

"But what does the scion *mean* to the creature?" Ottentus asked.

Anna was struck by the wise question. "Yes, what does the scion mean to you, Mopey? Come on. Turn around and tell us. Tell us what the scion could *do* for you."

Mopey sat unmoved, as if in thought, before turning his head. He flapped his wings and pointed skyward with a gargoyle finger.

"He wants to fly," Thomas said.

"Could you fly once?" Anna asked. "Is that the problem? You wish to fly again? Or have you never flown and now want to? I think I overwhelmed him with too many questions," she said when the little creature frowned at her, as if he were struggling to understand.

"Do you want to fly?" she asked more clearly.

For the first time ever, Mopey nodded.

"Then I can promise you this. After your quest inside this tunnel, I will take you on a little adventure of flight."

"How exactly do you intend to fulfill that promise?" Thomas whispered.

Anna ignored him. "Do we have a deal?"

Mopey stared at her for a moment before turning about and waddling down the tunnel, making the three warlocks breathe a sigh of relief.

As they waited for the strange little creature to return, the three discussed Mopey's possible history, theorizing he could be a Rivican construct, for some historical engravings suggested the Rivicans had known the secrets of flight. As time passed, Thomas excused himself to "get a breath of fresh air" and to visit the privy, located outside the excavation. The moment he was out of earshot, Thia got into a vicious whisper argument with Ralf. Besides the coming child, it seemed that there were as yet unresolved issues between them. Anna, knowing Ottentus was a scholar in the occult, realized this might be the perfect time to question the boy on that very topic—and see what Ottentus had to say on the matter, what with Ralf being his apprentice.

"What rituals did you perform with my daughter?" she asked Ralf, who had wandered over to Ottentus with Thia following him and hissing quiet accusations of him being a worm and a snake.

Ralf stared at Anna with wide eyes before narrowing them at Thia. "You betrayed me."

"Look at me not my daughter and answer my question."

"They were games," Ralf blurted.

"They were no such thing and you know it!" Thia shouted. "You tell my mom the truth!"

"What is this I hear of rituals, boy?" Ottentus pressed.

"They were consecration rituals," Thia explained. "Rituals to bind me *and* my child to him forever."

"Is that true, boy?"

Ralf only dropped his head.

Anna, infused with fury, did not know what to say or do. It took her some effort to squeeze out the words, "We must tell your father—"

"No!" Thia snapped. "No, Mom. I *forbid* it. I wish no one knew—I wish you hadn't even told your mentor, Ralf! Mom, you say a peep and I swear on the Unnameables I will run away and never speak to either of you again! This is between us only. I don't trust how Dad would handle this, but I *trust* you, Mom."

Anna, stunned by the iron in her daughter's voice, whispered, "Why, Thia?"

"Because ... because I've disappointed him enough."

"Do you not think he has a right to know?"

"Does he, though? Besides, you know what he would do."

"Kill me on the spot," Ralf muttered.

"And that would be his right," Ottentus declared, making everyone raise their brow in surprise at him, especially Ralf, who had gone quite pale. "And you will say nothing to anyone without the young Miss Stone's *permission*, boy," the man added coldly.

"Yes, Master," Ralf mumbled, head hanging.

It did not surprise Anna that Ottentus, who Ralf looked up to as a role model and father figure, knew what was transpiring with the boy — and there was more than a hint of disappointment in his tone. What she worried about was that they were right. Her husband had been fragile of late, and she had to admit she could not trust how he would respond. Many a necromantic ritual could only be absolved upon the caster's death. But Thomas might just kill him as a point of honor alone for "defiling" his daughter.

Niterra looked Ralf up and down, snarling, "I would slay beast who dare cast such spells on me."

"Let us calm down," Anna said, turning to Ottentus. "I have searched my daughter for signs of necromancy but have been unable to find any. Could you have a look at her?"

"If you like, I could do this for you now, yes?"

Anna exchanged a look with her daughter, who gave her approval with a small nod.

Ottentus then opened a hand before Thia, incanting, "*Examino potente morbus aurus persona.*"

As Ralf tensed, the hairs on Anna's neck rose. Ottentus hadn't cast Reveal as she had expected, but the 1st degree healing spell Diagnose! He was a dual wielder and she hadn't known — hadn't even *suspected!* So rare it was to come upon a fellow dual wielder that Anna only gaped at him, mystified. It would certainly explain how he had emerged from prior explosions without so much as a scratch ...

Ottentus took a long time with the spell, hand slowly drawing downward along Thia's body, making her squirm as she drew her robe close and held herself. Then he repeated the maneuver with Reveal, which further mystified Anna as the spell only allowed the caster to see surface tendrils. At last, he dropped his hand. "I am happy to report I have found no sign of necromancy whatsoever."

"But you do not know the 19th degree Arcanic Surgery of the Soul Humor spell," Anna countered.

Ottentus surrendered a nod. "This is true."

Still, Anna felt some relief. It seemed the boy had merely been playing mind games. Luckily, it also seemed that Thia had caught on.

"I *told* you they were just games," Ralf spat. "Symbolic. I … I didn't want to lose her."

"They seemed to mean more than that at the time," Thia countered. "But at least you admit you faked them to manipulate me." She spat a gob at Ralf's feet. "You will *never* have me. Do you understand that, you skeevy little worm? You creep? *Never*."

Ralf looked at Ottentus and Anna, as if he wanted to react a certain way but could not do so in their company, and so held his tongue — literally, for it stuck out between his teeth.

"You're a dual wielder," Anna blurted.

Ottentus shrugged. "One needs to learn a trick or two to survive to the 20th, yes?

But Thia wasn't done, hissing, "I want nothing more to do with you. We're done. Forever. And you will have nothing to do with my child. Do you understand? Look at me, you disgusting worm. *Look at me!*" she roared so loudly her voice bounced around the cavern. "Do. You. Un. Der. Stand."

Ralf refused to look at her, and even though his head was low, Anna sensed he was waiting to see what Anna and Ottentus would say.

After Anna glanced at Ottentus, the man straightened. "You heard the young lady. You will forget her. The matter is closed."

"Yes, Master," Ralf mumbled.

Yet Anna sensed Ralf would not easily let it go. He had revealed himself to be the typical controlling boyfriend sort, with the rituals being a way for him to symbolically control Thia. She had been about to reinforce the point that he stay away from her daughter when Thomas wandered back into the cavern.

"Did someone yell earlier?" he asked.

Thia stepped away from Ralf. "It was nothing, Dad."

Thomas snorted as he looked at Anna. "She get mad at you now too?"

"Yes," Anna said after a moment's hesitation, covering for her daughter — and hating herself for it.

"Oh, don't worry, her emotions are like the weather. They'll pass."

"Wish I could say the same for you, *Dad*," Thia muttered under her breath.

"Mopey return yet?" a chirpy Thomas pressed, having not heard. "Guess not, eh? What's with the long faces and awkward silence? Thia? Want to explain yourself?"

"Nothing, Dad. Forget it. Mom, I want to go home. This is boring."

Thomas snorted more derisively. "Everything is boring to you except for Drama class. Stick around and learn something, or are you bent on finding new ways of disappointing your parents?"

Thia glared at him but somehow managed to keep silent.

As an oblivious Thomas poked his head into the tunnel in search of Mopey, Ottentus made a shooing motion at Ralf, sternly mouthing, "*Go!*"

The boy glanced at Thia, face cut with deep hurt, before schlepping off. At the iron-doored entrance to a side room Ottentus had excavated to use as an office and lunch room, he turned about to stare at her again.

"Creep," Thia muttered, arms folded, turning her back on him. Only then did the boy enter the room, quietly closing the iron door behind him.

Ottentus gave Anna an apologetic look which she acknowledged with a nod. Being his master, it seemed the man was caught in between. Whereas Anna wanted nothing to do with the boy, the man could perhaps talk some sense into him. He was Ralf's final chance at redemption, the only person sparing him from a life of street villainy.

"Here he comes!" Thomas called, fiery palm lit before the miniature tunnel. "And he's dragging something!" He retreated, rubbing his hands in the same manner as Ottentus.

Mopey soon emerged—and he was dragging a large iron key with a complicated end bit. He heaved the key about and kicked it out of the tunnel. Thomas caught it telekinetically and splayed a hand over it to cast Reveal. "It's enchanted, all right."

"It is the key to the subterranean door below us," Ottentus declared. "Yes?"

Anna, following his logic of deduction, gave a vague nod. "Possibly."

Thia threw up her hands. "Good. Mystery solved. Can we go home now?"

"Soon," Anna said, pointing at Mopey. "Are you ready to enjoy the fruits of your labor? Here we go!" and she lifted him telekinetically.

He floated forth and began to flap his wings. She raised him higher and higher, and for the first time ever, little Mopey smiled—or that was what it looked like. It was hard to make out for sure what the gargoyle's face was doing, though it was definitely a new type of scrunch at the very least.

"Look at that, he's happy!" Thia said, clapping sarcastically. "Yaaay! Seriously, can we go home now? It's late and I have school tomorrow and it's been a *long* day."

Ottentus double-tapped Thomas on the shoulder. "Why don't you take your daughter home, my good man. I will have a talk with your wife, yes?"

Thomas glanced between Ottentus, the key, and Thia, before flipping the key into Ottentus's hand. "We *do* need to have a talk about your attitude, young lady."

"Ugh. I'm *so* not in the mood."

"That is exactly what I am talking about, Thia. Do you even hear yourself these days? It is as if the world has done you wrong ..." They walked off, with Thomas lecturing a sullen Thia, Niterra trailing just behind, head on a constant and watchful swivel.

"Come. Let us eat." Ottentus led Anna to the same room Ralf had entered, not even knocking before throwing open the door and barking, "Out, boy."

Ralf, in the middle of chowing down on half a loaf of journey bread, immediately got up and sheepishly skittered by. "Close the door and send for food—my favorite," Ottentus snapped. "And you and I will have a little chat later about propriety and respect, *Apprentice*."

"Yes, Master," Ralf mumbled, closing the door as quietly as he could.

Ottentus and Anna settled around a folding wooden table.

"You have faith in the boy?" Anna asked.

"I believe I can make something of him, yes."

"I hope so. I do not like to give up on anybody."

"He only needs something he has never received before—fatherly guidance."

"Mmm."

As they waited for the food, Ottentus chatted about the excavation and how excited he was to see them making real progress. He talked about his homeland and how he missed Franterran food, which happened to arrive in short order, carried on a silver tray by the hulking workman Ralf had lambasted earlier. Anna, not very hungry at the moment and impatient to get to the point, politely declined.

"You have led a very unique life, Arcanist Stone," Ottentus said, taking a small bite of *bwelfinion*, a Franterran delicacy consisting of beef, onion, eggs, and spices, mashed and pressed into a flat cake and roasted to perfection. The food, which had floated to his mouth to allow his hands to remain free to express himself as he was wont to do, floated back to a golden plate.

"Mmm," was all Anna toned, the mouth-watering scent waking her hunger.

"I confess I pressed your husband, Arcanist Stone," he continued, idly pushing aside parchment notes on the excavation. "A while back he said you were upset. I asked why. I hope you will forgive me, but you hardly talk about yourself. But maybe you will unburden yourself tonight …" He leaned forth. "… yes?" When a suddenly stiff Anna failed to reply, he let his flat cake settle back to the plate. "Let us make a pact. You tell me about this curse your mother put on your family and I—"

"I beg your pardon?"

"Arcanist Stone, please, I am an expert in the occult. Do not insult my work. This curse your husband speaks of, I can help. I am confident I can identify almost any curse. Maybe even—" He dabbed at his lip with the cloth. "—break it, yes?"

Anna looked the hairless old master up and down. "How *dare* Thomas divulge private matters he has no business divulging. I will have a word with him when I return—"

"Please, I implore you *not* to do that, Arcanist Stone. I have nothing but respect for you and your husband, and I have already confessed that it was *I* who did the digging, yes? You must forgive his inability to withstand the onslaught of my curious nature."

"I don't understand. Why would you inquire about our private affairs?"

"Give me a moment to be articulate for a change." Ottentus pushed aside his half-finished plate and wiped his hands on a white cloth embroidered with his initials in gold. He closed his eyes, took a deep breath, expelled it, and opened them again. "Because it is getting in the way of our work, Arcanist Stone. And—" He raised a finger, stalling her protestation. "—I cannot stand to see you both so troubled. Further, curses of that sort are no jest. Your mother was 16th degree when she inflicted that curse, yes?"

"That she was, but what does—"

"May I suggest that the death of your son was no accident."

Anna searched his eyes. "Where are you going with this?"

"Such curses—profound curses amplified by the raw emotions of tragedy—cannot always be found by standard means. You will let me explain, yes? The curse may have been embedded into the fabric of arcanery itself—the ether, hidden from view. There have been instances where such curses point to this theory. People knowing things they should not know. Seeing things they should not see. Hearing and feeling and tasting and so on and so forth, yes? What we simpletons call The Fates may simply be the consequences of our own decisions, played out in a manner beyond our understanding."

"I must say you are full of surprises tonight, Ottentus. First you casually reveal yourself to be a dual-wielder of the ice and healing elements, and now you reveal to me that you know about our private struggles."

"Yes, yes, but I repeat I have had to adjust who I am many times in life to survive, and learning the healing arts has been part of that struggle. You too will come to know this truth as you approach the 20th, yes? There are secrets on the path to mastery that will reveal themselves to you in due course, secrets only for you. As to your private struggles, yes, I admit that my interest in your welfare is partly driven by a selfish desire for success. Yet how could you blame me, your research partner, when we are on the cusp of making a breakthrough of such historical importance that it could change the very *face* of Sithesia? Of the arcane arts itself?"

Anna took a breath and exhaled. "You are most persuasive, Ottentus."

He smilingly patted her hand like an uncle. "Then let us return to the topic of this curse. Your husband—again, because of my nosy prodding—divulged that your mother spoke of the land of rock and fire. There is an old myth, Arcanist Stone. It says that those condemned in such a way—with such a curse—can be, how shall I put this … trapped."

"Are you suggesting Samuel's soul was—*is*—trapped in the land of rock and fire? In … in *Hell*?" The headache twinged up a notch. "Surely you must be jesting—"

Ottentus leaned back to stare at her. "Arcanist Stone, I have been working on such research for half of my life. To know death is to keep it at bay. That is how I survive, yes?" He stabbed the table with a finger. "I say to you now, this curse that your deceased mother cast on you, a curse too powerful for her to rescind, may have reached out to you from beyond the grave. From the sacred ether itself. The ether that knows arcaneological *intent*. Your husband fails to grasp this concept. But something tells me you understand it."

Anna was shaking her head. "No, I do not understand at all—"

"It is not just the soul that is taken, but the body. Now listen very carefully, Arcanist Stone." He leaned closer, dropping his voice to a whisper. "The land of rock and fire *is as real as Ley*."

"You are suggesting Samuel might still be alive …"

"Based on my knowledge of necromantic witchcraft in the old way and how those mechanics apply to the ether, I am only suggesting it is possible. But theory aside, your mother cursed you and your children, yes? Then you must be on guard with young Thia. She is in grave danger from this curse."

"I have tried everything to dispel it—"

"If it resides in the ether, as I believe it does, it will be almost impossible to dispel."

"Almost?" Anna leaned forward. "What do you mean *almost*?"

"We speak of a solution so ancient it is not even worth discussing —"

"Tell me. I must know."

The man sighed. "Very well. It is theorized — ah, but we speak of truly ancient things here, so the better word is *mythologized* — that a curse such as that cannot be undone — except in necromantic sacrifice. Kin for kin. A trade of souls."

"I would give myself in a heartbeat if it meant protecting my children." There, she'd said it. Said *children*, as if Samuel were still around.

Ottentus shook his head. "But in this case, you yourself may be cursed in the same manner, so even *if* it was possible, it would likely amount to nothing. Therefore, if something happened to your daughter, you would have to find another route, one with a higher chance of —"

"What do you mean if something happened to my daughter?"

"Your husband said your mother used the phrase 'dragged kicking and screaming,' yes?"

"He talked to you about all this?"

"Everything, yes. Kicking and screaming," Ottentus repeated. "I say to you now, as I said to him. Your daughter may be cursed — truly, in the old way. If so, the curse is hidden in the ether, beyond prying eyes. It is a powerful curse. A generational curse. You must take heed."

"But if it *was* possible to protect my daughter, or even —" She swallowed, daring herself to voice it aloud. " — or even to bring back my son at the sacrifice of myself, how would that work?"

"Ah the old trap. How easy it is for us all to fall into it."

"Indulge me."

"This is all theoretical, of course —"

"Of course. Go on … please."

Ottentus flicked an eye to the door and dropped his voice. "Well, then you would have to learn an ancient necromantic ritual that has long passed from memory. A curse so old that not even Occulus had been able to learn it, for he too tried to bring a loved one back. The knowledge is thus almost certainly lost to time — at least in *this* plane. But even *if* you somehow tracked that ritual down, and even *if* it worked in the mythologized way of old, and even *if* nothing else got in the way, that particular piece of arcanery exacts a certain …" He cocked his head. "… price."

"Death," Anna whispered.

Ottentus slowly nodded. "You would have to choose. You cannot protect both your daughter *and* bring your son back, for you only have one life to spare." He leaned forth a little. "Do you understand?

Anna stared at him, mind ablaze. He was still hinting that it was indeed possible to bring back her son. After all, it was how the 20th degree healing spell Resurrection worked—except that spell required the person the caster wanted to save to have recently died. The body needed to be fresh, less than a day dead. It was a spell that could only be successfully cast once.

"And hence the old trap," he added. "That path is the same path necromancers have tried treading for millennia. Regardless of how good the intent, that path leads, if you will forgive me for saying so … to darkness."

"And I have only but one life to give." After thinking about it, Anna realized he was right. Still, a seed about her son had been planted. "Then how can I stop the curse from taking my daughter?"

He sighed.

She grabbed his arm. "Ottentus? How can I stop the curse?"

"I am sorry, Arcanist Stone. But since your mother's passing, there is no known way to stop a curse such as this from taking its vengeance. Not without knowing the original arcane signature. Not without access to the mind that laid the original pattern in the ether. Were your mother still alive, and had you brought me in earlier, perhaps then …" He cleared his throat. "Forgive me, I speak so easily of things that are impossible and—"

Anna shot to her feet, her chair falling to the floor with a clatter. "I do not believe you. I cannot believe you! There has to be a way to save her! And-and-and my son is gone. Do you understand me? Samuel is *gone*! He is not in-in-in—" She pointed fiercely at the ground. "—some cage, crying and screaming and-and-and—" She stiffened in an effort to compose herself lest she lose it completely. "From now on, I would prefer that you did not discuss my family's private affairs without me."

"Arcanist Stone, I was only trying to aid you and your husband with a grave matter that is complex beyond—"

Anna was already gone, having stormed out of there and past a still-chewing and wide-eyed Ralf, head pounding. Despite her best efforts, she could not stop certain visions from breaking into her mind, visions of a shadow dragging her screaming children toward an iron cage …

* * *

Once outside the cave, Anna hurried to the snowy forest. The moment she was away from prying eyes and ears, she pressed her back up against an ancient pine and stared up into its snowy branches. She closed her eyes and saw the cage anew, this time with an arm dangling amidst shadowy others.

No. No, that can't be my boy, she thought, tears rolling from the corners of her eyes. Surely the curse, if it was even real, could not have had the power to capture Samuel's soul and drag it into an unknown realm …

"A realm some call Hell …" she whispered to the tree canopy. No, The Fates would never be so cruel knowing that the very *origin* of the curse was a false assumption on her mother's behalf. The gods—The Fates—surely knew her sister's death had been a true accident, and that Anna and her children did not deserve such a cruel fate. Surely there was some sort of divine justice with such curses … right?

But the more she thought about the history of necromancy the more she realized how unjust and unfair the craft was, especially when it came to afflictions. How many had been cursed unfairly over the eons? Preyed upon? Victimized? The texts were full of countless examples … so why would she think herself exempt from such cruel machinations of what felt like nothing more than chance? Than bad luck?

"But do I even believe in bad luck?" she whispered to that old pine, a question that begat further questions. If Ley was real, surely Hell should be too, right? What gave her the right to believe in the former but not the latter? Because she carried an artifact crafted in Ley? Was that it? Because her lineage had thus benefitted from *believing* in Ley? And what if neither existed?

Yet like a vein of coal amidst crimson clay, the underlying question remained. What if Ning and Ottentus were right, and her mother's demonic voice had been an expression of the curse, hidden in the ether beyond all known reach? What if the curse was real, and her son suffered in a cage in some hellish plane? *And what if her daughter was next?*

The more Anna thought about it, the more she wanted to retch. It was the fact she was unsure that caused her the greatest anxiety, for every moment she dawdled, her son was potentially suffering. Yet she needed to be here to protect her daughter too …

"Oh, what to do, what to do, what to do?" she whispered, chin trembling, head throbbing. She flicked a hand and the scion floated into view, its innards empty, reflecting only the forest, which curved fishbowl-like. "Papa … guide me. Is Samuel with you? Did I not see him holding Deya's hand in your presence? Or was that a vision my soul *wanted* to see? Is he safe, or is he in trouble? Tell it to me true, Papa. *Please.* And if he isn't safe, am I to find him? And how am I to do that? And is my Thia in danger? What can I do? Please, Papa, talk to me …"

The scion remained empty before slowly clouding over to opaqueness.

"What sort of answer is that?" she gibbered, slapping the cool crystal, making it spin in midair. "Huh? Don't you understand I have no time for vagaries? How painful this is to consider? How ridiculous?" When the scion remained clouded over, she slapped it aside completely, hissing, "Bah!"

But that only made her feel worse. Things felt like they were spiraling out of control. She was failing her family. Losing her husband. And now perhaps her daughter as well. One thing she was sure of—that boy would not triumph over her daughter. She would not allow it. Even thinking about Ralf and the way he had looked at Thia made the blood in her veins froth. How dare he. *How dare he!* Did he not know whose toes he was treading on? Did he not fathom that there was no moral line she would not cross to protect Thia? And if he had exacerbated the curse, or cursed her anew … well then, gods help the boy. Gods help him, for he would quickly learn what temper she could bring to bear with a scion in her possession, and wrathful Arinthian blood roaring through her veins …

Yet she still needed to keep her daughter safe. That had to be the first priority. It had to.

She thus took a deep breath to calm herself and dried her eyes with the sleeves of her robe. It was time to go home, to tend to her wounded family. For now, she would have to consider Samuel's soul safe. Thinking otherwise would quickly drive her mad. Stark, raving mad. Her family could not afford that. Not now.

But just as she readied Teleport on her lips in preparation to zip home, an alarm triggered in her mind.

Someone was trespassing on their home.

FAMILIAL TRIALS

Knowing exactly which alarm it was and where—south of the tower, near the street—Anna switched her visualization to an alley on that very street, choosing the end of the alley to muffle the telltale *thwomp*.

"*Impetus peragro*," she snapped, appearing between stacks of barrels. Heart racing, she rushed forth, slipping up to the entrance of the alley before peeking out. Other than an elderly couple taking an evening stroll, the street was empty. The snow-laden oaks and pines and cedars and spruces of the family grove stood still, the snow showing no unusual disturbances.

Anna splayed a hand, whispering, "*Un vun asperio aurum enchantus*." Nothing turned up other than the usual enchantments, which looked like giant colorful blankets laid out amidst the trees, as if awaiting a picnic.

Or perhaps someone is being devious, she thought. Conscious that her stamina had not fully recovered, meaning she would have to be ruthlessly efficient, she swept a hand down her body, incanting, "*Armari obscura chameleano traversa*." Then she stepped out into the street, barely a shimmer, a winter mirage—and that was to the trained eye. She moved slowly, a hand splayed with Reveal, feet carefully placed into previous footprints, a panther stalking potential prey. Was it the boy, coming to claim what he considered rightfully his? She tried not to let that thought linger lest it pollute her decisions, for she walked a knife's edge of brutal lethality. If someone strayed across that edge, they strayed into perhaps the most dangerous place in the entire kingdom in that moment.

Once underneath the canopy of a bare oak, her eyes found the spot where the alarm had been triggered. Twenty feet away, it sat amidst unbroken snow. Yet there was indeed a disturbance there—a subtle bump in the snow, as if someone had hidden a shield underneath.

Anna stopped to watch the mound, recalling once seeing something similar. It was a tragic tale of an 8th degree student, known for her gentleness, abruptly going missing one summer day. Speculation had run wild—a crazy ex-boyfriend, kidnapping, slavery, only for her to be found a quint later, when a groundskeeper stumbled upon a bump in the grass just north of the Student Wing. She had teleported two feet under, creating a bump in the earth. A classic misfire. Anna still remembered the shake of fellow arcanists' heads as they muttered how the poor thing had been too ambitious. In truth, anyone could have a bad day, a stray thought, an imprecision. Teleport was not a spell to be trifled with, and should only ever be attempted with a clear mind and iron intent—at least in theory, for in battle, there was no such thing as a clear mind. That was where experience came in.

In the dim light of the torchlit street, she saw something rising above the bump—steam. Rising as slowly as candle smoke. Then the bump rose ever so slightly—or Anna thought it did. When it fell again, ever so slightly, she knew something was there, something that *breathed*.

She glanced about in search of anything else untoward—watching eyes, hidden objects, anything. Finding nothing, she refocused on the slowly breathing bump. It was a trap, of that she had no doubt, and she had to trigger it lest it ensnare her daughter.

Anna extended two fingers and pointed to a spot near the potential trap. A snowy boulder rose from the ground and floated to hover above the bump. With a sudden withdrawal of the hand, the boulder fell onto the bump. The snow exploded as something dark sprang up, quiet and deadly. Nine feet in height with thick, glossy black fur and tree-trunk arms out of proportion to its body, it looked like a malformed ape. Its wide head glanced about, yet there were no eyes, only giant nostrils that flared whilst pushing foggy plumes into the crisp air.

Having never seen one in person, Anna recognized the thing only from books—it was a banyan beast. If she recalled correctly, they lived underground in the deserts of Sierra, and could only be tamed arcanely, meaning this one had a master. There was an export market for them. Hideously expensive, they were used as slave labor, enforcement, or assassination—oft all three.

Anna stood rock still as the eyeless beast's snuffling led it to focus on her. Although it could not see, it could certainly smell. Knowing nothing about its strengths and weaknesses, Anna considered her options. Teleporting away to seek reinforcements would be the prudent thing to do to save her hide—for the moment. But that would also give whoever controlled the beast time to retrieve it and try again at a later date. Further, she could not risk her daughter stumbling across it and—

There came a quiet giggle from the tower, and the beast's ape-like head swiveled toward it.

Don't you dare, Anna thought, muscles tensing in readiness to launch an attack.

The beast shot forth so fast Anna's heart jammed into her throat. As it galloped off on all fours, she thought of the doorway, infusing into the spell the usual demands to factor in positioning in case someone were already standing there. *"Impetus peragro!"* She vanished and reappeared with a *thwomp*—right beside Thia. The girl was standing before Jonah, who flushed as he squeaked, "I apologize but Miss Thia allowed me entry and—"

"Get inside!" Anna shouted amidst the sound of crashing branches.

The broad-shouldered young man reflexively spun about whilst Thia screamed, "Behind you!"

The beast blasted through a shrub like a ballista bolt. It was so quick that all Anna had time for was a reflexive shove, roaring, *"Baka!"* The scion buzzed in her pocket as the beast was sent slamming into an oak, which shook so violently that a rain of snow fell.

"Shyneo!" Thia called, lighting her palm with ivy in readiness to slap the portal rune.

Jonah squiggled out a five-pointed shape in the air, incanting, *"Summano elementus minimus!"* An earthen elemental appeared before him. As the banyan beast charged anew, he pointed, shouting, "Elementus—attack!" and the elemental thumped forth.

At the same time, two new alarms blared in Anna's mind, barely registering in the frantic moment. With her daughter's life at stake, Anna reacted out of panicked reflex and thrust both arms downward. Her scion flared with a great *buzz* and the charging beast, its head gripped in her mighty Telekinesis, slammed into the ground. It slid right to the feet of the elemental, which raised a two-handed fist and brought it down on the ape-like head, making a squishy *thud*.

Behind Anna, there came the sound of a hand slapping stone and Thia shouting, *"Thia Atticus Stone—fourth floor!"* followed by a portal flaring to life.

Meanwhile, the banyan beast swiped with a massive arm. Its claws, honed for digging, were so strong it disemboweled the elemental, and the summoned creature exploded. The shower of earthen flesh slapped into Jonah's face, blinding him and causing him to stumble.

Anna, who happened to be smacking her wrists as she roared, "*Annihilo dio!*" saw Jonah cross her line of fire, forcing her to adjust her angle of attack at the very last moment. There came a simultaneous quadruple *crack* of thunder as four thick bolts of lightning shot over his head—and obliterated the oaken trunk Anna had shoved the beast against moments prior.

As the tree began to fall toward them, Anna sensed Thia go for the portal behind her—only to hear the *thud* of two bodies bumping into each other. Thia yelped while the thick voice of Niterra Bladesong barked, "What in the gods—"

There was no time to think about the two women colliding, for the banyan next swiped at a fumbling Jonah, slicing his belly open with the same clawed hand that had disemboweled his elemental, sending him rolling. He landed with a gurgling scream in a nearby snowbank. Thia, having witnessed this, screamed behind Anna, almost deafening her.

The banyan beast reared up before Anna, ready to deliver a killing swipe. But now she had a clear shot and slapped her wrists a second time, roaring, "*Annihilo dio!*" Her scion flared with another loud *buzz* as a second attack of the Fourth Offensive siphoned what remained of her precious stamina—and went beyond, dipping well into dangerous overdraw territory. Three of the four bolts connected with a *sizzle*, punching a hole in the beast's stomach, blowing off one of its massive arms, and obliterating its face. Dead mid-swipe, it fell forward in harmony with the fall of the tree directly above. A gold-fringed crimson-robed arm shot by Anna's head, and with a mighty *creak*, the oak, which was about to smash into them, halted only feet away. A slew of rotten acorns tumbled from above, plonking into the snow and pinging off the stone steps of the tower.

There was a moment of panting stillness, accented by the pronounced smell of burnt copper and wood, before there came two simultaneous *twangs* from the forest. Anna, head throbbing to the point of bursting, reflexively threw an arm up, summoning a wispy shield. There was a *zip* quickly followed by a *thunk* from her shield—and a *shloop* directly beside her, the telltale sound of a bolt sticking into flesh. It was the latter that sent a thrill of horror through Anna's soul.

Yet she had to keep focused. Knowing herself already depleted, she dipped further into the limited well of overdraw and extended her black lightning crust shield to envelop herself and her daughter. This time the cold siphon brought with it a black horizon, making her soul shiver to its core. Not too many survived the abyss of overdraw. At the least, it meant arcane sickness, something Anna, having been a conservative and careful user of her stamina, had never encountered.

"Mom, Mom, Mom—I'm hit, I'm hit, I'm hit!" Thia gibbered.

Niterra shoved forward and down, and the precariously leaning tree swung at the attackers, cracking and splintering along the way.

Suddenly there came the sound of two new wrists slapping together from the right. "*Annihilo ito!*" roared Thomas, who must have charged in using a different route.

A fearsome battle broke out, but Anna's sole focus turned to her daughter, who had slumped to the ground behind her, hands shaking above a crossbow bolt wedged deep into her stomach. While she fought to keep her shield up—and sustaining thumps from spells—Anna made her daughter's hands press around the base of the bolt.

"Hold firm," she said, knowing she had to end the fight immediately. Being dangerously depleted, the only thing she could think to do was an age-old tactic—the feint. As the violence raged, she snagged the scion from her pocket and tossed it over her shield. Then she pointed around it and flared it. Lightning connected to everything, creating a globular spiderweb.

"Uncle, stop!" Jonah gurgled. "It's me … It's me …"

The violence halted. "*Johanas?*" a man called from the trees.

"*Ya, yava Johanas,*" Jonah replied in Abrandian.

The uncle loosed a bevy of what sounded like Abrandian curses at him.

"*Neine, ya neina eha hostaag!*" Jonah replied, before switching to Solian. "No, I'm not a hostage! And no, I'm not a doppelgang—"

Jonah's pleas were interrupted by the sound of two pairs of wrists slapping together—and they were immediately countered by two more pairs of wrists, so that four volleys of offensives flew back and forth. There came the simultaneous sound of fireballs and airy spears and bolts of lightning and jets of water that culminated in a quadruple explosion, followed by one brief cry of pain and a sickening *splat* before everything went quiet.

"Mine's down!" Thomas reported from the forest.

"Mine too!" Niterra, cocooned in airy armor, called out.

Anna, holding Thia with both hands, roared, "Get us to Antioc!"

Niterra hovered nearby. "But infirmary more reliable—"

"I want Ning!"

There was a brief pause. "Very well. I grab boy."

"It burns, Momma," Thia whimpered as Niterra floated Jonah over. "It burns real bad."

Thomas shoved into the circle. "What can I do what can I do what can I—" Upon spotting his daughter lying in a pool of her own blood, all the color drained from his face.

Anna, who had briefly looked up to lock gazes with her horrified husband, returned her attention to Thia. "Hold our hands and get ready to teleport," she said, cupping her pale cheek with a shaking hand. "Let go of the bolt."

"I don't want to. It hurts so much—"

"M-my uncle," Jonah croaked, hands crimson from his own blood. "Did ... did you kill my uncle?"

"Just for a moment, I promise," Anna replied to Thia, unable to reply to Jonah.

Thia wincingly reached her arms out and allowed Anna and Thomas to each take a hand. They linked up with Niterra and a shivering Jonah, who was holding his stomach and groaning as he kept glancing back at the trees where the men had attacked from. The Black Eagle then snapped off, "*Impetus peragro grapa lestato exa exaei.*"

The besieged group appeared on Gargoyle Bridge, right as a procession of white-robed Canterran Path missionaries were wandering by. The hairless men recoiled from the group. The eldest even dropped his incense burner, meant to cleanse the city of its sins—or so Anna remembered. She did not take much interest in what the various faiths were up to these days.

"Get out of our way," Thomas growled, picking Thia up and shooting through the middle of them. "Make way make way make way! We need to see the senior arcaneologist!"

Anna ran alongside, letting Niterra telekinetically carry Jonah, albeit at a much slower pace, for the woman's old legs could not quite keep up. The library's six sets of double doors, each exquisitely carved with depictions of gargoyles and books and historical scenes, were closed. But Anna didn't let that stop her as she thudded a fist against them, shouting, "Let us in! It's an emergency!"

Armed guards rushed to the doors. "Get you to the infirmary!" one shouted through the glass, brandishing a longsword drawn upon the sight of blood.

The lone warlock amongst them did a double take after seeing Anna. "That's Anna Atticus Stone! Open those doors!"

"But sir—"

The warlock shoved him aside and slapped the two main doors with a fiery palm, commanding them to open. The group rushed inside before the doors even fully opened, and they soon came to a skidding halt at the front desk of the library, encountering the same young man Anna had seen on her last visit, the one who hadn't recognized her.

"Where is she?" Anna snapped.

The young man blanched upon seeing Thia, then almost fainted upon seeing Jonah, who had fallen unconscious and was now a floating ragdoll dripping blood all over the clean floor.

"Lecture … Lecture Room seven," the young man squeaked, holding himself steady against the desk.

A man hurried out from an office, barking, "No, she's in the Trainer!" Anna recognized him as the same older attendant she had met whilst trying to help Jonah. "You go get her. I'll take them to the operating room."

"Y-yes, sir."

They raced to the portal room, with attendants and guards jumping out of their way as if the group were diseased. The senior attendant summoned a portal and they shot through it. Running down the halls was a blur to Anna, and before she knew it, Thomas was gently laying Thia down onto an operating slab. As he held her hand with one hand and the wound with the other, Anna held her daughter's other hand from the other side. Nearby, Niterra wrapped Jonah up with linen gauze the senior attendant had tracked down.

"Am I going to die?" Thia murmured, eyes roving about, forehead beaded with sweat.

"No, honey, you're going to be fine," Thomas replied, choking back tears. "You're going to be fine. Everything's all right. They'll take care of you. You just hang in there, sweetie."

"Is Jonah … is he going to die?"

Anna glanced over at the young man, whose robe was soaked with his blood. His lips were blue, face white as a sheet.

"You worry about yourself right now," Thomas said. "Jonah will be fine."

"They have to … they have to save the child."

"You worry about you now."

Ning burst in through the doors with the young man and a slew of attendants. "You cannot simply barge in here every time someone you know gets a scratch—" She briefly froze upon seeing Thia, before rushing forth.

"Bolt to the stomach," Anna began. "Certainly perforated, but with no additional—"

"Shut up," Ning snapped, pronging fingers at a pair of twin attendant women with healer's armbands. "You two stabilize the boy." As the healers went to him, she tilted her head. "Is that the same boy who I've already—"

"Yes," Anna blurted. "Jonah Ivanov."

Ning scowled as she pronged two more fingers at the senior attendant and the young man. "You two drag these entitled fools the hell out of my sight."

Thomas slapped the older man's hand aside. "I'm staying with my daughter."

"Not if you want me to operate on her," Ning hissed, glaring at him.

That was all it took for Thomas to allow himself to get dragged away by the elbow. The attendants took the three of them to the grandest office in the library, the towering round chamber filled with books that rose to a glass-domed ceiling.

As Niterra paced with folded arms and the senior attendant stood nervously by while the younger one returned to his duties, Thomas grabbed Anna by the arm and whirled her about to face him. "What happened? Anna?"

"We were attacked—"

"*Obviously!* What was that thing back there in the snow?"

"Let go of me."

Scowling, he released her arm.

"It was a banyan beast."

Thomas's shoulders rose and fell with his breathing. "Did you just kill our daughter?"

She wanted to slap him. "It was a surprise attack—"

"You could have teleported her away—"

"There was no time—"

"Like hell there wasn't!" Thomas roared into her face. "Like *hell* there wasn't …"

Anna searched his eyes, finding nothing but rage there. "I did everything I could to—"

He thrust a quivering finger up. "Don't. Just … don't. I don't want to hear another excuse. Not one."

"Which one you take down?" Niterra asked Thomas in her thick accent. "The uncle?"

"How the hell am I supposed to know?" Thomas roared, still glaring at Anna.

"Did both expire?" Anna pressed on Niterra's behalf.

"I don't know! I was aiming for the pair of them, but one stepped into my fireballs by accident to get out of the way of Niterra's four air spears. I think he blocked the view of his comrade, because that man took one of those spears directly in the face. I do not believe either survived."

Anna, full of self-doubt, looked away first. She chewed on a finger as she paced before the doors. Thomas continued to glare at her with a stare she had never seen from him before—a stare of utter loathing and utter disappointment. She wanted to plead her case yet also knew it would be utterly futile.

The older attendant cleared his throat gently. "The surgery could take some time. Perhaps if I bring you some tea—"

"We don't want anything!" Thomas roared, eyes following Anna as she paced.

Niterra nodded at the senior attendant, who bowed, murmuring, "I shall return shortly, m'lady."

"Is this how it is?" Thomas hissed when the man had left, looking between Niterra and Anna. "Three supposedly competent warlocks who can't keep one girl safe? What's the point? Huh? Look at me, Anna. How does ill fortune keep slipping in through the cracks?"

Anna, who had ceased pacing to stare at her husband, did not have an answer.

"Look at you chewing on your fingers like a little girl. You can't even give me a straight answer. Why can't you protect our daughter? Answer me, you damned woman!"

"Enough, Thomas!" Niterra said, standing in his way before he grabbed Anna again. "Enough."

Thomas pointed over Niterra's shoulder. "You failed her again. *Again!* It is the last time, so swear I to the Unnameables. The last time …"

Anna didn't know what that meant. Innards numb, she looked away and continued pacing.

"Coward," Thomas hissed.

Anna ignored him, her thoughts on Thia. She had no idea what to say to her husband, not that he would listen anyway.

The senior attendant came with a full tray. "My lord and ladies, would you like some—" but Thomas smashed the tray with the back of a hand, sending tea and biscuits flying and the cups smashing against the floor.

"Leave us be, man," Thomas hissed. "And leave the blasted mess."

The elder attendant hesitated before bowing. "My lord."

"Haven't you heard? I am no lord, but a former lordling turned noble-sniffer."

The man straightened in an attempt to keep his dignity and, after suffering Thomas's glare, promptly strode out. Niterra offered the man an apologetic nod as he walked by, one he did not acknowledge.

"I go check house and enchantments," Niterra said. "Check bodies too. Inform authorities of attack."

Anna nodded her thanks and Niterra excused herself. When she was gone, Anna turned on her husband. "Heaping rage upon servants is beneath you and will gain you nothing but disdain—"

"Oh shut your fool—"

"—and might only cause problems should we ever have to return to receive more healing—"

"That will never happen!" Thomas roared so fiercely that Anna backtracked. "Do you know why? Because I won't let you put her in danger again! Not ever. Having proven yourself incompetent in keeping our daughter out of harm's way, *you* have lost the benefit of the doubt. *I* will manage her safety from now on. Me. Not you. *Me*."

"We will do it together—"

"*We* will do no such thing!"

"We will do it together, and this discussion is over."

"It's over when I say it is over! Do you hear me, woman!"

"It takes two for a discussion to take place. Now I suggest you stop before either of us says something we regret."

Thomas's eye twitched, as if he were contemplating saying something quite foul. But he sucked in air through his teeth like a hoodlum and started pacing.

They waited in silence, pacing and brooding and avoiding each other's gazes. At long last, after what felt like forever, the doors flew open and Ning stepped out, her hands bloody.

"Both are fine," she said before either Thomas or Anna barked at her to deliver the news already.

Thomas threw up his arms, howling, "Thank the Unnameables!"

"Or you can thank the hand that actually saved your daughter," Ning snapped.

"Yes, of course. My apologies, Senior Arcaneologist Ning." Thomas bowed. "You have my deepest gratitude. I mean that truly. May I see her?"

Ning flapped a hand toward the door and Thomas rushed past. She then placed cold eyes on Anna. "This is the second time you have rushed to me, expecting me to drop everything to save your hide."

"I know and I—"

"Shut up. You wear a cloak of entitlement so thick it's a miracle people aren't tripping over it left and right." She took a step closer, searching Anna's eyes. "Let me be crystal clear. The next time you deign to drag your daughter, your husband, or any other blasted fool in here, rest assured that they will *die* from lack of attention. I am not an infirmary!" she roared so suddenly Anna jumped. Her voice then dropped to an acidic whisper. "Am I making myself understood, Stone?"

Anna dropped her eyes and nodded. She swallowed. "Thank you." When Ning did not reply, Anna looked up. "At least tell me, did her baby …" She opened an inquiring hand, not wanting to verbalize the remainder of the question.

"There it is." Ning nodded at Anna, a nod that kept going. "There. It. Is. You selfish brat. That's why you came to me. To ensure the bloodline survives. To ensure your precious little toy can be passed on."

"You misread me. I merely wanted to know if—"

"I misread *nothing.*"

Despite knowing her to be wrong, Anna did not want to drag this out. She stormed past to go see Thia, only for Ning to grab her wrist. "There is something else. And as much as I loathe your selfishness and entitlement, you have the right to know."

"Know what?"

"I found … a tether."

Anna felt a cold flush and yanked her hand back. "What … what sort of tether?"

"I am not sure. It is an echo beyond my reach."

"What about Arcanic Surgery of the—"

"—Soul Humor? I tried. Beyond my scope."

Anna knew what that meant. As far ahead as Ning had studied in the healing arts—legally, being the healing element—she had nonetheless fallen short, meaning she lacked not only experience but expertise in Arcanic Surgery of the Soul Humor, a spell so difficult the founders had placed it in the 19th degree, alongside the other famed healing spell—Arcanic Surgery of the Brain Humor.

"My mother's curse?"

"Possibly …"

"Probably?"

"I said, *possibly.*"

Anna dropped her head. "I should have pushed harder to convince her to renounce it."

"It could be ancestral, familial, or something else entirely. Like I said, it's beyond my scope, and there's no use in wild speculation."

Anna was certain it was her mother's curse, and tried not to think about the implications on her son. Even the shadow of the thought of him reaching out from a cage made her innards want to unleash a shrill scream of potent horror.

Ning sighed. "You do not deserve to hear this, but you did what you could, as did she. Had your mother been younger and cleaner of mind, she *might* have succeeded in reversing it. But such curses, conjured in such moments … sometimes they're irreversible no matter how repentant one is. Such is the nature of consequence."

"Did you … did you make any further identifications?"

Ning slowly shook her head.

"How strong was the bond?"

The shaking of the head continued.

"What about if you—"

"It's beyond reach, Anna. Infused into the ether itself, making separation near impossible. Not even a master could—"

"But I know a master. A dual wielder."

"And what color is his sleeve? Hmm? He does not have the expertise. One wrong move down there and—" Ning sliced the air with two fingers. "—cleavage. A total corruption of the soul, well beyond repair. Beyond salvation. See your mother in her last days and think of your daughter suffering in such a way, except there would be no back-and-forth between a kindly Thia and a demonic Thia. There would only be the latter. A festering wound that would soil any sweet memory of her. No dual wielder could get down that far, not even close. He *might* have a chance if his primary was healing, but even then, based on what I've seen and what I know, you'd have a better chance of being struck by lightning *underground*."

Anna bit her lip.

"You ask him and he tries then she's as good as gone," Ning went on. "And if you choose incompetence now …" She shook her head as she once more stepped to Anna, looking up at her due to her short stature. "No forgiveness. None. Not that it would matter seeing as the consequences for you would be … well, I need not put it into words, do I?"

Anna closed her eyes, not wanting Ning to be right. But she knew it to be true. "Is there anyone, anywhere, who could—"

"This is an arcanic surgery that should not even be attempted." Ning shrugged as she withdrew a cloth from a pocket to dab at her forehead.

"Who knows, it may not even trigger. Or it could be a remnant, an echo of a curse that was *already* triggered. Have you thought of that? Or it could be something else entirely—"

"It will trigger."

"You do not know that."

"My mother's original intent was venomous. She already killed my son."

"*That* was circumstance. And you ought to know the difference."

"But it wasn't *your* son, was it?"

The two women stared at each other before Anna swept past, muttering, "Thanks for doing your duty."

"Just because you couldn't hack it as a healer doesn't make me your personal healing servant," Ning snapped back. "Next time they die outside the library doors. You understand me?"

Anna stopped but did not turn around, wanting to say something vile. But unable to think of anything worthy of the moment—or herself—she continued onward, crashing through a pair of doors. She found Thia unconscious in a bed, one of two bathed in pools of low torch light. Attendants quietly fussed about in the background, dumping towels into a basin, whispering amongst each other as they stole glances her way.

Anna slid onto the bed, opposite her husband, to hold her daughter's hand.

"They said she needs rest," Thomas whispered, caressing Thia's hand. "My girl. My sweet little girl ..."

Anna fixed Thia's damp hair and caressed her cheek with the back of her hand. *I'm sorry*, she thought. *I'll do better from now on, that I promise you, my darling child. My baby.*

"Who is the father?"

Anna looked up to see Thomas staring at her.

"Answer me. I know you know."

"Did you kill ... my uncle?" Jonah croaked from the other bed.

Anna looked over at him. The boy was pale, his midriff bandaged, indicating he would have to have a second round of healing at some point. The wound must have been quite damaging.

"Is it him?" Thomas hissed. "Or that Turman boy? Or someone else?"

Jonah closed his eyes. "My uncle's dead, isn't he?"

"We don't know yet, son," Anna replied.

"And Thia? Will she be all right? Please tell me."

"Yes."

He opened his eyes and breathed a shuddering sigh of relief. "Mr. and Mrs. Stone ... with deep and humble respect ... I want you to know

I … I love her. I want you to know that. I love her and I will one day marry her. With your blessing, of course."

Thomas straightened. "She is with child."

Jonah swallowed. "I … I know that. She told me."

"So perhaps you ought to save your infatuations for someone else … unless it is *your* child."

"Alas, it is not my child, sir. And they are no mere infatuations, sir. I *love* her."

"Even if she is with someone else's child?"

Jonah paused before nodding. "Even if she is with someone else's child."

"And who are you exactly? An Abrandian whose uncle tried to murder her? Whose father was notorious scum? Who are you to dare ask for my blessing?"

"I … I am nobody. A humble peasant, sir. A former soldier. A student warlock who wants to do some good in his life to atone for his family's wrongs."

"Family? *Family?* You would exact vengeance on *this* family."

"I would do no such thing, sir. I swear to you, on everything I hold sacred, that I would be bound to you by honor and by love, even if my uncle was found dead by your hand. I renounce any such act for all time, no matter what. I would protect and care for Thia and the child as if it were my own. That I swear to you, Unnameables help me so."

"Even if she leaves you?"

Jonah shuddered, but nodded. "Even if she leaves me."

Thomas grunted, returning to holding Thia.

Someone stepped into the room. They all looked over to see that Niterra had returned. One look at her grave face told the tale—both attackers had perished.

"So he is dead," Jonah whispered. "My uncle is dead …"

"The one with beard perished by my hand." Niterra stepped forth. "Constables request confirmation from a relative."

Jonah could barely speak. "The bearded one was … he was my uncle."

Niterra nodded. "I sorry, boy."

Jonah placed his gaze on Thomas. "Although he treated me well, he was a fool and a criminal, and this would have happened sooner or later. My pledge to you, sir—" He looked at Anna. "—and lady, stands. I love Thia. There is nothing else."

Anna stared at the boy, who looked at her pleadingly. There was not a shred of indecency in those brown eyes. Only humility, honesty, and love. A love she once remembered feeling herself. A love she missed feeling deeply. A love she wanted her daughter to feel.

Anna gave him a small smile, yet that smile, as tiny as it was, was enough to put color back into his face.

Thomas grunted a second time before looking at Anna as well. "So only Thia knows who the father is."

Anna did not take the bait, and continued caressing her daughter's hand whilst avoiding that fiery gaze.

SUCKER PUNCH

Jonah cupped his face with both hands before the stone slab. "I can confirm that is my uncle. Gods help me, that is him. Oh, you fool, what have you done this time? What have you done?"

The attendant covered the body back up, one of a pair lying side by side.

"And if your uncle had gotten free and come after Thia again?" Thomas asked, staring at the outline with hard eyes.

Jonah thought about his answer. "I would have done everything in my power to stop him."

"Even if that meant—"

"Even if that meant killing him." Jonah stared at Thomas with iron resolve until the latter gave the slightest nod.

"Who is this man?" a constable asked, holding a tablet and quill under one arm whilst revealing a mangled face with the other.

Thia slid her hand into Jonah's to urge him on, only to quickly let go when she saw her father watching.

Jonah stepped up to the body. "This is Igor Advanenkov, the brother of Segor Advanenkov, and friend to my uncle. He is Abrandian and the second-worst man I have ever met, the first being my father."

The attendant, who had scowled at the mention of the word Abrandian, threw the cover back over the man. "I will submit my report today."

"Forgive me, sir, but will there be any repercussions for Mrs. Stone and her daughter?" Jonah asked, nodding at Anna and Thia.

The constable looked Jonah up and down as if he had crawled out of a sewer. "Seeing as it is a clear case of self-defense, corroborated by you, an *Abrandian* next-of-kin, I anticipate the investigation will come to a swift end. Lord Stone, Champion Stone, Miss Stone—thank you for your cooperation." He gave a curt bow of the head to Anna and Thomas. "Fair morn," he said, and left.

Thomas stepped up to the slab to stare down at the covered bodies. For a time, no one spoke. Anna had an inkling of what her husband was feeling, for it was his first kill. He had never slain anyone before. Were there not such a divide between them, she would have placed her arms around his torso and given him a warm embrace.

" 'Today a warlock I hath becometh,' " he whispered.

" 'Thus hath I becometh locked in war,' " Thia whispered in turn, quoting the rest of the lines from *A Baron's Blunder*, a famous play—and a tragedy.

Thomas did not acknowledge her despite surely having heard what she had said. Instead he turned on his heel and walked past them.

Thia watched her father go with melancholy eyes. "I did not like the way that man spoke to you," she said to Jonah as they left the room. "He judged a play by its title and he's a jerk, as is everyone who judges you for your kingdom's sins."

"You are a wise and kind girl."

They smiled at each other.

Once they stepped outside, Thomas wagged a rude finger at Niterra. "Don't let her out of your sight. Not in the academy, not at home."

"She volunteers her time, Thomas."

"And I am grateful for it. Thank you. Now if you will excuse me, I have a well-paying noble waiting for me to set alarms on his prized collection of rabbit feet." He pointed at Thia. "You stay out of trouble," though his look of warning was reserved for Jonah, who swallowed. Thomas then snapped off, "*Impetus peragro*," vanishing with a *thwomp*.

Anna stared at the spot he had been standing in a moment prior. *You once used to kiss me prior to leaving. You once used to say I love you.*

"Mom? Can we go to school now? We already missed half the morn."

"One of my key traps—the Paralyze one—was disenchanted," Anna said, still staring at the snow. "Was it you?" When Thia did not respond, Anna turned on her, throwing Jonah a nod. "To get him in?"

"It was the only way I knew how!"

"What about the alarms? How did you bypass those?"

"Er …" Thia mumbled something.

"I beg your pardon?"

"Since they don't trigger for me, I, uh, I carried him." She thumbed over her shoulder. "On my back. Which wasn't easy considering—" She patted her belly and winked. "I'm a warrior who called upon preggers strength." She shrugged. "Ugh, *fine*. I was determined to have him over, all right? Happy?"

"It's not funny, Thia." Anna rubbed her forehead. "You could have talked to me. We could have arranged something."

Thia folded her arms. "You almost sound as disappointed as Dad."

Anna was too tired to take the matter further. Besides, she had a whole school day ahead still, and who knew what her substitute arcanist was making her students do. The last one had made Anna's students jump ahead a chapter and learn it by performing rote memorization, which not only put half to sleep, but completely dispirited their will to learn the material when Anna returned to teach that chapter anew.

* * *

It was a long quint, which turned into a long month, and then three long months. Months of paranoia, academic toil, excavation, the occasional scroll work, endless cycles, deep excavation research, and, after countless hours of trial and error, the successful repair of Thesper the animated suit of armor, resulting in a big payday. Mercifully the high-pitched headache had deadened to a distant whine, and the nightmares had all but halted, now only fleeting images experienced between the occasional moment of reflection. By the time the spring peonies and hyacinths and bloodroots were in full bloom and the land lush and the air hot and the sky bright with the long sun, and Thomas had worked a good chunk of his gambling debt off, and Thia had grown quite the bump and Jonah had become her steady boyfriend and Ralf had seemingly vanished off the face of Sithesia, Anna thought herself finally ready for a glass of wine with Syanda.

Just as she was about to knock on her colleague's office door, she heard Syanda say, "I am glad you have informed me. Now I will in turn inform the authorities."

The door opened and Syanda jumped. "Gods, you startled me," she said, a hand pressed to her chest. Behind her, a burgundy-robed girl nervously fiddled with her hands.

"Everything all right?" Anna asked.

"You need to hear this," and Syanda grabbed Anna's robe and yanked her inside.

Once inside and with the door closed, Anna smoothed her robe, muttering, "Was that really necessary?"

Syanda folded her arms. "Tell her, young lady. Go on."

The girl's eyes went wide. "Is that—"

"Yes, that's who you think it is. Now cough up the story."

"But she's her—"

"Just tell it, girl."

The girl swallowed. "Hello, I'm Yennica and I'm in 2nd degree—"

Syanda rolled her hand along with her eyes. "We don't care one hoof about all that, girl. Just spill the salt."

Yennica cleared her throat. "I was in Drama and we were working on the play *The Necromancer's Folly*, which is based on—"

"We know what the play is based on. Move it along, girl."

"So, yeah, uh, we finished the play and people were leaving but I lost my earring—" She pushed her long hair back to reveal an emerald earring that matched her eyes. "—while jumping about doing a dueling scene and I was on all fours sniffing about like a rat under one of those long tables you know the one—"

"Girl, if you don't get to the point immediately—"

"Sorry yes so an argument broke out—someone had come in, someone I don't know, but the older boy in class called him Turdy or something—"

The hairs on Anna's neck stood on end. "Turman? *Ralf* Turman?"

"That sounds about right, yeah."

Syanda tugged at her curls as she grimaced. "Isn't that the kid—"

"—who got expelled, yes," Anna concluded. "Where was Niterra Bladesong?"

"Oh, she had to go to the privy, Arcanist Stone. You know how old people are."

"That privy is far from that class too," Syanda muttered.

Yennica drummed her cheek with pink fingernails. "Now that I think about it, I reckon that Turman boy was waiting for her to go to the privy."

"Go on, young lady," Anna urged.

"So this Turman boy starts shouting about how he owns, uh …"

"Owns who?" Anna pressed, already knowing the answer.

"Y-y-your daughter, Arcanist Stone."

The two arcanists exchanged a look before Anna nodded for the girl to continue.

"The two boys really got into the yelling after that, saying awful, *awful* things, and next thing I know Turdy—I mean, Turman—sucker-punches your daughter's boyfriend—"

"Jonah?"

"Yes, that's him. He went down like a sack of spuds. Turman kicked him for good measure but he was already unconscious. I saw it from under the table, right? Anyway, your daughter tried to shout but Turman cast a bunch of spells in a row and silenced her. Then he rifled through her pockets and tossed some stuff out—"

The tracking pebbles, Anna thought.

"—and he threw her satchel aside and then grabbed her by the hair and started marching her out, saying she was his and no one else's and she should have known better than to think he would let it go—I think he's her ex-boyfriend?—and that it was her fault he got expelled and she was silently begging and sobbing but she'd been muted and he just talked over her anyway. Like, frothed at the mouth, practically."

Anna could hardly breathe. "Tell me he didn't leave the academy with her …"

"Well see that's the thing as soon as he left the room with her I shot out from under the table and went to Jonah and managed to wake him—I'm healing element, right? So I knew how to bring him about by using smelling salts, which Drama happened to have because of this one play that—"

"What happened next?" Anna snapped, not meaning to sound so harsh.

"Yes, Arcanist Stone. Er, I got Jonah up and the moment he realized what had happened he bolted out of there. I ran after him. The halls were empty by then—it's in that quiet part of the school, right?—but he managed to catch up to Turman before he could wrangle your daughter outside, where I think he was planning on teleporting her out—and I only know that because he said so, that he had a Group Teleport scroll or whatever. Anyway, Jonah runs up to him and Turman hears him and whirls about and slaps his wrists with a First Offensive—" She slapped her own wrists here, hissing, "—*bam!* But Jonah blocks it with his shield—" She lifted her left arm up. "—*thwap!* And then—"

"Less of the theatrics and just tell us what happened, girl," Syanda said, once more rolling her hand in a *move it along* motion.

"So they go back and forth and are sort of evenly matched, you know? But other students started taking notice and someone said the arcanists were gonna come. They kind of tired, and that Turman boy said, 'If you never want to see me again, then you and I will duel for her in the old way,' and Jonah spat back, 'Anytime, anyplace,' and your daughter shouted—'cause his Mute spell died by then, you know?—how she would never, ever, *ever* accept Turman and that no such duel would take place. But the way the boys glared at each other, I don't know …"

"Where is Turman now?" Syanda pressed.

"Oh, he walked off."

"What? What do you mean he *walked off*? Did nobody chase him?"

Yennica shook her head. "They were too scared. He's deranged. You should have seen his face. All twisted with rage. *I* was scared. Deathly afraid he would do something terrible. He had those evil eyes, you know? The sort they write about but you never really see? There was just … nothing but spite there. Malice is the word. Malice. So, yeah, he walked off, all confident like, staring people down as he went. I shivered when he looked at me." She swept a hand over her forearm. "*Literally* shivered."

Anna moved to the door, readying to find her daughter. "Where are Jonah and Thia now?"

"I … I don't know, Arcanist Stone. I think they left together. Seeing as the arcanists never showed up—I think it was just a bluff and Turman knew it—I thought I would do the right thing and tell someone and Arcanist Mibukwa is my Written Word teacher so I—"

"You did the right thing," Anna said, flinging open the door. "Thank you," and she rushed out.

"I'll take a full report from her!" Syanda called after her.

Anna waved a thanks over her shoulder as she raced around a corner, thoughts frantic. Months of peace, with nothing happening. *Months!* She had been expecting perhaps someone to have a go at her scion, or maybe some outside calamity that would need her attention, like a pack of robbers or something, but Ralf Turman? And at the *academy*? They should have revoked his permission to enter. Yet it was unheard of for an expelled student to return due to the utter shame—there were few things as dishonorable in warlock culture as being expelled from the academy.

Despite having not been seen in months—not even at the excavation, with Ottentus saying he had not seen the boy either—Ralf Turman had in fact been plotting his revenge the entire time. As the father of Thia's child, he would have felt a burning attachment. Having been a Drama student himself, he would know about the class, what time it ended, and where to hide …

Just in case, Anna skidded to a halt in an empty corridor to splay her hand and focus on a certain pebble, which she had enchanted with Object Track and given to Thia. The tendrils connected with the ether and pulled her toward Drama class. She waited a moment to see if they would move—and to her surprise, felt them nudge. She raced in that direction, and almost careened into the couple—and Niterra Bladesong—as they departed the classroom.

"You heard, Mom?"

"I heard," Anna replied, checking her daughter over as she grabbed her arms. "Are you all right?"

"I'm fine, Mom."

Anna looked at Jonah, whose right cheek was swollen.

"I'm all right, Arcanist Stone. He got a cheap shot in, but only one."

"And that's exactly what would happen if you dueled." Anna raised a finger. "I forbid it."

Jonah dropped his gaze.

"Look at me, son. I forbid it. Do you understand?"

Jonah glanced at Thia, who was giving him an imploring look, and surrendered a nod.

"He was waiting for me," Niterra said. "Cursed boy wait in shadows for Niterra to be her old woman self. *Bah.*"

"It was not your fault," Anna replied. "He should have never been allowed back in the first place." If she took on the headmistress position, she would make it a policy for an expelled student to be arcanely prevented from entering. "I'll need you to submit a full report to the disciplinary committee, Jonah."

"I'll start on it right away, Arcanist Stone."

"Mom, can I talk to you for a moment? I'll catch up with you later, Jonah." Thia grabbed his hand and gave it a reassuring squeeze.

Jonah squeezed back, nodded, and walked off, with Niterra Bladesong stepping away to complain under her breath about her old body.

"You sure you're all right?" Anna asked.

"*Yes*, Mom."

"Because I'm here if you need me—"

"Well, that's the thing." Thia dropped her voice. "Can I ask you to do something for me?"

"Anything."

"This one is a big ask, Mom."

"I see. Go on."

Thia checked to make sure no one was within earshot before whispering, "Can ... can you find Ralf and wipe his memory?"

Anna gaped at her daughter. "I beg your pardon?"

"I don't want him to ever remember me. And I *especially* don't want him to remember whose child I am carrying. He doesn't deserve it. Not after ..."

"After what?"

"After everything he put me through. And I'm not just talking about today."

"Thia Atticus Stone, do you realize what you are asking me to do?"

"Mom, I'm only trying to protect—"

"Unlawful use of Memory Wipe—and there are *very* few lawful uses of that spell—is a grave crime, Thia. A grave crime. Do you really wish to turn your own mother into a criminal? I have a responsibility to the academy, the kingdom, and warlock-kind as a whole to—"

"I don't want anyone to know that *he*—that evil, cursed, horrible *thing* of a human—is the father of my child." She pressed her lips together as she shook her head, eyes distant. "No one, especially him. *That* will be my revenge."

"We must let the authorities handle him."

"*You* are the authority, Mom. You. All anyone in warlock culture understands is might. And you're kingdom champion. If anyone could get away with it, it's—"

"That's not the point, Thia. That's *not* the point. We have laws for a reason. Without them we are barbarians. And as kingdom champion, I am a standard bearer."

"No one has to know ..."

"I would know. *I* would, Thia. I cannot fathom you, girl. Never ask me this again."

"Fine, whatever, see you at supper," and Thia shoved her way past.

"Thia—"

Her daughter marched off, with Niterra trundling along behind.

Anna sighed and trooped after her, wanting to stay close while she wrote out a report.

THE SWAY OF CANDLELIGHT

———————

Anna strolled through the wooded grove that surrounded the Stone family tower, hand splayed, eyes on the alert for the slightest sign of ill intent. The sound of birds warbling pleasantries mingled sweetly with the rustle of oak leaves. Grass swayed in a gentle breeze, vibrant in the late afternoon sun.

After concluding that all was well, she padded up the tower steps, summoned the portal, and stepped into a silent living room—only to be surprised to find a monk sitting cross-legged before a dead hearth.

Except it wasn't a monk, but her husband, his robe hood raised, back rigid straight.

"Thomas …?"

Thomas raised a single finger. "Do you hear that?"

Anna listened. "Hear what? I hear nothing."

"Precisely. It is the sound of *silence*."

Anna smiled. "I see your new mentor has been making strides." Thomas had hired a monk to help him with his more destructive habits of gambling and drinking.

"He is a guide to the spirit. Usually, I'd be drunk by now. Instead, I'm here. I'm *now*." He turned. "Did I ever thank you for your help?"

Anna raised an eyebrow.

"With the debt."

She took off her shoes and placed them beside his. "We stumble and heal together, just like in our marriage vow." He had kept himself quite the busy bee taking whatever job was available in the enchantment and tutoring markets, where there was no shortage of work for a 15th degree, piling on odd jobs in between, such as starting a kiln fire with his fire element, or various other fire-related tasks.

"We both know you could have made me pay for it all—and would have been in the right doing so. Instead you chose to spend who knows how many hours fixing some ancient contraption. You are a kind woman, Anna. I married a kind woman."

Anna, having not heard a compliment from Thomas in some time, gaped at him. "Er … is Thia—"

"She's studying hard at the moment. That old warrior watches over her still. We have to do something for her after all this. For watching our daughter." His gaze returned to the dead hearth. "She too has found purpose in life again. It ought not to be without reward." He tilted his head. "Yet the monk said service is in itself a reward …"

Anna made a show of peeking into a broom cupboard. "Is he in here?"

"What are you doing? Is who in there?"

"My husband."

Thomas laughed.

Anna closed the cupboard door. "You will have to be patient with me as I adjust to this new man who wandered into my home." She fiddled with the end of her long braid as she watched him. "How are you and Thia coming along?"

"We're on speaking terms. But I have … I have a long way to go with her."

"You have much amending to do."

He nodded. "I know …"

She sighed, turned to an old oval mirror etched with ivy, and fixed her braid, but stopped when Thomas stepped up behind her to take over.

"Don't undo it," she said, squirming in his touch. "Takes forever to get it right."

"I have something I wish to celebrate," he whispered, the braid vanishing behind her back as he fiddled with it. "What do you have to do tonight?"

"You mean besides—"

"—*besides* the usual cycles and book learnings and marking student work."

"I was planning on training with Niterra, with a focus on Combat Portal. My dueling skills—"

"—are still legendary."

"I was going to say are falling by the wayside."

He undid her braid, making her smack her lips. "Ugh, you fiend."

"Look how beautiful you are," he whispered, fluffing out her long brown hair.

Anna picked up a frizzy streak of gray. "I was promised I would not age."

"You are aging beautifully. Gracefully." He glanced over her other shoulder, whispering, "But why doth the queen squirm?"

"It's just that …"

"The queen has not felt the king's touch in some time."

Anna nodded as she lowered her eyes. How she had missed this man, yet *this* man was a new man. The old Thomas was not so self-reflective. At least, not since they had started dating all those years ago. And certainly not since Samuel's death. Losing a child together had fractured them.

But it has not broken us, she thought, looking into the mirror at her handsome husband. Will this new Thomas stick? Or will he fall back on his old ways?

"I think you ought to drop those plans," he whispered, nuzzling into her neck.

"And why would I do such an irresponsible thing? My students—"

"—will survive. And because the king wants to take his queen out for supper as a reward for helping him with a burden that should have been his alone. A burden he no longer carries …"

"You … you paid the rest of the debt off?"

"Every last castle, spine, and crown."

For a moment, Anna gaped at him in the mirror before blurting, "I'm *so* proud of you."

"Thank you."

Anna dawdled. "But Thia—"

"—will be just fine with that old windbag."

"That's not very nice. She's helping us out of the graciousness of her own heart."

He patted her shoulders. "And that's how easily I forget myself. You're absolutely right. I owe her a great debt that I may never be able to repay."

Anna, having already seen a flicker of the old Thomas, sighed. "Don't start what you do not intend to finish, sir."

Thomas nibbled at her ear, making her squirm. "Oh, I intend to take this caravan the whole way, my lady. Ah, the heavens just parted to let the light seep through, for look at the wry smile I won."

Anna tried to bury the smile under a grimace. "You ruined my hair. How do you expect me to go out looking like some crone?"

"I want you to wash it, brush it, and put on your finest gown. Tonight, my dear lady, we *feast*." He adopted a snooty accent. " 'Let them dine, wine, and entwine.' "

"You're a terrible poet."

"And you're a gloomy wretch."

"Hoodlum."

"Wench."

They smiled cheekily at each other before he whirled her about and raised her chin with a hand.

"My lord doth be rather forward."

His lips graced hers. "Go. Change."

She shoved him away, muttering, "Teasing fiend."

He watched her go. "See you shortly, Anna Atticus Stone."

She did an awkward hip wiggle to tease him back and went to have a quick bath in their stone bathing room, made a little less primitive with the addition of an oval banded-wood tub. After washing up and brushing and straightening her hair, humming the pleasant tune to "A Maiden's Love," she opened the door to her triple wardrobe—one of a pair in their room, the other belonging to Thomas. Her hand traveled across four identical black arcanist robes and four identical turquoise robes with a single golden band on the upper shoulder, denoting that the robes belonged to an 18th degree. Long gone were the days when she could only afford one robe. But she had just a handful of dresses, usually worn to ceremonies. All seemed stuffy and out of fashion, and probably didn't fit her anymore.

Nonetheless, she chose a simple cream-colored dress with a V-shaped neckline, the edges of which were embroidered with five-petaled blue belias, Solia's mountain flowers. Yet when she tried it on, she did not like the fact that her ankles were exposed. "I recall you being longer," she muttered at it, twisting this way and that before a corner cheval mirror on a mahogany stand. The dress billowed nicely, but was still far too short for her liking. "I suppose it's better than the others," she concluded, picking out one of two purses she owned, a lovely miniature leather satchel dyed light blue, which clipped to a belt. She stuffed the scion inside, making it bulge, and smacked her lips. "Gods, that's ugly." As she fussed with it, the door opened.

"My turn, my girl, so I hope you're—" Thomas halted upon spotting her. "Who is this stunning vixen and where is my dowdy wife?"

"I beg your pardon, sir?"

"I mean … Unnameables help me, you look …" He swept a hand up and down as he shook his head. "Where did *that* come from?"

"I last wore this for that Antioc arena honoring ceremony, remember?"

"But that was …"

"Ten years ago, yes. It, uh, it still fits, it seems." She whapped the bulging purse secured to the side of her waist. "And this thing looks like I'm carrying a melon around."

"Oh, believe you me, *nobody* will be staring at the purse. Now get out. My turn." He tried to smack her on the butt when she left but she sensed it coming and parried it with a forearm before zapping him with a harmless bolt of lightning.

"Ouch!" he feigned, closing the door behind her.

"Whoa, Mom. What's with the getup?" Thia said when Anna paced into the kitchen. She reached for a sack of rice from a cupboard, only to groan and lean back while she grabbed her now large belly.

"Your father is taking me out to supper," Anna replied, flicking at the sack and floating it over. "You ought to use Telekinesis at home more."

"It's not natural for me like it is for you. And that's wonderful. I can't remember the last time you two went out."

Anna didn't mention she couldn't either.

"All right if Jonah comes over later? After my studies are done, of course."

"Sure. But you know the—"

"Yes, I know the procedure, Mom, yeesh. Niterra will shepherd us through safe and sound. Don't you worry. And at the slightest sign of trouble, I'll touch one of the bazillion alarms you set about the place."

Anna nodded. She and Thomas had each set an Object Alarm on the main places in the house—a certain book and a Tiberran vase in the living room, a painting and a statuette in Thia's room, and so on. There were at least eight scattered about the place.

"Your father says you two are on speaking terms."

"He's making some effort, but it's really hard for him. I catch him staring at me and my tummy and he just looks away. I ask him, 'Is there something on your mind, Dad?' and he just mumbles about having stuff to do or whatever."

"Your father will get there."

"Yeah, right. When, after the baby's born? When he stops thinking of me as a loose woman? When I get married to someone *other* than the baby's father? I'll give him this—at least he's stopped asking who the baby's father is."

Anna could only sigh.

"Sorry. I don't mean to ruin things for you. You look great, Mom. Almost fashionable."

"Almost?"

"It's, uh, a little old-fashioned, but I like how short it is. Oh, those noble hens are going to *tut-tut* though!"

"They can *tut-tut* themselves to the henhouse for all I care," Anna muttered, though when Thia poured some rice into a pot, she tried to drag the dress down.

When Niterra stepped into the kitchen and spotted her wrestling with the dress, she pressed the side of her fist to her mouth to stop herself from cracking up.

"Not a word," Anna muttered, though secretly wondered what the Nodian warrior's face would look like if she dared to allow herself such base amusement as a smile. She didn't wait to find out and instead marched back to her room to change into a different dress, only to run into Thomas, who had emerged wearing a fine royal blue doublet embroidered with golden swirls and pressed black pants.

"You ... you look great," Anna blurted, still tugging at the hem of her dress, feeling decidedly unlike herself. She *really* wasn't used to wearing dresses, and felt more at home in a robe than anything else.

"You're not allowed to change."

"How did you know?"

"I could spot that *I should present more dowdy* look from a league off." He grabbed her by the hand and dragged her forth. "The finest supper Solia has to offer awaits, my queen."

"A queen is not dragged, sir."

He gentled his hold. They waved at Thia and Niterra, who still had to suppress a laugh, promised they would be back at a reasonable gong of the city bell, and summoned the portal to the front stoop.

"Where is my lord husband taking his queen?" Anna asked once they were outside.

"Her ladyship is in for quite the treat, for her king doth takes her to, well ... you'll see." He opened a hand.

She took it. "I see we are gambling again."

He flashed her a confident smile. "I've been training diligently, my lady."

"Let us see the proof, then." She girded herself, trying not to imagine waking up embedded in a tree—or worse.

After a few concentrative breaths, Thomas incanted, "*Impetus peragro grapa lestato exa exaei!*"

The pair appeared in a bustling shop-filled street Anna instantly recognized as Banker's Lane, as nearby stood the imposing Black Bank, the warlock-guarded monetary power behind the throne and nobility.

As always happened when teleporting into the heart of the city, a few people yelped in surprise, with a middle-aged man hissing, "Watch where you 'port, fool 'locks!" Those who recognized Anna through her fancy getup did a double take or whispered behind their hands. A street artist with a sooty face and hands switched out his parchment and started sketching her on the spot—this despite an old woman sitting before him.

"How much for a portrait, good sir?" Thomas asked, approaching.

"Would you like both of you, m'lord?" the man asked, shooing the huffing old woman away.

Thomas enthusiastically threw an arm around Anna's shoulders and yanked her close. "Absolutely."

The man indicated to the lone chair and Thomas sat down, dragging a squirming Anna onto his lap.

"Hold still, please," the artist said as his hand started sketching with charcoal.

"Charcoal, how modern," Thomas noted.

"I find it allows for total freedom, if you allow me for sayin' so, m'lord," the man replied, biting his lip as he worked away.

"I feel rather foolish," Anna muttered, conscious of the gawkers who were assembling, many of whom were pointing and whispering behind their hands. She tried not to worry if one was an assassin. She tried not to think of the mental pictures people were painting of *the* Anna Atticus Stone, kingdom champion, sitting on her husband's lap with her ankles bare for all to see. Warlock women so rarely showed anything beyond their heads and hands that she practically felt naked.

"Aaaaand done!" The man yanked the parchment, bowed, and presented it with a flamboyant twirl of the hand. "I await m'lord and lady's verdict," he said, head remaining low.

Thomas held it aloft, his other arm around Anna's waist. Before them was a rather stylish couple, the man smiling broadly, the woman nervous but pretty. He looked distinguished, she youthful and energetic. His hair was a little unruly while hers fell in a curtain around her neck. He had eye and mouth crinkles while she had only one, in the furrow of her forehead. But it was what the artist had drawn behind them that caught Anna's eye.

"Why a giant circle, sir?" she asked.

"That represents the sun, which shines down on us all, lighting souls afire with passion."

"Ah." She had thought the man had been sly and drawn a large scion behind them, like a preying shadow. But his interpretation she quite enjoyed. "It is beautiful, sir."

The man bowed deeper. "I am your most humble servant, my lady."

"The last portrait prior to us becoming grandparents," Thomas murmured, eyes taking in the drawing.

Anna looked at him. "You are full of surprises today, aren't you?"

"All things pass. That's what my mentor is teaching me. Everything is fleeting. The only eternal thing is the moment."

Anna tried to reconcile this man before her with the man she knew, but was having a hard time doing so.

"Can we see it, m'lord?" a kid squeaked from the gathered crowd.

"Yes, do show us, Arcanist Stone!" a teenager Anna recognized from her classes called.

Thomas withdrew his hand from the parchment, leaving it to float. He then revolved his hand and the parchment turned in place, before giving it a flick and sending it shooting forth. It floated in a circle so all could "ooh" and "awe" at the work. A spontaneous round of clapping ensued, coloring Anna's cheeks.

"Really, this is all quite too much," she muttered, hiding her face behind her hair as if she were herself a teenager again.

"We shall cherish it forever," Thomas said upon its return, withdrawing a whole crown from his own purse and floating it to the man.

"My gods," the artist said, accepting it with both hands. "You humble me, sir."

"It is us who are humbled, sir," Anna replied, extending her hand to thank him.

He not only grasped it with both hands as he would a dove, but took a knee and kissed the top of her hand, whispering, "Your Grace, Champion."

"Mind those graces lest the constables cut that tongue off for abusing the royal title," Thomas said, allowing the man to delicately roll up the sketch and tie it with a blue ribbon before handing it over. It was illegal to call anyone by a royal title who was not a royal.

"Of course, sir." The artist circled his heart with a finger before tapping his chest. "I apologize to myself."

"That's a new one," Thomas said as they walked off, hand-in-hand. "Superstitions are strange."

"Some consider meditation a superstition."

"Only fools do. Ah, here we are." He squeezed her midriff as they looked up at a black-oak sign with fancy golden lettering.

" 'The Pine Garland Inn & Tavern,' " Anna read.

"One of the oldest in the kingdom. Ever been?"

Anna shook her head. "Too fancy for my purse." And too gossipy, for it was also where the nobles liked to mingle.

"Not today it isn't." He guided her into an old building with great arched columns that looked like they had been pilfered from some ancient tomb. In between were tables fitted with pristine white silk cloth and golden flatware and etched-crystal goblets that sat upside down on gold-rimmed porcelain plates. People dressed in their finest gowns and doublets sat chatting with low voices, a single candle on a golden sconce flickering between them. Giant chandeliers in the shape of dragons hung from trusses in the ceiling, casting a dim light on paintings of knights charging into battle or men holding scrolls before an audience or royals sitting for a group portrait.

One long table of plum- and cobalt- and crimson-attired men and women with sparkling jewelry and powdered faces was particularly loud—obnoxiously so. Yet no one paid them any mind, even as they laughed uproariously at a lewd jest. Circling them, standing in the shadows, were crimson-robed Black Eagle guards, indicating the group was royalty—perhaps princes and princesses, or some of the countless cousins that fluttered about the throne like mosquitos.

As Anna glanced about at the luxury like a curious little girl, a gaunt man with silver hair and a silken black robe embroidered with colorful flowers glided forth, his fingertips pressed together. "May I help you?" he crooned in a courtly drawl.

"Your finest table," Thomas crooned back.

"And you are …?"

Thomas yanked Anna close by the shoulders again. "Thomas, and this is my young secretary, Anna."

As Anna flashed her husband an alarmed *What in Sithesia are you doing?* look, the man glanced at Anna's naked ankles.

"One moment please, sir. I think we may have a large party arriving." He left to consult a ledger that even from a distance looked suspiciously empty.

"That man's posture is so rigid I think he once accidentally sat on a pole and never noticed," Thomas whispered as young servants bustled large silver trays of food and drinks, quiet as mice.

Anna pressed a hand to her mouth. "A little propriety, sir. One would think a man brought up in the nobility would carry kinder airs."

"The only airs that one carries are the ones that get stuck under his robe when he farts."

She whapped his chest with the back of her hand, grinning. It was somewhat refreshing for her husband to be so lewd.

The man soon returned. "I do believe we are rather full at the moment, sir."

"Maybe we ought to find someplace else," Anna whispered, subconsciously tugging at her dress.

"May I suggest the Diving Drake just down the street—"

"Nonsense. We're eating here," Thomas snapped, rubbing his hands together as if squaring for a verbal joust.

"Thomas!" a man boomed from the head of the long table, shooting to his feet.

Anna's heart sank when she saw none other than King Power Ridian the Second, his arms wide in welcome, a bejeweled cup in each hand. "Bring my dear friend over, you pasty ghoul!" the king hollered, beckoning with both hands, the cups sloshing wine about.

The man paled as he gibbered, "Right this way, my lord and lady."

Thomas grinned as he strode forth. Anna sighed … and trailed.

"Theeeeeere's the old goat," Thomas sang as the men clasped arms and drew each other into back-clapping hugs. "How's the hunting arm? Still sore?"

The king winked. "Not sore enough to take your money again in another hand of cards," and he roared a red-faced laugh, quickly echoed by the others.

"I see you've assembled the usual miscreants," Thomas said, chortling along. "Lady Taylor. Lady Haught. Lord Slimwealth. Even my devious sister doth attends."

"Brother," Lady Samantha Blackflower said, taking a sip of wine from a gold-rimmed goblet. She looked regal in a silk dress with lace cuffs. The others inclined their heads and mumbled greetings, though more than a few exchanged looks Anna read as, *What are they doing here? Aren't they broke?*

"And there is my former mentor," the king sang, throwing both arms open, inviting Anna in for a hug, which she pretended not to notice by fixing her dress for the umpteenth time. "What a divine sight she is, Thomas. You old dog, how did you snag such an eternal beauty?"

Thomas scratched the back of his head. "I ask myself that question all the time."

"But you simply *must* join us," the king sang. "We have missed your company, old friend."

"Thank you, but I am afraid we were planning on—"

"I insist, sir. It is a royal decree. Or is it edict?" The king glanced around with a pretend lost look, and the table erupted with laughter. He raised a wagging finger above the crowd, roaring, "It is a royal order, sir! Sit, sit, sit, sit!"

The tavern host—now aided by two young men—quickly brought two more chairs, squeezing Thomas and Anna in beside the king, with Anna sharing elbows with Triana Taylor, clad in a crimson dress and matching ruby rings.

The two women nodded curtly at each other, Anna reminded of the awful piece the woman had published slandering the Stone name—and her daughter. Her daughter had suffered at school because of it, too, something Anna would never forgive the woman for.

"I hear it on good authority that someone had paid his debt, is that not so?" the king asked. "Slimwealth! Call it so."

"The Stone name has indeed been redeemed," Lord Reginald Slimwealth replied, the taxman looking decidedly uncomfortable discussing someone else's private affairs.

"Excellent!" The king elbowed Thomas. "Then shall I dare tempt thee in a hand of cards later? Hmm? *Hmmmm?*"

Thomas chortled as he washed his hands in a bowl of steaming lemon water held by a servant.

"By the gleam in his eye, my man here may indeed be interested," the king declared. "I know you're in, Slimwealth, you degenerate gambler you."

"And how is your daughter?" Mayda Madeline Haught asked, head dancing about as the men bantered loudly. "Surely she must be enormous by now."

"She is coming along," Anna replied, not knowing what else to say. Although a few choice words came to mind, none should be shared in royal company, as uncouth as that company was.

"Despite my best efforts, *my* daughter adores you," Triana threw in.

"Kimani is a talented and ambitious student," Anna said.

"Yes, well, the little witch can't keep her mouth shut half the time," Triana said, cracking with laughter.

"You ought to put the whip to her," Samantha Blackflower said. "The *snap* will keep the little tart in line."

"I used to have an old servant do it when she was younger, but that man drank himself to death. Kimani used to call him Big Bloat. He hated that. But he had a firm hand. Gods know her father lacked it, useless turd that he was. You believe she wants to be a lowly constable? After everything I've worked for to keep her station, she wants to be a lowly squealer. Practically a hoodlum. She's even signed up to become a reserve constable and trainee. I cannot fathom her."

"There is honor in being a law-abiding constable," Anna said, purposely implying that too many constables were corrupt, paid off by either the street, or especially the nobility.

Triana's roving eye dialed Anna in again. "It has not escaped my notice that you do not ever mention our mutual history to my daughter," she said, taking a long sip. "Why is that? Too proud, are we? If it were me, *I* would gloat about beating a 6th degree as an aspirant."

" 'The sins of the father are not the sins of the son.' "

"A convenient proverb for the Arinthian line." Triana scoffed. "Hoarding a scion all to yourselves for two thousand years. I suppose it's in that pumpkin-sized purse?"

Anna's cheeks colored. With all her warlock responsibilities, she did not have the luxury of exploring her femininity, and even when she did wander beyond her comfort zone on nights like this, she rarely got things *just* right for the discerning eye of the nobility, which had little better to do than dress for occasions and gather arrows for the gossip quiver.

"Imagine sounding so graceful even as you slag the entire nobility," Mayda Haught drawled. "This woman here lives in a witch's tower and owns a castle—which she leaves abandoned." She leaned forth, swirling her goblet, fingers glittering with rings. "If it weren't for that scion, she'd be a lowly arcanist barely scraping by. Probably long hit her ceiling like the rest of us."

"She's drunk," the king boomed, thrusting himself into their conversation. "I like a drunk woman. Loosens the tongue. Let the gossip flow, ladies, so say I! Speaking of gossip, would you be so kind, Arcanist Stone, to regale these foul-mouthed harpies of a tale of how awful I was as a student?" He leaned forth, eyes traveling around the group. "Do you know she made me grovel before her?"

The women pressed fingertips against their chests as they gasped a mockingly dramatized, "*No!*"

"That she did. Your wife, Thomas, was quite the academic harpy herself. It be true, so say I. Made me smash a pitcher—or was it a cup?

Yes, I am certain it was a pitcher. Anyway, she made me smash a pitcher, repair it, and then smash it again! And it was the best thing she could have done." He slapped the table. "The best thing, so say I." He grabbed a goblet in each hand and raised them. "To the harpies of Solia! May they curse us all with progress!"

"To the harpies," the other three women said, sharing bemused looks.

They think him an idiot, Anna thought, looking on without reacting. *But then I think the same.*

"Pour it liberally, man!" the king snapped at a servant who had come to refill Thomas's goblet, which Anna hadn't noticed he had finished already. She glanced back at the many empty tables, longing for one with her husband. A candle to share between them. Whispers of love whilst holding hands. Candlelight falling on a nearby charcoal drawing of them. She sighed, dreaming the dream of a teenager-turned-woman. Why could that not be the norm for her?

"Remember that one game," King Power crooned. "The one where I made that singer sit on your lap as she belted out that song?"

Anna's head snapped about so sharply she felt it *crick*.

Thomas chortled nervously as he repeatedly wiped his hands with a cloth. "You mean the one I threw off? That was a dirty trick."

"Dirty is right! What was the name of that devilish song again?"

"Certainly wasn't 'A Boy and his Cat,' " Triana muttered with a sly grin.

The king slapped the table. " 'Those Wiggling Hips'! What a fine prank that was indeed!"

"Men and their boorish games," Mayda said underneath the men's raucous voices. "If only they weren't so predictable, we'd have a ball of a time." She narrowed her eyes at Anna. "Speaking of balls, how come you no longer grace us with your presence at them? Surely it is not because my brother accidentally spilled a tomato drink on your fancy dress at that old dance now, is it?"

"I hardly concern myself with events that happened thirty-five years ago," Anna retorted, hating the fact the vile woman got it absolutely right—having been humiliated so publicly by her sister, who had been dancing with Mayda's brother at the time and purposely bumped into her, it was exactly why she avoided such balls. That and she tended to be a favorite target of gossip.

"Dare I suggest you have hardly touched your wine," Lady Blackflower noted. "You can try relaxing around us, you know. We do not bite—hard."

The harpies snickered.

The woman played with a lace cuff. "Tell me, my dear sister-in-law … does it gall you that you had to pay my oafish brother's debt?"

"He paid half by working hard. I believe it is important for a family to share burdens and blunders. The gods know he had to share in mine."

"Helping protect a scion is hardly much of a blunder. You know, as head of House Blackflower, he could have been powerful and filthy, *filthy* rich. Instead, he is forced to debase himself for scraps around the nobility. Much like a lapdog, would you not agree?"

"You talking about me, Sister?" Thomas interjected. "I thought I heard my name."

His sister put on a simpering smile. "Only with the fondest of sentiments, dear brother."

"Good, because otherwise I'll have to put you into another headlock."

"Those days are long over." Her eyes went cold, but Thomas didn't notice and resumed jousting with the king and Lord Slimwealth.

As the first course came — sweet-sauced quail eggs beside creamed sweet potatoes and a breast of roasted pheasant — Anna, annoyed by the two-faced games and bored by the same old jabs, glanced about in search of a distraction. She found it in the dazzling robe of a woman, the embroidery of which *moved*. The woman was older, likely in her seventies, and sat with a young man, perhaps her son.

"Ugh, but did you see what Lady Scarson wore to the high fair ball?" Mayda asked. "Scandalous to wear royal purple when you hardly have two castles to rub together. She ought to be conscious of her station in high society."

"Who does she think she's fooling?" Triana added. "And glad you reminded me. I'll write a piece about her impropriety tomorrow."

"Excuse me," Anna muttered, dabbing her lips with a cloth and getting up. She moved quickly away just as Mayda opened her mouth and raised a hand after her, as if her sole audience were departing.

"Forgive me for intruding," Anna said, coming to the older woman. "But I couldn't help but notice your robe and how beautiful it is."

The woman smiled. "My son said the same thing," she said in the sophisticated accent of the Canterran court. Yet unlike the nobility Anna had been interacting with on that eve, there was only kindness in her voice. "I enchanted it myself, my dear."

"Really?" Anna watched as two dragons fought on her robe. One was green and threw a vine rope at a red dragon's neck, while the latter slapped its wrists and shot a fireball at the former. The stitching fluidly undid itself and adjusted moment by moment, quickly and efficiently, and seemingly without tearing *or* wearing away.

"It is absolutely *stunning*," Anna added. "And how imaginative to have dragons use arcanery!"

The woman batted the air. "It was but a fancy, taken from old mythology. Some story about Arcaners."

Her son, dressed in a fine linen shirt with golden buttons, leaned forth. "Forgive me, my lady, but are you by chance *the* Anna Atticus Stone? Solia's champion?"

"Er ..." Anna still found it hard to reply to such questions. Saying yes always felt like she was putting on airs.

"Let us not embarrass the esteemed lady," the mother said. "And I am surprised you know, my boy."

"I may be a lowly Ordinary, but knowledge of other kingdom warlocks is a prerequisite for my position."

"My son is one of our kingdom's ambassadors," the woman said proudly. "He has spoken to your king, who is having quite a time tonight it seems, on many an occasion."

"Trade and budgets and taxes and surplus," the man threw in. "Trivial and boring to one such as you."

"Such affairs are hardly trivial," Anna replied. "I am sure your efforts have bettered *both* our kingdoms."

"Would you like to learn how I animated the stitching?" the woman offered.

"Oh, I couldn't possibly ask such a—"

"I insist. It would be an honor to teach such a paltry thing to someone held in such high regard. Please, have a seat." The woman pointed at an empty table nearby and had one of its two chairs slide over.

Anna glanced back at her own table and, finding it in the midst of obnoxious laughter, with Thomas clinking cups with the others, smoothed her dress underneath her and sat.

"Are you by chance familiar with ancient animation arcanery?" the woman asked.

"A little bit," Anna replied, choosing not to divulge her triumphs with Mopey and Thesper.

"I had the privilege of studying a practice dummy at Castle Von Edgeworth," the woman went on. "And amidst the vast complexities, I discovered an interesting line of arcanic progression. Mind you, I'm not the only one who uses the knowledge of arcane stitching. It's just that my casting route is simpler. The standard methods to animate threading are complicated and convoluted, and I fear purposely so—"

"Because they keep the clothing frightfully expensive," her son interjected. "Ten thousand crowns a robe. I know because I checked."

"And the tailors tend to keep such knowledge to themselves, creating generational dynasties. But as with many spells, there are variants, and this one is certainly as off-the-books as you can get. Now let me demonstrate the base ideas and we can delve into some nuance, which you can extrapolate on at home."

And so the woman explained how the arcanery worked, starting with the root spell work and working her way up the chain of complexities. The spell would have to be explored in further detail at home, but Anna was sure she could get there now that the map had been laid out in front of her. The woman was so succinct in passing on her ideas that Anna couldn't help but ask what she did for a living.

"I'm a teacher," the woman replied.

"So am I!" Anna readjusted herself in her chair. "Excuse me for my outburst."

"And rumor is you are to be the next head of the academy," the man added.

"I have not yet accepted the position."

"Ah. Now you must excuse *me*, my lady, for there is another rumor, an old one, that you once used to date our kingdom champion, Scadius Von Edgeworth."

"That one is true, and indeed old. We were 9th degree at the time. He was an exchange student from the Iron Feather Academy, and I was an insufferably ambitious know-it-all and arena dueler. Alas, any love I had for him died when I found another woman in his dorm room bed."

"And in the end, he couldn't keep any of them," the old woman said. "Now although he is a strong dueler, he is a shell of the man he used to be, always arriving drunk at our pageants and balls and oft making quite the scene."

"Isn't he in the city?" her son asked, looking between the two women.

His mother shrugged while Anna cocked her head, asking, "On what business would he be in town for?"

"Why, for his business of dueling, of course. It is how he makes his income."

"I see." How vexing that he had returned when she had warned him once already.

The woman glanced past Anna, who turned to see her husband approaching.

"*Honey*, you are embarrassing me," Thomas sang whilst putting on the same simpering smile she had seen his sister flash him earlier. "You've left me all alone with those vultures."

Anna, having a good mind to deliver a tongue thrashing over who had left who with vultures, nonetheless smiled at her hosts. "You gave me a wonderful little secret," she said to the woman. "How ever can I thank you?"

The woman smiled. "Consider it a gift from one arcanist to another."

"Then I am deeply honored, and hope we get to speak again someday."

The mother and son inclined their heads, with the mother saying, "That would be lovely, Champion Stone," and the son adding in jest, "Perhaps you two can start a stitching circle."

Thomas took Anna by the elbow and guided her back to the raucous gang. On the way, she politely snagged the attention of the head server and told him she wished to pay for the mother and son's meal.

The man gave a stiff bow of the head. "Of course, my lady."

"They must have made quite the impression," Thomas said as he brought her back to the king's table, which greeted her with drunken applause led on by the king.

As Anna sat down for the table's third course, she noticed the charcoal portrait lying open amidst a puddle of spilled wine, its ribbon lost, and thought it an apt symbol of how her husband had yet again let her down. Instead of rescuing it, she let it be, leaving it to her husband to salvage. Something told her she would never see the drawing again.

Uninterested in the topic at hand of banal slights committed against various lineages, she kept her mind occupied with thoughts of animating threading and Scadius Von Edgeworth. She gave vacant nods, placating smiles, and lackadaisical variants of "Mmm." The women, finding her a boring target, moved on to more salacious morsels—who cheated on whom.

It was whilst she was wistfully staring at an older couple at a far table, their heads together as they whispered, gazing fondly into each other's eyes, that an alarm blared in her head—and it was coming from *inside* the family tower.

Anna shot to her feet, whispering, "Thia …"

A wavering Thomas looked up with red eyes, blubbering, "What's that stupid girl done now?"

Anna, knowing he'd only be a drunken liability, ignored him—and the giggles of the women—and focused on home. "*Impetus peragro!*" she incanted, rudely vanishing from her place at the table with a loud *thwomp*. Back at the tower's steps, after a quick glance about in case of enemies, she lit her palm, slapped the rune, summoned the portal, and shot through to her daughter's floor.

"Thia? Thia!" Anna shouted as she raced to her room.

"I'm fine, Mom!" Thia called, meeting her out in the hall. "It's Jonah."

"What about him? Where is he? Does he need healing? Where's Niterra?"

"Here," Niterra said, emerging from Thia's bedroom.

"Jonah isn't hurt—at least not yet."

"What do you mean? Explain."

"He was here—you allowed him to visit, after all—but then he had to leave, saying he had something to take care of—but it was the way he said it that made me think and because I was thinking I couldn't do my homework and then it hit me I can't believe I didn't see it coming with him being all secretive today—"

"What? Spit it out, girl."

"He's gone to face Ralf. He's gone to duel him."

"Where?"

"I … I don't know for sure, but there's word of an underground tournament tonight, with open slots prior to the main event. I think he and Ralf arranged to meet there."

Anna instantly knew her ex-boyfriend Scadius Von Edgeworth was involved.

"Mom?"

They'll have chosen an even more discreet space this time, Anna thought, meaning it would be more difficult to find.

"*Mom!*"

"Mmm?"

"Where's Dad?"

Anna looked away.

"Did you at least have a good time together?"

"Let us not worry about that right now."

"Aww, I'm sorry, Mom. Fine. Anyway, I'm coming."

"No."

"Mom—"

"Absolutely not."

"*Mom—*"

"*No,* Thia. And that's final." Her daughter had no idea what awaited. "I'll bring Jonah back."

"It's a duel of honor in the old way, Mom. You know what that means, right?"

"I do." The terms would have been agreed upon—the terms being her daughter. But such agreements meant nothing to her as their foundations were dishonorable.

"You can't let him lose, Mom. All right?"

Anna didn't know what to say to that so she looked at Niterra.

"I will watch like hawk," the woman said, wrinkled face as alert as ever.

Anna said her thanks, kissed her daughter on the forehead, and whisked off.

"Mom—you forgetting something?"

"What?"

"You can't wear that."

Anna glanced down at her dress. "There's no time," she snapped as she tore the scion free of the purse and tossed it aside as she summoned the portal. Knowing she had to be as efficient as possible, she stepped outside and incanted, "*Impetus peragro,*" reappearing at the door of a constabulary in the heart of the city. Memories of herself as a teenager of about Thia's age wandering through that very door flooded her mind, and here she was doing the same thing all these years later, playing constable. But this time her daughter's future was at stake.

Anna swooped inside. "Get all the warlock constables together," she snapped at the junior constable behind the desk, the same one who had helped her take her statement after the fight at Castle Arinthian. "Starting with Captain Peters," referring to the senior constable who had a reputation for being incorruptible.

"What? Why? And who are—wait, is that *you,* Champion Stone?" the young woman asked, large forehead shining with candlelight under a bloom of pinkish hair. "I didn't recognize you in the dress."

"Get every warlock constable who isn't on the dark payroll here *now,*" Anna said, scion clutched in a fist.

"Er, forgive me, but why should I send messengers out to fetch them all? And what should I tell the captain?"

"That we're going to shut down the tournament ring once and for all."

THREE CHALLENGES

After gaping, the young constable blurted, "But there's only, like, thirty of us—"

"I'll be lead." When the woman still hesitated, Anna cocked her head. "Do it."

"Yes, m'lady," and the young woman raced into a nearby office, and soon three junior constables—some still chewing, all with crumbs on their robes, apparently having been eating—hurried out.

A cat-call whistle came from a nearby cell. "Well 'ello there, little dove," cooed a burly man with an exposed hairy chest and a sun-wrinkled face. "Fancy a tankard later?"

Anna stared at him. The scion began to buzz in her hand.

"Oh, you is got a hard face, lass, a hard face indeed. Don't match that pretty little dress though, does it?"

The young woman emerged from the office, smacking the man's cell door on the way. "Shut up."

"But I only want to have me a wee chat and maybe see if—"

The young woman whirled about to clench her fist at his throat, hissing, "*Voidus lingua.*"

The man turned puce as he shouted at her, yet not a sound came out.

She returned to the desk. "They're on their way and should be here any mo—"

There came a *thwomp* from beside her.

"Champion Stone."

"Captain Peters."

"I was on my way here anyway and caught one of the messengers." The gray-haired senior constable didn't so much as glance at her dress, yet there was tension in his voice. "At long last, someone with the courage to shut those awful tournaments down, permanently. I must confess that I have long waited for this day ..." He looked beyond her, as if seeing a phantom. "... perhaps even dreaded it."

"There's little time, Captain Peters, as I fear a student of mine may have accepted a duel of honor."

He refocused on her. "Then he would have chosen an open slot."

"What's that mean?" the young woman asked.

"There's usually room for one or two duels, called open slot duels, to settle grudges and gambling debts and the like."

Other warlock constables started to appear, most of whom Anna recognized as former—or even current—academy students, the latter usually being on a trial period or in apprenticeship training. The majority were so low in degree that they ran in through the door instead of teleporting. More than a few did a double take upon seeing Anna, and in a dress no less. One of them was none other than Triana Taylor's own daughter, Kimani, who gave a confused smile upon seeing her teacher.

"The problem is I don't know where," Anna added, ignoring them all.

The man looked at the other constables, men and women in their twenties and thirties, with a handful of older ones mixed in. His lips moved as his fingers wiggled at heads. "Twenty-eight. Where's Selmak?"

"Sick, sir," answered a young woman.

"And Wilkins?"

"Visitin' his grandma, sir," said a young man.

"Any idea where?"

The young man shook his head.

The captain sighed. "Great." He rubbed his chin, his eyes finding that distance again.

He's distracted, Anna thought. *He better focus, and right quick.*

"What's the quest, sir?" a young man with a snake-tattooed hand asked.

The captain seemed to catch himself. "We're shutting down the tournament ring." He swallowed, evidently conscious of Anna watching him. "Once and for all."

The constables glanced at each other uncertainly.

"You know what that means," the captain went on. "This isn't going to be pastry—it's going to be meat. *Raw* meat. But I've trained you for this. We'll fan out in squads of four, with seniors taking point. Cobalt, you've got Rose Quarter, north district. Kowalski, you've got the south. Smith—Market Quarter, north district. Littleton—that puts you into the south. Cheng—Stone Quarter north, and I want Basra in the south. My squad will take north Shanties. Start by querying the usuals. Word will spread like a filthy rumor, so keep it quiet. Once someone digs up where the tournament's being held, scoot on back here as quick as you can and we'll throw up a flare. Someone in each squad should keep an eye on the sky at all times, get me?"

"Yes, Cap," the group chorused.

"Good. Once you see the flare, hurry back here and we'll coordinate a raid. These things usually kick off after supper, so we don't have much time." He clapped his hands twice. "Hop to it, people."

The constables sprang into action, with the leaders quickly choosing squads familiar to them.

"Excuse me, sir, but you forgot South Shanties," Kimani said.

Captain Peters pointed at her and some stragglers. "Taylor, Meeks, Strides—you're with the champion. South Shanties."

Kimani glanced over at one of the boys and quietly groaned.

"I haven't done this sort of thing in a while," Anna told the captain as people bustled about.

"Something tells me you'll be fine," the captain muttered.

Two men in their early twenties and Kimani, who was her daughter's age, scurried to Anna's side, each mumbling a variation of, "It's an honor, Champion Stone," with Kimani using the word arcanist.

"Two fives and a six," Peters said, nodding at the three youths. "You get the freshies."

"I'm 7th now, sir, remember?" Kimani corrected.

"But they're competent," Peters went on, seemingly not caring about such details. "Show them a trick or two. As for you lot—watch and learn. This woman might look like your loving supper-cooking aunt, but she's a lioness who's been about in her day."

"We know, sir. She's our teacher," Kimani said.

"*Was* in our cases," the taller boy mumbled, referring to the pair having hit their ceiling.

"Two very different occupations, as you'll soon discover. Make your introductions and get out of here. Oh, and you might want to keep a distance should things pop off." Peters then turned to three other young constables he had picked for his team, and Anna turned to hers.

The shorter of the boys gulped as he traded a look with the other, mumbling, "Whelp, he's never said *that* before …"

Kimani slapped her own chest. "Kimani Taylor, 7th, ice. I have Sword & Sorcery class with you, Arcanist Stone. You taught me some killer angles." She whapped the shoulder of a tall boy with sandy hair. "This is Chev Baker, who we call Strides—"

"—on account of my long stride when I walk," he said. "6th, lightning. I'm sure you remember me from class, Arcanist Stone—and writing me up for insubordination."

Anna nodded at him, recalling him being a bit of a misfit in the academy who had been lucky not to hit his ceiling earlier.

Kimani then whapped the other boy's arm, a chubby and short fellow with drooping shoulders Anna barely remembered. "And this here's Meeko Sanders, who we call Meeks. He's 5th, earth."

"Hello again, Arcanist Stone," the boy mumbled without making eye contact. He had a protruding gut and the scruffy beginnings of a beard on his neck.

"Just call us by our nick names, Arcanist Stone," Strides said, shrugging. "We're used to it."

"Good. Meeks, you're on flare-watch duty."

"Yes, Champion," the boy mumbled, still unable to make eye contact.

Just like in class, Anna remembered. Even the arcanists had called him Meek Meeko behind his back.

"Rest of you keep your eyes peeled. Now stick close, and let's go." Anna led them outside, where she bid them to hold hands with her. Since her dress didn't have pockets, she had to let the scion float free. Being tuned to her, as long as the scion was nearby, it would teleport along—it just had to be mentally communed with during the moment of teleportation.

In that moment prior to teleportation, the three young constables stared at the scion in their midst with eyes that reflected its silent inner lightning. Eyes filled with awe … and fear.

"*Impetus peragro grapa lestato exa exaei*," Anna incanted, sending the group hurtling through the arcane ether.

They appeared on a cobbled street lined with three-story homes that perched over the street like haggard vultures. An old gap-toothed woman in nothing but rags ran up to them, hands together as she silently mouthed, "Alms … alms, please."

"Can't help you today, Bertha, sorry," Kimani said, shooing her away. "Poor thing fell for fraud years back," she added as the woman tottered into an alley. "She paid a caster to sweeten her voice and the seedy bastard ended up frying it. It's a miracle Ordinaries trust us at all."

Anna, well remembering the myriad tragedies of the streets, watched the old woman sit herself down amidst a pile of trash she used as shelter. Had she time at the moment for *proata mentora*, she would certainly help the woman out somehow.

"This way," Anna said instead, and guided them over a short arching bridge made of crumbling stone, sludge trickling by underneath. A quarter of the houses in this district were boarded up or burned out, the remainder locked up tight. The occasional iron-banded lantern flickered with torchlight, looking like a miniature prison cell—and reminding Anna of a certain cell in Hell.

"Forgive me, Arcanist Stone, but were you having supper or something?" Kimani asked as they stalked the cramped but quiet street. "Only asking because of the dress."

"Indeed I was. Happened to be with your mother's crowd."

"Not by choice, then," Kimani muttered. "I suppose the topic of yours truly came up?"

"I am afraid your mother disapproves of your fondness for the constabulary," Anna replied, eyes searching the shadows.

"I couldn't care less what she thinks. She's a snob gossip with nothing better to do than write slag pieces about people. I sincerely apologize for all the horrible things she's written about you, Arcanist Stone. And about your daughter, who I consider a better friend than ever because we relate so well together. So I guess I have *that* to thank my mother for."

"I said this to your mother and I will say it to you. 'The sins of the father are not the sins of the son.'"

Kimani thought about the proverb. "Thank you, Arcanist Stone. That actually means a lot to me. Too bad not everyone thinks that way. Some *kingdoms* don't even think that way …"

"'Locks on a walk!'" a kid-like voice shouted from a three-story rooftop, quickly echoed by others, some using the slur *squealers* instead.

Anna looked up in time to see a head dip behind a chimney.

"There they go," Kimani said. "No matter what we do, they always spot us."

"Be right back," Anna said, envisioning herself one foot above clay tiles, stacked sooty brick, and openness above. "*Impetus peragro*," she snapped, reappearing a foot above the roof near the chimney—and directly behind a young boy, whose scruff she snatched with a hand even as her feet landed on the tiles.

"Gotcha," Anna said, disappointed to find one so young.

The boy, who had to be no more than ten years old, immediately began to cry as he burbled, "*Eep!* Don't turn me into no cockroach …"

"I mean you no harm, child. I only want to know where the tournament is being held."

"I don't know. They don't say nothin' like that to us 'cause they knowin' you is goin' to be askin'."

She sensed he was telling the truth. "I figured, but I still had to ask. Where's your momma?"

"Drinkin'."

"And your papa?"

"Dead o' fever."

"I'm sorry."

"Why? You didn't kill 'im."

"Do you have a home you can go to?"

The boy nodded, wiping his tears with his sleeve.

"All right, run along now, and don't let me catch you roof-hopping again." She let go and the boy raced off, hopping onto the first roof he found. Knowing there were hundreds of kids just like him in the Shanties alone and that he would likely return to trouble tomorrow, Anna sighed and teleported back.

"Anything?" Strides asked.

"After the last raid, they expect their underlings to be questioned on the tournament's location."

"So they told the kids nothing," Kimani concluded. "Clever."

Anna nodded, thinking. "Let us change tactics." She herded the group to a nearby alley and stole a peek out of it to make sure the coast was clear. "We'll have to get our information by guile. And I have an idea on how we might be able to do that."

"Ooh, are you going to cast Metamorphosis on us?" Meeks squeaked. "I want to look like a girl—"

"It'd take a whole hour to cast it on all four of us, time we cannot spare."

In the dimness, the faint outline of a coy smile graced Kimani's lips. "You're going to cast it on yourself, aren't you?"

"Only if the opportunity presents itself. For now, hold still." She dragged a hovering hand down the length of Kimani's body, incanting, "*Armari obscura chameleano traversa othra persona.*"

"Holy Unnameables, she just cast *two* extensions to Chameleon," Meeks whispered. "You all know how rare that is?"

"Shh," Anna said, enchanting the boys next before turning the spell on herself with the shortened, "*Armari obscura chameleano traversa.* The trick here is to hold hands and move slowly. I've got lead." Anna grabbed Kimani's hand and waited for her to grab one of the boys.

"Ugh, why's your hand so slimy?" Kimani hissed.

"I'm nervous," Meeks replied.

"Gross."

"Quiet now." Anna led them down the street, moving slowly but methodically, eyes watching the rooftops and the alleys, one of which she took, judging it a shortcut.

"You're not taking us where I *think* you're taking us, are you, Arcanist Stone?" Meeks squeaked when they paused before another bridge.

"It's the quickest way to find out what we need to know."

"But those are the meanest types—and the best prepared. It's the heart of the lion's den."

"Did you forget who you're talking to?" Strides interjected. "And the lion's den is fitting for a lion*ess*, don't you think?"

"Yeah, but there's, like, *hundreds* of them. Ain't no scion gonna help us with that many if they feel like going hunting."

"See him?" Anna cut in, focusing near a battered sign that read "Rough-spun Wool." It squeaked in a wind that had kicked up.

"See who?" Kimani whispered, adding under her breath, "Can't even see myself."

"Stay still. First alley after the bridge, under that sign."

"Still don't see nothing," Strides whispered.

"Keep watching. There—that tiny light." A small light outlined a silhouette in an alley near the sign, followed by a puff of smoke.

"He's piping," Kimani said.

"Did you see that his pipe showed his hand? I mean that quite literally. That warlock has a hand splayed with Reveal. They're already well prepared here. This whole district will be a dead end."

"How do you know that, Arcanist Stone?" Kimani asked.

"They wouldn't make themselves that obvious if it was the real location of the tournament."

"Sorry, but why don't you just teleport in and throttle one of them?" Meeks asked whilst peeking over his shoulder at the sky above the constabulary. "No sign of a flare," he muttered. "Everyone's coming up empty."

"Because if I get found out in any way, word would spread quickly and they would lock the tournament up."

"What does that mean?" Strides asked.

"Withdraw everybody to inside," Kimani replied. "That way the tournament can still happen, but nothing can be seen from outside. We'd be left standing about, scratching our robes."

"We need a different plan altogether," Anna said.

"I'm in Drama with your daughter and we're sometimes tasked with reacting to spontaneous scenarios."

"I don't quite follow …"

"Earlier the topic of Metamorphosis was brought up. Thinking along those lines, what if we, you know, pretended?"

"You mean like act out a scene?" Meeks asked, unimpressed.

"No, I mean pretend we—or maybe just one of us—are somebody we're not. What about a variant of Thieves-Constables?"

"The childhood game?" Strides said.

"Yeah, sort of. What about if Arcanist Stone plays a stern constable who drags one of us in by the ear and dumps us into a tavern or something? Broken Hilt's nearby, if I've got my map sense right."

"I volunteer *you*," Meeks said.

"And I accept," Kimani immediately replied. "Let's say she's had a long day and needs some ale to wash it all down, and I got dragged along after she caught me stealing a warlock's robe whilst looking for the tournament."

"And you weasel your way into finding out where the tournament is being held," Strides said.

"No way that'll work," Meeks threw in. A ruffle of his chameleonic robe indicated he had folded his arms. "No one's going to fall for that."

"You haven't heard how persuasive I can be," Kimani countered.

"I have," Strides muttered.

"And I wish you'd be as meek as you usually are instead of suddenly being so opinionated, Meeks. Cynicism doesn't impress anyone, let alone a Champion."

Meeks unfolded his arms. "I wasn't … I mean … I'm not *that* cynical. Besides, you *told* me I need to speak up for myself, so here I am speaking up and all you do is—"

"Quiet, please," Anna said, and the pair fell silent so she could think. Running out of ideas short of accosting random people, which had its drawbacks, she thought to give the young woman a chance. "All right, we get close to the Broken Hilt, where I'll morph myself. But you'll need a getup to make it work."

"You leave that part to me, Arcanist Stone."

Anna could almost hear the girl grin.

AMIDST THOSE IN NIGHT
ETERNAL

❧━━━━━━━━━━━━━━━━━━━━━━❧

"Even *I* was a little skeptical, but that's actually pretty convincing," a still-chameleonic Strides said a quarter of an hour later, looking Anna and Kimani over. They were in an alley near a raucous establishment named The Broken Hilt Inn & Tavern.

Kimani indicated Anna. "The disgruntled old street hag of a constable, long corrupt and sick of everybody—" She next indicated herself, her supposedly stolen robe torn from a supposed chase, cheeks sooty, frizzy hair filthy with dirt. "—and the young hoodlum *only tryin' to catch us some fun*," she added, adopting the accent of a girl raised on the streets.

"You're only missing one thing," Meeks said, and there came the sound of him digging about in a nearby barrel overflowing with trash. An empty bottle of wine soon floated over to Kimani, who caught it.

"This'll do fine, thanks," she said, and sprinkled what remained of the bottle's dregs onto her robe.

"You stink," Meeks said.

"That's the point." She held the bottle up as if performing a toast. "Shall we do this, Arcanist Stone?"

Anna took a deep breath. "You two going to be all right here?" she asked in her old hag voice, one that matched the fictitious sixty-year-old woman she had metamorphosized into, complete with faded constabulary robe—she was adept enough with the spell to craft objects—and leather coin purse *just* large enough to hold the scion and some coins, items Kimani and the boys had lent to aid the ruse.

"As long as Chameleon holds," Meeks replied.

"It's cast at 18th degree strength," Strides countered. "Of *course* it'll hold."

"Good, because neither of us knows how to cast the basic version."

"You just *had* to hint at our incompetence, didn't you, Meeks? I'll keep us quiet, Champion Stone, and good luck."

"Like she needs it," Meeks muttered.

Kimani flicked a hand skyward. "Just keep an eye out in case they send a flare, and come fetch us right quick if you spot one."

Meeks rolled his eyes. "Obviously."

Kimani nodded at Anna. "Ready, Arcan—I mean, Constable."

Anna took hold of Kimani's arm and led her out of the alley.

"Harder, Constable," Kimani whispered as she pretended to struggle. "Be rough, like you're sick and tired of today's youth."

Anna jerked her about. "Like that?"

"There you go. Your voice is raspy, but pepper your words with more street."

"I'll try. My quest is simple, though. It's yours that holds the challenge."

"I'm up for the challenge, Constable," and then Kimani raised her voice as they neared the tavern, shouting, "I ain't done nothin', you stupid old hag!"

"Shut up, you weasel," Anna croaked, jerking Kimani about like a ragdoll. "You'll stay still or I'll whip ye raw."

"You ain't got the nerve!"

"You try me, witch." Anna opened the door and shoved Kimani in first, keeping a tight hold of her upper arm. The place was filled with ruffian people of all ages, from kids drinking gigantic tankards to leather-faced stragglers in fishing frocks.

"Sit down," she snapped, shoving Kimani into a chair. "I'm sick and tired of you lot and I need a stiff one. What you got, 'keep?"

The barkeep, an old woman not unlike herself who spat tobacco into a brass spittoon, leaned on her battered counter. "We don't take to squealers here."

"I'll be stayin' out of yer way just fine," Anna drawled, keeping a pretend eye on Kimani, her terrible acting only masked by her raspy voice. "Been a long one, so can ya spare this old hag mercy?" She pronged two copper castles with two fingers of each hand, readied for just this occasion as per Kimani's suggestion to add believability, and slid all four across the counter. "One for the robe thief too, which ought to shut her up. Ain't suppose' to be drinkin' on me shift." Anna almost cringed at how bad she was at this.

To her surprise, the woman, seeing the coins, slid them off the counter, grunted, snatched two tankards, gave them a twirl, and tipped one against a huge cask.

Meanwhile, Kimani kept up a running complaint. "… ain't right to treat people like they is nothin' … all I was tryin' was ter get me some fun … ain't no harm in that … look at me, lookin' all fancy, like a real 'lock … the only spell I'd cast on *you* is ter make you fetch me some ale," she told a young fisherman her age whose attention she had caught. He was at the table over with a bunch of rowdy friends.

The barkeep slid two tankards at Anna, who caught herself prior to almost telekinetically picking them up. Instead, she grabbed one in each hand and hauled them over, slapping them onto the old wood, sloshing them a bit.

"Shut that yap and drink," Anna said.

Kimani squealed. "Now *that's* what I'm talkin' about," and guzzled a third of the ale right off the get-go, earning a few whistles from leering men.

Anna tried not to gawk at the display, feeling guilty for what she had gotten the girl into and trying not to envision the headline the girl's mother would write were she to catch wind of their antics.

Kimani kept shooting her mouth off and drinking, and was soon swaying, though Anna didn't know if it was real or playacting. Her own ale sat practically untouched, which was contrary to the plan—*she* was the one supposed to get drunk to let Kimani "slip away." But the ale tasted so awful she could barely drink it, not to mention she realized she could not afford to let it affect her arcanery—the situation could get dangerous fast if things went sour.

Her lack of thirst drew the attention of a burly man, who elbowed another burly man whilst nodding at her tankard. Anna gathered the courage and guzzled a large swig, making it loud and obvious, before slamming the tankard down, sloshing a good bit onto the table. Kimani, having proudly downed the last of her ale, made a show of licking the spill off the table. She flashed eyes at Anna, telling her she was gawking. Anna lightly cuffed her on her frizzy head, snapping, "Don't be such a pig, girl! And don't get nothin' on that there robe seein' as you will be returnin' it." She was starting to get the hang of the twang.

"Can't you just let me keep it? I promise I'll return it after the tournie. All I wants to see is some 'locks flyin' spells at each other. Gots to be thrillin', don't it? Come on, squealer—"

"You can't take 'lock robes, girl!" Anna countered, pretending to take another swig and wiping her mouth with her sleeve after. "And for the last time, there ain't no tournie!" she roared, adding in a bemused mutter, "And if there was, you bet your hide I'd be there watchin'," and then channeled the king by employing a booming, albeit a raspy, laugh.

The boy at the table over received a bunch of elbows and encouraging whispers before leaning toward Anna. "Hey, squealer. Squealer—how much to get 'er off yer hands?"

"What's it to ya?" Anna snapped at the same time as Kimani asked, "You goin' to the tournie?"

Both women subtly cringed at talking over each other.

"I suppose we could make it a date," he said, suddenly red in the face.

"He ain't taken a girl before," one of his mates said, to much snickering from the others.

"How much, squealer?" one of his more serious and older friends asked.

Anna, unable to fathom what the bribe should be, hesitated.

"Ten back-crunchers," Kimani blurted. "That ought to let the boys take me, eh, Squeals? Come on, Squealy, Squealy, Squealy … let the lad 'ave himself a proper date with a sweet little princess like me." She pressed a hand to her heart. "I swears on me mom's drink-ridden soul I will return this here robe after."

Anna, having no idea what back-crunchers were as she hadn't kept up on the street lingo, still knew enough that she ought to haggle. "I can't come back to the 'stabulary light-pocketed.

The boys got their heads together, pooling their money on the table. "Make it fifteen, then!" the oldest called.

Anna shrugged and waved a hand. "Bah, she's yers."

The boys and Kimani cheered and the oldest one handed Anna fifteen spines, so-called because they were silver and had the Solian pine on the reverse of the king's head. Anna figured the back-crunchers had to be a clever pun on the word *spine*, making slang out of slang. She slid these into her coin purse, which now hung heavy on her belt.

"Don't let me catch you again," Anna drawled. "And you best return that robe, or else …" Having no better threat to employ, Anna shook her fist like she imagined a common hoodlum would, but that only made the boys snicker.

Kimani took the elbow of the young man. "I will, and I'll be sweet as sweet can be, squealer, so don't get your robe all ruffled worryin' 'bout me." She giggled. "Hear that? I made me a rhyme."

"Kimani?" someone called. "Kimani, that you?"

Anna glanced over her shoulder to see a student standing behind her, one she recognized from her classes. He was a lightning warlock named Julian and had hit his ceiling at the 6th degree last term, having failed his third and final try at the academy. She recalled him having slipped after taking to towder—Tiberran nose powder. He used to fraternize with Kimani's group, but Anna couldn't recall much else as students changed friend groups like they changed robes.

Kimani hesitated only a moment before launching into a tirade. "I *told* you not to talk to me ever again, Jules! We're over, finished, done. Let's head on out before my ex throws another fit," she quickly added, dragging the young man away. "What's your name again?" she asked over the bewildered former student, who was asking, "What's gotten into *you*? And why do you look like the street ate you up and spat you out? And I thought you—"

Anna pointed two fingers at him under the table, whispering, "*Hoodvinka*," loudly adding, "Seems she ain't want nothin' to do with you no mo', young 'lock. You just let 'er be."

"Yeah, let our boy's new girl be," the older of the friends called.

Julian, already confused, muttered, "Guess I got her all wrong, then," telling Anna her on-the-spot Bewitch casting had taken root.

"Darn right you did," Anna spat, turning her back on him.

Julian wandered to the bar in a daze, sat down, stared at the doorway and, whilst scratching his head, mumbled under his breath. Anna had to wait a little bit anyway as per the plan. But after a time, he got up and returned to Anna.

"I reckon something don't add up," he said. "Where did she go?" Perhaps the Bewitch casting hadn't taken after all.

One of the heftier of the fisherman's friends stood from his stool, snapping, "Don't you be followin' them! You get yourself back to that counter there." He hitched two thumbs behind the straps of his brown fishing trousers. "We ain't afraid of no 'lock 'ere, boy."

Julian, who Anna remembered as having a temper of his own, especially after getting into the towder, ballooned. "What'd you just call me, you bloated pissant?"

"You gonna do somethin', squealer, or do I 'ave to deal with it?" the barkeep woman shouted, her well-practiced voice cleaving through the loud tavern like a butcher's knife.

Anna knew she had to act lest things spiral, and she had to do it quickly as she needed to catch up with Kimani. "You boys calm down," she said, standing. She placed herself between the two boys and gave her half-empty ale to the burly friend. "Drink instead, son." She then flicked two fingers within the sleeve of her robe at Julian, muttering, "*Hoodvinka*," before saying to him, "You just want to go and have yourself a calm drink at the bar, don't ya?"

"No, I want to mash that little pup's face in," Julian snapped back, sniffing and rubbing his red nose.

The second casting had failed—not an uncommon thing with the spell when cast against a warlock, seeing as warlocks were trained to fight such spells off. Despite Anna having figured out the 14th degree Bewitch spell's secrets, it still only tended to work three times on Ordinaries, twice on low-degree warlocks, and maybe once on the higher degrees if their guard was down or the casting was particularly potent. It didn't help that Anna only ever used the spell on practice dummies really, enchanted to make a sound or give a visual cue if the spell had been cast properly.

"Oh *yeah*?" the fisherman said, his friends standing behind him.

"Yeah," Julian snapped past Anna's shoulder.

Just as Anna opened her mouth to tell them to back off, a fist flew past her head and smacked Julian square in the nose. Julian howled in pain but managed to claw a hand toward the fisherman, hissing, "*Dreadus terrablus!*"

The fisherman screamed the scream of a child caught in nightmarish terror, silencing the entire tavern. The two men stood there, one bleeding profusely from the nose, and the other howling like a banshee from the Fear spell.

Then the fisherman's friends launched themselves at Julian. For some reason Anna could not fathom, this gave permission for another man to throw a fist at the back of *her* head, hissing, "Always wanted to take a piece out of a squealer!"

"Don't hit old ladies!" another man shouted, smacking the first upside the head with a beefy hand.

Next thing Anna knew she was in the middle of a full-on brawl, with others using the opportunity to settle old scores or try to rob a neighbor or steal an unattended tankard or grub.

Overwhelmed and realizing she couldn't lose Kimani, Anna did the only thing she could think of in that moment, and that was to quickly draw the outlines of the worst nearby offenders, incanting, "*Paralizo carcusa cemente dio!*" Four men—including Julian—froze in place, their fists stuck in midair. Then she turned on the other brawlers and repeated the spell, paralyzing them on the spot too.

Panting from exertion, Anna turned in place to face the eerily quiet tavern. "On second thought, I think I ought to have me a drink elsewhere," she said, and strode out, bewildered mutters following.

"Thanks, I guess," the barkeep said as she passed. "Will make it easier to toss 'em out."

Once outside, Anna checked the street for any sign of Kimani and the boy.

"Champion Stone!" came a whisper from an alley. "Over here!"

Anna scurried to the alley and bumped into a still-chameleonic body.

"It's Meeks. I know where Kimani and that boy went. Strides is already after them. Follow me."

"Any sign?" Anna asked as she ran alongside Meeks, who had turned visible from the effort.

"No flare yet, Champion." He looked down at himself. "Oops, didn't mean to."

"Doesn't matter," Anna replied.

"Want me to sprint to the constabulary to send up a flare?"

"Only when we get confirmation of the exact location."

They came to a grimy intersection of stinking, run-down fish shops that were closed for the night. "Which way?"

"This way, I think," Meeks said, choosing a cobbled road.

"I should have alarmed her," Anna said, the pair jogging along the cobbles.

"She doesn't scare easily, Champion Stone."

"I meant the spell."

"Oh." They passed lanterns decorated with posters of a coming fair before Meeks spoke again. "I don't think it's fair that girls can get boys so easily."

"What?" Anna huffed, eyes darting about in search of Kimani.

"I fancy her yet she just … throws it in my face."

"Now's not the time. Where are they?" she pressed as they came to another intersection.

"Probably making out in an alley," he muttered. "I'm so angry at her. I can't believe she would do this. It's so blatant. She turns me down repeatedly then—" He flipped a hand to the right. "—*this*."

Anna, incredulous at the random tangent the young man was going on yet determined to focus on the quest at hand, took the hand flip as an indication of direction and shot that way.

"Wait up, Champion Stone!" Meeks called.

Anna was now at a near sprint and left him behind. Unlike Chameleon, Metamorphosis did not snuff itself from a vigorous run, and so she remained as the old constable woman, figuring she would snuff the spell later when she had a chance—or keep the facade up if needed.

She skidded before a bedraggled old man collecting rags from the street. "Excuse me. Have you seen a girl and a boy walk by this way?"

The man looked up with sooty eyes before pointing to a cemetery with a bony finger.

"Thanks," and Anna shot off again, slowing to a jog and then a standstill as she came upon gigantic wrought-iron gates not unlike those found at the academy. Scrolling across the top, in rusted iron lettering, were the words, "Here rest souls in night eternal." The gate itself was festooned with charms against the undead—amulets, wards, and certain flowers and vegetables such as garlic and onions, most long dried out. History books were filled with variations of such practices, yet only real arcanery protected against curses, which were beyond the reach of superstition, and only wisdom and intellect and education prevented the rise of a necromancer.

The cemetery was near the south end of town, surrounded mostly by small generational orchards, old oaks, and the deep silence of the forever. Beyond loomed the high wall of the city, with its stone watchtowers. A pale knife moon lit the tombs and sarcophagi and obelisks. Since few could afford burials throughout history, those interred here were oft of the noble or merchant classes, Ordinary and warlock alike. Anna always thought the relatively few warlocks who chose burial over burning in the sacred blue flames secretly wanted themselves preserved in the hope they would be resurrected if such knowledge came to light. Unfortunately for them, that wish sometimes came true—albeit in the form of being risen as the undead to serve a necromantic master. The smarter Ordinaries preemptively hired warlocks to perform the 16th degree Memorial Ceremony for themselves or their family members to prevent a necromancer from snatching their souls.

What was most interesting about the old cemetery to Anna was what it sat atop of—an ancient underground Rivican temple, which had been sealed off by the authorities for preservation purposes, as no one could make sense of the structure. Like everything Rivican, scant evidence of what that race and society looked like had survived the eons of time after their extinction. One could get a permit to enter this particular structure, but it was expensive. Mainly, it was hoped future arcaneologists would decipher the temple's meaning and use. Some even speculated it wasn't a temple but something else entirely.

"Like an arena," Anna said, eyes scanning the vast cemetery in search of movement.

Meeks finally caught up. "You see them, Champion Stone?" he wheezed, hands braced on his thighs as he bent over to catch his breath.

"No." *They must have already entered*, Anna thought. *Which means Strides will find us to report on the entrance, giving us confirmation.*

"Then we're hooped," Meeks said. "I knew that Strides was an idiot. Never should have trusted him to carry out the quest. Bet you he's making out with her now too."

Anna glanced at him. "Have some patience, young man. And I do not appreciate the way you speak about your colleague."

"She's the one who owes me—"

"She owes you nothing. What you owe *her* is what she is already giving you, which is respect." She held up a hand to stave his argument off. "Silence. I have no patience for such foolery. Do you understand me?"

Meeks dropped his head, mumbling, "Yes, Champion."

Jogging footsteps approached through the darkness, and a figure soon emerged from behind a line of stone sarcophagi. "They're inside," Strides huffed.

"So where exactly is it then?" Meeks snapped. "And what took you so long? You kept the champion waiting."

"Can you confirm there's a tournament being held there?" Anna pressed.

Strides nodded. "I overheard them talking on the way as Kimani was being purposely loud even though the boy kept shushing her. Based on what she said, I can confirm there's a tournament happening here underneath the cemetery. The entrance is behind King Northsword's tomb."

"The founder of Solia," Anna muttered out of interest. The tomb was symbolic, erected posthumously many years later in recognition of the man's accomplishments. The choice of location made sense to Anna because he happened to be a lover of blood sport, having commissioned many warlock tournaments that had oft culminated in death. This was in the time prior to The Founding, meaning arcanery had been wild and far more volatile, making it quite the spectator sport. He was also said to be the first to make his mark upon the Black Arena, building it up from a Rivican stronghold, although that part of history remained highly contested by historians.

"They closed shop just after Kimani entered," Strides went on. "Some little kid ran in there to warn them."

"No doubt from our snooping," Anna said, wondering if it was the same kid she had caught on the rooftop.

"They're ignoring latecomers, but I saw a rich noble get ushered inside, so there're secret eyes on the entrance."

"All right, I want you both to race back to the constabulary and have them send up a flare. Tell Peters everything."

"Yes, Champion," Strides said, and took off without waiting for Meeks, who frowned and asked, "Wouldn't it be faster if you teleported, Champion?"

"I'm going to scout ahead." She ran a hand down her body and said, "*Morpha null,*" turning back into herself.

"You're going in wearing *that*?" He ran his eyes up and down the dress she had worn to that disappointing supper. "Er, Champion Stone?"

Anna ignored him as she mentally prepared for what awaited. The last thing she was worried about was her dress. "Make sure they don't go in without a plan."

"It's just a bunch of hoodlums who are probably scared of a fight. We mash their faces in all the time on the street."

"You could not be more wrong. What awaits here is great danger. Do as the captain bids and nothing else." It disconcerted her that the boy spoke more like a vigilante than a constable, as if the constabulary were trying to replace the vilified and banished Arcane order. The Arcaner order had oft been accused of vigilantism, although at least they had had an iron self-governing code of honor that severely penalized misbehavior, making Arcaners nearly incorruptible.

Meeks shrugged. "We'll do as we're told, I guess. Always do."

Anna, wondering why he was dilly-dallying, gave him a questioning look.

"Right, I should go. Er, good luck, Champion … not that you need it." He finally ran off.

Anna focused on a tomb near Northsword's that she had visited on an academy excursion for History class back when she was a student. She hoped her memory was sharp enough to prevent a misfire, for that excursion had been over thirty years ago.

"*Impetus peragro,*" she snapped, reappearing with a *thwomp* that echoed off nearby tombs. She had been strategic in choosing a location far enough away from Northsword's tomb that the sound ought to dissipate well.

She stood listening before the tomb of the famous Solian explorer Codus Trazinius, remembering herself as the still-precocious teenager, with William and Jordan by her side, the three fresh from a romp in the cloud cavern under the Black Castle. They had been 5th degree back then and in the thick of a strong friendship, spending time together in places like the secret hangout den under the academy's also secret 6th degree Trainer. How adventurous that all had felt! Now everything seemed drab and routine in comparison. Maybe Thia was right—maybe adulthood *was* boring.

She read the epitaph on the tomb. *I, who hath seen the sacred and enchanting plane of Ley with mine own eyes, long to rest as a pebble amidst the sandy shores of eternity.* She sighed, remembering how that epitaph had so deeply affected her all those years ago. Now it reminded her of Roth and Panza and her father and her son ... and the quest to come.

Hearing nothing, she cast her usual spells—Reveal and Chameleon, the latter with the travel extension. She then padded up behind the tombstones, eyes trained on a large structure ahead—only to freeze upon spotting a puff of smoke emerge from just beyond an obelisk.

The pipe-smoker, Anna thought. He must have spotted them earlier and come to watch in person. He would certainly have Reveal lit, with eyes of a hawk. Probably 13th to 15th degree, he was likely no slouch, perhaps even a dueler himself. In fact, she had yet to find a slouch among those who watched with alert eyes. They were oft the dangerous ones. The ones she least had to worry about were usually those with big mouths. The arena had taught her that bravado was parchment foil when it came to arcanery, hence why she let her spells do the talking.

The pipe-smoking guard was facing the back of the tomb, a towering marble structure that showed a great king holding the hilt of a sword, the point of which rested against the ground.

Just as Anna was about to slink closer, a giggle echoed off the tombs and the man snuffed his pipe and glanced about, forcing her to duck behind a tombstone. She peeked out to see a couple wander in, the man wearing a long coat and the woman a white mink throw.

"Black knight charging!" the man called out.

"Shield formation," came the immediate reply. It had to be a passphrase, for two men—warlocks by the cut of their robes—emerged from out of nowhere and shepherded the couple into an open tomb.

As Anna waited for them to return to take their places so she could note their positions, she happened to read the inscription on the tombstone she was hiding behind.

Here lie husband and wife Morton and Capsella Othington
Having died holding hands at the ripe ages of ninety-three, in the year 2998
Resting in love unconquered

The nearly three-hundred-year-old marker made her think of Thomas. Where was he right then? Was he with Thia, reflecting on his choices that evening? Or was he still slumming with the king and his harpy entourage? Would he and Anna grow old together and, if so, be burned together in the sacred fires? Or would they choose to be buried under a tombstone in the vain hope of living a second life in some forward-thinking future? Most would say that everybody died alone, yet this tombstone begged to differ.

She shoved those thoughts aside and refocused on the men, who had retreated into two separate tombs, the doorways of which were open, the innards dark. The entrance was underground, down a series of steps. The three men triangulated their watch, meaning there was no way for Anna to slip by. Spells of stealth would be noticeable to someone adept with Reveal, which left either guile … or violence. The latter would have the organizers calling reinforcements while they themselves fled. Hostages might be taken, and then things could spiral once the constables got involved, and the last thing Anna wanted was a bloodbath. She had to be smart, yet time was also of the essence, for the duels would have surely already begun.

Knowing that either way she had to get closer, Anna dropped to the ground and slithered forward in the grass like a snake, not caring one lick about dirtying her dress. When she was but ten feet behind the pipe-smoker, she heard one of the men ask something that froze her in her tracks.

"When should we expect her?"

"The captain said any time now," the pipe-smoker replied.

The incorruptible captain had been corrupted.

ANCIENT BLOCKS

❧————————————————————❧

Anna lay frozen in place, hearing nothing but a loud buzzing in her ears. How could the one constable she had faith in have allowed himself to become a pawn? What had they offered—or threatened him with—to make him turn on her, on his own kingdom? By gods, students were in there! His own *kid* could be—

That had to be it. They got to his kid. That's how they *always* won. And she was sure the young constables had no idea—at least Kimani didn't.

Feeling lonely, Anna considered retreating, leaving it be. Then she remembered Thia's pleading eyes. Yet what could she realistically do? It was a duel of honor, and as such—

A voice pierced her roiling thoughts.

"I'm the girl! The one they're fighting over!" Thia wheezed between huffing breaths, having apparently run there.

It took everything Anna had not to bolt to her daughter.

"Which ticket?" the pipe-smoker asked. Anna noticed his eyes were alert, hand still splayed with Reveal. This man was no fool.

"What?"

"Which draw?"

"Uh … Ivanov versus Turman."

"We don't have a Turman, but we have an Ivanov versus a Narsus."

"That's it! Has it started yet?"

"Probably, little miss. Wait a moment—aren't you *her* daughter?"

"Yeah, so? Why, is my mother here?"

The man glanced pointedly down at her big belly. "You ought not to be here in your … condition."

"I have a right to be here if they're fighting over *my* honor!"

As Thia pled her case, Anna ruminated on her options. Storm in there and snatch her daughter and teleport her to safety—or let her go inside. The first decision might lead to violence—and her daughter, being with child, would be highly vulnerable. The second decision would at least allow Anna to come up with a plan.

The man, seemingly tired of listening to Thia, beckoned. The two men, one stout and the other lanky, emerged from the shadows. Moonlight glinted off numerous small blades on their leather-wrapped torsos, indicating they were night stalkers—initiated members of the thieves guild. Some were warlocks, but all were well trained in the night arts—the small blade, the stalk, gaining illicit entry, the blowpipe, among other nefarious talents.

The pipe-smoker whispered something into the ear of the lanky one, who nodded and ran off. The only word Anna had made out was "Peters," telling her the man had been dispatched as a messenger. She wondered what the captain would do, before realizing he'd probably do nothing.

The pipe-smoker flicked his head first at Thia then at the open tomb. "After you, young lady. Renner, see she makes it in safely, would you, chap?"

"This way, miss," the stout man said, taking her by the arm.

"Let go of me!"

"It's for your own protection."

"What is this? What are you doing?"

"You want to see two men kill each other to win you over, don't you?" the pipe-smoker asked. "Here's your chance."

"*Kill* each other? B-but I thought—"

"We know you're here," the leader said aloud to the surrounding tombstones. "Thinking you could use your daughter as bait was … ill-conceived."

"What? I came on my own! My mom forbade me from coming! I even slipped a sleeping potion into my guardian's tea and ran like a fool to be here—and I'm with child! I wouldn't risk it if I—"

"We know about the plan to shut us down, miss. You coming will be extra insurance in preventing that, so thank you. Now I suggest you hurry inside if you don't want to miss the fight." He nodded at his cohort and the man half-dragged, half-walked Thia to the doorway. And it was that half-dragging that made the blood rage in Anna's veins. She could be lightning quick, yes, but that would mean whisking her daughter off to safety and leaving Jonah behind. Besides, perhaps her daughter *did* have a right to be there—perhaps even to try to intervene. She was a woman grown and had the right to determine her future. One man was the father of her child and the other a pursuer of her heart. And it was the latter who Thia loved.

But she was also Anna's daughter. If this was going to happen, it would happen *supervised*. With Reveal still lit, she rose like a cobra from the grass and stepped out into the open, the scion floating above her head like a miniature lightning sun. "Let go of her," she said.

"Mom, what are you doing! I'm not leaving—"

"I know." She looked to the leader. "I will escort my daughter myself."

Three more leather-clad men emerged from the shadows and drew knives and daggers—but surreptitiously, so Thia could not see them. This was in addition to having a warlock on their side, meaning the night stalkers had great confidence in their blade arts. But then, they also had Anna's greatest weakness within range of a single blade stroke, confident that Anna would not dare gamble with her daughter's life.

The pipe-smoker looked at the scion. "I always wanted to see one up close."

"Now you have." Anna tilted her head to the side a little. "And it sees you."

The man swallowed, unnerved. Then he smiled unkindly. "Alas, having made your intentions clear about shutting us down, I would be a fool to let you wander in without insurance. If you want to enter, we will do it together. That way we can avoid certain, how shall I put this … shenanigans."

Anna took the men in with one swift glance. If they were to act, all it would take was an eye blink for them to forever silence her daughter—a moment no amount of vengeance or skill or pleading or healing could undo. This particular battle had already been lost. But they also had to know that even wounding her daughter would cost them dearly.

"Then we all go in together," she said, seeing little choice in the matter. Her daughter insisted on being here, the captain was corrupt, and a young man's life was at stake—as was her daughter's.

The pipe-smoker smirked. "You dirtied your dress."

"The supper was hardly worth the effort anyway." She hoped keeping things light might soothe their unease. The men were wound drum-skin-tight, and she didn't want any accidents.

He looked at the scion.

"It will stay neutral as long as you do," she said. "There is no reason we cannot solve this amicably."

"Oh, I heartily agree." The man grinned in a manner that gave Anna the creeps. He opened a hand, indicating for her to lead. "After you, ladies."

"How'd you get to the captain?" Anna asked as she stepped by, taking her daughter's hand, which felt clammy and cold and clutched hers with the fear of a girl out of her depth.

"The same way we got to you."

"Family?"

"Family. You cost the guild a lot of money the last time you spearheaded a raid. This time we thought to take precautions. The threat of a blade combined with a purse of crowns can buy anything these days."

It was just as Anna had suspected. She walked, acutely conscious of one of the night stalkers sticking very close to Thia and feeling profoundly vulnerable knowing these men could strike first—and easily succeed. The only thing that prevented them was fear of her, which meant she had to show she was at total ease. Only complete confidence—and the certainty of a merciless death—would stay their hands.

An opportunity to show that confidence came as she finished descending the stone steps of a narrow passage, at the bottom of which was a sarcophagus, its lid Reveal told her was enchanted with a basic locking passphrase. With her hand hidden from the men and her feet purposely scuffing the stone floor to mask what she was about to do, she pointed at a key tendril of the enchantment and murmured, "*Exotus mia enchantus duo dai ideum exat.*" After surreptitiously pinching it loose, the entire tendril web dissolved. Anna stepped aside with her daughter, who had widened her eyes at her, having heard what she had done.

Anna ignored her as a night stalker shoved by, leaving his cohort to hold Thia by the neck as he splayed a hand at the sarcophagus. "*Entarro—sarkas.*" Nothing happened. The man repeated himself, this time barking the password. Still the lid refused to open.

"Allow me," Anna said as the pipe-smoking leader tried to squeeze by his two other men in the narrow stairwell. She raised an arm and connected telekinetically to the sarcophagus. The scion buzzed as the space around her warped, making one of the men gasp, and the entire sarcophagus ground aside, revealing a hole—not just in the floor, but hopefully in the men's confidence as well. The distant cacophony of a large crowd in the thrall of watching something exciting filtered into the small and dingy room, along with the fetid odor of sewage and brick and decay.

Having demonstrated her arcane might, Anna calmly stepped aside. The pipe-smoker squeezed by his men, but all he could do was glance between the shoved sarcophagus, Anna, and the scion.

"The air warped," one of the men mumbled. "Never seen nothin' like it."

Anna, wanting to project confidence, said nothing.

"Stay sharp," the pipe-smoker snapped, glaring at Anna. "She's a wily one."

Thia danced from foot to foot as if she had to go to the privy. "Please, can we hurry? The duel must have started already."

The pipe-smoker took up position on Thia's right, opposite his colleague. He nodded at Anna. "Go on, then."

Anna stepped into the hole and descended a rusted ladder that went down quite a ways, second-guessing herself at every rung. Was this truly the best course of action? Should she have simply snatched her daughter's hand and teleported her to safety, leaving Jonah to his fate? This wasn't just about Thia either, but the child she bore. Anna wondered if she was gambling with the Arinthian line's entire future, all for some seventeen-year-old Abrandian Thia hardly knew anyway—and would surely get over in time. Was he really worth it?

By the time she got to the bottom and looked up to see the burliest of the night stalkers holding Thia by the scruff as he guided her down the ladder, a dagger between his teeth, her waffling resolve turned to iron. This fight was not about her, but her daughter. That made it personal. These men … they had no idea what she was capable of. Of how she could wield the scion and her vast reservoir of knowledge like the most potent of weapons. In fact, only those she had slain knew the true extent of her power, and their lips had been forever silenced.

The pipe-smoker flicked a hand down a brick passage covered with white deposits of lime and calcium and lit by guttering torch lamps. "Go on, then."

Anna met her daughter's eyes.

When the girl looked past her, anxious to get to Jonah, Anna turned to lead with a quick stride. The echoing noise of the crowd got louder the farther along the ancient sewer she went. With that noise came the familiar tingling nerves of the arena. It was mixed with the air of history, for they walked underneath the tombs of the dead and the shrine to the founder of their kingdom. There were three layers of history here—the time of the Rivicans, the time after King Northsword's reign during which the tomb above had been erected, and the time of the rise of the city of Blackhaven, when the sewers had been built.

The passage forked into three wider sewage canals. Two went left and right and the third seemed to have been dug out not too long ago — judging by the excavation tools and carts nearby. The arcaneologist in Anna was appalled at the sight of what surely had to be an illegal operation. Who knew what ancient history had been damaged or lost by these ham-handed efforts? But such concerns, being trivial against her daughter's life, were swept aside like leaves in autumn.

"Go on, then," the pipe-smoker said for the umpteenth time.

The passage ahead angled twenty degrees down and forced them to dip their heads under a low ceiling of hard clay. All pressed against the ceiling as they went, for the footing was precariously slippery. At the bottom was a gurgling brook of filth, and judging by the splash marks, many a visitor had already graced its muddy waters with their body. Under any other circumstance, Anna would have found the sight amusing.

The passage cleaved through a wall of blocks, which Anna recognized as the smooth workmanship of the long-extinct Rivican empire. It opened into a vast underground dome made of gigantic blocks of basalt, the bottom of which was lined with rows of descending stone bleachers well-worn from ancient use. A crowd of hundreds pressed in around the center, a large pit recessed into the earth. It seemed the thieves had broken into an ancient Rivican arena — and the first thing they'd decided to do was use it for blood sport.

They pressed forth together, with Thia held by the arms from both sides. The audience roared ahead, where a vine shot skyward from the pit. It smacked the concave ceiling, polished to such a mirror shine — and enhanced arcanely, judging by the tendril geometries — that the spell rebounded toward the pit. The crowd hooted about a near miss, which was followed up by a low-angled vine punch which also missed, instead smashing into a shield hastily summoned by a warlock spectator.

Thia struggled in the men's grips, pleading for them to let her get near, for Jonah Ivanov and Ralf Turman shared the same element of earth — it had to be them dueling. The pipe-smoker nodded at his men, three of whom led Thia closer. But just as Anna moved to join her daughter, the pipe-smoker grabbed her arm. "You stay here!" he shouted over the crowd.

Anna nodded at the pipe-smoker that she would obey, and he let go. She used that freedom to edge closer so she could see the combatants. The pipe-smoker perhaps allowed this only because he himself also could not see, yet he stayed behind Anna, watching her more than he watched the show, his goon alongside, meeting Anna's gaze with paranoid eyes whenever she glanced back.

For Anna, it was no longer a question of stopping the fight. With her daughter as hostage and the constables compromised, she could only watch helplessly as the two duelers, indeed Ralf and Jonah, battered each other with spells. Jonah kept up a steady onslaught of direct attacks while Ralf used feints and guile, reminding her a little of a man she had faced thirty years ago … The Reaper.

And that was when she spied him. Her ex-boyfriend of long ago, Scadius Von Edgeworth, now a prize-purse dueling champion, stood on a makeshift plank platform. He mingled with fellow scarred arena duelers, corrupt soldiers and officials, and night stalkers. And with chiseled warriors of the sword—Ordinary arena duelers. Men in full armor, proud to wear it. All looked on, cups in hand, chatting and betting and laughing. Yet Scadius spoke most with the jewel-fingered leader of the thieves guild.

Anna narrowed her eyes. So Scadius also held some responsibility in all this. To what extent did not matter anymore. He had taken a certain path in defiance of her and her kingdom. An unforgivable path.

Scadius looked up to meet her gaze, and the sociable smile—a smile she saw her husband oft deploy amidst company—slipped from his face. His eyes hardened, the eyes of someone who loathed her as deeply and profoundly as he still loved her. A noble with a peacock-feather hat elbowed him and the smile returned as they greeted each other like old friends, before the pair struck up a conversation with the leader of the thieves guild. Yet Scadius kept stealing quick glances at her.

Anna eventually returned her attention to the duel. Jonah was tiring, and Ralf pressed his advantage. Thia was screaming at them to stop, but the crowd drowned out her cries. As nerve-wracking as it was to watch what would usually be a thrilling duel, something about how the pipe-smoker and his goon were standing behind her put her on alert. Both had tensed up, angling themselves a certain way. When she looked at the platform, she saw that both Scadius and the leader of the thieves guild had stepped forth to stare at her, as if she were the most interesting thing in the kingdom.

In that moment, Anna realized she was about to be assassinated.

IN THE BLINK OF AN EYE

In the span of a heartbeat, Anna saw the potential consequences play out, all of which culminated in her daughter lying in a pool of her own blood.

All but one. The lone recourse she had to take, an act that might condemn a soul to death and shatter her daughter's heart. Such was the price for the decisions all involved had already made.

Anna whirled and telekinetically snatched both blades as they shot forth. In one swift movement she angled the pipe-smoker's dagger up, slamming it into the base of his jaw, burying it to the hilt. At the same time, she angled the other man's dagger at his heart. Whereas the former had been too slow to do anything but gasp, the latter grabbed the dagger with his free hand and tried to turn it around. His face went purple from the strain of his Ordinary muscles fighting against her Telekinesis. Then the floating scion buzzed loudly as she lent the spell its might and the dagger sank into the man's chest. As his leader fell to the ground beside him, he stared at her with disbelieving eyes. She gave him the courtesy of staring back, for she would be the last person he ever laid eyes on, before letting him fall. There they lay on the grimy floor, two nameless assassins, with a lone pipe between them.

Anna whirled, snapping, "*Impetus peragro*," and appeared directly behind the three night stalkers holding Thia, only one of whom had the wherewithal to check back on their captain, as if unaware of what they had planned. The next events happened in moments. Anna shoved at the air, roaring, "*Baka!*" sending that lizard-eyed fool flying into the pit. The remaining pair, both of whom had hold of Thia's upper arms, reacted swiftly. The first thrust forth with his dagger, which sank into Anna's side. She ate the hot pain that would have usually made her scream and instead flicked at the second night stalker, who was about to murder Thia. His dagger, which had been aimed at Thia's face, instead shot over her head and stabbed the first in the eye. As that man howled in agony, both let go of Thia. Anna used that moment to kick the second stabber in the gut, sending him tumbling back into a crowd of gawkers, grab Thia, and snap off, "*Impetus peragro grapa lestato exa exaei!*"

The last thing she saw was Jonah looking up at her as Ralf "Narsus" Turman grabbed the fallen man's dagger and plunged it into Jonah's chest. It was the last thing Thia saw too, for when the pair appeared outside their home tower, Thia loosed a blood-curdling scream. There was only one time in Anna's life she had heard such a scream—from herself, when she had lost her son, Samuel. It was so jarring, and so vivid a moment, that Anna staggered, the pain in her heart far greater than the one in her side.

"No, no, no, no, no!" her daughter gurgled between sobs, beating on her mother with her fists. "Why did you have to attack them!"

Anna withered under her daughter's blows, one of which glanced the hilt of the dagger, dropping her to one knee. She had to check the wound. "I had no choice," she wheezed, splaying a hand over the hilt. "*Examino potente—*"

But her Diagnose casting was cut short when her daughter slapped her hand aside, roaring, "Answer me!"

Anna tried to explain they had been about to assassinate her but Thia refused to hear a single word, instead pummeling her with her fists as she shouted, "You killed the love of my life! You killed him! You have to take me back! I need to hold him! You need to heal him before it's too late!"

"I will, I will! But *I* must heal first. Thia! Do you understand? You must let me heal!"

The portal behind them flared. "What is commotion?" Niterra Bladesong croaked, rubbing one eye with the heel of a hand. "What happen? Why you outside, girl?" Then she spotted the blood and shot over. "Stone—"

"Thia slipped you a sleeping potion. She will explain. Has my husband returned?"

"He has not."

Cold dread seeped into Anna's soul. He had let her down most profoundly. But there was no time to dwell on it now. "I must make haste in healing and return," and she thrust a hysterical Thia into the old woman's arms, freeing herself to perform the critical Diagnose. After seeing that the blade had miraculously slipped by her pancreas, she knew the dagger could stay in place. It would save time, allowing her to possibly save Jonah.

She envisioned the floor of the arena, its sand soaked with ancient blood. The writhing bodies of two men, one shoved, the other stabbed. And the one who called himself Narsus looming over his victim.

"*Impetus peragro!*" Anna roared, reappearing exactly where she intended.

There indeed stood Ralf Turman. He held a bloody dagger in his fist, chest heaving as he stared down at Jonah. The way Jonah stared at the polished ceiling, how empty his eyes were, instantly told Anna that the kind young man who had captured her daughter's heart, the one who had somehow escaped the bonds of an oppressive childhood, was gone. There was nothing she could do to bring him back.

Ralf looked over at Anna. "As per the traditions of old, your daughter now belongs to me," he boomed in an amplified voice, having apparently prepared his speech. "I am the rightful winner, and thus champion of Thia Stone's destiny. I have been witnessed, and so shall it be."

Anna's eye twitched. "You will never have my daughter's hand, *ever*. This was an illegal bout, and instead of making your opponent take the knee, you chose the path of murder."

" 'The sword calling the dagger sharp,' " Ralf said, quoting an old proverb about hypocrisy.

From the stands above, men demanded her death.

"She murdered our comrades!" a night stalker shouted.

"Vengeance is nigh!" called another.

Ralf glanced up at the unruly crowd with a smirk. Onlookers were either crying hysterically, talking in low voices, gawking with horrified faces, or fleeing altogether. Shadowy figures moved behind those who remained—guards and night stalkers, thugs and miscreants. Faces popped up only to vanish, watching, circling, waiting for the mob to form before they could gather the courage to strike, for none could match her strength one on one.

Anna was about to declare that Ralf was under arrest, when the awful truth of the matter settled in. The captain, the one remaining constable she had thought she could rely on, might have had a hand in her attempted assassination.

"Arcanist Stone!" shouted a voice.

Anna looked up to see none other than Kimani, Strides, and Meeks rushing down the ancient bleachers.

"Arcanist Stone!" Kimani hollered, shoving through the crowd to the edge of the pit. "The captain's—" She froze upon seeing Jonah, the color draining from her face.

Anna had been about to teleport them out of there when night stalkers seized them from behind, pressing daggers to their throats. Each gasped and raised their hands.

"My turn," said another amplified voice, "since these fools show their ineptness, as I knew they would."

Anna looked opposite to see Scadius Von Edgeworth descending a narrow line of carved steps slicing through the arena wall.

"Anna Atticus Stone!" he boomed, taking a swig from a bottle before tossing it aside. It landed on the drag marks where Ralf had pulled Jonah to unceremoniously dump him by the wall before climbing it to join the crowd. "Anna Atticus Stone!" Scadius repeated, arms wide like a master of ceremonies. "How long I have waited for this day …"

As he droned on about his own vapid destiny, Anna, knowing what he wanted, and knowing how they had all cornered her by working together, merely opened a hand over the dagger, incanting, "*Anesthelatestranaga o nerva arregando au bona ata au flaeho au o chessa*," using the 5th degree Anesthetize spell to numb the wound, the translation being *anesthetize the nerves around the bone and the flesh of the chest*. Then she took a deep breath, grabbed the hilt of the dagger with both hands, and yanked it out, refusing to cry out from the sensation that had jarred her body nonetheless.

"Yes, I will allow you to heal," Scadius said, hands at his hips. "For I want you at your best." He smacked his chest with a fist. "And you will give it to me!"

She dropped the dagger to the sand before once again splaying her hand over the wound, this time incanting, "*Remedia binda arregando min finateo*," using the knowledge she had gained from Diagnose to bolster the Remedy Elementary Wound spell. She worked with patience, slowly repairing each bit of flesh until it was whole, not letting anything disturb her concentration. Scadius droned on throughout.

"… to avenge my honor, for this woman here gave my family's rightful inheritance to another, betraying my kingdom and *me*. The Fates have brought us together so that I may repair that old wound. Today we settle our old score once and for all, kingdom champion against kingdom champion!"

After healing the wound, which had bloodied an already dirty dress, she glanced over at Kimani and Strides and Meeks. All were terrified, hands still in the air, hostages to the agendas of others. She could not walk away from what lay ahead. She could no longer run or hide or make excuses, for the last bastion of the good constable had been breached. Now it was up to her to show that hope remained.

"Look at me," Scadius declared. When Anna finally did so, he once more opened his arms, this time to the crowd, although his eyes were on her. "Thus speaketh I the sacred words!" he boomed, and the crowd, which had thickened once again, hushed. "Anna Atticus Stone, today we duel in the old way. Not as servants of others, but as free warlocks. Let us bow, so I may avenge the wound to the Von Edgeworth honor! I call on thee to show thy stripes and duel me *to the death*!"

"To the death!" echoed some men in the crowd, beginning a chant, "To the death! To the death! To the death!" This was not a crowd of supporters, but outcasts and miscreants and those who longed for and gambled on blood. The crowd also rapidly thickened, meaning some of those who departed did so merely to fetch others.

Seeing Ralf pound his fist against the stone wall as he chanted along with the others stiffened her spine. At stake was the last vestige of incorruptibility, the Arinthian line's future ... and her daughter. She could not let him or Scadius or any of them triumph. *Would* not. She was out of practice, yes, and he a seasoned arena warrior, but he had made the mistake of placing everything she cared for on the line. It would be the last mistake he ever made.

"To show how confident I am, I shall grant her the use of the scion!" Scadius roared, smiling at Anna in a way that suggested he had planned all this ahead. As if conscious it was being spoken of, the legendary ancient orb flickered with silent lightning as it moved to float on the other side of Anna.

Another mistake, Anna thought, for she would have been prepared to do the honorable thing and set it aside. Now she knew he must have planned for her to use the scion's greatest power—ring snuff. His best response would be an instant teleport away, beyond the reach of the rapidly expanding ring snuff bubble. Quite achievable at his competence level.

Scadius took a deep breath, savoring the moment, before his eyes swirled with whirlpools, a basic display of strength that told the crowd he had achieved the mythic Settling—and one that strengthened the crowd's chant of "To the death!" Only then did he bow, flaring eighteen watery rings around his arm.

Anna, who had yet to say anything to him, finally asked, "How would your son feel if Papa never came home?"

"I will not lose. Besides—" He shrugged. "—*she* took him," referring to his ex-wife.

Anna, glad the boy would at least have a home, calmly walked to Jonah's lifeless body. As the crowd booed and hissed, thinking she was about to decline the challenge, she slipped off one of her shoes, causing them to roar—for all knew what it meant. She slipped off the other one and placed both neatly beside the young man's body, knowing she would have to pass on to her daughter the awful news.

Ignoring Ralf, who was trying to get her to see the glee on his face, she looked at the three young hostages. Finally, she looked at Scadius Von Edgeworth, who had straightened, face mocking, confident, arrogant. For a moment she heard nothing as memories of old duels flooded her mind. She remembered crawling through a summoned darkness cloud as she waited for a 6th degree Triana Taylor, whose own daughter was held captive here tonight, to make her move. She recalled running bare of foot through the snow as her deranged sister chased her, and then confronting her staff on staff in the grove before their now abandoned home. And she remembered pressing forth with Burst, sending blast after lightning blast at The Reaper, the greatest foe she had ever faced … until tonight.

She walked back to face a man she had once shown affection, a man who had called her sweetie, with her calling him Scadie in return. Calmly, she placed a hand to her throat, incanting, "*Amplifico*. Scadius Von Edgeworth—I have asked you to leave this kingdom in peace. Instead, you have chosen to machinate a plan that resulted in the death of a student." She looked to Jonah once more as the crowd became a mixture of boos, with a few whistles of what could be mistaken as support. She refocused on him. "I have also asked you to let me and the past go. Instead, you have chosen to revel in it. To use it as tinder for a fire you should have extinguished long ago."

Anna raised her chin. "Scadius Von Edgeworth, I will mourn you *but once*." She let the implication settle in, watching his arrogant grin slip before squaring her shoulders, raising her chin ever so slightly, and making her eyes burst with lightning. As the crowd roared, she flared eighteen rings around her arm, bowed whilst never taking her eyes off her opponent, and added, "I accept thy challenge."

Scadius slapped his wrists, roaring, "*Annihilo!*" sending a jet of water at Anna, who nimbly danced aside and slapped her own wrists in turn, hissing, "*Annihilo!*" A bolt of lightning crashed into his large watery shield, which he had summoned in anticipation prior to her wrists connecting.

He slapped his wrists a second time, "*Annihilo bato!*" this time sending two watery prongs, one of which she ducked and the other she blocked with a quickly summoned shield of her own. She countered by slapping her wrists a second time as well, incanting, "*Annihilo bato!*" Two bolts of lightning pronged at him. As a testament to his instinct and skill, he turned sideways, allowing them to fork by, then responded by slapping his wrists a third time, roaring, "*Annihilo ito!*"

Anna replied by latching onto the wall and yanking herself aside— an expert dodge that caused the audience to hoot and clap in appreciation. With the buzzing scion floating attentively alongside, now it was she who slapped her wrists a third time, incanting, "*Annihilo ito!*" shooting three massive bolts of lightning. Two smashed into his resummoned shield and the third crackled into the wall behind him. The shield held strong—he didn't even grunt.

"*Annihilo dio!*" Scadius shouted, slapping his wrists a fourth time and sending four monstrous jets of water. With nowhere to hide, Anna resummoned her shield and fattened it. The scion buzzed as two of the jets smashed into it. The shield slammed into her face in turn—his castings were immensely strong, stronger than any she had ever encountered in—and out—of the arena.

Trading wrist volleys for the sake of bravado had run its course and, sensing the coming advance the moment of hesitation had provided, Anna snapped off, "*Impetus peragro*," and vanished and reappeared with a *thwomp* in an empty spot on the right side of the arena. Just as she had predicted, Scadius had shot forth, readying to summon a weapon. But seeing that she had moved, he changed tack and wiggled first his left and then his right hand and back again, incanting, "*Flustrato! Flustrato! Flustrato!*"

Anna bobbed and weaved, replying with her own Confusion castings, wanting to match him, show him she was not afraid despite her innards buzzing with terror, a terror she remembered all too well from the arena—albeit one infused with the real fear of death.

Whereas he was used to organized duels in relatively safe confines, Anna had battled out in the wild against unpredictable and clever opponents. Further, she oft had practice duels against her students, showing them only the mercy of feathered castings. Thus she had kept up on which spells were in and out of fashion and which moves were making the tournament circuit, and she learned new moves from her students all the time. Little tricks here and there, making her an all-around strong dueler. Yet having underestimated a teacher's experience, he could not know that.

Anna made a graceful but quick *S* motion with a hand. *"Effectus xadius!"* To her surprise, he replied by doing the same but reversing the motion, pairing it with the reverse pronunciation of the spell too — *"Suidax sutceffe!"* instantly nullifying it.

"Yes, I'm *that* good," he said, catching her momentarily gaping. Counterspells were no longer officially taught in the academies because they required extreme gestural and pronunciative precision. Heck, Anna could count on one hand the number of students to have ever bothered to learn even one off-the-books counterspell extension.

Despite the showmanship, it was a rather customary beginning — the dance of getting to know your opponent. Whose spells were stronger, whose were faster. Who took shortcuts, who was more methodical, sacrificing speed for strength. Anna tempered her spells, conserving her energy, looking for weaknesses. He did the same, as she discovered upon allowing a Deafness casting to smack into her Mind Armor — and finding it featherlight. She cast Reveal after that, paying for the relatively slow casting by taking a blow to the stomach from a mild jet of water. At least she could see what he was up to in the arcane spectrum.

That was when she noticed he was encased in a thin blue membrane, the telltale sign of a 17th degree Immunity ritual casting. It was a clear and dishonorable break in the rules of a duel, for he had prepared it prior without allowing her a chance to do the same. Perhaps it was his way of balancing the scales against her scion, which buzzed with every thrust and counterthrust. Luckily, these days Immunity only reduced ten to thirty percent of the spell strength of the chosen element — depending on the competence of the caster. It was a pale comparison to the days of old, when warlocks had been measured at reducing fifty percent of an incoming attack. Arcaneologists theorized the originating versions could reduce up to ninety percent.

Throughout, the audience was a constant roar pierced by occasional whistles and random shouts and the like, all lost to the chaotic din of people craving blood and death, people wanting to see history made before their eyes.

And so it went. He shoved. She jumped. He clawed a hand, casting Fear. She dipped, countering with Mute. He hurdled the tendrils, attacking with another jet. She angled her shield, letting it carom off, telekinetically snagging his leg underneath. He spun away, shoving right back. She dodged, countering with Deafness. He let it smack into his Mind Armor, correctly guessing that it was tempered, and used the speed advantage to dump a deluge of water from above, forcing her to teleport away *twice*, the second time after he had sent a jet at the spot she appeared in—untempered too, judging by the awesome crash it made against the wall.

They traded some mind spells and ducks and dodges and offensives, keeping their voices amplified to intimidate the other with verbal onslaughts, something the audience appreciated. Both tried to strip each other of their shields, but found themselves too wily, either resummoning it right away or using the momentum to counterattack. Scadius knew enough not to flood the area as her lightning would fry him on the spot. In fact, he had to be careful with his water as it was a natural conduit, giving her options other elements did not present.

The crowd called for her to run along the wall like in the poster, but she kept things simple. Water versus lightning, aggression versus patience. He pushed, she countered. He proved himself adept with his shield, lowering and raising it and dancing behind it, while she nimbly prodded at him with her mighty Telekinesis, arguably her greatest strength—besides her creativity, which she rationed like a starving castaway.

She drew on a bit of that creativity when he slipped up by casting an offensive she recognized as a feint. Instead of wasting time dodging this fake attack, she repeatedly flashed lightning using a 6th degree off-the-books spell known as Blinding Strobe. As the audience winced and Scadius turned away whilst preemptively jumping aside, as if expecting to be attacked with an offensive in turn, Anna, expertly blinking in rhythm to the strobe so as to avoid it, instead telekinetically caught hold of his left foot and his right hand. She then stretched her arms apart, and like a ragdoll, Scadius's right arm and left leg went taut in opposite directions. The lioness in her roared, and the space around her warped fishbowl-like. The scion buzzed so loudly the sound filled the arena, joining the fresh roar of the crowd. With her telekinetic might, all she needed was one more heartbeat and she would have torn his limbs from his body. But Scadius did not hesitate, snapping, "*Impetus peragro!*" and vanished and reappeared to his right, frustrating Anna's attempt. He immediately whirled an arm, hissing, "*Voidus vis!*" and a black cloud filled the pit with a *whoosh*.

Anna instinctively ducked and froze, hands at the ready, numerous spells on her lips. She had drained half her stamina, but judged him to have drained two-thirds as he lacked a scion, which naturally fattened one's reserves. Yet it was difficult to have any certainty as she wasn't sure how many of his spells had been tempered feints.

"Break time, darling!" Scadius sang, much to the amusement of the crowd, which chortled amiably as if everyone were friends. "You may not be familiar with our ways, but we like to pause the more drawn-out duels to have ourselves a cup." There came the sound of him taking a long pull from a bottle. "I'm not sure if you could tell, but I've been toying with you, my dear woman. I'm not like one of your pupils. When it comes to spilling blood on sand, I am a—" He burped, the sound amplified, making people laugh. "—professional." More laughter. Scadius took another drink. "Weapons?"

Anna, having caught her breath, stood within the darkness cloud. "Weapons."

"*Voidus null.*" The cloud vanished with another *whoosh*, leaving Scadius standing thirty feet away, holding a bottle of wine by the neck, his watery rings and whirlpool eyes snuffed, which Anna followed suit by snuffing hers, leaving the scion to float by her head.

"You're not as good as I thought you'd be," he said, tipping the bottle back to his lips and taking a third pull, all while staring at her with gleaming eyes.

Anna didn't reveal that she had been holding herself back, waiting for a critical opportunity that had yet to present itself. It was a gamble, of course, as such a moment might not come, and he could catch her slipping any time before then. All it would take was one bad move, and he'd have her. For the strategy to work, she had to be conservative—for the time being.

"You *are* the professional," she thus said, playing to his ego.

"But you haven't tried any of your tricks. No—" He made two fingers run along the air. "—flitting along the wall, no dancing about in the air, not even that rapid-fire arm-scrapey thing of a spell."

The audience chortled once more, with a spectator sniping, "Yeah, show us some fancy tricks, lass!"

"Maybe I'll show you one next," she told Scadius.

"No, you won't, because you're not that stupid. Those might have worked in the arena of old, maybe against a goon out on the street, but this is the underground. This is blood sport, and we don't mess around here." He took another pull, then snorted. "You know I'm better than you now, right?"

Anna did not reply. He was stronger in certain respects—his shield, dodging, even some fluidities. But such things did not always translate to a win.

"I know you know it. I know you *sense* the inevitability to come."

"You shouldn't have involved my daughter."

"That all came together—" He waved a hand about whimsically. "—rather naturally."

"And taking hostages …" She glanced at the three scared young constables. "I thought such things were beneath even you."

"I had to force your hand. You owe me."

"I owe you nothing."

"On the contrary, you owe me *everything*." His eyes fell on the scion, hovering around her body. "And everything I will have." He took another pull, guzzling long enough to finish the bottle. "Ah, what divinity," he said, wiping his mouth with the back of a sleeve. He waved the empty bottle about by the neck. "It's a mistake to treat me like one of your students."

"That is how we teachers learn from our students."

Another snort. "Your students. What do they know? Solian arcanery is weak these days. None of you are truly battle-hardened."

Anna did not reply, wondering if he was lying, for she had more experience out in the field than a whole squad of military warlocks put together. Perhaps it was a ruse, or perhaps he truly did not know her or her history. She recalled instructing on such moments in class, telling her students to always study one's opponent regardless of what one had heard about them. After their last encounter, she had studied about him in great depth. But how much had he studied about her?

Besides, one of us drank a whole bottle of wine, she thought, and wondered how it would affect his performance.

" 'Long peace makes weak men,' " he declared, quoting a well-known Canterran proverb.

"But happy children," Anna countered.

"Until war comes knocking." He idly tossed the bottle aside. "Play time's over." Whirlpools flared around his eyes and watery arm rings returned to his arm, drawing a roar from the audience. He flexed both arms, hissing, "*Summano arma*," and a watery short sword appeared in each hand. "Three touches, but I'll only need one."

"And you will honor them?"

"Why wouldn't I?"

"The Immunity you cast."

He nodded at the scion floating above her head. "Only fair, all things considered. But as I said, I will honor the touches."

Anna nodded, agreeing to return to spells after three successful hits. She re-flared her eyes and arm, drawing a second roar from the crowd. Then she flexed both arms whilst making to grip something, incanting, "*Summano arma*," and a long staff of pure lightning appeared in her hands. As he whirled his blades left and right, she slowly whirled her staff in her right hand. He paced to his right, as did she, so that they circled each other, steadily closing the space. She saw herself doing the same thing in Dueling Club, teaching her students how to use the angles of approach. Amidst the steady clamor and roar of the audience, she waited for him to make the first move.

Grinning, he hopped onto a foot, spun, hopped onto the other foot, jumped, and whirlingly slashed at her with both blades. There came two electrified watery *thunks* as Anna smacked both blades aside with opposite ends of her lightning staff. Scadius sprang back and they resumed circling, she slowly twirling her staff, he his blades.

When they came together again, he stabbed forth with his right hand, pulled back at the last moment, and feigned a strike at her abdomen while slashing at her neck with his left. She countered the first two with smacks of the staff and barely managed to dip her head under the slice of the left-handed strike.

That was a close one, she thought as he jumped to circle again. *Now to test him*, and she spun her staff quickly before halting it to rest on her shoulder, one end pointing at Scadius's feet as she announced, "Diving Heron," and shot forth to jab at his stomach. When he tried to parry it aside with a sword, she whizzed the end in an upward Z pattern, forcing him to use his other blade to whap the staff away with a watery *thunk*.

"Get with the times, Anna," Scadius spat over the audience's roar, circling like a shark. "Monk positions have long gone out of fashion."

Anna didn't counter with a clever retort, choosing to save all her creativity for that precious moment that would hopefully reveal itself soon.

"Here I come," he said, and danced her way, blades whirling.

She prepared by rapidly spinning her staff, creating a steady and crackling *whoosh*. He slashed at the left and right with each blade, horizontally halting her spin with a dual watery *clunk*. He then kneed the staff upward, sizzling the robe at his knee where it touched the lightning, and thrust the sword tips forth and inward, attacking both arms. She sprang back, yanking the staff and horizontally rolling it around her waist to meet his right-hand thrust with a *thwap* before snapping the other end at his other thrust. He used the momentum of each parry to bring the blades about, slashing at her center with a dual thrust, forcing her to twirl aside. She kept his follow-up advance at bay by spinning her staff in a figure eight, but he waited out the spinning by feigning advances, drawing defensive reactions from her. He used his head and shoulders to make as if he were about to advance, only to rear back and do it again, albeit in a different direction. He did this four times, forcing her to react each time, annoying her, before finally slicing at her with an X pattern. She countered with a Z pattern of blocking, as she had before, but then he thrust a leg forth, causing her staff to smash into it — and used the opening to slash at her. She squirmed aside from one strike, but the other sliced her left forearm open. She gasped from the sting, and the audience went absolutely crazy. It seemed the wine had not affected him as much as she had hoped. Perhaps he had indeed been only toying with her.

"Been waiting for a repetition," he said amidst the roar of the crowd, hobbling back a step, leaving a trail of blood from the leg he had used to parry with. "That's one."

"That's one *apiece*," she corrected, conscious of the blood dribbling onto the sand from the gash he had made in her forearm. He'd gotten her, but at the sacrifice of his own leg.

"Fair enough. Here I come again," and he shot forth. Even with a hobble, he was quick, ramping up the pressure by whirling his blades this way and that, feigning strikes and jabbing, forcing her to expend a lot of energy just to parry them aside. Both were panting and grunting, with Anna wincing from pain and him from effort. With *whaps* and *sizzles* and *smacks* and *thunks*, they danced the dance of death, trying to tempt the other into a fatal mistake.

But what Scadius failed to understand was that she had also kept up the *staff* arts with her students, who, being so different from each other, had evened out her skill, allowing her to put up a robust wall. Having been struck and annoyed, the more he pressed, the less she gave — and the more both tired. Nonetheless, he kept pressing and she kept retreating. He kept finding openings and she kept closing them. It went on like this for many rounds, with Scadius pressing her at every turn, keeping her on her back heels. Just when he thought he got through, she would slam the door with an artful twirl or parry or dodge. Although she comported herself with grace, he was relentless, and she knew she could not keep up with his artful arena experience.

Finally, just as she thought this would not end well, he cursed in frustration, spun away, let his blades vanish by letting go of them, smacked his wrists together, and roared, "*Annihilo!*"

Anna instinctively summoned her shield as the jet of water shot forth.

Except the strike had not come at her.

Anna looked over her shield to see everyone looking at one spot. She followed their gaze and saw Strides staring at her with wide eyes. The young constable glanced down at his chest, which pulsed with blood.

And then he fell.

MARGINS

A hushed silence fell over the crowd, which had only gotten larger since the beginning of the duel. Scarcely anyone could believe what had happened, that an arena combatant had murdered someone in the audience—and a young constable at that. Not even the thieves and lowlifes knew what to say, or how to react.

"You want to keep playing about or are you going to hit me!" Scadius roared at her, pacing back and forth, leaving a trickle-trail of blood in the sand.

Anna, weakened from her own blood loss, could barely contain her rage. But knowing she only had a moment, she let her staff vanish, tore the remaining sleeve of her dress, and bound it tightly around the wound, choosing classic healing over the arcane version so as to conserve precious stamina.

"See? Even *she* doesn't care about some corrupt constable!" Scadius shouted to the crowd, who stirred uneasily at the display. Many had not been aware that three young constables had been taken hostage. Now word was spreading, and spreading fast.

"Kick his ass, Anna!" a random girl shouted.

"Yeah, kick his ass!" a man added.

The audience piled on after that.

"Kill him!"

"Dishonorable fiend!"

"Canterran loser!"

"Murderer!"

Scadius snarled at Anna. "What are you going to do about it? Huh? *What are you going to do about it?*"

Anna looked up to see Kimani bawling and a trembling Meeks gaping down at the lifeless body of his colleague. Despite what had happened, the night stalkers holding the remaining pair of hostages stuck close by, no doubt spurred on by her downing two of their own earlier.

Anna thrust her left arm out, hissing, "*Arcanis rapidio baersto!*" charging her arm with lightning.

"And there it is," Scadius snapped as Anna sliced her right hand down that injured arm, roaring, "*Baersto thub! Thub! Thub! Thub! Thub!*" With each slice, a bolt of lightning shot forth. "*Thub! Thub! Thub! Thub!*"

Scadius danced about like a jester. Every time he jumped or dodged or ducked a strike, he shouted, "Hey! Ho! And now high! And now low!" making a mockery of her scion-amplified attacks.

He jumped and shoved at the ground, roaring, "*Baka!*" sending himself flying up. Anna instinctively followed him with her attacks, only to realize that he was trying to goad her into accidentally killing a spectator. She cut off the attack, but not before a bolt of lightning struck the stands between a young woman and man who had been holding hands, singeing their sleeves.

Still in midair, Scadius lashed out telekinetically with his left hand, snagging Anna's midriff, lurching her forth. He summoned a watery spear into his right hand and hurled it at the spot she would be in. She summoned her shield, and while the spear smacked into it with a hissing splash, she used the momentum of the lurch to telekinetically snag the nearby arena wall and yank herself away, breaking the hold.

The crowd, now a mix of rage and excitement, roared at witnessing one of the maneuvers she was famous for—wall running. Anna barely heard them. Guiding herself telekinetically whilst perpendicular to the floor, her bare feet slapping the cold stone, she took several quick steps and launched herself at Scadius, who had by then hit the sand and was blasting jet after jet at her. But instead of lashing ahead, she reached back, latched onto the opposite side of the arena, and yanked, shooting herself toward Scadius. She flew like an arrow, shield out front and taking hit after hit, and slammed into him—just as her shield exploded from his last strike, a Fourth Offensive composed of four massive jets of water.

They rolled, grappling like cats before she sent lightning coursing through her body. He must have sensed it coming, for he kicked away from her, rolling backward in the sand. Her lightning fingers crept after him like the needy hands of a child, albeit a deadly one, before she switched tack and swept both hands forth, incanting, *"Laitna furia potam!"* A veritable *river* of lightning cascaded forth. But during the switch-over, he rolled up to a ducking position, dug his heels into the sand, and lunged over the river. In midair, he slapped his wrists together, roaring, *"Annihilo bato!"*

"Impetus peragro!" she countered, reappearing to his right just as two jets of water drilled holes into the sand where she had lain a heartbeat prior.

He gurgled, *"Vomitus piutra!"* and opened his mouth wide, vomiting green bile at her. Anna summoned a huge shield to ward away the famously disgusting—and some argued borderline necromantic—12th degree off-the-books water element spell, which slapped into the shield and began hissing as the acid ate away at the lightning crust. He kept up this wide stream for a few moments before yanking and roaring, *"Disablo!"*

Anna, who had been expecting the Disarm maneuver based on their earlier testing of each other, had already cocooned herself in the Elemental Armor spell, so that when her shield vanished, the remaining acid splattered that armor instead of her flesh.

Finding it cumbersome, warlocks at their degree rarely cast Elemental Armor, prompting the bloodthirsty audience to howl.

With both low on stamina and desperate to end the duel prior to hitting that arcane wall, the attacks came quick. He shot a jet. She rolled and yanked at his injured leg. He twisted free and shot two more jets. She twirled between them, letting the hem of her dress get shorn, spitting the Fear spell. Only feet away, he did the same. The pair of spells slapped into each other's Mind Armors, and both combatants continued the onslaught. Wrists and hands jiggled as each spat mind spells at the other—*"Flustrato! Dreadus terrablus! Voidus lingua! Voidus occa!"* Neither bothered to dodge; each only wanted to wear the other's mind armor down.

In a strange fashion, they were harmonious in the way they mirrored each other. He the grizzled arena dueler, she the teacher. He the murderer, coveting the scion, she the defender of the kingdom's last vestige of honor. As he had promised upon their first meeting, he laid siege to the castle of her mind. What he did not know was that that mind had been fortified by not only a studious love of the craft, but by her own students, the ones he had ridiculed. Countless hours of asking pupils to attack her mind so as to judge the attack's merit now paid off against a professional dueler—in the form of even footing.

And so it was that, amidst that harmony of onslaughts, both combatants finally struck true, with an arena-honed Fear casting penetrating Anna's dented Mind Armor and a scion- and teacher-honed Confusion casting penetrating his. She saw it in his eyes, which abruptly rolled about uncertainly, and felt it in herself when she heard the echo of her daughter's blood-curdling scream neatly slice through the roar of the audience.

Each stumbled back, trying to make sense of things—Scadius desperate to regain focus through the Confusion casting, and she searching for Thia in the audience, totally convinced that her daughter had been captured and was being tormented then and there. The perpetual headache she always felt in the background heightened to a high-pitched whine.

Then she spotted a cage in the center of the arena, from which dangled shadowy limbs. But one limb, pale and small, was fleshy.

"Momma!" she heard her son sob. "Momma, help me!" Samuel's voice turned into a pained scream. "*Momma—!*" His scream morphed into a high-pitched sound, as if a boulder had slammed into her brain, knocking her senseless. That sound blocked out her thoughts and made her face scrunch in pain, yet through slitted eyes she could still see the ground open up, revealing a fiery glow. From within that glow emerged a giant and shadowy hand.

"No!" Anna screamed, scrambling along the sand as the hand grabbed hold of the cage.

"Momma!" Samuel shrieked. "Momma! Momma! Momma!"

"Momma's coming, baby. Momma's coming!" Anna tried latching on telekinetically, but the hand was too strong, and all she could do was grimace and thrash from the telekinetic effort as the shadowy hand dragged the cage down into Hell. The rift quickly closed, leaving her to rabidly scratch at the sand, hearing little but that cursed high-pitched noise.

Then she heard a voice she thought she recognized as Kimani's. "Arcanist Stone! Behind you! Watch out!"

Anna turned to see that Scadius had overcome the Confusion. He jiggled a hand at her head, hissing, "*Dreadus terrablus!*"

Anna flinched against the second Fear casting, but the high-pitched noise was so loud and offensive that she misjudged the flinch, and the spell truck true, slapping into her unprotected mind like a thousand needles.

Thomas stepped up behind Scadius, and in his arms he was holding their limp daughter.

"What are you doing!" Anna screeched, as a second fiery fissure opened up at his feet. "Stop it!"

Face lit from below with the fires of Hell, Thomas dumped Thia into the pit, hissing at her, "I'm so sick of your lazy whining!"

Anna screamed. A shadow rose to her left. A young man, who she recognized as Jonah Ivanov, stumbled into view. He fell, turning into lumps of writhing maggots that cascaded toward her. Wrapped in the prickly embrace of Fear, Anna could not look away.

"*Annihilo!*" someone roared, and Anna felt the last vestige of her armor blow apart. The violence of it sent her tumbling—tearing her attention away from the maggots and her husband, who had morphed into a shadow.

"*Annihilo!*" came the follow-up, but nothing but a fizzling *sizzle* occurred.

He's out! she thought, even as she saw those maggots tumbling toward her, each with the face of one of her children, and even as her husband drifted forth, wanting to dig out her brain with bloody shovel hands. *He's out of stamina! He's out he's out he's out!*

Just as she tried to scrape together the focus for a counterattack, Scadius was on her, a rabid dog that was punching and mauling and screaming bloody murder. It was such a ferocious and violent barrage, knocking nearly all sense from her, that the only thing she could do was point at a nearby object she barely recognized—an empty bottle of wine.

Somehow, she grabbed its neck and, summoning what strength remained, smashed it across Scadius's scalp. As he staggered back with a moan, the maggots finally caught Anna and overwhelmed her. Their squishy flesh felt real, the faces of her children twisted in agony. While she writhed against these maggots, unable to see beyond their globule thickness, she saw a hand hook two fingers at the air and yank, hissing, "*Voidus occa!*" For a fleeting moment, before she went completely blind, Anna saw her own eyeballs dance away from her.

Yet the maggots, enlivened by sheer imagination, crashed through the darkness, burrowing themselves into her mind. As if seeing her own brain from within, she saw a noodle of pink flesh unwind and get devoured.

Still having some stamina, Anna gritted her teeth and forced her ever-weakening willpower to sweep her arms forth, roaring, "*Laitna furia potam!*"

"*Flustrato!*" Scadius shouted in the same instance.

She heard her lightning river cascade, and although she envisioned her maggot children get fried in that lightning, she *heard* Scadius fall and thrash, screaming in harrowing pain throughout. Simultaneously, his 18th degree Confusion casting smashed into her mush brain, and it was as if someone had taken the sculpture of her thoughts and put a hammer to them, breaking them into a million pieces that tinkled in the darkness of total blindness.

For a moment, all she heard was that peculiar sound, not unlike shards of tiny glass, as they cascaded across what she imagined was a black stone floor, at the end of which rested a cage.

Soon that too disappeared, as did the whine, and the roar. All that was left was nothing in particular. Perhaps a dull throb, a fleeting and fragmented thought … or two.

Then two became three, and then five and ten and twenty, until she started to weave the tapestry of reality back together. With that reality came the return of her maggot children, the only things now visible to her. Although she had retrieved the sense to know that the lightning wave had passed through Scadius, she now had to grapple with those maggots feasting on her thoughts, each child nourished by her terror, their maggot bodies getting bigger and juicier, until they developed rows of teeth and multiple eyes that reflected her terror. When she picked one off her face, another would mow down. She saw nothing but their eyes and undulating white bodies, heard nothing but their shrieking and feasting, felt nothing but their teeth and squishy flesh.

Anna had no idea how long that lasted. For all she knew a lifetime passed in which she was the subject of her maggot children's torments, writhing throughout, a mouse caught in the paws of two hungry cats.

And then, like a fog blown away by the wind, the harrowing visions retreated. The feasting children let go and writhed away, leaving a trail of her blood in the sand — she could see again! And the sound of their chewing had been replaced with the steady roar of an audience.

Only moments had passed. *Only moments!*

She saw Scadius stumbling about, robe hanging in strips, body and face visibly scalded by the telltale branching effect of lightning. A watery shield clung to his arm, for he no doubt expected another attack from her. Somehow, he had maintained a low pool of stamina. His wandering gaze eventually found her. He squared his shoulders and readied to end her with one last strike. And there she was lying in a sandy pool of her own blood, scratched and bleeding and barely conscious of what she had to do.

That was when she noticed the most peculiar thing, a thing straight out of arithmetic class.

An angle.

This angle, however, was special, for it showed a particular path born from precision. In her delusional mind, she saw herself before a blackboard, chalk in hand, drawing a line. She heard herself say to the class, "The warlock shoots her offensive up, like so—" She drew a line straight up from a crudely drawn figure at the bottom. "Now watch as it hits the concave ceiling at this point here—" She tapped one side of a curve with the chalk before continuing the line. "The strike rebounds at a perpendicular angle of forty-five degrees, strikes the other side of the concave curve at, you guessed it, class, another forty-five degrees, and commences down like so—" Another double-tap of chalk against the blackboard, this time over a second figure. "—striking her opponent from above."

As Scadius moved to slap his wrists, Anna beat him to it, slapping her own whilst roaring, "*Annihilo!*" As she had expected, Scadius reacted by jumping behind his shield.

But the attack did not come from the front. Instead, the bolt of lightning connected with the polished concave ceiling, caromed off at a forty-five-degree angle, hit the other side of the curve—and reflected straight down on his shoulder.

His scream pierced the roar of the audience. Scadius Von Edgeworth stood wavering, eyes in wide disbelief, before he fell back in the sand like a plank.

Yet he still gasped.

Anna stumbled up to him, a bloody mess in her own right. He had been her greatest opponent yet, a dueling master who had managed to even the odds against her scion-amplified prowess. Now he lay vanquished, his shoulder torn open along with the front of his chest, exposing part of his heart—an injury well beyond her healing arts.

Their eyes met. He opened his mouth, struggling to breathe. The words came in a croak. "Then mourn me ... but once."

Anna stared at him, watching as yet another life saw her face as the last thing it would ever see. The menace of the arena, the protector of the underground, a foreign champion ... was gone.

A moment passed during which she closed her eyes and looked skyward, as if seeing the stars through the ceiling. The cacophonous and confused roar of the audience melded into the background along with her headache. The scion's buzz quieted. For that brief moment, she felt the peace of a warrior overcoming her greatest challenge yet.

But the night was not done, and when she opened her eyes once more, she turned her attention to Kimani and Meeks, who were being dragged away by armed men.

"*Impetus peragro*," Anna snapped, and with a *thwomp* appeared ten feet before them, bare of foot, dress torn, the scion buzzing angrily by her head. She was low on stamina, but had plenty enough left for ones such as these.

"Cowards," she spat, eyeing the four night stalkers up and down. People streamed around them, hurrying to get out of there, fearing a raid by constables that would never come. Two of the four did let go—of Meeks, who bolted away along with the crowd. The remaining pair clung to Kimani as if she were all they had left in life, albeit under the threat of cold knives pressed to her neck.

Anna tilted her head and the hands bent back and away, and the next thing the fools felt was the daggers sinking into their own flesh. They screamed the scream of children and staggered off. They were not mortal wounds, but would certainly need attending to.

Kimani shot to Anna, who embraced her, with the frantic girl repeating, "Oh my gods oh my gods oh my gods …"

The pair lurched back to Strides, who lay contorted between a row of ancient stone bleachers. Anna picked him up telekinetically and floated him to lie alongside Jonah.

Back up top, shadowy men began ganging together. Anna recognized one amongst them—the squat, jewel-fingered leader of the thieves guild, barking orders at others. Perhaps he wanted her captured. Lacking the strength to take them all on, she decided not to stick around to find out. She could have used ring snuff then and there, but it would hardly do much good if she could not take advantage.

She stared at him—made sure he saw her fearless face—before she spat the incantation that whisked her group to the supposed safety of the family tower.

Kimani pressed the sides of her head as she stared down at Jonah and Strides, lying at the foot of the steps of the tower. "What just happened? Unnameables, *what just happened*?"

"Kimani. Look at me, Kimani."

Kimani's wide eyes fixed on Anna. "Y-yes, Arcanist Stone?"

"You are all right. Do you understand?"

Kimani stared with glazed eyes before nodding.

"Are you sure?"

"Yes."

"Listen to me. After you take stock of what you have seen, I need you to go to your mother and convince her to write about the corruption in the constabulary."

Kimani stared at Anna with eyes that barely saw her.

"She needs to convince the king to do something. You saw what happened tonight. There needs to be a purge. Order must be restored. And it must be published tomorrow morn. Do you understand?"

Kimani swallowed, but nodded. "I will do it. So help me, Unnameables, I will do it. And if she ever—*ever*—wants to speak to me again, she will write it." Kimani looked at the two bodies. "I don't care if I have to write it for her and she publishes it, I will make sure it is done. Peters will not get away with this treachery. None of them will. I'll do this for you," she whispered to the dead boy. Then she burst with a cry, gurgling, "I'm sorry. And I'm sorry to you too, Arcanist Stone. We let you down. We all let you down …"

Anna hesitated, then gave the poor thing a gentle hug, whispering, "Just remember that Peters may not have had a choice as they likely kidnapped his child." Kimani returned it, whispering, "I will." She drew away, looked at the dead boys, and sniffed. "They will be judged." She nodded to herself, mouthing, "They will be judged," and raced off into the night.

"Mom?"

Anna looked up at Thia's window.

"Mom? Is that you? Who's down there? I can't see."

"It is me."

"Where's Jonah? Mom? Where's Jonah?"

"Thia, I'm … I'm sorry …" Anna didn't know what else to say.

"M-mom … what are … what are you saying …? I'm coming down."

Anna sighed a troubled sigh, nodding to herself in the same manner Kimani had. This was how it had to be. There was no other way.

The portal soon appeared and out stepped Thia, followed by her guardian, Niterra Bladesong. Thia gasped upon seeing the state of her mother. Then her eyes saw what lay behind her and she slapped both hands over her mouth, stifling a scream that sent tingles down Anna's spine on behalf of her poor daughter.

Thia stumbled down the steps and bent over her fallen young companion. She embraced him with shaking hands and sobbed. Anna went to her daughter but was promptly shoved away.

"I'm sorry," Anna said, adding in a murmur, "I tried. I really tried …"

She felt a hand on her shoulder. "You ought to heal," Niterra said.

"Where is Thomas?" Anna looked at Niterra. "Where is her father?"

Niterra shook her head, indicating he had yet to return home from his frivolity.

As if The Fates had been listening, there came a *thwomp*, and there Thomas stood—or rather wavered. The stench of ale and strong liquor hit Anna.

"What is this?" he slurred, trying to take in the scene before him. "Thia? What did you do? What did you do, girl?"

A bawling Thia, enveloping her dead companion, stroking his cheek with the back of her hand as she stared into his face, ignored her father whilst she cried on.

Anna stepped between them to face her husband. "You will find another place to sleep tonight."

Thomas eyed her torn and bloody dress. "What happened to you? Get into anotherrrr brawl?" He scoffed. "Of courshe you did. And this is the reshult. A constable and a shtudent … dead. Word shpreads quick in this city, you know. I'm sure the—" He burped. "—heralds will make a feast of it." He looked down at his hands. "Shorry, honey, but I think I losht that drawing …"

"The drink gives your cruelty permission, but that is no excuse. You are not wanted here. Leave. Now."

"But I ought not to teleport a second time—"

"Then *walk*!" Anna roared into his face. "Walk the walk of shame, you damned fool! Stumble if you have to!" She wanted to shove him, but instead pointed. "Go!"

Thomas tried to focus on her except his eyes kept roving. He tried to pat her shoulder but missed and his arm went through the air, telling her he saw more than one of her. "Fine, whashever. I'll find me an inn," he slurred, and stumbled off.

Anna watched him weave off, feeling he had let her down for the last time. She would no longer put up with his antics. She would mourn him too.

She looked to Niterra, whose eyes were ever on the alert—on her whimpering daughter, who kept brushing Jonah's cheek, and to Strides, whose family she would have to inform as soon as she had healed up, changed, and made sure her daughter was safe.

It would be a long and difficult night for everyone.

A SOARING MELODY

Anna stood on a wide field of grass around the academy. Above trawled bulbous gray clouds that, no matter how much she tried not to think about them in that way, reminded her of maggots. Before her was a pile of wood, above which rested two wrapped bodies. Assembled beyond was the entire school, students, arcanists, and members of the public. Everyone was either dressed in black or had draped over their shoulder a black sash of mourning.

Together they waited in windy silence, their robes ruffling gently in the cool summer breeze. Many a person held on to a *Blackhaven Herald* or an *Academy Herald*. Against all odds, Kimani had persuaded her mother to write the piece, and even helped write portions herself. It had been published in all three major heralds, including the *Antioc Herald*, and pleaded for the king to put "a firm hand to the corrupt injustice that continues to spread like a cancer," artful words that Anna knew would not be enough to persuade the nobility. But she had a plan for that too, and that was why she had insisted she be the one to address the crowd.

"Today we gather to mourn two of our own," she boomed in an amplified voice. "Two whose lives were taken prematurely. Chev Baker, a young man with a heart of determination and valor whose colleagues affectionately nicknamed Strides, and Jonah Ivanov, a young man who chose Solia as his home and remained pure of heart despite having faced great hardships." She looked at the quietly sobbing Baker family. Near them stood Kimani, her mother Triana Taylor, Thia, hands over her big tummy, and Niterra Bladesong, composed, eyes roving over the crowd, alert for any sudden movements. Notably absent was Thomas, who was probably retching from the drink in some hovel of an inn.

As the first of eight morning city bells began to gong in the distance, Anna, eyes puffy from lack of sleep, raised her chin to the massive crowd. "We will not let their deaths be in vain. After the ceremony, we will walk together to see the king." She ignored the stir of the senior arcanists, who had no knowledge of the plan she had concocted, a plan she had only shared with the student council and select trusted arcanists. "He will hear our voices cry out as one for change, for the corruption to be stamped out. As we walk, let us call on Ordinaries and warlocks alike to join us in a peaceful demonstration, one that will tell the powers that be we are sick and tired of it!" She slapped a fist into an open palm, shouting, "No more!"

The crowd roared in agreement, stirring with eagerness to commence the march.

Anna calmed them down with a single raised hand, and they fell silent to hear the last of the eight gongs ring. She kept that hand raised as she took a ceremonial step toward the body-laden logs, robe ruffling in a stiff wind.

After uttering the sacred words of the 16th degree Memorial Ceremony spell, married with the correct imagery and gesture, the woodpile burst with a high blue fire.

"Hear the cry," Anna said, and began to sing. Like a small bird, the melody warbled gently, rising above the blue fire that steadily consumed the bodies of two young men. It floated above the crowd and into the heavy clouds above.

As Anna sang, she saw everything turn white, and out of that white stepped people. It began with Jonah. The young man walked out alone, smiling kindly. He raised a single hand. Next came Strides, a young man she barely got to know. But others came as well, including the nameless ones she had stricken. Lastly, Scadius Von Edgeworth appeared, hands in his pockets as if he were out on a stroll. He looked at Anna with a strange pride, as if he had nothing but respect for his vanquisher. He nodded, casually withdrew a hand from a pocket, and raised it in goodbye.

With tears rolling down her cheeks, and with her melodious voice continuing the fragile tune, she nodded at them all, mouthing her goodbyes, letting them return to the eternal whiteness. And with their departure, that whiteness faded away, replaced by the first patter of rain.

Anna's soaring voice faded to a whisper before dying altogether. Usually people would depart upon their vision ending, but this time, the crowd stood in wait with her. When the rain turned into a downpour and snuffed the flames, leaving behind nothing but ashes, Anna swept them all with an iron gaze … and marched.

And they followed.

THE THIRD SLAB

❧⸺⸺⸺⸺⸺⸺⸺⸺⸺⸺⸺⸺❧

The cool winds of autumn ruffled Anna's black arcanist robe as she padded down a tunnel, the gravel crunching underfoot, her scion floating alongside a pumpkin-sized lightning lamp. The excavation work had finished by then, the final slab revealed deep under Mount Barrow. All that remained was a puzzle on how to open the door.

She wondered if her husband would be there too. He had been helping with the puzzle, but only on days when Anna was busy teaching at the academy—not that she visited the excavation often, what with her busy schedule. That fateful night when he had stayed at the inn had turned into three, then a tenday, then a month—and now, another month later, he had yet to return home. Anna suspected it was from shame, for she had divulged to Ottentus what had happened, knowing he would counsel her husband. The shame of having let his wife and their daughter down after learning how close to death both had come. The shame of not being there to help protect them. The shame of being hungover through a Memorial Ceremony important to Anna and Thia. The shame of missing out on a historic protest that had gathered half the city.

When the king had seen the masses and who was at the fore, he made a speech filled with promises from atop the castle gates, from where many a man had been hanged. To Anna's relief, a cascade of raids, coordinated by none other than the Black Eagles, began, starting with the thieves guild, whose leader was hanged from the very gate the king had made his speech from, sending a strong signal to all. Following that came a great purge that saw constables, officials, and even some nobles arrested and replaced. Mercifully, Captain Peters's daughter was freed, but the captain himself had yet to face trial. The king even smoothed over the kerfuffle with Canterra that rose after Anna had slain their champion. He reminded Anna of the promising young man the king had been, when he had taken her advice on eliminating slavery. Nonetheless, had Anna had the strength, she might have pushed for the return of the Arcaners. But her daughter had needed her, as had her students, and she knew such a thing would be too great an ask of a nobility already under fire for corruption. One step at a time.

One step at a time, she thought as she walked, thinking about how big her daughter's belly had become. She would soon be a grandmother, The Fates willing. The girl had suffered a bout of serious illness after Jonah's death that had her mumbling that she was caught in a nightmare. The healers had worried about a miscarriage from the stress. Anna had summoned the best of the best, from Ohmish monks to Canterran specialists—to even Ning, who despite her earlier protestations, found enough mercy within her heart to not only see the haunted girl, but ease some of her suffering. Anna had fed Thia soups and warm milk and honeyed tea and love—so much love, cradling and caressing and whispering, steadily nursing her daughter back to health, until all that remained was an occasional dry cough.

The date of birth steadfastly neared. Anna and Niterra had kept a watch for the father, Ralf Turman, to make an appearance. But after Anna's now legendary victory over Scadius and the march on the city center and the numerous raids, and despite claiming her as his rightful property as the victor of a duel of honor in the old way, the boy had gone into hiding, no doubt because there was a warrant out for his arrest, with a threat of arcastration at the end of it. For, after hearing much testimony from witnesses, the authorities, by then replaced by proper constables, had concluded that the duel had been illegal, and the final dagger blow murder.

Still, Anna had not let her guard down, doubling the number of enchantments around the tower, unsurprised to have found additional enchantments crafted by her husband, probably out of guilt, yet without showing his face or taking any credit. She had even considered whisking Thia away to Castle Arinthian, as it could be fortified better, but she did not possess the knowledge of how to open the castle fully. Nor did she have the time to uncover its many ancient secrets, which would have to remain unexplored … for now. And nor did she have the heart to isolate her daughter further. At the tower she was at least able to receive classmate guests, namely her friend Kimani Taylor.

The farther down the excavation tunnel Anna went, the mustier and warmer it got. The deep silence of the underground was soon punctuated by the unmistakable sounds of spells being flung. Anna, thinking the puzzle had been solved and Ottentus, and maybe her estranged husband, was under attack, bolted forth.

Yet her footsteps slowed to a halt as she entered the final cavern, for down in the central pit, well before the gigantic slab of the final door, was the master warlock Ottentus Maledius Anavictus—and he was dueling himself.

It was unlike any duel Anna had ever seen, for the pair of identical hairless men moved as fluidly as water. Taking shelter by a nearby support beam, Anna cast Reveal. Ice spells, mind spells, off-the-books spells—all flew back and forth. His shield work was on another level. His dancing this way and that reminded her of Scadius. His feints of The Reaper. It occurred to her he had to be performing cycles, for each spell cast was different from the one prior. Which also meant—and sure enough, at last he cast a spell she had never seen in person before, one that made both of him a blur.

"Slow Time," she whispered, holding the nearby pillar with one hand, the other splayed with Reveal, feeling like a child spying on dueling grownups. The two men whizzed about the chamber, shooting spells—untempered spells at that!—at each other with almost reckless disregard for safety. Yet every spell was dodged, blocked by shield, or parried by a longsword of pure ice. But Anna couldn't always tell as the blurring of the figures was so pronounced.

Then the men halted. Both turned to Anna and in that distinct Franterran accent, chorused, "Come in, Arcanist Stone."

Caught spying, a startled Anna hesitated, wondering if she ought to snuff Reveal. She chose to keep it lit, figuring he would understand.

"Your Doppelganger spell is the most advanced I have ever seen," she said as she paced down a gentle slope. Other than the two identical men, the slab, and a slew of excavation equipment—carts, pickaxes, chisels, sacks, and the like—the chamber was empty, making echoes of their voices.

"Thank you," the men said in unison.

Anna paced around both men, her hand raised as she inspected the arcanery. "Even with Reveal, I cannot for the life of me tell who is who. Remarkable."

"That is because I doubled the telltale giveaways onto my real self as well," the two Ottentus's replied in unison, their heads swiveling as they watched her, their chests heaving from the exertion.

Anna found it creepy to have both men staring at her. It was like seeing hairless arcane twins—master ice warlocks at that.

"That blur effect from Slow Time," she said. "I take it that is the principle of arcanic relativity?"

"It is," the men replied.

Anna swallowed her pride. "I hesitate to ask this, but would you consider practice dueling sometime? With me, that is?"

"Perhaps," the men chorused. Then one of them flicked a hand, and the other silently vanished. "But I prefer practicing on my own, yes?" Ottentus said.

Anna snuffed Reveal, for there was nothing left to see. "Against yourself."

"As you have already witnessed, my Doppelganger is highly advanced. Besides, I find myself to be my greatest challenge."

"Mmm. If you do not mind me pressing further, where did you uncover the knowledge? I do not believe much of what I saw can be read in books."

"I had … strong mentors."

Anna nodded, choosing her words carefully. She tilted her head at the man, more curious about him than ever. "You could overthrow kingdoms with such knowledge."

"I could."

"But that does not interest you."

"It does not." He looked at the slab. "*That* interests me."

"Because of the destination."

"Because of the destination, yes." He looked at her. "Your husband and I have made progress. As always, we lack the depth of understanding to solve the final puzzle. Your brilliant mind must come to our aid, yes?"

"He was here earlier?"

Ottentus nodded.

"But he left to spare me pain."

The nod continued.

"I am embarrassed that you have to put up with our private struggles."

"Nonsense. To err is to learn, yes? I have had more than my share of such struggles."

"You have a family." She felt a flush of shame for never inquiring about them.

"A daughter. A wife. A son. All murdered."

Anna gaped. "I ... I am so sorry."

"I caught the offenders, who taught me that sometimes ... sometimes morality can be a hindrance." He cleared his throat. "But that was a long time ago, and time dulls all wounds," he said before she could inquire as to what had happened to the perpetrators. He stepped aside, indicating the slab. She silently accepted his invitation and the pair started a thoughtful stroll.

"No word from your apprentice?" Anna asked.

"*Former* apprentice. I do not suffer fools."

Is that what you call a murderer? But she kept that thought to herself. "I am surprised this did not draw the boy out," she said instead. "What with his thirst for power and acknowledgment. I half expected him to try to talk his way out of his predicament, perhaps offering some form of contrition in exchange for being allowed to participate."

"His ambitions lie in a different sphere."

"Necromancy."

Ottentus nodded in that nonchalant manner of his. He looked back at the tunnel entrance. "This one took a while, yes? Many months. The workers are happy it is finished."

Now it was Anna who nodded along absently, her eyes taking in the slab as a whole for the first time. A rickety wooden scaffold laced up the surface, obscuring some detail, but most of it was visible.

"Your husband translated five distinctive groupings amidst the general work." Ottentus pointed five times to separate sections of the slab. "The remainder were meant as distractions. Nonsense carvings."

"They are arranged in a circle."

He nodded. "That they are."

Anna stepped up to the lowest of the five groupings of runes, which were the most accessible, the others requiring the scaffold to read. She hovered her fingers over the ancient carving, almost hearing the master builder's voice as she translated them. " 'Thus would you show faith, to cast light on falsity, perhaps craft simplicity, if not to persuade, then to change.' " She grimaced. "That makes no sense whatsoever. What makes Thomas think it's a grouping?"

As was his habit, Ottentus gesticulated enthusiastically. "The runic commas, yes? And the periods at the end of each runic grouping. Look you to the other groupings, Arcanist Stone."

"No runic periods. No commas. Mmm."

"The master builder wanted us to pay attention to these—and only these, yes?"

Anna had been about to climb the scaffold to read the others when Ottentus interrupted her with, "No need, Arcanist Stone." He pointed to a nearby campaign table, from which floated five scrolls. "The groupings, fully translated." They unfurled themselves before Anna. She recognized her husband's handwriting, causing a tinge of hurt to flit through her soul. She had to compose herself before reading one of the pages.

" 'To change the past, enter the oval, conceal not four prongs, or take command of another, to bring to heel the great arbiter.' " Two fingers danced above the translation. "These last two words ... great arbiter ... they allude to time."

"Yes, we believe so too."

She moved to the next page. " 'Silence thy mouth, blacken thine eyes, make strong thy dreams, froth not small, but protect and destroy.' " She shook her head, mouthing, "What does that even mean?"

She turned to the fourth page. " 'Start with movement, block a noise, follow a prong, dread not the night, or go stiff with danger.' " *Dread not*, she thought. *Could that possibly allude to the Dreadnoughts? No, too random, thus coincidental, or perhaps intentionally divertive.* The head shaking continued as she stepped before the final page, the most interesting one as it was the longest. " 'To see the aether's fingers, mix the up and the down, manipulate the many, make space where there be none, to reverse the great arbiter ... all insignificant against five prongs.' " She tapped the three dots. "A runic ellipsis."

"The only one in the translation. And that grouping is the only one with six lines."

"Interesting." She stepped back to look at the whole. "It's a riddle. A spellcraft riddle."

"Yes, I believe this too. Your husband and I have already overextended ourselves with theories, and have started running around in circles. We are most frustrated, yes? These lack sense. I would thus very much appreciate your analysis, Arcanist Stone."

"That would take some time."

"Please."

"Very well then." Anna took a deep breath and began her analysis, standing for a time before each scroll, thoughts a blur as they whizzingly searched for patterns. Ottentus stood by, watching with complete patience. After an hour of grueling and deep analysis, the conclusion became inescapable, and Anna's eyes narrowed.

"They're not supposed to make sense," she declared.

Ottentus's chin rose, but he said nothing.

"The groupings allude to the tiers of our craft." She picked out words. " 'Movement, block, noise, follow, prong, dread, night, stiff, danger.' These are synonyms for spells found in the Lesser difficulty tier—" She used a finger to underline the word *movement*. "Telekinesis—" She underlined the word *block*. "Shield—" and then went down the line, naming Slam for *noise*, Object Track for *follow*, First Offensive for *prong*, Fear for *dread*, Darkness for *night*, Paralyze for *stiff*, and Summon Weapon for *danger*.

By then, Ottentus was standing beside her, head shaking in awe. "Yes, of course ..." he whispered, hands waving about with excitement. "Yes, yes, do go on, Arcanist Stone, please do go on ..."

She pointed to another page. "Silence thy mouth, blacken thine eyes—synonyms for Mute and Blind and so forth."

"The mid-ranged tier, yes?"

She flicked a hand at the translations. "Showing faith alludes to Reveal, casting light on falsity—"

"Compel Truth, yes, yes, *yes!*"

" '—perhaps craft simplicity, if not to persuade, then to change,' refers to Create Simple Object, Bewitch, and Metamorphosis."

"The advanced tier ..."

" 'To change the past, enter the oval, conceal not four prongs, or take command of another, to bring to heel the great arbiter.' These of course refer to Modify Memory, Portal, The Fourth Offensive, Possession, and Slow Time."

"Ah, the Spells of Legend tier." Ottentus pumped his fist as if having won a duel.

She stepped before the final page. "And these ..." She shook her head—not out of bewilderment, but out of awe. " 'To see the aether's fingers,' that must allude to the master spell Tendril Sight—' "

"More of an ability, but let us not digress," Ottentus threw in.

"Yes, yes," Anna whispered, fingers moving to the next phrase. " 'Mix the up and the down ...' that has to refer to *Gravis Isisio Ipulato Taerak*, no?"

"Gravity Manipulation, yes, I agree! Oh, how blissful it is to repartee with someone able to conjure the ancient names of spells! I am honored, Arcanist Stone, to have an equal of the mind!"

"Mmm," Anna toned. *If you were so honored, you would invite me to be your apprentice*, she thought. But she continued working the problem at hand. " 'Manipulate the many,' has to refer to the various *Mass* spells—Mass Frenzy, Mass Doppelganger—"

"—Mass Possession—"

"—Mass Telekinesis, and so on. And 'make space where there be none,' well that could only refer to Expand Room. And then this …" She circled a phrase, whispering, " 'to reverse the great arbiter …' can that possibly refer to what I think it refers to?" A lost spell found only in ancient parables.

"Yes, I rather think it does, Arcanist Stone," Ottentus whispered, adding, "*Annocronomus Tempusari* …"

"The arcaneologists refer to it as Cron, as it has no proper name—"

"—other than its ancient name."

Anna nodded. "Other than its ancient name." The spell was mentioned far too infrequently to have earned a common name. "Many of these have been lost to time. Cron itself is thought to be a parable about ambition and greed. If it ever existed, it is presumed to be Rivican, and off-the-books."

"This is remarkable, yes? Utterly remarkable. The implications …"

But as he droned on about the historic nature of the text, she tilted her head at the ellipsis. " 'All insignificant against five prongs,' " she whispered. *All insignificant* …

She stepped back. "Oh, how clever."

"You have made a breakthrough?"

"How clever indeed …"

"Please do explain, Arcanist Stone."

"Patterns within patterns. Puzzles within puzzles …"

"Arcanist Stone, please, I cannot bear any more riddles …"

"These are all a distraction. A brilliant distraction. It's so simple—"

"I must know, Arcanist Stone! *I must know!*" For the first time that she had heard, petulance entered his voice.

Anna allowed a tiny smile to grace the corner of her mouth. "The riddle is solved within the very last line. Everything, the entire tapestry of engravings, the clever wording that alludes to the five tiers—Lesser, Mid-ranged, Advanced, Spells of Legend, and Spells of Mastery … are all distractions. *All* of them. Meant to misguide, deceive, demanding only focus." *Puzzles within puzzles.*

"Arcanist Stone, please, how can you torture me so?"

"A single spell holds the key. A spell I do not know—" She turned to him. "—but you might."

His eyes widened.

" 'All insignificant against the five prongs,' " she quoted.

"The Fifth Offensive."

Anna nodded.

His mouth, open in awe, slipped into a graceful smile. "As a matter of fact, Arcanist Stone, I *do* know that spell."

"I thought as much." No 20th degree master could truly call themself a master without having learned the quintuple blast. Anna looked up. "The scaffolding is blocking—"

"No matter," Ottentus snapped, swiping at the air with both arms. The entire scaffolding shoved itself aside, creaking and cracking in protest as it crashed into a pile of splintered wood. Then without warning, he slapped his wrists together, roaring, "*Annihilo lito!*"

"Wait. We need to—"

Five huge bolts of ice slammed into the slab.

Yet nothing happened.

"I would have preferred to take time to prepare," Anna said, annoyed.

Ottentus dropped his hands. "Forgive me, Arcanist Stone. I allowed my excitement to get the better of me." His eyes pored over the slab. "I need a target."

Anna and Ottentus stepped back to take in the whole slab.

Anna pointed. "Note the last period in each of the runic groupings."

"They are slightly larger …"

"And with a deeper divot." This time she grabbed his arm before he could recast the spell. "Should we not …?"

"That is up to you, Arcanist Stone."

"He deserves to be here."

"Then you ought to fetch him."

Anna hesitated. "Yes, I suppose I ought to. Regardless of what he has done in our personal life, this he has worked for. This he has earned."

Ottentus nodded. "Please do not take too long, Arcanist Stone, for I do not know if I have the patience or self-governance to stop myself from opening the door on my own."

"You won't open it if you respect that the accomplishment earned here is mutual," and Anna strode off in search of her husband, who she hadn't spoken to in months.

PUZZLES WITHIN PUZZLES

"Dad was here, Mom."

"When?"

"Earlier. Looking for you. Apologized—" Thia paused to cough dryly. "—for the umpteenth time. When are you going to forgive him? Even he and *I* speak more than you two do, and you know how he grates on my nerves with his constant jabs. Mom? Are you even listening? When are—"

"I don't know, Thia!" Anna snapped, only to sigh as she pressed her eyes shut and rubbed them, whispering, "I don't know."

"I guess I just *expect* Dad to constantly let me down, so it's easier for me to forgive him. Must be much harder for you, though." When Anna did not reply, Thia, sitting in a dining chair, hands folded over her big tummy, sighed as well. "Kimani's here. That all right?"

"You don't need to ask me permission for your friends anymore."

Thia shrugged. "Old habit. She's teaching Niterra to wear her rope belt backward to look fiery with the youth." She scoffed. "Which is going about as well as you'd expect. I don't think those two get along. But then I don't think *anyone* gets along with that old bat. Except for you maybe."

Anna went to the nearby window that overlooked the oaks before the tower, absently chewing on a thumbnail. Was she ready to face Thomas? Was she ready to forgive him? The more she thought about it, the more it terrified her. Mostly, and just as Thia had said—that he would let her down again. Maybe she could just tell him to come and that she did not want to talk about anything yet.

"Where is he? Tavern?"

"No. He's with the monk."

Anna nodded.

"He's really trying, you know."

"Mmm."

"Mom—"

"Enough, Thia."

"All right, all right. I just think ... I don't want you two to, you know ..."

Anna thought of her parents' divorce and how it had affected her. "Neither do I," she murmured. "Neither do I ..."

"Well then, good luck ... I guess."

Anna swept past.

"Wait, Mom."

"Hmm?" Anna toned as she slipped on her shoes near an oval portal etching.

"Did you make a breakthrough? The excavation."

"Yes, I rather think we did."

Thia smiled. "I'm happy for you, Mom. Both of you."

Anna forced a smile. "Mmm," and summoned the portal.

* * *

"Our daughter tells me this is where you have been spending your time."

Thomas, sitting in a cross-legged position amidst the peaceful silence of a monastery, whirled about. "A-Anna—!" He promptly got up, one hand smoothing his robe, the other trying to make something of his unruly hair. He was unshaven, but there was color to his cheeks. "I ... I wasn't expecting you. Er ... hello, Wife." His voice echoed gently in the monastery.

Anna stepped up to a miniature red maple set in a rectangular terracotta pot. She remembered Scadius telling her how such trees were pruned every season, sometimes to near death, then coaxed back to life by masters of the leaf. "Hello, Husband."

His gaze went to his feet as he wrung his hands. "I am glad you still think of me as such."

Anna paced between ancient columns carved with Ohmish monk poems, stopping before each one, recalling her old mentor Panza reminding her how all things pass. "I do not know why, but I still have faith in you. In our marriage. Maybe I also don't want to turn into my parents. Maybe I don't want to put Thia through that."

"I … I have not had a drop since that morn. I swear."

Anna nodded, wanting to believe it would last.

"And one day I will tell you I am sorry in a way you will know is final. But for now, I have much to repent on. I might not be ready to come home, but I am ready to start making things up to you. Truth be told, I thought you'd never want to see me again."

"I still have faith in you, Husband," she repeated, tracing her fingers over a delicate floral arrangement of purple bell and lanceleaf and blanketflower. "And I hope I always will."

"Er … why *did* you come?"

She gave him a coy smile.

His mouth fell open. "No …"

The smile remained.

"You cheeky thing, you solved the final slab." He rushed to her and grabbed her limp hands. "I knew you could do it! I *knew* it! It was a spellcraft puzzle, wasn't it?"

"A riddle."

He jumped like a little boy, smacking a fist into a palm. "I knew it! The groupings, they were …?"

"Clever obfuscations of a single simplicity."

"What? Are you telling me that all that intricacy was nothing more than—"

"—a distraction, yes."

"Unnameables, wish I could have been there to see the slab open."

"Well, as it turns out …"

"You're waiting for me?"

Anna gave a smiling nod.

Thomas took a breath as he smoothed his robe once more. "Then we better hurry as he's not exactly a man of patience when it comes to these things."

* * *

Husband and wife teleported to the excavation and ran inside, with Thomas chasing and pinching at the robe of his giggling wife, barking, "I knew you'd do it, you brilliant woman you! I *knew* it!"

"Thomas Bran Hubert Stone, if you think your antics will open the door for you to return home, you are sorely mistaken."

Thomas pulled back a little. "It has been some time since I have heard you use my full name."

"I still remember learning it just before our wedding. A most toady of a noble name."

"And *I* remember you wielding it like a scythe after I angered you for wanting to invite half the city."

She smiled crookedly. "I took some small pleasure in watching those gossiping, pasty-faced nobles hovering by the gates, hoping for a peek."

"You certainly enjoyed your moment."

"*Our* moment."

"Of course." He sighed. "I know I have a lot of making up to do, my beloved Anna, but I promise you I will get there."

She allowed him to slip his hand into hers as they ran, and a sweet wedding memory surfaced of the pair of them running across a Solian meadow, hand in hand. They had spoken of building a home together and having two children and traveling and working together and so many other things. Many had come true. One had turned into tragedy.

Their footsteps halted at the chamber entrance.

The huge slab stood open.

Beyond was a giant stone dais—and it was empty.

"That impatient, selfish, bald wretch," Anna muttered, striding forth, only to stop a few steps later, feeling it fruitless.

"He must have gone back to the first door," Thomas said, voicing her thoughts. "But I'm not comfortable teleporting through all that rock."

"Then I suggest we run."

And run they did, with each waiting for the other when one got winded. It was a long way and made them sweaty and tired, but at last they pantingly stumbled into the first chamber where the arcane battering ram had obliterated the golem. There they saw Ottentus standing before the open slab door that led to the explosive spiral stairwell—and beside him stood a gigantic golden crest shield far too large for a normal-sized person.

"Ah, there you are," he sang, arms wide. "Husband and wife reunited. Just a small marriage spat, yes? Come, come, I was about to take the next step. Had you been any longer, I fear I might have blown myself up. Oh, don't look at me like that, Arcanist Stone, for I meant no disrespect. Since I was a child, I could not keep my hand from reaching into the sweets jar. You will forgive me, yes?"

Anna, still catching her breath, only sighed. Even now he was as giddy as a child, and his wide grin was almost endearing.

"I didn't ask in our haste, but how did he open the third door?" Thomas muttered at Anna as they approached the shield.

"Fifth Offensive."

"Ah, the last line of the riddle. Hence the simplicity you mentioned."

"Mmm."

Both cast Reveal prior to stepping up to the gigantic shield, emblazoned with the master builder's personal crest—a plumb bob, a hammer, a measure, and a chisel, all overlaid atop a labyrinthine spiral. Inscribed underneath were the words *Patteri vat patteri*—patterns within patterns.

"It turned out to be a literal shield *with* a crest," Thomas said, pacing around the artifact, hand splayed over the metal. "Albeit one made for a giant. A shield is ... quite symbolic, all things considered."

"Precisely," Ottentus said. "A shield represents guarding knowledge."

"And its size represents great responsibility," Anna noted, tilting her head. "But it's also his personal crest, which means—"

"Yes, yes, it could still be his tomb. But I do not believe that will be the case. Now let us not dally a single moment longer, for this coming puzzle—" Ottentus looked expectantly at Anna. "—we know how to solve, yes?"

"Because we don't need a giant to wield it, but merely a 17th degree," Anna said as she inspected the flawless workmanship, referring to the 17th degree Incarnate spell, a spell she had first seen an Abrandian champion cast near Devil's Gate but could now cast herself. "Arcaneologically speaking, the tendrils hint at relatively simple key-lock arcanery. The webbing tells me that, once the shield is wielded by an incarnated warlock, the shield *turns on*, so to speak, and can then amplify one spell, and one spell only, in a specific way."

"Disenchant," Ottentus said. "Nullifying the explosive stairwell."

"But temporarily. These third-order tendrils here indicate timed reversion, meaning everything resets. And these second-order tendrils here point to teleportation. Once reversion is triggered, the shield will teleport back to its dais and the stairwell traps will reset. Whoever remains inside would either be exploded—" She looked at him. "—or trapped. But almost certainly the former."

Ottentus smiled. "I volunteer myself to be the one."

Anna hesitated.

Ottentus raised a hairless brow. "You want it to be you?"

Anna looked at the explosive stairwell that had stymied them so thoroughly. One wrong move and Thia would be without a mother. "I will defer to your experience, Ottentus."

He clapped Thomas on the shoulder. "You married a wise woman."

"Darn right I did. Now I just have to get her to forgive me for my antics."

"She will never forgive you. Oh, look at your face. I jest, I jest, yes? We men must thrust and parry to keep the swords of wit sharp. Now I suggest you take shelter as my impatience may get me killed. Don't need husband and wife blowing up too."

Anna and Thomas retreated behind a pile of excavated stones near the entrance, which afforded much stronger shelter than their shields. Both kept Reveal lit.

"Does he even know how to work it?" Thomas asked.

"This one should be intuitive."

"He didn't even want to discuss it though."

"He might if he runs into difficulty."

Thomas snorted. "You get the feeling he's just using us?"

"Are we not using him too?"

"I suppose. You *do* know what this means, right? If he's successful?"

Anna nodded. It would either be the ancient builder's tomb, or The Hall of Sacred Doors, and one of those doors would lead to Ley. If it was the latter, she might be able to fulfill her father's dream of bridging the two planes and the knowledge within—or at least take a big step toward fulfilling it.

After a long think during which he stood focused on the entrance, Ottentus summoned what all warlocks coveted and respected—a full sleeve of his element, in this case, ice. Ottentus's sleeve glowed with brilliant cool light and ran from the base of his wrist all the way up his shoulder. Dry icy mist billowed from it in slow waves, lending him a sense of power not unlike the one people described upon seeing Anna's field warp or her scion.

"Have you ever noticed that he hasn't achieved The Settling?" Thomas whispered as the man took deep breaths in preparation for casting the spell that would allow him to wield the shield.

"Huh. You know, that never occurred to me, but you're right." Even when he had been dueling the doppelganger of himself, his eyes had not lit up, meaning he had never exceeded the expectations of any one spell.

"Interesting, isn't it? Points to a methodical mind that always does what is needed. Methodical at least when it comes to the craft. When it comes to many other things, it seems as if he flies by the hem of his robe."

"Mmm."

After concluding his breathing exercise, Ottentus made a series of complex but precise hand gestures whilst uttering the incantation of Incarnate. The moment the final gesture was completed, he exploded into a giant version of himself.

Anna and Thomas craned their necks.

"Can't wait to learn that one," Thomas muttered. "I really ought to spend more time training with you. Maybe that's how I'll start making things up to you."

"I'd prefer a husband over a pupil."

He snorted at that.

A giant Ottentus flicked a finger at the shield, which rose off the ground and flew to his waiting hand. After grabbing hold of it, he turned it around and slipped his forearm through its back handles. "A perfect fit," he boomed. "Here I go, yes?" He moved to the entrance of the giant spiral stairwell, every wall of which was enmeshed with explosive trap arcanery. Anna and Thomas hunkered lower, only keeping their eyes and Reveal-splayed hands above the detritus.

Ottentus raised the shield and said, "*Exotus mia enchantus duo dai ideum exat,*" the incantation to Disenchant. With one fell swoop, every fiber of tendril arcanery in the stairwell beyond the slab door vanished.

Anna and Thomas exchanged one look before shooting forth, running like a pair of giddy schoolchildren. The thought, *We're in we're in we're in!* kept bouncing around Anna's brain. They followed Ottentus—who had cast Shine to light the way with his icy hand—down the stairwell. Whilst holding their breath in anticipation, they soon entered a huge round chamber with a polished but dusty stone floor— only for both of them to let that breath loose through flapping lips.

The chamber was empty.

"No," Ottentus boomed, running forth. "No, no, no, no, *no!*"

"I refuse to believe it," Thomas said, moving his Reveal-lit hand about. "All that work … for nothing."

"*Shyneo lampa,*" Anna incanted, creating a ball of lightning that floated nearby as she searched the area for any sign of arcanery. What had they missed? Surely the complexity of the challenges had been beyond the reach of warlock tomb raiders … right? The answer had to be here. The mystery *had* to continue.

She kneeled to examine the floor. After brushing aside the dust, she saw it was made of granite, a hard stone difficult to work with. And upon closer inspection, she saw thin lines of a different stone, most likely basalt.

"There's workmanship here," she declared. "Under the dust."

"I got this," Thomas said. "Might want to jump," and he swept both arms forth along the floor, incanting, "*Fiero braesos.*" A low fire swept forth from his position, consuming the dust as it expanded.

Brushfire, Anna thought out of trained reflex, hopping over the advancing line of low flame. *7th degree, off-the-books, elemental.* It was nice to see the spell being used ethically. Although its primary purpose was for farming—to burn sagebrush or dead leaves or grass—it had been co-opted by the occasional pyromaniac, a perennial problem for the fire element, giving it a bad reputation amongst Ordinaries.

The ruffling flames fanned out, gobbling up the dust, which made for great fodder. Ottentus didn't bother to jump, and the flames licked harmlessly around his giant feet. Underneath the dust, a faint pattern emerged, for although the granite and basalt were both black, their slight difference was discernible to the eye. What made the pattern stand out was texture and gloss—the basalt was shinier against the granite, creating a shimmer-like offset. Anna, seeing the pattern, immediately thought of the spiral portion of the master builder's crest.

"It's a gigantic fingerprint!" Ottentus boomed.

"Then it must be the fingerprint of a giant," Thomas said, for it filled the entire chamber floor. "Or a god," he added in a mutter.

Anna took a knee to examine the breaks between the lines and noticed another pattern. "This isn't a fingerprint." She looked up, incredulous at the scope of the task before them, for the width of each miniature corridor was no wider than a finger. "It's a maze."

"Heavens spare us mercy," Ottentus whispered.

"Unnameables, this will take forever to solve," Thomas added.

Anna craned her neck up at Ottentus. "Can you see a beginning or end of the maze from up there?"

"No. I am too high up to see detail." He started running a hand down his body to nullify Incarnate, only for Anna to shout, "No!" halting him and adding, "We do not know what will happen if you take the shield off."

"Nor do we know how much time we have before the enchantments return," Thomas threw in. "Don't want to blow us up, do you, Ottie?"

The man grimaced, seemingly not wanting to be left out of the fun. But he remained incarnated, the shield still on his forearm.

"Let's hunt for a beginning and an end," Anna said.

"You take that side. I'll take this one," Thomas replied, and the pair took up opposite ends of the room.

Ottentus tried helping by crouching, but even from that height and with squinting he still had a hard time making out the lines, evidenced by the stream of Franterran curses coming from under his breath.

Anna crawled on her hands and knees, looking for a thumb-sized entrance. She might as well have been searching for a particular pebble amongst a beach of them.

Thomas rushed along on his hands and knees while she took her time, not wanting to mistake an opening for a looping dead end. When her eyes hurt from the strain and she was certain she was seeing double, she spotted an opening near where Thomas had started.

"Found one!" She marked it by removing her shoe and placing it on the spot.

"I still got nothing," Thomas replied, and continued on.

Anna traced after his steps, double-checking him. He soon did the same, but after Anna worked her way to her original starting point, she knew what they were dealing with.

"It ends inside the maze," she declared. "The opening I found is the beginning. The ending is somewhere in there." She nodded at the quizzical mess of lines before them.

When they both tried following one internal edge of the maze, starting from the entrance, by tracing a finger along the floor through the intricate passages, they found it quickly split into myriad more passages—and some floated like little islands, nullifying the classic trick to solving a maze. In other words, this wasn't a maze where one could merely follow a wall due to the breaks and crossing corridors. That and all it took was the slightest lack of attention for them to lose their way.

"This is impossible," Thomas said.

Anna rubbed her eyes. "We need a way to mark the paths we've tried, but even then …" She shook her head.

"We're talking thousands upon thousands of avenues," Thomas concluded for her. "We don't have that sort of time."

Or evidently the patience, Anna thought, seeing Ottentus on his hands and knees, eyes so close to the floor it looked like he was kissing it, an odd sight to see. *A master groveling before a puzzle crafted by a man long dead.*

She considered bringing in one of her classes, as maybe thirty people working at it at once to trace the route would yield results, but she also didn't want to put anyone else at risk, let alone her students. Nor was she certain that the knowledge contained here should even be shared until they knew exactly what it was they were dealing with.

"What if it's another obfuscation?" she whispered.

"Hmm?" Thomas toned as he crawled along, following the trace of his finger. "Bah, another dead end. This is hopeless … utterly hopeless …"

"As with one of his prior puzzles, such a puzzle might not be intended to be solved, but to obscure the actual solution," she said more to herself than anyone else. She thought long and hard about the master builder's personal crest and how it could relate. Finding no solution there, she searched for another way. Checked the ceiling, the smooth walls. Even telekinetically latched onto the ceiling and hauled herself up to look down on the gigantic fingerprint. Whilst she hung in the center of the space staring down at the maze, she recalled Thomas muttering how it could be the fingerprint of a god. It dwarfed even the incarnated Ottentus, who looked like a child against its size. *And my husband a mouse against both*, she thought.

Yet the longer she hung there, dangling like a Sierran fly trap, the more she noticed something off near the beginning of the maze. The lines were different there, almost as if …

Goosebumps rose on her skin as she whispered, "*Patteri vat patteri.*"

While the men continued following the maze, cursing under their breath whenever they hit a dead end or lost their way, she silently lowered herself to the floor and hurried to the entrance of the maze, marked by her shoe. There she squatted, placed her finger on a slightly wider maze passage by the entrance, and traced that passage upward, until she outlined the letter *E*. She looked to the right and saw that along the edge of the maze were other wider passages. She thus moved on to the next closest one, outlining the letter *N*. The ones after that were *D* and *A*. "*Enda*," she whispered, arcanic for *end*. It continued from there. "*A, U …*" *Au* translated to *of*. And then, "*M, E, Z, I, L*." She stood up, tilting her head, translating in a whisper, " 'End of maze.' "

She looked at the men, who had been so absorbed in their task that they hadn't noticed what she was doing. "Except there *is* no end to the maze, is there?" she whispered to herself. She thought about it. *End of maze. Patterns within patterns. Puzzles within puzzles. What if … what if it is literal? End of the word "maze," perhaps?* She crouched at the end of the word *mezil* and studied the very tip of the letter *L*. And sure enough, there was a tiny oval the size of a thumb. It was the only closed oval in the entire maze.

She smiled, licked her lips, and pressed her thumb into the oval. She felt a thrill zip up her spine when her thumb went right through the floor—or rather there was a miniature latch underneath that made the oval swing down like a hatch. She held the hatch open with a second finger, withdrew her thumb, made her lamp float over, and goosebumps again rose when she finally spotted what she had been so eager to find.

There below the floor of the maze … was a keyhole.

THE PULL OF BEYOND

Anna explained to the gob-smacked men how she had solved the puzzle.

"So it was another distraction," Thomas concluded. "Imagine crafting an intricate and gigantic maze in the shape of a thumbprint just to obscure a tiny keyhole. If it wasn't for your smarts, we could have spent years trying to solve it."

Ottentus, still incarnated, withdrew the key from a pocket. Unlike the rest of himself, the object had not been enlarged. Pinching it, he dropped it into Anna's hands. "I think you have earned the honor, yes?"

"She certainly has," a grinning Thomas said, head bobbing up and down.

Anna held the key with both hands, allowing herself to feel its historic significance, before slipping it into the hole. She took a breath, tensed, and twisted it. There was a *click*, and the ghostly bottom hem of a robe appeared before Anna.

She looked up to see an olive-skinned stout old man with a beard so long it reached his belt. He had a slight hunch and rested a trembling hand on a walking stick. "*Mio nominos io Dragoon Vilnius,*" he said in a gravelly voice that echoed softly in the great chamber. "*Arcan languino?*"

"Right, because he's an Arcaner," Thomas whispered.

Anna, having risen to compose herself—she was, after all, facing the master builder himself—cleared her throat. "*Commona languino Solianos, Dragoon Vilnius,*" she replied, voice echoing as well.

"Greetings through time. You have followed the breadcrumbs I left for posterity, and I welcome you." He stared straight through Anna as he spoke. "My name is Vilnius Vivictus. I was a builder. A husband. A father. A son. A brother. An Arcaner. I was blessed to have lived in the time of great men like Atrius Arinthian and great women like Rebecca Von Edgeworth. In a time of evil men like Occulus the Necromancer, who smote many an innocent soul."

He shifted his weight on the stick. "Although we vanquished Occulus, there was a terrible price to pay for that victory. The Leyans, fearful of how their knowledge was being used, withdrew, raising the drawbridge between our planes. In so doing, they deprived us of the knowledge only a handful of bad seeds had utilized to corrupt ends. In my belief, it is inevitable that this deprivation will result in us backsliding as a people into the arms of superstition and fear ... and thus barbarity."

He raised his chin as he glanced around the chamber. "After the withdrawal of the Leyans, I committed the remainder of my life to a secret pursuit—reconnection. I applied every morsel of wisdom and knowledge toward this pursuit. Finally, after much toil—" He finished turning about to once more stare vacantly through Anna. "—I discovered a means to reach them."

He let that thought settle as Anna, Thomas and the incarnated Ottentus exchanged wondrous looks.

"But that momentous discovery begat others. As it turned out, the knowledge I used to craft a door to the Leyan plane ... could also be used to craft doors to *other* planes."

"The Hall of Sacred Doors," Ottentus whispered.

Thomas swallowed. "Gods, we found it. We actually found it ..."

"Unfortunately, I was only able to craft a handful of these doors, for I ran out of lifespan. I begged my colleagues to help extend my life so I could continue my work crafting these planar doors, but they said that such things lead to corruption." He nodded at the floor, beard trembling along with his hands. "I ... I do not disagree." He raised his head once more. "There are restrictions, however. Each door requires a key, and these are no ordinary keys, for they are demanded by the plane beyond. They are keys of the soul."

"What does that mean?" Anna asked during the lull.

The master builder ignored her. "If you should open a door, be sure to close it behind you, lest the unwanted follow. Be warned, for now that you have discovered my final masterpiece, The Hall of Sacred Doors, its existence will have to be guarded against those who wish to corrupt or abuse the knowledge contained within. If the day should come when such a person comes along, you must destroy the chambers under this mountain as well as The Hall of Sacred Doors, raising the drawbridge once more. I have built into my work a means to do this, and have left detailed instructions underneath the keyhole." He raised his chin, voice a trembling whisper. "I pray you never need to use this knowledge, for it will undo all my work."

"We understand," Anna replied with a grave nod, despite not seeing any indication that the man was aware of them. He was but an echo of a person's intent, crafted almost two thousand years ago.

"Now you must answer me clearly. Should I open the portal to The Hall of Sacred Doors?"

"Yes," Ottentus boomed, without consulting Anna and Thomas.

"Are we ready, though?" Anna asked.

"I was born for this," a mesmerized Ottentus said as the master builder's left arm flared with a full sleeve of glowing ivy, leaves and branches.

"I warn you that the shield must stay in this room to prevent the portal from closing, and my protections from spawning. Now, behold! I summon the portal to my masterpiece, The Hall of Sacred Doors. *Portus ea ire itum ancro hass au portio!*"

A large portal appeared with a *whoosh*, shooting a strong wind from its deep blackness. It floated two feet off the ground, its edges rippling with dark energy.

Through the roar of the wind, Anna heard a great *clang*. She turned to see the shield rolling to a halt, and a normal-sized Ottentus beside it.

Anna instinctively splayed her hand, voice lost to the din as she incanted, "*Un vun asperio aurum enchantus!*" Tendril geometries appeared around the shield, but there was one area she had been concerned about before. Sure enough, the tendrils there were slowly winding down, or rather decaying.

"The hourglass is trickling!" she shouted.

Ottentus either did not hear her or did not care, for he stepped up to the portal and dove inside.

"How much time until reversion!" Thomas shouted.

Anna took a moment to carefully judge the speed of tendril attrition. "By my estimation, three days!"

"That's plenty enough time!"

"Maybe! We don't know how time flows beyond the portal! There could be arcaneological relativities involved!"

"Right!"

Both looked at the portal. Thomas girded himself before shouting, "Here I go!" and he jumped through the void.

Anna unsuccessfully tried to calm her beating heart as questions swirled. What if they couldn't get back? What if it was a trap? What if someone stole the shield in the mean? What if what if what if?

But the precocious student of the craft that she had been since picking up one of father's books as a little girl refused to let the fear of the unknown triumph, and so she followed her husband into the portal.

She emerged in darkness, feeling a hard floor beneath her, the silence deafening compared to the prior cacophony. Amidst that darkness were two lines of strange floating ovals, each with a different texture. There was something else strange too—far above, as if she were an ant looking up at a tree canopy, was a landscape. Directly in the center was the bottom of a two-legged structure, one she immediately recognized.

"That's Devil's Gate!" Thomas declared, voice echoing. "Unnameables, we're leagues underground …"

Anna glanced about with her Reveal-lit hand. They were in a long hall, with the back acting as the entrance point that would lead them back to Mount Barrow. The hall led onward into the darkness, but there were only a handful of portals, each twice her size. The arcanery was ancient, tightly bound, and obviously crafted by a master on account of the sheer complexity. The central castings were a potent Invisibility enchantment and an Expand Room enchantment. The Invisibility made the room feel as if it were floating amidst a great void. There were no visible walls, and no earth or clay or stone to see beyond the portals. The floor was invisible, or black, or empty, or however one wanted to think about it. It simply wasn't there, only a surface to stand on, like finely polished glass.

Ottentus already stood before one of the ovals. "Doors to other planes," he said in a hallowed whisper. He raised a hand before a surface shifting with a windy desert landscape, a low orange sun on the horizon. "This is Ley."

Anna stepped before a door showing a wild jungle beyond, careful to keep her distance. The part of her that would forever remain a teenager feared being sucked in, as if it were a door from the academy's Hall of Rapture. *Papa, if you could only see this*, she thought.

Another door showed only an azure sky with a pinkish hue. The slightest tuft of a cloud lingered near the base of it, giving the impression that one could step onto clouds. Yet another door showed a rolling grassy plain, with puffy blue trees, except there were *two* suns in the sky. Another still, with crimson mountains and golden rivers, showed three moons, a brilliant star-filled sky, and no sun.

"This one wasn't completed," Thomas said, stepping up to the farthest portal. "It's dark, and the casting traces are incomplete."

"Unless the master builder passed it on or succinctly wrote it down somewhere," Ottentus said, stepping up to a portal glowing like hot coals, "I suspect the knowledge to complete that door and craft more is lost to time."

"That one looks like it goes to Hell," Thomas quipped.

Anna joined the men to stare at the glowing embers, which turned out to be veins of lava amidst obsidian. She could almost hear the distant burbles of molten rock, the quiet crackling of stone under pressure.

But there was another noise that fought its way through, a high-pitched whine. When she blinked, she spotted a shadow, a certain cage … and an arm.

"We should go back," Anna said, stepping away from the portal, fearing her own feelings and impressions. "We have a lot of research ahead before we can attempt to open one of these doors."

"Yes, we should go back," Thomas agreed. "Before we're trapped here forever."

Ottentus, who had been watching her most keenly, looked at the portal he had said led to Ley. "*Ei sola del quera au pathos*," he whispered, then looked to the lava portal. "*Ei sola kusu*. The others, they would be guesses …"

"A soul in search of peace," Anna translated. "A soul cursed." She tilted her head, brow furrowing. "You've researched ahead. You know about the keys, don't you?"

"I am surprised you do not. The clues have been there in the mythologies the entire time. The master builder himself said the keys are based on the expectations of the plane."

Anna blinked. He was right. She could have followed the breadcrumbs in the mythological archives.

Annoyed with herself, she stepped up to the return portal, but seeing that neither man followed, she added, "We do not know how time flows here. Arcaneological dilation has been proven with Slow Time and Gravity Manipulation, among others. We ought not to play the fools gambling with what we do not understand. It would be wise to return early."

Thomas, who had been transfixed by the supposed door to Ley, blurted, "I can hear it! I can hear the wind. I can hear the sand …"

Ottentus rushed over to listen. "That is your imagination, yes? I hear nothing."

A troubled feeling settled over Anna's heart. This place, so deep underground with its mysterious doors that reached places beyond all imagining, at distances beyond comprehension, frightened that same part of her that initially wanted to explore it. The precocious child within, having felt the pull of the beyond, now wanted to return to the safety and comforts of home and call out for her papa to hold her close and tell her that everything would be all right …

Yet this *was* for her father. He would have wanted to be here, to see such doors with his own eyes.

"Come, Thomas, let us return home," she said.

Thomas turned away from the portal. "Do you mean that?"

"I do."

He glanced back at the desert, hesitating.

"Come, Husband. Duty calls."

"Duty calls," he whispered, stepping away from the portal.

Another portal kept stealing Anna's attention. Even from that distance, she could hear the faint crackling of the molten earth and the rustling whisper of fire, sounds which frightened her as to their meaning. She could hear that high-pitched whine that defined her background headache, except this time, she swore it was coming *from* that particular door, raising goosebumps on her flesh.

Sweat trickled from her brow. All of this was wrong. It was wrong to be here, to even stand before these doors. It was too soon. The time was not right. None of it felt right at all.

She noticed Thomas had halted halfway to her and turned around to face the desert door.

"I'm not leaving without you," she said. "Thomas?"

"Yes?" He did not turn around.

"Come home."

"Home …"

"Thomas."

"Yes?"

"Come home to me."

"To you."

"To your daughter."

"To my daughter …"

"Thia."

"Thia …"

"Thomas."

"Yes?"

It took Ottentus grabbing him by the arm and sharply jerking him about. "Back we go, yes?"

"Yes," Thomas blurted, shaking his head. "Sorry, was just … thinking."

Ottentus guided Thomas back to the portal, where Anna took hold of her husband's hand and the pair stepped through together, Ottentus following just behind.

Once back inside the chamber with the thumbprint maze, Anna stepped up to the key and withdrew it, instantly snuffing the portal — and plunging the chamber into blissful silence.

Ottentus pointed at the shield, which lifted off the ground. "The hourglass tendrils indicate that the same amount of time has passed here as in there."

"Then dilation is not inherent to the hall itself," Anna concluded. She turned to Thomas, who still had a glazed look in his eyes. "Are you all right?"

He nodded, staring at the spot where the portal had been.

"Are you sure?"

"I saw …"

Ottentus cocked his head. "Yes …?"

"Hard to describe. A life. Eternity. Me."

"You're scaring me," Anna whispered.

He looked at her. "There is nothing to fear."

"That makes me even more fearful."

"I saw clarity, Anna. I saw clarity. It was the most beautiful thing I have ever seen." He looked away again. "I felt a serenity I had never dreamed existed. A serenity the monks speak of in the abstract. And there it was, only feet away. It was the serenity of *acceptance*."

"What sort of enchantment would create such a feeling?" Anna asked Ottentus.

"There are many, mostly ancient incantations."

"They can be tricks, right?"

"They can, yes." Ottentus looked away, as if seeing that very hall once more, before focusing in on her with a most intense stare. "The door called to you."

"I'm sorry?"

"I saw you. You were *listening*."

Anna, feeling caught out, shook her head. "I am not sure *what* I heard."

Ottentus studied her before nodding, though it was obvious he did not believe her.

"This wasn't the master builder's tomb," Thomas noted. "He didn't even mention it. As if it didn't matter."

"Because it doesn't against such great knowledge, yes?" Ottentus swept his splayed hand around, as if searching for eavesdroppers, whispering, "We cannot speak of what we have seen. Not to anyone. Not in whispers, not even in thought. Are we in agreement?"

Anna and Thomas nodded.

"We must research. I will hold on to these items." He reached out for the key in Anna's hand, but she withdrew her hand before he could snatch it.

"If you don't mind, Ottentus ..."

"You do not trust me."

"Forgive me, but you *have* proved to lack patience in ... certain regards."

"Being a true statement, I accede the point. You may keep the key, to keep peace. Let us deepen our research and confer on the regular."

"Mmm," Anna said, watching her husband closely. His mouth was slightly open, eyes a little wider, their focus on something distant, something well beyond this plane. "Come, Husband. Let us see our daughter. I am sure she will be most glad to have her parents home together."

"Our daughter. Thia. Yes ..."

MEMORIES AMIDST YELLOW GRASS

"Let's go. Keep up," Anna said, leading a class of giddy burgundy-robed kids through the castle-like halls of the Student Wing. She searched over her shoulder as she walked, making sure her teacher's assistant hadn't let a single straggler lose their way in the labyrinthine passages.

Kimani flashed a thumbs-up from the rear, and Thia, waddling along beside her, smiled a pained smile, her belly so large she struggled to walk.

Satisfied, Anna continued on. Thia had asked to be allowed to come along, as their destination was a family tradition, and Anna had been all too happy to allow it. Besides, Kimani had become a bosom friend to her daughter.

"This is really exciting," she heard one fourteen-year-old girl squeal to another from behind her.

"Can you believe we have *her* as our Arcaneology teacher?"

"No, pinch me." There was a shriek. "Not *that* hard! Jerk."

Every year, the aspirants seemed to get younger and smaller, albeit ever so slightly. This year was no exception. They looked fragile and puny and fickle and squeamish, and Anna worried for the future of the kingdom. She recognized it was irrational thinking, suspecting the thoughts were more a mirror of her own fears about the future than anything.

"First excursion!" a boy whispered.

"I'm *so* excited," a second boy replied.

"Where do you think she's taking us?"

"Somewhere super daemonish, I bet. Like the Black Castle—"

"—or the Black Arena—"

"—or even her own castle, Castle Arinthian."

"No way. She owns a *castle*?"

"Of course."

"Daemonish."

There's the flavor-of-the-term's new lingo, Anna thought as she led.

"Didn't you know that already? She's an Arinthian."

"I don't believe you."

"Ask her."

"No way. *You* ask her."

"Settle down, people," Anna snapped as the gigantic portal to the courtyard appeared ahead. She glanced back over her shoulder, doing another quick count. *Ten fewer kids than last term. The steady decline of warlock enrollment continues.* Perhaps her research might put a stop to that. That had been part of her father's dream—a repopulation of the craft, but only after the knowledge of Ley was freely shared. It was that, or warlock-kind as a whole would go extinct, leaving Ordinaries to fend for themselves against their own vices—and whatever evils came along.

"Will going through the portal hurt, Arcanist Stone?" the first boy asked, voice breaking awkwardly with squeaks.

"Did it hurt the last time you walked through?" his friend said.

"Oh. Right. Never mind. Sorry, Arcanist Stone."

"Dare you to ask her to show her rings," the other whispered.

"Dare *you* to ask her about the scion."

"Shut up. I'm not stupid."

Anna glanced back at the boys with the mildest look of annoyance and both instantly went silent. A variation of that same banter happened in almost every aspirant class at the start of every term.

She led them through the massive and silent portal and waited in the breezy autumn courtyard for Kimani and Thia to catch up, doing a silent head count as each student stepped outside.

Almost at all times, those young eyes gawked at her with undisguised awe. Anna, being long used to such things, especially from aspirants, simply ignored them.

"Everyone's here, Arcanist Stone," Kimani reported, and the women set off once more, their ducklings in tow in between.

"Anyone know the names of these steps?" Anna asked once they had reached the teleport boundary.

One boy jumped up and down with his hand raised, hair bouncing. "Ooh, ooh, ooh, I know! I know!"

Anna nodded at him. "Chubbuck."

"The Steps of the Crescent Moon! So named because of their shape."

"Correct. Now let us form a big circle. I want everyone to take the hand of their neighbor."

They quickly did as they were told, with many a kid squealing in excitement.

"Does anyone know which spell I am about to cast?"

Chubbuck's hand waved about once more. "Ooh! Ooh! Ooh! I know, Arcanist Stone!"

There's the class bookworm, Anna thought. She had a special place in her heart for all the bookworms, for they reminded her of herself. But she was careful not to show special treatment, only encouragement.

She nodded at the boy, trying not to smile. "Chubbuck."

"Group Teleport, 17th degree, standard."

"Correct."

Mutters of *bookworm* and *suck-up* abounded, though were quickly silenced with a single eye sweep of the circle. "I will not tolerate such nonsense from anyone," Anna snapped. "You will either encourage each other, or you can find yourself deluged with extra homework. Your choice." *Some things never change,* she thought, though was glad to hear more than one muttered apology. "Now ready yourselves, for teleportation can be a little nauseating to the unprepared."

The students stiffened, with both hands Anna held becoming clammy with sweat.

As Thia and Kimani giggled at a jest across the other side of the circle, Anna thought of a vast plain of tall yellow grass surrounding an old gray barn. After a final check that everyone's hands were holding on tightly, she incanted, "*Impetus peragro grapa lestato exa exaei.*"

They appeared in the exact spot she had envisioned. She quickly took stock of everyone, flicking a finger to Kimani and Thia to see to those who had doubled over to vomit. As the young women comforted the distressed, Anna turned her attention to the farm, warmed by the sight of a chimney wafting smoke. She remembered echoes of laughter, the crinkles around her father's eyes, a bright sun, and a large and loving family. She remembered holding the little ones and getting teased by the older ones and she remembered games and feasts and people sharing stories around a crackling hearth.

A stiff autumn breeze swayed the grass, blowing away the putrid stench of vomit. *Burgundies*, Anna thought, bemused. *What mercy that it's a windy day*.

"Everyone all right?" she asked, searching their green faces. "You'll get used to it." She received non-committal nods, many students still holding their stomachs. "Onward, aspirants!" she said, and led them toward the farm.

A kid peeked from one of the windows and waved. Soon a gaggle of kids spilled out the door. Then emerged an older woman with a pot belly, who leaned against the doorframe, hands folded.

"Go on and introduce yourselves," Anna said to her throng. "And be polite!"

"Yes, Arcanist Stone." The kids ran toward each other, attracted like lodestones.

The woman in the doorframe smiled. "Well, well, well, if it isn't *the* Anna Atticus Stone come to grace us with her eminence."

Anna smiled back. "Marybel.

Marybel opened her arms and the pair embraced. She smelled of a mix of coffee and earth and chicken coop. When she pulled back, she held on to Anna's shoulders and beamed with a wrinkled face. "Gods, I missed you so much. Really wish you'd come around more than once in a red moon."

"I know. I'm sorry."

"And there's that sweetheart. Come here, girl. Give Auntie Marybel some love."

"Hi, Auntie," Thia mumbled, accepting an awkward hug before retreating to talk with Kimani and some of the older teenagers.

"What's with her cough?" Marybel asked after Thia turned away from them to cough into a cloth.

"Stubborn thorn from a bout of sickness."

"But she's on the mend, right?"

"It's just a cough. I'm sure it'll go away on its own."

Marybel glanced about at the kids. "Look at this flock. Reckon they're smaller than last term, aren't they? And there's less of them too."

"Tell me about it," Anna muttered.

"Gabe. *Gabe!*"

A sleepy-faced teenager in loose brown pants emerged from within, scratching his behind. "What, Ma?"

"Find the girls and get the tea ready."

He grunted and disappeared inside.

"Are we having tea, Arcanist Stone?" a student asked.

"The best pine needle tea in the whole kingdom," Anna replied. "Kimani, make sure they wash their hands and take off their boots. I don't want them tracking mud into the house."

"Yes, Arcanist Stone. Line up at the well! Let's go, people!" Kimani herded them like the cattle grazing in a nearby pen, while Thia took a seat on a bench with a great groan.

"She looks about ready to pop," Marybel whispered.

Anna nodded. "We're watching her like hawks."

"Where's that old buzzard, anyway? The grouchy Black Eagle?"

"I insisted she take a day to herself. The gods know guarding a sullen teenager's every move has to take its toll."

"I bet she loves guarding her. Maybe 'cause she ain't got no family to herself no more."

"We are grateful to have her kindness."

"So diplomatic. Have an opinion, would you."

"My students think me *too* opinionated."

Marybel scoffed. "I bet." She flicked Anna's shoulder as they watched kids line up by an old stone well. "So the big five-O is coming for you soon. Gods, we're getting old. Or at least one of us is. You don't look a day over thirty-three. Witch."

Anna only grunted.

"Still haven't taken the job, have you?"

"Haven't had the time to decide."

"What's there to decide? Isn't it your dream job?"

Anna sighed, which was enough for the perceptive Marybel to change the topic. "And how's that unruly man of yours?" she pressed. "Still wet on the tongue?"

"He's managed to dry up."

"That's unexpected. They usually like to bathe in it until they croak." She shrugged.

"I'm sorry you lost him," Anna replied, remembering the funeral held in the barn. "He was a good man."

"Was until a bull trampled him on account of him being too drunk to realize you can't make a huge beast do what you want by slapping it around."

"Mmm."

A little girl tottered over. "Can I say hello, Grandma?"

Marybel placed her hands on her knees as she loomed over her. "Why, of *course* you can."

The little thing extended a paw. "Hello."

Anna took it. "Hello. And who might you be?"

"I'm me."

Marybel ruffled the little girl's hair. "She means your name, sweetie."

"Oh. I'm Anna."

Anna raised an eyebrow at Marybel, who shrugged. "Don't look at me. *You're* the reason that name became popular."

"Mmm." She nodded at the little girl. "It's a pleasure to meet you, Anna. I'm Anna too."

"Who's the first one?"

"Not Anna *two* as in the number two," Marybel corrected, "but too as in *t—o—o*, meaning *as well*."

The girl blinked. "Oh. Nice to meet you *too*, Anna." She flopped a hand about with a clumsy wave. "Okay. Bye," and tottered off.

"Precocious little thing," Anna said, watching her go.

"She's smarter than a bunch of the kids put together, and she's still wearing nappies. Believe that? Where do these smarts come from? Her mother and father are country bumpkins."

The women sighed.

Marybel nodded toward a lone tree, underneath which were the markers of Marybel's parents, the kindly Mr. and Mrs. Plowman. "Want to go say hello?"

"I do, but after."

"Of course. Jon's on his way. You know he looks forward to this every term. He's very grateful you let him take Papa's place. It's amazing to see a man develop the craft for a single spell. Gives me hope for my own dying arts. He's been working hard at it too."

A girl of about thirteen emerged in a long polka-dot dress with frilly edging. She curtsied before Anna, too nervous to make eye contact. "Mrs. Stone."

"Hello, Jasmine—it *is* Jasmine, isn't it?" Anna whispered to Marybel, who nodded whilst whispering, "I lose track myself."

"I've been practicing, Mrs. Stone," Jasmine blurted, twiddling a blond pigtail. "And, and, and if I can just get the timing right, I'm sure I can be ready for next term's entry exams."

"That's wonderful. I look forward to seeing you there. But I shan't take it easy on you just because your mother and I are old friends."

"Of course not. Er … Mrs. Stone, do you think I will be teased because of my country twang?"

"I hardly—

"'Cause every time we visit the city they talk all precise-like and I feel like the cat's got my tongue and I stumble over them words 'cause I don't know the fancier ones but I'm a fast learner and I can pick 'em up right quick you know, Mrs. Stone." The girl snapped her fingers. "Right quick."

"I can see that," Anna said. "We get a lot of country folk, so don't you worry."

"That's a huge relief, I must say. A *huge* relief. I hope I'll get to know some of them."

"You'll make plenty of friends. So many you won't know what to do with all of them."

"Just don't you be forgettin' where you came from, missy," Marybel threw in. "Not gonna pretend like you don't know your old country bumpkin of a mom when she comes to visit, are ye?"

"I wouldn't *dare* do such a dastardly thing, Ma! Never ever! I'm as proud as a preening hen to be comin' from this here farm."

The two old women nodded their approval.

The teenager glanced back inside. "Er, I guess I better help with the tea, seeing as the Waxmans are coming and all." She curtsied again. "It's a real honor, Mrs. Stone," and she ran back inside.

"She fancies a Waxman boy," Marybel said, watching her daughter go. "You should meet them. Great family."

"She's a spitting painting of you," Anna said.

"Got her father's fool smile. She gonna get into trouble, I know it."

"They all do at one time or another. It's a beautiful family."

"When they're not unruly. But Jon and his kids swing by to help often, and the neighbors are nice."

"Even though they're two leagues off?"

"You ever heard of horses? Because that's what we ride out here."

"Smart ass."

"You know it."

"Any of the little ones showing the gift?"

"Here and there. I'll be sending them your way. Don't you worry." Marybel clicked her tongue in that contemplative country way of hers. "So how's that excavation coming along? Make any breakthroughs?"

"It's coming along. But enough about me. How's Jon's health? How are your brothers and sisters? Tell me everything."

"All right, I get it, I get it." Marybel shaded her eyes to peer at the horizon. "And there's his wagon." She smiled. "It's good to see you, my old friend."

* * *

Marybel, red-faced from so much laughter, leaned closer to a wide-eyed Kimani, who had been pestering her about Anna's past. "Then Anna—

and mind you Anna was younger than almost everyone here at the time—"

"The youngest to *ever* blossom," a gray-haired and wrinkled-as-an-old-apple Jon threw in, surrounded by his own grandkids at the head of the table.

The room was full of people, from the young to the old, everyone with a steaming mug of tea, riveted by the story unfolding before them. The smallest of the aspirants even shared the occasional chair, for they had run out.

Marybel raised dramatic hands. "Anna said, and I jest you not, she said, 'I can *absolutely* repair that horse! And Papa said, 'I don't believe it!' Then *her* papa whispered—and mind you her father was a proud and accomplished man in his own right—anyway, he whispered, 'Just you watch!' Then we all gathered 'round and, to our utter amazement, watched an eleven-year-old girl repair a rocking horse."

"That's not quite how it happened," Anna muttered amidst the whispers of amazement.

"But the repair *did* happen," Marybel said. "It was like … it was like history had come to life right before our eyes. It was like watching a *miracle*."

There was a collective "Ooh" from the captivated audience.

Anna's lips thinned. "I am not sure it is wise to fill my burgundies with such nonsense."

"Oh, and there it is, too!" Marybel said, pointing. "See that rocking horse in the corner? That's the very one."

"It's a piece of family history now," Jon threw in. "A story we tell every Endyear 'round the fire."

The students and kids all looked at the beaten old rocking horse as if it were a museum piece.

"Been repaired a hundred times since," Marybel added. "We use it as a miniature Trainer now."

"Must have been amazing to watch someone so young make history," Kimani said, with many nodding along.

"We were honored," Jon said. "After that moment, every single one of us knew that Anna was special."

"Most definitely," Marybel added, staring at the horse. "That was almost forty years ago and it feels like it happened yesterday."

"This was a mistake," Anna muttered. "I swear it's the last time I'm doing this."

Marybel ignored Anna, who had made that empty threat on every such occasion. "Even that young she was smart and ambitious and kind. *So* kind, it hurts your heart to hear what she went through after."

A teenage girl, blushing fiercely, raised a tentative hand as if in class. "Sorry, but, er, Miss Thia, how is it being the daughter of the most famous woman in the kingdom?"

"Reckon it must be interesting at the least," a scruffy teen boy blurted, causing a ripple of laughter.

"It, uh … has its challenges," Thia mumbled.

"I bet!" the boy said, nodding his encouragement for Thia to continue, but Thia's eyes traveled to her belly and stayed there.

"You should have heard the stories of her triumphs in the arena," Jon said, whistling whilst making his head travel about in a circle. "She *constantly* made the heralds. The Settling—that's when her eyes turned into lightning—happened in the arena itself, in front of a packed crowd!"

Anna wanted to melt through her chair and then the floor and then dribble into the earth itself.

"And when she ran along that wall the very first time, I swear the whole kingdom went wild. There was this excitement wafting about, like—" Jon pinched at the air with both hands, eyes closed. "—like, 'What is she going to do next?' You know?"

The kids all leaned forth, eyes wide.

"The only one to ever be unbeaten. And she calls herself a teacher and a bookworm first, but her fame came from the arena. And then on top of all her brilliance in the sandy pit, she became a healer too."

Marybel nodded along. "We were all so very proud—and still are, of course. She was head of student council and an assistant arcanist and—"

"Enough!" Anna slapped the table a little harder than she meant to, clattering dishes and startling some. She cleared her throat. "Enough blowing smoke up my robe. Let us get to the main event." She stood up. "Jon."

"Yes, I do believe it is time," and Jon ceremonially stood up as well. "Anna."

The kids squealed as the pair walked outside, with everyone scrambling to get a good spot to view the excitement from.

On the way, Thia squeezed Anna's arm. "I'm really glad you're doing this, Mom."

Anna did a double take. Her daughter looked exhausted, her forehead beaded with sweat, as if she was fighting a low-grade fever. "Are you all right?"

Thia coughed dryly and sniffed. "Hanging in there. You had two kids, so you know how it is. Anyway, I'm proud of you, Mom." Then she did something that was all too rare for her to do—she slipped her hands around her mother's waist and drew her into a hug, whispering, "I love you, Mom."

Anna squeezed her warmly, closing her eyes as she whispered, "I love *you*, my sweet child. I love you so very, very much." For a moment, amidst the giddy yakking and whistling of children and teenagers, and the bubbly talk of the elder farmers and their older sons and daughters about Anna's exploits in the arena, Anna only felt the peace of holding her daughter. She felt beyond precious in her arms. Here was this giant family, and it was all Anna could do to nurture her little sapling of a family and keep it alive against the overwhelming odds of history and expectation and danger. She felt like a storm was coming, and she had to batten down the hatches. But she didn't know what shape that storm would take.

Just like that, Thia's arms slipped away from Anna's waist and the budding young mother went to join Kimani. Anna watched her help arrange some of the younger kids in a circle alongside the burgundy-robed aspirants, all eager to witness what the farm boys and girls whispered about, a tradition that had been carried out for about four decades now, off and on. She saw the children gaze at those burgundy robes with awe, some even flexing their own arms, pretending to have rings. Others poked each other with sticks in mock duels. A few grimaced at pebbles, hoping they would move, despite being far too young.

Jon waddled into the procession, carrying a familiar boulder, and dumped it in the center of the large circle of people with a dramatized grunt.

Anna took her place and looked about. "These are the words of two great men … our fathers. This is their lesson." She raised her chin at Jon. "Ready, you ol' scoundrel?" she asked in such a poorly executed twang—done on purpose, of course, for it was in honor of her father's own poorly executed twang—that the children laughed.

"I am most ready indeed, young lass," Jon replied in an equally poorly executed highborn accent, also done on purpose.

They raised their hands, rings exploding around their arms.

The boulder lifted.

The crowd went wild.

BETWEEN THE PLANKS

"Headmistress Anna Atticus Stone."

Anna, deep in the study of a huge old book open before her in the dark academy library, recognized the voice even before looking up. "Headmaster Bowbrick," she blurted in surprise, standing. "To what do I owe the honor?" She had heard the quiet swish of robes approach, but had assumed it was a colleague also keeping late hours.

The man stepped into the circle of blue light cast from her floating lightning globe lamp, the only source of light in that part of the library. "At least that is what I would like to call you. I am old. Exhausted. It is your name they chant at the assemblies. It is you they follow with their eyes. How can an old fool like me compete?"

"Forgive me, Headmaster. I have tried to calm them, but—"

"Not at all. It is important that you maintain the fame." He stepped closer, fingertips pressed together. "Nurture it. Use it for the only thing it is good for."

"And what's that, Headmaster?"

"The interests of the academy. Your kingdom. Warlock-kind. Knowledge."

"I have been trying, Headmaster. I have been trying …"

"I know. You grin and bear the banquets with grace, the tedious ceremonies honoring some past achievement they dug up in the archives, your mind ever on your duties. You accept the awards and accolades with humble gratitude and an eagerness to get away. You put your energies into the young, the future hopes of this kingdom. Even now, you study at this late hour, pushing forth your craft, no doubt to advance the kingdom's interests. And while the rest of us are corruptible in some form, you pursue with iron resolve. I am old and very, *very* tired. I expect your answer sooner than later."

"Headmaster, I ..." But she didn't know what to say to the venerable old man.

His gaze wandered to the tome before her. "*The Book of Dark Things*. Cozy night-time reading, and no doubt the reason I find you in the restricted section of the library. Is there a necromancer about who will soon reveal himself to us?"

"This is mere field study, Headmaster."

"For the excavation. I rather thought that particular pursuit involved the master builder's tomb."

"If by tomb you mean legacy, I suppose it does."

"And what is that legacy?"

Anna hesitated. "Passing on the torch of knowledge."

"You choose your words carefully."

"It ... it is a complicated endeavor, Headmaster."

"Someone choosy with their words is exactly the sort of person needed to take my place. Do not make *me* choose the unqualified. And everyone is unqualified." He tapped a finger at the book, whispering, "Everyone but you." He lingered a moment, letting her absorb the point, before inclining his head. "Arcanist Stone." He departed her circle of light with a swish of his robes.

Anna inclined hers in turn. "Headmaster." Still undecided on the matter of her future, she expelled a long breath, sat back down, and returned to her studies, turning the delicate page to the next chapter. Her lightning lamp crackled gently as it floated above the ornate golden script.

" 'Symbols and Meanings of the Dark Arts,' " she whispered, reading the chapter title. " 'The dark arts have been so duly labeled due to the moral implications of their use. Even the innocuous Shine spell could be considered a Dark Art if it were used to torture, for example.' Blah, blah, blah, we know all that," she muttered, a finger skimming down the page, eyes searching for something of relevance.

" 'Common terms, listed alphabetically. Alchemy ... Ape ... Ashes ... Ax' ... yadda, yadda, yadda ..." She skipped paragraphs quickly now. " 'Bahbell ... Bird ... Bleed ... Bleeder ... Blood'—wait a moment—" Her finger returned to a particular word, the following paragraphs of which had caught her eye.

" 'Oft confused as *extractors*, *bleeders* are another subset of necromancers who in a way *also* desire to squeeze the maximal essence out of ideas—but take the principle quite literally. The difference between the two subsets is as follows. A benevolent or well-meaning necromancer would pursue an idea to its finality, perhaps resolving a question about death in order to further life in whole—hence the epithet *extractor*. The latter necromancer's core intent, on the other hand, is selfish and malevolent in nature. Let us use an example from olden times: the drinking of blood, or blood essence, was thought to reinvigorate the soul, and with enough ingestions, even induce immortality—hence the epithet *bleeder*. In this case, the aim is to further one's own life at the expense of another's.' "

She paused to take a breath, reading quicker now, anxious to get to that word that had flashed across the page. " 'This core belief resulted in many ritual sacrifices in the search for purity in blood. It was further thought the ingestion of greater quality blood from a more intelligent or wise person would increase the quality of the effect. Warlock blood was considered of the highest quality for numerous reasons. Because the intent was the extension of one's life at the expense of another's, such pursuits were almost always selfish. Historically speaking, the vast disparity between a selfless and a selfish pursuit has greatly overshadowed the contribution of the former, resulting in the banishing of necromancy as the eighth primary element, a fault that could be laid at the feet of the selfish.' "

At last, the word that had caught her eyes waited for her in the next sentence, which she whispered. " '*Bleeder*, as translated from the Rivican original, *narsus*.' " She sat back, whispering, "Narsus means bleeder." Ralf Turman had nicknamed himself after a subset of necromancers—a bleeder. And judging by his actions, not the benevolent sort.

Anna sat digesting what this could mean. When she realized that one of the things the boy might have asked—or perhaps done—was to drink Thia's blood, she found the thought so disturbing she shivered and promptly shoved it out of her mind.

He's gone now, she told herself. *And if he has any sense at all he will never dare show his face again in this kingdom.*

After composing herself, she continued her research. " 'Chain … Cicada … Circle …' No, no, no, let's look for *door*. 'Darkness … Death … Devil … Deer … Dew …' Here we go. 'Door. Doors, as they pertain to the Dark Arts, have myriad symbolic meanings including the transition from one stage to another, or the passage from life to death. But perhaps the most interesting symbolism relevant to this composition is of the door as a representation of forbidden knowledge. Historically speaking, the necromancer was responsible for his or her own morality. Left to their own devices, what would a person choose? History has shown us a deluge of selfish and malevolent acts, but there are outliers, principled users of the Dark Arts who opened doors for the good of all, sometimes even at the sacrifice of their own souls. Devil's Gate, in some arcaneological circles, is but a euphemistic door to secret knowledge, particularly knowledge derived from Ley and Hell. The benevolent necromancer argues that forbidden knowledge can be put to the use of goodness, whereas the malevolent necromancer corrupts that use. Any knowledge can be used for either means; it is thence the *application* that is the crucial divider. Doors therefore must be constructed to ward away the weak, to ward off—and this will surely rankle the malignant—those with malicious and covetous natures.' "

Anna readjusted in her chair, whispering, "The selfish sort," before smoothing her robe and continuing on. " 'These doors are thus often protected with puzzles or trials inaccessible to those weak of mind and soul. The most basic example of this is the warlock degrees, where only the strong of mind advance in degree, though this has hardly stopped the malignantly ambitious. But the principle can be expounded upon. For example, one could guard whole planes with a single door. The Hall of Sacred Doors is such a construction.' " Anna swallowed, throat suddenly dry. Of all the books in which to read about The Hall of Sacred Doors …

" 'The historical record suggests that master builder Vilnius Vivictus's last great work was constructing The Hall of Sacred Doors in answer to the withdrawal of the Leyans (and therefore the withdrawal of knowledge itself). The master builder's point was that access to forbidden knowledge needed to remain for benevolent use, for he himself was a benevolent Arcaner. Although some records exist of this construction (work receipts, construction plans, and the like), the actual location has been kept secret, perhaps even purposely lost to time. It is theorized that the master builder, a man fond of puzzles, hid the location of The Hall of Sacred Doors as a puzzle itself, to be discovered by those intelligent and wise enough to solve its hurdles. Even those with exigent need would therefore have to take time to ponder these puzzles, which are theoretically biased in favor of those possessing a more thoughtful nature.' "

Anna had to take another breath, for this was a lot to take in. She was also proud that it was her, Thomas, and Ottentus, using knowledge gained from Anna and her husband's research, who were the first to crack the riddle to the true location of The Hall of Sacred Doors.

She continued reading aloud to herself. " 'Once solved, entry to The Hall of Sacred Doors would thereafter be granted. But that only allows the *opportunity* to petition each door. Entry beyond, into realms of sacred and forbidden knowledge, usually come at a price, oft paid but once. The most prevalent example of this is the mythical door to Ley. Doors—or portals—to Ley have been constructed throughout history. Regardless of means of entry, being accepted as a Leyan induces a price. In the case of Ley, that price is mortality in the resident plane. Thus a Sithesian citizen, once accepted as a Leyan, could not return without facing death. That said, it is possible to visit and return without incurring that price, as long as the enterer does not *become* Leyan. Mythology states that three knocks begin the inquiry and—' "

Anna had read about Leyan expectations in other texts, and so skipped to the portion relevant to her. " 'The second most prevalent example is the mythical door to Hell (a term oft used for planes of forbidden knowledge). Obscure ancient mythology says this door requires two keys, one of which is for the aspiring entrant to have been cursed.' "

The hair on the back of her neck rose as she distinctly remembered her mother throttling her whilst screaming words Anna would never forget, words that echoed as clearly now as they had then. "Anna Atticus Stone—I hereby denounce you in the old way! Thou art no longer a daughter of mine! I denounce thee! And I *curse* thee! Thy children shall know only woe! This I swear on the Unnameables! They shall know only woe! I damn thee! *I damn thee!*"

A numb Anna slumped in her seat. The door to Hell had called to her because she met *one* of the requirements …

She bolted upright. Her mother's dying words spoke about how her daughter would be dragged, kicking and screaming, to Hell. This thought was met with another. What if Ralf had performed a ritual with her daughter that involved drinking her blood, perhaps in curse form, so as he could gain entry into Hell?

But for what purpose? she asked herself. The answer was obvious. *To gain forbidden knowledge, of course.* Yet the more she thought about it, the less sense it made for someone so young to shoot that high, and the more her thoughts spiraled to paranoia and fear, until that cursed high-pitched ringing returned, as if someone had knocked her head with a bell hammer and stepped back to watch it ring.

She continued reading the text, but the only mention of the second key was a simple note at the end that said, " 'The second key shall not be detailed or even revealed in this text for obvious reasons.' " Anna suspected those reasons had something to do with preventing people from attempting to open such a door. She wondered if it could be deduced, however …

The academy bell gonged three times. Anna rubbed her eyes and took calming breaths, beating back the high-pitched noise. It was late, the hour of the cricket, and her fears were getting away from her. She ought to return home. She would speak to Thia on the morrow on the subject of Ralf, and see if she could have her daughter recount any nefarious rituals that awful boy had performed.

She closed the book and returned it to the old woman at the front desk, who in turn had Anna sign a ledger of receipt. Few books were allowed out of the restricted section of the academy library, even to arcanists. Just as she thanked the crotchety old woman for her late hours in readiness to return home, a particular alarm rang inside her head. An alarm that could only mean one thing.

Thia was in labor.

* * *

Anna burst into the family living room and passed two hearths lit with low fires. Her husband stood in the dining area, with Niterra sitting in a seat at the supper table. The old Black Eagle rose upon Anna's stormy entrance. Rain lashed the window behind them, and the exterior sound of wind-battered oaks competed with the creaking of timber within the ancient tower.

"What news?" Anna asked, rushing forth without taking off her shoes.

Thomas raised a hand and pressed it downward. "Calm yourself, Wife. All is well. The midwife has no less than three attendants, and you yourself ensured she is the most competent one in the whole kingdom."

Anna had wanted Ning, but the woman had refused, saying a common birth was far beneath her precious time. Anna knew it to be true, but selfishly wanted her near in case something went wrong.

"Any complications? How far along? What is the state of—"

"All is well," Thomas repeated.

"Does she want me with her?"

"No, she *specifically* said she only wanted the midwife and attendants. Do *you* want someone here?"

"I do not want to bother anyone."

"Not even Marybel? Shall I fetch her?"

"She has a huge family to worry about and it's awfully late—"

"I'm going to fetch her anyway. You said she told you she wanted to be here, despite the hour."

"Is this farm woman?" Niterra asked in her thick Nodian accent. "I get her. You stay."

"Thank you, Niterra," Thomas replied. "You grace us with yet another unpaid kindness."

The woman grunted before standing with a groan. "I return soon," she said, and left.

In the mean, despite Thomas reassuring her that all would be well, Anna couldn't relax, and paced like an anxious bird, chirping now and then about why there was no news, this despite an attendant girl coming to deliver it often.

"This is going to go wrong. I know it," Anna mumbled as she wrung her hands, her pacing route now so short she was practically turning about in place. "I have a bad feeling about this. A bad, *bad* feeling."

"Let us not jinx what needn't be jinxed," Thomas replied, though he too was pacing, albeit slowly, more thoughtfully.

Passing each other, they traded points.

"But the family curse—"

"Your mother's words were just that—words."

"Words carry weight, Thomas."

"I know they do, but—"

"Words wield arcanery and bend reality, particularly words of intent."

"Obviously, but—"

"And intent affects the ether—"

"Anna—"

"And the ether has memory—"

"*Anna—*"

Anna halted, breaths coming shallow and fast. "Words killed our son. Our *son*, Thomas."

Thomas sighed. "That was bad luck, and nothing more."

"Bad luck? *Bad luck?* This is not one of your games of dice, nor do The Fates care about luck or circumstance! You do not understand. Not at all!"

"But I *do* understand. He was my son too. Now settle yourself. Our daughter will be fine, and we will be grandparents and all will be well. You mark my words."

"Oh, suddenly words matter, do they?"

"Anna, you're being irrational—"

"I know that, damn it! I *know!*"

Thomas stared at her. Anna ran a hand through her hair, feeling the braid coming undone. But she couldn't care less. Couldn't care less about the bags under her eyes, about not having removed her shoes, about her research, about anything or anyone, other than her daughter.

"I don't want your pity," Anna snapped, resuming her pacing, annoyed by the sad look he was giving her. "I only want to hear that she and the babe are well. Anything else—save it."

And save it Thomas did, saying nothing more, letting her pace herself into muttering loops of worry.

Time crawled to a halt, driving Anna crazy. "Where is Bladesong?" she barked. "And why isn't that blasted attendant giving us news?"

"The attendant was here a heartbeat ago," Thomas replied.

"That was ages ago."

"No, it was literally heartbeats ago. Perhaps some cold water would do you well—"

"I don't need water! I need news!" But she accepted a cup of icy water with shaky hands and drank the whole thing.

"Feeling a little better?" Thomas asked, taking the cup from her.

Anna, wincing from a brain freeze, bobbed her head about noncommittally. "A little. And I apo—"

"I know. You needn't even say it."

Anna swallowed, whispering, "Thank you. This all just … It feels so inevitable," she said as Thomas put the cup away in the kitchen. "Like I'm having my own story of horror read back to me."

"It's a story of hope and redemption, Anna," Thomas said upon his return, wiping his hands on a cloth. "Not a tragedy."

Anna bit her lip as she stared at her husband, wanting desperately to believe him. "Birth is the greatest danger a woman goes through," she blurted instead.

"Outside of being a warlock," he replied, sitting down to rub his face with the cloth.

Anna couldn't help her temper from flaring. "At least you're *here* this time."

"What is that supposed to mean?" He threw the cloth into the kitchen. "Have I not shown enough contrition!"

"Moments cannot be undone."

"Oh, so you want to bring the past into it?" He shot to his feet, throwing up his hands. "Fine! Taint this sacred occasion, why don't you! You're highly advanced with *that* skill, aren't you?"

"And what is *that* supposed to mean?"

"You're cursing the moment! You're *willing* the curse to come true!"

"How *dare* you—"

Thomas opened his palms. "Let's stop. I don't want to fight. All right? Let's hope for the best. Pray to the Unnameables—heck, beg The Fates if we have to. Whatever. Let's … settle down. All right? Anna? Want to pray instead of fight?"

Anna, who had never truly prayed to either, not even once, gaped, at a loss for words.

Thomas dropped to his knees before the rain-lashed window. He placed a hand over his heart and a hand to his forehead. "Unnameables, hear me now. Please lend my daughter strength. Please ensure our grandchild survives and is healthy. Please do what you can to help our still-grieving family. May The Fates watch over them both. May The Fates watch over us all."

Anna looked on trying to fathom the man she had married. Who *was* this man who had taken to the ways of the monk and now prayed to gods he had never seen or heard?

Yet, after watching him do two rounds and just prior to him starting the third, Anna reluctantly dropped to her knees beside him. She placed a hand to her heart and forehead, and repeated what he said. They kept this up together until there came the sound of a portal flaring behind them.

"Didn't know you were the type," Marybel said, moving to hug Anna, who had stood to greet her.

"Neither did I," Anna muttered, squeezing her friend.

"Hello, Thomas."

"Marybel. Thank you for coming. You will be a great solace to my Anna. She is most distressed."

"It is an honor to be here after everything Anna has done for my family."

Anna looked away, her nerves frayed by the ordeal of waiting for news. In that moment, pleasantries felt like obfuscations.

"And thank *you*, Black Eagle Bladesong," Thomas added.

Niterra nodded as she sat down at the table with a weary groan.

"I'll make tea," Marybel said, and whisked herself off to the kitchen, where she continued talking. "Ugh, the young ones bleat like sheep, I tell you. Hard to get a wink of sleep in that house. Who's the midwife? She any good?" She continued talking, no doubt trying to help, and Niterra and Thomas replied, but Anna returned to pacing and worrying, eyes flitting to the hallway. They were using Thia's old bedroom at the end of it, so that the sound would not carry and worry them further.

"… and that little turdling, you know what he does?" Marybel returned with a tray holding cups and a pot of steaming tea. "He flings the turd at his sister. *Slap!* Right in the face. Instantly grounded, and he's lucky his father's *in* the ground, otherwise he'd have gotten the belt. For now, all he'll be doing is shoveling manure for a tenday. Anna—tea."

"Thank you," Anna mumbled, accepting the cup. But her hand shook so much that she had to set it down after the first sip.

Marybel noticed, but only gave Anna a bittersweet smile. She continued talking about this and that, filling in the void of tension as best she could, trying to poke at Anna to answer the occasional question. How's the excavation? How's your research coming along? The academy? The kids the craft her colleagues the nobles the—

"I don't know!" Anna snapped, repeatedly scrunching her robe. "I don't know, all right?"

Marybel turned her cup in her hands. "I'm sorry. I'm being pushy."

Anna rubbed her forehead. "No, it is I who am sorry. Truly." She placed her gaze on each of them in turn. "To all of you. I am grateful for everything. For *everything*."

Before any of them could reply, an alarm sounded in her brain. "Perimeter breach!" she spat, dropping her cup and racing to the portal etching, knowing who it was.

"I shall go to the room," Niterra replied, whilst Thomas took up position beside Marybel.

Anna summoned the portal and stepped outside into a bitterly cold night. The oaks swayed and cracked as rain pelted the old stone walls of the tower. Anna, blood raging with readiness, shot forth, not bothering to cast protective spells. The trees lit up with blue lightning, as her crackling eyes and the eighteen rings around her right arm emitted light. The scion freed itself from her pocket and rippled with lightning, which with a flick of the hand spidered through the forest, lighting up the area. She was ready to annihilate and pulverize.

Anna arrived at the source of the alarm, roaring, "Show yourself! Show yourself if you dare!" She whirled in place at every *crack* of a branch or tree trunk. But nothing showed itself. Not beast nor man nor ghost. And Reveal uncovered nothing either, only that someone or some*thing* had triggered a perimeter alarm.

"She is *not* yours!" Anna roared. "Do you hear me, boy? And if I ever lay eyes on you again, so help me—"

Another alarm cut her off, this one from inside the tower. It sliced through her like an ice arrow.

For it came from the midwife.

A high-pitched ringing ever present in her ears sharpened.

"*Impetus peragro*," Anna snapped, appearing at the door. She slapped the oval, hand lighting subconsciously as she roared, "Anna Atticus Stone, fourth floor!" The moment the portal appeared, she zipped through it—and found the dining area empty of people.

Heart seizing, she shot forth, thoughts a frantic blur as she careened through doors. It felt like it took forever to get there, and the closer she got, the louder a certain sound became. The cacophonic sound of many voices … mixed with someone screaming. It was a particular scream that sent a jolt of sheer horror ripping through Anna's soul. A scream she never thought she would ever hear again.

Then she saw Marybel and a slew of servants and the old midwife and some of them were holding Thomas back and the midwife was holding a bundle and Thomas was thrashing about like a madman, screaming, "No no no no no no no no no—!"

When Anna realized it was her husband who was screaming, all her strength left her as if sapped by a spell. She stumbled to a halt, falling to her knees. Somehow, she knew. She knew what had happened. It was, of course, inevitable. In a dead mother's words, carved in the stone of the ether. In the curse that mother had inflicted on her daughter and her daughter's future children. For the death of a sibling. This was the price. The inevitable price. The eternal price.

Niterra stepped into view, half enmeshed in shadow, half in hearth fire. Beyond her lay a still bed. That stillness was a nightmare, but amplified as if by a scion, beyond even delusional childhood nightmares brought on by acute fever.

Anna, hearing nothing, feeling nothing, looked to the scion, longing to use it in a manner it had surely never been used in—self-extinction. It would be quick. All she needed to do was tap into wild arcanery, amplify it, and aim it at herself. The lightning would surge from within, exploding her against the walls. It would be an echo of what had happened to her son. It would be a mercy.

Niterra walked forth, ebony chin held rigidly, as if forged of iron, eyes cold. Anna watched her approach like the reaper from a children's tale. Maybe she could get away. If she got away, the news could not be delivered! If she got away, the truth would never come to be, and all would be as it was, a memory of old. A memory she could cherish.

Anna got up and ran like a child eager to escape consequence. To shut herself in her room. Maybe to pound on the doors in frustration and anger, her argument to be heard and acknowledged … and rectified.

But her legs barely worked, and all she could do was stumble into the dining area, a puddle of a woman whose soul splashed across the planks.

Her hands scrambled at those planks, her fingernails digging between the boards. If she could pry them apart and slip underneath them maybe she could find safety. Maybe she could find solace.

A shadow appeared in the door. Anna, seeing the female specter of death in the flesh, of how unafraid and silent the woman was, floated away from herself. Drifting along the ceiling like pipe smoke, she saw a girl rolling about, scrambling to open the floor with bleeding fingers. She heard that girl mumble inanities. Obscenities. Curses. Don't you touch me. Don't you dare. You foul witch. You cursed, evil witch. You are death incarnate. Such things. She floated above it all, unsure of who or what she was. A spirit lingering amidst rotting old timber and stone, a ghost haunted.

Floating, she turned her attention to the rain. Each drop was a lonely patter against panes of old glass. If she could only become one of those drops, then she would rest amidst the others, and in the light of the morn, evaporate with the morning dew …

But the bleating of that poor wretch on the planks drew her back. The old woman waited in the doorway, saying nothing, as the girl on the floor roiled about as if someone had splashed her with a bucket of acid. Except Anna saw that it was her soul that had been seared, branded by the hot iron of catastrophe.

The pull became too strong. She tried to squirm away, but she found herself getting dragged back into that possessed and crazed girl. When the girl she had been and the woman she was now melded, Anna felt oily black horror once more race through her veins.

Then she remembered that stillness.

Its essence.

The curse itself, distilled into the very absence of sound.

That stillness *was* the horror.

Anna had no idea how much time had passed. Time itself became an abstract. Whereas before it had come to a halt, now it seemed to vanish altogether. Time was herself, this specter of a woman in the doorway, the pitter patter of rain tapping glass, and the distant animalistic screaming of a father in dire anguish.

Then the woman took a single step toward her, and with great grace, put forth a hand, opened in invitation. Anna stared at it, unable to control or hear what she said, barely able to fathom the obscenities coming from her own mouth. She was a pitiful and cornered creature, hissing, spitting, frothing, with its tail puffy, in fear of being devoured.

Yet the hand remained, the fingers crinkled like old parchment. Anna stared at it as her words stumbled over themselves, finally succumbing to the silence of inevitability. With the sound of rain and a distant screaming, she slipped her hand into the one offered. The hand lent her strength, and hauled her to her feet.

Only then did Anna see the venerable old Black Eagle's face … and the streaks of tears. The woman turned in place, holding Anna's hand, the pair continuing eye contact like two actors in a play, until she had turned Anna to face the doorway. Then she let go, again with grace, her hand returning to her side, yet leaving that grace with Anna.

The pair of women stared at each other, and it was then that Anna knew that the old guardian's self-ascribed watch had ended. Filled with overwhelming gratitude for her, Anna did the only thing she could think of … she bowed. It was a solemn bow, a bow full of that same grace and dignity. It lasted until the woman acknowledged it with a nod. Anna then straightened, turned around, and drifted toward the calamity that awaited her.

Halfway down a hallway broken up by open doors, Anna turned to look back at Niterra Bladesong. The venerable woman stood with poise. She had never looked wiser and kinder and older. They stared, woman to woman, each knowing the other, before the retired Black Eagle silently departed the tower for what Anna knew would be the last time, as there was no longer a reason for her to return.

Letting the moment linger, Anna stared at the emptiness left by the woman's absence before continuing the walk onward to the end of the hall. By then Thomas had devolved into a rolling mess of his own, and it was all Marybel and the young attendants could do to hold him. Anna looked past them to the midwife, who stood just beyond, holding a bundle while she mournfully tried to explain how sorry she was and that Thia had died from preeclampsia, or some such nonsense. For Anna knew the truth of the death. It was the curse. The curse had taken her daughter. Was the child alive or dead? She did not know. Her eyes were for her daughter, who rested in a bed that had been remade—bless the midwife for the precious dignity she had lent. Tucked under Thia's arm rested Bun-Bun. At least he had been there for her in her final moments …

Thia lay with her hands folded atop her chest, hair matted but swept aside, forehead still beaded with sweat. Her face was pale—frightfully pale—as if she had given all she had had left in the battle of birth. Her chest was still. The stillest thing in all existence.

Anna stood beside the bed for a time, taking in every detail of her, from the loose threading of her gown, to the way stray hairs stuck to her cheek, to how Bun-Bun seemed to nuzzle her even now, having surely lent her great comfort.

Having memorized every detail, she slipped in beside her daughter, took her still-warm hand, placed it between both her own, and pressed her cheek to hers. "My baby girl," she whispered with closed eyes. "When you hugged me at the farm, I somehow knew. My soul knew, even if I didn't. You were saying goodbye, in your own way. Oh, my baby girl, I will always love you. Always. Forever and ever and beyond. Please take care of Samuel. See that he knows we think of him every day, as we shall think of you. Wait for us, for one day we too will come. I am sorry for letting you down. For not protecting you. I tried everything, and it all failed. Now here you lie in your last repose, and everything I wanted for you lies in ashes."

She heard the cry of a babe. The babe had lived. *The babe had lived!*

"As per your wishes, if she is a girl, I will call her Lividia. And if it is a boy, Lividius."

She felt a gentle hand and withdrew to see the wrinkled face of the old midwife. There was a withered peace in those light green eyes, which glinted as if they had seen it all. But the face was also troubled, as if she had seen something new, something she could not yet form into words.

The woman offered the bundle, and Anna accepted it with a trembling arm, the other refusing to let go of her daughter's hand.

"It is a boy," the woman said. "A healthy baby boy."

"Then his name will be Lividius," Anna whispered, staring at the little miracle.

"The liver of life in the old tongue."

Anna looked up in surprise.

"Your daughter told us."

Anna nodded, returning her attention to the baby. He was small and tender and red and couldn't stop crying. She tickled him with a finger and rocked him, but nothing stayed his wailing. She couldn't blame him, for his mother had died giving life to him, and he was mourning her in his own way.

The midwife sat down beside Anna, hands wringing in her lap. "Champion—er, Mrs. Stone."

"What is it?" Anna asked, holding the babe and her daughter, composing herself for the child. He ought not to see any more calamity.

"In her last moments, your daughter feared …"

"Feared what?" *Spit it out, woman.*

"A shadow. She feared … she feared being taken. She started to kick with her feet. It was all we could do to deliver the babe. In all my years, I have never seen anything like it."

Anna felt a clammy flush as she remembered her mother's words. Dragged, kicking and screaming … The high-pitched ringing got louder. When she blinked, she saw a cage. She looked at her daughter's face, and was it her imagination, or did she see struggle there?

Thomas's own struggles with his minders petered out, his raspy voice having devolved into a gurgling weep. "Let me go," he croaked in resignation. "Let me go so that I may join my daughter."

The women holding him warily let go, and he hauled himself to his feet, a blubbering wretch of a man. As if someone had cut the legs out from his soul, he hobbled to the other side of the bed and slipped in beside his daughter. He took her other hand and pressed it to his breast, eyes on her face the entire time. Then he placed his head on her chest and quietly wept, now and then whispering his own final words to her.

Marybel kneeled beside Anna, placing her head on Anna's lap, while the attendants and the midwife withdrew into the hall. For a long time, with the rain lashing at the windows and the hearth crackling away, Thomas lay weeping, whilst Anna held their crying grandson with one hand and her daughter with the other, her thoughts as blurry as the windows. Marybel quietly wept on Anna's lap, saying nothing, providing quiet comfort with her touch and tears.

Thomas eventually sat up, Thia's hand pressed between both of his own. He looked at Anna with a gaze bereft of life. He appeared old and tired, and the gulf between them felt impassable, as if a Devil's Gate-sized fissure had opened up at their feet. They stared at each other, tears flowing freely, before he looked away to stare at Thia's face. Anna did the same, and so they sat, listening to the baby, to the rain, and to the fire, until a pale dawn graced the windows, and the rain settled, replaced by a stiff wind that made the old timber of the tower creak and groan as if its old joints gave it pain.

The midwife, having dismissed the attendants, lingered in the doorway. Sensing the old woman had something left to say, Anna passed little Lividius off to Marybel and joined her in the hall.

"Mrs. Stone, I fear it is my duty to …" The old midwife swallowed, hands wringing once more.

"Go on."

"It is my duty to confer your daughter's last words."

"Her last words." Anna smoothed her robe, readying herself. "Go on. Please."

"She said … she said, 'Don't let him take me.' "

Bumps rose on Anna's arm. Thia's soul had been captured. And Anna knew exactly where she was.

Behind a door of crimson cinder.

In a place straight out of ancient tales told in the dark of night.

Her daughter was in Hell.

CIRCLE OF CANDLELIGHT

Anna drifted through the following days like a ghost lost in a haunted forest, the light having been snuffed from her life. She knew only heartbreak and toil, feeling as if she would never meet that old stranger that was joy ever again. Even a simple smile felt leagues away.

She accepted condolences with grace on behalf of herself and her perpetually distraught husband, who accused her of not feeling anything, of being "Stone cold," maliciously intending the pun. She had tried explaining to him that Thia was being held captive in Hell, but he only accused her of having lost her mind to grief, roaring, "How can you be so callous! Do you not realize what happened? Can you not *fathom?*"

They second-guessed and shouted and threw things and were as cruel as they could be and stormed in and out while Lividius cried. Marybel stuck nearby, tending to him when Anna wasn't, and people came and went, but nothing mattered, for Anna's gaze went beyond them all, to her daughter, who waited for her mother to save her. Perhaps alongside her son. That thought gave her a small measure of comfort, for she imagined Thia holding Samuel protectively in her arms, keeping the shadows at bay. It was the only thought that kept the madness from winning completely.

The Memorial Ceremony was performed by a senior warlock, as Anna, believing it was only the husk of her daughter, knew she could not fulfill her duties. Instead, she stared through the blue flames that leaped around her daughter's body, knowing that her precious girl was still alive, held captive in a plane of fire. She did not see the sacred smoky whiteness or feel even the remotest balm that grieving through that whiteness would lend. Having been cursed, she held one of the keys to enter that cinder door, and was resolved to throw herself into research and find the other key that would allow her full entry.

The others who stood in the circle — Marybel and family and Anna's colleagues from the academy and Jordan Winters and Senior Arcaneologist Ning and her attendant entourage and Thomas beside her and even the little baby in her arms — all cried during the ceremony. But Anna felt nothing, feeling them all fools in a way, for how would they all react when she returned from Hell with her son and daughter in tow?

But what they would think didn't matter either. They could curse her as a witch of old for all she cared. She would bring her children back. Save them from the abyssal flames. People would of course denounce such a miracle as necromantic witchcraft, meaning the family would have to adopt new names and a new home in a distant and exotic kingdom where nobody had heard of them. *It'll be worth it for the kids*, she thought. *It'll all be worth it for the kids*. Nothing else mattered.

Except little Lividius. The baby was a crier. He cried all day and night, as if profoundly conscious of the wrong done to him. Motherless and fatherless, he was, for all intents and purposes, an orphan.

"But you have me," Anna whispered one winter's eve, the rocking chair beneath her creaking as she tried to soothe the baby's incessant crying. Snow brushed against the window of the old tower room, the only light coming from a nearby hearth. "You have me, and I will do my best to overcome the curse. To bring you up to be a good man. Teach you compassion and kindness. You will know your mother. I promise you that. But not your father. Never your father. Now please, *please* stop your crying. Shh, little grandchild, shh …"

No amount of soothing did the trick, and she had to wait for him to cry himself to sleep, as he had done every day and night since his birth. She rocked while she waited, staring out the window or at the fire or at the floor, beneath which she could practically see Thia's room. It had been left as was, with a rumpled robe in a basket, scattered school books on a disheveled desk, a sock on the floor. Anna had been down there only once, to collect Bun-Bun, but the battle on whether or not to send him with Thia, so that he may look after her in the Great Beyond, had lost to powerful imagery of Thia waiting in Hell. And so Bun-Bun sat alone on Thia's pillow, waiting for his companion to return, for Anna had refused to let him burn in the sacred fires as she had let Bear depart with Samuel.

Thia wasn't gone, after all! At least not to where people thought. And perhaps Samuel too.

The rest of the tower felt empty and cursed. Everywhere Anna looked she remembered a moment with her daughter as if it had just happened. The hearths, in which Thia had singed her hair. The bookshelves, where she had accidentally pulled a book down onto Samuel. The dining table, where a little Thia had pointed at an apple and said, "Aww-pull." The hallway, where a freshly teenage Thia shouted out in joy, celebrating her acceptance into the Academy of Arcane Arts. The kitchen, where Thia had hugged her mother not too long ago. In every room, Anna heard the echo of her daughter's laughter, her words, even her complaints. She saw her smile serenely, think with chin on her fist, nap with her head on folded arms, a schoolbook oft beneath. All of it rang special. All of it was to be cherished.

At last, the baby's cries petered out, replaced by a restless sleep. The planks creaked.

"He carries the curse," Thomas said, leaning against the doorframe, a half-empty bottle of Nodian fire whisky in hand. "All that crying ... I know he carries it. *You* know he carries it."

"Have you even held him yet?"

"Why, so that he can cast a spell over me too?"

"I don't know what that means. And keep your voice down lest he wake again."

"It matters not. Our lives are over. All of this—" He indicated with the whisky, the amber liquid swirling. "—is meaningless. Utterly meaningless."

"You have always succumbed to despair too easily, Husband."

"Husband." Thomas snorted.

"You wish to say something else. Say it, then."

Thomas took a swig, lingering about. "You look old."

It was true. The last time she looked in a mirror, she had aged a decade, practically overnight. It was as if her body had ignored her son's death, truly believing it an accident, only to succumb to the hard truth of the curse when her daughter passed.

Anna glanced at her husband. His hair looked as if he'd gotten into a scrap with it. His face was unshaven, he was thin, and he had the appearance of an aged farmer. She could easily wound him. Part of her wanted to. After all, all they had done of late was wound each other, and effortlessly so.

In this moment, Anna chose a different path. "But that's not what you wanted to say ... is it?"

He took a guzzling pull, staring at the fire. "First Samuel ... now Thia." His eyes found hers. "Yet you don't believe Thia is dead. You somehow think you can just—" The fingers of his free hand danced about in a whimsical fashion. "—resurrect her. What are you going to do, sweep into Hell, drag her soul back, and stick it into some poor wretch's body? Huh? Is that your genius plan? Are you going to turn into a necromantic witch? That it? Maybe snatch a recently deceased body from the infirmary, some bloated wretch of a thing, and put our little girl's soul into it? Huh?"

She returned her attention to Lividius. "You're drunk."

"I haven't stopped *being* drunk."

"Find the hope."

"Because it's all you have?"

"And why do you wish to destroy it?"

"I only want you to face reality."

"Our daughter is alive. Captured in a plane *some* call Hell."

He took another swig. "Of all the people to fall for that stupid myth ..."

"The curse was real."

"Maybe. But the plain fact remains, Anna. *Anna*—"

"What!"

"Look at me. It. Was. Preeclampsia."

"Her last words—"

"Delusion brought on by fever. You heard the midwife."

Anna looked away.

"You still can't face it. I guess I don't blame you." He sighed heavily. "I don't think I will ever face Samuel. I don't bring him up with anyone. Too painful. Always will be. He has ceased to exist. And I want it that way. My only son. My only boy. Erased ..."

"Stop talking."

A long pause. "Fine. I'll be at the tavern—"

"I don't care."

"I know you don't," he said from the other room, where she could hear him tugging on his boots. She wanted to curse him out for being so useless and unwilling to help, for not believing a *little* bit that their daughter was still alive. Trapped, but alive. Maybe taken hostage, who knew. Maybe alongside their son. What little faith her cursed and drunken knob of a husband had!

But there was one person who might believe—Ottentus. They had communicated by letter only, using cryptic language to discuss their learnings. He had made strides, but Thomas had stopped caring about anything after Thia's death, whereas Anna had buried her grief under a mountain of research, learning multitudes about planes, about relevant myths, about the histories and trials and spells and necromancy and old witchcraft and countless superstitions conflated with spellcraft. It was hard to tell which nuggets held the truth. It was hard to see anything beyond that still bed.

"I'm going to see him," she declared, only to realize Thomas was gone, leaving behind that stillness, tinged with that perpetual high-pitched ringing.

She tickled the crying baby's chin, who had been startled awake by Thomas's departure. "But only after we change your nappy, you stinky boy you. Then you're going to visit Auntie Marybel." The kindly old friend had insisted Anna drop little Lividius off any time she needed a reprieve, or for no reason at all. The Plowman family would take care of him as if he were their own. After everything Anna and her father had done for her family, it was the least they could do, Marybel had said. The very least.

For once, with Thomas forsaking his duties as a grandfather, Anna knew she needed help.

For she was readying for a sacred quest.

A quest into Hell.

* * *

After dropping little Lividius off with the Plowmans, Anna stepped into the foyer of the Library of Antioc, drawing eyes as usual.

"Greetings once again, sir," she said to the old desk attendant. "You have twice now been kindly helpful to me. I hope you will forgive me for being a bother once more."

The man pressed his fingertips together and inclined his head. "Greetings again to you too, Grandmage Stone, and it is no bother at all. I am honored to serve the kingdom's illustrious champion, but please allow me to say on behalf of myself and the humble servants of the Library of Antioc, that we express our deepest condolences on the tragic loss of your daughter."

Anna tried not to sigh. "Thank you."

"Now how can I be of assistance, Grandmage?"

"I would like to speak with Ottentus. I believe he is in the restricted section."

"The only living master warlock. He causes quite a stir among the young attendants every time he graces us with a visit. We have to—" He flicked a wrist. "—whip them every time they pester him with inanities." He smiled cheekily, telling her he was jesting, before abruptly straightening and clearing his throat. "Forgive my impertinence, Champion. I forget myself."

"Not at all."

The attendant opened a hand toward a nearby hallway. "Master Anavictus is indeed in the restricted section." The hand swiveled toward the ceiling. "Shall I inform Her Brilliance that you are on the premises?"

"You are going to do it anyway, are you not? As per her instructions?"

"How … how did you know?"

"She was once my mentor."

"Ah." He bowed. "Nonetheless, forgive me."

She waved the matter aside. "Please take me to see Ottentus."

"I'll have a junior attendant escort you immediately. Unless you'd prefer to take a portal …?"

"An escort will be fine." Anna enjoyed seeing the library, for it reminded her of better times.

Soon a young ebony-skinned attendant with short, curly black hair led Anna through a stone-block hallway of bronze sculptures of mythical figures and tapestries of ancient scenes. Anna kept spotting little gargoyles hiding amidst the tapestries, and remembered solving some of the library's more adventurous puzzles years ago.

"They're said to be a riddle," the young lady noted. "Clues pointing to the labyrinth beneath the library. I understand you have passed its trials."

"In my twenties and thirties, yes."

"Fewer and fewer even dare to attempt them these days on account of how dangerous they are. People really did think differently in the old days, didn't they?"

"Mmm."

"Were the trials, uh, were they …"

"Difficult? Some of the later ones, certainly."

"But they have earned you access into coveted research rooms."

"Which was the reason for me solving the puzzles in the first place."

"Forgive me for pestering you, Grandmage, but why did so many figures of history use puzzles?" the attendant queried as they stepped into a vast hall with two rows of thick pillars, a high arched ceiling painted with ancient scholars, and a gigantic central statue of a gargoyle sitting with its chin on a fist in thought. Beyond the pillars stood rows of doors that led to libraries open to all, including Ordinaries. Men and women streamed in and out, many doing a double take upon seeing Anna, some whispering behind their hands and pointing excitedly at her.

Anna ignored them all, instead remembering pacing around that very room years and years ago, a stuffy tome open in her arms as she attempted to decipher old clues.

"A great question," Anna replied. "The answer lies in access. The theory is that only the wise and intelligent could solve such puzzles, and so there was a higher chance that the knowledge hidden behind the puzzles would be used wisely."

"Ah. You are a wise woman, Champion Stone. And it is an honor to meet you."

They came to a pair of huge doors. The attendant placed a hand to one, said her name, and the door slowly and silently swung open. They stepped through, with the attendant gently closing the door behind them. After a walk down some wide steps, they entered another hall, this one silent and vast and high. One side held only one pair of ancient doors, which led to an invisible bridge that traversed an abyss and led to the labyrinth she had explored in her youth. But it was the other side, lined with doors so tall and thin they looked like stretched planks, that she took interest in. In front of each door stood a giant gargoyle statue.

"It is an honor for me to have met one of the few to have earned permanent access," the attendant whispered, as if not wanting to disturb the silent peace of the hall.

"Mmm."

They stepped up to a gargoyle.

"Here you are, Grandmage. Will that be all?"

Anna nodded her thanks, and the attendant bowed and departed. Anna turned her attention to the gargoyle, lit her hand, and pressed it to the gargoyle's palm. "Anna Atticus Stone," she said. Having already completed the requirements of entry many years ago, the gargoyle inclined its head and stepped aside. Anna walked past and pushed on the door, which opened silently. She closed it behind herself and moved on through an antechamber into the library portion itself, passing two gigantic stone golems who stood by the entrance as guardians. They were impervious to arcanery and wholly unforgiving should a warlock dare to remove an item. Further, teleportation here was impossible unless given privileges which were rarely doled out. Not to mention almost all the master-level arcanery protections had long sunk to permanence, making them nearly impossible to disenchant or destroy.

The room was cave-like and smelled of ancient dirt and decaying parchment. The shelves here were made from crudely hewn rock, filled with ancient tomes and tablets and scrolls and artifacts and jars and all sorts of oddities, each arcanely chained to a mooring and labeled underneath. Anna had spent many a day and night inside this room, learning secrets she sometimes thought she ought not to learn. Secrets of the arcane arts, bygone times, forgotten histories, names not uttered in centuries.

She set her sights on a single hooded candle flame in a distant corner, throwing a pool of light on a battered round table.

"You prefer the candle," she said, voice absorbed by the books, which lent the place a tomb silence that seemed to magnify the perpetual high-pitched background headache that stalked Anna like a hungry mirko.

"I feel it appropriate when studying ancient history, yes?" Ottentus replied in his Franterran accent without looking up from a slew of open books, a quill in each hand, each scribbling on a separate parchment.

"You are ambidextrous."

"It is a spell. A rather complicated one, but I find it better than dictation."

"And how do you avoid her snooping?"

"I keep the doors to my mind shut tight."

"Is she listening to us now?"

"I always assume she is."

"Is that why you did not attend the Memorial Ceremony?"

The hairless man put both quills aside, folded his hands on top of a book, and looked at her. "Because the person who died was not in those flames."

Anna stepped into the candle's pool of light. "What makes you believe that?"

"Arcaneological interpretation. And I know you believe it too. Allow me to pose a theory, yes?" He stood and began casually pacing, a favored habit of thoughtful warlocks, perhaps because it created a calming and silky *whoosh* from the bottom hem of their robes dragging. "A malignant presence weaves its way through history, looking for weakness, probing, exploring. This presence seeks only to enrich itself, yes? And by that, I mean make itself more powerful." He stopped before a bookshelf to inspect a particularly ornate tome before continuing his pacing. "At last, this presence finds an opportunity in the form of a mother grieving the loss of a child, who in turn curses her own bloodline. The question then is …" He opened a hand at Anna.

"Who is the presence?" Anna replied.

"But you know the answer."

Anna did not want to verbalize the word on her lips.

"Known by many names throughout history," Ottentus went on. "Names like Bazu. Soti. Azmat. Vanta. Xie Da Lo. Mephisto. The

Guardian of the Dark. The Father of Demons. The Arch Fiend …" He stopped to place his hands on the back of his chair. "… the devil."

"I know this tale." Now it was Anna who paced, examining the bookshelves. "You speak of the myth of the two brothers. In the beginning of time, two brothers were charged as keepers of all knowledge. But one brother wanted it all for himself. They fought. The victor charged himself with watching over Ley—"

"—condemning the other to watch over Hell."

"That tale is but *one* myth. Another says there are infinite planes, and these two happened to be one of only a handful we discovered. We made up narratives to explain what we did not understand …" She stopped her pacing to stand across from the desk. "… and *still* do not understand."

"A cynical path."

"Merely a counterpoint."

"Yet the evidence suggests a conscious malignance, yes?"

Anna said nothing.

"Allow me to, as you Solians like to say, cut to the chase." Ottentus straightened. "I want to gain entry to the cinder door." He raised a finger, forestalling her. "Why? Because *He* was a hoarder. I want to retrieve the stolen knowledge on behalf of us all."

"The door spoke to you."

"It did not. None of the doors spoke to me. Which means I must piggyback my way in." He raised his finger a second time, forestalling her once more. "And a door spoke to each of you." He gave a casual flap of the hand. "Alas, I have no interest in Ley at this time. But the plane of fire and what it hides … *that* intrigues me. And in return, of course—"

"You will help me free my daughter." She did not dare mention her son as well, lest he think her truly mad.

"We must be wary. He may want to absorb what we know, adding our knowledge to his hoard."

"If what you're saying is all real, and we find a way inside, what if—"

"—we bump into the Arch Fiend himself?" He turned away, hands behind his back.

Anna scoffed. "You think we can defeat him, don't you? The two of us, working together. Despite us struggling with a golem, requiring a literal battering ram to triumph."

Ottentus did not turn around.

"I have never had cause to say this to you, Ottentus, but I think you have lost your mind."

"Then please allow me entry," Ottentus said into the darkness. "Give me the scion. Give me time to tune to it. Learn how to wield it. Then you open the door, and I will enter on your behalf, and free your daughter."

"How would I be able to trust that you would fulfill your promise? There is no morality in Hell. No laws. No anything."

"There is no assurance I could lend that would give you satisfaction. I could tell you I would return you the scion—after all, were I to want one, there are six others out there—but my word would mean nothing. My actions, however, would speak on my behalf."

Anna nodded to herself, idly flicking the corner of a parchment. "I will have to think on it." *Long and hard.* She rubbed the sleep from her eyes.

"The boy keeps you up."

"He is a crier."

"Crying from the harm done to him." He tilted his head. "You wanted to know how to get in …"

Anna froze, mind blazing from the implication. "You found the second key."

He turned, a mysterious smile on his lips.

"Well? What is it then?"

"We know that one of the keys required to open the door is to be cursed—truly cursed, yes? The other key I will reveal to you once you commit to either entering with me or allowing me entry. Either way—" He took a step forth, face turning fierce. "—I swear to you on everything I hold sacred that I *will* find your daughter and return her to you. I know she's there. The puzzle pieces all match. But it would be easier if we went together, for as a master warlock, *He* would want to absorb what I know first. And as he wastes time hunting me …"

"I could free my daughter," Anna whispered.

"Precisely. I would be bait, lending you the most precious resource of all … time. The only challenge would be for me to evade him, for I suspect that should the Guardian of the Dark catch me and comb over my soul, he would find me … vapid. Uninteresting. Boring. And he might be able to do that without ever revealing himself."

Ottentus looked down at the floor as if ashamed. "Whereas you … you are an artist, yes? He could learn from you. I have little to offer, other than maybe some shortcuts. Variations of spells he might find—" He twirled a hand whilst expelling a breath through flapping lips. "—mildly amusing. You have something beyond my understanding … pure arcaneological creativity. That, to him, would be worth a great price. And so you would be in greater danger than me."

"Am I to be your backup, then?" asked an approaching voice from the darkness, startling Anna—but not Ottentus. Senior Arcaneologist Ning stepped into the field of candlelight. "You knew of my snooping and wanted me to hear this."

Anna glanced between them, wondering if Ning had heard every tidbit.

"You coveted—and still covet—the scion for your own research," Ottentus said.

"How do you know about that?" Ning snapped.

"Deduction."

"Elaborate."

Ottentus tapped the top of his chair with a fingernail. "No."

"May I remind you—"

"That I am a guest? How petty." He chortled as he paced to a bookshelf, running fingers along ancient spines. "Look at us. Probably the three greatest minds in the entire kingdom, here in this silent room, yes? Surrounded by ancient knowledge. Yet it pales in comparison to what awaits. *Nosiqiuous ani enitrios*—" He turned to face Ning. "—knowledge is forever. You want answers to deep arcaneological questions. I can provide them."

"You believe you can defeat the Arch Fiend."

"No. But I can stall him."

"While we rob him blind."

Ottentus raised a finger. "Reclaim only that which he has stolen from us. From our people. From history."

"You are mad."

"Am I?"

"Yes. And you have cleverly convinced my colleague that her daughter is trapped there."

"I have convinced her of nothing. It is not *I* who covets her artistry, but the Arch Fiend himself."

Ning folded her arms across her chest. "Is that so?"

"That *is* so."

"Then open your mind to me."

Ottentus scoffed. "So you may steal my secrets? You, who desperately covets knowledge beyond your grasp? And you think *me* deluded …"

"Then I reject you and hereby revoke all your privileges and expel you from this library. Be gone, serpent."

"You disappoint me, for I had hoped you would consider my offer to attend and advise." His eyes trawled the ancient spines. "Luckily I have already learned all I needed to learn from your horde of carefully guarded knowledge."

"I am sure you have," Ning spat.

Ottentus looked to Anna. "I will await your word, Arcanist Stone." He bowed. "Senior Arcaneologist Ning. Arcanist—"

Ning flicked her head. "Get out."

He said nothing more and, with a swish of his robe, left.

Ning turned to Anna. "He needs to be banished."

"Why?"

"Because *he* is the malignance."

"No more malignant than any of us pursuing knowledge."

"No one who takes such great pains to hide what they know—"

"Pains that I take?" Anna countered. "Pains that *you* take?"

"That is different—"

"Is it?"

"Yes."

"How?"

Ning struggled to respond.

"That's what I thought," Anna snapped. "You continue to covet. And I know what you want, and the answer is still *no*."

"But if it's just you and me, we could ensure—"

"I said, *no!* You are not a dueler. What are you going to do, run like a mouse, acting as bait against the second-most powerful being in mythology? I am going for one reason and one reason only—My! Daughter! Do you understand that?"

"So you *are* intending on going."

"No—" Anna turned away. "I ... I don't know."

"It's not even Hell. It's probably some fiery plane he mistakes as Hell. Do you know how common that has been in history? For planes to get mistaken as others? Ley is *not* Heaven, and whatever place this is is certainly not—"

"I am aware of the mythologies, thank you."

"Really? Because all I see is a grieving woman *hell*-bent on wanting something to be true. Something impossible. I bet you think your son is there with your daughter, don't you? Pathetic. You realize that, right? How pathetic it is that you of all people fell for this ancient trap of a thought? Eternal life never held any sway over you, but this ... this I cannot fathom. The sheer gullibility required."

"I never asked for your counsel on this point!" Anna snapped, her back still turned. When Ning did not reply, she forced herself to calm down. "We know some arcanery is out of reach, enmeshed in the ether itself—"

"That is not proof enough and you know it!"

"I will not give up on her!" Anna roared, spinning about, thumping her chest with a fist. "I know what I saw and heard. I *know*!"

"You know what you *wanted* to see and hear. What others wished you to—"

" 'Don't let him take me!' " Anna roared. "Those were my baby's last words! 'Don't let him take me …' "

The two women glared at each other.

"I am sorry for your loss," Ning whispered.

"Like hell you are—"

"How could you say such a thing?"

"You think yourself different from him? Where there is loss, *you* see opportunity!"

"How dare you imply—"

"Dare? *Dare?*" Anna stepped up to Ning so suddenly that Ning almost tripped backing away. Anna stabbed the woman's chest with a finger. "*You* want to replace him. *You* want entry as much as he does. But guess what the difference is between you two—he's honest about it!" Anna stormed past.

"You can't trust him. Anna? You can't trust him!"

Anna halted past the circle of candlelight. "I can't trust you either, can I? Your intentions with the scion prove that."

"And I regret doing that to this day."

"Is that you asking for forgiveness?"

Ning said nothing.

"Your pride has always been your curse."

"Damn you, Anna Atticus Stone. *Damn you!*"

"Too late for that," Anna spat, and strode off, leaving Ning to stand alone in the circle of candlelight.

CRIMSON VEINS

~⚬————————————————⚬~

Anna padded down ash steps split with crimson veins. The hot air, infused with rank sulfur, made everything shimmer—the columns of twisted black rock, the tables filled with steel implements, the caged unfortunates hanging above pools of lava, and the fiery horizon looming above it all.

A figure in one of the cages stirred, whimpering, "M-mom?"

A smaller figure in a second cage perked up. "Momma, is that really you?"

"Thia! Samuel!" Anna rushed forth only to bounce off an invisible wall.

Thia and Samuel rattled the bars of their cages, each hysterical.

"I'm here!"

"Help me, Mom—"

Both yelped as their cages dropped a foot.

"The chain, Mom!" Thia called out. "The chain—!"

Anna spotted a chain running from the top of her cage to the ceiling, pivoting from there to the hands of the one who called himself Bleeder—Ralf Turman. He was smiling maniacally as he kept pretending to lose his grip on the chain, making it jolt toward the lava. Samuel's chain was held by a shadow.

"Stop him, Mom! Stop him!" Thia shouted. "I want to go home! Please just take me home ..."

In the mean, Samuel devolved into an uncontrolled crying fit as he slumped against his cage, almost accepting of his destiny. His shadowy captor trickled out the chain in short slips, jolting the boy.

"I'm coming, my loves! I'm coming!" Anna blasted the invisible wall with four bolts of lightning. It reverberated with waves, but remained standing. As she pummeled it with everything she had, an enormous horned shadow rose on the horizon, blocking out half the fiery light. It was so large it made her feel like an ant facing an elephant.

During one of Ralf's feints, the chain broke. There was a yelp and a "*Mom—*" followed by a heart-stopping *splash*. It was quickly followed by a boyish shriek and a second *splash* when the shadow let go.

Anna yelped like her kids as she bolted up in bed, panting as if she'd run a league. Her breathe fogged in the cold air, yet she was soaked in sweat.

She groped about the bed in the dark, as if hoping her son and daughter had made it out with her. But there was no one there, not even her husband.

Another nightmare. The nights had been refusing her any semblance of peace or rest, tormenting her with variants of Thia and Samuel held captive.

Groggily rubbing puffy eyes, she rolled out of bed and thumped bare of foot on starlit planks to the privy, where she splashed her face with stale water. She looked up in the darkness at her mirror image and saw a woman she hardly recognized.

"You look old," she croaked, echoing the words of her husband. "Old and flailing. Old and angry." She batted the water in disgust, splashing the mirror. The rivulets distorted the dim view and made her look like she was crying. "Old and sad." She leaned forward, whispering, "Yet full of hope. They're alive. And they're waiting for you …"

After washing up, Anna thumped out of the privy and changed into a clean arcanist robe before a window blushing with a yellow dawn, readying for perhaps her final school day ever. And there was hope in the boy, too. Baby Lividius was at the Plowmans. She wondered if she would survive her quest and see him again. But she also knew Marybel would care for the child as if he were her own.

Before leaving, she looked into the bedroom, at the empty bed. She lingered in the morning stillness, eyes poring over the loose socks and undergarments, crumpled robes tossed into a corner, a book on Leyan thinking Thomas had left behind, still open to a chapter he had been reading. It reminded her of the many unfinished books her father had left behind after his death.

She dropped her head, nodded to herself, and left.

* * *

School offered little reprieve. Anna drifted through her lectures like a shadow, doing only what was required of her, saving what energy she could for the trial ahead. An absurd trial. An impossible trial. Everyone noticed she was a ghost of herself. And everyone understood.

As she corrected students and answered questions with as few words as possible and minimally acknowledged those who gave their condolences, she waffled and second-guessed herself and ran through the possibilities and the repercussions ... to little avail. There were no concrete answers, no certainties to be found. The myths and histories involved seemed too nebulous for the mind to fathom.

Yet life was meaningless without her son and daughter. Only blind hope allowed her to finish the school day. It was that hope that led her to a plain old door in the snowy forest surrounding the city. With a creak of protest, that door opened of its own accord.

"You've come," Ottentus said, standing at the far end of a small cabin, side profile lit by hearth fire. "I knew you would come."

"Why a shack in the woods?" Anna asked, stepping inside. While the door creaked closed behind her, she stomped her shoes, kicking off the snow. It was a cramped cabin with only a cot and a desk strewn with scrolls, books, parchments and quills.

"A shack hidden in the woods is easier to protect than a visible tower in the city."

"Fair point. Judging by the enchantments, the place is a tiny fortress, yet there is nothing here but research notes few would understand."

"Ah, but it is not the notes that are precious, yes?"

"Mmm." He valued his life above possessions. As everyone should. She knew that was the answer; she had only wanted to hear him say it.

Ottentus's head bobbed as he glanced past her. "And your husband?"

"You make a show of looking when you know he has no interest in what he perceives to be a fool's quest."

"You have grown terse, Arcanist Stone," he said, closing the door. "But I fault you not, all things considering. That terseness will aid you well when you become headmistress."

"If I live." Anna turned to face him. "We will enter together. You will distract—" She waved a hand about, not wanting to say the name.

"The Black-sooted One?"

"Whilst I save my daughter." *And son, if he is there too. Unnameables please return them both to me. Please ...*

Ottentus studied her as he nodded. "Then we must prepare. Let us meet here in one month at the hour of the witch."

"Why such a long wait?"

"It is my estimation that it will take you about that long to illegally learn a spell of ill intent. And that is a compliment, for someone less astute would require four times that amount—if not significantly more."

"I don't under—" She took a step forth, whispering, "The other key …"

"To truly understand the light, one must understand darkness. That is the other half of the requirement—the proverbial key, if you will. You must be cursed, and you must show true ill intent, which can only be expressed in the form of a spell. Only then will the door open."

"And you will train me—"

"No. I do not know any such spells. The spell must be an individual effort. Besides, even if I could, I cannot take part in such an endeavor. It is unethical. I merely study the necromantic arts for historical and research purposes, not actively pursue them."

"I find it hard to believe you do not know such spells considering you seek out forbidden knowledge in a hellish plane. Is necromantic knowledge not considered forbidden?"

"Vivictus famously said, 'Let me make my own judgment on what I ought and ought not to know.' "

Anna bit her lip as she nodded. It was the perfect reply. "So I must bear the burden."

"That is the price."

"How do I know this is not some elaborate scheme to have me arrested, the scion confiscated?"

To her surprise, his answer was to flare his full sleeve of ice. He raised it, turning it in place like a sculpture to be admired. "One of the sacrifices of gaining mastery is that everyone loses trust in you. All think you have a secret agenda, yes? It is inevitable."

Anna, mesmerized as always with the full sleeve, nodded at it. "How did it happen?"

"It happened on its own. The craft itself saw me ready, and chose me as its recipient, so to speak. But I find I am still so very mortal, and so very fallible. I make mistakes and still have much to learn. That tells me mastery is only a beginning step."

"A step to … what?"

"It is a great question. What lies beyond mastery?" He snuffed his arm and walked up to the fire, basking in its warmth. "You must have faith, Anna. Only faith in the quest will see you through. Only faith will bring your child back to you."

"In return, you can continue your quest for knowledge. To what end? Power?"

"I wonder if you are familiar with an ancient tale written long before The Founding," he said, staring deep into the flames, voice distant. "An allegory, really, about a man who is relentlessly mocked for his stupidity—"

"—and he undertakes a quest to the fabled Library of All Knowledge to become smarter," Anna said. "I am familiar with it, yes."

"Of course you are. He learns everything there is to know and returns to show he has become learned. Except everything he knew is gone, his family long turned to dust." Ottentus looked up at her, half his face in shadow, the other in firelight. "I *am* that man. Not literally, but in spirit. The difference between us is that my family has already turned to dust. I am thus free to pursue knowledge to its logical conclusion."

"Eternity?"

"Perhaps, but I suspect that would be incidental to the great pursuit before me."

"Which is why you do not covet my scion as others do. You believe the knowledge you gain will more than compensate."

"Precisely." He looked back at the fire. With an idle wag of a finger, the logs resettled themselves, releasing crackling sparks. "I do not know what insights gleaned from a forbidden library will lend me, but I must believe they will lead me to other libraries, perhaps Leyan or Rivican or who knows what sort. Many peoples—exotic races we have yet to uncover—have secreted banks of knowledge through history, which is far, *far* older than we think. The end resolution must therefore be a benevolent one, for how can knowledge be evil? Like arcanery, it is but a tool. Now imagine that man, full of knowledge, returning to the world—not to rule it, but to aid it, for we suffer so. In our ignorance. In our depravity. In our short lifespans." He looked up and smiled. "My curiosity begs me to try. Besides, I have achieved everything I have wanted to achieve in this plane. There is nothing left for me here. I might as well put myself to some use for us all."

Anna could not argue with his logic.

"And while you learn a spell of ill intent, I will learn a spell that will make me interesting to the Arch Fiend, one that will keep his mind on me, not you."

"*If* he exists."

"If he exists, yes."

He had passed her final test. Now she could pursue the quest without restraint. "So be it."

He gave her a bittersweet smile, perhaps the most genuine smile she had ever seen him employ. "You and I are very much alike, Anna. I wish you luck in the challenge ahead."

She went to the door, placing a hand on the old iron handle. "Where am I supposed to find a spell of that sort?"

Ottentus padded up to stand beside the door. "Your kingdom has invaluable archives in Blackhaven and Antioc, among others. I am sure the kingdom's champion will have little trouble gaining access."

Anna grunted, opening the door, letting the cold in. "You will be here?"

"When you are ready, I will come."

Realizing he meant she would have to step on his alarms again, she nodded, and departed without another word.

* * *

The answer to the riddle of where she would find a dark spell came when she got home, after laying eyes on a certain black book.

"Providence … or circumstance?" she asked herself, picking up the old tome. Red slashes crisscrossed the thick black cover, just like in her nightmare. "Perhaps the nightmare stole this imagery, yes?" She snorted at herself for talking like Ottentus. Yet he was right—she *didn't* fully trust him, even despite him answering her questions to her satisfaction. He was also right that it would happen to her too if she ever achieved mastery. Even possessing the scion caused distrust. Who knew how it would be in combination …

She ran her fingers along the cracked binding of demon skin, the intertwining clawed hands that made up the latch mechanism. She wondered if this was how necromancers began. With mere curiosity …

"But this is not curiosity, is it?" she whispered. "It is necessity." The dire necessity of a mother wanting to save her children. "How to open you, you little villain?" She had exhausted all ideas on how to open the book, to the point that it had sat untouched for months, forgotten …

"What have I *not* tried?" She took the book to her office desk, lit brightly by moonlight streaming in through the window, and splayed a hand over it. "*Un vun asperio aurum enchantus,*" she incanted, revealing a dense tapestry of gray and black and red tendrils. She'd tried using Telekinesis to move the puzzle pieces around, she'd tried casting spells on them that necromancers had used historically, she'd thrown countless variants of solutions to classic kargeyasnaras—yet this necromantic kargeyasnara remained unsolved.

"The door requires malice ..." Her splayed hand floated above the tendril workmanship. "And these castings are infused with malice. What if..." She took a seat before the book. "What if that's also the secret ingredient?" It seemed implausible, yet intent was one of the backbones of arcanery. "It's certainly something I haven't tried ..."

She straightened in her chair, trying to think of a way to infuse malice into Telekinesis. "Hate. It has to be hate." But she did not hate anyone. Everyone had a story, a reason for being who they were. The closest person who would match that feeling was the father of her grandson, a young seventeen-year-old man. A misguided orphan with possessive tendencies. A boy who might have had a hand in Thia's death ...

"What choice do I have?" she muttered. "Let's dive into it," and she pointed a finger at the largest tendril piece that interacted with the locking mechanism and thought about how much she disliked the boy. The piece did not budge, but there was a slight crimson blush to one edge of the tendril webbing.

"Hmm," she toned. "Me thinks it doth requireth a leaning," and she leaned into the spell, thinking of how much she loathed Ralf Turman for treating her daughter like chattel. For using her in rituals and possibly drinking her blood.

The piece flared and vibrated ... but still refused to budge.

Anna resettled in her chair. "So malice is the right path. Now to amplify it." She had a bad feeling she knew what the puzzle wanted of her. After a deep breath, she leaned close, grimacing with utter hatred. She thought of grabbing the young man by the collar and violently throttling him. Instantly, guided by her Telekinesis, the piece began to move, albeit at a snail's pace. Knowing she had to increase the intensity lest she sit there for a whole tenday, she visualized lightning coursing through her hands and enveloping the boy. At last, the puzzle piece slipped along. Having already studied the shapes, she knew where it had to end up—alongside a piece with a matching edge. After she imagined Ralf convulsing within her lightning, crying out in pain, it slipped into place, sealing with a flash of light.

Anna expelled a breath and sat back, admiring the work ... and feeling awfully guilty for such potently vile thoughts. Yet it was merely one piece of many, and the work had only just begun. She rubbed her eyes, resettled into position, and began another round of intense hatred.

By the time the last piece was sliding into place, a fictitious Ralf Turman had experienced many agonizing deaths ... and Anna was on the verge of an emotional breakdown. Tears rolled down her cheeks, tears of guilt and sorrow for her daughter—and it was those emotions that ground the piece to a halt.

"I can't do it," she blubbered, head flopping onto the book. "I can't finish it …" The scion, floating beside her, flared with silent lightning. *Do it for my grandchildren*, she could almost hear her father say. *Do it for Samuel and Thia.*

Anna sniffed, sat up, cleared her throat, extended a finger, and thought of eviscerating Ralf Turman with the shortsword Burden's Edge, feeling it strangely appropriate. Every limb she sliced off, the piece nudged forward. An arm. A leg. Another arm, another leg. She could hear him screaming as he lay in a puddle of his own blood, pleading for her to stop. After a shuddering breath, she raised the blade high, and with trembling hands, lopped off his head.

The final piece slipped into place, sealing with a flare of light. There was a *click* as the claws unclasped. But Anna had slid off the chair to the floor, crying like a newborn babe. Crying harder than she had cried in many years. It all came pouring out. Samuel. Thia. Her husband. The potent loneliness. The emptiness. The loathing at herself, at Ralf, at the gods, at The Fates for putting her family through such cruel circumstances. So worn down was she that she cried herself to sleep there on the old plank floor.

A NEW PAGE

Anna, still on the floor of her office, woke to a sunbeam on her face. With a groan, she raised herself up to a sitting position. Today was her fiftieth birthday and her bones ached, but not as much as her soul. The aching lingered amidst bitter loneliness and sweet sorrow. Yet it had been a surprisingly deep sleep, devoid of nightmares. In some strange fashion, unleashing the hate had given her a reprieve.

"A dangerous precedent," she muttered, rubbing the sleep from her puffy eyes. Seeing the book unlocked on her desk, she hauled herself to her feet with another groan, using the chair as leverage.

"You are getting old," she muttered. "So old." It wasn't true. Fifty wasn't that old. She only felt like it was because of how horrendously awful a year it had been. It was a deep ache that bled from her heart and settled into her joints and bones.

After straightening her arcanist robe, she hooked a fingernail underneath the edge of the book and flipped open the cover. Written in clean and large script, in ink that looked suspiciously like blood, were the words *Morba Minad*. Those two simple words brought back her fourteen-year-old self. That aspirant girl stood amidst debris, before a gigantic bull demon that was laying waste to the city. She remembered a black tendril web slapping into her, eating through her Mind Armor like acid. She remembered octopus tentacles slithering their way in. She remembered searching about for a brick to bash her own head in, wanting only to die.

"Morbid Mind," Anna whispered, a finger tracing above the crimson wording as she heard the echoes of a battle that had happened thirty-six years ago. "I was so young then …" *Now I must take the place of the demon and learn its spell.* She flipped the cover back over, wondering if the skin was from a bull demon, careful to keep a finger inside the pages lest she have to do the kargeyasnara all over again. Judging by the separation between the creases, she suspected it was. But she couldn't tell for sure, nor did she remember what the bull demon's skin had looked like up close.

"Could be any demon," she muttered. Just as she opened the tome once more, there came the sound of a portal flaring in the living room, and she threw a blanket over the book, hurried out of her office, and found a hairless man standing in the living room, clothed in a freshly cleaned purple robe. She was about to ask what Ottentus was doing there and why he was wearing that color, when the man opened his mouth.

"Hello, Wife."

Anna had to brace against the wall, for her heart had sunk to her knees. Instinctively, her body knew what this meant. Yet her mind refused to believe what it saw.

"I can hardly recognize you," she mumbled. He had even shaved off his eyebrows …

Thomas said nothing. Instead, he walked forth with the lightest ease, stepping up to the sunlit dining table. As if painting memories, he lightly brushed its dusty surface with a hand. "Look how beautiful the sun is today."

Of all the things he could have said, of all the days, those words confirmed her deepest fears, and she collapsed to her knees.

"Do not fear, Anna. Do not fear."

"I have lost you …"

Thomas padded up to her. "I lost myself," he whispered, offering a hand. She took it, allowing him to drag her back to her feet. "That old me died along with our daughter. There is but a shell now, to be filled with only one idea … the moment."

"But … but what of our future?"

"You know the answer to that."

She *did* know the answer to that. Had known it every time she'd placed her gaze on him. Whatever they had between them that had barely survived the death of their son had crumbled upon the death of their daughter. Except he did not know the hope she had, the power the coming quest offered …

"I can make it right," she whispered, placing a trembling hand to his cheek. "I can put it all to right …"

Thomas closed his eyes and leaned into her hand. He took a deep breath, as if inhaling her love, before opening his eyes and returning to the sunlit table. "She's gone, Anna. She's gone."

"You don't know that. You don't *know* that!"

"I do. I see it in the sun in this very room. I hear it in the silence. I feel it in my heart." He glanced around, nodding to himself, before turning to face her directly. "I have decided to move to the monastery."

Anna raised her hands as if to ward off a blow. She shook her head. "No, I forbid it."

"I want you to know I will always love you."

"I forbid it …"

"Anna."

"Don't you abandon me. Don't you dare do it. And on my birthday! My *fiftieth* birthday! We were supposed to celebrate it together! Renew our love, remember? Remember that promise you made to me all those years ago?"

"I do. And I am sorry. I truly am. But we both know there is nothing here for us."

"No. You don't understand." *I can bring our children back …*

"But I do, Wife. I do."

"Stop it. Stop it! I won't let you. I *can't* let you. Please don't … don't abandon me …" Eyes unfocused, she grabbed feebly at the air, as if trying to snatch a ghost. She saw her mother leaving the house for the last time. She saw her father shoving her away before he too turned his back …

Thomas stared at her with pity and a peace that hurt even more. "I will gather the things I will require. The remainder you may do with as you please."

Anna shook the memories off. "Why would you say such hurtful things? Do you not still love me? I'm still here … yet you're leaving me. I … I don't understand …"

"I will always wear the ring. I will always be your husband. But the life we had is over. Even now I cannot say their names. My own son. My own daughter. But particularly our boy. He didn't even have a chance to become a warlock, to attend the academy, to climb the degrees and make warlock friends and experience that camaraderie and to have a manhood ceremony and a graduation. All that lost potential …"

"I don't understand …"

"You will in due course. I have a journey. A journey with one sole aim—to transcend the moment. To *become* the moment."

"Stop talking in riddles!" she snapped, straightening. "I will suffer none of your foolishness, Thomas Bran Hubert Stone. You will cease this nonsense immediately."

"I am not a child to be berated, Anna. I am your husband. I ask you to respect my wish."

"I can bring them back!" she blurted. "I can bring them back ... both of them."

"Oh, Anna. Do you even hear yourself?"

"We can move away—"

"How utterly mad and delusional you sound?"

"No one will understand, that much I know, but we can start a new life together as a family in a distant kingdom—"

"My dear wife, what have you done to yourself? What foolish belief have you fallen for?"

"I will show you. I will bring them back. You will see. You will *see*."

Thomas shook his head. "This is a dead end that will only cause you more pain. Acknowledge the grief. Feel it. Let it filter through your soul like a prism. It will take time for you, as it will for me. But I urge you to quest for peace, Anna, not delusion. Do it for yourself. Do it for your grandson. That is the only way."

Anna, whose trembling hands were still raised in a defensive position, slid around the corner and stumbled down the hall. "You've lost all hope," she mumbled. "You've lost all hope ..."

"There is no hope to be had, Anna. Do you hear me? Anna ...?"

Anna did not respond. She thumped back into her office, slammed the door so hard some books tumbled from a shelf, and slid into her chair. There soon came a quiet rustling from the hall, indicating Thomas had begun packing. She sat there, watching the ray of sunlight crawl across her desk. Even as Thomas came to the other side of the door and she heard his hand press against it as he said something that meant nothing to her, some useless monk riddle that served only to distract her from the sacred quest ahead, she continued sitting there, staring at nothing. Only when her husband had left their home for what felt like the last time and the ray of sun had departed did Anna slip the blanket off the open book.

"To truly understand the light, one must understand darkness," she whispered.

After staring at the title to Morbid Mind, she turned the first page.

A FOND FAREWELL

It was a dark and snowy morning when Anna appeared amidst tall yellow grass, little Lividius bundled in her arms. The boy's crying immediately intensified, as it always did after a teleport. She'd changed his linen nappy and fed him and spent all morning cooing at him, trying to get him to stop crying even for an hour.

"It's your soul. It's injured without your mother," she said, tickling his chin. "I will bring her back to you. This I swear. But for me to do that, I will have to leave you with the Plowman family, all right? You know them. They're friends. Now you behave lest we give another poor impression."

Her words, as always, fell on deaf ears, and she sighed, fearing the look on Marybel's already tired face when she would once again accept the crier who surely had already caused her family many nights of lost sleep.

Anna looked up at the overcast sky, closed her eyes, and let the fat flakes of snow prick her cheeks. After seeing great success in the academy and in the arena and in her teaching and research, and for a few precious years even in her family, life had not turned out at all how she imagined it would. A life spent in sorrow was no life at all, but a puddle of misery and toil.

She trudged onward through the snow, keeping the babe close to lend him warmth. The home soon appeared amidst the swirling snowflakes, its windows cozy with candle and hearth light. She could hear playful jostling and laughter from within. The Plowman family had grown, whilst hers had gotten obliterated.

Anna had raised her hand to knock when the door burst open.

"I said I'd check on the sow and see if—" The young lady—a Waxman girl—yelped when she saw Anna. "Mrs. Stone! Oh my, what an—" But her face fell when she saw the bundle. "Oh."

Anna, ashamed, tried to back away. "I'm sorry. Maybe I ought to—"

"No, no, no, it's fine. I apologize, Mrs. Stone. I'll just have to study in the barn. Please, come in. Please. Mom! Moooom, it's Mrs. Stone!"

Marybel hurried into the hall, joined by a slew of kids and a few older folks, probably neighbors or friends of the family. There came a bunch of hellos and nods and bows and curtsies. Marybel didn't even flinch, throwing out her arms and shouting, "Anna!" and hugging her gently before drawing back to have a look at her. "You're wearing your arcanist robe. Is it a school excursion?"

"Er, no. I'm afraid not."

"Then let's have us some tea."

"I can't—"

"Nonsense. Jasmine!" she called over her shoulder. "*Jasmine!*"

Thirteen-year-old Jasmine poked her head out from the hall. "What?"

"Don't you *what* me. Take little Lividius."

"But *Mom*, I have studies—"

"Now, Jasmine."

"Ugh." The girl gently took Lividius from Anna, mumbling a "Hello, Auntie Stone."

"I'm so sorry to put this burden on you," Anna said.

"It's fine," Jasmine muttered. She tried to nuzzle his nose with hers, but the baby spat a loud cry and whapped her on the side of the head with his little paw. "Ugh," she said again, and thumped to the living room.

"You look exhausted," Marybel said.

"And you look spritely. How do you keep up with them all?"

"I look in the mirror every morn and say to myself, 'It will be a beautiful day.' Now come on, one tea will not kill you."

"I really can't." She could, but it would be too painful. Seeing such a happy family reminded her of her own failure and loss.

Marybel took a second look into Anna's eyes and her face softened. "Lot of you, out. I said away with you, and that means you too, Uncle!"

The gawking kids and teenagers and adults and one old geezer with a scowl and a cane waddled off, though some of the younger ones remained within earshot, until Marybel chased them off with a bevy of well-honed but gentle curses.

"Something's happened since last you came to pick the little one up," she said. "And you were all tight-lipped back then too. I won't have it this time. Spill it. What happened?"

Anna stole a look at the living room, full of people carousing and chatting and laughing and glancing her way. At least Lividius's crying blended into the chaos.

Marybel noticed and grabbed Anna by the elbow and led her to the dim parlor room that had been Mr. Plowman's study. Snatching flint and steel from the mantel, she dropped to her knees before a cold hearth.

Anna held herself as she paced the room. A dusty Endyear candle sat on a window ledge, waiting to be lit for the upcoming festivities. Outside, snow had piled up against the nicked glass. She examined shelves of old books, recognizing some titles as once belonging to her father, who had donated many to the Plowmans when she was young. She picked out one about a little girl having her own castle.

"I remember reading this," she whispered, flipping the crinkled pages. "Must have read it three times. And then when it came true for me, I realized the castle was nothing but a tomb."

Marybel kept striking toward a pile of tinder. "Blasted thing won't light. Sorry, we don't use this hearth much."

Anna put the book back. "Let me."

"Have at 'er."

Anna reached down and sparked a finger. The fire caught instantly, spreading light into the dark corners of the room. She still remembered learning the extension from a hoodlum in an abandoned part of Shoptown what felt like a lifetime ago …

"Thanks." Marybel hauled herself to her feet with a groan and gave Anna a pained smile. "It's that fool of a husband, isn't it? What'd he do now?"

Anna's throat went dry and she couldn't get the words out.

Marybel wilted. "Oh, sweetie … he *left* you?"

Anna surrendered a single nod, and Marybel enveloped Anna in a hug. But Anna stood listlessly.

"Hug me back, will you!"

Anna lamely did so, then tightened the hug, until she found herself quietly weeping. "I thought we'd be together until we died," she blubbered, withdrawing and turning to a dark window, watching the snow sweep past the glass.

"He found himself a comely little wench, didn't he? I'll kill that son of a—"

"It's nothing like that. He'll keep the ring, but he's ..."

"He's what?"

"He shaved."

Marybel pressed a hand to her chest. "He's taking the line," using the euphemism for becoming a Northern Monk.

"Looks that way."

"Maybe that's just his way of dealing with the loss. Maybe he'll snap out of it ..."

"I don't think so." Anna sighed heavily. "Look, I'm sorry, but I can't stay."

"Anna, come on, some tea and company would do you good. We can chat about the old days and you can complain and we can sup and—"

Anna grabbed Marybel by the shoulders. "You've been a good friend to me. If something happens, will you watch over my grandson? Rear him up as your own?"

Marybel cupped her mouth with both hands. "Gods, Anna ..."

"I know it's a lot to ask, especially seeing as he's such a crier and all, but—"

"Of *course* I'll do it! It is the least we could do after everything you and your father have done for us. The very least! And I promise you that, no matter how much trouble he gives us, he will be well loved." She tapped the side of a fist against Anna's chest. "But you make sure it doesn't come to that, right? *Right?*"

Anna dropped her arms and head. "Right."

"Where are you going, anyway?"

Anna looked at the fire. "I'm afraid I cannot say."

"It's something to do with that excavation, hasn't it?"

"I cannot speak on the matter. I'm sorry."

"Oh, Anna. What have you gotten yourself into this time?"

Anna wanted to reply and tell her how she was in way over her head, that she was afraid she was wrong about everything and was walking into something she might eternally regret. "Thank you," she said instead. "Thank you." After all, her children were worth any price.

Marybel pressed her lips together and gave a pained nod. "You should say goodbye to him."

Anna was about to take up that advice, only to change her mind at the door. "I can't."

"I understand. Too painful."

"I said my peace outside, anyway. But I can't go into that living room knowing …"

"That you might not return?"

Anna nodded, and for a time, amidst the clamor of a family playing a friendly game of Keep Away, and a babe crying in an exasperated young girl's arms, the pair of friends only stared at each other. At last, Marybel hugged Anna, and Anna hugged her back.

"Good luck," Marybel whispered. "We will be praying for you."

"Thanks." Anna slipped away, and walked out into the snow for a while to give herself the space to cry alone. When she turned to face the house, she saw Marybel still standing in the doorway. Her friend raised a hand and gave a single wave. Anna returned it before quickly snapping off, "*Impetus peragro.*"

She appeared in a snowy wood, before an ancient manor. The windows were dark, but that was how its owner, a certain retired Black Eagle, liked to keep them. Yet Anna knew she would soon be greeted, for she had purposely teleported directly into an alarm enchantment. She intended to ask one last favor—a practice duel, with the intent of having the old woman throw everything she had at Anna.

She waited in the snowy quiet, and waited, and waited. Yet the old woman did not appear. Growing curious—and mildly concerned—Anna splayed open a hand. "*Un vun asperio aurum enchantus,*" she incanted, and saw *some* enchantments appear, but not all. Had the remainder been disenchanted?

Heart dropping, Anna raced to the door—and found it unlocked.

"Niterra?" she called as the door creaked open, hand still splayed with Reveal. "Niterra, are you home? It's Anna. I'm going on a quest and was hoping we could have a friendly duel and one last lesson …"

Her voice was met with silence. The place was frigidly cold too, so much so that a nearby glass of water, half empty, had frozen solid. The sight made Anna hurry through the house, calling out the old woman's name.

"Niterra are you—" Anna halted in the expansive living room, seeing a figure slumped in an armchair. Anna stood frozen in place like the glass of water, heart splintering into a thousand smaller pieces, before making a quick circle with a finger. "*Shyneo lampa,*" she whispered, and out popped a floating ball of lightning. It lit up empty bottles and old wine goblets and half-open books and a thin film of dust over everything.

And it lit up a woman, head slumped forward, a bejeweled goblet lying on the floor beside her, the wine frozen into the hide carpet of a Nodian red bear. The side of the cup caught her eye, for reflected in her stark blue light were the words, *"Loyaltos, creatos, vira."* Loyalty, ingenuity, strength.

Anna stepped before the old warrior. "I should have come sooner," she whispered. "I should have come sooner …" She'd visited twice since Lividius's birth, and both times the woman had seemed all right, if not a little restless and melancholy, as if she had nothing left to do. They'd talked about the past, sparred some, and traded tips, with Anna taking more than she had shared simply due to experience, especially when it came to Combat Portal.

Anna snuffed her lamp, plunging the room into dim silhouettes, and stared at the body of her friend, who appeared as if she had died in her sleep. She took a knee before her and gripped her hand, cold and frozen and stiff with death, between both her own.

"You have led a good life," she whispered, tears streaming down her cheeks. "I thank you for everything you did for my family. You may feel it was not enough, but one survives. A little boy, and he is the future. I had hoped we could spar one last time. I had some questions about a few spells. But I guess those will have to wait until I join you in the Great Beyond." She bowed her head and remained in that pose for some time, acknowledging the venerable woman and everything she had done.

"I will send a letter to the king explaining things," she said, standing. "I know you don't care, but you will have a funeral in the old way. In the tradition of the Black Eagles, in the way of the warrior. You *will* be honored. That much I promise you."

Anna took a step back and gave one last bow, this one deep and filled with gratitude, before straightening. "Now I go to the plane of rock and fire in search of my children. If I fail, perhaps we shall see each other sooner than later. Fond farewell in the mean, old friend. Fond farewell …"

LEAPING

❧━━━━━━━━━━━━━━━━━❧

For the final time and just before midnight, Anna appeared by a certain cabin in the snowy forest that surrounded the city like moss around a boulder. The cabin, resting snugly underneath a sprawling pine, sat dark and empty.

Anna, purposely having appeared in a spot that tripped an alarm, waited, breath pluming in the frosty night air, fingers drumming the strap of an old rucksack. She had packed everything she thought she might need, including a tenday of rations, a blanket, a tent, two skins of water, and the key to the thumbprint maze.

And Bun-Bun. She figured her daughter would need him. The little old bunny rested snugly amidst the blanket, waiting for his companion to nuzzle and kiss him once more.

And of course the scion, which weighed heavily in her pocket, as if anxious to be utilized.

"You must be wondering why we meet specifically at the hour of the witch," Ottentus said from the darkness.

A startled Anna whipped about. "How long have you been there?" she asked, still failing to locate or see him.

A shimmer briefly moved at the trunk of a massive old pine. "A long time preparing, meditating." Steps formed in the snow as he approached. "I hope to be as proficient with Chameleon as you are one day," he said. "They say you are the best, yes?"

"Why *did* we have to meet at this particular cursed hour?" As an early riser, it was a tough adjustment knowing she might not get any sleep tonight.

"*Chameleano null*," he said, making himself visible before her. He too carried a rucksack. "The answer lies within your question."

Referring to the word cursed, Anna thought. She closed her eyes and flipped through the meticulously catalogued pages of her memory. "Old mythology. Witchcraft. The *cursed* hours, also known as the witching hours, began at midnight, as that was the hour the witch of old was said to begin accepting human sacrifices." She opened her eyes.

"And thus midnight becoming forever known as the hour of the witch," Ottentus added. "Have you learned a spell of ill intent?"

"I have."

"As promised, I too have learned a spell."

"The one that will keep the devil's attention on you."

He looked up at the moon. "It is full. Behold its beauty."

Anna looked up at the silver moon. "It is larger than I remember."

"Focus amplifies." He stepped away from her, bent down, and used a finger to draw a circle around himself in the snow.

Anna splayed her hand. "Do you mind?"

"Not at all."

"*Un vun asperio aurum enchantus*," she incanted, and a slew of protective enchantments lit up around the cabin. But she kept her attention on what he was doing.

"You would make a great apprentice, Anna Atticus Stone."

"I *am* an apprentice."

He took a moment. "An apprentice of knowledge. You are wise." He reached into a pocket and withdrew a doll made of rough burlap, dressed in an identical miniature opalescent-white robe to the one he wore. His hand shook as he placed the doll in the center of the circle, stepped outside its boundary, withdrew a small knife from a pocket, and shakily sliced his hand.

Anna watched as he dribbled his blood on the doll, wondering about this dark ritual he was about to cast.

Ottentus next dribbled his blood on the circle's perimeter. Upon closing the circle, he stood up and splayed both hands, one over the doll, one over his heart as he began a long incantation, "*Goho ah ga ahu ioa ehi eha nah* ..." and it went on and on. The words were unfamiliar and sounded like inanities. Throughout, he stared at Anna with a determined gaze, unnerving her. What was she getting herself into? But it was too late to turn back, what with her children waiting for her. At this point, she would become a necromancer herself to save her daughter. Nothing else mattered. Nothing.

She witnessed black tendrils weave their way between the doll and his heart. Upon closer inspection, the energy flowed from the ground into the doll and *then* to his heart. Were it a different situation, she would have guessed it was an armor spell for the heart, and therefore the soul, for the heart was said to be the gateway to the soul.

The doll burst into flames, yet Ottentus's chanting strengthened. Only when the doll turned into a smoking crisp did the chanting stop, and Ottentus gasped as he fell to his knees, where he clutched his heart with both hands and wept.

Anna did not know what to say to comfort him, so she honored the moment by remaining present in it.

"Forgive me," he blubbered, sniffing, robe still scrunched with both hands.

"Is there something I can do to ease the suffering?"

"Nothing. The price is beyond our reach."

"May I ask what that price was?"

"Please do not. I cannot bear to think on it a moment more."

"But it armored your soul."

Ottentus shuddered with renewed weeping. "A ... necessary ... precaution."

Anna waited until he calmed down a little. "If I may, against what, precisely?"

Ottentus hauled himself to his feet and looked at her with new eyes, the whites of which were now as black as the night. "Cruelty."

"Your eyes ..."

Ottentus used the blade of the dagger to check his reflection. "By gods, that is most ghastly, yes? I apologize for my frightful countenance. Hopefully they will return to normal after we cross the barrier."

Anna certainly hoped so. Yet it did not escape her that becoming a Leyan meant having one's eyes turn completely black too. She wondered why that was, and how it all tied together.

He tossed the dagger into the circle and looked past Anna at his hut. She glanced back at it but saw nothing untoward. Then she realized he was saying goodbye to it.

"A home away from home is still a home," he said, as if reading her mind.

"And where is home? Franterra?"

"Home is ... home is long gone." He nodded to himself, those black eyes distant as he seemed to recall something from a long time ago. Then he slapped his hands together. "Onward, Arcanist Stone. To the excavation. *Impetus peragro—*" and he vanished with a *thwomp* before Anna could reply.

She followed him nonetheless, appearing outside the excavation … and found the entrance had been buried back up, and all traces of the exterior encampment gone.

"A sensible precaution," she said.

"I thought so," he replied, striding up to the wall of rock that was Mount Barrow. He placed a hand on a particularly large section and whispered, "Ottentus Maledius Anavictus Anna Atticus Stone." It opened inward with a grinding noise. He stepped inside and waited by the door.

"The password is our full names said together?" she asked upon joining him.

He nodded as he flicked a hand at the door, which swung shut with a deep thud, plunging them into pitch darkness.

It did not escape Anna's notice that he had listed himself first. Then again, had he not earned that right as a master? Part of her wanted to leave that password somewhere where it could be found, particularly by Thomas. But another part did not want anyone following in their footsteps. The knowledge contained within was too dangerous and powerful, and had to be hidden and protected before it became accessible. Arbiters would have to be appointed. It might take decades for people to be ready to accept Leyan wisdom into the world once more. Maybe even lifetimes. Having existed almost two thousand years without the Leyans, people had had much time and practice in strengthening their beliefs in the Unnameables, among other gods and goddesses. Reintroducing such a door to the unprepared—especially the rabidly superstitious—could plunge all seven kingdoms into a catastrophic war none had ever seen. And that was only regarding a door to Ley. The other doors would be a whole other challenge …

The reservations won, and Anna summoned her lightning lamp. The pair walked past discarded mining equipment and retrieved the master builder's golden shield. Ottentus then cast Incarnate to get them through the explosive hall, where Ottentus put the shield down on the floor and nullified Incarnate.

"The arcane hourglass has begun to trickle," he said. "We have three days."

"Understood." As if it were routine, Anna withdrew the key and inserted it into the thumb-sized slot within the fingerprint maze. The portal appeared, and after exchanging a single look, they stepped through it. As before, they found themselves in a long and see-through room with a few portals, floating far beneath Devil's Gate amidst a sea of darkness.

Anna stared up at the distant pair of legs that made up the base of the mammoth horseshoe-shaped structure.

Ottentus, meanwhile, glanced around at the planar doors. "We stand before perhaps the greatest discovery in all of recorded history."

"It must be guarded," Anna replied.

"It *is* guarded. It took a team of us to unwind the master builder's secrets. None will follow, yes? *We* are the arbiters." He took a deep breath and exhaled. "Do you hear that? That silence is the sound of endless possibilities. In time, this will change everything."

"It must be done responsibly. And that might take lifetimes."

"If done responsibly, lifetimes we will have."

Anna replied by striding to the portal and stopping a foot away from it. Its black surface bubbled with molten globules, and she could hear the quiet hiss of steam from within ... along with a distant and chilling sound that mingled almost sweetly with her high-pitched headache. Anna leaned closer with her ear. It was a chorus of screams. A prolonged and shrill chorus of a thousand voices in simultaneous agony. Unable to help but fear that her children were among those voices, she recoiled away from the door. What she had heard almost came out of a book about Hell, of things that should frighten. Or perhaps a story told around a campfire to scare children into behaving.

"You hear something," Ottentus said, placing his ear near the door. "I hear nothing. Yet your face says it is something terrifying, yes?"

Anna did not quite understand how the arcanery worked for only her to hear the sounds.

"Allow me a quote from one of your Solian kings," Ottentus went on. " 'When faced with the most dreaded of dreads, the heart longs for peace.' It is not too late to turn back, Arcanist Stone ... Anna. We do not have to enter."

"Two of those voices ..."

"You hear voices?"

"Screams. I hear screams."

"You believe two of them are your children."

"Do you think me mad?"

"It would take a great deal more for me to believe that. We have seen things Ordinaries could scarcely fathom. Knowledge itself can be a curse."

"Sometimes I think I have gone mad," she whispered, absently staring at a crimson vein cracking the molten black surface. "Sometimes I think everything has already ended and this is a nightmare …"

"Perhaps this will be a new beginning."

"Perhaps."

"We do not know what we shall face on the other side. It may be a swift death."

"That would almost be a mercy." Then she could join her children in the Great Beyond … assuming it existed. But it had to, for she needed something to look forward to. The starkness of a vast nothing, the implication that her children could truly be no more, frightened her more than anything of this world.

"Then I am ready." He waited for her.

She took her time to consider the ramifications of proceeding before nodding. "As am I."

"Let us begin." He stepped back. "On you. Remember I will have to enter first."

"On me." Else the door might close behind her, as it would for a regular portal. But this was no regular portal. She summoned so much inner loathing, focusing it on the gateway itself, that she snarled. After coalescing the necessary arcaneological thoughts required of the complex spell, and thinking how a victim of the spell would crave death by any means necessary, she thrust both hands forth, roaring, "*Morba!*" She imagined the invisible tendril web smacking into the portal. Amazingly, the lines of that webbing created a diamond-like pattern against the molten mass, suffusing it with crimson veins. Those veins split apart, until the whole door was crimson. The steaming hiss grew louder and louder, forcing Anna to back up, until the door went all black—and a monstrous and windy suction began.

Ottentus leaped into the suction. Anna, instead of opposing that suction, closed her eyes and surrendered herself to it. Her body was yanked forth, and she hurtled through light so bright it penetrated her eyelids. She opened her eyes and saw colorful rivers of light streaming by amidst a vast infinity she could barely fathom. Light bent around her as if she were a fishbowl flying through a prism. The noise was something else, like a thousand bison charging by, stampeding over her thoughts. And the sensation was that of accelerated falling, moving quicker and quicker, her body—her very bones—drummed by the cacophony.

A black and crimson mass loomed ahead, getting larger. It quickly took up the entire horizon, and everything went black and dense, with the noise coming to a fevered and screaming pitch. For a brief moment, she thought she was dead—until she felt the stomach-lightening sensation of being in midair.

And before her was a landscape of fire.

Rock and fire.

She landed rather gently beside Ottentus, on black cinder rock that was surprisingly cool on the feet. The air was frigid cold, frosting their breath, and stank of acid and sulfur and ash. The ground had a craquelure look to it, with crimson veins spidering along the surface. Jagged spires of mountainous rock jutted into a sickly yellow sky like teeth biting into a lemon. Between the spires leaped enormous columns of fire, and behind was the darkness of night. Opposite that horizon was one filled with stars—millions of them, each a pinprick against a rich canvas of gases and swirls and strange creations, as if a painter had gone wild with splatter.

Anna's stomach felt strangely light. She looked back up and saw that the raging portal that had spat them out was thirty feet off the ground—yet she had landed softly.

"Imagine if someone were to close the door on us, yes?" Ottentus said with a chortle, staring up at it. "Of course such a thing would be quite improbable. No one alive, other than your husband, knows what we are up to."

"Mmm," Anna toned, finding that an odd thing to say. The last thing she feared was someone following them, especially considering all the precautions they had taken. She turned her thoughts to other things, and having an idea of what effect was involved in this plane, she jumped—and found her stomach wanting to climb into her throat, for her jump was four times higher. She landed like a feather.

"Gravity Manipulation inherent to the plane," Ottentus noted, giddily jumping in the same manner. "I feel like a child. How fun! How fun indeed …"

Anna wasn't smiling, for amongst the quiet hissing of the ground she could still hear that terrible distant screaming, now perfectly tuned to her perpetual headache, so that the two were one. She splayed a hand, incanting, "*Un vun asperio aurum enchantus*," unsurprised to find no evidence of arcanery whatsoever. "This way," she said, following the distant screaming, knowing every step brought her closer to her children.

Ottentus watched her carefully. "You are following the screams, yes?"

"They are having a nightmare," Anna said. "My son and daughter are having a nightmare, and I will wake them up."

"*We* will wake them up."

Anna, too focused on the awful sound of torment, did not reply.

They trekked for hours without seeing anything other than formations of rock and dried lava. Anna identified obsidian and granite and pumice and ash mud, but there were other rocks that were unfamiliar, ones embedded with rich crystalline structures that she swore were gems—ruby and amethyst and turquoise and opal and topaz and sapphire and emerald and diamond. They trekked over mesas and dried-out lava beds and snaking canyons, taking sips of water often from their waterskins, until a grand light crested beyond the spires. That light, brighter than any sun Anna had ever seen, made the spires glow and the air heat up rapidly.

Anna, staring at the distant glowing tips, halted to a stop amidst an enormous valley between two bulges of old lava. "We need to find shelter."

"Why?"

As if the gods had dropped a floor plank across the sky, a beam of white light pierced the spires and shot overhead. The beam lit up a nearby spire, and that spire began to smoke.

"Because we're two eggs about to be tossed into a frying pan."

The spire, the color of which rapidly changed from yellow to red to white, burst with enormous flames.

Ottentus took a step forth. "Gods ..." he whispered, repeating, "Gods ..."

Anna ran through her arsenal of spells, yet quickly realized she could not rely on any of them to protect her against such intense and prolonged heat, for it would last all day—and they had no idea how long one day was in this plane.

A second beam shot across the sky, this one from a totally different angle. It lit up an entire range of peaks, which also began to smoke.

Anna felt the color drain from her face. "Unnameables ... there are two suns here."

MOLTEN

As the sky brightened and the horizon smoked, Anna and Ottentus scrambled to search for a place to hide, for the air heated so rapidly that by the time they stumbled into an empty cave halfway up the side of the valley, Anna thought she would suffocate.

Inside, Ottentus drew a wide circle with a finger, incanting, "*Sfaera au praentergo buboa*," enveloping them in a giant dome of ice, more than large enough for them not to run out of air anytime soon. Safe inside the Sphere of Protection spell, the gasping pair collapsed from the exertion, with both grabbing for their waterskins and taking gulps of water. The cool water quenched her parched throat, and the insulated space gave her reprieve from the screaming of her children.

"I shudder to imagine what would have happened had we come during the day," Anna noted.

"Or if one of us was not an ice warlock," Ottentus threw in.

Outside, the sky got brighter and brighter, becoming hard to look at. They had to squint to even peek outside the cave. The nearby peaks burned, creating curtains of flame. The earth shook as distant geysers plumed crimson lava. Where the plumes fell in shadow, new spires formed. Older spires melted, creating lava rivers that cascaded down valleys. One of those rivers crept through the way they had come from. It soon merged with a river crawling in from the opposite direction. When lava began dripping from overhead, Anna grew worried.

"My casting will protect us," Ottentus said. "It's strong enough."

"I am not concerned about the bubble failing, but about being buried alive."

"Ah. Yes. That would be a problem."

Taking small sips of water, they watched helplessly as the entire basin steadily filled with lava. Ottentus cast ice spells to keep things cool inside the bubble, beyond which the air wavered with heat. Smoke soon rose behind them … followed by a crimson light.

Anna, staring at the advancing light, blurted, "We're in a lava tunnel." Her palms were clammy with sweat, despite her standing beside a block of ice that billowed vapor.

Ottentus, who had been fiddling with the contents of his rucksack, whirled about. He strode forth to stand beside her at the edge of the bubble.

"Can you ice the ground?" she asked.

"I can try, but I doubt it will work." He took a knee and swept his hands along the ground, muttering a phrase under his breath. The ground froze up underneath him, but failed to penetrate the bubble. "I will do this, though," he said, standing and sweeping a hand about in a circle whilst incanting, "*Isikili codola arregando marjorus*," which Anna recognized as the 10th degree off-the-books spell Major Cool Area. The inside of the bubble instantly cooled to the point of fogging their breathing.

By the time the lava gurgled into view, Anna was shivering.

"Now a battle of the elements, yes?" Ottentus said, standing well back of the bubble wall.

Anna joined him in the center, and they watched as the lava steadily rose, until it lapped against the base of the bubble, where it hissed against the ice, forming a crust. Outside in the valley, the lava had risen to the cave's height and spilled into the entrance. The glow made everything orange.

"Your eyes are still black," Anna noted.

"As I feared they would be. I must look like a demon to you. I am sorry."

"Is it permanent?"

"I cannot deny it may be. My price of entry."

"Mmm." She supposed he worried about how he would appear to others when he returned, but she didn't have the energy to delve into it. Only her children mattered. "Should I cast a secondary bubble?" she asked.

Ottentus was as cool as his element in his response as he watched the lava hiss against the bubble. "That will not be necessary."

Anna nonetheless readied the spell on her lips. Any teleporting out of there was certain to end in a molten bath. This had to be their stand.

The ice bubble kept cracking from stress, and the air inside once again grew hot, forcing Ottentus to cast the cooling spell a second time. He would keep recasting the spell as the lava level rose to fill their line of sight, plunging them into an ever-darkening orange glow.

"*Shyneo lampa*," Anna incanted, summoning the floating lightning lamp. She paced, wondering how many hours had passed. "Do you think time flows differently here?" she asked, fishing for distraction.

"I think it flows the same. But how long is the day? There was no mention of multiple suns or the length of day in my research. I fear for the timing enchantment on the golden shield."

"Hell is supposed to be filled with monsters, yet we have seen none," Anna went on, breath fogging as she paced. "Perhaps this plane is not what we think it is."

"Perhaps. Yet what of the voices?"

"What of the voices indeed ..." She imagined her son and daughter. Could almost feel their souls crying out for their mother. *I'm coming, children. I'm coming ...*

As time passed, the exterior stabilized to a solid, and the interior air remained cool from the castings. The pair took turns napping, realizing they would have to do their trekking at night. Sometime later, a crimson light began to emanate from the cave-entrance side of the dome—the lava there had begun heating up.

"What is happening now?" Ottentus whispered, studying the one-sided glow.

Anna thought about it. "Sunset, I believe."

Sure enough, that side began to bubble and ebb away, and soon a white light pierced the crimson-glowing rock, forcing Anna and Ottentus to cast their shields for shade.

"This land is not meant for humans *or* warlocks," Anna muttered as Ottentus recast the cooling spell.

"Yet a portal door was built."

The sunlight melted the lava away, which retreated, leaving behind an even larger hole. When the fiercely bright suns slipped behind distant spires, Anna saw that the lava in the valley had also retreated, leaving an oblong basin loosely matching the original. New holes had sprung up from lava geysers and miniature volcanoes, creating a bulbous environment that steamed and hissed and cracked. The lower the suns set, the more splitting and cracking came from cooling rock and lava, until the ground was a near-constant rumble. Only when a dense fog enveloped the valley and the interior of the bubble went unnaturally cold did they agree they could chance dropping the protective sphere.

"I will have mine ready on my lips," Anna said, giving him the go-ahead nod.

Ottentus whipped a finger about, snapping, "*Sfaera null,*" and the bubble vanished. The cold and fog swept in like an ice bath.

Anna took a tentative sniff. "It is survivable," she reported, her nostrils burning a little.

"Let us hurry, then, as we do not know how far we have to travel."

After taking sips of water, they set off, watchful of their steps. The ground was still hot, sometimes even singeing the soles of their shoes, but it was walkable. The lava had mostly retreated down its tunnels, leaving behind only the most virulently bubbling pools, usually around geysers or miniature volcanoes, which they gave a wide berth. The remainder had crusted over, creating new formations. Although the fog remained, pungent and acrid and heavy, it cleared after a couple of hours, revealing a brilliant star-filled sky.

Hours later, as they made their way through a freshly carved lava canyon only a human-length wide, Anna halted.

"I hear something," she whispered, trying to discern the noise from the screaming.

"A snuffling," Ottentus whispered.

They pushed on, hands in attack position, until they came to the mouth of the miniature canyon. It opened into a shallow valley dotted with boulders. One of these boulders, which rested about fifty feet away, was embedded with gems that gleamed different colors in the starlight. And it was that boulder from behind which the snuffling was coming.

Anna and Ottentus shared an inquisitive look. What manner of creature would they find in this mysterious plane?

The boulder rolled a couple of feet, making Anna and Ottentus stiffen. The snuffling got louder, and a paw grabbed hold of the boulder—but it was unlike any paw Anna had ever seen, for it was made of pure silver, with black diamond claws. Soon a snout emerged, followed by a body the size of a raccoon. The snout was long, with a tongue that licked at the gems, each lick taking a slice off as if it were butter. Yet there appeared to be no eyes. In the book of monster mythologies, this creature's appearance would fall somewhere between a miniature bear and an anteater.

The beast's trumpet-like nose caught onto a new smell, and it went still and silent.

Anna held her breath, wondering what it would do. Could their spells defeat a beast made of pure silver? Or was that simply its armor? Just in case, she readied offensive spells on her tongue. At worst, they had already agreed that, should anything happen, they would attempt to teleport back to the cave.

"It's watching us," Ottentus whispered.

"It has no eyes," Anna replied.

"Then it smells us. Perhaps if we—" He made to adjust his position, but in doing so, accidentally kicked a piece of obsidian.

The beast dove into the ground, burrowing so ferociously and quickly that it threw up debris aimed in their direction, forcing them to summon shields.

"It did that on purpose," Anna said when the onslaught had died down. "It sensed danger—"

"Meaning there is danger to be sensed," Ottentus concluded. "There are predators here. We must be wary, yes?"

They walked onward, taking a wide route around the gem-encrusted boulder. Yet gems were of no interest to either of them, wealth being immaterial to their goals.

"The alchemists would love this plane," Ottentus muttered, head on a swivel.

Some hours later, with the sound of screaming slightly louder, they stopped to eat.

"And you still can't hear that?" Anna asked, chewing on a square of biscuit beef as she sat on an obsidian boulder studded with turquoise shards.

Ottentus looked up at the star-dense sky. "I cannot. It calls to you and only you, yes?"

"Yes." Anna nodded, repeating, "Yes …" She looked at the horizon where the sound was coming from. If the suns rose in the east and set in the west, they would be traveling south. Though direction meant little here. Only the destination mattered. But how long until they got there?

"We must find water soon," Anna said, wincing after accidentally splashing the ground. "Clumsy fool," she muttered. "I am three-quarters empty and—"

She froze, hearing a sniffing underneath her. Just as she was about to spring away, the ground exploded underneath Ottentus, throwing him into the air. A snout shot toward the spot where the water had fallen, followed by a silver claw thrust at Anna. She instinctively leaned back, her reflexes saving her from evisceration by seven black claws.

She slapped her wrists together, roaring, "*Annihilo dio!*" The scion in her pocket buzzed as it lent its amplifying strength to four massive bolts of lightning, two of which slammed into the relatively small beast with four simultaneous *cracks* of thunder. There was a great *sizzle* and a metallic yelp, followed by the thing jamming itself right back into its hole. By the time Ottentus floated back to the ground, it had burrowed away like a mole.

"My lightning did not kill it," Anna blurted, stunned she had thrown everything into the spell yet the creature had not been blown apart, as she had expected.

"That is most ominous," Ottentus said. "It has been hunting us, yes?"

"Or it's a new beast," Anna countered. "It knows where water is," and she explained what she had seen its snout do, and how it only attacked after she had spilled water on the ground.

"It would be too dangerous to follow it in its own tunnel," Ottentus said.

Anna sighed. "Alas, if only the Shrink spell had not been lost to time …"

Ottentus answered by throwing his rucksack over his shoulder. "Let us move on."

And move on they did. At one point, as Anna hopped over a small ravine, she made a simple revelation, which was to *keep* hopping after landing.

"Oh my," Ottentus said, catching on, and the pair were soon making great leaps at little energy expenditure, for the weak gravity allowed it.

Had Anna been younger, not searching for her captured children, or hearing that awful screaming, she would have enjoyed the thrill of such a strange feat.

Like children, they leaped over valleys and dried rivers and small hills and huge boulders and great fissures. At long last, just as the horizon blushed with fire once more, Anna glimpsed something different in the distance during one of her leaps.

"I see something!" she called, aiming for a higher jump. With each leap she made out a little more. It was a jagged black shape thrusting into the starry sky, but a shape that was distinctly flat. A transparent blue dome surrounded it, with a strange oblong shape sitting just outside its base.

"It's warlock-made!" she reported as she passed Ottentus on the way down.

"By gods, do you know what this could be?" Ottentus said on his next jumping pass.

I don't care. All I want are my children, Anna thought.

The closer they got, the more detail they could make out. The oblong shape at its base was a statue of a lion with wings, albeit one as large as four side-by-side barns.

A winged lion, Anna thought, unable to recall the name of such a beast from mythology, probably because it was rarely mentioned in the books. *And likely a guardian.* It sat outside the dome, waiting who knew how long for an intruder. *Or perhaps guarding it from the beasts inherent to the plane …*

"The sky is brightening," Ottentus called as the pair landed on top of a jagged mesa surrounded by sheer cliffs. In the valley ahead, like a great monolith of ancient times, stood an upright slab enclosed in a dome as wide as five barns. Inside the dome, in front of the large slab, floated other small slabs, much like students before their teacher.

Anna squinted and saw lines—no, cubbies—set into each slab. She gasped. "It's a library …"

"Yes," Ottentus said, licking his lips like a starved man. "By gods, it is indeed a library!"

The largest slab faced east, toward the coming double sunrise, and rose as high as a ten-story building. This was no ordinary slab either, but a wall filled with thousands upon thousands of cubby holes, each crammed with tablets and scrolls and books—an ancient repository of knowledge. Yet there were no ladders between shelves and the other floating smaller slabs, as if the reader were expected to fly.

Or jump, Anna thought. She focused on the ground in the center of the forcefield, where the screaming was coming from, calling to her. Sure enough, the blood in her veins quickened and her heart jammed in her throat, for there in the center of the dome was a tiny cage filled with squirming people—and Samuel and Thia had to be among them!

Her son and daughter were *right there*! A mere teleport away …

She envisioned grabbing hold of her kids, squeezing them tightly, telling them that everything would be all right, that momma was here and would take them home and their father waited for them and all would be well once more …

Except that high-pitched sound, incurred from the excavation explosion, reared up stronger than ever, jarring Anna's thoughts and forcing her to focus on something else to gain a reprieve.

"Who is the winged lion's master?" Anna whispered, wincing from the noise in her head. Would the devil himself show? Did the beast *have* a master? What *was* this place?

The entire dome began to slowly rotate on its circular base, the low grinding noise so loud they could hear it from that far out.

"Unnameables," Ottentus whispered. "The library is turning its back to the suns. Fascinating …"

The winged lion statue did not move along with the library. Just as they were going to take a leap forth to get closer, it sat up and looked about, focusing on something small approaching from the east. From that distance, the little beast looked like an insect. When the beast sniffed at the base of the dome, the winged lion raised a paw and smashed it like a gnat. The lion then yawned, flexed its enormous wings, and sauntered around the library to stretch its legs before resettling in a spot at the back of the great wall, facing the sun side.

"Just like a cat craving sunshine," Anna noted. "How do you want to approach it?" It was incredibly difficult for her not to recklessly teleport down there and pound her fists against the dome like a woman possessed.

"Let us deliberate, yes? We must be quick, for the suns soon rise."

They strategized, settling on a two-fold plan of query and retreat, choosing another lava cave nearby, but out of view of the winged lion's line of sight. It would do them no good to retreat to a spot the beast could discover. As mighty as the pair were in the arcane arts, nothing was certain against a monster of such size—especially considering how effortlessly that tiny silver beast had survived Anna's amplified Fourth Offensive. The arcanery in this plane was of a whole other nature and strength, and the relativities involved did not favor the pair of otherwise highly accomplished warlocks.

With the eastern sky quickly going orange with fire, they leaped forth, and kept leaping until they were three hundred feet from the winged lion, at which point one of the beast's great eyelids opened, halting them on the spot.

"Here we go," Anna said, keeping an eye on the cage inside the center of the dome. It was blurry, as if she were seeing it through a glass of water. The screaming coming from it combined with the high-pitched headache were now almost as loud as her own voice, forcing her to speak up just so she could hear herself.

The winged lion sat up, an imperial beast of an unknown epoch, of an unknown race.

"*Aziz ogo nok zoa ga?*" it boomed in a deep growl that reverberated in Anna's innards. The question was interspersed with sharp clicks of the tongue, as if there was a clacker in the beast's throat.

"Does the language sound familiar to you?" Anna asked. Casting the 12th degree Tongues would be useless against a language so incredibly different and foreign.

"It does not," Ottentus replied. "But we can guess it is old. Very, *very* old …"

"*Aziz ogo nok zoa ga?*" the winged lion repeated, a little more aggressively, adding a derisive snort at the end.

For the first time, Ottentus was speechless with hesitation. After glancing between the winged lion and the library, Anna had an idea. "*Dos yon saeka arcan linguino?*" she asked.

"Do you speak the arcane tongue?" Ottentus translated under his breath.

"*Yon chessa yeva o linguino arcan, mortus,*" the winged lion click-growled.

"You have chosen the arcane tongue, mortal," Ottentus translated, adding in a mutter, "It understands the old tongue. Brilliant, Arcanist Stone. Brilliant …" He cleared his throat. "Who made you, ancient one?" Ottentus asked in the arcane tongue. At their degree and proficiency in the language of arcanery, neither needed to cast Tongues.

"Birth is not a choice," the winged lion boomed. "The creation of the self, however, is."

"I … I do not understand," Ottentus replied.

"We beg entry into the library, ancient one," Anna interrupted in the arcane tongue, not caring one hoof about its history.

"Entry must be earned, mortal."

"How do we earn entry?"

"By answering a query."

"No doubt a riddle," Anna muttered. "And if we fail to answer it correctly?"

The beast only tightened its paws, the threat of destruction apparent. "Do you wish to hear the question, mortal?"

Anna looked past the beast, at the blurry cage within. The screaming and the ringing begged her to do something. She could already feel the heat on her back from the brightening sky. At any moment, the suns would pierce the horizon of mountainous spires and fry them to a crisp.

"Yes," she blurted without consulting Ottentus.

"The question I pose thus follows." The winged lion raised its gargantuan chin slightly. "Why must all knowledge be free?"

Before either warlock could even consider the question, a monstrous ray of blinding white light shot across a swath of the sky, instantly heating the area up and making the pair of warlocks stir in discomfort. Both began sweating.

Anna turned to Ottentus to confer with him, but this time it was he who blurted, "*Beka osiqiuous ani enitrios!*"

"Because knowledge is forever," Anna whispered, translating the ancient proverb, supposedly Tiberran.

"That is correct," the winged lion boomed, raising a paw at the dome, which vanished with a mighty *whoosh*. "You have nineteen grains of sand before sunrise."

Anna understood the winged lion to be referring to particles of sand in an hourglass, and shot forth. As they sprinted past the monstrous beast, a second ray pierced the sky, and Anna felt her skin burning. She kept her focus on the blurry image of the cage, not understanding why it was still blurry despite the forcefield being down. The screaming was shrill, the high-pitched ringing obscene, drowning out all thought.

The tips of nearby spires burst with flames. Anna sprinted past the dome line first, followed by Ottentus, who tripped at the last moment. She heard him roll and the contents of his rucksack sliding along the black stone floor, free of dust and polished to a mirror shine. The largest bookshelf slab cast a long shadow. In the dark of that shadow floated variously sized smaller bookshelf slabs, each cubby hole stuffed with tablets and tomes and scrolls.

There came another *whoosh* as the dome returned, plunging the interior into utter silence. Outside, the world burst with fire.

Anna kept sprinting, but the closer she got to the cage, the more ethereal it became, and the quieter and more echoey the screaming and ringing inside her head. For a brief moment, like portrait paintings floating beneath the surface of a river, she saw her son and daughter's blurry faces. By the time her steps faltered to a halt, the cage, filled with squirming people, had vanished in a wisp of smoke.

"No," she mumbled, falling to her knees. "No …"

Behind her, a voice complained. "I could not take the stuffy confines of the rucksack anymore, Master. I am sorry."

"It matters not," Ottentus replied. "Our quest has all but been fulfilled. Only one obstacle now remains."

"I am ready, Master. You have trained me well."

Anna, too absorbed in the catastrophic failure before her, could barely comprehend the implications of that failure, let alone what was going on behind her. She did not even notice that the headache had completely gone away. Samuel and Thia were not here. Her son and daughter, her beautiful and precious children were not here. And that meant something she could not fathom.

Thia was dead.

Her daughter truly *had* died.

Just like Samuel.

Like her marriage.

In one fell swoop, the light of hope extinguished.

"Now, Master. Strike now!"

"Quiet, fool!"

Some vestiges of vague interest made Anna turn her head. She saw Ottentus rushing at her, readying to cast a spell.

Running behind him was none other than Ralf Turman, the father of her grandson, and the one who called himself Narsus.

MASTER AND APPRENTICE

"Annihilo!" Ottentus roared, slapping his wrists together as he sprinted forth.

Anna, unable to comprehend what was happening—and unable to bring herself to care—summoned her lightning shield out of sheer reflex. A strong bolt of ice smashed into it, splintering against the shield and knocking her back a step. Everything that happened next continued out of reflex, as if she were her usual Dueling Club arcanist self—except lecturing a class of bored students.

Ralf slapped his wrists, roaring, *"Annihilo bato!"* and two vines shot forth.

Anna angled her shield, allowing the vines to harmlessly carom off.

Ottentus began a barrage of mind spells, hands a blur as he launched one after another in quick succession, with Ralf joining in, the pair's voices overlapping. *"Flustrato! Flustrato! Voidus aurus! Voidus lingua! Effectus xadius! Voidus vis! Dreadus terrablus!"* and so on, focusing heavily on Confusion.

Anna, unable to summon the motivation to counterattack—survival mattered less and less with each thought—dipped, dodged, and wove about like a practice dummy on a swivel.

Hit after hit dinged and dented her Mind Armor. The barrage was so ferocious and her grief-stricken mind so woefully unprepared to deal with reality that one of Ottentus's master-level Confusion castings eventually punched through. Suddenly she found herself wanting to tell these recalcitrant students that they weren't trying hard enough, that they weren't penetrating her Mind Armor. Heck, how would they fare if she chose to draw on the power of her scion? Had they no thought to the danger they were putting themselves in? She swore students were getting dumber and dumber these days …

With determination lending her focus, she summoned her staff and flipped over a tempered ice bolt, wanting to show how it was done. She whapped aside a vine, slapped a donkey-sized elemental summoned by the younger of the two students, and jabbed the older student in the chin when he teleported behind her, idly wondering why he was hairless—maybe he had a condition, not unlike her Dueling Club mentor Niterra Bladesong, who suffered from skiniligo.

Anna couldn't wait to take that class again. That woman was brilliant and had already taught her so much! But wait until she saw the new tricks Anna had learned last term—Anna might even earn herself a smile from that old crabapple of a woman.

"Too slow," Anna snapped, hopping over a clumsily cast Second Offensive double bolt of ice. *At least they are appropriately tempered*, she thought, giving the pair of students a nod.

"Good ferocity," she noted when the younger managed to entwine her foot. "But not tight enough," and she discarded the vine with a flick of her foot.

"The coot thinks she's in class," the younger one blurted, laughing as he slapped his wrists together.

Anna knocked his vine punch down with her summoned staff, creating a loud *sizzle*. "Don't be rude, Initiate, unless you want to be sent to the disciplinary committee. And you there—how dare you wear the robe of a master. Go home and change this instant! I do not appreciate you bringing Drama class costumes to Dueling Club."

"She's lost her marbles," the younger student snapped.

"Shut up and keep at her, boy," the bald student snapped, circling her.

Anna nodded at a nearby girl she recognized as Kimani. "Tell my daughter I will be late for supper."

Kimani nodded. "Yes, Arcanist Stone."

"And tell that boy Thomas I've still got his books!" she called after the girl, who had run off. "And that he's cute!"

There was a *whap* to the back of her head, making her stumble forth. She turned to see her mother standing in the kitchen. "Idiot girl, how many times do I have to tell you to put away your dishes!"

"Sorry, Mama, I forgot, I was busy studying—"

Another *whap*. "Shut up!"

Someone said words that should have been familiar to Anna, but they did not make sense. A bright light zoomed overhead not unlike her floating lamp. She felt a jab below her, and when she looked down, she saw her own shadow attacking her.

"What sorcery is this?" she mumbled, trying to get away.

But the shadow kept attacking. She parried with her staff. To her surprise, that somehow worked, yet the shadow, with its long ponytail flopping about, pressed. There was the crackling thud of her lightning staff meeting a shadow staff as she danced a most unusual dance trying to avoid herself.

Finally it occurred to her what to do, and she focused on the floating lamp above her and squiggled a hand at it, incanting, "*Exotus mia enchantus duo dai ideum exat!*" She tore out its tendrils like the vocal chords of a throat, disenchanting the shadow just as it launched another poke.

Amidst dancing away from other arcane attacks, a reptilian part of her, perhaps out of memory, scraped a hand down her arm as she muttered, "*Arcanis rapidio … arcanis rapidio baersto!*" She then tried making a peeling-carrots motion, but all she managed to do was fizzle out some lightning flares.

"Now, Apprentice!" the bald student in his fake opalescent robe shouted. "Do it now!"

The attacks came in fierce. At least they were playing fair, tempering them. She danced like a marionette, taunting and goading throughout, shouting things like, "Is that all you got? Go on and try to hit me! You can do better, Fungal! Not even remotely good enough, Spigot! I expected more from you in particular, Pedworth! Too slow, all of you!" She felt strangely at ease, a lioness back in her true arena—that of a teacher showing her students how it was done.

There was a tearing sound and she felt her satchel get torn away, spilling a waterskin and biscuit beef, which made no sense —what would that stuff be doing in her arcanist's satchel? But something else escaped her satchel as well—a thing that also made no sense in the context of a Dueling Club class. Lying on its side on the polished black stone floor was a rumpled bunny, one ear brown, fur well-worn from all the love.

In the brief moment during which Anna stared at Bun-Bun uncomprehendingly, she felt a hot sharpness slip into her back. Whatever it was struck her innards, brought a jarring clarity, and made her entire body tense up. She gasped, unable to move … and crumpled to the ground.

"*Flustrato null*," said a voice, and clarity washed over Anna like acid. She stared at a bright sky, the edges of which burned with gargantuan but distant leaps of flame. Amongst those flames, she thought she saw her son and daughter.

I never got to say goodbye to you, Thia, she thought, comprehending she was truly in Hell. *Will you ever forgive me?* The profound gullibility required for her to have fallen for the ruse made her face flush. She could not recall feeling such a deep sense of self-hatred. How could she have been so consumed by grief as to believe such a far-fetched notion? How could she have allowed this level of betrayal to happen to herself?

A figure stepped into view. "A Blade of Paralysis," Ralf said, panting. "Do you know how rare such a blade is? How expensive?"

Ottentus stepped up beside him. "Lucky you had one crafted, Apprentice." He patted him on the shoulder. "Good work."

"Thank you, Master, that was an incredible duel. Her movements were so natural and fluid. I saw the arena dueler she used to be." He closed his eyes, smiled, and sighed. "I am honored to have helped bring down the legendary Anna Atticus Stone, a moment I shall cherish until the end of my days."

"As you should, dear boy. As you should. Now the true work begins." He flicked a hand and Anna heard metal scraping across the floor, until something clanked into her side.

Ralf stooped down and picked up a pair of manacles, then kicked her over onto her side to get at her hands.

Anna, the fight drained from her now that she was forced to face her daughter's demise, didn't bother resisting—not that she could anyway after being paralyzed. At least she got to see the spot where her son and daughter should have been. Except in the place of the cage sat a rumpled old bunny.

Poor Bun-Bun. You did not deserve this. I failed you too, my dear old friend. She watched as he sat in lonely silence amidst a backdrop of leaping flames. How out of place he looked! How lost and lonely and sad!

Ralf slipped on the manacles, pressing his lips close to the metal so he could whisper the incantation without her hearing. Even as she felt herself cut off from the mighty reservoir of arcanery, Anna strained to listen, only to receive a shoe to the face from Ottentus.

"Wily thing," he said, stretching out his shoulders. "This form of paralysis allows you to speak. So amuse me and grovel for your life. Or perhaps speak your sorrow. Cry, beg, or curse me. It is a rare privilege to humble someone who holds herself in such high esteem."

Anna groaned, eyes still on Bun-Bun and the barren spot in the center of the floor where her son and daughter should have been. It had been a mirage. A powerful, *powerful* mirage. Perhaps this itself was a nightmare, and she would soon wake …

"I do not hear much contrition." Ottentus crouched beside her and fished the scion out of her robe pocket. "Won't be needing this anymore, will you?" He tossed it from hand to hand. "Do you know that, upon first reading about the cinder door, I thought to entice a curse by taking the lives of warlock kin, much as you were cursed. I murdered so many. So, so many. Men, women … children. I even tried killing them in, let us say … *creative* ways. I heard screams of agony that would—" He made an exaggerated shiver. "—shrivel the spine." He shrugged. "At least the spine of someone who cared about such things. For me, it was all a means to an end. You understand, of course."

He sighed. "Alas, none could muster the courage to curse me in that particular way. That is, to *truly* curse me. Sure, they swore and begged and drooled and bargained and cried, but loathing—the sort of loathing I so desperately craved—failed to grace me with its presence. Instead, all I managed to coax from them was a deep terror I could hardly make use of. And pain. A lot of pain."

Ottentus stood, smoothing out his robe. "But you know what my problem was? I could never be genuine. I can't feel things, apparently. Or so one of my wives told me. Everything is, as the Sierran proverb goes, *kwento kwa*—transactional. I suspect that is why I cannot absorb a proper curse. But I do feel something I think you would call pride, for the complexities involved in getting *you* to believe the myriad falsities …" He shook his head. "… it would be difficult to explain all the layers to you. Even adopting that stupid uncle persona … such tedium, I tell you. *Yes* this and *yes* that and pretending to be kind. Empathy is terribly tedious. It will take a while to drop that persona."

He tugged at the creases of his robe, smoothing them out. "You may have thought your inquiries into dispelling powerful curses would go unnoticed, but I have quite an inquisitive mind myself. So when I, in my quest to curse my soul, discovered your research notes, I deduced what might have happened to you. Some further inquiries—much quieter than yours—confirmed my suspicions, and I knew then that my search for a soul that had been truly cursed had come to an end. What delighted me though was the subject of the rest of your research. The more I gleaned, the more inspired I became, until a most devilish plot unfolded before my eyes. If there is any creativity in me, I suppose it is in crafting plots."

"You know, Anna, you were right about something most profound." He stepped on her fingers, making her squeal with pain. "In this plane, we are not shackled by morality. I do not even have to apologize. Here, *we* make the laws." He stepped off, allowing her to suck in air, the only thing she could do to ease the pain. "In truth, there is only one law. The law of survival. Everything else is but a—" He twirled a hand. "—means to that survival."

"You should consider yourself honored, *Anna*," Ralf said, sneering her name, seemingly enjoying the disparity of a seventeen-year-old using a fifty-year-old teacher's first name—especially a teacher who had instigated his expulsion. "You get to witness a miracle performed by the only living master."

"He speaks of your soul, my dear woman," Ottentus threw in. "There is a spell here that I am determined to find. A ritual that will allow me to absorb all of your knowledge. Once I have robbed you of your past, your deductions and observations and learnings and decisions, you will be a hollow husk of rotting meat. And this—" He held up the scion. "—will tune to me. A little bonus, not that I need it. But it's nice. A trophy, even. What do I want of your soul, you wonder? Let me answer that for you. You see, I do not have the one thing you possess in droves ... creativity. And I want that, woman. I want that. I want to know what that feels like, to craft out of joy instead of necessity. To feel deeply and creatively. To think beyond the transaction. Perhaps even to love." He sighed wistfully, yet that sigh felt forced and disingenuous.

Anna felt herself drooling blood onto the floor from a cut tongue. She wanted to tell him to go to hell—if it wouldn't be so ironic.

"That is just the beginning, Arcanist Stone. There is another spell we already once discussed, a spell so powerful it can reverse time itself. A spell that would make me invincible in any duel."

"That spell is either lost to time or a children's story," Anna croaked. "A parable. And even if it weren't, such spells come with a great cost." It was interest that had pushed her to speak. Pure interest in the past, where she took shelter in her mind. Even now, she saw herself amidst tall yellow grass, her daughter jumping on her husband's back, their son running about, hands outstretched as he pretended to be a bird. How she longed to join them! *Mercy let this be quick*, she thought. *That is all I ask of you, Unnameables—The Fates—whatever—whoever—is listening. Let my suffering end soon, for I am done.*

"I beg to differ," Ottentus replied. "The spell is real. And invincibility is worth almost any price. Further, I suspect that there is another spell here in this library, one I am sure would pique your interest. Imagine trading your life to resurrect one of your children. Hmm? Imagine that!" He chortled. "But of course, I require your life for my own purposes, so this cannot be, but still, the idea is quite tantalizing, isn't it? But musings aside, do you know *why* I think such spells exist here? Do you not recognize the obsidian workmanship? The casting involved in creating the winged lion? They are *Rivican* constructs, proving the long-held theory that the Rivicans traveled amongst the stars. And that time reversal spell … it is a Rivican spell. It will be here. It will be up on that giant slab."

He wiped her cheek with a greasy thumb. "You need not cry for your daughter, Anna. Your delusions are your own fault. You wanted them to be true. For a time, I gave you that solace. All I can now offer you … is acceptance. Take it. Bathe in it. It will be your only sanctuary in what is to come." He leaned forth, whispering, "I read that the ritual will be painful. Very painful." He patted her back. "But you will have plenty of time to prepare for that." He slipped the scion into his pocket, turned to the largest library slab, and hitched up his rope belt. "The only challenge is finding it first. That might take a while, yes? Ugh, there I go again with the stupid *yes*. I *loathe* that persona. I do. *Loathe* is a good word. It has tremendous power, you know." He chuckled. "I guess you *do* know now, don't you, having learned a certain spell to get into this plane?"

"Master, did you notice that the library slowly rotates?"

"Huh, look at that. So it does. Almost imperceptibly too. It's set so that the large slab always has its back toward the suns, casting a shadow over the library, protecting it from the light. Now *that* is irony."

"We ought to start with water, Master. There is precious little here."

"Upon nightfall, Apprentice, until I find a way to safely travel during the day. In the mean, take what you need from her waterskin."

"Thank you, Master, I will. Will you follow one of those creatures to a source underground?"

"Paying attention, were we?"

"I had little else to do in that stuffy rucksack."

Ottentus waited for Anna to say something before throwing his arms open. "Oh, come on, woman! Ask us how I slipped my apprentice in. Go ahead, ask us—I know you're curious."

Anna's reply was to spit a gob of blood onto the floor.

"Well, *I'm* proud of the accomplishment. You know why? Because the Shrink spell was lost to time, but guess who purchased an ancient and uncast scroll of that very spell? That's right—*me*. Apparently dug up from some warlock crypt in some hovel of a town in Canterra. Cost a veritable fortune, too, but the results speak for themselves, don't they? I went on a search for it after the second slab quest, just to see if I could explore that miniature tunnel myself. But as with many things, the spell eluded me … until months later, when I got lucky. By then, I had a better use for it. And so here we are. Why *not* bring my acolyte, my faithful little servant along? I will need servants in the era to come, and he is most willing."

"I certainly am, Master."

Anna's grief-stricken mind took shelter in memory. She saw herself coming home to see her husband serving supper to the children. He smiled at her.

"Came home on time for once," Thomas said, ladling a roast chicken breast onto gravied potatoes. "Books not interesting enough?"

"Everything I want is right here. Have I told you I love you lately?"

Thomas danced his way over and pressed himself up against her. "You did, but say it again. I love hearing it."

Thia rolled her eyes. "Ew, you two," while Samuel giggled, mouth covered with food.

"She's lost her mind," a voice rudely broke in. "Will that affect your work, Master?"

"I doubt it. Besides, wait until you see how she reacts when the rituals begin."

"I very much look forward to that, Master. It will be entertaining to watch the one who ruined my life feel the sting of karmic justice."

The pain of the betrayal was acute. She had to know how he had done it. *She had to know.* "You … you broke into my mind."

"And it was a *masterpiece* of arcanery, Anna. A masterpiece. It had to be done carefully, though, for there were many complex pieces to the ruse. I went so far as to shave my eyebrows and hair to get you and that insufferable husband of yours to trust me. But meticulously manipulating you to do most of the work whilst still bringing you here was one of my greatest challenges. Luckily, after much planning, an opportunity presented itself in the excavation."

"When I was buried."

"Yes. I considered letting that oaf of a husband of yours die, for your sake, so you could focus. But I knew you would pull through in accepting the illusion. I had faith because you so desperately wanted the illusion to be true. Unfortunately—or rather fortunately, my oafish apprentice here managed to bless your daughter with a child. And that complicated everything. *Everything.* But where there was tragedy, I dug up fortune. I thought I would have to strong-arm you into opening the door. That would have been a gamble, for I wasn't sure how you would react. You are a renowned dueler, after all, and I don't like taking unnecessary risks. No, a more brilliant plan was in order. And all it took … was capitalizing on your mother's curse. After that, it all fell into place. Just. Like—" He snapped his fingers, mouthing, "—*that*."

He smiled. "The triumph was convincing—" He stabbed her temple with a finger. "—that mind that a cage existed. A cage in a place I did not know how to describe. But I had maps. Yes, I did. And old texts that provided descriptions. It was enough. But I shall give you credit. Do you want to know how strong you are? Even while unconscious, your Mind Armor vigorously defended you. It was something to behold. But I broke through. In the end, I *always* break through. Oh, and remember that ritual I performed that supposedly drew the devil to me? It was actually a ritual of protection. Had the so-called Arch Fiend actually made an appearance, he would have feasted on *you* first, allowing me time to get away."

Anna looked up into his fully black eyes. "You are the essence of evil."

"If morality mattered, the craft would have taken away my mastery after I poked and prodded all those poor wretches, trying to goad them into cursing me. After all, it granted me mastery, deeming me fit. Even now, look—" Ottentus reached behind her and twisted the knife. Anna screamed. Then he flared his full sleeve of ice. "See? It is still here. If anything, the craft approves. Besides, spellcraft itself is highly unethical, if you think about it. Most of the spells are violent or manipulative. Every warlock is morally compromised by the fact *they* are a warlock."

"Master, I worry that she is bleeding to death as the wound is making a puddle under her."

Ottentus sighed deeply. "Such tedium. Lucky for the both of us I am a dual-wielder like you, eh, Anna?" He stepped behind her and she soon felt the hot pain of the dagger getting yanked from her flesh, causing her to scream a second time. "Oh, hush. You're a big girl. Eat the pain." He waited, listening to her whimpering before smacking his gums. "*Fine*, I'll knit you back up just to *shut* you up."

As the man worked to heal her, Anna stared at Bun-Bun, remembering leaning against her daughter's bedroom door as the little girl made the bunny bounce across the bed toward Bear, held by little Samuel. She remembered thinking how she and her old friend Samantha had done that very thing.

"Do you want to come see my castle?" Thia squeaked in the voice of Bun-Bun.

"Oh, yes! I very much do!" Samuel squeaked back, making Bear bounce up and down. "Can we look for treasure?"

"We sure can!" Thia turned to look at her mother. "Mama, do you think we can visit the real castle soon? You promised we would."

Anna smiled. "That would be lovely." That smile slipped when she felt a double pat on her shoulder.

"There, all healed, my dear lady," Ottentus said. "Now I begin my first quest—to find the ritual of knowledge absorption. Keep watch, Apprentice."

"Yes, Master."

Anna looked on as Ottentus moved to the base of the great slab of scrolls and tablets and tomes. By the time he actually got to the base of the structure, he was but an ant compared to its mammoth size, revealing just how much knowledge rested here. There had to be handholds in the obsidian between the shelves, for it was easy for him to climb and search the contents of the cubbies. He moved like a spider up the slab, the low gravity allowing him to jump higher with ease.

With the Blade of Paralysis removed, a manacled Anna could have sat up, but she remained lying on her side in defeat, staring at Bun-Bun. She remembered, sometime after her wedding, hoping for two children. She remembered asking the gods to break the curse and grant her two blessings. And she remembered imagining letting both Bear and Bun-Bun go, watching them spin off into the ether, until they turned into children. Into real, soft, laughing children. With her husband's face and hers. And even her sister's and mother's and father's faces. The Fates, or the Unnameables, had granted her wish of two blessings, only to cruelly recant it. She had lost all faith. In everything and particularly in herself. It made it easy to give up. There was nothing left to fight for. The future of the Arinthian line lay in a cursed child. Hope? There was no hope. None at all.

Anna lay like that for a long time, lost to memories of the past, until a hard kick to the stomach jarred her from her reveries.

"I said, *get up*."

A coughing Anna groggily sat herself up.

"Entertain me." Ralf sat down ten feet from her, watching her like a hawk. "Don't make me kick you again, *Arcanist Stone*."

She fixed her gaze on him. "What do *you* get out of all this?"

"Master will teach me the library's secrets. I will be his greatest apprentice and servant."

"Are you his son?"

Ralf scoffed. "No, but I wish I was."

"Do you not care for your own child?"

Ralf shrugged. "I'll get to him later. When he can speak. That hovel of a farm you left him at can bother with him for now. We could hear his cries a league off, and I can't handle criers."

"What did you do to my Thia?"

He shrugged again. "Nothing. Only made her *think* I had cursed her. We needed you to believe that, either way, she was cursed."

"Was she?"

"Cursed? Yes." He thumbed over his shoulder. "Master ensured it. Hid it deep in the ether. Probably even hinted at it, knowing him. He likes his little games. Found some ancient witch curse that ensured a corrupt birth."

"He murdered my daughter so I would bring him here."

"Pretty genius of him if you think about it." Ralf smiled. "Oh, look at those eyes and how full of hate they are," he cooed. "You too are a murderer. How many have you silenced eternally, anyway? Five? Ten? Fifty? Huh? I guess it doesn't matter," he said when she did not answer. "Your only purpose now is to serve me and my master. You have no other purpose. You are a tool." He chuckled to himself. "A tool. Like a shovel or hammer. I like that. I can be quite brilliant sometimes, you know. Really."

"You let him murder the mother of your child."

Ralf's smile faltered. "She deserved it." He slammed a fist into his chest. "She *rejected* me! Do you understand? *Rejected!*"

"As was her right."

"It *wasn't* her right! I made her swear to serve me forever! It was a sacred oath!"

"Was it an oath made under duress?"

Now it was Ralf who fell silent, a loathsome scowl splayed across his face.

"You allowed the murder of the mother of your child because you were too weak to—"

"Shut up!" Ralf roared, shooting at her and punching her in the mouth. She fell to the ground and spat another gob of blood up. "Shut up!" he repeated, his voice echoing.

"Quiet!" came a distant voice from up high. "I need to focus!"

"Sorry, Master!" Ralf kicked Anna in the stomach again before retreating, muttering, "Crazy old witch. Can't *wait* to see you shrivel up like an old apple when master sucks you dry of everything you know. Can't wait to hear about what secrets you've been hiding too. I bet there's all sorts of juicy stuff in that brain of yours."

Anna fought to sit up again and observed the manacles in her lap.

"You won't get out of them. The master ensured they work by testing them on me."

Anna spotted a tiny rune stamped into one of the cuffs, which translated to "terra." It had to be the unlocking word, which only a viable warlock could incant. This pair, made of bronze, looked particularly old. That gave her an idea, as some of the older sets did not require a thought pattern but the mere incantation of the phrase or word, along with the touch of a hand. But to orchestrate that would take some serious cunning. Not to mention she would have to wait until nightfall ...

She glanced at the dome, beyond which was a molten hellscape, a stark contrast to the cool and quiet interior. Were it any other circumstance, she would have considered the library peaceful, with its black floor and towering shelves and ancient smell of books and scrolls and its spectacular scenery.

Anna heard something soft slide across the ground.

"I miss her, you know."

"Don't you dare speak about my daughter, *Ralf Turman*," Anna said, staring at a river of lava flowing by the protective blue dome.

"You do not get to dictate anything to me ever again. And my name is *Narsus*."

Anna trained her eyes on him and saw he was holding Bun-Bun, having fetched him telekinetically.

"Don't you narrow your eyes at me. Drop your gaze, woman. *Now*."

Anna stared defiantly, until Ralf shot over to her and slapped her face, causing her to fall. Then he kicked her, then again—and kept kicking her all over, hissing, "Witch! Witch! Witch!" until she was wheezing and bloody and barely conscious.

"*That's* for getting me expelled." He sat back down, panting as he watched her gasp for breath. "Sucks to lose, doesn't it? Guess you're not familiar with that sensation, are you, seeing as you've never lost before ..."

Anna thought of her son. Her daughter. Her husband. Her father, mother, sister. She wanted to tell this unruly boy about them, about how much she had cared for them all—and still did. How deeply she had loved her family. How hard she had fought to keep everyone together. How great her failure truly was. Loss? She knew loss. Knew it all too well ...

"Did you honestly think you were going to show up, open some cage, take your daughter out, and hand her a stupid toy and everything would work out?" Ralf tossed Bun-Bun aside as Anna faded out of consciousness. The last thing she heard him say was, "And I thought Thia was naive …"

INNOCENCE REGAINED

Anna felt another kick to the ribs and groggily opened her eyes to find Ralf crouching before her. It was dark behind him, and the dome was mysteriously open to the air, revealing a brilliant field of stars.

"Good news," he whispered, picking up Anna's braid and idly whipping it against each of her cheeks. "Master found the ritual of absorption. The hourglass has begun to trickle for you." He threw the braid against her face and stood. "Hungry?"

She nodded.

"Then get up."

Anna struggled to sit up. Her stomach hurt as did all the muscles he had pummeled. She was black and blue, but no bones had been broken. "I was having a dream," she said, accepting a chunk of biscuit beef.

Ralf sat down opposite. "Let me guess. You were lecturing a class, probably putting someone in detention."

The manacles clanked as she took a bite. "As a matter of fact, I was indeed teaching. But I was happy. And so were the students."

He scoffed.

"And I dreamed my son and daughter sat in those seats, and they were staring happily at my grandson, only a little boy, but oh so eager to learn ..." How she wished he had let her sleep and enjoy those precious moments with her children!

Ralf roared with knee-slapping laughter. "That's so stupid," he said between snorts. "So utterly stupid ..."

Anna, staring off at nothing, continued in a murmur under his laughter. "I realized … I realized that some things are worth living for …"

"It's going to be *so* fun watching you get robbed of all your knowledge and memories," Ralf said, having not heard.

Anna focused on him and tilted her head, trying to sound nonchalant. "Where is your master?"

Ralf flicked his head sideways between bites. "Just left to find water."

She looked out into the wasteland of dried lava and steaming vents — and spotted a four-legged beast not unlike a bear, albeit one with stone teeth, stealthily approaching. She glanced back and saw that the winged lion was napping on the opposite side.

Ralf took notice. "What are you looking at the lion for?" He glanced about. "Ah, look there. See that little beastling stalking us? I guess you thought you could use it for your gain. Well, think again." He cleared his throat before belting out, "*Geh geh aka ach ahi geha nah!*" The dome reappeared with a tremendous *sizzle*.

Anna couldn't stop her hopes from crashing.

"What a tough incantation. Sounds like sneezing, doesn't it? Master learned it by asking the winged lion."

Anna did not reply, and they watched as the bear-like beast neared. A huge shadow crossed overhead, and next they knew the winged lion had silently smashed the toothy monster into bits. Only the ground gave a slight tremor. With its task complete, the winged lion stretched and sauntered back to curl up in its spot. Anna spotted her waterskin that had rolled out of her rucksack during the earlier melee, though only one bundle of biscuit beef remained, hinting that Ralf had fed her from her own stash.

"That was interesting. But I prefer the stars, not to mention we don't want Master getting suspicious, do we?" He craned his neck. "*Geh geh aka ach ahi geha nah!*" and the dome vanished with another *sizzle*.

The repetition helped her commit the phrase to memory.

"Strangest language I've ever heard, isn't it? Master thinks it's Rivican." He continued throwing her scraps.

"He might be right." Getting him to trust her, even slightly, might be her only opportunity to try what she had concocted, for she would only grow weaker from here on out, and who knew if she would ever get another opportunity …

She finished everything he gave, then gulped from his waterskin which he had passed her, until he snatched it back, slapping her face for her greediness.

"Feels good to slap a teacher," he said, taking a greedy slurp himself. "Every student ought to try it at least once. They should make it mandatory. Have a Slap Your Teacher day or something. That'd be a hoot, wouldn't it?" He drummed his fingers against the waterskin. "You know, I thought you'd be a better dueler. Guess you've been spending too much time teaching. Out of practice and all that."

"I've heard that before," Anna muttered, thinking of Scadius Von Edgeworth. Satiated, she girded herself for what she had to do, hoping it would work. It had to begin with a question. "You don't actually believe he'll keep you alive, do you?"

"Shut up before you annoy me."

"He'll use you like he's used everyone else in his life. Then he'll spit you out, grind you under his boot, and leave you to die. You're nothing but a puppet to him."

Ralf bit his lower lip before hissing, "What did I just say?"

Now the push. "I do not fear you. You *do* know that, right? I do *not* fear you. You are a scared little boy, desperately craving a father. But all that man will ever give you is a spanking."

Ralf stood, fists balling. "You don't fear me, huh?"

Yes, take the bait, she thought, looking up at him as he hovered near. "Not in the least, Ralf Turdman—" and she thrust forth both fists into his stomach, being sure to keep the manacle chain taut. Sure enough, he grabbed that chain and yanked it, roaring, "*Dreadus terrablus!*"

The spell walloped Anna's unprotected mind. But she also heard a *click* and felt the manacles loosen, instantly unlocking her vast reservoir of arcanery. Her hunch had been correct—the ancient and rather crude manacles needed only to hear the trigger word "terra" whilst being touched.

In that split moment, Ralf's eyes widened. But because his Fear spell had taken root prior to her Mind Armor activating, she saw his teeth elongate and his nails turn to claws that shot out at her and pierced her flesh. Blood poured from his eyes and mouth and ears and from his long fingernails. Narsus meant bleeder, she remembered.

He wiggled a hand at her, incanting, "*Flustrato!*" The spell slapped into her now armored mind—and slid off like slop. He might as well have been flinging dirt for all the good a spell flung at 7th degree proficiency would do against the might of an 18th degree warlock.

Anna, snagged in a web of delusional terror, stood up. She loomed over Ralf, controlling her face and eyes, watching through the nightmare before her. Having seen his Confusion casting fail, the boy had frozen stiff, terrified she would fry him on the spot were he to move a muscle.

His face kept contorting, with his own teeth piercing through his skull, dipping about like white worms. His skin kept sloughing off, only to return, gliding back up his body like a flat snake.

Anna glared at him throughout, almost daring him to act. Her resolve, rage, and the fact the spell was so weak in relation to her degree allowed her to control her countenance. The moment his eyes flicked to the world beyond and he opened his mouth, no doubt to cast a spell or perhaps to cry out for his master, she lashed out with a hand toward his throat, hissing, "*Voidus lingua.*" The incantation caught in his mouth and she followed up by drawing his outline with a finger, incanting, "*Paralizo carcusa cemente.*" All of him but his bleeding eyes went rigid. They darted between her and the world beyond, pleading for freedom.

"But freedom you shall not have," Anna hissed. "At least not the sort you think." She closed her eyes, trying to locate the scion, but could not feel it through the terror of Fear. She had to wait the spell out, which she patiently did. When Ralf's body stopped gruesomely morphing, indicating the spell was abating, she closed her eyes again and felt the scion somewhere to the west.

"Mmm," she toned.

She opened her eyes to stare at him, pointed at his rope belt, where the Blade of Paralysis was, and had it float free and tuck itself under her own belt. "Now let us see what you know, boy." She placed a hand on top of his head in preparation to cast the 4th degree healing spell Empathic Transmission.

His eyes went saucer-wide.

"*Empatinio minad communa enhana historia.*" A flood of imagery rushed at her. Being well-practiced with the spell allowed her to delve into that which interested her—to begin with, how he came to be a certain way.

She saw herself as a little boy lying on the ground, with a bigger boy looming overhead and slamming a fist into his face. They were in a cornfield, with a group of boys gathered around, cheering him on. "Get that weirdo!" one of them called. "Bleed 'im good!" shouted another. "What a creepy loser," said a third.

"Why is you so weird?" the big boy asked between punches. "Huh? Why is you so weird?"

"I ain't weird," Ralf cried.

"Yes, you is. No one else talks to themself like you do, makin' up dumb stories and all."

"I only make up stories for fun! They don't do no harm—"

"And you is ugly too."

"No, I ain't!"

"Oh, you is ugly, all right. Look at that nasty hair." He grabbed Ralf's hand, raked it through his hair, then slathered his face with it while his friends cackled. "Could light a bonfire with all this grease."

"I curse you to hell!"

"Hell? What you know 'bout hell, boy? And I don't take no lip from weird freaks!" The bigger boy then reared back and punched Ralf so hard everything went black.

Anna moved on to see a slightly older Ralf sitting before an open book Anna recognized from the pages alone, having read it herself when she was his age. He was near the end, and kept checking the hallway, implying he should not be reading this particular book.

She moved on. Now he was a burgundy-robed fourteen-year-old stepping up to a pretty girl with raven hair.

"Hi," he blurted. "Want to go to the Endyear dance with me?"

"Thank you, but I've already got a date," she replied, looking about as if searching for friends to get her out of there, but there was no one else in the academy hall.

"No, you don't."

"Yes, I do."

"Then who is he?"

"Uh … Jonathan," she blurted.

"You're lying. Why don't you want to go with me? I'm a nice guy."

"I …"

"I *deserve* a chance, you know. You're not taken. You need to give me a chance."

"I … I … I don't know. I—"

"All you girls are the same. Wenches. You're a wench, you know that? A stupid wench."

The girl was breathing quickly, looking for an escape route.

"You go out with stupid dumb bricks instead of decent guys like me."

The academy bell began to gong.

"Got to go, class is starting, bye—" and she bolted off, leaving Ralf to fume.

Anna moved on to how he had manipulated her daughter, Thia. The visual sucked her into his dorm room, which she knew he had snuck Thia into. She wanted to gasp, for she saw herself staring through his eyes at her daughter. How desperately she wanted to reach out and hug her one last time!

"You're going to marry me," Ralf declared.

Thia was sitting on his bed, fiddling with her hands in her lap. "I'm not sure I'm ready to—"

"No buts. You're mine. You know how much I love you."

"I know, but—"

"I said, *no buts*! What are you, deaf? I'm the man here. You understand?" Anna saw Ralf's hand slap his own chest. "I'm the man. We're going to have a traditional marriage. You're going to do my bidding. That's the way of old, and that's what you agreed to in the sacred ritual."

"I'm not chattel—"

There was a *slap* as he smacked her. "But you're just a *woman*. Therefore, you *are* chattel. Aren't you? Say it!"

It took everything for Anna not to yank herself out of the vision and throttle him. Except she needed to know more, and dipped away, skipping over memories that included bleeding or her daughter or anything of that sort, choosing instead a memory in the excavation, with Ottentus. The hairless man held a whip in his hand, and a worker was bent over a log before him, his back raw and bleeding.

"Master, I bring news, and I am not sure how you will feel about it," Ralf said, huffing from having run.

Ottentus whipped the man once more. "You so much as put a pebble in your pocket and you will rue the day. Now get back to work." He kicked the worker, who scrambled to find his shirt and ran out of there. Ottentus tossed the whip aside. It fizzled before even hitting the ground. "What is it?"

"Er …"

"Spit it out, boy. I worked very hard for these plans to come to fruition. What have you done now to foul them up?"

"I …"

Ottentus opened his hands. "You …? You *what*? Say it before I put the whip to you too."

"I blessed her with a child," Ralf blurted.

Ottentus kept his hands apart, gaping at him, before dropping them. "Idiot boy …"

"I know, Master. I'm sorry. But I want the child. I … I want an heir, and I think I could use this to—"

"You want an *Arinthian* heir. I suggest you speak plain, my boy. *Very* plain, lest I lose my temper."

Ralf straightened. "I want their castle. I want the prestige. I want the *respect*."

"And you want the scion."

"Only if you don't, Master. And I promise you I have no feelings for the girl whatsoever. We can still sacrifice her. She's a useless wench who betrayed me the moment she broke her sacred promise to be with me forever."

Ottentus squeezed his nose three times before he began pacing. "This might work to our benefit," he muttered to himself. "The grandmother's curse could be manipulated. It would be a matter of making the mother believe her daughter is in peril. Bewitch, cast at 20th degree after consecutive onslaughts at Mind Armor until a penetration occurs … it would have to be vague enough that she doesn't suspect us … a moment of weakness … but constructed properly, it could indeed work …"

"I'm glad to hear that, Master."

"Shut up," Ottentus barked, startling Ralf. "I need to think." He continued pacing and muttering to himself. "That still leaves the keys of entry … but how to make her learn the crucial one? Perhaps a plant … a book slipped right under her nose … Yes, I think I see a path …" After some more brooding and mumbling, he stopped to stare at Ralf. "You sure you haven't developed feelings for the girl?"

"She's a toy, nothing more. And she deserves to be punished for rejecting me."

"But you still want to possess her."

Ralf surrendered a reluctant nod.

"Then I suggest you let go, and double quick."

"I'll distance myself from her at the right time. I swear, Master. She'll be nothing but amusement in the mean."

"Good. And you share a Drama class with her, is that right?"

"I do, sir."

"Excellent. I'm going to give you a book. A very special book you will use as a prop, with a provenance I will craft so that your story is unimpeachable even if pursued by the authorities. I have a plan I want you to carry out, but it must be done very delicately. The pieces to this puzzle must align just so, otherwise the sheep might go astray."

"I will be as delicate as a spring flower, Master. And consider me your wolf shepherd."

Having heard enough, Anna tore herself away from the vision. She found herself glaring at Ralf, whose eyes were wide in awe at her. Wanting to hear what he had to say for himself, she squiggled out his outline, incanting, "*Paralizo null.*"

He went limp, dropping his head in submission. "I … I saw you fighting your legendary duels, how you vanquished The Reaper … I saw you take on Apoc and Endius and Totillus … and-and-and I can't *believe* how incredible you were and there are so many others not in the books and—"

Typical that all he had been interested in were her duels. "What were your intentions with my grandson?" Anna barked, cutting him off. "Answer me true."

His eyes remained on the floor.

"Answer me!" When he still refused, she took a step forth, hissing at his bowed head, "To take the Arinthian line's name. Secure the castle. Take the scion. Is that not so?"

Ralf hesitated. "Y-you're an amazing d-dueler and I b-beg your mercy …"

"Mercy? You want mercy after murdering my daughter?"

"P-please, don't kill me—"

Anna glanced out into the wasteland, considering doing just that. Then she remembered her daughter's desperate wish. "I'm not going to kill you," she said, looking back at him to see him relax. "But you will not remember your son, or even the mother of your son—the woman you murdered." *My daughter* …

His face went ashen. "N-n-n-n-no—"

"You will not remember your ambitions with necromancy. You will not even remember having gone to the academy." She leaned close, whispering, "Your son will *never* know his father. No one will know. Ever."

"N-n-no … you can't … M-M-Memory Wipe might as well be arcastration … and-and-and it's illegal …"

"Not here it isn't," and she made a claw with her hand and latched it onto his face, yanking it up. "My daughter sends her regards," she spat, venom dripping from each word.

His voice was muffled through her palm. "Oh, g-g-g-gods, no, I'm sorry. I didn't m-m-mean it—"

"Oh, but you did. You *did* mean it, you foul worm," and Anna began the complex process of the thought alignment required for the infamous—and usually highly controlled—13th degree Memory Wipe spell. She began with the present and worked backward, scrolling through time in her mind by reversing particles of sand up the hourglass—but destroying each one before it reached its destination. Each year eliminated coldly drew a swath of stamina. "*Erassa memora*—"

Ralf screamed.

"—*au o minad.*"

He went silent, eyes vacant as he stared straight through her, mouth agape.

Anna took his arm and bid him to sit down with her. Having drained an immense amount of stamina—the spell would have taken multiple castings if Ralf had been older—she had to meditate before Ottentus returned. First, she needed to know how successful the spell had been, for she had never cast it on a living person before, only training dummies.

"Ralf?"

He looked at her and blinked, eyes plain. "Yes?"

"How old are you?"

"I'm ten. How old are *you*?"

"Five times your age."

Ralf scrunched his face as he looked at his fingers. "So ... you're ... fifty?"

"Correct."

He glanced about. "This place is weird."

Anna watched him carefully.

He pointed past her with a clumsy finger. "Can I go outside and play around that giant statue?"

"Ralf."

"Yes?"

"What do you know about arcanery?"

"I know lots. I've read ... I've read ..." He grimaced trying to think.

"*The Rudiments of the Arcane Arts for Beginners.*"

His eyes went wide. "How did you know that?"

"Why did you read that book?"

"I ... I want to be a warlock one day, I guess."

"Do you know who I am?"

He shook his head.

"Do you know where you are?"

He glanced about with an open mouth. Another shake of the head. "It looks scary here. Am I dreaming?"

"No."

"Have I been bad?"

Anna did not reply.

"Do I have to go back?"

"Back where?"

"To the orphanage."

"I'm not sure. Is there a place you would *like* to go? Do you have a home somewhere else?"

"I ... I don't know. No, I guess not." Ralf looked down at his lap, only to start. "My hands! Why are they so *big*?" The more he saw of himself, the more he panicked, until he began crying out of terror, forcing Anna to place a hand on his forehead and incant, "*Calma o sola au persona balan,*" the incantation to the 2nd degree healing spell Calm.

Ralf relaxed, his concern turning into interest.

"I'm so big," he said, drying his tears with his sleeve before inspecting his hands. "Am I a giant?"

"No."

"What am I, then?"

"A big boy."

"Why?"

"Why what?"

"Why am I so big? I don't remember being so big."

"The Unnameables made it so." She had no better answer at the moment.

"Are *you* an Unnameable?"

"No."

"So … who *are* you?"

"Someone who will take you home."

"The orphanage?"

"I don't know yet."

"I'm dreaming, aren't I?" He thought about it. "Can I make my own home?"

"I don't know."

He stared at her. "You seem kind. Would you like to be my mother?"

"No."

"Why not?"

"I'm afraid that's impossible, Ralf."

"Why?"

"Because."

"Because why?"

"Because I already have a family." It hurt to say it, for she no longer had a family thanks to him, but she couldn't think of a better explanation he would understand.

"Oh. They must be very lucky."

Anna could not reply through the lump in her throat.

"What's your name?"

"Ralf, I need to ask you something important."

"Yes?"

"Haven't you already become a warlock?"

"What?"

"A warlock. Aren't you already one? Show me your stripes. Go ahead." Theoretically, Memory Wipe should have obliterated the body-infused tendrils of the 16th degree Convery Degree, as they were also bound to one's memory of spell knowledge. But she had to be sure.

Ralf frowned at his forearm. He grimaced and strained, but no rings appeared. "I'm not a warlock," he whispered, disappointed. "Am I?"

"You are not." The casting had worked. And a second casting later should put his memories beyond the reach of the 14th degree healing spell Rectify Memory.

"Can I become one though?"

"If you want to."

"Can I go live with you?"

"I'm sorry. I need you to be quiet now, Ralf. Please do not be concerned, but I cannot have you wandering about." She traced his outline, paralyzing him anew. Due to the Calm spell's lingering effect, he took it well, sitting and watching her. In the mean, she lay down to pretend as if she had not moved, hid the dagger in her sleeve, and placed the manacles loosely over her wrists. Then she closed her eyes to rest and meditate.

While Ralf sat in stone silence, and between deep thoughts of distant and peaceful places and times with her family, Anna put together a trap for Ottentus.

PUFFS OF SMOKE

When the sky began to yellow in the east, the *thwomp* she had been waiting for at last arrived.

"Success, Apprentice!" Ottentus crooned, followed by the *slosh* of waterskins getting dumped to the ground. "It was some trial as I had to follow a slippery thing quite a ways into the hot earth, but in the end I found a cache of water interestingly protected by a hard shell of rock, so the quest was a success. What's with the dull look, Apprentice?" He padded closer, his steps hesitant. "Why aren't you—"

Anna, a coiled viper, lashed out with the blade the moment she glimpsed his robe. He instantly reacted by yanking a hand and incanting, "*Disablo!*" The dagger twirled out of Anna's hand, but she transitioned to slapping her wrists, roaring, "*Annihilo dio!*" figuring the close range was enough to land a blow—and one *did* land, albeit against a hastily summoned shield of ice. The remainder flew off into the yellow sky.

Gods he's quick, Anna thought, eighteen lightning rings bursting to life around her arm as she incanted, "*Impetus peragro!*" vanishing just as four bolts of ice smashed into the spot where she had lain. She appeared twenty feet behind the master warlock, whose arm had burst with a full sleeve of ice. While his eyes remained black and unlit, Anna's had flared with lightning—The Settling—a testament to the "creativity" he so longed for.

"Wait!" he said, holding up a hand. "If we are going to do this, let us do it properly. Let us do it in the old way."

The rage bubbled like lava. "To the death."

"I rather meant with a bow, but I suppose that will do as well. What a waste of your talents, which I would much rather absorb. But why not—to the death it is!"

Anna, under no illusion he would not still suck her soul dry if given the chance, hissed, "You have something that belongs to me." She flicked a hand and the scion, which had been in his pocket, tore through the fabric and zoomed toward her.

"That's a little rude," he jested. "You ruined a perfectly good robe."

But Anna wasn't smiling, and she snatched the scion out of the air, only to toss it right back up, so that it floated nearby, its innards flashing with silent lightning. "It took us thirty-six years to get to this point together, old friend," she whispered to it, never taking her eyes off Ottentus, who for some reason bothered to arcanely repair the stitching of his robe pocket. "The time has come for me to ask everything of you. Lend me your strength, Papa. Lend it all."

The scion buzzed, flickering wildly, silently.

Ottentus glanced at the manacles lying by a frozen Ralf. "How did you slip out of them? You conned him, didn't you?" he added when she did not reply. "Ah, well. He was dutiful, but a bore to be around. Thought himself smarter than he actually was. I would have disposed of him in the end."

She padded to the center of the circular stone floor. "I know."

"People are so easy to manipulate—" and he snatched Bun-Bun. It took a lot for Anna to restrain herself from reacting. He chortled, wiggling the creature about as he sang, "I have a hostaaaaage!"

"He's already dead," she lied. "He died the moment you murdered my daughter."

Ottentus shrugged. "I suppose," and tossed Bun-Bun aside.

Anna silently breathed an immense sigh of relief.

He padded forth, stopping twenty feet away. "Shall we dispense with the pleasantries and get right to it? A bow and a kill? I shan't take it easy on you this time."

Anna narrowed her eyes.

"Oh, feisty. And let us avoid casting spells that might damage the library. Agreed?"

She nodded.

"Shall we, then?" He made a ridiculous bow, accented with a twirl of both hands.

Anna gave only the barest of bows, and waited until he made his move, which came in the form of slapping wrists even as he straightened.

"*Annihilo!*" he roared.

Anna, having expected the breach of etiquette, stepped aside, and the single bolt of ice, which she suspected was tempered to conserve stamina, *sizzled* by. She countered by slapping her own wrists and sending a bolt of tempered lightning right back, curious how he'd react. He summoned his shield and batted the spell aside, a clever response as it allowed him to feel that it had indeed been tempered.

They exchanged various low-degree spells in this manner. Like a Rivican mechanism, he was relentless, casting spell after spell with fluid precision and impeccable timing. He pressed, anticipating all the standard counters, keeping her on her heels, never allowing her to take the initiative. Throughout her defending, she realized that although he might best her on the ground, there was one arena she thought she could beat him in—the air.

As she did a backflip over a dual prong, she lashed out at a floating barrel-sized slab of cubby holes and yanked herself skyward. The low gravity assisted, and she shot away, the scion flying after her like an attentive hummingbird. Even before she reached that slab, she snatched the one beyond, propelling herself forth, beckoning him—no, *daring* him to join her. Interestingly, despite floating in free space, none of the slabs moved, as if they were anchored to the ether.

"Clever girl," he said from below, "but let's see how you deal with this—*muerto tempus ideus deo didaeiee!*"—the incantation to the mighty 20th degree Slow Time spell, which slowed time for the caster, but no one else. To observers, the caster appeared to zip around like a blur, while to the caster, everyone else moved in slow motion, lending great advantage in combat. The better one was with the spell, the slower everyone moved, and the longer the duration. It was a spell Anna greatly feared. There was only one logical response to it, too, which she had already planned for during her meditation.

"*Impetus peragro!*" a still-flying Anna snapped as he finished his incantation, vanishing and reappearing with a *thwomp* on top of the mesa from where the pair had seen the library. She focused on another mesa and loaded the same incantation on her tongue, ready to deliver it within an eye blink. Sure enough, the moment she heard the beginning of a *thwomp*, she snapped off, "*Impetus peragro!*" and vanished again. When the *thwomp* followed, she again snapped, "*Impetus peragro!*" this time appearing on a thin ledge on the side of a towering spire.

The man raced around in a blur of frustration across the last mesa, trying to locate her teleport tendril evidence. Anna watched like a clinging lizard, noting where he had appeared was far farther than where she had appeared on the mesa, meaning her tendril evidence had a chance of expiring before he could get to it and properly analyze it.

Ideally, the Slow Time spell would lapse by the time he caught up to her—the casting duration was notoriously short, after all, at least for those *not* under the influence of the spell.

With her ledge being too small for another person, there was only one other spot he could possibly teleport to catch up to her—another ledge located just below, creating a perfect trap. She prepared by balancing herself precariously on her ledge and aiming both arms in that direction, her wrists a mere finger's width apart. Apparently he'd gotten to what had remained of her tendril evidence before it vanished into the ether, for she soon heard the beginning of another *thwomp*. She slapped her wrists, quickly hissing, "*Annihilo!*" Her scion buzzed, for she had used it to throw everything she had into the spell. As quick as she was, she witnessed his blurry form try to dodge the thick bolt of lightning. By doing so, he lost his footing—and caught a bit of the bolt in the shoulder. The force of it sent him twirling into the air, blood spraying like a cloud from the wound, the movements sped up due to Slow Time, making an almost comical display.

"*Impetus peragro!*" came a mousy voice, the words said so quickly they came out as a squeak. He vanished well before he hit the ground, but she did not see where he had gone.

"Gotcha," she said, and focused on a spot behind the main slab. "*Impetus peragro,*" and she appeared exactly where she had intended. There she took shelter behind a giant boulder of dried magma, knowing the only way to survive at the moment was to stay out of sight and wait for the spell to time out. He would have hidden himself too to lick his wounds—that was, to heal himself.

Just in case though, she splayed a hand and incanted, "*Un vun asperio aurum enchantus.*" She checked herself over for hostile enchantments— and discovered a small blue tendril web at the back of her shoe.

"Clever man," she muttered, recognizing an Object Track enchantment, which he must have cast after she had succumbed to his initial onslaught alongside his apprentice. But just as she was about to disenchant it, a better idea came to her, and she slipped the shoe off and left it behind the boulder. Then she retreated between two nearby boulders offering a limited view of the shoe. There she drew a hand over her body, incanting, "*Armari obscura chameleano,*" making her body indistinguishable from the black rock. She waited, a camouflaged lioness ready to lunge, Reveal still lit in a hand.

It wasn't long until he slunk into view, his body camouflaged, his hand lit with Reveal, healed, and moving in normal time—the Slow Time spell had lapsed.

Just as he spotted the shoe, she slapped her wrists together, roaring, "*Annihilo dio!*"

He jumped out of reflex, but not quickly enough, and a bolt slapped into his thigh. He yowled before snapping off, "*Impetus peragro!*" vanishing with a *thwomp*.

"Gotcha again!" Anna said as she quickly examined the tendril teleport evidence and gave chase, teleporting about the various mesas. Unable to find him, she returned to the library. He had evidently found a spot out of view where he could heal a second time.

That's all right. I'll use the time to replenish my reserves, she thought, chest heaving from the exertion, eyes darting about. Alertness meant no meditation, but she still aided the replenishment by being as still as possible, an open target. In the stillness, with a field of strange stars above, she became aware of the vast emptiness of this place. The loneliness was sweetened by a lone boy, sitting paralyzed, unsure of where he was and what had happened to him—and by a lone little bunny, lying on his side, waiting to be cuddled and loved.

If I live, I will annotate both duels, she thought. Not just for posterity, but as teaching moments for future generations. She would just have to do it in a way that hid the true location …

Eventually there came another *thwomp*, this one directly ahead and on the opposite side of the library floor.

"You are a worthy opponent," Ottentus said, voice echoing against the floating slabs. "Two hits to none. I now see why they called you the Arcane Artist. It is your ability to improvise that sets you apart from other duelers, who use the same tired old tricks, the same thrusts and counter-thrusts. Were I not an accomplished healer in my own right, this would have been over already, with you the victor."

She kicked off her remaining shoe, choosing to go bare of foot, just like when she was a young girl. "They *still* call me that."

"The Arcane Artist? Ah, you must mean your students. How quaint. What's next, your father always said you were brilliant?"

Anna raised her chin. "I will destroy you. It will not be a pleasant death."

He chortled, striding forth. "I take it you are ready for round two. Or I suppose it's round three now, isn't it?"

Anna was more than ready. In fact, she had a surprise—she only hoped it would work. As he began an incantation that came with a complex series of gestures, one she recognized as a powerful off-the-books ice spell, she tried something she had only practiced—a double-armed gesture, the left arm creating a whirling spiral, and the right an angry clawing, as if she were raking a brain. Her mind spliced both spell visuals into one while her mouth split the wording, interweaving the incantations together. "*Summano dreadus laitna terrablus virli!*" She felt a double cooling draw from her stamina, with additional stamina sucked, as the arcaneological texts predicted.

Ottentus cut his spell off before she finished. He ducked the Fear incantation and, after looking up to see a massive lightning tornado crackling to life directly above him, he snapped off a teleport, appearing on top of the giant slab that provided shadow in the day.

"You performed a simulcast!" he shouted from above, smiling broadly. "Anna! I am *so* proud of you! That was a true feat of legend!"

Anna, despite performing her first ever true simulcast in the field, was annoyed. She had chosen poorly, for the 18th degree off-the-books Lightning Tornado spell had been too slow to form, and the Fear spell too quick.

Ottentus grabbed his head, screeching, "Damn it, woman! Don't let it destroy the library!" The tornado swallowed up a floating shelf, the contents of which were ripped from its cubbyholes and strewn about, lightning frying some on the spot, creating puffs of smoke amidst small *cracks* of thunder. "Those are irreplaceable!" he screamed, and began a series of gestures aimed at the tornado that Anna recognized as part of the Disenchant sphere of arcaneological influence.

Anna used the time to telekinetically snatch Bun-Bun and a still-paralyzed Ralf and slide them away from the raging maelstrom. Amidst the roaring wind, she shoved Ralf against the main slab, jammed Bun-Bun into his lap, secured the little creature by pinning it with one of Raf's arms, and telekinetically lashed out at a nearby floating slab of cubbies, launching herself into the air. Before her ascent slowed, she lashed out at another slab and yanked again, hauling herself toward Ottentus like a shark rising from the depths.

By the time Ottentus neared disenchanting the tornado, Anna was forty feet away and lobbing mind spells. Each hit snapped his head back a little, slowing his progress, but not halting it, showcasing the toughness of a master's Mind Armor. After another twenty feet of forward momentum and three more mind spells, Anna yanked telekinetically, this time latching onto his leg. In that same moment, the roar of the tornado quieted, indicating a successful disenchant. To her surprise, he let her shoot him toward her, and although he was sent hurtling on his back, he managed to slap his wrists at her, roaring, "*Annihilo lito!*" Five massive shards of ice blasted at her.

She instantly thought of the mesa and snapped, "*Impetus peragro!*" Just as her body yanked, she felt a searing tear in her thigh. She appeared on top of the day-seared stone, took one look down at her leg, and screamed, for it was twisted at an awkward angle and barely hanging on. There was a huge hole in the robe, and a pool of blood was forming rapidly underneath her.

She was in serious trouble.

First, she needed to find shelter from him, so she envisioned standing in the first spot her eyes fell upon—an out-of-view valley beyond the mesa. "*Impetus peragro!*" she hissed through gritted teeth, and heard a *thwomp* just before hearing her own *thwomp*. She appeared in the valley and immediately looked for another spot, for the savvy Ottentus would surely be examining her tendril trail. She spotted a ravine, at the bottom of which was a dried-out river of lava pocked with boulders. "*Impetus peragro!*" she hissed again, appearing behind one of those boulders. There she collapsed in time to hear the distant echo of a second *thwomp*. She grabbed her thigh, pressed it with all her might, and dared to peek around the boulder.

She saw Ottentus running toward a spot, hand outstretched. *You're too late*, she thought, hoping the teleportation tendrils had dispersed enough for him to have to guess her direction of travel.

Either way, with the tunnel of consciousness rapidly closing, she did not have the strength to teleport a third time. She turned her attention to the wound, splaying a hand over the mess, knowing she had to be quick. That meant no unnecessary spells like Reduce Pain or Anesthetize.

First came Diagnose. "*Examino potente morbus aurus persona*," which revealed a clean slice through the femur, and a huge hole through the thigh flesh—and the *lafus loga*, a main artery in the leg. The stark realization that she had heartbeats to live quickened her heart, which was good as she needed to keep her blood pressure up lest she pass out or suffer heart failure altogether. Either meant certain death.

She had to start with Bone Heal first. "*Apreyo explithica sysali amtrenervo bona*," she incanted, and began to fuse the thigh bone back together. Guided by her sheer lust for justice, she somehow managed not only to heal the bone, but avoid screaming from the jarring pain.

"I know you're neeeeaaar," Ottentus sang from afar, voice amplified and bouncing off the spires. "And I know I wounded yooooou!"

With the bone healed, she moved on to the artery. Because of the clean slice, it should be possible to heal it with Remedy Elementary

Wound. "*Remedia binda arregando min finateo*," she incanted. Using the index finger of each hand, she telekinetically grabbed both ends of the squirting artery and carefully spliced them back together. The moment there was a small flash of sealing light, she continued the same spell, repairing the flaps of flesh until they too sealed with a small light.

Then, trembling, she flopped back, gasping from the memory of the pain and trauma. It had been by far the worst injury she had ever repaired on herself, and it took some time for her to battle off the tremors. Throughout, Ottentus kept singing out to her, taunting her to reveal herself, how he could "smell her blood" and looked forward to "finishing her off." All as the sky to the east brightened. Dawn would soon come and set the world aflame.

"You haven't got me yet," she muttered. Parched and starved, she knew it was crucial to replenish her energy reserves. After visualizing her waterskin lying on the floor of the library, she incanted, "*Impetus peragro*," and appeared exactly there. She grabbed the waterskin, snatched the remaining bundle of biscuit beef, and teleported off just as another *thwomp* came. She teleported twice more before settling behind a spire, where she devoured the beef and guzzled the water like a famished beast.

After satisfying her hunger and thirst, she glanced down at the gaping hole in her robe. Even though she remembered thinking it odd that he had repaired his own robe earlier, she found herself doing the exact same thing.

"It's about dignity," she muttered after the robe had finished repairing with a white light. "Dignity and unity. Unity and strength. Strength and power." She looked to the scion, which zipped into view, having been floating above her head. "Are you ready, old friend? Let's go. *Impetus peragro!*"

She appeared on top of one of the floating medium-sized slabs—and spotted Ottentus throttling Ralf, who was crying hysterically. "Snap out of it, you little brat!"

Anna, unable to shoot a spell without possibly hitting Ralf, shouted, "Leave him be!"

Ottentus stepped behind Ralf and placed the Blade of Paralysis to his throat. "How about I kill him instead?"

Anna extended an arm and pointed at the great slab. "How about I send lightning coursing through every scrap of parchment here?" She was conscious of the horizon blushing fiercely, readying to engulf the world with fire anew.

"You wouldn't dare!"

Anna's arm swiveled to point below her. She reared her hand back and made an idle tossing gesture, incanting, "*Bola lauba.*" A ball of lightning spilled forth and ruptured against the cubbyholes, instantly igniting a slew of ancient scrolls.

Ottentus sprang away from Ralf, who somehow maintained a clutch on Bun-Bun. "You *witch!*" he screamed. "You cursed, cursed witch!"

Anna pointed both arms at the great slab, ready to cast a Fourth Offensive. "You keep the battle between us only and I *might* spare the parchments!"

Ottentus took a step forth, face crimson with rage. "After I'm done sucking every juicy piece of knowledge you possess, I'm going to tear you limb from limb, like a boy dissecting a fly!"

Anna's response was to reach over her shoulder with both hands and make a dual javelin-like throwing motion, incanting, "*Kuranta spaera!*" Two tempered spears of lightning hurtled at Ottentus, who smartly stepped in between them. Both slapped into the floor, dissipating with a *sizzle.*

"*Impetus peragro!*" he snapped.

Anna, anticipating his coming, had already charged her arm by spitting out, "*Arcanis rapidio baersto!*" By the time he appeared on top of an opposite floating bookshelf slab, she was making a carrot-peeling motion down the length of that arm, roaring, "*Baersto thub! Thub-thub-thub-thub-thub!*" sending blast after blast of lightning at him. He jumped and yanked himself and teleported from slab to slab, but Anna merely changed her arm angle and followed, until her arm abruptly sputtered out. Her thesis spell, crafted during her last term at the academy thirty-some-odd years ago, had always been a fickle thing—and too complex for her liking.

Sensing an incoming strike, Anna jumped off the bookshelf as it exploded with shards of ice. Pieces of parchment rained. She yanked herself this way and that between floating bookshelves, dodging his ice blasts. One of those blasts obliterated another bookshelf, causing him to hurl a slew of enraged expletives.

As she soared toward another floating bookshelf, she marshalled her thoughts and started circling a finger, whilst incanting, "*Portus ea ire itum combata lina,*" charging up a certain spell. Immediately upon landing on the shelf, she drew an oval behind it, incanting, "*Portus da.*" When a black portal appeared there, she jumped off, hooked on a passing shelf, and swung outside of the dome. Once her feet connected with dried lava, and while Ottentus began incanting a complex ritual, she drew another oval behind a boulder, incanting, "*Ata ei portus da*," creating the exit point to the Combat Portal spell.

She glanced eastward and saw the sky turning molten. She only had one chance to get this right.

Ottentus finished his ritual with an ostentatious flurry of five-pointed gestures, and no less than *one hundred* ethereal soldiers appeared with a massive simultaneous *thwomp*.

Summon Army, 16th, elemental, the trained warlock in her thought out of reflex.

Each soldier was dressed in ancient bronze armor and had the same face—that of an enraged Ottentus, albeit in common soldier form, and with hair and eyebrows. They spread out, crowding the entire floor of the library. Anna recognized what he was doing—hoping to either trap her outside the dome, or inside. Both would serve his needs.

"Clever," she said, striding forth a few steps before drawing a five-pointed shape and incanting, "*Summano elementus marjorus!*" A huge lightning elemental *sizzled* into existence amidst the army. It immediately stomped out one soldier and punched another into smithereens. She could have cast the 16th degree Summon Army spell as well, but would have only been able to summon a fraction of the forces. It was a ritual that demanded tremendous hours of field practice and concentration to up the numbers, and she had never felt the need, trusting her prowess as a dueler instead.

Ottentus waved his arms apart, splitting the forces. A third went after the elemental, a third spread out on the floor, and a third charged at Anna.

She cracked her knuckles and began sweeping her arm. Each sweep caught a soldier, who was then used like a battering ram to bowl over others. As soldiers tumbled, the scion buzzed, lending its strength. Using her telekinesis was the route with the least stamina draw.

By the time she finished destroying the third soldier that had attacked her, Ottentus finished a second ritual—which was to craft two copies of himself.

Doppelganger, 19th, standard, double casting. Gods he's good, she had to once again admit. All three Ottentuses teleported, appearing on various floating slabs, with one taking the high position atop the largest slab. *And very clever*, she thought, realizing he was goading her. But what choice did she have? She could run back to the exit portal from the plane, but doing so would allow him to live and learn unrestrained from the library. It would be the cowardly way out, not to mention leave justice unmet— and that was assuming he would let her exit.

A quick glance eastward told her that sunrise was imminent, as was the return of the dome. Once the first plank of light burst across the sky, she would have maybe twenty heartbeats before the dome appeared. Already the library began to rotate with a low grinding rumble, preparing the massive rear wall to face the sunrise and protect the innards from the light and raging heat.

Spell possibilities scrolled through her mind. Chain Lightning ran the risk of spreading to the point of killing Ralf and frying Bun-Bun. It was the same with Lightning Tornado and Thunderstorm and all the other mass-impact spells, not to mention they would destroy the library, which would in turn stoke Ottentus's wrath, putting Ralf and Bun-Bun in greater danger.

No, this had to be done the old-fashioned way—directly. Besides, she still had one trick up her sleeve …

She made a twirling gesture, hissing midway, "*Summano arma,*" and a huge lightning staff appeared in her hands, which she halted underneath her armpit, pointing it forward like a lance as she roared, "Charging Knight!" She ran forth, shouting a battle cry. The summoned soldiers streamed her way. Meanwhile, Ottentus used the time to summon a champion elemental, which tore into her lightning elemental, causing titanic rumbles.

A barefooted Anna reached the first wave of soldiers, lancing the first man she came across, running him down like a bull. He screamed ghoulishly, and after his back smacked against the obsidian floor, he vanished in a puff of icy smoke. She spun the staff and smashed it into numerous faces, obliterating each with a *sizzle*. Throughout, the scion *buzzed* and her arm rings and eyes *crackled* with lightning—all while bolts of ice rained down from above, interspersed with the occasional mind spell. Fear, Confusion, Mute, Slow, Blind—all the basics peppered the ground around her, sometimes bonking off her Mind Armor, with a couple denting it.

She dipped and dodged and parried and smacked aside sword strikes, countering with jabs and pummels and whaps. She performed monk martial arts positions she hadn't tried in years.

But she needn't destroy all the summoned soldiers, just whittle them down a bit. It was all about timing. When the champion ice elemental put a fist through her lightning elemental, making it vanish with a great *crackle*, she prepared to make her move. Sure enough, the entire army made a run for her—and a slew of sky attacks descended.

"*Impetus peragro!*" she incanted, teleporting to a spot outside the library, away from Ralf. She glimpsed the spot she had been standing in explode with shards of ice that rebounded so strongly that one shard impaled a soldier, vanishing it into a puff. Once the army was well clear of Ralf, she pointed her arms at the rushing horde, shouting, "*Cani linka laitna!*"

A bolt of scion-amplified lightning ripped forth, smashing into the first soldier. It immediately fanned out to three nearby others, then three more from each of those, until every soldier was connected. The scion screamed with a thousand bees as the army lifted as one, their feet dangling, bodies shaking as they began to smoke. Throughout, she kept her hands aloft, holding the lightning, her Mind Armor absorbing mind spell after mind spell. Multiple shadows formed as ice spells from above converged on her. She held the spell until the last moment, then teleported out of there just as the spot exploded in a burst of shards.

She appeared at the base of the great slab, and the ice spells halted, once more replaced by mind spells—Ottentus didn't want to damage all that precious potential knowledge.

The sky above was turning fiery. The stars had disappeared. The elemental rumbled toward her, raising its fists. All three Ottentuses were wiggling their palms, casting the same spell—Confusion, judging by the gesture. He still wanted her immobilized to suck all her knowledge, turn her into a husk he could then gleefully dissect.

The time had come to play the card up her sleeve.

Anna imagined snuffing all three sleeves as she pointed at the scion and roared, "*Extingui!*" She *felt* the spell go off, ballooning in a great invisible bubble. At the same time, her head snapped back from a triple Confusion. Her Mind Armor caved inward—but held, albeit barely.

Still in the fray, she imagined standing atop one of the higher bookcases and snapped off, "*Impetus peragro!*" She appeared in time to see two of the Ottentuses' sleeves go dark—they did not have the wherewithal to dodge the oncoming invisible bubble. But the third, the one atop the wall, had vanished with a *thwomp*.

Anna looked down at the remaining pair, whose sleeves she had snuffed. Far below, a giant ice elemental waited. She aimed at the closest Ottentus, who was gaping up at her with a rather stupid look, and slapped her wrists, incanting, "*Annihilo!*" A single scion-amplified bolt of lightning sliced through his chest. His torso slid to his right, his legs to his left, and the two parts tumbled off the shelf, vanishing before they hit the floor. She repeated the spell against the second Ottentus, catching his shoulder. He twirled off the shelf, one arm flying opposite of the body, until he too vanished.

Anna searched for her Combat Portal entrance—but couldn't locate it. Yet the exit portal remained. That was when it occurred to her that the entrance portal had stayed in place while the library had turned. All that training with the spell for nothing!

It was too late to worry about it, for as the sky went yellow, readying to reveal an apocalyptic double sunrise, there came another *thwomp* atop the main slab. Anna looked up, and their eyes met. There was a windy moment of silence as the pair of panting combatants faced each other before both began hurling spells.

It was the full gamut. Push and Disarm and Fear and Deafness and Confusion and Paralyze and Mute and Darkness and Slow and Blind and countless others, with both casters using every trick in the book, from off-the-books spells to ambidextrous castings to silent castings to feints to simulcasts. There were teleports and telekinetic yanks and ducks and dodges. Offensives were hurled and counter-hurled, blocked and parried and dodged. Ice and lightning tore the sky open, sometimes obliterating whole shelves.

Midway, Anna switched tack. She focused *only* on mind spells, mostly vacillating between Fear and Confusion, the simplest of the lot. Her arena skills kept her clear of hits, but there came more and more close calls, until he landed a blow—a thin shard sliced clean through the side of her abdomen, making her gasp and take a knee on top of the floating bookshelf she was perched on.

He capitalized by incanting, "*Muerto tempus—*"

Anna's mind shouted, *You let him cast Slow Time again and you're dead!* and so she did the quickest thing she could think of, which was to lash out telekinetically at his leg—and *yank*.

"*—ideus deo di—*gah!" He flipped backward, fizzling the 20th degree spell on the spot. At the same time, a gigantic swath of the sky lit up with a white light. Instantly her skin heated, and the peaks of numerous spires exploded with flame.

Twenty heartbeats.

Anna, abdomen screaming with pain, stamina near empty, eyes aglow and scion buzzing by her head, put everything she had into one simple onslaught. She wiggled first her left wrist then her right and back again, over and over incanting, "*Flustrato! Flustrato! Flustrato! Flustrato! Flustrato!*"

His head kept snapping back as he flopped about like a fish, trying to evade, yet there was little space on top of the slab, and she was so quick, so determined, that she didn't give him a moment to teleport out.

At ten heartbeats, knowing she had enough stamina left to cast a certain spell, and amidst a flurry of Confusion castings, she went for it, thrusting both arms forth whilst incanting, "*Morba!*"

The spell slapped Ottentus upside the head.

Anna, drained of stamina, lowered her arm and pressed the hand to her abdominal wound.

Ottentus rose, staring at her with eyes darker than obsidian. Behind him, a second plank of light speared the sky. The horizon sweltered, the heat coming in a great wave of fiery death.

Ottentus raised his chin, eyes wild. "I need to die," he said, as if stating a mere fact he had read once. "*I need to die!*" he repeated in a roar. Anna could almost see his mind racing. She remembered the spell's effect from her youth—remembered wanting to smash her head in with a brick, to end it as soon as possible.

Ottentus turned toward the light. He raised his arms skyward, as if greeting his maker.

Then in a moment Anna would forever remember like a vivid painting, he jumped skyward. Due to the low gravity, he shot straight up. As he reached the apex of his jump, a beam of light hit him square on.

He screamed.

There was a horrendous *sizzle*.

And a final puff of smoke.

HAND IN HAND

The dome appeared with a great *whoosh* in time for the light of the rising suns to reflect off its surface. Once more absorbed in peaceful silence, Anna dropped to her knees on top of one of the higher floating slabs of shelves, gasping, panting … and crying. She cried deep and sorrowful sobs, knowing it was over. The man who had murdered her daughter, who had orchestrated such a fiendish plot … had been consumed by sunlight. It had been an appropriate end. Yet what had her daughter died for? Access to ancient knowledge?

She knew it was more than that, for that knowledge would have led to power and, likely, eternal life. She looked up at the main slab of shelves. Gods collected such knowledge … yet it meant nothing to her now. Less than nothing. The quest had been a total failure, the truth having cleaved through the desperate illusion. And even *if* she scoured every tablet and scroll and tome and found an ancient necromantic ritual that would see her sacrifice her life to resurrect one of her children, she now knew that the end result would be nothing short of corruption.

She picked up a piece of parchment that had fallen onto the floating bookshelf. The words were written in an old arcane tongue, but she could make out a recipe for deviled eggs. *Deviled eggs!* Anna let the parchment go, watching it flutter out of sight. It all felt … so needless. So terribly, *terribly* needless.

Above, beyond the dome, a world burned.

"Hello?" echoed a voice from below. "Is anyone here?"

Anna peeked over the edge of her slab and saw Ralf standing amidst a floor littered with debris. He held Bun-Bun by his brown ear like she had as a child, and like her daughter had when she was younger. The elemental was gone, having vanished after his master's death, leaving Ralf to amble about.

He spotted her and gave her a flopping wave. "Hi."

Anna gaped at him as if he were an apparition.

"Are … are you all right?" he asked.

Unable to speak through her tears, Anna could only nod. She sniffed, peeled back the torn and bloody cloth of her robe, and began the healing process, which took a lot of time as she had to wait for her stamina to replenish a little.

After healing, and after repairing her robe for the second time, she hopped down, floating in the low gravity, until her bare feet touched the floor.

"Hi," Ralf mumbled.

"Hi."

"Are you hurt?"

Anna shook her head.

"Where is that man?"

"He's gone."

"Where'd he go?"

"It doesn't matter."

"Why?"

"Because we'll never see him again."

"How do you know that?"

"Because the light took him."

"Where did it take him to?"

"The Great Beyond."

"What's that?"

She looked up at the dome. "A place beyond places."

Ralf followed her gaze. "Are we going there too?"

"One day. But not yet. Not yet …"

They waited for sunset together all day, talking. Anna spoke freely about herself, about her daughter, her son, her husband, her father, her mother, her sister, her friend Samantha, even the scion. Ralf questioned everything, a child enthralled, wanting to consume knowledge. He asked about himself, but she had few answers. She told him anything he wanted to know, for she also knew it meant nothing as she would have to rob him even of all this. The talking was to benefit her and her only, to lighten the heavy load on her shoulders. He would never know her daughter, in whose murder he was complicit. Never know he was a father. He would not know Bun-Bun, this plane, and would not remember Anna. That was the plan, and the only way forward for the boy. The only chance he had at a normal life.

Throughout, Anna did not touch a single book, scroll, tablet, or parchment. For her, the knowledge here was tainted. She refused to profit off her daughter's death, even considered destroying it all—and how great a temptation that was!

Except she felt that destroying a library, even one as dark as this, felt profoundly wrong. After all, what was once forbidden could end up saving. What was dark in the past could be light in the future. So she let it be. But nor did she clean anything up, choosing to leave the library in a state of disarray.

"Let it be proof," she whispered, staring at the mess as dusk took the sky, "to whoever cometh in the future, that I, Anna Atticus Stone, battled here … and faced my nightmare." Something told her this was only one library of many. A stash, hidden amongst the stars. One piece of a great whole.

"Will you ever see your daughter again?" Ralf asked, holding her hand, Bun-Bun in the other.

Anna dropped her head. "No."

"Is she with your son?"

Unable to speak through the lump in her throat, she surrendered a nod.

"I'm sorry."

Anna looked at him and saw genuine sorrow in his eyes. Ralf Turman, at ten years of age, was capable of compassion. She kneeled in front of him. "You will not remember any of this. But in case you do … in case somehow, in some way, you rediscover a part of yourself that longs for the darkness …" She pressed a hand to his chest. "I hope you find a way to return to the boy you are now, and not the abandoned boy they bullied …"

Ralf stared at her, mouth agape. There was no light of understanding behind his eyes, only a hurt confusion. She forced a small smile and stood. "Come, let us watch the sunset for the last time. It will be unlike any sunset you will ever see again."

She took him to the top of the main bookshelf slab, and together they watched as two distant suns vanished beyond the horizon, slowly plunging the world into darkness. When the stars twinkled above and the cold air solidified the lava and turned steam into fog, Anna craned her neck and said, "*Geh geh aka ach ahi geha nah!*" and the dome vanished with a *sizzle*.

She stepped outside the library and sniffed about for the Blade of Paralysis, but didn't see it. Likely it had been consumed by the light, or lay lodged somewhere out there in that hellscape. Before leaving, she glanced back at the library. The dome would return on its own, protecting the contents for who knew when and what. She wondered how long that would be. She thought about her son and daughter and how she had so naively hoped that both would be there. And for a time, that hope was what carried her onward. Now it was gone, replaced by hollowness, and by a deep grief she could finally start facing.

"Why are you crying?" Ralf asked as they walked back, one hand clutching hers, Bun-Bun dangling from the other by a brown ear.

Anna wiped the tears that had flowed and averted her face. "I miss my daughter."

"Where is she?"

"She's gone."

"What happened to her?"

"You. You happened to her."

"I don't understand."

"Nor should you."

Ralf let go of her hand. "I'm sad."

Anna retrieved it. "Let us speak no more. And keep an eye out. It's dangerous here."

She had wanted to teleport back to the portal, but realized the landscape might have changed. Why take the risk of teleporting into dried lava? And so together they walked, she bare of foot, he clumsily plodding along, a ten-year-old in a seventeen-year-old's body, Bun-Bun swaying as he had swayed when she was a little girl. They walked past the silent winged lion, past canyons and valleys and mesas and lava tunnels. They walked unperturbed, unencumbered, and free. She sped up the journey by teleporting from ridge to ridge, using only clear sight lines, taking no risks. At last, they stared up at the portal that would take them home.

"Why won't I remember any of this?"

"So you will have a chance at a future."

"I feel like I did something bad."

Anna said nothing.

"Did I hurt you?"

Still, Anna said nothing.

"I hurt your daughter, didn't I?" It was a whisper. "Are you going to punish me?"

She patted his hand. "Come. You have a long life ahead. Let us start you on the right path."

"Was I on the wrong path?"

"Yes."

"Why?"

"Choices."

"I don't understand."

"I know."

She took him through the portal first and, after another tumbling trek through a twisting and light-filled ether, stepped out into The Hall of Sacred Doors. The moment she walked out, the portal closed behind her. With Ralf safe and holding on to Bun-Bun, she turned to the cinder door.

"I ought to destroy you," she whispered. The master builder had left a mechanism to do just that. But there was no rush, and she supposed she could always trigger it later.

"What are those?" Ralf whispered in awe.

Anna glanced down the hall at the various portals waiting like hungry mouths to devour their next unsuspecting victim. Maybe she would destroy them all. Maybe warlock-kind wasn't ready. She had much to think on.

"Doors," she replied.

"Doors to where?"

"Distant places."

"Like as far as the next town?"

"Farther."

"Like to the next kingdom?"

"Much farther."

"Oh." He thought about it. "Are we going to enter one of them?"

"No."

"Why?"

"Enough questions."

"Okay."

When her eyes settled on the desert door, she realized that, at least for now, these doors would remain on account of a daughter making a promise to her late father …

Holding Ralf's hand, Anna led him through the end portal. Back in the thumbprint room, she put him to sleep, cast Incarnate, picked up the golden shield and the boy, and walked onward, keeping the key in a pocket and leaving the slab doors open—for the time being. Then she returned the shield to its alcove deep under Mount Barrow and retraced her steps back through the excavation.

As she walked, with the sleeping boy floating alongside, she contemplated how she could discreetly protect it all—and in such a way so that only she could return. The knowledge in The Hall of Sacred Doors was too dangerous. Additional protective layers had to be added, even if that meant filling the excavation tunnels back up. After all, who knew how many unknown workmen and battering ram soldiers had seen the interior. The final room should only be accessible through competent teleportation, after unlocking secrets meant only for the good-natured— and she wasn't sure that would include Senior Arcaneologist Ning. It would take years to learn the requisite arcanery, but years she had.

Anna stepped outside with a floating Ralf and closed the doorway, ensuring it was indistinguishable from the mountain. She then swept a hand at Ralf, whispering, "*Senna null.*" As he slowly woke, she placed him back on his feet. He blearily rubbed his eyes, looked at her, at the mountain, and then up at a starry night and a full moon that lit up the snowy pines.

"Is this a dream?"

"Sort of."

"I don't understand."

"I know."

"Have I been here before?"

"You have."

"Will I come back?"

"No."

He thought about it. "I won't remember you, will I?"

"You will not."

"Will you ever forgive me for whatever it is I did?"

Anna looked at the moonlit forest. "I don't know."

"Will I still become a warlock?"

"That's up to you." She patted his hand again. "Ready yourself, for I now take you home."

"Can I not stay with you? Will you be my mother?"

"No."

"Why?"

"Because my children are ..." Even then, she couldn't say it. "I too shall start anew. Now hush, child."

"Oh. Okay."

She closed her eyes, visualized a certain building in the city, and incanted, "*Impetus peragro grapa lestato exa exaei.*" With a *thwomp*, the pair appeared before a quiet manor amidst a grove of thick elms. The windows were dark, and above a pair of oaken double doors was the sign, "Blackhaven House for Boys."

"The orphanage," Ralf whispered, stepping away. "Please … no …"

Anna grabbed his hand and gently tugged him onward. She took hold of Bun-Bun and tried to take him back, but Ralf held a death grip on the little creature. "Please, no. Don't …"

"He has another quest. A quest to watch over my daughter."

Tears streamed down Ralf's face. "The girl I did a bad to …" He let Bun-Bun slip from his grasp.

"I am sorry, but this is the only way. You promise to be a good boy, all right?"

"All right …"

"Promise?"

"Promise."

She straightened. "Goodbye, Ralf."

He looked up at her. "Goodbye."

She made him face away, for he could not glimpse her after the completion of the spell. He had to start a new life, a life unfettered by what he had done, and what he had seen. A life without a son. That was the price for his deeds, a kinder price than death, which was what the kingdom's laws demanded.

After steeling herself, Anna placed a hand on top of his head and incanted, "*Erassa memora au o minad,*" destroying the precious grains of hourglass sand that denominated all the relevant moments that led up to this moment, so that the last thing he would remember was being ten years old. And to mitigate against some well-meaning future healer casting the 14th degree healing spell Rectify Memory, she went over the blank parts she had already erased, erasing them anew. There should now be no memories to be salvaged. Her daughter and her grandson should forever be safe from the thoughts of this boy.

With the spell complete, she let go of Ralf's head and quietly stepped away, her bare feet making no sound against the soft grass. Ralf stood alone, gaping at the doors before him. From behind a tree, she raised a finger and made the brass door knocker *clang*. Candlelight soon lit up inside, brightening the window by the door, until it was opened, revealing a plump woman in a nightgown.

"Oh, hello there. And what might you be doing here, young man? Hmm?"

Ralf stared up at her.

"Can you speak, my son?"

"Yes."

"What's your name?"

"Ralf."

"And how old are you, Ralf?"

"Ten."

"That cannot be. You look at least eighteen!"

The boy shook his head. "I'm ten."

"Then you are the biggest ten-year-old I have ever seen. Something must have happened to you."

He looked down and started. "My hands!"

So it began anew, the quest to discover himself. Anna only hoped that the quest did not lead the boy astray. Clutching Bun-Bun with a heavy heart, she withdrew into the shadows, leaving Ralf Turman to whatever fate awaited him. Perhaps, in time, she would see him again at the academy as a kinder boy. In truth, she never wanted to lay eyes on him again.

ORANGE SUN

As dawn blushed in the east, an exhausted Anna stepped into the monk monastery. The place was dim and quiet and smelled of sandalwood incense. After taking in the rows of candles and statues and paintings of holy men and women, she walked toward a hairless man. He sat cross-legged before a large bell that hung above a pond.

"You are up early," Anna said.

"These days, yes," Thomas replied. He was dressed in his usual purple robe of the 15th degree. The robe was spotless, freshly ironed and cleaned so well it shone, giving him the appearance of being wrapped in silk.

"You were right. It was a fool's errand. I, the great Anna Atticus Stone, am the *greatest* of fools." She pressed a hand to her mouth, the facade she had been hoping to keep intact cracking like a stone. "She's … she's gone …"

He stared for a while into the pond in which red and white fish slowly swam about, occasionally nibbling at a floating bread-like nugget. A bowl of those nuggets sat half empty beside him.

"Aren't you going to say anything?" Anna pressed. "Didn't you hear me? Our daughter is dead!" Her words rudely echoed off the walls.

"What is there to say?" he asked in a gentle voice that starkly contrasted with her shout. " 'I told you so?' How could I say such a thing to a grieving mother? You did what you needed to do to cleanse the demons haunting your soul. You did it for our children. I fault you not, dear wife. I could have argued more against the quest, but in truth, I too had a faint hope that you were right." He added in a whisper, "By gods, if only you had been right …"

Anna opened her mouth to argue, but in light of his words felt her anger had no place—especially here, and so it dissolved like incense smoke. She watched him pick up a nugget and toss it into a pond. A fish swam up to it, gave it a nip, and swam off.

"I was blinded by my longing," she whispered. "I wanted it to be true …"

"I know."

"Desperately …"

"I know …"

"She's gone. And our son is gone. And we—" She swallowed, unable to articulate the depths of loneliness that ate at her soul. For a while they stood watching the fish.

It was Thomas who spoke first. "In the river of time, paths often diverge."

Now the anger flared. "What's *that* supposed to mean?"

He stood, hands moving gracefully even as he pushed himself off the ground, and turned to face her. Although hairless, the wrinkles ran deep, and he looked older than she ever remembered him looking.

"And now we are both bare of foot," he said before tilting his head. "But you have seen combat."

"I have."

"Triumphant."

"Triumphant would have been returning with our children."

He nodded. "You look like you haven't slept in a month."

"Don't prance about like a fool, Thomas. What did you mean?"

"You know what I meant."

She searched his eyes, finding them unreadable. "What about your grandson?"

Thomas looked away. "I have accepted that his path does not involve me."

"Then he will be worse off for it. You would be neglecting your duties."

"Perhaps. But I had two children and had them taken away from me. I am not as strong as you are, Anna. I cannot go through that again. And I cannot exist like this. I cannot watch another child succumb to your mother's curse. I cannot watch another child take on the burden of the scion. I have seen how it has been nothing but a torment in your life. To constantly have to watch over your shoulder, to mistrust those who speak well of you. I … I cannot do it. Any of it. In truth, I have been waiting for you to step through that entrance. I cannot live here anymore. My time here has come to an end."

Anna's lip quivered as she whispered, "Damn you, Thomas Bran Hubert Stone. You will speak plain and true to me and stop with riddles *this* instance!"

"I am not a boy to be scolded, Anna."

"Then stop acting like one!"

"My dear wife, I have something to tell you."

"Spit it out already, you old fool!" How he enraged her suddenly!

"You do not mean to be cruel. It is the grief."

She knew it to be true, but held her chin rigid out of sheer pride.

Thomas walked up to her, robe swishing quietly, and took her hands, even whilst she held on to one of Bun-Bun's ears. He dangled between them, and she could almost hear him squeaking in protest.

Thomas looked her in the eyes and whispered, "I am going to knock on the desert door."

Despite hearing the strength of his resolve in his voice, she shook her head, trying not to collapse to the floor. "No. No no no no no—"

"Anna—"

"I forbid it—"

"Anna."

"I will not let you—"

"Anna. Listen—"

"No!"

"Please. Anna—"

"I refuse your request—"

"It is not a request."

"You won't."

"I will."

"You can't."

"I must."

"You *must* stay. That is the only must you are allowed."

"Anna. I am going to knock on the desert door."

"You can't … no … don't leave me alone … don't you do it …"

"But I have already left. I was half out the door upon our son's death. The very moment our daughter died, the other half went with her. Let me go. My sweet wife, my Anna … let me go. Let me find the peace I long for." He closed his eyes and kissed her forehead. "Please …"

She wanted to shove him into that stupid pond and rage and scream and cry. Instead, she drew back, her hands slipping from his, barely holding on to Bun-Bun's ear. She stared at her husband's bare feet, nodding to herself, trying to fathom the loss and what it meant. A thousand arguments and curses and denunciations came to mind, which she wanted to hurl at him. Then she looked into his eyes and saw her sorrow mirrored in them. And how handsome he still looked, even after all these years! Thus, the most absurd question stumbled off her tongue.

"Do you not find me beautiful anymore?"

The question broke through, and he burst with a tearful scoff. "Oh, Anna … you are an eternal flower, and the most beautiful woman I have ever seen …"

"Good. Good! Then you will stay and we can start to fix our divisions and—"

"Anna—"

"—we can rebuild and start a new life and—"

"Anna. Stop. Stop it, Anna. Please. Don't do this. Don't."

She nodded, more so to herself than him, and kept nodding even as salty tears rolled over her lips and dripped off her chin.

Thomas watched her as if from afar. "Never have I seen a woman look like a little girl, a teenager, a woman in her middle life, and an old woman at the same time. As if the gods forgot about you and let you slip through time unopposed, so that you may return to any point in your life."

"If that were true, I would return us to before our son died and take us far, far away …"

Thomas nodded, saying nothing. She wanted him to say more too. His silence annoyed her. She wanted to hear him speak his mind as much as he dared.

She smoothed her robe to compose herself, raised her left hand, and pinched her wedding ring between the fingers of her right hand. "I will never remarry. I will honor everything we were … until my dying breath."

Thomas, face streaked with tears, raised his hand and mimicked the gesture. "I too shall wear mine, and honor everything we were … until my dying breath."

Their right hands intertwined, and they drew each other close, embracing. She inhaled his scent for what felt like the last time, and refused to let go, until he gently pushed her away.

"Now I have one last thing to ask of you, Anna."

Anna stood staring at her feet, already knowing what it was.

"Please take me to the desert door."

For a time she stood, desperately seeking a final way out. In battle, it would always be a clever move or spell she had been saving. But this was not a battle. It was life. And it was his ardent wish. The only path forward. He was right. He wasn't as strong as her. Were he to join her in normality, the drink would consume him. That much she knew. Thus, he deserved peace from the torment of living beyond his children. He truly deserved that.

And so, with the greatest reluctance, she surrendered a heavy nod.

"Thank you," he whispered. "Thank you …"

"Will you need anything? Is there any place you would like to see before you … before you go?"

He shook his head, and she reached out to him. He accepted her hand, and she led him through the doors, remembering leading him in such a way from their wedding spot. Just the two of them to experience a life together. But that life together had ended, and soon it would only be her, alone to face an uncertain future.

As the first ray of sunrise pierced the sky, reminding her of moments in that hellish plane, she turned to face him. "Are you ready?"

He looked back at the temple before gazing long and hard at his last Sithesian sunrise. "Look at the golden glow," he whispered. "That is the most beautiful sunrise I have ever seen."

Anna nodded, not wanting to taint the moment with words.

At long last, her husband looked at her. "I am ready."

She nodded. "So be it. So be it …" She let the sun bathe them together before finally incanting, "*Impetus peragro grapa lestato exa exaei.*"

They appeared in the shadow of Mount Barrow. Thomas glanced around at the trees, silently saying his goodbye, before the pair stepped up to the mountain, neither commenting on the coldness of the snow against their bare feet.

Anna placed her hand on the rock and whispered, "Ottentus Maledius Anavictus Anna Atticus Stone." A cavity in the rock rumbled open inward.

"He placed his name first," Thomas noted. "Why am I not surprised …"

Anna, remembering having the same thought, was nonetheless too troubled to comment on such an insignificant matter, and simply stepped in after her husband. Once inside, they turned to watch the door rumble closed behind them, as if sealing them in a tomb. Thomas lit his palm with fire and they strode onward into the deeply silent innards of the mountain.

Anna walked in a daze, still trying to come to terms with what was happening. The fire from Thomas's palm played off the rock, creating jagged shadows and making her feel as if they were in caveman times. They had a long walk ahead of them, for they had to retrieve the shield first.

"Will you tell me a little about what you saw?" Thomas asked, as if trying to distract her.

"I wouldn't know where to begin."

"I suppose I don't need to know. But it exists."

"Hell?"

He nodded. Their voices echoed into silence.

"That wasn't Hell. It was … a place. A hot place. A place of two suns."

He raised a hairless eyebrow. "*Two* suns?"

She looked up, as if seeing the sky through the mountain. "A place far, far away. A desolate place. A lonely place."

"What did you find there?"

"A library. I suspect one of many others, hidden like tiny islands on a vast ocean …"

"A library."

"A beautiful one of floating bookshelves that turned in place to ward off the light of those two suns."

"I wish I had seen it. And was it, as was foretold, a library of forbidden knowledge?"

"That it was."

"And … did you destroy it?"

"No. But I might. I might …"

He sighed. "That would almost be a shame."

"I may hide it and protect it instead, as the master builder did. I know I will never return there no matter what. Everything else … I don't know. I don't know …"

"And Ottentus?"

"Ottentus betrayed us."

Thomas nodded, as if having expected this. Anna wanted to tell him how badly he had betrayed them, about Ralf and how she had let him live and that he was the father of their grandchild … but strangely, Thomas did not pursue the matter, and they walked together in silence. She retrieved the shield, used it to pass safely through the explosive stairwell, summoned the portal to the Sacred Hall of Doors, and walked up to the desert door, with its perpetually low orange sun. There, Thomas turned to her for the last time, and they stared at each other, each knowing their truth, each appreciating the moment.

"I'll miss you," she whispered.

"And I you, Anna Atticus Stone. My beloved wife."

"It's not too late, you know. You can change your mind. Stay with me and help rear our grandson and—"

"Anna—"

"—and we can start anew, maybe live somewhere else. Heck we can renew our vows and—"

"Anna."

She held Bun-Bun close.

"You look so young," he whispered. "Yet so old. I know, I know, I repeat myself." He sighed deeply, sorrowfully. "Take care of our grandson as best you can, but do not be afraid to let him go should he choose a path of darkness."

Anna opened her mouth to ask what he meant, only to close it, for she knew exactly what he meant. Knew it better than anyone could. But that didn't mean she would not try to turn the boy into a good man. She would put everything she had ever learned into that particular challenge …

Thomas turned to the scion, cupping it with a gentle hand. "And you, ancient one. Please take care of my beloved wife. Lend her strength when she needs it, hope when she lacks it, light in darkness, shield against despair, and guide her to a fruitful life. To you I say goodbye as well."

He smiled at Anna, and she forced a smile back. Then he turned to the desert door, raised a hand, and knocked three times. When he lowered his hand, the door-portal opened.

"Salutations, Husband Thomas and Wife Anna Stone," said an echoing voice from the other side.

"Who are *you*?" Anna blurted, curiosity taking the reins.

"Go by multitude of names, this soul does. But pertinent that is not. Pertinent is that thou hast queried the door. In riposte, I pose a monumental query. Who amongst thee seeks enlightenment?"

"I do," Thomas boldly replied.

The door waited, as if hoping for Anna's reply.

"Thomas Stone, I deem thee worthy of trial. Enough particles of sand from the hourglass of time have trickled for a new beginning to spawn, a beginning that shall commence with thee. I thus grant thee permission to enter, on the condition of comprehension that there shan't be return should Leyanhood be granted."

"This I understand."

"So be it."

"So be it," Thomas whispered, turning to Anna. Once more they stared at each other, the door to the sacred desert of Ley beside them. "Farewell, my wife, my Anna." He offered a hand.

She took it, finding a handshake strangely appropriate, as a hug would have broken her. "Farewell, my husband, my Thomas." She squeezed, and let his fingers slip from her grasp as he stepped into the void, leaving her forever.

It was quick. Too quick. One moment he had been holding her hand, the next he was gone. Just like that.

"Just like that ..." she whispered.

Alone, Anna clutched her heart and closed her eyes, Bun-Bun hanging heavily in her hand. She deeply missed her husband already. Missed his counsel, his wisdom, his smile, his wit, his playfulness, his touch ...

"Anna Atticus Stone," the voice boomed, startling her. "To thee an invitation I also extend. Is it thy wish to become Leyan?"

Anna saw her father's face, feeling the joy he would have taken in hearing his daughter receive such a historically prestigious invitation. But the time was not right. "I ... I am honored, but I do not wish to become a Leyan ... yet." The *yet* surprised even her. But it also felt right. After all, that *yet* held a father's hope. A hope of recovering lost knowledge. Of bridging the gap between the past and the present. Between Ley and Sithesia ...

"The question shall linger until the last light of your last sunset. And with thee, a new beginning too shall dawn."

"Who ... who *are* you?"

"Thou seeks a word that defines the indefinable. But a name I can provide. That name is Krakatos."

"The brother in myth ..."

"I have gone by many monikers ..." His voice started to echo again.

"Wait, I have questions!" *So many questions* ...

"I grant you leave to ask but one."

"Devil's Gate—the Arcaneum—I know it's a Trainer for Ley. How can I open it again for the generations to come?"

"Only when the bridge between our worlds is rebuilt can the Arcaneum reopen. Until we meet again, Anna Atticus Stone. Fare thee well."

"Fare thee well ..." Anna whispered. "Fare thee well ..."

THROUGH LOVE AND LOSS

It was supper time when Anna stepped up to the old plank door of the Plowmans. She could hear Lividius crying within—and had heard him while walking all the way up to the house. Having slept in that lonesome tower for the first time in days, she felt rested, yet her heart was heavy. She knew she would eventually sell the tower and move, though maybe after Lividius was all grown up. Having thought she would want to let the past go, she had found herself wanting instead to hold onto it in some ways, and the tower would do that for her, for within lingered many pleasant memories she was not willing to let go of just yet.

She raised a hand and was about to knock, only to hesitate. She saw the cinder door, and then the desert door. She saw possibilities and selfish futures and freedom from the pain of this life. She saw travel and exploration and learning.

Then she thought of her students and the academy, and inside the babe cried even louder, and Anna sighed and knocked three times. The door opened to reveal Marybel, eyes puffy from lack of sleep. She expelled a great sigh of relief upon seeing Anna, and enveloped her in a hug.

"Merciful heavens, I'm *so* glad you're all right," she whispered, squeezing her tightly.

Anna squeezed back, not wanting to let go. Marybel's adult children and young grandchildren and nieces and nephews started to crowd in the background, but Marybel quickly shooed them away with a hand.

When they barely moved back, she smacked her gums, dragged Anna outside, and shut the door behind herself.

Marybel then tilted her head and shook it. "My word, woman, you look awful."

"Let's just say I've been to hell and back. And you look like you haven't gotten a wink of sleep since I left. He's been that bad, has he?"

"We haven't been able to get him to stop crying. Only to eat and sleep. We called all sorts of medicine men and women and midwives and healers and every crackpot that wandered through these parts. Tried countless remedies …" She shook her head. "Nothing worked. The consensus is that he has to get bored of crying."

"That's what I was afraid of," Anna muttered.

"Some of the, uh, crazier loons think he's, uh …"

"What?"

"Cursed."

Anna sighed. "Ah."

Marybel brightened. "How's that old fool of yours, anyway?"

"He's …" Anna dropped her head. "He's …" She couldn't bring herself to say it. Not yet. It would be too final. Yet the finality had already taken place …

Marybel only nodded. "Then he is a fool. A damn fool. Have you eaten?"

"No."

"Come, have a proper family meal. And you can speak as much or as little as you like."

"That would be wonderful, thank you," and Anna allowed her old friend to usher her inside, where she would go on to catch up on the latest gossip, including who snagged what job and who traveled where. Anna let them do all the talking, merely enjoying having a large family about, pretending she was one of them.

* * *

Anna stood atop Mount Barrow, holding a crying Lividius in one arm, Bun-Bun by the ear in the other, the scion floating nearby. It was twilight, and the entire kingdom, laden under a blanket of fresh snow, sprawled in every direction. A wind ruffled her robe and made her long ponytail dance, whistling as it grazed the jagged black rock of the mountain, sweeping Lividius's cries along with it.

She stepped up to the bonfire she had assembled and raised Bun-Bun before her. He was worn, missing patches of fur, one ear still brown from her father's blood. "My beloved old companion," she whispered, caressing his face with a thumb. "I charge you with a sacred quest. Your last and most important quest. Go to my daughter. Watch over her. Care for her. Love her. Tell her I will see her when the sun sets for me too. Tell her to watch over Samuel. Tell her I love them both so very, very much. Will you do that for me?"

She nodded. "Thank you. Thank you so much. And I will miss you too. Until we meet again, my beloved friend." She kissed his little snout, smelled his mustiness, made him kiss Lividius's nose, and placed him on the logs. Then she stepped back, organized her thoughts so that the arcanery of the 16th degree Memorial Ceremony spell would trigger at the right time, raised her free arm, and said, "I call upon the spirits of the dead to listen to the cries of the living, and to remember those they left behind, those who still breathe the air and walk above ground. Dearly departed, allow us a final goodbye as we mourn your passing from this life." The woodpile burst with a high fire that reminded her of a certain place, until it settled into a guttering blue flame. "Hear the cry," she said, and began to sing a fragile and lonely melody that, along with baby Lividius's crying, shepherded her into a foggy whiteness.

From that whiteness emerged a girl, already holding Bun-Bun by the ear. Her daughter, looking fresh as a daisy, squeezed the little creature tightly, raised a hand, and smiled. Anna raised her hand and smiled back. In her mind, even as she sang in the real world, she told her daughter how much she loved her, asked her to forgive her for her many failings, and to watch over Samuel and Bun-Bun and Bear. She said she would look after little Lividius to the best of her ability, and not to worry about her, that she would be fine. Samuel soon emerged alongside Anna's mother, and then, to her great surprise, Niterra Bladesong stepped in behind them, as if to continue her watch over the family. That was when she knew they would all be protected, forever and ever, and that they would wait for her and Thomas to join them when the time allowed it so. Throughout, she kept waving and waving, and even waved as her daughter was the last one to meld back into the white mist and the mist faded, leaving Anna standing with a tiny babe, a hand raised in a final farewell, her voice cracking, until she could sing no more.

The blue fire had consumed Bun-Bun completely, marking the true end of what remained of her childhood. She watched the fire until it too died, leaving a smoking trail the wind stole. Having lost a son and daughter and husband, she knew she would never get close to anyone ever again. Except maybe her grandson. She would try with him. Truly try.

Already the detachment from her husband began. In time, that love would get covered with moss and lichen. In time, she would let him go …

When the stars glimmered alongside a pale moon, and a bank of dark clouds marched toward her and Lividius, indicating a storm, she turned and walked to the edge of the mountain.

"Want to see something neat?" she said to the baby, gently rocking him up and down. "See that ledge down there? Your mother and I discovered it together. Come on, let me show you," and she teleported down to the spot, finding it untouched since her last visit. She found the hidden box and read aloud the poem for her grandson.

" 'For many a year, through love and loss, I returned to this ledge, sun rise and set. None that are born escape untorn, yet at final bell I fare thee well, for I declare'—" She paused to sigh wistfully just as her daughter had done upon first reading the poem aloud. "—'that I have lived.' "

She bounced him up and down, whispering, "Beautiful, isn't it?" She put the poem back and stepped up to the hollow. "What do you think about making a cave here and turning it into our home? Or maybe I can retire here after you move out of the tower, surround myself with books and research and thoughts and memories and silly musings, like exploring the other elements. It'd be so peaceful and quiet. Or maybe after I pass you the scion …"

Yet already doubts crept in. Would the boy have the right skill and temperament to take on the ancestral responsibility that had caused the lineage so much heartache? How would she train him? What element would he be? Would he even *become* a warlock?"

She turned to look at the horizon. "A storm is coming. Isn't it beautiful? Well, *I* think storms are beautiful." She readjusted him, trying to make him more comfortable, but his crying did not abate. "You long for your mother. I do, too." She sighed. "Or maybe you want your father. Alas, as per your mother's wishes, no one shall know who your real father is, not even you. Until the end of time. No one." The boy would know only that his father had abandoned his mother, nothing more.

"So be it." She patted his tummy. "There's lots to do. Come, let us get you to bed."

* * *

It was sometime after an interview during which Anna had allowed herself to be debriefed about her journey to that hellish plane, conducted by a notable arcaneologist sworn to secrecy for certain events, that Anna stepped before a pair of doors that led to the Room of Masters in the Academy of Arcane Arts. She could already hear the other arcanists discussing the latest formalities.

The doors silently opened for her, but Anna remained at the doorway. Inside, a slew of old black-robed arcanists turned to her, many raising their brows in surprise. Behind them, a thunderstorm silently raged beyond the great invisible wall that rose to infinity.

"Arcanist Stone!" Headmaster Bowbrick said, arms wide. "What a pleasant surprise! We were just conversing on the day's business. Please, do come in. There is much to discuss—"

"I'll take it," Anna said as lightning silently flickered outside, lightning up the great room.

"I … I beg your pardon?"

"The job. I'll take it. Assuming it's still available."

The headmaster looked back at his startled cohorts. "Why, of course it is! This is most wonderful news indeed! I will step down immediately and—" Yet when he turned back, Anna was already striding down the hall, seeing a whole new future. Her kids were gone, but there were still hungry minds she could nourish as headmistress.

And as she strode, she couldn't help but do something she had not done in what felt like forever.

Anna smiled.

* * *

PERSONAL THOUGHTS
FROM THE AUTHOR

Thank you for reading *Flames of Stone* and partaking in Anna's journey. Before I delve into my personal thoughts (and once you've had a moment to take a deep breath after that rollercoaster), I wanted to briefly mention that this entire saga was a prequel to *The Arinthian Line*, which starts with the book *Arcane* (in case you want to get to know Anna as a 101-year-old woman).

One of the interesting things about writing a prequel is you have a destination you know you need to get to, but only a loose forest path to get you there. It certainly had its challenges, yet I greatly enjoyed the journey.

Now I was quite prepared to write Anna as a kid and teen in *Prodigy of Thunder* and *The Arcane Artist*, for I had already written *The Arinthian Line* and *Fury of a Rising Dragon*, and both dealt extensively with that age range. But sitting down and writing Anna Atticus Stone as a 49-year-old teacher, wife, and mother was a whole other challenge. Truth be told I was terrified upon first glimpsing the full scope of the project before me that was to become *Flames of Stone*.

For I am not a teacher. I am not a woman, a mother—nor even a father. I have not experienced the death of a child, let alone two. It thus felt arrogant and presumptuous to think that I could walk in Anna's shoes.

So why *did* I choose to write *Flames of Stone*? After all, there was no shortage of interesting times in Anna's life, like juggling being a headmistress whilst rearing her grandson and battling Narsus, for example. But I felt that was already discussed in *The Arinthian Line* series. Besides, were I to explore the depths of her and Narsus, I feel it might kill some of the mystery *The Arinthian Line* offered when discussing Anna's past. I could have chosen her early twenties, but I plan to write from that point of view next with my first beloved characters of Augum, Bridget and Leera. I could have chosen a time that *overlapped* with the trio. But that whole timeline was already covered in *The Arinthian Line*.

I wrote *Flames of Stone* because it was the most influential and tumultuous time in Anna's life, by far. The tragic events that Anna experienced in this book solidified who she became as a much older adult. She was scarred and hardened and changed in tangible ways that explained how a warlock prodigy became the cantankerous hermit mentor in *The Arinthian Line*.

Also, the idea about this timeline had actually been born in *Riven*, with Thomas uttering the following line: "The children need feeding," when referring to his younger years as a father. It was that small clue that was the genesis of this book, published eight years later.

Further, I chose the subject matter long before what happened next. In a twist of ill fate, the tragedy in Anna's story intertwined with one in my own life. Our beloved cat, Buddha, died a month into the writing of this book. Just shy of fifteen years of age, she got critically ill over the span of a weekend and passed Monday, January 30th, 2023. On her final day, my wife and I stayed up all night cuddling her, watched the sunrise together for the last time, before taking her to the vet to have her put down. She was a four-year-old stray when we adopted her in 2012, and her vet gave her the birthday of February 2nd, which coincidentally is also Augum's birthday. Perhaps you've seen some of Buddha's photos, as she inspired Sir Pawsalot in *Fury of a Rising Dragon*.

Thus the emotions and grief that Anna experienced interlinked with my own grief. I recognize just how fortunate I am not to have experienced such potent grief in my life until now — and hope for a long respite before inevitably experiencing it again. Of the countless contributions Buddha gave me over the years, the impact of her passing was a final parting gift, as it aided me in writing the tragic story Anna demanded of me. And so I thank my late little companion for that bittersweet gift, and will forever think of her as being part of this work. Lastly, I hope I lived up to Anna's expectations — and yours, dear reader.

What happens with Anna after this point and until she meets the trio is implied or mentioned in *The Arinthian Line*. Sure, there are some mysteries left that could be explored and extrapolated and solved, but I like those mysteries, which I feel lend depth to the work as a whole. Besides, I can always write a fourth book in the future (even a fifth!) if I feel like there's a need for it (maybe even well after she had met the trio, and any adventures in an as-yet unwritten future). After all, the saga *is* called *Chronicles of Anna Atticus Stone* for a reason. For now, I'm content with how everything ties together within the body of my work.

Stepping back, *Flames of Stone* was my twelfth book and my third series. *Chronicles of Anna Atticus Stone* was my first series from a female point-of-view, and my first prequel. Yet that was all incidental to wanting to sincerely express Anna's own journey, regardless of my own preconceptions or biases. Did I do Anna justice? That's for you to decide.

For now, I'm done with prequels. Next, I'm going to write a saga about a certain rambunctious trio you may already know.

Because of the length of my books, I only write one a year. It is thus difficult to express my gratitude, for I am acutely aware of how rare it is to survive publishing a single book a year. That is solely possible because of you, the reader.

As for me, I'm proud of the work. I'm proud of the team, the friends around me. The fans. It was a mutual effort. We could never have gotten this far alone. It was done together (see the acknowledgments).

Some of you have been here since the beginning, others joining the journey along the way. Many of you have written me (and continue to write) incredible letters, some of which I published on my website. Some of you have read and reread my books *multiple* times. Some of you have even started a fan-run Discord server about my work, where you discuss fan theories, duel as warlocks, role-play within the world I have crafted, and mingle (you are, of course invited to drop by—the link can be found on my website in the Discussion page). Heck, the fans at the Discord even helped me brainstorm the Black Eagle motto (among other things)!

But perhaps most difficult for me to articulate and comprehend is the sober fact that some of you have passed on during the writing of my work. I sometimes return to letters sent from those souls, and the follow-ups sent from their loved ones announcing their passing, in an attempt to understand the big picture. It is a humbling experience every time.

To those these particular words will never reach, I hope you know that your absence is felt.

Thank you for reading. It means more than these mere words could possibly convey.

Until we talk again, and feel free to reach out to me at severbronny@gmail.com with any thoughts.

All my best to you and those you love,

—Sever
P.S. Honest reviews play a vital part in readers discovering new books. Please consider leaving one on Amazon for *Flames of Stone,* or any of my works you have read (Goodreads too if you feel like it). Also, I mostly rely on word of mouth, so if you enjoy my work, consider sharing something on social media. Thank you so much for your kind support.

P.P.S. To receive email notice of my new releases, as well as bits of news relevant to my work, subscribe to my newsletter at **severbronny.com/contact**. I don't email often, so you don't have to worry about mailbox clutter.

P.P.P.S. Although Buddha could never be replaced, we now have a little cat named Miso, photos of whom you can find on my social media.

Advance Reader Team:
Want a chance to read my next book before its retail release? Consider joining my Advance Reader Team at severbronny.com/team (spots are limited, as is the application window).

Connect:
Want to tell me what you thought of the book, ask a question, report an error, or just say hello? Email me anytime at sever@severbronny.com

Visit severbronny.com to see a list of spells, class schedules, FAQ, the lore of Sithesia, duel in the arena as a warlock with fellow fans, and converse with readers and the author.

Or connect with me on social media:

Home:	severbronny.com
Facebook:	facebook.com/authorseverbronny
Reddit:	reddit.com/r/severbronny
Instagram:	@severbronny
Discord:	Link can be found at severbronny.com/discussion
Amazon:	Hit the "Follow" button on my author profile

ALSO BY SEVER BRONNY:

THE ARINTHIAN LINE
Arcane
Riven
Valor
Clash
Legend

FURY OF A RISING DRAGON
Burden's Edge
Honor's Price
Mercy's Trial
Champion's Wrath

CHRONICLES OF ANNA ATTICUS STONE

Prodigy of Thunder
The Arcane Artist
Flames of Stone

Arcane (The Arinthian Line, book 1) **blurb:**

Fourteen-year-old Augum and friends Bridget and Leera dream of becoming warlocks. But with a kingdom in chaos, it will take great courage to make that dream come true.

A vicious tyrant has overthrown the king in a quest for seven mythic artifacts—and Augum's mentor, the legendary Anna Atticus Stone, possesses one. Forced to take shelter in a mysterious castle with a brat prince and his unruly entourage, the aspiring warlocks must learn the arcane arts—before the tyrant finds them.

But not everything is as it seems, and when a sudden betrayal plunges the trio into a terrifying ordeal, survival will hinge on their aptitude in the arcane arts … and on a friendship forged in fire.

An enduring bestseller, Arcane is the beginning of an epic coming-of-age fantasy saga beloved by fans the world over.

Audiobooks narrated by Grammy and Hugo winner Stefan Rudnicki. Nominated for the Epic Fantasy Fanatics Readers Choice Award. Suitable for ages 10 to retiree.

Available from Amazon.
Check severbronny.com/books for the latest releases.

ARCANE

THE ARINTHIAN LINE BOOK ONE

SEVER BRONNY

ACKNOWLEDGEMENTS

My work could not have been possible without the love and support of many people. And that starts with my beloved wife, Tansy, who believed in me and my work every single step of the way. You had a choice, Tanz, and you chose the path of support. You helped me build something that will outlive both of us. Love you so much, babe.

The editorial team:
Tansy Bronny (sound-boarding, developmental editing, proofreading, all books)
Elizabeth Darkley, Arrowhead Editing (line edit books 1, 2, 4 *FoaRD*, book 1, 2, 3 *CoAAS*)
Drew Mildon (beta reading, all books)

The audiobook team:
The Arinthian Line narrator Stefan Rudnicki + team, courtesy of Skyboat
Fury of a Rising Dragon narrator Gary Furlong + team, courtesy of Tantor
Chronicles of Anna Atticus Stone narrator Moira Quirk + team, courtesy of Podium

The cover design team:
Sever Bronny (*The Arinthian Line*)
Deranged Doctor Designs + team (*Fury of a Rising Dragon, Chronicles of Anna Atticus Stone*)

Additional special thanks:
Thank you to my friends and family, much love to each of you. Thank you to the Advance Reader Team (you know who you are)! Thank you to all those who participate in discussions on my website and in the fan-run Discord server, especially Atticus Monroe for all his contributions over the years. And thank you to the thousands of you that have written me over the years. I cherish your letters.

Last but certainly not least, thank you to every single reader out there. It is because of you that I've been able to be a full-time author since 2015, a career I am grateful for *every single day*.

ABOUT THE AUTHOR

Sever Bronny has been a full-time author since 2015, having published the bestselling coming-of-age series *The Arinthian Line (Arcane, Riven, Valor, Clash, Legend)*, the follow-up series, *Fury of a Rising Dragon (Burden's Edge, Honor's Price, Mercy's Trial, Champion's Wrath)* and *Chronicles of Anna Atticus Stone (Prodigy of Thunder, The Arcane Artist, Flames of Stone)*. He has also released three albums with his industrial-rock music project Tribal Machine, including the full-length concept album *The Orwellian Night*. One of his songs can be heard in the feature-length film *The Gene Generation*. He lives in British Columbia, Canada, with beloved wife, Tansy, and house panther Miso. Connect with him at his website severbronny.com, subscribe to his newsletter to keep up on events, and duel as warlocks and discuss fan theories in his fan-run Discord server.